The Mayflower Marriage

Arminal Dare

Matador
9 Priory Business Park,
Wistow Road, Kibworth Beauchamp,
Leicestershire. LE8 0RX
Tel: 0116 279 2299
Email: books@troubador.co.uk
Web: www.troubador.co.uk/matador
Twitter: @matadorbooks

ISBN 978 183859 289 9

British Library Cataloguing in Publication Data.
A catalogue record for this book is available from the British Library.

Printed and bound in Great Britain by 4edge Limited
Typeset by Troubador Publishing Ltd in 12pt Adobe Jensen Pro

Matador is an imprint of Troubador Publishing Ltd

In memory of my mother and father,
and for my sons,
Thomas and Peter.

We are such stuff as dreams are made on;
And our little life is rounded with a sleep.
Shakespeare, *The Tempest*, Act IV

'Having undertaken, for the glory of God, and advancement of the
Christian faith, and honour of our king and country, a voyage to
plant the first colony in the Northerne parts of Virginia, doe, by
these presents, solemnly and mutually in the presence of God and
of one another, covenant and combine ourselves together into a
civill body politick, for our better ordering and preservation and
furtherance of the ends aforesaid; and by virtue hereof to enacte,
constitute, and frame such just and equall laws, ordinances, acts,
constitutions, and offices, from time to time, as shall be thought
most mete and convenient for the generall good of the Colonie
unto which we promise all due submission and obedience...'
From *History of Plymouth Plantation*
by William Bradford (1590–1657), second governor of Plymouth.

I have a dream that one day this nation will rise up and live out the
true meaning of its creed; 'We hold these truths to be self evident:
that all men are created equal.'
Dr Martin Luther King, Jr., Lincoln Memorial, Washington, 1963

The audacity of hope.
That was the best of the American spirit, I thought – having the
audacity to believe despite all the evidence to the contrary that we
could restore a sense of community to a nation torn by conflict; the
gall to believe that despite personal setbacks, the loss of a job or an
illness in the family or a childhood mired in poverty, we had some
control – and therefore some responsibility – over our own fate.
It was that audacity, I thought, that joined us as one people.
The Audacity of Hope – Thoughts on Reclaiming the American Dream by
Barack Obama, 2006

CONTENTS

CHARACTERS

Colonists
William Mullins
    Alice, his wife
    Priscilla, his daughter
    Joseph, his son
John Alden
Deacon Carver
    Catherine, his wife
    John Howland, the Deacon's servant
    Desire Minter, Catherine's servant
Elizabeth (Lizzie) Tilley, marries John Howland
Edward Winslow
    Elizabeth, his first wife
    Susanna White, his second wife
    Resolved and Peregrine, Susanna's sons by Mr White
    Josiah, son by Susanna
    Elizabeth, daughter by Susanna
William Bradford
    Dorothy, his first wife

Alice, his second wife

John, his son by Dorothy

William, his son by Alice

Captain Miles Standish, military leader of Plymouth Colony

Rose, his first wife

Barbara, his second wife

Alexander, his son by Barbara

William Brewster, founding Pilgrim

Mary, his wife

Jonathan, Love and Wrestling, his sons

Patience and Fear, his daughters

John Billington

Goodwife 'Goody' Billington

John, his older son

Francis, his younger son

Reverend Lyford, Anglican minister

His wife

His son

John Oldham, Lyford's cohort

Roger Williams, free-thinking, anti-doctrine teacher

Mary Mendome

Constance, her daughter

Arthur Howland, John Howland's nephew

Christopher Martin, governor of the Mayflower appointed by Thomas Weston

Thomas Prence , married Patience Brewster

Elizabeth Prence, their daughter

Charles Prence, twin brother of Thomas Prence

Benjamin Church, commander in King Philip's war

Mr Peabody, William Peabody's father

John and Priscilla Alden's surviving children and their spouses
>Elizabeth marries William Peabody
>John (Jack), spouse unknown
>Joseph, spouse unknown
>Priscilla (Pris), does not marry
>Jonathan marries Abigail
>Sarah marries Alexander Standish
>Ruth marries John Bass
>Mary does not marry
>Rebecca marries Thomas
>David marries Mary

John Winthrop, governor of Massachusetts Bay Colony
John Endecott, governor of Massachusetts Bay after Winthrop

Other interested parties

Thomas Weston, Chairman of the London Board of Investors
Master and Commander Christopher Jones, Skipper of the Mayflower
The Mayflower's Bosun
Officer Clark, First Mate on the Mayflower

Indians

Samoset, the first welcoming Indian
Squanto, speaks English, helps settlers survive their first year
Massasoit, Big Chief of local tribes
>Alexander and Philip, his sons
Hobbamock, Massasoit's most trusted advisor
Tinsin, Hobbamock's son
>Aijana, Tinsin's wife
>Chitsa, Tinsin's daughter
Tokamahamon, helpful brave in Massasoit's tribe
Corbitant, troublesome petty chief
Kekut, John and Priscilla's adopted Indian son

Part 1

1620-1621

Leaving England's Shores

Chapter 1

March 1620

The Star Inn – London

It was the close of the day, the time when dusk melts into darkness, the hour of shadows and blurred moving shapes. On this evening, a soft, cold March rain fell straight from the sky. William Mullins, head bowed against the heavy drizzle, encouraged his tired mount through the north gate of London Bridge.

'Not far now, not far.' He leaned forward to pat the mare's neck. *Second turning on the left, leads almost directly to the Star.*

'Hie, Hie! Dismount or your life. Your purse, man. Gi' us your purse and we'll let you go.' Two beggars leapt from the shadows. Scrawny, barefoot and ragged, they moved with practiced agility.

Damn no! My future's in my purse.

One man caught the bridle and reins. The other thrashed with a stave while tugging at Mullins' leg to drag him from his horse. Pulled sideways, Mullins' face came close to his assailant's snarling mouth: foul breath, spittle cracked lips, a few black teeth.

Losing his right stirrup he dropped the reins and caught the stave. Gripping the flanks of his horse with his knees, he drew his dagger from its sheath and slashed at the man's hands, then his neck. A gash poured blood; the man screamed. His grip loosened. He fell. Shaking, dripping with sweat, Mullins righted himself on his jostling horse.

'Gee up; gee up… come on, girl!' The horse reared, kicked, and whinnying, set off at a gallop along the nearly deserted street. After a short distance Mullins slowed her to a trot. 'Easy now, easy. Good girl.' There, in the mist and drizzle, he could just make out a turning to the left. About five hundred yards on, after a dogleg in the road he spied the barely visible hanging sign of an inn. A hundred yards more, still trembling and breathing hard, he turned his mount into the open cobbled yard.

Safe at last, pray God. He made the sign of the cross. A young ostler hurried from the shadows to take the reins. Thankful that no one was about to see the decrepitude of his old mare, Mullins dismounted.

'Here.' He pressed two farthings into the lad's open palm. 'See you give her a good brush down and feed. She's trekked all the way from Dorking this day.'

The lad nodded. 'Aye, I will, sir, she's all of a sweat.' He led the horse away to the stables.

Weary and stiff, Mullins straightened his back, trying to reach the height of his youth – about five foot, ten inches – a good height. He stood a moment to regain his composure. Shaken as he was, he was grateful for his strength of limb. The street stench of sewage and rotting carcasses permeated his nostrils and rain dripped from his graying beard. Anxiously, he peered into the silent shadowy mist, and strode to the door of the inn. Taking a deep breath and keeping one hand on the dagger by his side, he lifted the latch and pushed. The heavy oak door yielded to his weight and he stepped into a warm blast of loud talk and a pungent haze of pipe smoke, blended with the steam rising from wet doublets and coats. Candle flame punctuated the dimness, and the savory odors of ale and beef pie chased the stink from his nose. He turned to close the door.

'Master Mullins?'

He jerked round, hand dropping to his dagger.

'Deacon Carver. Welcome.'

Mullins faced a slender man slightly taller than himself, dark hair cropped short, dressed in black homespun breeches and jacket, adorned only with a broad, flat white collar: the style of a religious non-conformer. Above the severe garb a welcoming smile and kind brown eyes greeted him. Mullins nodded. 'Aye. Good evening.'

'Master Weston and I are seated over there.' Carver gestured toward the far side of the room. Mullins followed as his host, with a natural grace of movement, threaded though small groups of men, some standing, some seated on stools round tables, drinking, eating, talking, and laughing. As they reached their destination, Weston stood.

'Master Weston, Chairman of our Board of Investors… Master Mullins,' Carver said.

Mullins returned Weston's nod of greeting. Weston was a short man of pallid complexion, clad in a velvet doublet decorated with silver buttons, a crisp white cartwheel ruff at his neck and white lace cuffs setting off his sleeves. Mullins regretted his worn velvet and hoped his ruff hadn't gone limp and gray in the rain. He noted Weston's well fed paunch and round face, squinty green eyes restlessly glancing here and there. His hands rested on the table: thick fingers, short stubby thumbs, soft and white, unlike his own, muscular, hardened and brown from years of tanning hide.

'Do be seated.' Carver drew up a stool. Mullins sat, arranging himself to appear at ease, shoulders relaxed, face adopting an expression of confident well-being. He did not want to betray his weariness or any traces of fear.

'Goodwife!' Carver called and beckoned. The innkeeper's wife, plump and red faced, hurried over, weaving in and out through huddled groups of garrulous men. 'May we please have another tankard and a trencherful of pie for three?'

Mullins was pleasantly surprised at the Deacon's courtesy, unusual toward a woman of lower social status, especially in a hostelry such as this.

'Might as well keep this flagon.' The goodwife set the large jug of ale down with a thump. 'Gets busier and busier here with all the planning and preparing for voyages. Ye'll be another I wager?' She mopped her perspiring brow and cleavage with an already damp handkerchief. ''Tis good for business but runs me off my feet. Back in a trice.'

Taking his seat, Carver addressed Mullins. 'You have come to learn details of our proposed voyage?'

'It interests me,' Mullins replied.

Carver lowered his voice, bending his head. 'I represent a group which has withdrawn from the Anglican Church. Suffering many trials and betrayals we escaped to Holland where folk have religious freedom, and established our own Church of Christ. A great balm it is to be free from persecution.' Carver held Mullins' gaze. 'But as you may have heard, the Catholics are on the rampage. Holland has been a safe haven but you watch, we'll all be suffering papist persecution before long.' Carver spoke with quiet fervor. 'We must find a place where we are free to worship without fear of persecution; where we can build a new Godly England, free of the corruption that infects this country.'

Mullins twisted his hands under the table and leaned back, crossing and uncrossing his legs. He had not risked his life this day traveling a long road, besieged at every turn by thieving beggars, to join a flight from religious persecution. Where religion was concerned he could bend with the wind. He was also very hungry.

Weston placed a restraining hand on Carver's arm. 'The strength of your faith does you credit, my friend, but I think Master Mullins' interest lies more with business concerns.'

'Aye,' Mullins said. 'I am a master craftsman shoemaker. Footwear ranging from sturdy boots to fine shoes, my specialty, for merchants, magistrates, nobility. I need superior hide from Spain, silver buckles and laces. Scarce as hens' teeth. These days peddlers have naught to offer but news; news of wars in Europe, no money, folk starving, so no trade. And with sheep farming replacing crops, out of work farm laborers come into the town desperate for work, begging for food. Only a few days gone by a group of vagabonds broke into a goodman's house. Smashed the heads of all the family with an axe – crazed with hunger. They'll hang for sure.' Mullins suffered a surge of fear for his own small family left behind.

Weston leaned forward, resting his forearms on the table. 'Our venture may be the very opportunity you need. We have a plan, a far advanced plan, to build a colony for the Crown in North America, land of endless riches. A land where industrious men like yourself can prosper. You would be the colony's only shoemaker, unfettered by wars, the recession and,' he lowered his voice, 'the whims of the Crown.'

'A land free of popery and corruption.' Carver leaned into the conversation. 'Our Crown has emptied its coffers with profligate spending on male lovers. Whores they are; Buckingham the worst. Drain the King dry. I tell you, Master Mullins, the comet that streaked across the sky two years back. Accepted wisdom that it was a portent of disaster, God's wrath.'

Mullins gaped in alarm at Deacon Carver's dangerous talk.

'Hush!' Weston hissed. 'Spies everywhere.' He refocused all his attention on his guest. 'Our plan. We have formed a venture company and recruited almost one hundred colonists: tradesmen, women, children, hired hands and servants. Just over half are religious protestors. The others are folk like yourself, men of business who do not want their hard earned prosperity to be swallowed up in the economic crisis that is upon us. We've commissioned a ship, the *Mayflower* skippered by Master and Commander Captain Christopher Jones.'

Deacon Carver interrupted. 'Our people in Holland will commission a smaller ship and rendezvous with the *Mayflower* in

Southampton. We'll sail in tandem to America. The *Mayflower* will return to England and the smaller vessel will remain as the colony's trading ship.'

'Ah!' Weston looked past Mullins' shoulder. 'A welcome sight.'

Mullins turned. The goodwife was struggling across the room bearing a large tray, holding it aloft above heads and her ample bosom. She squeezed through the crowd and fairly collapsed her burden onto their table. 'Phew! Here ye be. Hope 'tis to your liking. Ye've plenty of ale?'

'Aye. Thank you, goodwife,' Carver said. 'You do us proud.'

In concentrated silence they ate, Mullins being careful not to take more than the third that was his portion.

'Ah, delicious!' Carver said, relaxed now. 'A man can use his mind to better advantage with a full belly.' He placed the empty trencher under the table and poured from the flagon, refilling their tankards.

'Thank you,' Mullins said. 'That was excellent fare and most welcome.' The steak pie was clearing the fog from his brain.

Weston then outlined details of their planned venture; to set up a colony in the fertile Hudson River valley, a land brimming with fish, beaver and endless trees. Colonists would export timber and beaver pelts to England where they would fetch a handsome price. Guaranteed prosperity.

In response to Mullins' anxious questions regarding the dangers of the sea crossing and rumors of massacres and scalpings by savages, Weston reassured him that their skipper, Master Jones, was one of the most experienced sea captains in England. 'He's sailed the North Sea many times – the most treacherous waters in the known world. If anyone can take a ship safely across the ocean it is he. And as to the savages,' Weston reached across and clasped Mullins' arm, 'I know. Peddlers peddle such stories across the country along with their wares. Exaggerated – greatly exaggerated. In fact traders report that the natives are more often welcoming and eager to learn our ways. They are very keen to trade beaver pelts, desiring such novel trinkets as we can offer.'

Nodding in agreement, Carver said, 'As it is God's will we should build a new England, it follows the savages should belong to His kingdom too – through our ministry.'

'Or our firearms will defeat them,' Weston said. Carver flinched. Weston leaned back and smiled. 'It is hard to imagine a better prospect. Think of it. Your own large house…'

Weston and Carver stared past Mullins' head toward the door. The loud hubbub of the room gradually dimmed to silence. Mullins swiveled round.

A young man stood in flamboyant pose, legs astride, one hand on his hip, the other resting on the hilt of a heavily engraved sword. He wore an emerald green doublet of fine satin, embroidered in gold silk. His hose were silk, his legs shapely. A black velvet cape embroidered with gold thread hung on his shoulders, held in place by a large gold chain.

'One of the King's courtiers,' Weston muttered, barely audible. 'Damn waste of time and space.'

The courtier's arrogant gaze roved around the room as he swished his long dark curls. Seeing the object of his quest he pushed men out of his way, striding toward a lad, fresh faced, blushing and eager, not of courtier status but well clad nonetheless. The youth stood and received his lover's long kiss. Seemingly oblivious of where they were, or perhaps enjoying the silent consternation surrounding them, the courtier embraced and fondled his lover, not heeding the passing minutes. *It is as if he relishes putting on a spectacle. How long before a protest erupts?* Mullins had difficulty stopping himself from fidgeting.

Flushed with arousal, the courtier took his lover by the hand. 'Come… my carriage is waiting. Out of the way, rabble.' He led his companion through the wave of men stepping aside. On reaching the door he faced his audience; flourishing his hat he bowed, 'Adieu.'

As the door swung shut a swell of voices, excited, indignant, disgusted, filled the room.

Mullins was shocked. *Queen Bess kept her courtiers under control. Whatever they did behind the scenes, in public they behaved impeccably. King*

James seems not to care what his subjects think and if a soul dares protest he's had for treason. Slowly he turned back to face his hosts.

Carver spoke softly but with vehemence. 'England is a stinking mess of corruption and disease. Master Mullins, surely you want your children to grow up in a land free of depravity, founded on godliness, honor and virtue. Where men elect their leaders. No more blind subservience to a king proclaimed to be next to God.'

'You are talking treason,' Mullins whispered. 'The King **is** next to God.'

'Some would disagree, Mr Mullins, and our leader, William Brewster, is in hiding for printing such ideas.' Carver breathed his words. 'But once we are on the other side of the ocean there is nothing the King can do.'

'No,' Mullins said, keeping his head lowered. 'I'll not be party to a treasonous plot. I don't want to endure the rack and be hung, drawn and quartered.' He raised his head and sat back on his stool, hands pushing against the table, grateful for the sheltering volume of talk and laughter.

'You need not fear.' Weston leaned forward, quiet, reassuring. 'There is no plot. And in America we'll be free of spies and royal dictates. Our colony will be a settlement where men prosper through their own ability and hard work. Not through birth, trading favors with men in high places, or bribery. Equal justice for all; where murderers and charlatans do not walk free because they have connections. Think on it. A land where every man has the chance to better his lot. What say you, Master Mullins? A man of your understanding and experience would be a great asset in building and administering our colony.' Weston leaned back slightly, sitting straight, hands folded on the table. He assumed a dignified, somewhat detached demeanor, his features composed, a half-smile conveying confidence as if to say, 'I have what you need. You would be a fool not to accept.'

Mullins recognized the manner and ploys of a man practiced at persuasion. He looked past his hosts at the oak paneling behind their heads. He stared into the veining glowing deep brown in the wavering candlelight. English oak. Solid English oak. He turned to Weston. 'Who else is on the Board of Investors? How much have they contributed? How well funded is this venture?'

Weston leaned forward. 'It is not our practice to divulge details of our investors' finances.' He drew a deep breath and let it out slowly. 'But for you... I'll give you a notion.' Weston named six investors beside himself who had each invested five hundred pounds. Mullins knew of several; wealthy, canny men. 'Shares are ten pounds each,' Weston continued. 'With seventy investors so far, many of them men of accomplished status like yourself, buying upwards of ten shares, you can see we are well funded.'

Feeling giddy with the enormity of his decision, Mullins gazed again into the oak paneling. He had reviewed both sides of the argument, again and again, back and forth. His estate was leeching away in high prices and taxes, even as business dwindled. He couldn't bear to see his family reduced to poverty. But at least if they remained here in England they would be in a familiar life, amongst kith and kin, not cast upon the vast ocean to sail to an unknown wilderness with only strangers as companions. He sensed Weston staring at him, fidgeting; twisting his hands, shuffling his feet. Let him wait. Carver sat still, head slightly bowed. Carver is right. This country stinks of corruption and disease. In America he could build a new life, prosperous, clean and just.

No risk no gain. I would prosper, being the only shoemaker. My lass, Priscilla, an adventurous spirit, would thrive on the challenges. Fine looking; she'd have the pick of suitors. Young Joseph. Already showing intelligence, fleet afoot, sporting. They would have space to grow, make good lives of their own. And Alice, dear wife. I know she'll be apprehensive. But I reckon she'd give it her all, and I would build her a fine house.

His eyes met Carver's honest gaze. He liked the man, and sensed that for all his suspect beliefs, he was a sensitive man and trustworthy. He did not warm to Weston. But Weston was a man who made things happen, keen to make money and nothing wrong with that. *The venture seems solid. That is the important thing.*

Mullins drew his hand across his eyes. Slowly he reached into his doublet, fingering the threadbare velvet of his money pouch. 'I'll pay two hundred pounds for twenty shares and passage for five.'

'Did I hear you right?' Weston flared. 'Ridiculous. How can we finance a venture on chicken feed?'

Mullins stared into Weston's face. Small beads of sweat gathered on the merchant's upper lip. He thrust his stubby thumbs into his waistcoat.

I reckon they need me. 'I'll offer two hundred and twenty-five pounds. That's all I've got.'

'To have a man of your experience in our number,' Weston said, 'agreed.'

Mullins withdrew his money pouch and holding it out of sight on his lap, counted out two hundred and twenty-five pounds. He kept back enough money to pay for his lodging and to buy gifts for his family; gifts to celebrate the start of a new life.

Chapter 2

June 1620

Thames Street – London

The air hung heavy with dockside smells: rotting fish, rotting carcasses, men's sweat mingled with the acrid smell of the river. John Alden's nostrils and throat cloyed. He sweated in the sultry evening heat, as wearily he trudged along a narrow alleyway that ran parallel to the quay. The upper stories of the houses leaned inwards creating a tunnel with shafts of light filtering through. He glanced around for pickpockets and robbers lurking in shadowy doorways and looked up, preparing to dodge objects and slops flung from windows above. A woman ranted; then came the crash of splintering pottery on the cobbles behind him. A filthy ragged child stepped out from a doorway; stretched out a flea-bitten arm.

'Please, sir.'

John reached in his pouch and at arm's length dropped a half-penny into the cupped hand. Hurrying on he caught the toe of his boot on a loose cobblestone and stumbled. *Strewth. Time to seek refuge.*

Pushing open a tavern door, he stooped to enter and shuffled through the sawdust into a dim, dusty room permeated with pipe smoke, the pleasant smell of ale, sounds of raucous laughter and hands slapping thighs and tables. The room was filled with sailors disembarked from ships moored in the Thames. Removing his hat he asked the tavern-keeper for a jug of ale. A call from one of the drinkers rose above the surrounding din. 'Look at that head 'o hair. Yeller as cornsilk. Must be from strange parts.' John spun on his heel to face a heavy belching lout staggering toward him. He wasn't bothered. He could flatten any man in a brawl. However, the tavern-keeper shoved the drunkard back onto his stool.

'Shut yer mouth or I'll throw ya out.'

Jug of ale in hand, John seated himself alone at a small table, and staring into space, pondered his predicament. Here he was, a skilled cooper, taught by his father from a lad in a time when there was work aplenty. But now, with wood so scarce and expensive, no one wanted a wandering cooper. Merchants made do with the barrels they already had. Nigh on a year he had traipsed through towns all along the coast. No work. He gazed into his tankard. Would he have to beg? So far he'd survived doing odd jobs on farms, but farmworkers were a penny a dozen.

'Mr Alden! John!'

John started. A wave of ale spilled over the lip of his tankard. That deep hearty voice. 'Master Jones!' He stood in greeting. The sea captain clapped him on the shoulder.

'I'll get another jug.'

John flushed with surprised delight as his gray-haired friend drew up a stool.

'How many years? Here's to you.' Master Jones raised his tankard.

'Reckon about two. Finding work here and there but almost none the past year. And you, sir?'

'Been plying the seas, to Flanders, France. The usual. Until now. Been commissioned to take a load of discontents to North America. Took my fancy. Always wanted to cross the Atlantic.'

''Tis a long way,' John said.

'Aye, but sail in the summer, before the westerlies blow, should only take a month.' Master Jones went to the bar to light his pipe. 'New horizons,' he said, settling again. 'Captain John Smith was telling me 'tis a wondrous land. Endless forests, fish, rich soil.' He leaned forward, forearms resting on the table. 'Good fortune to find you here, John. The organizer, man called Weston, has asked me to find someone to maintain the barrels in the hold. You're just the man. Deal is, sign up to stay for a year, help get a colony built, and then you can return if you wish. Passage and victuals free. Give you work and a chance to start afresh.'

John peered into his ale as if it were a fortune-teller's crystal ball. *Crossing the Atlantic. Fearsome. A land of endless forests. Could make a good living if I liked it there. Could marry and make my own home: a solid, loving home.* He looked up into Master Jones' crinkly eyes. 'You reckon?'

'Aye, for sure. With your skills in woodworking you could build your own business, with no interference, probably no competition for a time.'

John gazed again into his ale.

'Your uncle was dastardly.' Master Jones reached across and put a hand on John's shoulder. 'But there's nowt you can do to be rid of him – except wait for him to die, and that could be many years hence.'

John looked up. 'I keep hoping for word he's met his end; sickened or been murdered, but 'tis a vain hope. I'll never get my father's business back. Damn.'

'You're young and strong – in your prime. Surely the new world is worth a try. As I said, you can always return after a year if you want.'

Don't relish the sea crossing; a hell of a long way – but what sort of man am I if I can't take a risk? 'Agreed.'

'Good man. I'll have you on my ship once more.'

'Still the *Mayflower*?'

'Aye, fine little vessel. We sail a month from today – 3rd July.'

'Aye, sir. I'll be there.'

'Promised my dear wife I'd not stay out. I miss her and the children, so many months away. We moved to London a year ago – please call by. Harwich House, Candlewick Street. Mistress Jones will give me no end of trouble if she doesn't set eyes on you, and you're most welcome to bide with us.' He touched his hat. 'Goodbye, John. Hope to see you soon and don't forget – we sail a month today.'

'Aye, sir.' John stayed, seated, sipping his ale. He closed his eyes against the sting of pipe smoke and, wrapped in the comforting blanket of men's voices, let his mind drift back into memories he usually kept at bay; his father's long, slow death from consumption; John aged fourteen, taking on his mantle to be master of his trade, foremost coopers in Harwich. Even while his father was still alive, John witnessed his mother and uncle kissing, fondling and fornicating in secret corners. They wed before the earth had settled on his father's grave.

Then the beatings. On the slightest pretext ten to twenty horsewhip lashes, sometimes more, and when his uncle was spent with whipping, the kicking boot, in his stomach, groin, face. *Was he trying to kill me?*

He remembered the day when, recovered enough from a beating to stand, he stumbled out the front door. A familiar voice called, 'John! My lad.' Master Jones strode to his side. 'John, what has happened to you? How fares your father?' With Master Jones supporting him they walked to the quay and John told his story.

'I was always uneasy about your father's brother. Something about him smelled bad. Your father was a good man. Many an hour we passed by your hearth exchanging yarns. You sat still as a stick, listening.' Master Jones put an arm round his shoulder. He flinched. Raw – red raw pain.

'You're not to go back to that house. Come bide with us. Mistress Jones will treat those wounds and feed you. Skin and bone you are. Come with me when I next sail. Learn the ways of the sea. Who knows, you could become a sea captain – have your own ship.'

John opened his eyes, took a last swig of ale. *Pity I couldn't take to it. Three years I tried. Wanted to succeed for Master Jones. However, he understood. Some men are meant for the sea, some for land. So I've been wandering and now, just at the moment when I'm so far down, almost penniless, Master Jones appears with a way forward. Is this a sign?* John shuffled through the sawdust to the door.

Chapter 3

July 1620

Dorking to London

It is so hot. I wish I weren't laced up in this thick gown. And poor old Dolly, pulling our heavy load. Priscilla Mullins wriggled amongst pots and pans, kettles, rugs and chairs, trying to make a comfortable nest. She looked up at the blazing blue sky and longed for a soothing breeze. *How many hours will we have to endure this grating noise of wheels on chalk and choking white dust. But I must not feel cross. We are on an adventure.*

Mother and Father sat on the cross bench, looking straight ahead, Mother swishing at flies with her willow bough. Her young brother, Joseph, slept; a welcome respite from continual storytelling.

Priscilla reached into the small pouch at her waist and pulled out a parcel wrapped in her handkerchief. Her secret treasure. Given to her by Father when he returned from London, to celebrate their coming voyage on the *Mayflower*. He'd also brought her a gardening book, a book of recipes for Mother, and a small musket for Joseph.

But he'd given her the sash when she was alone, milking Bessie in the field behind their house.

'This is for you, lass. I want you to have something of luxury and beauty. Keep it safe. Your mother wouldn't approve of the expense, as there is no practical use.'

Making sure that no one was looking, Priscilla unfolded the sash, only partway. Gazing at the wide black satin embroidered with gold silk, she stroked the fabric and imagined. *How lovely around my small waist against a deep blue gown. Harry said my eyes are midnight blue pools. He had charm, Harry, but not much wit. And he would only ever be a tenant farmer. I don't fancy being a farmer's wife!* She traced a finger over her nose, cheekbones and full lips. *Surely my features are too fine to be seen only by livestock and babes. Or a gown of emerald green. My hair would go well.* She gathered a curl of her rich dark auburn hair round a finger and inspected it. *Yes. Or a gown of deep crimson – would set off my fair skin, neck and bosom.* She peered down at her curved breasts, pushed up with a tightly laced bodice, her neckline low, almost exposing a nipple. *I wish I had a mirror. If I marry a nobleman I will have a mirror. Pity I'll have to wear a high neck when I marry.* She refolded the sash, wrapped it in her handkerchief and replaced it in her pouch, smarting with the memory. She had made good use of her beauty and wiles enticing James. Tall, handsome, son of a magistrate, he'd been attending the grammar school and was a good catch. She was the envy of all her friends and betrothal was expected any day. Then, in the evening, walking home from milking Bessie, she'd spied him and her cousin Eliza behind the hedge, making love, about to… Priscilla brushed away a tear. It was unbearable, inexplicable. At least now she could escape the humiliation. *When we reach America, I'll show them. Father will build a grand house – he promised – and I'll be courted. There must be some worthy young gentlemen on this voyage.*

Resting her head against a rolled up rug, Priscilla lapsed into a dreamy doze, drifting through images of tearful goodbyes to visions of fine houses, walled gardens and gentlemen coming to call.

'Are we nearly there? How much longer?' Joseph's high pitched questions roused her. The sun was halfway down to the western horizon. A soft breeze eased her discomfort and stirred the petals of wild roses twined in the hedgerow. Frail pink-white petals, delicate as a butterfly's wing. Small birds now had the energy to twitter and flit about. Looking down to the right Priscilla saw a stone marker 'London VI Miles'.

'Only a little over an hour now. Come on, Dolly, I know it has been a long hard day,' Father encouraged the old mare. Dolly put her ears forward and tried to quicken her pace, but she stumbled.

'Father, what will happen to Dolly?' Priscilla had the fearful thought she might be butchered.

'Don't worry. When I was staying at the Star Inn I arranged for a man to have her. Master Mathewe. He'll meet us at Galley Quay.'

Priscilla's stomach churned with nervous excitement. Wondering and wondering about what lay ahead, she hardly saw the last of the hedgerows and fields. They all passed in a mist. And then they were in sight of London Bridge!

'Look – look – look!' Joseph jumped up in excitement.

'Joseph, hold still! You'll make it harder for Dolly.' As they approached the massive Great Stone Gate to cross the bridge, Father said, 'Look to the left.' Priscilla was amazed. So many boats and barges. A person could go from one side of the river to the other by climbing across them.

Joseph called out, 'There's a glass boat!' Priscilla looked further to the left upstream and sure enough, floating among the smaller wooden boats, some carrying passengers, some transporting casks, barrels and timber, was a huge glass barge. A high dragon-head bow adorned a vessel of grace and beauty. From the dragon-head the line of the barge followed a long gentle curve to the stern where a banner fluttered in the breeze. From bow to stern a patterned strip, glistening gilt, decorated the side of the boat.

''Tis like a magical ship!' Priscilla clutched her hands.

'That is the King's barge, and those are the King's swans swimming all around,' Father said.

Priscilla imagined herself amongst the lords and ladies of the King's court, lounging on cushions, listening to the King's musicians as a crew of oarsmen rowed them smoothly, gliding along the river.

Now, about to pass through the Great Stone Gate, Priscilla looked up and gasped. Too late she put her hands over Joseph's eyes. Mother hid her face in her hands. But there was no protection from the sight and stench of rotting heads and skulls stuck on tall spikes. 'Why?' came Priscilla's hoarse question.

'This is what happens to traitors,' Father said. Frowning, he urged Dolly on through the gate and into the midst of a noisy, jostling crowd of horse-drawn carriages and carts, folk on horseback and on foot. Priscilla and Joseph held onto the sides of the cart so as not to be thrown about and bruised. The bridge was lined with tall, three-story houses and shops, and Priscilla marveled at an enormous, brightly painted timber house with glass windows, built right across the bridge with a passageway through the center so traffic could pass.

'Father, when will we get to the other side?' Joseph asked.

'It will take a while, lad. A man at the Star Inn told me this bridge is eight hundred feet long! And with all the folk and horses jostling about and getting in the way it might take some time.'

Market folk called out, 'Buy my fine sausages. Finest in all London Town!'

'Hot puddings and pies! Here, dearie, have a nice pie. Ye look peaky.' A plump untidy woman thrust a pie at Joseph.

'No thank-ye,' Mother replied sharply.

'Rosemary, rue, bay, lavender.'

'Ribbons and laces.'

As they passed through the final gate at the northern end, Father steered Dolly's head to the right. Priscilla gazed through a forest of masts and sails, stretching down the river as far as she could see.

'Oh, William!' Mother exclaimed. 'All those ships! There must be hundreds and hundreds!'

'This is the main port of London. It is deep enough here for big ships to moor. Upstream, the other side of the bridge is for smaller boats and barges,' Father said.

Burly, rough men hurried everywhere, shouting as they heaved and tossed barrels and crates across from barges to big buildings on the left.

'Father, what is in all those?' Joseph asked.

'That'll be goods from far shores: wine from France, spices from hot lands t'other side of the world, cloth from Flanders. The stevedores are loading all those goods into the warehouses where merchants will come to collect them. Now, here we are at Galley Quay. See that ship anchored yonder?' Priscilla followed Father's gaze and gesture. 'That'll be the *Mayflower*.' He shaded his eyes. 'And I'm sure… yes, there's Deacon Carver.' He handed Mother the reins. 'Hold Dolly, Alice, while I greet the Deacon and find a sailor to unload.' Priscilla watched as Father strode across the quay to meet a tall, slim man overseeing provisions being loaded onto a barge. She gazed at the ship. It seemed enormous: three masts reaching way up into the sky and a towering castle-like structure at the stern, rising as high as a three-story house. Attached to each mast was a latticework of ropes rising from the deck up to the tapering top.

Vile odors from the river hit her nose, and the noise! The shouting and banging, catcalling and cursing of stevedores reeled round her head. After the long hot journey, the excitement of crossing London Bridge, and horror of the gory heads on spikes, Priscilla felt giddy and faint. 'Mother, the stench. I feel unwell.'

'We must be strong, Priscilla,' came the terse response.

Priscilla thought back to the day Father had returned from London. He'd thrown his hat into the room, caught Mother in his arms. 'We'll be going to America!' Eyes sparkling, with the excitement of a young man, he told them of the plan to build a new life in a land full of riches. 'Don't you fear, Alice,' he responded to the look of shock and dismay on Mother's face. 'I'll build you a fine house and you need never be cold again. America has endless forests for the taking.'

'When do we depart?' Mother had asked.

'July.'

In the months that followed, as they sorted and packed, Priscilla had spied Mother weeping when she thought she was alone. She wished Mother were like Father, keen to set out on an adventure.

Just now she wished Father would return to the cart. Glancing to her left she noticed narrow stairs and a passage that cut through the warehouses to the streets beyond. It was dark and, she imagined, dank and stinking. A woman leaned out of an upper story window to empty a chamber pot, the contents splashing onto a man passing below who cursed and shook his fist. Joseph sat very still, wide-eyed and silent. Priscilla put an arm round his shoulder. She was glad their servant, Robert, hefty, young and strong, was seated behind.

'There's Father.' Joseph pointed. Far down the quay amidst the shouting stevedores, Father appeared, accompanied by three burly sailors.

'These are our possessions,' Father said as they reached the cart. 'All labeled 'Mullins'.'

'Aye, aye. Heave to,' one sailor commanded the others.

Robert and Father helped Priscilla and Joseph climb down from the pile. Within minutes their household goods and trunks were in a heap on the quay. Father explained which items were to go in the hold and which to be placed in their living space.

'Aye, aye. Cursed landlubbers. Take up room – always seasick,' the lead sailor muttered.

Priscilla raised her chin. *Vile man, way above himself. If he's in the Mayflower's crew, he had best keep out of our way.*

'Ah! Master Mathewe,' Father called to a bent elderly man stumping along, with a limp and a stick. Priscilla knew it was time to part with Dolly.

Master Mathewe raised his hat. 'Good-day, ladies. Now don't you fear, your Dolly will have a good home with me. She'll be well fed and not worked too hard.' Mother handed the reins to Master Mathewe and Father gave her a hand down. Priscilla and Joseph went forward to stroke Dolly's muzzle for the last time. 'Oh, Dolly, Dolly,' Priscilla murmured softly, stroking the old mare behind the ears and down the neck as she had always done ever since she was a child. The mare pricked her ears forward and nodded with a soft whickering sound. 'Farewell, Dolly.' She pulled Joseph away, wiping the tears from her cheeks.

'There, me old beauty, thee'll come along with me now.' Master Mathewe climbed up onto the cross bench and gently persuaded Dolly to 'Gee-up', pulling the empty cart behind.

'Now,' Father said, clearing his throat, 'we'll go up these stairs and through the streets to the Star Inn. Tomorrow we sail!'

Chapter 4

July 1620

London - Southampton

'Aboard! Aboard! Y'beggardly landlubbers!'

Priscilla's gaze traveled up the *Mayflower*'s hull, up the rope ladder, to a huge sailor standing feet astride by the ship's rail. Her heart sank as she recognized the surly man who had unloaded their cart.

'Wretched scum. Nothin but trouble ye'll be.' The man muttered and cursed as one by one, the passengers cautiously stepped from the barge to climb the rope ladder. Priscilla followed Father who had helped Mother and then Joseph to begin their ascent. Trying to curl her feet round the rope rungs she struggled not to trip on her skirts and keep her balance as the ship's hull rocked in the waters of the Thames. When she was one rung down from the deck rail the sailor taunted, 'There's a fair wench. Hurry on, hurry on or we'll sail w'out ya. Ya wouldn't want that now.'

Horrible man. As Priscilla grabbed hold of the rail the sailor took her arm. 'Don't touch me!' She yanked her arm out of his grasp, and felt herself falling. She clawed at the rail posts. A strong, unseen hand held her waist from behind, keeping her steady, guiding her over the rail onto the hot noisy deck where sailors called out, tossing barrels and trunks, hurrying, knocking into passengers.

'Thank you. Thank you, sir.' Priscilla grabbed hold of the rail and turned, feeling herself blushing. A trickle of sweat traveled down her neck toward her bosom.

'Close call. Easy to lose your balance,' the man said, his voice deep and genial.

'Yes.' She took a deep breath. 'I… It was that vile sailor. So disrespectful… how dare he…'

'Sailors can be a rough lot, but I can tell you Master Jones will be sure you ladies come to no harm.' The man doffed his hat letting loose a tumbling mass of blond curls. Priscilla looked into his open, inviting face, noted his strong arms and physique. Her tummy flipped. But his garb. Lowly. Brown leather jerkin and breeches, holland shirt. *And his bootlace is untied. No.*

'Setting sail for a better life?' The man leaned against the rail, one foot across the other, arms folded across his chest.

'Yes. Father wants us to prosper.'

'Your father a farmer?'

'No! My father is a member of the shoemakers' guild. He makes footwear for the nobility.' Priscilla raised her chin.

'Ah. Great asset. We'll all need sturdy shoes and boots.'

'I'm sure my father will have an apprentice to make footwear for the common folk. He specializes in fine boots and slippers for those of superior status. They pay a handsome sum. Our house has glass windows. Father says in the new world we'll have an even grander house with more glass windows than the one we've left.'

'Oy!' A sailor bumped into her from behind. Her rescuer reached to steady her. She snatched her arm away and took a step back.

'A house fit for a fair... elevated lass like yourself.' A smile hovered on his lips as he leaned back against the rail. His glance traveled down her body and back to her eyes. 'You'd perhaps be wanting a cooper such as I for a servant?' He raised an eyebrow. His eyes laughed.

'Sir! I never.' Priscilla tilted her nose and looked away. 'I must find my family.'

'Mr Alden, Mr Alden... Good, good.'

'Master Jones!'

Priscilla's savior eased past her to meet the hearty greeting. Tall, solid, with gray hair and gray-blue eyes, the *Mayflower*'s Master and Commander wore a deep blue tailed coat with shiny brass buttons, crisp white breeches, tall polished black boots and freshly brushed black hat.

'Come along to my cabin.' Master Jones put a hand across Alden's shoulders and led him away.

How dare they! Positively rude. Didn't even... ignored me, as if I weren't here! Flushed with anger, Priscilla pushed her way into the jostling crowd, standing on tiptoe to search for Mother and Father. The upturned ship's rowing boat, lashed between the mainmast and the fo'castle made it impossible to see across the deck.

'On wi' ya – git up there – faster, faster.' Hearing the crack of a whip above, Priscilla craned her neck, squinting against the fiery sun. A lad no older than Joseph was scrambling up the rigging chased by a grown sailor; up... up. The whip flicked his legs drawing blood.

Priscilla swayed and covered her eyes. Something banged into her legs, throwing her off balance. A dog. A massive dog, wagging its tail, slobbered on her skirt. 'Get off! Get away!' *Oh where is Mother? The stench. Must get across to the rail; I feel sick.* Tears pricked her eyes.

'Out o' the way... move!' A sailor carrying a trunk on his back pushed her aside. With tears blurring her vision, Priscilla pushed and shoved her way to the rail, collapsing against it. Holding on, she closed her eyes, swallowed hard and steadied herself. Opening them again she stared at the huge ropes holding the *Mayflower* at anchor. Thick as a man's wrist, they were covered in dead fish, seaweed and filth. In the river she saw floating feces, dead vermin, even a dead sheep. A gull swooped down and pecked at the carcass. Far over to the left a human corpse, bloated and purple, bumped against the ship's hull. Mercifully she didn't retch but grabbed the rail and twisted round, concentrating all her effort on searching for Mother and Father. *Where could they be?* Fear gripped her; she became a small child again, parted from Mother, lost in the marketplace, abandoned. *Would they have gone off the ship and left me?* She knew Mother wasn't happy about this voyage. *Ah! Father's hat!* Priscilla elbowed her way across the deck to her family, standing by the stern rail.

'My dear, you're white as chalk.' Mother clasped Priscilla's hands. 'Cold and clammy. What has happened? Are you unwell?'

Before she could answer, the sailor bellowed, 'All passengers below! Hurry! Out o' the way wi'ya!'

Priscilla followed Father to the hatch and the ladder that led to below decks. Only halfway down the air became dim and dusty. After the bright sunlight above, she could not see. In their half-blind confusion passengers jostled into one another garrulously searching for their belongings. *How will we ever all fit?* 'Ouch!' She whacked her head against a beam. 'Only a midget or a child could stand up straight down here.'

'Ach – I've banged my elbow,' Mother tut-tutted. 'Where's Joseph?'

'I'll search.' Priscilla clambered through the jumble of trunks and boxes. 'Joseph, where are you?'

'Boo!'

She jumped and whirled round, tearing her skirt on a protruding nail. 'Oh bother!'

Joseph grinned at her from behind a cannon. 'Scared you!' He taunted as he chased after a calico cat picking its way among skirts, legs, and the multitude of human belongings. The cat slithered out of his grasp as Priscilla grabbed his collar.

'Come with me and stay put!' She scolded and hauled him back to where Mother sat, slumped, on a trunk. 'Mother, where is Father?'

'Over there, behind that cannon with the gentleman who was on the quay yesterday, overseeing the loading of goods. What is his name?'

'Deacon Carver.'

Father was nodding as the Deacon gestured toward Priscilla and Mother. He then picked his way through the chaos to join them. 'We'll have this space near the hatch,' he said. 'More air here. Not so fetid as farther back toward the stern.'

Joseph, his arm hooked around a stout post, swung in a circle. 'What are these posts, Father? They're like tree trunks growing through the roof.'

'These three are the masts and this is the capstan, for raising and lowering heavy cargo.' Father put a hand on Joseph's shoulder and gave a kindly squeeze. 'Now hush,' he said as Deacon Carver raised his hand for attention.

Gradually folk fell silent, all eyes on the Deacon's face.

'Welcome. As you may know, I am responsible for the care and management of all passengers for the duration of the crossing. In due course I will give details of rules and procedures, but for the moment our priority is to establish order. Therefore, would you kindly pull your trunks into your allotted spaces?'

'We'd best stand over by the ladder, out of the way.' Mother carved a path through trunks, baskets and bedding rolls. Priscilla followed, grasping Joseph's hand. A sharp bark and pawing at her skirt halted her. Another dog. A spaniel. 'Don't pet it, Joseph. You never know. Why these dogs? How many more? Go away – off.'

The two dogs barged about, tails wagging, while excited children leapfrogged over barrels and each other. The chickens and goats penned near the fo'castle squawked and bleated and a sow grunted.

'Can you please hold those dogs still – and the children?' Deacon Carver called out above the din. 'We cannot shift these jumbled piles of stuff in all this commotion.' Priscilla chuckled.

Finally, when all was in order, the Deacon spoke again. 'Thank you. When we reach Southampton we'll put up walls so each family will have some privacy.'

'Reckon I'll go down in the cargo hold and check our belongings are stacked together,' Father said.

'We'll sort the trunk.' Mother took a key from her pouch.

'Please may I go and play?' Joseph pointed to a cluster of children gathered round a cannon in the far corner.

'Yes, but no mischief!' Mother said.

Priscilla pushed back the heavy trunk lid and unpacked bedding, a chamber pot, a trencher, knives and tankards. 'Look. I've found your little bag of rosemary, lavender and rue.'

'Good. We are so crowded, likely to all die of disease before we ever reach America. Need every remedy and protection we've got.' There was a crash and wailing. Mother wheeled on her heel and hurried toward the children.

Priscilla bent over the trunk and dug down to retrieve their Bible, psalter and almanac. She wished she could bury her head in the linen to get away from the high pitched chatter and thumping and raucous sailors' calls. She was shoved from behind and stood abruptly.

'So sorry. Sorry, dear.' Leaning into her was a large woman. 'I'm desperate... desperate for... ' She pointed at the chamber pot. 'I can't find ours.'

'Here.' Priscilla held the woman steady as she squatted.

'I've been waiting so long.' When at last she'd finished, Priscilla helped her to her feet. The chamber pot was almost full to the brim.

'Thank you. Goody Billington. And you?'

'Mistress Mullins.' Priscilla raised her chin.

Goody Billington raised her chin. 'Mistress are ye? Sorry to leave you with that.' She nodded toward the chamber pot and slowly shuffled down the deck.

Priscilla seethed. *How dare she!*

Gingerly, carefully, Priscilla picked up the offensive pot full of urine. She would have to climb the ladder and empty it over the side of the ship.

Rung by rung, struggling not to trip on her skirts, holding onto the ladder with one hand, grasping her foul smelling burden in the other, she climbed as quickly as she could, fearing a sailor would come and push her away. Sweat covered her face and neck and made her hands slippery. Once she almost dropped the pot, and urine spilled onto her skirts. It felt like a miracle when she climbed onto the upper deck, hurried to the rail and poured the liquid into the Thames. Suddenly hands grabbed her waist. She screamed, whirled round and bashed a sailor's face with the pot.

'Thought m'be y'd be wantin somethin, comin up'ere against orders.' The man leered, grinning, eyes fixed on her breasts, unperturbed by the clout he'd received.

Priscilla wielded the pot again, ran to the hatch and almost threw herself back down the ladder. She looked for Mother, who was now at the far end of their quarters talking with another woman; then sank onto a pile of bedding, taking deep breaths as she wiped the sweat from her face and bosom. *What has Father done? Why are we down here in this filthy dark place? Why do we not have our own private cabin?* She thought of their room in the Star Inn. She knew no cabin on a ship could be as comfortable and pleasant as that – but this. *We might as well be cattle – though the sailors would show more respect to cattle than they do us. But Father must know what he is doing. Only a month. When we are in America he and Robert will build a big house and in no time at all we'll have a fine town with wide streets.*

Priscilla delved into the trunk and took out her own small box of treasures. Unlocking it, she took the sash from her pouch and laid it carefully beside her lace handkerchief. *One day.* Sighing, she locked the box and buried it deep down near the bottom of the trunk, keeping her gardening book handy near the top.

'Have you found our Bible?' Mother's voice made Priscilla jump. 'What have you been doing?' Priscilla recounted what had happened with Goody Billington but said nothing about the sailor accosting her on deck. It would only cause worry.

'Hmpf. I can see this voyage is going to be a trial. I must ask your father to request pails. How else are we to manage?' Nodding in the direction of excited babble and scolding coming from behind a pile of trunks, Mother said, 'Those children are going to be a handful. There's a mischief maker amongst them, called Francis. You're not to be led astray by him, Joseph. And there are four little mites, all hollow-eyed and thin, without a mother or father. Poor things.' She looked to inspect Priscilla's unpacking. 'Good. Everything here we'll need for the night. We've got bread and cheese left from breakfast and I'm sure we'll be given a ration of ale.' Hands on hips, she declared, 'We'll be a whole month with scarce a hot meal. Mistress Carver said the only fire is in the fo'castle, where the ship's cook prepares meals for the crew.' She shook her head. 'Nor able to sit at table. Here. Take this hunk of bread and cheese over to Robert. He's worked hard. Look… he's over there.'

'But he's our servant. They're all servants over there. Surely I shouldn't…' Priscilla tilted her nose.

'Priscilla. This is not the place to have airs.' Mother thrust the bread and cheese into her daughter's hands.

Priscilla struggled along the narrow pathway to where Robert sat with a group of single men. 'Do you all have to share this small space? All dozen of you?' She handed Robert the food.

'Aye, we're at the bottom of the heap, Mistress,' Robert smiled ruefully. 'And we'll be piled in a heap, sharing this patch.'

Priscilla felt a sudden unwelcome pang. *A dozen of them, in that tiny patch, hardly as big as a pig's sty. No matter. We are all crowded and they are only servants.* She set about picking her way back, taking care to keep stooped over and not trip.

'Out o' the way – move!' The jeering sailor barked from behind and pushed her aside. 'Take up all our space, vermin. Us crew can't bring truck to trade with the Indians.' He glared at Priscilla. 'Stealing our rightful gains, you are.' He spat. A large glob of spittle hit her skirt. He kicked at bedding, rugs and small stools as he lumbered to the ladder to climb up on deck.

Shaken, Priscilla stumbled in his wake. Mother comforted her with a hug. 'Poor lass. He's a beast! Gives orders to the other sailors. Hope they won't all be that bad!'

'Splendid, splendid.' Father emerged from the cargo hold. 'All our belongings are together, everything in order. Alice, even you would be impressed with how all the provisions are arranged, the farming and hunting gear, and all the crates and trunks and pieces of furniture and carpets. Amazing. Priscilla, it's the young man who saved you from falling in the Thames. John Alden, he's called. Signed on for a year. Cooper by trade.'

He may have saved me but he was unforgivably rude, not introducing me to the captain. Who does he think he is? Priscilla frowned, pursed her lips and rounded on Joseph. 'Hold still. Stop that poking about and fidgeting. Time to learn your letters.' She ferreted down through the trunk 'til she found Joseph's slate.

'No souls on deck. Stay below all o' ya!' The sailor's face appeared in the hatch. He slammed it shut.

'Too dark, too dark, can't see,' Joseph crowed.

Priscilla stood still, grasping Mother's arm. The darkness brought a hush of waiting. A loud deep voice called out, 'Man the windlass.' Shadowy shapes of sailors appeared, just a few, gathered round the windlass, operating it with wooden staves. Hearing a clunk she squeezed Mother's arm, whispering hoarsely, 'What was that?'

'Hauling up the anchor,' Father said.

Then from above the command, 'Make fast and cat the anchor.' The sound of hurrying feet and the order, 'Loose the main s'l, the fore s'l.' This was the moment; they would be carried away, imprisoned in this vessel with frightening sailors and sounds: timbers creaking, the slurp and gurgle of the river as the ship, loosed from her anchorage, tilted slightly to the side, sailing down the Thames.

'Here, we'd best sit on the trunk lid.' Mother pulled Priscilla to sit beside her. Father leaned against the masthead. 'Where is Joseph?'

A dim shaft of light revealed a small figure at the top of the ladder close against the closed hatch. 'Joseph?' Priscilla called.

'I want to hear the first mate's orders.'

'Come down from there this instant,' Father said.

Joseph climbed down and groped his way to stand beside Priscilla. 'I wish I could be on deck to see how we sail down the river with so many boats in the way.' Priscilla thought of the lad she'd seen being chased up the rigging and hoped he was safe.

A soft, light body jumped onto her lap. Purring. Priscilla stroked the silky fur. Even in the murky shadows she recognized the small calico cat. 'Where did you come from? You pretty thing.'

'Will it be ours?' Joseph asked.

'I expect it's the ship's cat,' Mother said. 'I hope it doesn't have fleas.'

'It is probably seeking refuge from the dogs, and boys like you, Joseph, who give chase.' Priscilla hoped the cat would adopt her.

On and on. It seemed the ship was creeping along until at last Priscilla felt a swing and pull as the wind filled the sails.

'Here we go,' Father said. 'We've left the Thames. We're sailing straight down the Channel.'

Chapter 5

July 1620

London – Southampton

A sailor opened the hatch. 'Ya can come up now. See how many can stand. Ha!'

Priscilla pushed to be among the first to climb the ladder. The deck rolled and pitched under her feet, one instant rising to meet her, the next, falling away. She grabbed whatever rope, post or rail she could get hold of and waited until she got her balance enough to stagger across to the outside rail. Around her folk were slipping, falling, calling out. Holding tightly to the rail, she gazed up at the high white chalk cliffs rising on the right, topped with green turf, vivid against a bright blue, cloudless sky.

'France is over there, across the water,' Father said as he and Mother and Joseph lurched their last few steps to join her. 'Mr Alden told me the *Mayflower* has sailed to France many a time, fetching cloth and wine. The spilled wine is why our ship smells sweet.'

'I wondered why the air below isn't foul,' Priscilla said, grabbing Joseph's arm. 'Hold on and stay still or you'll slip overboard!'

'Because of the wars and high prices,' Father continued, 'folk no longer have enough money to buy fine cloth and wine. A good reason for us to go to America, land of endless riches.'

Priscilla caught Mother frowning, shaking her head.

'Father.' Priscilla spoke just above a whisper. 'Who is that fine couple in such elegant garb?'

'Ah yes. Deacon Carver introduced them to me. Master and Mistress Winslow. Wealthy. Apparently he leaves behind a large estate. They've joined the religious group and Winslow prints all their pamphlets; writes some of the discourses. He's been in trouble several times; printing machines smashed.'

Priscilla sighed, examining Winslow's jacket of fine velvet, lace collar and cuffs, a silk tassel at the neck and small silver buttons all down the front. She appraised his stature: medium height, compact build, dignified. He was in conversation with his wife and smiled, revealing a gap between his two upper front teeth which gave him an endearing boyish air. *If only there were other men like him on board, younger, unmarried.*

'Order! Order!' A deep resonant voice called out over the deck. Chatter died down and eyes turned toward the half-deck where Master Jones stood looking down on the passengers. His crew hastily gathered in formation.

'I am your captain. The first mate is second in command followed by the bosun. He gestured toward the vile sailor. 'Dear Lord, no,' Priscilla murmured.

'My orders for the navigation and sailing of this ship must be obeyed at all times. No exceptions. And you must all follow my regulations for good behavior, as instructed by the first mate. Any seaman who disobeys will be flogged.' He stared hard at the passengers. 'My word is law for every man on board this ship.'

'Aye, aye, sir,' responded crew and passengers.

Priscilla nudged Joseph who stood mesmerized, staring up at the captain eyes wide. 'Don't gawk,' she whispered.

Master Jones climbed down the short ladder. Women gathered their children in close and men doffed their hats as he passed. He stopped for his crew to doff their caps and Priscilla had a chance to look at him closely. She thought he looked remarkably like Father; a decent height, standing straight, sturdy build, with a kind face and capable air. She imagined if her father were in a position of authority, folk would respectfully attend to what he said. The captain proceeded until he stood facing Deacon Carver. As the two men conversed, the Deacon nodded repeatedly, indicating… what? Understanding? Agreement? *I wish I could hear.* Priscilla kept her eyes on Master Jones as he walked back along the deck and was surprised when he stopped beside her family. There was something magnetic about him. He wasn't young, but had a handsome dignity. She noticed laughter creases at the corners of his mouth. She curtsied slightly.

Master Jones addressed Joseph. 'Your name, lad?'

'J-Joseph, sir.'

'How'd you come by that shiner?'

'A fight, sir. I told the lads we were going to sea and they said I was lying. So we fought.'

'I have a lad your age and he fights. But there'll be no fighting on my ship. Understood?' Master Jones' tone was gruff but Priscilla discerned a twinkle in his eye and a twitch of his lips.

'Yes, sir. No fighting, I promise.'

'Well said. Now. I'm due for an inspection of my ship. Like to accompany me?'

'Oh! Yes, sir!'

Priscilla felt a glow, watching her little blond-curled brother trotting to keep up with Master Jones' long strides.

'May I make your acquaintance?' The man's voice was velvety, well spoken.

Swiveling round and taking a step backward, Priscilla faced a dapper gentleman, standing slightly shorter than Father. He doffed his hat, his greeting encompassing her parents.

'Master Thomas Prence,' he said. 'Carriage-maker, London.' The ship lurched and Priscilla caught hold of Mother's arm.

'Master Mullins,' Father said. 'My wife and daughter Priscilla. Our son Joseph…'

'I saw,' Prence cut in. 'Favored by our captain,' he said; his eyes on Priscilla.

She noted his velvet doublet and breeches, lace collar and cuffs, fine linen hose, and a manicured goatee and small moustache, deep brown like his shoulder length hair. Not a Puritan. However against her will, her gaze riveted on his sallow fleshy face, drawn to a large mole tucked into the corner where his slightly bulging nose met his right cheek. A single hair grew out of this reddish protuberance.

Mr Prence tilted his head slightly to the right, thus removing his blemish from Priscilla's line of sight without abandoning his own focus. 'May I congratulate you on your beautiful daughter, Mr Mullins?'

Priscilla blushed and looked down at her feet. He wore black shoes of fine leather with a small heel. *A man of status.*

'What brings you on this voyage, Mr Prence?' Father asked.

'As with everyone I'm sure, the promise of prosperity…'

Before Mr Prence could continue Deacon Carver stepped up to face the passengers. He raised his hand for order. 'I suggest we go below for evening prayers.'

By now the hot yellow sun was taking on the gray-purple hues of pre-dusk light, sinking to meet the horizon; the wind gentler. Priscilla wanted to stay on deck. 'Must we?' she asked Father.

'Oh, aye,' Father said. 'The Deacon is our leader.'

'After you, Mistress.' Mr Prence placed his arm behind Priscilla's waist, guiding, without taking the liberty of touching her. Dutifully, she climbed down the ladder into the dusty half-light of their living space.

As the passengers assembled below deck Mr Prence stood beside Father, leaving her beside Mother. *He behaves well. He behaves as a gentleman should.*

It was some minutes before the children could be made to stop running about, playing hide-and-seek. Priscilla studied Deacon Carver as he stood and waited. He seemed a kind gentleman. His face, with well-spaced deep brown eyes, was sensitive and thoughtful, often smiling but never laughing outright. Eventually the company stood quiet, ready to listen, though most wore an expression of resignation. She heard a whisper, 'I hope this won't be long.'

'Before we pray, I wish to say a few words about procedures we must follow for the sake of our well-being on this voyage,' Deacon Carver said. 'First, to protect against disease we must keep our living quarters clean. No food left lying about, no dirty linen. And most important, use of chamber pots must take place on deck. This of course includes the dogs, and you should keep them well brushed – also to be done on deck. Equally important, we must all co-operate, and help one another in times of adversity. It would be advisable to show goodwill toward the crew. Do not respond to insults, should there be any, and at all times obey Master Jones and obey ship's regulations. We will follow a routine of morning prayers before breakfast, evening prayers before supper, and of course the Sabbath will be devoted entirely to religious observances. And now, let us pray. "Our Father, which art in Heaven…"'

Priscilla listened to his deep, calm voice, *I'm glad he is our leader, but I hope prayers won't occupy too much time.*

'Down wi' ya, varmint.' The bosun's snarl ushered Joseph's descent down the ladder into the praying group.

'Master Jones took me all over the ship!'

'Ssh! Hush!' Priscilla pulled her brother close.

By the time prayers were over it was difficult to see. In the darkening shadows Mother set out bread and cheese for supper, using the trunk lid as a table.

'I be a sea captain when I'm grown,' Joseph said. Then after a pensive moment he asked, 'Will I be flogged if I'm naughty?'

'No, Joseph.' Father hugged him. 'Only grown men who have done something bad get flogged. I'm sure Master Jones would never do that to you. Now, it's so dark I cannot see my own hand. Bed. Tomorrow, Southampton.'

As she lay beside Mother, waiting for sleep, Priscilla prayed silently. *Please God, please may we not remain long on this crowded frightening ship. Please may we reach America soon.*

Two images chased one another in and out of her mind. Mr Alden; handsome, strong clean features, laughing eyes, inviting smile. But lowly and disregarding her when Master Jones appeared. Mr Prence; fleshy face, that repulsive mole, but an eloquent voice, well-dressed, the manners of a gentleman. He was properly attentive. Exhausted, lulled by the rocking motion and the sound of water lapping against the hull, she drifted into sleep.

Chapter 6

July 1620

Southampton

Returning from his sojourn in the town to buy provisions, John Alden rowed rhythmically across Southampton harbor toward the *Mayflower*. Only mid-morning but a hot sun beat down on the back of his head and there wasn't a breath of air. Seagulls cawed and wheeled, some diving close to his head. The plop, plop of the oars, usually a calming sound, did nothing to dispel his irritation with the heat, the pesky gulls, and the wait. An entire week lost. What had happened to the ship from Holland? He wanted to set sail across the ocean, not be stuck here. Having decided to come on this venture, John wanted to quit England quickly; leave his past behind, forget it if he could, and immerse himself in building a new life. He hated this idleness, which allowed memories and guilt to invade his mind; the guilt about his friend, left behind, rotting in prison. As he drew near the *Mayflower* he could hear laughing and raised voices. He secured the rowing boat to the ship's hull as a crewman lowered a tackle to lift the crate of spices. When the crate was safely hoisted aboard he climbed the rope ladder up onto the deck. Straightening his back and shading his eyes, John searched to find the source of the commotion. *Can it be? Mistress Mullins!* Holding the end of a rope, pulled by her little brother, she dodged amongst passengers, ducking and weaving, laughing, gasping. *Well I never! Not so high and mighty now. She's playful, spirited. Be gad she's beautiful.* He whistled softly as her coif slid off spilling a cascade of rich auburn curls. A rogue wave tilted the deck. She fell and rolled down until she hit the fo'castle bulkhead.

John ran to her, elbowing folk out of his way, racing against a strapping youth, equally intent. He won, offering a hand to his quarry, who was still laughing and gasping for breath as she freed her feet from her skirts.

'May I?'

Looking up, Mistress Mullins smiled and took his hand. He was surprised at how easily she rose, using his hand only to steady, not to lift.

'Thank you, sir.'

John started to speak but stopped, obeying her fingers pressed against her lips and following her upwards glance toward a small group of sailors tending the rigging up on the fo'castle.

'Don't like this delay,' a sailor said.

'Naw. Isn't good. Much longer and we'll be sailing into westerly gales.'

'Craziness taking all these strange folk. I'm afeared they'll jinx us.'

'Aw well. Nowt we can do but take what comes. Least we 'av a good captain.'

'Up ye go, lad. I'll follow.'

As they listened to the sailors above, John stood silent, gazing into Mistress Mullins' face; pert nose, deep blue eyes, arched eyebrows.

'Are you hurt, Mistress?'

'No, thank you, sir, 'twas nothing.'

John smiled inwardly as she gathered her dignity, standing straight, her nose slightly elevated.

'Priscilla, more, more!' Joseph bounced between them. 'I am Master Jones, the *Mayflower* is towing *Speedwell*.' He pointed to his sister. 'To escape pirates.'

'No more now.' Priscilla bent to untie the rope round Joseph's waist. 'Now coil it, as Master Jones has taught you.'

'Do you know how to coil a rope, Mr Alden?' Joseph looked at John.

'Yes, Master Jones taught me.'

Joseph gazed at him, wide-eyed. 'Did he? When?'

'When I was, oh, about five years older than you. He taught me seamanship. We both come from Harwich. That's on the east coast. By the North Sea. Sailed under his command nigh on three years.'

'Father says,' Priscilla interrupted, 'that you keep the cargo hold in good order.'

'I want to see it,' Joseph said. 'I'll be Master Jones and inspect.'

'Pleased to hear it,' John said.

'*Speedwell*! *Speedwell*! Harbor entrance!' The first mate called out from the half-deck, his voice booming above the hubbub below.

John forged a path leading Priscilla to the deck rail. They stood side by side, waving and calling to the ship as she sailed through the harbor entrance.

'I'm curious to meet these folk from Holland,' Priscilla said.

'Aye. They are a brave lot that I know.' From the corner of his eye John noticed Mr Prence standing nearby, edging closer.

'Are they all religious protestors like Deacon Carver?'

'Reckon so, though I'm not sure.' *Speedwell* sailed across the harbor and when she had anchored, passengers surged up onto her deck, hailing folk on the *Mayflower*.

In the midst of the melee and excitement Priscilla asked, 'Where is Joseph? He was with us.'

They searched amongst the crowd.

'We'd have heard if he'd fallen overboard. But he couldn't have. The rail is too high,' John said.

'Perhaps he is in our cabin – or – he did say he wanted to see the cargo hold.'

'No!' John exclaimed. Turning, he hurtled down the first ladder, then the second. *Please God, he mustn't find… mustn't uncover… we could all be doomed.*

The hold was quiet. Not a soul to be seen. John called, 'Joseph.' Silence. *Is he here, hiding?* He began unstacking trunks and sacks, searching behind barrels.

'Joseph – are you here?' He heard Priscilla call. *So she has followed.* No answer.

'My father was right, Mr Alden. Peas, beans, salt-beef, butter, barley and corn for planting. All properly labeled.'

John glanced behind. 'No time to dally.'

'All these sacks. If you ever should have an empty one, could I have it to make dolls for the girls?'

'Aye, aye. But we must find your brother,' he replied curtly.

Showing no sense of urgency, Priscilla peeked behind the barrels, almost singing, 'Joseph, Joseph, where are you? Ale, wine, aqua vitae, brandy…'

'Hurry!' John worked his way down the hold. This was taking forever. He pulled away stacks of carpets, furniture, and bedding, all neatly stowed. Drops of sweat stung his eyes. Only halfway. Fie. Crash. Metal on metal. John froze. He leapt to the far end of the hold, Priscilla scrambling behind.

Crouching down, Joseph was ferreting in a pile of armaments and farm equipment. John grabbed him by his collar and yanked him backwards.

'Come away from there. What do you think you're doing?'

'I want my musket.'

'Fie! Who said you could… you meddling rascal. Now be gone and don't ever come down here again.'

'Mr Alden.' Priscilla cringed. 'Why?' She grabbed Joseph's arm and hauled him up the ladder.

'Fie!' John kicked a sack. Wearily, he then set to re-stacking the hold. *I was hoping to know her better. She won't want anything to do with me – not now. Wish I hadn't been so angry, but this is life or death. Praise be I was in time. Wish I could have told her, explained; but I vowed I'd say nothing.*

Eventually, when the hold was in order again, John climbed up into a crowd of excited welcomes, embraces, children playing tag among skirts, dodging a clip on the ear from masculine hands. *Where is Mistress Mullins? There, with her father and mother near the rail.* He positioned himself nearby, within her line of sight. When she saw him, she turned her head away, nose in the air, giving all her attention to boarding passengers, so he did likewise. A handsome, buxom young woman climbed on board, blond curls escaping from under her coif. *There's a wench*, he thought. Enjoying the sight of flouncing hips he ignored other newcomers until he heard a stifled gasp and murmur from the man by his side. *What?* He saw a spectacle he could scarcely believe. Four personages stood in a row facing the crowd.

The first was a short man, dwarfed by a vibrant yellow long-tailed coat with wide lace cuffs. A bright green waistcoat pulled at its brass buttons, struggling to hold in a bulging stomach, and a crisp starched ruff propped up a double chin that resided on a short neck. And the breeches! Lavender, tucked into pointy toed knee-high black boots. As if he believed himself to be the picture of dignity the man held up his hand for attention. John was amazed that no one laughed.

'I am Christopher Martin. I have been appointed Governor of this ship by the venture company and you all will obey my commands.' He cast an encompassing glance up at the sailors spectating from the half-deck.

What an oaf. What a podgy-faced conceited oaf. John snorted.

'Captain Miles Standish, your military commander.' Mr Martin gestured to a short, red-headed florid man in full military dress, sword at his side. His brass helmet, held next to his chest, sparkled in the sun. The captain saluted the gathering and bowed to the plump, merry faced woman at his side. 'My dear wife.' She answered murmurs of welcome with a dimpled smile and a curtsey.

'And Mr Weston, chairman of the venture company funding this voyage.' Weston stepped forward.

'I wish to meet with Carver, Bradford and Winslow in the great cabin.' No greeting. No smile. No word of encouragement or good wishes for the coming voyage.

John watched as Deacon Carver and Master Winslow pushed through the crowd; two men he admired. He reckoned both were men of integrity, prepared to risk all for this venture they believed in. He respected Carver's solid authority in managing the *Mayflower*'s passengers, religious and non-religious folk alike. And Winslow; with his poised bearing and deferential manner. John wondered how many hundreds of pounds of his own money Winslow had donated to the cause of printing and promoting Brewster's discourses. He shivered and his skin prickled at the thought of Brewster, the founder of this religious movement, wanted for sedition and treason, entrusted to his care, hidden under the pile of armaments below. Pray God they set sail soon to speed far away from England's shores, out of reach of the King's men.

Carver and Winslow halted by the Mullins family and Carver asked Mr Mullins to join them. At the same time a slender serious-faced young man jostled against Priscilla. *Must have come on Speedwell.* There were apologies, introductions; 'Bradford... my wife Dorothy.' Folk stood aside as Mr Bradford hurried to the great cabin. *He seems young, has an untried, innocent air about him.* John turned his attention to Priscilla and Dorothy, who seemed distraught, wringing her hands, head bowed. Dressed in dove gray, she was so slight of figure she could have been mistaken for a child.

Talking earnestly, then jovially, Priscilla put an arm round Dorothy's shoulder and gestured to the half-deck. John looked to where she was pointing.

Christopher Martin faced a group of sailors. 'Low-down vermin: you will obey my orders!' He stamped his foot. 'Or I'll have you flogged!'

The sailors sniggered and made mocking obeisance. 'Aye, sir; your very *Highness*, sir.'

'What?' The bosun leapt through the hatch and up onto the half-deck. He shook his fist in Mr Martin's face. 'Stupid puffed up bully. Puffed up like a bullfrog. Bullyfrog. That's what you are. Leave my men alone. Master Jones is our captain. Me and my men'll take orders from nowt but 'im.'

The sailors chorused 'Aye, aye.'

'You all are to obey my… ' Mr Martin stepped back from the bosun's fist. 'I'll inspect you this afternoon.' He scuttled down, getting tangled in the tails of his bright yellow coat.

John grinned and shook his head. *Silly pompous fool. Governor indeed. He'll only be a laughing stock, I'll wager.* He glanced at Priscilla and saw she was stifling her laughter. Dorothy was smiling, a hesitant smile as if she hardly dared.

Minutes later, just as he was about to return to the cargo hold, the doors of the great cabin were flung wide as Weston marched out, his face flushed and contorted. 'I'll see for myself the quantity of your supplies, whether you are as impoverished as you claim. Take me to the cargo hold.'

Deacon Carver beckoned to John.

'Aye, sir.' John stepped forward. 'Come with me.'

Weston slipped and stumbled down the ladders, his paunch slowing his progress. He landed in the hold, belligerent and puffing, pulling at his waistcoat, scrunched up around his chest, several buttons popped. John waited while the little man rearranged himself, wiping his sweaty pimpled face and fat moist lips with a large silk handkerchief pulled from an inside pocket.

'Show me all that these religious rebels have purchased – with my money.'

Not only your money. I know enough to know that. John led Weston along the stacks of barrels, chests and sacks, giving details of the contents. The merchant peered at the labels.

At the far end of the hold, where the armaments and farm equipment were neatly stacked, Weston stopped. Kicking at the pile he said, 'Sell some of these. Fetch a good price.'

John drew his hand across the back of his neck and wiped his brow.

Weston turned on his heel. 'You've plenty to sell. I'll hear no tales of hardship.'

Studying the backside of the merchant as he followed on his heels up the ladder, John thought, *You are a scoundrel. A low-down scoundrel. I feel it in my bones. Why did anyone ever trust you? I pray the other backers are men of their word.*

Emerging through the hatch John saw Weston straightening his waistcoat and jacket, assuming a dignified posture. He held up his hand commanding silence. 'Y've more than enough to sell. Always said you overbought. You can fend for yourselves. Y'll not have a penny more from me. I'm off, back up to London to deal with honest folk. He stomped across the deck and clambered down into the rowing boat.

'T'isn't fair,' a man called out. 'He promised.'

'Aye, we've been duped. He's pocketed our money and scarpered.' A burly man pushed his way to the front. 'I say we go after him. Lower the ship's boat, run him down and hold a knife to his throat.'

'Goodman Billington, desist. Gentlemen, gentlemen.' Deacon Carver raised his hand. Gradually the angry passengers stopped their mouths to listen.

'As you have seen, there is a disagreement with Mr Weston over the terms of our contract. Also, on inspection, Master Jones says *Speedwell* will have to be re-rigged before we can set sail.'

'What? Again?' Billington stamped his foot. 'We had to stop and re-rig her coming from Holland – caused our delay.'

'Therefore,' Deacon Carver said, 'we will have to sell some of our supplies to pay for the repairs to *Speedwell* and the harbor fees.'

He raised his voice over the groans and shaking heads. 'But we are strong, of good heart, and with God's help we will all pull through together and succeed.'

John glanced at Priscilla and her family.

'Yes!' Mr Mullins said, punching the air with his fist. John smiled to see Priscilla do the same, although his smile became a grimace as he watched Mr Prence sidle up beside her and speak softly in her ear. She gave him a glance but John couldn't read her face. She didn't smile, nor did she look displeased. *There's another rat. Prances and apes the gentleman but I can smell a fake.*

'Let's us pray.' Deacon Carver raised his voice.

After prayers it was time for the midday meal. The *Speedwell* passengers returned to their ship and John descended to the cargo hold to dole out victuals. Tomorrow he and the ship's carpenter would start work re-rigging *Speedwell*.

Crossing the Ocean

Chapter 7

September 1620

Challenges

Priscilla grasped the rail as the *Mayflower* sailed out of Plymouth Harbor. *September 6th. We should be in America by now.* For the third time in four weeks she stood with her family, silently saying farewell to the disappearing green slopes of England. She saw Mother wipe a tear from her cheek. Mother had always been fearful of this venture and when Master Jones declared the *Mayflower* would sail leaving the leaky *Speedwell* behind she had begged Father to be among the passengers who would remain in England. Now most of *Speedwell*'s passengers were squashed into the *Mayflower*.

During the hot weeks of trouble with *Speedwell*, Mr Prence had become increasingly attentive. He treated her like a lady and was always on hand to protect her from the unwelcome attentions of Mr Martin, an obnoxious pest. So why could she not warm to him? Was she so frivolous as to be put off by his ugly mole? She tried to ignore the issue, concentrating on teaching Joseph, helping Mother look after the children, and on her friendship with Dorothy Bradford, always sad and fearful, as if something haunted her. *I wonder if she'll ever tell me what troubles her so.*

Against her own wishes, Priscilla had begun to share Mother's fears of storms, illness and death, and now she had her own fears. One day, a few days before they finally set sail this third time, she had come on deck seeking relief from the fetid heat below. Apart from a small cluster of sailors up by the fo'castle there was no one about. She stood by the rail longing for even the faintest breeze to waft across the still harbor.

Of a sudden she felt herself gripped round her waist from behind; a vice-like grip pulling her hard against a man's body, his head buried in her neck, kissing her ear. She smelled a sickening mix of perfume and sweat and opened her mouth to scream when a hand fastened over her lips. With all her strength she bit.

'Aaah!' The man gasped and, throwing her down, ran off. As she fell, Priscilla's head knocked against the rail and she blacked out.

When she came round she was lying on the bed in their cabin, Mother soothing her brow with a wet cloth. 'Ah, poor love. Have a sip of brandy.' Mother told her Mr Alden had carried her down, and no one knew who the culprit was. Mr Prence came quickly to inquire after her safety. Speculating about who could have done such a thing he said that Mr Martin was with Master Jones most of the afternoon. Perhaps it was one of the sailors, but knowing the punishment that lay in store... he doubted they would risk it. 'No, I'm sorry to make such a suggestion.' Mr Prence looked down at his folded hands. 'But given his tendency to unprovoked violent outbursts, I think it could have been Mr Alden.'

She did not know why, but Priscilla was distressed to think Mr Alden would do such a thing. She put her head in her hands.

Mother intervened. 'Please, Mr Prence, Priscilla needs to rest.'

Prence bowed. 'I pray you may soon recover from this dastardly act, Mistress.'

There had been almost no communication with Mr Alden since he'd been so angry with Joseph in the cargo hold. It seemed like years ago. However, on the few occasions when he was on deck taking the air, she noticed him looking at her in a searching way. For her part, she felt unaccountably drawn to him and wished she didn't.

Whoever had accosted her was on board this ship. Would he try again? Now, even under the close protection of Mother and Father she felt uneasy. She wished she could be rid of the memory; trust that whoever it was wouldn't dare try again. She wanted to feel brave, excited to be going on this adventure to make a better life. For there was a nugget inside her, of curiosity and eagerness for new horizons.

Priscilla looked up into Father's face. His jaw was set firm, determined.

He smiled at her. 'Third time lucky. Fine day.' Together they admired the white sails billowing out against a sun-filled blue sky, a brisk wind pushing from behind. Cawing gulls ushered their departure as the ship plowed through the sparkling ocean and slowly her fears gave way to a surge of exhilaration. She spied Dorothy and William Bradford standing further along toward the bow. Dorothy, as ever, hunched her shoulders in worry, her face slightly pinched in a frown. Priscilla had never seen William smile. His entire demeanor radiated earnest religious endeavor. They were both pale. With them stood Mary Brewster, wife of the long missing founder of their new church. Tall, gaunt, she braced herself against the ship's rail. Taking on most of *Speedwell*'s passengers meant the *Mayflower* was terribly overcrowded; a hundred and one passengers, with three pregnant women on board, Father said, and about thirty sailors. However, she and Dorothy were on the same ship and that was good. In their days of waiting in Southampton, they'd grown close, although Priscilla sometimes felt impatient with Dorothy's inability to be merry. Like her husband she hardly ever smiled, except when they were playing with the little children. Then she became a different person, entering their world of games, delighting in their individual quirks and ways. Otherwise she seemed always to be anxious; worried about absorbing William's teaching, and about pleasing Mistress Brewster. Also, she was fearful of the voyage and adventure into the unknown. But Dorothy was warm and loving and Priscilla felt a bond. She knew Dorothy needed her.

Priscilla turned her back on the deck to look out over the ocean. Waves danced with frothy white caps as if saying 'Hurry, hurry, we'll help'. She lost track of time until she became dimly aware of Mother saying, 'No, Joseph, not now. Master Jones is busy. Be still.' She was about to offer to take Joseph below to learn his letters when there was a stirring amongst the passengers; shuffling feet, folk pushing and jostling in semi-hushed excitement. 'Is it really? Can't possibly be. 'Twould be a miracle.' The murmurs gradually crescendoed into an explosion of shouts, 'William, William! Is it really? Elder Brewster!'

'Amazing. Who'd have believed it? Their adored minister and leader!' Father exclaimed, joining in the jubilant stamping and clapping.

With a slight scream Mary Brewster pushed forward, folk standing aside to clear a path. As Mary flung herself into her husband's arms, Priscilla stretched on tiptoe to see better. Standing side by side with Mr Alden, almost as tall, gray hair reaching his shoulders, Brewster wore the garb of a Puritan gentleman. Despite the pandemonium his demeanor was dignified, restrained. He smiled and a tear rolled down his cheek. In response to his raised hand, folk hushed their shouting.

'I salute you all,' Brewster said. 'I am full of joy to see you. I especially want to thank Mr Alden who kept me hidden in the cargo hold during all the delays. A challenge for him at times, I know.'

Cheers erupted. Father shouted, 'Hoorah!' The deck exploded with joyful noise. Priscilla looked at Joseph. *Is that why Mr Alden was so hostile? Was Joseph about to dismantle Elder Brewster's hiding place? And from that moment I've been disdainful of Mr Alden, scorned his attentions. But how could I know?*

'Silence!' Faces turned upward. Master Jones stood on the half-deck. No longer dressed in his fine blue coat and white breeches, he wore a rough brown woolen coat and breeches with a holland shirt. His working garb, Priscilla supposed, but he was no less imposing for that. 'What in God's name?' he thundered. 'Your name, sir.'

'William Brewster, sir.'

'The same William Brewster who is wanted by the Crown for publishing seditious literature?'

'Aye, sir.'

'A stowaway. I could have you thrown overboard.' Mary Brewster's moan was echoed by all on board.

'Come with me,' Master Jones commanded. Brewster climbed up to the half-deck and followed the captain to his cabin.

William Bradford held his hat to his chest, looking to heaven, praying, and a woman put her arms around Mary Brewster. Mr Alden disappeared below.

Against her wishes, Priscilla's thoughts fastened on him again. She recalled the moments during the weeks of repairs and false starts when he was courteous, kind, and she had rebuffed him. Rumors circulated that it was he who accosted her. But that didn't make sense and Father was sure Mr Alden would not do such a thing. Yet still no one knew who it was. One of the sailors? She remembered the peculiar smell. A sailor would not wear perfume. Nor would Mr Alden, she imagined. Only a gentleman… She shook herself. What did it matter? Mr Alden was beneath her, not worthy of her attention. She listened to Mother softly repeating Hail Marys, 'Have mercy, have mercy.' Father paced in circles clearing his throat. She saw Captain Standish's red head cutting a figure of eight as he paced.

'Mistress Mullins.' She started at the voice soft in her ear.

'Mr Prence.'

''Tis a tense moment.'

'I pray Master Jones will be kind.'

'A rough place, this ship. Vile sailors. You've had no more trouble?'

'No, Mr Prence.' She caught a whiff of scent, but no, it wasn't the same. Rather pleasant, musky.

'I hope you don't mind; I've taken it upon myself to keep a protective eye on you.' His arm hovered at her back. 'You are fair, prone to unsavory attentions from… sailors… and those who work in the lower parts of the ship.'

Joseph tugged at her skirt. 'When will Master Jones come back?' his treble voice rang out. Priscilla cuffed him. 'Sssh!' She looked up at Master Jones' cabin and, with all the passengers, waited in hushed dread until the door opened. Master Jones emerged, escorting Elder Brewster down a short ladder to stand on the half-deck looking down on upturned silent faces.

'I have decided Elder Brewster may stay on board,' he announced.

'Hoorah! Hoorah for the captain!' a man called out.

'Thank you. Thank you, sir!' The deck reverberated to shouts and the noise of clapping hands and stamping feet. Sailors stopped and stared. Master Jones raised his hand in acknowledgement.

Priscilla grasped Mother's hand. 'Praise be the captain was lenient. The thought of sending a man overboard to drown.' She shuddered.

Joseph tugged her arm. 'Master Jones is good. I want to be like him when I'm grown, in command of a ship. I want to be with him now, in his cabin.'

'I know, but he is far too busy. It is tricky sailing 'til we get past the headlands. Now come below and learn your letters.'

'Oh no. That's dull.'

'You'll need to know your letters if you want to be a sea captain. Now come along.'

'Good day. Mistress.' Mr Prence doffed his hat and with a nod to Master and Mistress Mullins, moved away.

★ ★ ★

'No, Joseph, 'b' is this way with the circle bit on the right and 'd' the other way.' Hearing voices below Priscilla stopped to listen. She recognized the bosun's snarl.

'Master Jones let 'im off? Too soft. Should've dropped 'im in the waves. Go on. Go on up and celebrate. Useless landlubbers.' The ladder creaked and then Mr Alden stood by their cabin. Priscilla got to her feet, blushing.

'You're not celebrating?' Mr Alden asked.

'Joseph was bored. We are all very relieved Master Jones…'

'He is good,' Joseph cut in. 'I want…'

'Hush,' Priscilla said.

'You are right, Joseph. Master Jones is a fine man. I knew he wouldn't send Elder Brewster to die in the sea. He has to be fierce but he is a kind man. He was good to me when I was a lad.'

'I…' Priscilla knew she was blushing and looked down, twisting her hands. 'You were responsible to keep William Brewster hidden. I see now. Joseph, he might have caused…' she looked up beseechingly, not knowing how to say what she wanted to say.

'Aye. I was harsh. I had to be. And I'll admit I was afraid. Is that why you have been so aloof? Because I was harsh? The cargo hold is my responsibility, with or without William Brewster.'

'I'm sorry if I've been ill-mannered.' Priscilla's voice was low. She looked down again and took a deep breath to collect her wits. When she raised her eyes she found Mr Alden regarding her with a raised eyebrow, and half-smile, head slightly tilted. 'Tell me, Mr Alden, when did Elder Brewster come aboard? Who brought him to you?'

Alden leaned against a post, thumbs in his belt. 'It was when we were anchored in Southampton; the night before *Speedwell* arrived. Dead of night, I was sleeping in the hold; less crowded and cooler down there, when I was woken by someone shaking my shoulder.' Alden shifted his weight and grasped a beam to lean slightly closer toward her. 'There was Deacon Carver with this fellow. He introduced William Brewster and said he was trusting me to hide him and see he had victuals. I wasn't to say a word to a soul. I said yes, of course. I was honored to be trusted.' He looked sideways and gave a nod. 'Your lad's escaped.'

Priscilla took her eyes from Mr Alden's to see Joseph's legs disappearing through the hatch. 'Oh, well, 'tis no matter.'

Alden let go of the beam and stood straight. 'I made a place behind all the piles of armor and weapons and tools and such.'

'The very pile Joseph was pulling down.'

'Aye, it was a close call. At night when all souls were asleep I'd help him stretch his limbs and we talked a bit. He is a brave man, I can say. He helped found the new church these folk believe in. He has been with them from the beginning, through terrible trials, in hiding nigh on five years. Not even his wife knew where he was or if he was still alive. He says he wants more than anything to lead his followers to America and build a Godly colony, free from corruption. He said he wishes he was younger. He's fifty-four. Too old to go exploring, but he will be our religious leader and will give advice and counsel.'

'And you never said a word! All that time we were delayed. And when *Speedwell* arrived. And he had to keep hidden even from Mary!'

'Aye. We had to wait 'til we'd left England for sure, when there was no chance of being searched by the King's men. He is a wanted man. He'd hang if they found him.'

''Tis to be admired, Mr Alden, you keeping him safely hidden; six weeks we were, with repairs and then to-ing and fro-ing with *Speedwell* always leaking.'

''Tis to be admired Elder Brewster stayed calm and patient. It was painful for him, cramped up all day long. He got terribly stiff and sore.'

Priscilla stood quiet a moment looking at the floor. *Dare I?*

Alden didn't move. She examined his gaze. Open, steady. 'Mr Alden, there is something I want to ask.'

'Aye?'

'You must know of the rumors…'

'Aye. The rumors that I accosted you.' Now Alden's mouth was unsmiling, his eyes hard in their earnestness. 'I swear to you by Almighty God 'twas not I. I'd put the hold in order after the midday meal, came on deck for some air, and found you lying as if dead. 'Twas a terrible moment 'til I found your pulse.' Alden's neck flushed red. 'Please believe me, Mistress. 'Twas not I. I would never do such a thing to any woman, and… and especially not to you.'

Shaken by his fervor, Priscilla clutched her arms around her waist. 'I, I think I believe you.'

'Please. You must,' he said with pleading eyes.

Priscilla looked to the side in the tense silence.

'Shall we join the celebrations?'

'Aye,' she said.

'After you.' He motioned to the ladder.

Priscilla and Mr Alden emerged into a scene of undiminished excited babble. Dorothy pushed through the melee to reach Priscilla. 'Good. You're here. I've been searching. William is with Elder Brewster. Please come with me.'

Priscilla cast a look to say goodbye to Mr Alden and went with Dorothy to stand by the rail.

'This is like a miracle,' Dorothy said. 'Surely a sign from God that our way is the true way – to have Elder Brewster, our founder, restored to us, alive and well.'

'What does your church believe, Dorothy? I've never quite understood. In prayers you keep asking God to help you search your souls. And you make up your own prayers. It does seem strange.'

'Not really. It's like this.' Dorothy faced Priscilla. 'Everything that happens, all good fortune and bad fortune, is God's will. There is a reason behind everything. If we have good fortune it means we are in tune with God's plans for us.'

'But what if something bad happens? Does that mean you are being punished?'

'Perhaps. It means we must search our souls for the reason. It means God is testing us for a higher purpose.' Dorothy's tone became earnest, almost urgent. 'You see, God has chosen us, as He chose the Israelites long, long ago. We are special, the true Church of Christ. God has a purpose for us. We are His saints, His Pilgrims. Just as God led the Israelites out of Egypt to the Promised Land, He is leading us to a new promised land, free of sin. Our mission is to build a new England where our truth and way of worship are free to fulfill God's will. We must be constantly vigilant, attending to the state of our souls. To work for salvation – 'tis the whole purpose of our lives.'

Priscilla frowned slightly, taking a step back. 'But what of us who are not in your church? Are we not part of God's purpose?'

Dorothy looked down at her feet and twisted her hands. She looked out over the sea. Facing Priscilla again she said, 'Anyone who stays with the false, idol-worshipping ways of the Catholics and Church of England is a "stranger" to us.'

She speaks as if reciting words she's been taught. Priscilla searched Dorothy's face. 'So am I a stranger to you?'

Dorothy shook her head, her frown deepening. 'Oh dear, I don't know. I would have to ask William. He studies the Bible hour after hour. He is even learning Hebrew to better understand the Holy Scriptures.' She continued twisting her hands, turning her head, eyes downcast. 'You are a good person, I know, and I feel I can trust you. Surely that is what matters.' Her gray eyes looked into Priscilla's.

Priscilla grasped Dorothy's hands and smiled. 'You are right. Trust is what matters. Trust and care.'

'Dorothy, there you are.' William Bradford joined them. 'Come, dear. We need to prepare for prayers.'

Standing alone, looking out over the sea, Priscilla's thoughts returned to Mr Alden. She had to admit she felt drawn to him. She sensed he found her attractive and she wanted to respond but he was not a gentleman, not worthy of her status. A cooper. No.

Impossible. Mr Prence behaved and dressed like a gentleman, with decorum and concern for her welfare. But she did not desire his company, and she wished she did. *What is the matter with me?*

★ ★ ★

Priscilla shivered with delight and pride. It was rare for a daughter to be accompanied by her father, but here she was on deck with her handsome father, drawing looks. Perhaps being confined to the ship was causing him to loosen up. She glanced at his profile; neatly cropped beard and hair (thanks to Mother), thick dark locks turning gray. Strong cheekbones and nose.

The evening autumn sun cast dancing auburn rays across the dark water and soaked their backs with warmth.

"Tis fine, 'tis fine,' Mullins said. 'Pray these easterlies hold. We're making good progress.'

They rested silent a time, looking across the sea.

'May I ask you something, Father?'

'Aye.'

'What sort of man would you choose for your daughter?'

'That is a question.' Mullins laid his hands on Priscilla's shoulders, turning her to face him. 'You know why I've come on this voyage; to prosper. We were gradually sinking into poverty in England, and there was nothing I could do. I have always wanted to provide well for my family, and liked to imagine you, lass, a lady in a large house with servants and fine gowns to enhance your beauty.' He looked out over the sea for a moment and faced her again. 'I still want that for you. However, during our time on this ship I've spent many hours conversing with Deacon Carver, Elder Brewster, Winslow and Bradford about their church. I don't hold much truck with their religious doctrine, but their ideas about folk electing those who govern, equal justice for all, a society where folk behave honorably; such ideas I've always considered to be against the natural order of things, but now they appeal to me.'

Priscilla thought she'd never seen Father so intense, and he was talking to her as an equal. She felt a tingle of excitement.

'Deacon Carver and Winslow reckon that although I do not share their religious beliefs, my experience of governing our shoemakers' guild would be of value in helping to govern the colony. I tell you, daughter, this venture excites me much. I am eager.'

'Aye. I see that, Father.'

'You wonder what all this has to do with your question.' He took Priscilla's young hands in his strong, weather-worn grasp. 'I want prosperity, but not at the expense of others. Therefore, the qualities I would look for in a mate for you are truthfulness, the desire to protect and care for you, a willingness to work hard – and an appreciation of your spirit – for in truth you are spirited. You need someone strong minded, my lass, to be a match for your feisty nature. I've come to believe, Priscilla, that the quality of a man's character is more important than his appearance or status.'

Priscilla's head reeled. She swayed.

'Steady, lass. It is a lot to take in. Perhaps you are shocked.'

'Not exactly, but it is different from… I've always thought status was most important.'

'Some men combine a good character and status. Master Winslow is such a man. And Deacon Carver. However, I'd say they aren't ten a penny.'

'I'll ponder it, Father. Thank you.' Priscilla squeezed his hands and stretched up to kiss his cheek.

Chapter 8

September 1620

Lizzie Tilley introduces herself

Priscilla huddled beside Dorothy, soothing her brow, holding the chamber pot while her friend retched and retched; by now bringing up nothing more than bile. With the stench of vomit, the cloying air, and bodies all crammed together, Priscilla felt she would vomit too.

'Ha. Said ya'd all be seasick, useless landlubbers, worthless cargo, taking up space.' The bosun clambered through and over the passengers.

Priscilla ignored him. 'I'll not be long, Dorothy. I'm going to ask Mother if she has a remedy to help you.'

She found Mother in their cabin. 'Dorothy is no better. Can you think of anything?'

'Chamomile is what she needs. If only, and fresh air.'

'Good day.'

Priscilla turned to face a plump blond woman about her own age.

'We've not been introduced. Elizabeth Tilley, but I'm called Lizzie.'

Priscilla felt small beside Lizzie, with her large hips, buxom bosom, her bodice laced tight so a nipple peeked provocatively through the lace border. 'Priscilla Mullins,' she said.

'Good to see you are not seasick. Poor wretches who are. Oh the stench!' She held a handkerchief to her nose and continued on, picking her way through prostrate bodies and their belongings.

Mother tutted. 'There walks temptation.'

'Where is Father?' Priscilla asked.

'Gone down to the cargo hold.'

Priscilla climbed down the ladder to the hold. Mr Alden and her father stood together, their backs to her as Mr Alden checked the spigots on the barrels were airtight, his head bent in concentration. 'Good. No problems.' He lifted a barrel to place it on a stack above head height. Priscilla marveled at the grace and ease of his movements. Effortless strength, as if he were carefully lifting a small child. She breathed in the refreshing scents of wood, grain, liquor.

'So you've known Master Jones since a lad?' Father asked.

'Aye. He and my father...'

Priscilla stirred and cleared her throat.

The two men turned. 'Mistress Mullins.' Alden smiled, inviting.

'Pardon me. Father, could you ask Deacon Carver, could women be allowed on deck more often? Dorothy is so sick. She'll never recover stuck down in our foul quarters. And she's not the only one.'

'I could speak with Master Jones,' Alden said. 'If you'll keep an eye here, Mr Mullins, I'll go now.'

'Oh, thank you,' Priscilla said.

'He's a good young man.' Father glanced up at Alden's disappearing feet. 'Prepared to work hard and wants a just society.'

Crouching again beside Dorothy, Priscilla clenched against the feelings Mr Alden stirred in her. If only he weren't... if only he were… of a good position. She remembered Father's words, and felt confused.

'All clear.' She raised her head to see Mr Alden standing beside them. He gestured 'thumbs up'.

'Poor Dorothy,' he said. 'Come. I'll help.' Priscilla followed as Mr Alden guided, half-carried Dorothy up the ladder. *He's so gentle.* A slight shiver ran through her.

On deck she said, 'Thank you, Mr Alden. I can take her now.' She stood looking into his eyes.

'I feel better already. Thank you so much.' Dorothy placed a hand on Alden's arm.

A bright blue sky softened with puffs of white cloud arched overhead and a light breeze stirred the air, soothing bodies hot and clammy from retching.

'Thank you, Priscilla,' Dorothy said. ''Tis a balm to be up here, away from the thick foul air.

The first mate was taking advantage of the light breeze to exercise the crew, practicing maneuvers. 'Port watch aloft to reef top s'ls… starboard watch to the braces … haul! … port watch loose gaskets … starboard watch sheet 'em home.'

'Isn't nat'ral, all this praying, twice every day.' The bosun's voice broke through, 'Church on Sunday, that's nat'ral, if ya be on land.'

'Aye,' came an answer. 'And they pray strange … not real prayers … they speak made up words … just spouting off … has to be the devil in 'em.'

'These strange ways'll jinx us,' the bosun again. 'The devil's on board. A cursed ship … the hex … send us to the bottom for sure.'

A look of panic came over Dorothy's face. She gripped the rail. 'Surely they don't think we're the devil? How could they?'

'My dear. How good to see you standing. Are you better?' William Bradford strode across the deck to Dorothy. Although he was greeting his wife, Bradford's eyes, set under prominent brows, had a faraway look, Priscilla thought, as if he were looking through her to some place beyond. As for herself, she might as well have been invisible.

'Aye, thanks to Priscilla,' Dorothy said. 'Master Jones relaxed his regulations so I could come up into the fresh air. 'Tis so good.' She breathed deeply.

'Actually, 'tis thanks to Mr Alden,' Priscilla said. 'He's a friend of Master Jones from a long way back.'

'Oh?' Bradford's curiosity was short lived. He turned his earnest attention to Dorothy. 'We can do an hour of comparative study up here in the open air. I've got my Bible and commentaries.' He patted the books under his arm.

Back down below deck Priscilla found Mother sitting on their bed alone, mending.

'Where is Joseph?'

'Having a lesson with Master Jones. He does love his lessons with the captain.'

Priscilla settled herself beside Mother to help. As if waiting for Priscilla's lap the calico cat jumped up, taking possession.

'On deck with Dorothy just now we heard the sailors grumbling about our strange religious ways, all the praying and how anyone can "spout off". They think it's the devil. Will jinx the ship. What do you make of it?' She kept her voice low.

Mother put her needle down. She spoke barely above a whisper. 'I summoned up the courage to ask Mistress Carver about the way they pray. She's a lovely woman, reminds me of my mother, same luxurious dark hair, elegant features. She explained their church believes people should pray from their hearts, not just recite; that reciting prayers can lead to chanting spells, like witches do. I said I love our prayers to the Virgin. When I pray to the Holy Mother it *is* from my heart.' Mother hastily wiped her eye. Priscilla put an arm around her shoulders. 'Mistress Carver said she understood, but I should take care; not say my prayers aloud.'

'But Mother, that is wrong. You should not have to pray secretly. Who dictates thus? Surely not Deacon Carver. He seems so kind, understanding.'

Mother put her finger to her lips. "Tis not the Deacon. Elder Brewster is revered. In his view folk should all follow the practices of the Church of Christ, even if they don't convert. Bradford is like a son to the Brewsters; follows their ways and Mistress Brewster is the most strict of all.'

'It is wrong. We should not be so shackled. And Mother, there is something not right about Dorothy. She is lovely, gentle, and so good with the little ones. But she is like a shadow. I keep wanting to shake her; find her substance. She devoutly follows William's teaching, but I sense it doesn't sit easy.'

'Aye. She does seem strained. Young and old at once. Strange. Ah well. We'd best keep our heads down and cope with the situation as we find it.' Mother dug her needle through the thick fabric of Father's breeches.

In the quiet, Priscilla heard voices below. A light lilting feminine voice. 'Oh Mr Alden. I've come down for Mother. She has the headache. Could I have some aqua vitae, just a few ounces? And while I'm here, perhaps a tour of your cargo hold. I've heard how orderly and well laid out it is.'

A deep chuckle. 'Aye, Mistress Tilley, just a few ounces, and a tour.'

Priscilla felt her cheeks flush hot. The back of her neck prickled. *How dare he?* He'd pleaded with her to believe. A vision of James and Eliza behind the hedge filled her head. What were Mr Alden and that Tilley woman doing down there?

'Mother, I'm so hot. I must go up for some air.'

Emerging on deck, Priscilla saw Father leaning against the fo'castle bulwark conversing with Winslow and Deacon Carver. As she stepped forward, balancing to adjust to the roll of the ship, Mr Martin pranced by, doffing his flamboyant hat. He halted and bowed.

'Mistress Mullins. May I escort you.' With a lurch of the ship he swayed, struggling to stay on his feet.

Priscilla grabbed hold of the half-deck bulkhead. Keeping her eyes averted, she dismissed him with a cold 'Good day' and made her way to a place by the rail where she would be within Father's protective line of sight. She stared into the ocean waters. Dark, dark blue, verging to black. Rolling waves. This far out, the ocean had no other color. She must put Alden out of her mind, cut the thread that pulled her toward him. In spite of his words he is not to be trusted. If he really wanted her to think well of him he would not flirt and… with another woman.

Father was excited about their future. But for her? What lay on the horizon? She lifted her gaze to the indistinct gray line that separated sky from sea.

'Sir, I think I've never laid eyes on a man… so strong… so strong as you.'

Priscilla spun round. *What is that silly girl up to? Flaunting herself so. She can only be thirteen or fourteen years. And to a sailor! Perhaps she is aping Lizzie Tilley.* The lass tossed her red curls, swiveled, hands on hips, in a come hither movement. Pivoting, casting a glance over her shoulder, she tripped and fell, banging her head against the mainmast. Priscilla lurched across the deck to kneel beside her inert body. Folk gathered round. 'Brandy,' Priscilla said.

'I'll go.' Father climbed down through the hatch. Priscilla cradled the girl's head; slapped her cheeks. Her eyes opened, hazel, unfocussed. 'I'm dizzy.' She swooned. Priscilla slapped her again.

'Here.' A hand offered a small jug. It wasn't Father's hand. Priscilla looked up. 'Mr Alden.'

'I'll get the brandy down her while you hold her head.' Alden held the jug to the girl's lips. She sipped. The stimulant worked.

'My head. My head hurts.' The girl put her hand to her right temple.

'You'll have a bruise for sure,' Priscilla said.

'I'll take care of her now.'

Priscilla looked up into Mary Brewster's eyes.

'Yes, Mistress.'

As Priscilla was getting to her feet the bosun charged into the group. 'What's this? You harlots keep away from my sailors.' He looked at Priscilla. The enticed sailor was nowhere to be seen. 'I never.' *What is the use?* Turning her back on the angry bosun and babbling passengers, Priscilla moved over to the rail.

Mr Alden followed close behind. 'May I?' He stood beside her.

'Are you not required in the cargo hold?'

'Your father kindly offered to take my place awhile, so I could breathe the fresh air. How did the girl come to fall?'

'She was flirting, shamelessly, with a sailor and tripped.' Priscilla kept her gaze fixed straight ahead. 'But you are no stranger to women who flirt, Mr Alden. I fancy you quite enjoy it.' She raised her chin.

'What's that?' Alden drew his hand across his brow. 'Who? You don't mean Mistress Tilley?' He shook his head laughing. 'How can you be so – like a silly girl? Surely you know more of the world – or have you lived a cloistered life and kept the innocence of a child?'

Priscilla whirled to face him. 'Mr Alden, you are unforgivably rude. And you call this loose wench *Mistress* Tilley?'

'Her father is a silk-worker, master craftsman like your father.'

'Her behavior doesn't deserve the status of mistress. But perhaps 'tis suited to a man of your position.'

Alden's face darkened into a deep flush. His eyes turned hard and his lips tightened. 'I think 'tis time for me to return to my place – below – Lady Mullins.' He doffed his hat, turned on his heel and strode across the deck.

Scoured by his sarcasm, Priscilla clenched the rail, stared out across the sea, all a blur through her tears; unwanted tears. *What is the matter with me? How could I be so rude? I didn't mean to say those things. The words just tumbled out. Never mind. He is of no account.* She wiped her cheeks. *I hate being locked up on this ship. Please God, let us see land soon. Surely there will be good folk already settled to welcome us. I want nothing more to do with Mr Alden or the Tilley family.*

'Mistress Mullins.' Priscilla recognized the velvety voice.

'Good day, Mr Prence,' she said facing him.

'You are upset. I could not help overhearing a few words. I pray you, do not be distressed. You do not deserve such rude disrespect. You have too fine a nature, housed in a noble bearing.' He made a slight bow from the waist, gently sweeping his lace-cuffed arm the length of his body and across her own. 'Your rightful place is in a spacious home, supplied with servants, furnished with elegance: carpets, silver on the table and you, adorned in gowns of satin and silk. Nothing less would be fitting. That is what I shall provide for the maid I marry.'

'What drives you from England, Mr Prence?'

''Tis a sorry tale.' Mr Prence stepped to Priscilla's right, looking out over the sea, positioning himself so she could not see his blemish. 'I and my twin brother are the youngest of three brothers. It was my fortune, or misfortune, to be cleverer than they. I learned carriage-making, our father's craft, and far exceeded their capabilities. Our business grew and I was about to secure a contract with the Duke of Buckingham when my twin brother pretended he was I and swindled me. We bore a strong resemblance, so it was easy. He did not stop there.' Prence wiped his cheek. His voice caught. He cleared his throat. 'My two brothers set about spreading false rumors, too foul for your ears, Mistress. They defamed my name. I was ruined. Mercifully I hadn't yet married my beloved.'

'So sad a story.' Priscilla looked down into the waves. 'I am sorry, Mr Prence.'

'Ah well.' Mr Prence straightened, adopting a more hearty tone. 'We are sailing to new beginnings, new prosperity, for I will prosper, and my good fortune has already begun, Mistress Mullins, for I have met you.' He bowed again and took his leave, as a gentleman should.

Priscilla felt a glow that he saw her as deserving of elegant surroundings, and was warmed by his story. *Poor man.* She was also relieved he did not wait for her to respond. But she felt an unaccountable twist in her stomach. *Why?* She recalled Father's advice; don't judge by appearance. *It is wrong of me to be put off by a blemish which is not his fault.*

★ ★ ★

'Ring a ring of roses, a pocket full of posies, a'tissue, a'tissue, we all fall down.' Priscilla and Dorothy circled and sang with the littlest children on deck in the warm sunshine and gentle breeze. The ship lurched and orphan Jasper, only four, did fall down. He stretched out his arms crying, 'Doorty, Doorty.' Dorothy swooped over and scooped him up, holding him close with comforting murmurs. Priscilla saw her eyes grow misty and her face cloud over with sadness. She seemed far away. Then she straightened and came back, all laughing and playful.

'Hie! Hie! A whale!' Deacon Carver's servant, Howland, shouted pointing from the bow rail. Holding fast to the little ones, Priscilla and Dorothy hurried to see. Rose Standish came scrambling, following Joseph and the older boys as they leapt across the deck, cup and ball competition abandoned.

'Look, Joseph,' Priscilla pointed. 'Way out. The fountain of spray.' As they sailed closer, the whale grew and grew into an enormous black creature. Diving and surfacing, it slapped its huge tail fin down onto the waves and puffed and blew fountains of spray from its spout.

Joseph clung to Priscilla. 'Will it come and bash our ship? Please don't let it do that.'

'I think if we leave it alone it will leave us alone,' Priscilla said with a confidence she did not entirely feel. 'And I am sure Master Jones would not put us in harm's way.'

The whale swam away and other creatures appeared: a huge sea turtle and a strange, floppy round creature about a yard wide. 'What is that?' Joseph pointed.

'That'd be a jellyfish,' a man said from behind. 'Ain't it weird? Look now, look. Porpoises.' He thrust his hairy arm and wart-covered hand, two fingers missing, between their heads. Just a few in the distance, dipping and diving, then more and more until about a dozen porpoises played and cavorted up close to the *Mayflower*'s hull. 'They be lovely creatures,' the sailor said. 'But a bad sign. Porpoises come, storms follow. A bad sign. Like you lovely lasses. Ye'll jinx us, lest we tame ya,' he sneered.

Priscilla wheeled round, confronting a misshapen face with a twisted nose and hair lip.

'Be gone!' she snapped. 'Be gone or I'll call for Master Jones.'

'Easy now, easy does it. Y're a spirited filly, eh?' He crab-walked off, grinning.

Chapter 9

October 1620

A storm

'All a 'ya stay below!' The bosun shouted down through the hatch and slammed it shut. The ship lurched, corkscrewed, dived bow down, then stern down. The wind whistled and roared, whirling round so it felt as if the ship would be lifted from the ocean and dropped again. Waves rose high above the gunnels, pounding down onto the deck.

Three days later John Alden had given up hoping this tempest would blow through quickly. In the cargo hold he struggled with ropes and straps making fast barrels and chests and stacks of belongings to the floor planking. Water seeped into the bilges. Seasick, Mr Martin lay limp in his bunk above. The bosun was occupied manning the ship in the midst of the wind and waves. There. Job done. Everything secure for the moment.

Unsuccessfully, John tried to keep his mind off Priscilla. He wished to forget her. It was not only her beauty, though looking into her eyes made his insides churn. Her fiery spirit? *I want her and I don't know why. She is not always so high and mighty. I'll not be spurned, but I'll not give up. My gut tells me she is drawn to me, and I sense Mr Mullins favors me.*

John often left the cargo hold to tend the sick passengers, wiping brows, holding them while they retched, pouring the contents of chamber pots into a pail for the sailors to empty overboard. It was miserably cold. No hope of a fire. Folk huddled in blankets, cowering against the icy water dripping through the deck onto their heads, down their necks, soaking the bedding. The place reeked of vomit, wet linen and stale food. In spite of Priscilla's refusal to look at or speak to him he often lingered at the Mullins' cabin, watching as she tended Joseph, struggling to hold the chamber pot steady to catch his vomit. Day after day the storm raged.

"Tis there nothing can be done?' Mr Mullins implored.

'Sadly no,' John said. 'Impossible to hold a course.' He was concerned Mr Mullins looked unwell. He wasn't seasick but he coughed and was pale with deep dark circles under his eyes. John brought extra rations of ale for Joseph to prevent him dehydrating, but he wished there was more he could do to ease their misery. He sensed that Elder Brewster's constant praying brought more irritation than comfort to the Mullins family. Brewster was one of the few who wasn't sick.

Back down in the hold, John was checking his straps and ropes hadn't worked loose, tightening where necessary.

'Mr Alden.'

He straightened to face the first officer.

'Please report to Master Jones.'

'Aye, sir.'

'Bring your jacket and take off your shoes.'

By the time he'd clambered up to the half-deck and then to Master Jones' cabin, John was soaked, blasted with wind and slicing rain. As a rap on the door would go unheard, the officer opened and announced him.

'John. Thank you for coming. Sit down.' Master Jones gestured to a stool opposite his own chair. John glanced round the tiny cabin. Onto one bulkhead was fastened a small desk with a rolled sleeping pallet strapped underneath. Opposite was clamped a small pail.

John sat down. 'Sir.'

'I don't want to ask this of you, but I must command it.' The captain leaned forward, elbows resting on his knees. 'Lost a sailor overboard. Only a lad. Poor blighter. I need another hand on deck. I know you for a good sailor.'

'Aye, sir.'

'I've instructed the ship's mates you're to assist on deck, not go aloft.'

'Aye, sir. Will that be all, sir?'

Master Jones nodded.

The ship's mate stationed John to haul ropes on the port side. He could barely see in the lashing murk, and sensed an uneasiness in the other sea hands. Well, he'd do his best.

'Clap onto that line there,' the mate ordered.

He joined two other sailors hanging onto a straining rope on the port side and looked up at the dizzying sight of sailors perched high aloft to reef the top sails, bending over to grab and secure the flapping canvas as crew on deck released the ropes. Then to unfurl a bit in a lull, only to reef again as the winds worsened. With every muscle John balanced, hauled and released ropes, willing the *Mayflower* to keep on course.

The little ship soared up over a vast roller and slithered down, down, corkscrewing as she went, staggering as a rogue wave lashed her side. Again and again and again. Increasingly exhausted, John became vaguely accustomed to a haphazard rhythm, when suddenly a mountain wave crashed over, blanketing the sails. The *Mayflower* reeled and ducked into the sea. Green water engulfed the deck. His limbs tangled with those of his companions as they all hung onto the rope, floating, immersed in seawater. He knew not whether they were on board or in the sea. As the little ship surfaced, heeled over, and the sea slid away, he felt the deck sliding under his feet as they were thrown down against the scuppers with the draining seawater. Still hanging onto the rope they scrambled back to resume their task. So it went on hour after hour. Unused to manning ropes his hands blistered and bled, unfelt in the fury of a crashing sea and torrential sky. John focused only on his officer's commands.

'Furl the sails! Stow the ropes.'

John halted; listened again.

'Furl the sails,' the officer shouted. 'Lie a hull.'

John almost fell to his knees, faint with exhaustion and relief. He coiled and secured the ropes in his charge until satisfied they would pass inspection.

'Mr Alden,' the officer called. 'Relieved of duty.'

Staggering, dripping, John made his way back down to the cargo hold. Passing the Mullins' cabin he noticed Priscilla bent over Joseph, soothing his brow, talking… 'Once upon a time…' She did not look up.

When he had changed into dry garments he poured a small jug of ale and climbed back up to the Mullins' cabin. Still Priscilla kept her head bowed.

'Mistress Mullins. Ale for Joseph.' He handed the jug to Priscilla's mother.

'Thank you, Mr Alden.' She handed the jug to Priscilla. 'Mr Alden. Your hands – what has happened – blistered and bloody. Oh for clean linen. Here, I have a strip or two of pillowcases, torn up for bandages.'

'I'm most grateful,' John said as she bandaged his hands.

'Good to see you in dry clothes, Mr Alden,' Mr Mullins said. 'You looked near drowned as you passed by just now.'

'Master Jones needed me to do a turn on deck. Man the ropes – hands not used to it.'

Priscilla looked up slightly. He cast a sideways glance at her. 'Master Jones has decided to lie a hull. He has fastened the whipstaff and the tiller tight so we're pointing away from the direction of the wind. As she's not fighting the wind, our ship is bobbing up and down like a duck. Up to the crest of a wave and down the other side. It will give a gentler motion.'

'Could Joseph go on deck for a spell?' Mistress Mullins asked. 'Have a breath of fresh air?'

'Absolutely not.' John was firm. 'The sea is rough and wild as ever. You couldn't stay upright on deck.'

'How do the sailors?' Priscilla looked up and then bowed her head.

'Years of practice. Some do fall overboard and drown.'

'You might have drowned,' she blurted.

'Aye. How long has Howland been behaving thus?' He gestured with his thumb toward a muscular young man his own age. Like a caged animal, Howland paced, fell over, cried out, paced again. 'Let me out, let me out.'

'Is he mad?' Mistress Mullins asked.

'Reckon he's got cabin fever,' John said. 'Comes on some who cannot bear to be shut in.'

'If only I had an infusion of lime,' she said, 'to calm him.'

As John had predicted, the ship's motion soon changed from corkscrewing to a gentler bobbing up and down. Howland began to quieten.

'I must get back to my duties.' John glanced at Priscilla and caught her surreptitiously looking in his direction before she hurriedly gave all her attention to Joseph. Hiding a smile, he went below.

Chapter 10

October 1620

Kittens are born

As Howland calmed, sitting quietly, and Joseph's retching eased, Priscilla gradually unclenched muscles tightened against the heaving and rolling, the cold and wet. Water still dripped through the deck onto their heads, but she sat up straight, pushed her shoulders back. *If only…* she longingly looked up at the hatch, the doorway to fresh air. What? Two feet disappearing. A gust of wind blew down before the hatch slammed shut. An instant later she heard 'Man overboard!' and the sound of running feet. Folk gasped, stunned into silence. Then came more shouts from the crew. Priscilla strained to hear against the roaring wind. 'Pull, pull him in. Hang on… got you. Boathook – pull, heave – grab him!' The sound of a thud. Minutes passed. The hatch opened and a sailor slowly climbed down the ladder with Howland slung over his shoulder. 'Where to?'

Deacon Carver leapt forward. 'John Howland! My servant. Over there.'

Priscilla and Mother stepped back to let them through.

'Aye, his servant, but he loves him like a son, having none of his own,' Mother commented softly. The sailor carefully lowered Howland onto Deacon Carver's bunk.

Priscilla's head spun. 'It's a miracle he didn't drown.'

'Aye,' Mother replied, turning and bending low to gather up their blankets. 'I must go tend to him. Priscilla, please go down to the cargo hold and ask Mr Alden for some brandy. Be quick and don't tarry!'

'Must I?'

'Priscilla! Go!'

Priscilla climbed down the ladder, kicking her skirts out of the way. Mr Alden was at the far end of the hold, his back to her, checking supplies. She cleared her throat.

Alden turned. 'Mistress Mullins?' He wove his way amongst stacks of trunks and sacks to greet her.

'Mother sent me. For brandy. For John Howland. He fell overboard. The sailors rescued him.'

'Overboard? How?' Alden exclaimed as he poured a portion of brandy from the barrel.

'He escaped up through the hatch, and… and…'

Alden held out a small jug. 'Are you alright, Mistress Mullins? You're shaking.'

'I, yes. It is just…' Her head was spinning.

He was tender, not angry. She felt ashamed, dizzy. The barrels and sacks seemed to spin round. She grabbed at the ladder as her knees gave way.

''Tis you needs some brandy.'

Through her haze his voice was soft, kind, and she hadn't the strength to pull away from his arm round her waist as he held the jug to her lips. Nor could she hold back the tears.

'There – never mind.' He put the jug down holding it between his feet and fished a handkerchief from his pouch, to wipe her cheeks.

'Priscilla!' Mother's voice.

'Can you manage the ladder? I'll bring the brandy for Howland.'

'Aye, I'll try. Thank you, Mr Alden.'

Her head throbbing and stomach churning, Priscilla welcomed the demand to deal with a group of squabbling children. She did not want Mother to see her flushed cheeks and distracted manner.

★ ★ ★

Several days later, Priscilla sat in the Mullins' cabin alone. Mother and Joseph were at the other end of the ship with Mistress Carver and the children Joseph's age. Father was, as ever, sequestered in conversation with the Pilgrims' leaders about how to build a colony. She leafed through the pages of her gardening book, turning to October. Drawings of hedgerows festooned with boughs of blackberries, hazelnuts, rosehips, and old man's beard. Mushrooms in the fields. *Would America have these English fruits?*

'Mistress Mullins.'

She jumped, startled.

'Mr Alden.'

'Would you come with me a minute? I've something to show you. Mr Martin is with Master Jones so it's safe.' Priscilla followed Alden down the ladder into the cargo hold and along right to the other end, past barrels of drink and food, and trunks of belongings stacked high, and there, in amongst the piles of armor and tools, was the calico cat and three newborn kittens! 'Oh the darlings!' Priscilla knelt down and stroked the mother.

Alden spoke softly. 'She found a quiet place away from the dogs and crew. If anyone finds these kittens they'll be thrown overboard. So it must be a secret.'

'I'll say nothing.' Priscilla stood. 'You will try to keep them safe?'

'I'll do my best,' he said, searching her face. Neither moved.

Priscilla looked down at her clasped hands. Then, meeting Alden's direct blue eyes she asked, 'What made you decide to come on this voyage, Mr Alden?'

Alden glanced down at the kittens, pressed into their mother's belly. 'Several things. Some years back my father died. My uncle married my mother and took over our family business. There was no place for me.'

'Oh – I'm sorry.' Priscilla studied Mr Alden's fine thick blond hair, falling in waves to his shoulders. His beard and moustache were short and neat.

'Master Jones took me on his ship to see if I fancied going to sea. Sailed with him three years. Good captain, but I'm too much a landlubber.' He smiled. 'Couldn't take to it. Wood is my trade. I went to London looking for work, but with the shortage of timber, jobs for a cooper are scarce.'

'Aye,' Priscilla said. 'We've not had enough wood to keep warm these past few winters. When I was little we sat by roaring blazes, but recently only at Christmas and I know Father spent more than he should. He does so want the best for us.' She stopped. 'But you, Mr Alden, you were on board in London.'

'Aye, I happened upon Master Jones and he offered me a place on this ship. But it wasn't only lack of work. Another thing decided me.' His usually playful expression changed to a look of serious intensity. He leaned against a stack of trunks and folded his arms across his chest.

'What was that?' Priscilla held onto the top of a crate to keep her balance.

'I had a friend, Will. Been friends from a lad. He too was a cooper, was with me looking for work in London. Betrothed to a pretty lass – happy as turtledoves, it seemed. Of a sudden, she jilted him. Said she'd found someone with better prospects.' Alden arched his left eyebrow.

Priscilla looked down at her feet.

'Will went addled in the head. Wandered in his sleep, wouldn't touch food. In a terrible state. One day he came back from his wanderings, face radiant, beaming. "I've found the Lord, the living, risen Christ." It turns out he and another young man gave themselves to following a preacher who claimed he was Christ come again. He preached in public places. They passed the hat, receiving coins from the crowds. Damsels swooned. Some accompanied "the Christ" to his lodgings.'

'The fraud!' Priscilla stamped her foot.

'Eventually the King's officers caught them. The preacher escaped but my friend and his companion were thrown into prison.' Alden shook his head and looked down, poking at the planking with the toe of his boot. 'His companion had a friend on the Privy Council and was released. Will was left. I hadn't enough money to bribe the prison officers or the connections to free him. So he rots and starves, no doubt goes mad in a filthy rat-infested prison. Expect he'll die of the plague, unless I can earn enough money in time to pay for his release.'

Priscilla felt her insides lurch. 'That is terrible. Truly terrible. Was the fake Christ ever caught?'

'No, got off unscathed, and report has it he now sports fine garb and a big belly.'

'Is that why you came on this voyage? To get away from...'

'Aye. When Master Jones offered me this chance I grabbed it with both hands.' Alden looked into Priscilla's eyes and held her. 'I tell you, Mistress Mullins, I want to live in a land where laws are just and apply equally to everyone, no matter if they be poor or of lowly status. Where good fortune doesn't depend on being in the right person's favor. I want to make my way on my own merit, build a place where I can raise my children in a good home, secure community, where they can learn unfettered and prosper.'

Alden's earnest face and words shook Priscilla. She felt the power of him, his honesty, conviction and strength. This wasn't the man/woman game of chase and be caught. He had shared his feelings and convictions with *her*, a mere woman! Unheard of. A weakness in her knees traveled to her head and voice. Hanging onto the crate, still looking into his eyes, she could only reply, "Tis well said, Mr Alden,' her voice husky. She felt herself melt in his gaze, unable, not wanting, to look away.

Alden spoke first. 'Happily, no lords and ladies on this ship. Making a settlement will be tremendous hard work. We must be prepared for that. Do you agree, Mistress Mullins?'

Priscilla looked down and turned her face aside. 'No lords and ladies,' she murmured. She raised her head. 'I think most would say I am a good worker.' She wanted him to believe her. 'I must go back up. Mother will be wondering.'

Up through the hatch, Priscilla collapsed onto their bench, giving thanks Mother was somewhere else.

Needing to hide her blushing face, she fetched the mending from their trunk and bent low over a tear in Joseph's breeches. Her feelings were roused as never before. *Mr Alden has spoken true, strong and true. I like what he says. However, he is only a cooper; respectable, yes, but would he ever provide a grand enough house? No lords and ladies on this ship. I was hoping for a lord. Would I have beautiful gowns and wear my lovely sash? Would I have the pleasure of refined surroundings as Mr Prence promises? Not likely.* 'I want to make my own way on my own merit,' *Mr Alden said. But he never said how high he wanted to rise; nothing about becoming a magistrate or a governor.* And yet, she wanted him to want her. *I want him. I know I want him.*

Chapter 11

October 1620

Singing

Priscilla was sitting with Joseph on their bunk, telling him a story, when, 'Hark…' She inclined her head toward the hatch leading down to the cargo hold.

'I can't hear anything.'

'Be quiet. Listen.' Priscilla thought she heard a faint sound of singing coming from below. Yes, a man's voice, as if far away. 'Come, Joseph.' They climbed down the ladder.

''Twas in the month of Maying…' It was John Alden singing as he inspected barrels at the far end of the hold. Priscilla couldn't resist. She knew the song. Signaling Joseph with a finger on her lips she crept forward.

'When merry lads are playing…' Alden started and whirled round.

'Mistress Mullins! You've a fine voice!' He started the song again and Priscilla joined him. The delight. It was a merry song, and for a few moments, savoring the pleasant smells of wood and grain she was transported to the May time in England: the fresh spring green leafing, fields of grasses dotted with buttercups, wet with heavy early morning dew, dances round the Maypole on the green, choirs singing madrigals.

'S'what's this?' The fat florid face of Mr Martin appeared at the hatch. 'By Jesu, what do you think you're doing?' He hurled down the ladder. 'You harlot!' He yanked Priscilla's arm. 'And you, Mr Alden – any more of this singing rubbish and you'll be flogged. There's a cat-o'-nine-tails lying idle, just waiting for a backside to whip.'

'Mr Martin, forbear.' That smooth controlled voice. Mr Prence climbed down following the podgy governor in his yellow coat. 'I heard singing and harsh words. Don't worry, Mr Alden. Simply a bit of misguided childish fun. I'll not report you. Elder Brewster and Deacon Carver would be vexed but your secret is safe with me.' He put a hand under Priscilla's elbow. 'I'll escort you to your mother's care.'

Mr Martin stamped his foot. 'Mr Prence. You have no right. Mr Weston appointed me governor of this ship.'

'We all know that counts for little. Remember, if you should say anything, Mr Martin, it is your word against mine. I'm sure you know who would be believed. You wouldn't want to be defending yourself in front of Deacon Carver and Master Jones.'

Joseph clung to Priscilla's skirt. Her cheeks and neck were on fire. She stared at Alden, still as stone, fists tight, face suffused in a deep blush, eyes glaring hard blue, jaw clenched. She bowed her head and dutifully led Joseph to the ladder, Mr Prence behind her.

Startled from her mending, Mother said, 'Mr Prence? What has happened?'

'I rescued your daughter from a troublesome...' Mr Prence flicked his wrist, ruffling his cuff in his search of the precise word. 'A troublesome *affaire, une petite betise.* All is well now.' He bowed.

When Mr Prence was out of earshot, Priscilla sank onto their bench. She put her face in her hands and let hot tears flow. 'All is *not* well. We were not doing anything wrong. Only having some pleasure singing. Both Mr Martin and Mr Prence seem to think singing is a crime. Are we in a shipful of mad folk?'

'Sssh.' Mother put a comforting arm round her shoulder while cradling Joseph on her other side. 'I don't know. It seems some of our leaders are severely strict. Perhaps Mr Prence is under their influence. It is hard but we must do as we're told and be patient.' She heaved a weary sigh.

Priscilla nodded and pulled out the trunk to find her gardening book. She stopped short. 'What is *une petite betise?*'

'I don't know. Sounds French. Perhaps Mr Prence was trying to impress us. I'll ask Mistress Carver. She might know.'

'Oh, please no. The Deacon mustn't know we were singing. Mr Prence said we would be in grievous trouble. Please, Mother. Mr Prence said he would keep it secret.'

'Did he?' Mother frowned.

Alone, Priscilla stood on deck, looking out over the ocean, wanting to catch the last rays of the evening sun. As the red sliver disappeared down behind the dark rim of the sea, the skies clouded over and the wind picked up causing a mounting swell of dark waves. Peak, trough, peak, trough, never ending. Would her hunger ever end? She was so tired. Her mind felt empty, sucked into the rolling water, carried, full of nothing but the dark sea. So easy, tempting to let go, be submerged, and sucked away from the misery and strife on this ship. She leaned, responding to the mesmerizing pull. The waves called, 'Come, come away... come, come away.' 'Aah!' Priscilla jerked back into herself, pulled her shawl tighter.

'Merry month of Maying...' softly humming rich voice behind her. She froze. 'That could be our song, Mistress Mullins.' He stepped up beside her, his arm around her waist.

'Mr Prence,' she gasped.

'My dear.' He pulled her closer, whispered in her ear. 'I know that song and many others. We could sing together secretly in our own home. Just you and I. Our voices go well together.'

'Mr Prence, I beg of you. I am feeling unwell.'

'I'll take you below. I'll see you are safe.' Mr Prence insisted on climbing down the ladder before Priscilla to be sure she didn't fall. She felt his hand on her ankle, his arms reaching up to hold her waist.

By the time they reached the planking he was enfolding her, his face pressed to her cheek.

'Mr Prence.'

'Father!' Priscilla sprang to his side.

'Good day, Mr Mullins. I found your daughter on deck feeling unwell. I was helping her down the ladder.'

'Thank you, Mr Prence. Good day.' Unsmiling, Father doffed his hat, stifling a cough.

Mr Prence nodded to Priscilla. 'Good day, Mistress, I pray you will be recovered soon.' Stature erect, he made his way through piles of belongings toward his own space near the Brewsters.

'Hmph.' Father leaned against a masthead, taken in a coughing fit.

'Priscilla, you do look peaky, pale as if you've had a shock.' Mother drew a flask from the trunk. 'Have a sip; Mr Alden gave us our own supply.'

Priscilla sat down, gratefully sipped the brandy and felt the color coming back to her cheeks. 'Father, please have a sip. You're looking pale.' She handed him the flask.

'Seems Mr Prence is becoming Elder Brewster's star pupil. Swallowing scripture and spouting doctrine like a divinity whale.'

Priscilla choked back a giggle and then wondered, *If he is so devout why was Mr Prence saying we would sing worldly, courting songs together?*

At that moment Captain Standish descended the ladder from the upper deck, muttering. He addressed Father. 'I've just had to rescue a damsel from the unwanted attentions of Mr Martin. That man is nothing but a troublesome fool. Cannot think why Mr Weston appointed him governor. Only person thinks he's fit to govern is himself.'

'Aye,' Father said. 'Not a soul on board respects him, not even the dogs.'

'You fare well?' Standish bowed with an inclination of his head toward Priscilla and Mother.

'Thank you, yes,' Mother said.

'I'm going down for a visit with Mr Alden,' Standish said.

'Reckon I'll come with you.' Father followed the captain.

Priscilla settled to help Mother with the mending. Joseph was practicing his knots before his next lesson with Master Jones. 'I don't like that man.'

'What man?' Priscilla asked.

'Him. Carried you down the ladder.'

Priscilla studied her stitches. 'Do you like him, Mother?'

'My dear. Why do you ask?'

'Mr Prence offers everything I've wanted; but...'

'But?'

'But I feel repelled, and feel I shouldn't be. Father said a man's character is more important than his appearance.'

'Perhaps it isn't only Mr Prence's appearance that repels you. Perhaps something in his nature makes you recoil.'

Priscilla stopped stitching and stared at the masthead. *When I sang with Mr Alden I felt delight, and longing. With Mr Prence I felt sickened. He tried to push himself into me, onto me, assumed he was superior, assumed I should want him. He was arrogant. Arrogant. Like me. Mr Prence is of higher status than Mr Alden, but Mr Alden's nature is far superior. That is what matters, a person's nature.* She recalled Father's words, took a deep breath and stretched her back. 'Thank you, Mother,' she said. 'I see now.'

Chapter 12

October 1620

A beam cracks – Priscilla trusts

A report like the sound of a cannon being fired shot through the ship. The *Mayflower* shuddered. Joseph covered his ears and bent his head down to his knees. Mother crossed herself, rapidly murmuring prayers to the Holy Mother. Priscilla clutched her arms round her waist. *Is this it? The end? Please God, no.* The passengers waited in stunned silence.

Father was threading his way back toward them when the hatch opened and Mr Martin almost fell down the ladder in his haste.

'Stay below all of you and don't move!' His face flushed red, and then paled. 'A main beam has gone. The ship might split.' Now women screamed, moaned and wrung their hands. Children wailed. The dogs barked and whimpered. Elder Brewster pleaded for quiet and prayer.

Huddled over, her arm round Joseph, Priscilla struggled not to weep from fear and dizzy nausea, a constant companion to permanent hunger and the stench of their quarters. Joseph scratched his arm, red raw from flea bites, lice and itchy garments damp with saltwater.

'Stop that,' Priscilla hissed and then raised her head to watch as Father, Bradford, Winslow, Deacon Carver, and Mr Alden, climbed up through the hatch to the great cabin. Father said the previous storm had weakened the ship and they were meeting with Master Jones to decide whether to go on or turn back. Elder Brewster's prayers were barely audible through the howling wind and crashing waves. Priscilla listened to the calls of commands and hurrying footsteps overhead. Waiting... waiting. Head bowed, she became immersed in a numb fog.

A blast of cold air and spray jolted her upright. Deacon Carver climbed down the ladder. 'Master Jones has decided we will not turn back,' he announced. 'Mr Alden suggested using the screw jack to secure the beam back in place. He is getting a crew together now.' Priscilla heard murmurs of approval and dissent in equal measure: Standish punched the air, 'Aye!' Mother shook her head. 'I think we should turn back. Your father has been marking the days in his almanac and he says we've been at sea nigh on six weeks. The good Lord knows how much longer we can survive.'

In spite of Mother's words, Priscilla felt a surge of hope.

Through the open hatch to the cargo hold she could hear Mr Alden giving instructions and sounds of heaving and pushing as the screw jack scraped across the floor. She remembered seeing it; a massive iron screw with handles set into a stout, oaken frame. It would be unimaginably heavy.

'Heave.' The ascent began. Up the ladder, from the cargo hold one sailor pulled and steadied. Then Alden and Howland appeared, supporting and pushing, dripping sweat, grunting, balancing against the rolling and jerking of the storm-tossed ship. Clunk as they rested it on the floor next to the Mullins' cabin and paused to get their breath before heaving it up the next ladder. Priscilla stared, transfixed. Through the open hatches she could hear Mr Alden directing the men where to stand, some to lift the beam, some to shove the screw jack into place. He called out, 'One, two, three, heave!'

Desperate to watch, Priscilla ducked round a group of women and scurried up the two ladders before anyone could stop her. With just her head poking out above the hatch, she saw the beam lifters straining every muscle, sweat streaming down their faces, slowly, painfully, raising the massive oak beam high enough for the screw jack to be slid under. Then two men wound the screw until the beam was in position. The ship's carpenter wedged a bracing post between the deck and the beam, and another on the other side. Then slowly, carefully, Alden and the carpenter unwound the screw. They waited. No one uttered a sound. The beam held. Only then did Priscilla see Deacon Carver standing right by the hatch. She scurried back down the ladders like lightning, and in the nick of time joined the silent crowd of women and children before the Deacon climbed down.

'They did it! They did it!'

'Hoorah, hoorah, God be praised.' Priscilla joined the chorus of exultation. *And Mr Alden be praised for having the idea. I do want him to favor me. I hope…*

Returning from a visit with Dorothy, in the quiet time before prayers, Priscilla settled Joseph to practice his letters. Hearing steps on the ladder she raised her eyes to see Lizzie Tilley emerging from the cargo hold, smiling as someone who savors a special secret. Priscilla's heart curled in confused misery. *I cannot trust him. I must put him out of my mind.*

'Just enough time before prayers,' Mother said as she pressed a fresh poultice on Father's leg and wrapped a linen strip around it. 'Wish we had clean linen. I fear these soiled strips do more harm than good.' She tut-tutted.

'Mistress Mullins.' The ship's doctor stood by.

'Sir.' Mother stood in greeting.

'I'm told you have much knowledge of remedies. The bosun is in delirium with fever – sorely afflicted. Do you have a concoction that might help? I've none left.'

'Only one small jar. Belladonna.'

'I beg of you, could you bring it to him?'

Priscilla fumed inwardly as Mother brought the jar out from the trunk. *Don't waste our precious remedy on that vile creature.* She ventured to protest. 'But Mother, what if Father?'

'The bosun is a person in distress.' Mother went with the doctor.

'My leg will be fine,' Father said. ''Tis only a sore and with your mother's attentions…'

Priscilla noticed a tall, coifed figure standing half-hidden behind a masthead. She craned her neck for a closer look. *Mary Brewster. Strange. Oh well.*

She jabbed at her mending. *It isn't right. This horrid man said he wished we would all be washed overboard so he could grab our belongings. How can Mother use our precious remedy on him?*

It wasn't long before Mother stumbled back and sat down heavily on the bed. She wiped her brow. 'I've rarely seen a body in such a state. Ranting, thrashing in his own filth. Not a soul dared go near him. Mercifully, as I approached he calmed, said "Holy Mother of God" and took the concoction like a babe. Please God it gives him some relief. I fear he won't live. Gangrene too far advanced. Seems he cut his hand splicing a rope in the storms. A deep gash. Wrapped his neckerchief round it and carried on. Never told the doctor.'

Next morning when folk were gathered for prayers Deacon Carver announced, 'Our bosun died in the night – peacefully, the doctor says.' He looked at Mother. Priscilla supposed she should be sorry, but felt only blessed relief to be free of the bullying monster.

Bradford raised his voice, 'We see how this man's curses have fallen on his own head, and now he himself is the first to be thrown overboard. 'Tis the just hand of God at work.'

Priscilla heard a hissing whisper behind. 'Sacrilege to waste a precious remedy on him. Should have been saved for God's own.' Glancing back she saw it was Mary Brewster. She shuddered, and realized she herself had thought the same.

Gradually the winds eased. Folk could enjoy some respite from seasickness and fear, and have more time on deck in the fresh air. But Priscilla fretted about Mr Alden and longed to visit the calico cat and her kittens. *Had Mr Alden shown Lizzie Tilley the kittens?* She sought refuge in Dorothy. Dorothy needed her and was steady; didn't bounce her around.

One afternoon when the winds were gentle, Priscilla decided to see if Dorothy would like to come with her up on deck. On approaching the Bradfords' cabin she thought she heard stifled sobbing behind the curtain – so quiet she couldn't be sure. Softly, she called, 'Dorothy? – it's Priscilla.' Silence. After a moment a small hand drew the curtain aside and Dorothy's white face appeared, eyes red. Priscilla sat beside her on the bunk. 'What is it, Dorothy? Why are you so sad?' Dorothy drew the curtain across so they were hidden.

'My little boy, my John.'

'You have a child?'

Dorothy could hardly whisper the words, shaking with quiet sobbing. 'I can see him… standing on the quayside… his arms stretched out trying to reach me… they had to hold him back or he'd have jumped. He couldn't understand. He's five years old… other children coming… thought he should come too. He is dearer to me than my own life. I can't bear it. I long for him so. But William mustn't see me like this.' She shook herself. 'He is a kind man, a good husband, and he says it is God's will that we do this. I pleaded, begged. He said I was thinking only of myself. Little John must stay with Pastor and Mistress Robinson. They will cherish him, keep him safe. We must do what's best for John and suffer for the sake of God's will.' She shoved her knuckles into her mouth to stop her words, biting so hard she drew blood. Priscilla held her close. There was nothing comforting she could say. Gradually when the sobs and shaking stopped, Dorothy said, 'Promise me you won't speak of this to anyone.'

Priscilla promised. 'Come with me. Let's get some fresh air.'

She led Dorothy up the ladder and over to the rail, an arm round her thin, shivering shoulders. 'I've always wondered why you are so sad. It's terrible what you've suffered. Your own dear child, and you cannot know how he fares.'

'I do know Pastor and Mistress Robinson are goodness itself and John is fond of them. I have to trust he fares well.' Dorothy stared at her feet and gripped the rail. 'I was only sixteen when he was born. With William always studying or in religious discussion, my John gave me such happiness.' She choked.

'Aye, and when we have built a settlement then surely your lad will join you.'

Dorothy looked out over the sea. 'Endless waters. It is hard to imagine the day will ever come when we have built a colony. I need you to remind me, Priscilla, to encourage me,' she implored.

Priscilla hugged her. 'Of course I will. Of course.'

★ ★ ★

'It's a boy,' Mother called out. The wail of the newborn babe sent a surge of joy through Priscilla. 'The mother and babe are well.' Mother collapsed onto the bed. 'They're calling him Peregrine.'

The screams of birthing pains had kept all souls awake through the night. Now, in the early hours, Mother was settling into sleep, but Priscilla was wide awake and restless. She waited until she heard Mother breathing the deep breaths of slumber, then pulled on her skirts, wrapped her winter shawl tight and climbed to the deck above. Good. Only a few crew about and no one near 'her' place by the mainmast, tucked into a corner next to the ship's boat.

Weary, hungry and gnawed by a growing fear and sadness, she looked down into the sea lapping past.

Why am I sad about Mr Alden? Why do I keep wishing?

Haunted by Dorothy's sad story, she thought of the orphans.

Mistress Carver said they aren't orphans, they're bastards. Love children. When the husband realized, he took them away from their mother and sent them to America. Mistress Carver said it happens a lot. Wonder if Dorothy knows. Day after day we sail. Are we lost? Will we sail on and on and die of starvation and disease? No mistaking the signs: bad breath, red spots, bleeding gums. Scurvy. Her gaze followed the ship's wake, past the stern toward the east, where Dorothy's son lived, far across the ocean. Dorothy: despairing and now showing signs of scurvy. Joseph, thin, coughing, pale. *Is this all part of God's plan? Surely not.* The red rim of the sun edged up over the horizon, sending blood-red spears into a golden fan, up and up, chasing away the misty gray. *What beauty.*

'Mistress Mullins.'

Priscilla whirled round. 'Mr Alden!'

''Tis a splendid sunrise.'

'Aye.' She grasped hold of the rail.

'You haven't come down to see the kittens, weeks old now.'

'Does Lizzie Tilley know about the kittens?' Priscilla blurted out the words before she could stop herself. She felt her cheeks grow hot and looked aside over the rail into the sea.

'Mistress Tilley does not know about the kittens. I made sure.'

His voice was calm, gentle. His hand rested on the rail almost touching hers. Priscilla dared look at him. He smiled.

'You can trust me, Mistress Mullins. I promise.'

Chapter 13

November 1620

Land ahoy!

Why is it taking so long? Two weeks since the last storm. Holding Joseph's hand, Priscilla stared dumbly into the water. *Why would anyone choose to go to sea?* As she stared she started and rubbed her eyes. Stared again, searching. *Was it truly? Changing color? Not so dark – wait, wait.* She held her breath. *Yes, truly – lighter blue, blue with hints of green –* and then to proclaim she really was seeing true, the distant cawing of a gull. A hush settled on deck, as passengers listened for the call from the crow's-nest. Long minutes went by. 'Land ahoy!'

Joseph jumped and hopped and squeaked his joy. 'Land! Will we go ashore soon, and hunt?' He doubled over, coughing. Priscilla held him upright as the deck filled with jubilant voices and stamping feet.

William and Dorothy Bradford hurried toward her but Mr Prence intercepted them, reaching her a few paces ahead.

'May I be the first to share this joyous moment with you, Mistress?' He reached for her hand. 'Not long until we can make our home together in this new land.'

'Hoorah!' Bradford looked to heaven. 'God be praised.'

Priscilla withdrew from Mr Prence's grasp and hugged Dorothy.

'Priscilla...' she heard Father call.

'Here,' she waved.

Supported by Mr Alden, Father slowly, painfully, limped toward her. Mother followed. Mr Prence quickly pushed through to her father's side.

'Allow me, Mr Mullins. You may return to your duties in the hold, Mr Alden. I'll care for...'

'No,' Father said. 'I prefer Mr Alden should support me.'

Prence said nothing, and bowing slightly, backed away as gracefully as he could, returning to Priscilla and the Bradfords.

'Dear gentleman. I fear the pain is affecting his mind.'

Taking hold of Joseph, Priscilla threaded through folk to join her parents and Mr Alden, indicating they should find a place to stand away from Mr Prence.

An expectant hush enveloped the deck as folk waited for the first sight of land. It seemed to Priscilla the *Mayflower* was crawling.

Then, as if the ship had been climbing a hill and reached the top, there appeared, in the distance but clearly visible, a cascade of colors: red, gold, bright yellow, orange, pouring down to the shoreline.

'What?' Her question echoed round the deck.

'Trees.' Mr Alden hoisted Joseph up onto his shoulder. 'We are coming to a vast land full of trees, never ending.'

'Are we landing? May I go ashore? Please?' Joseph squirmed.

'Not yet awhile, lad.' Alden put Joseph down. 'Master Jones says the storms have driven us off course, way north of the Hudson. He's consulting now with Deacon Carver whether to anchor here in Cape Cod or head south.'

'Our contract is to settle in the Hudson valley,' Father said. 'But if we do go south, I hope it won't take many days.' He winced and grasped the rail, using it to support his weight.

The answer came with the first mate shouting orders, the crew hurrying, pushing folk out of the way, adjusting the sails, as gradually the *Mayflower* turned to the left to sail south along the coast. The ship's motion was steady with a cool wind pushing from behind. Priscilla breathed deeply, ''Tis glorious.'

'Aye. Puts hope in the breast. Looks a land to bring health, to prosper in,' Alden said, ruffling Joseph's hair.

'Pray God it's a good omen,' Mother murmured.

'We're into November and the air is warm. If these lands are as plentiful as we're told, we will surely prosper,' Priscilla said. 'Do you suppose there are natives amongst the trees, watching us, Mr Alden, and wild beasts?'

'There may be, but remember, the natives will be keen to trade. If we show goodwill there should be no trouble.' Alden spoke with confidence.

Priscilla glanced up at his profile. 'Will there be folk to greet us?'

Alden looked into her hopeful face. 'Did you not know?' He spoke softly. 'We are the first. The first from Europe to settle in this virgin land north of Virginia.'

'Oh,' Priscilla twisted her hands and glanced at Father. What else had he not told her – and Mother?

'Don't fear,' Alden gestured as if to take her hands. 'I'm sure we'll land soon and with food inside us we'll build quickly.'

Priscilla and Alden stood quietly together looking out at the brilliant foliage. Of a sudden they saw logs, twigs, debris from land hustling round the *Mayflower* as her bow swung out to sea. The ship swayed, rushed with the current as sails flapped and luffed and ropes slapped and banged.

'All souls below!' the first mate shouted.

Priscilla's stomach clutched. *Please God, not more danger.* Joseph pulled at her skirt.

Mother came beside her. 'My God. My God, what now?'

Priscilla and Mother and Joseph hurried to be the first down the hatch. Alden helped Father down the ladder. He sat down heavily with a grimace.

'We're caught in shoals,' Alden said. 'It's a rip tide. Pulls out so fast there's no warning and it's ferociously strong. We may have to anchor and pray we don't get dashed to pieces. We desperately need the wind to shift round to the south.'

'Alden? Where are you?' Mr Martin shrieked from the cargo hold below.

Alden raised an eyebrow. 'I'd best go see if I can settle him.'

We were so near. We could have landed. We survived the storms and now we could all drown within only a few miles of land. Priscilla sat with her arms around Joseph, leaning into her, weak and stunned into silence. She stared down at the floor planking as the hull creaked and tilted. Teeth clenched against the sound of turbulent surf, she watched and waited for the rushing water to surge up through the cracks. She imagined the ship being broken to pieces, herself being thrown and tossed against the rocks, helpless, hearing Joseph cry out, their bodies battered to death. This would be worse than drowning in the storm, silently disappearing into the deep. Her terror became angry. How dare these people talk of God's will, His testing? She hated Elder Brewster's incessant praying and bit her lip to stop herself shouting 'Shut your mouth'. Joseph whimpered. She hugged him tighter and rested her cheek on his blond curls, now lank and coarse from lack of food. The passengers stayed still and mute as if afraid that any movement or vibration might further destabilize the ship.

Father sat with his hourglass. Slowly, slowly the sands passed through. He turned it over for the second time. The last grains of sand passed through the neck and he turned it again. Two hours.

'Attention! Attention!' Priscilla's nerves jangled. That horrid squawk. Mr Martin stood amongst them, hand raised. *He does look like an inflated bullfrog with his swollen belly and bug eyes and little spindly legs. The bosun was right.*

'Master Jones has decided the *Mayflower* will not try to reach the Hudson. We are in uncharted waters. Too dangerous. The wind is shifting round to the south and the tide is turning. With wind and tide in our favor we will head back to Cape Cod.'

Priscilla could have whooped with relief. She gave Joseph a hug and, seeing Mother's drawn face relax into a smile, squeezed her hand.

'Master Jones is a good, wise sea captain. Pity there are some who disagree.' Father nodded toward a group of noisy men.

'Cowardly,' a man said. 'The Hudson valley is where we should settle. Guaranteed to prosper there. If he was worth his salt the captain would continue south.'

Priscilla twisted round. She remembered; when they were anchored in Southampton. It was John Billington, the big burly man who had wanted to chase after Weston with a knife when he'd said 'No more money'. She shuddered. He frightened her.

'Permission to go on deck,' Mr Martin barked.

Only a few climbed back up the ladder, Priscilla amongst them. She found her preferred spot by the mainmast in the shelter of the ship's boat. *Good, no one here.* She put an arm around the mast and laid her cheek against the cool, age-polished pine, feeling reassured by the ship's steady carriage, the support of a southerly wind billowing the sails and a favorable tide. *Hurry, Mayflower, hurry.* Hearing footsteps she turned. 'Mr Alden!'

'Mr Martin has relieved me in the hold so I could catch some light and air.'

'I'm glad he has an ounce or two of kindness.'

'He's fuming we're not heading for the Hudson.'

'Well I'm relieved.'

'I agree, but it looks like the Dutch have won.'

'What do you mean?'

Alden leaned against the hull of the ship's boat. He glanced around and lowered his voice. 'Don't speak of this to anyone, but not long after we'd set out from Plymouth, Master Jones summoned me to his cabin. He has taken quite a liking to your little Joseph, by the way. Says he is a bright lad and always asks after his well-being. Anyway, Jones questioned me closely about the repairs to *Speedwell*, where the hull leaked having already been put right. He said the ship was carrying too much sail and the strain caused the seams to spring and leak. It all seemed to confirm a rumor he'd heard that *Speedwell*'s captain had done a deal with the Dutch to delay our departure so they could reach the Hudson first.'

'But we might have all drowned in those terrible storms! And now we'll be having to explore and build a settlement with winter coming on.'

'It's a harsh world, Mistress. Some folk will do anything to seize the best land. The Hudson is a rich and fertile part of this world.'

Priscilla thought of Joseph, so thin and weakened from the storms. Everyone was haggard and hungry. She looked down at her own figure; her gown hung loose. When the voyage had started she'd filled it out handsomely. She looked at Alden's face. He too was gaunt with dark circles under his eyes. Weary as she was, Priscilla sparked. 'Well, we'll just have to show them.'

Alden smiled, straightening his drooping shoulders. 'That's the spirit. But not a word, mind. I'd best go below again. Mr Martin will be getting impatient.' He lingered, running the palm of his hand along the mast as his eyes joined hers. He cleared his throat. 'I must go.'

Priscilla's 'Aye' was soft and husky. She let her gaze follow him as he left her. Looking again toward the shore, she began to shake. Her teeth chattered, her legs wanted to give way. Clinging to the mast she wondered if she was falling ill. A small flock of gulls cawed and wheeled close to her head, intent on any scrap of food. Sailors called as they adjusted sails to catch the southerly wind. She wished the warmth of the late afternoon sun would ease her shivering.

Mr Alden had shared another confidence with her. He had asked her to trust him. She wanted him, so much it frightened her. Keeping hold of the mast she breathed in and out, slowly, deeply, gazing across the water to the colorful shore. Gradually the shivering ceased. She walked carefully to the hatch.

Chapter 14

November 1620

The Mayflower Compact

Priscilla descended the ladder into a commotion of men's voices, loud and angry, arguing, threats. Father was in their midst, trying to bring calm as John Billington shook his fist, shouting.

'We are under contract to colonize the Hudson River valley. Not be stuck up here in a backwater. The Hudson valley is fertile land and we know fish and furs are plentiful there. Why should we stay with this Church of Christ lot? They waste half their time praying. We'll do better on our own.'

Priscilla edged her way through the crowd.

'Be reasonable,' Father said. 'How will you fare without protection? How will you survive the harsh conditions of winter, an attack from Indians? There is safety in numbers. Far better to be part of a large group all working together. That is the way to prosper. And why have we all risked crossing the ocean if not to prosper?'

Bradford and Winslow joined Father, Bradford saying it was God's will they should stay farther north, Winslow arguing the practical advantages of no longer risking their lives on the sea. Instead of bringing calm, their remonstrations only further incensed the rebel group.

'Will o' God, will o' God. That's all we hear. Stop praying all the while and consult us when ya decide what ya'll do.' John Billington hopped and punched the air.

Father stepped closer to the man's large bulk. 'Cease your ranting and think, man. Do you want to destroy this venture? If you want to be consulted you should behave in a more civil manner. Can you not see?'

Billington's fist struck Father's jaw. He staggered and fell. Mother gasped, and with Joseph tugging at her skirt, Priscilla pushed through bodies to kneel beside her father. 'Joseph, go fetch Mr Alden. Brandy.' Joseph darted and ducked on his mission.

Mr Prence knelt beside Priscilla. 'I'll help you, Mr Mullins; get you to your feet.'

'No,' Mullins said. 'Keep off.'

'You heard.' Mr Alden was there with a small beaker.

'Thank you.' Mullins took a sip.

Gently, Alden lifted Priscilla's father and guided him to their cabin where he could sit.

'Mr Alden, we are very grateful,' Mother said.

Feeling faint, Priscilla swayed. Alden's arm was round her. She didn't move, closing her eyes a brief instant against the uproar of shouts, screams and barking dogs.

John Billington bellowed, 'Join me. All you who want to go to the rich Hudson.' Priscilla stood straight, stepping out from Alden's embrace. 'Are you going to allow a few heretics to spoil your prospects? We outnumber them.' He punctuated his words with his fists. 'We'll persuade Master Jones to carry out our orders.'

Bradford, Brewster and Winslow hung back. Priscilla could not see Deacon Carver anywhere. She spied Mr Prence half-hidden behind a large trunk.

Captain Standish squared up to Billington, drawing his sword. As Standish prepared to strike, Alden leapt between him and Billington. The butt of a musket hit Billington over the head from behind. Priscilla saw it was Howland.

'Silence!' A deep voice commanded above the din.

Priscilla watched as Master Jones descended the ladder, the first mate following him.

His face dark, eyes glinting, their Master and Commander spoke, his voice quiet but hard and sharp as the blade of his cutlass. 'A rebellion down here I'm told. On board ship it is called mutiny. Which of you wretches struck with his fist?'

Fingers pointed to Billington.

'Clap him in irons. I'll take him back to England for trial. No doubt he'll be hanged.'

'No, no, please, sir,' Goody Billington wailed.

'Hush, woman.' Master Jones silenced her. 'If there is any more trouble, this oaf won't be alone.'

He and the first mate ushered Billington up the ladder.

Stunned, sickened, Priscilla responded weakly to Mr Alden's concern. 'Will you be alright? More brandy? Anything?'

'Thank you, Mr Alden. We'll manage now.'

He is a good man, she thought, watching him disappear down to the cargo hold.

Hearing a sob, she looked down to see Joseph rubbing his fists into his eyes, his thin shoulders shuddering. 'He was so angry. Is he angry at me? Will I be in irons?'

'No, no. Master Jones wasn't angry with you. You won't be in irons. I promise.' She hugged him to her. 'Almost time for prayers and then we'll have our victuals.'

However, the shock of the fight and Master Jones' punishment had chased Priscilla's hunger. A heavy blanket of misery and fear hung over the passengers as they gathered for prayers. Elder Brewster prayed a long time, urging folk to pull together, work together, not forgetting their purpose, to build God's kingdom in this new land. Priscilla fidgeted. *That is exactly what the rebels do not wish to hear.* She noticed Deacon Carver was absent until the Elder said 'Amen' and sat down. Then the Deacon stood before them and spoke.

'I have been in consultation with Master Jones. He has promised that if all of you who have caused disturbance agree to co-operate with our plan he will grant Billington a reprieve.' He raised his hand against the rising swell of, 'Praise be... Bless the captain.'

'Silence. It is our intention to establish a community with an elected set of governors. There will be no ruler and no religious authority like the Church of England. Laws will be passed by the governors and will apply equally to everyone. We will disagree at times but we cannot allow disagreement to split us or we shall all surely perish. We cannot know what dangers lie ahead and we must always pull together.

'We, your leaders, will draw up a document setting out terms of governance as I have described and no man will be allowed on shore until he has signed, promising to uphold the terms laid out in the document. Furthermore, if there is any more trouble, Master Jones will see you returned to England to stand trial. Remember, the *Mayflower* is his ship and his word is law. His crew is one hundred percent loyal and you have no hope coercing any of them.'

Because of Father's bad leg, Mr Alden brought the Mullins their victuals. He stayed while they ate their meager rations.

'Mr Alden is going to help me up the ladder to the great cabin,' Father said. 'I have been asked to help draw up the document which Deacon Carver described just now. It is a great honor.' Even as he finished speaking, the leaders gathered at the foot of the ladder, carrying rolls of parchment, quills, pots of ink and candles.

Priscilla sat still, unable to take her eyes from Mr Alden as he carefully helped Father climb the ladder, at times bearing his entire weight when he had to raise his good leg to the next rung. *He makes it look easy, effortless.* She stared in wonderment, and wiped away tears of exhaustion. *Please God... may we have a rest from trouble.* As she stirred herself to help Mother prepare their bunk for sleep, Mr Alden slid back down the ladder, his feet barely touching the rungs. Priscilla smiled.

'Good night, Mistress Mullins.'

'Thank you, Mr Alden,' she spoke softly, 'for all you do for Father, for us.' She clasped her hands.

'I want to.'

'Look!' Joseph pointed to the hatch.

Tapered shoes, spindly legs and yellow coat-tails began their slow careful descent. Mr Martin disentangled his coat-tails from both the rungs of the ladder and his feet. He reached the bottom without mishap and disregarding his greeting of jeers and mocking laughter he raised his hand. 'Attention!'

'What now?' a man's voice called.

When the grumbling had quietened Mr Martin announced, 'Word from Master Jones. It is too dark to sail into the cape tonight. He'll fix the sails to drift with the tide 'til morning. Coastal waters can be treacherous, as we've seen.'

That night Priscilla could not sleep except in fits and starts. Fearful and exhausted, she hardly dared believe that tomorrow the *Mayflower* would anchor in the coastal waters of the new world, their new home.

As soon as there was light enough to see, Father opened his almanac. 'Today is Saturday, November 11th.' Even as he spoke, sounds of the ship getting under way filtered from the upper deck: the first mate's commands, padding of running feet, the sailors' calls as they set the sails. In spite of her fatigue, Priscilla thrilled to the tug and pull as the *Mayflower* began her work, plying the waves.

'Are we nearly there? I want to go on deck.' Joseph fidgeted and pleaded.

'No. We may not go on deck until Mr Martin says. So please stop asking.' As impatient as Joseph, Priscilla was sharp. 'Now sit here by me and we'll work on your spelling. Try the word *almanac*. You can sound it out.'

Joseph tried but he squirmed, kicking his legs. 'I would rather be in a lesson with Master Jones. He was teaching me to plot a course. But now he is so angry...' Joseph's lip quivered. 'I'm afraid he won't want to teach me anymore.'

'I'm sure he will. You must remember he is sailing in unknown waters. He hasn't time for anything else now. Find your rope and practice your knots.'

'Remember, Joseph.' Father was stern. 'In this new land you will not be sailing. You will need to learn to shoot, trap, and fish, prepare land for planting. Not much use knowing how to plot a course.'

Joseph's lip quivered again. 'Yes, Father.'

The hours dragged on. Priscilla sat with Mother, mending and telling Joseph stories. An expectant tension hovered in the fetid air. A sailor called the bells; again, again, again; and every time, Priscilla wondered, *Now?*

'All hands... all hands... furl the sails!'

Priscilla held her breath. *Is this it?* She felt giddy picturing the sailors climbing aloft, working their way out along the yards, reaching down to grab and haul up the flapping sails, the ship rolling in the long, regular swells.

'Anchor away!'

She thrilled to the splash and the hum of the anchor rope running through its hawse hole.

Below decks erupted into cries of 'Hoorah! Hoorah!' A tumult of shouting, cheering, dogs barking.

Deacon Carver demanded silence. 'Mr Martin will indicate when we are permitted to go on deck. When that moment comes the men are to go first, to the great cabin where they all must sign the Mayflower Compact. No one is allowed off the ship until this is done.'

The hatch opened. Instead of Mr Martin, the first mate climbed halfway down the ladder. 'Joseph Mullins, come with me.'

Wide-eyed, trying not to cringe, Joseph looked pleadingly at Father. 'Must I?' A hoarse whisper.

'Yes. You must follow the officer's orders.'

Priscilla watched Joseph's thin legs disappear up through the hatch. It shut.

When the hatch next opened, Mr Martin called down, 'All men to the great cabin.'

Before anyone could stop her, Priscilla dodged through the gathering men and bolted up the ladder. She hurried along the deck to the fo'castle and stood alone, looking across the bay to the shores of America. Out in the middle of the harbor a school of black whales cavorted and frolicked, diving and blowing spouts of spray as a flock of herons swept up from the marshes, their broad wings flapping and whooshing. Under gray skies the bright autumn colors were faded. The land was flat.

Priscilla drew her shawl tighter. *Thank God we have safely crossed the ocean. But home is so far away.* She thought of the friendly innkeeper's wife wishing them Godspeed as they left the comfort of the Star Inn. *There is no friendly soul here to greet us. No inn where we can find warmth and food. No safe place. Only beasts and wild men live here.*

Finding a Place to Settle

Chapter 15

November 1620

Washing day

Shivering in the damp gray wind and not wanting to gaze on the unwelcoming wild land before her, Priscilla returned to their cabin. She found Mother tidying as best she could, trying to keep their small space neat and orderly in the surrounding sea of mess.

'Where is Joseph?' she asked. 'He was so frightened.'

'Not returned from his summons.'

Priscilla bent over to pull the mending out of their trunk when a body thumped into her from behind. She jerked up, banging her head. 'Joseph!'

'He wasn't angry with me. Only with the rebels.' Joseph beamed, fairly dancing with delight and then dissolved into coughing.

When he got his breath back Priscilla said, 'Sit down and tell me quietly.'

'Master Jones was kind. He said he had to be fierce with the rebels but we are still friends. He showed me how to plot a course.'

Joseph's eyes took on a dreamy, faraway look. 'When my lesson was over he saluted me and I saluted him.'

An icy draught whistled down from the hatch. She wrapped Joseph in her shawl and looked up. It was Mr Alden, climbing down the ladder, carefully easing Father, taking his weight.

'That's almost everyone's signed the compact,' Father said. 'We chose Deacon Carver to be our governor. Captain Standish is at this moment selecting sixteen men to go on a first expedition. Check out the lay of the land.'

'The ship's carpenter and I will begin repairs on the shallop,' Alden said. 'She got bumped about and damaged in the storms. Master Jones has chosen a good anchorage here. We could sit out a gale and barely move.'

'What is a shallop?' Joseph asked.

Alden squatted so he was eye level with Joseph. 'It is an open boat. Not big like the *Mayflower*. Couldn't cross the ocean. For exploring rivers and coastline. Ours has oars and sails.'

'May I sail her?'

Alden put a hand on Joseph's knee. 'Got to put her together first.'

Dorothy struggled through the strewn belongings of passengers. Stepping round an upended stool, she negotiated the last few paces and sat beside Priscilla on their bunk. 'William is going on this expedition. Please come up with me to wave him farewell.' A pinched frown drew her forehead tight.

'I'll come too.' Rose Standish struggled across, barely able to stand.

'No,' Mother said. 'You are too unwell. You must stay out of the wind. I know Captain Standish would be upset if I allowed you to go up.' She put her arm around Rose and led her back to her bed.

The deck was crowded with men, women and children braving the freezing wind to bid farewell to Captain Standish's exploring party, about to set foot on American soil for the first time. Master Jones came down from his cabin and stood beside Standish at the bow rail, scanning the coastline with his spyglass.

Alden maneuvered through the crush to stand beside Priscilla and Dorothy. 'Wish I could go,' he said.

'Oh please do. Please go in William's place.' Dorothy put her hand to her mouth, too late.

'Ah, Mistress Bradford, not in your husband's place. He is one of our leaders. We need his opinion of the places we explore. As it is, I am needed here to repair the shallop.'

Priscilla turned to look up into Alden's face and saw Mr Prence standing several paces away watching.

As Captain Standish called his men together, Priscilla, Alden and Dorothy edged closer to hear his instructions.

'Our task is to reconnoiter the immediate area and bring back fresh water and firewood. I want you to stay together, muskets primed and in hand, at all times. There may be Indians lurking and we do not have enough daylight hours left to be searching for lost men.'

The troop climbed down the rope ladder into the ship's rowing boat and headed across the cape. Alden stayed with Priscilla and Dorothy as they stood by the rail waving farewell. Priscilla was thankful he was there. She did not want an encounter with Mr Prence. To their surprise the boat stopped while still a good way out from the shore. One by one, the men climbed out, muskets held high, and waded to a pebbled beach.

'The water is up to their thighs! They'll be wet and freezing before they even set out. Oh, I pray they all return safely. What if they're attacked by Indians? Killed? What will we do?' Dorothy wrung her hands and bowed her head as if her fears had already come to pass.

'They have muskets, and they're wearing corselets made for battle. Good protection against arrows.' Alden put a fatherly arm round Dorothy's shoulder. 'Remember, Captain Standish is a well tried soldier.' He escorted Priscilla and Dorothy to the hatch.

The afternoon of waiting seemed an eternity. Priscilla and Mother sewed. Dorothy paced back and forth, praying, hands clutching her cheeks, her hair, her shawl, shrugging off Priscilla's efforts to comfort her.

'Child. This will never do. You will spread fear. What would William think? Come and sit with me and Elder Brewster.' Mary Brewster, thin lipped and severe, put her arm round Dorothy's waist, in a guise of kindness, forcing her.

Priscilla cringed.

Darkness had fallen when, 'Musket shots! The signal!' The women hurried to put away their sewing and rushed up the ladder, over to the rail. They watched closely as the boat returned, and one by one, the explorers boarded to a happy and excited welcome.

'God be praised, you are safely back,' Dorothy hugged William.

'What did you find?'

'What was it like?'

'Did you spy Indians?'

The questions swirled around, everyone speaking at once. Captain Standish raised his hand for silence.

'We learned we are on a slender piece of land between the bay and the ocean. Sandy. Reminded me of sand dunes in Holland, but there is a topsoil of rich dark earth. Trees everywhere, not much undergrowth. Sadly we found no freshwater streams. And we must find somewhere with running freshwater. However, we have brought back juniper branches. There was no sign of Indians. Very odd.'

Priscilla's gut contracted in worry. *Please, please, they must find a place to settle soon. Winter is upon us. Joseph... so many folk are sick. But they are back safely, and as soon as the shallop is ready a place will be found. And now we'll be warm!* That evening she soaked up the strong sweet scent of the burning juniper and reveling in the glow and heat of the fire felt hopeful that it would not be long before the explorers found a suitable place to build.

However, at the end of the next day, when the ship's carpenter and Alden climbed down from working on the shallop, Alden was downcast, scowling, as Priscilla had never seen him before.

'Bad news. We'll have to rebuild her – could take weeks. And tomorrow is the Sabbath.' He shrugged his shoulders and shaking his head, hastened down into the cargo hold.

Priscilla's heart plummeted. She saw Mother's face cloud over as she looked down at Joseph, then at Father.

'Husband, this is a time for you to lie abed with your leg up, as I've been begging you. If you don't you'll have a peg leg or none at all!' Mother assumed the authority of a commanding officer.

In a half-whisper Priscilla turned to Father. 'I know it's right to give thanks and to pray, but to lose whole days for the Sabbath when the shallop needs putting together and we are desperately short of time before winter sets in – just doesn't seem right.'

'Priscilla, you have seen how close we came to losing good strong young men who wanted to go off on their own. We have drawn up and signed an agreement to co-operate and we've chosen Deacon Carver to be our governor. Co-operating means following the religious ways of Carver and our other leaders.'

★ ★ ★

Monday was a crisp autumn day. The sun, high in clear blue skies, still had a good heat and a light breeze freshened the spirits. The ship's carpenter and Alden chose a small group of men to take the shallop ashore, where there was more space to re-build. On deck, Priscilla breathed deeply, drinking in the bright air. Alden came over to her. 'I'm glad to get out of that cargo hold and go ashore! Mr Martin has agreed to take my place.'

Priscilla smiled. 'We'll be going ashore too, with all the dirty linen. Are the kittens safe?'

'Yes. I had to tell Mr Martin about them. He's bound to see them as they're beginning to crawl about. I said we would take them onto the plantation and he promised he wouldn't drown them.

Surprisingly agreeable about it. Must be off.' He raised his hat and hurried to help lift the pieces of the shallop down into the ship's boat. Priscilla watched the men row to shore and unload all the planks and tools. Then one of the sea-crew rowed back to collect the women and children.

Gathered together, they were ready with their piles of unwashed linen and the two dogs. To stand guard against Indians and wild animals, John Howland and two young men had armed themselves with muskets, and they now escorted the women, helping them climb down the ladder into the ship's boat with their washing.

As she watched the first boatload of women cross the cape, Priscilla pinched herself. The longed for moment, the moment of leaving this ship and setting foot on land, the land where she would live; it felt like a dream. In some peculiar way she felt outside herself, looking down as if she were a bird just arrived looking for a place to alight, as if the long terrible journey hadn't happened.

Priscilla, Mother, Dorothy and Joseph were amongst the last to be rowed across. When they climbed out of the boat the other women called and beckoned.

'Over here. Freshwater!'

They struggled through the icy sea, stumbling, trying to hold up their skirts and not drop their washing in the water. As they lugged their piles of linen across wet sand and pebbles, Priscilla's legs felt peculiar, not her own, behaving as if they were still on board ship, balancing against the rocking motion. *We must make a strange sight, lurching and stumbling as if we were drunk.* Reaching the edge of a large pond they dropped their linen and Mother fished a cake of soap from her pouch.

'Why did Captain Standish say there wasn't freshwater?' Goody Billington called out. 'Here's plenty o' water.'

'It has to be running water, a freshwater brook flowing from a spring. Otherwise it isn't safe to drink,' Mistress Carver said. 'Captain Standish is right.'

Priscilla laughed aloud. 'Oh joy! We can rinse the salt out of our linen. We'll have fresh bedding and clothes. No more itching.'

'That will be bliss. Since the storm I haven't been able to sleep for itching and my man and little ones tossing and fidgeting, scratching and sore,' Goody Billington said.

'Aye, aye. Let's get rid o' this salt!'

Priscilla stood still a moment, taking in this new place, so unlike England. She breathed in. The air was thinner, lighter; the sun brighter, quickly burning off the morning frosts that had covered the deck in recent days. The land bordering the cape was flat, dense with trees, the occasional boulder rearing up amongst them. The amazing colors that had greeted them on first sight were, almost a week later, still vibrant in the sunlight, but the frosts had loosened stems from their branches. Stirred in the light breeze, leaves fell, dancing gently as they floated to the ground. *Were there Indians lurking amongst the trees, watching, unseen*? She strained, searching. *A moving shape? A shadow? We are so vulnerable. Would the men on shore be enough to protect us?* She glanced across at Mr Alden and fell to scrubbing her linen.

Catherine Carver and her maid servant, Desire, carried armfuls of linen to work beside Mother and Priscilla. Scrub, rinse, scrub, rinse; it was heavy work. Every so often Mother and Mistress Carver stopped to draw breath and chat. Desire, plain and rather meek, had kept herself out of the way on board ship so Priscilla scarcely knew her. She was amazed at the lass' tireless, devoted energy.

The children ran about, arms and legs all akimbo, delirious with the joy and excitement of frolicking on a surface that didn't pitch and roll but stayed still and firm under their feet. The dogs scampered in the wavelets, sniffing and barking at the small surf. Priscilla and Mother looked up from time to time, keeping an eye out. They'd not been long at work when Francis Billington took to throwing stones at the dogs. He missed them but nearly hit one of the girls.

Mother hurried over. 'Francis! You mustn't throw stones. Someone could be badly hurt.'

Priscilla looked over to the group of women where Goody Billington was so absorbed in gossiping that she'd never noticed her son's mischief. She saw Joseph, no longer running here and there, but sitting on a large rock, alone. She went over to him. Poor lad. He was weak from lack of food, shivering, even in the hot sun. His blue eyes, that used to sparkle and dance with excitement and fun, were now glazed over with hunger. She wrapped her shawl around him. 'Try to keep moving about as much as you can. It will help you to warm up.'

As she trudged back to the pond Priscilla scanned boulders and the treeline. 'Mother, this is eerie, not sight nor sound of Indians. I pray we can find a place to settle soon, a safe place. Joseph desperately needs good food. Father said this land is full of fowl and deer and fish in the sea. We need this food soon or…'

Her mother nodded, her lips set in a grim line, a frown running down her forehead.

'I'll have a word with my husband,' Mistress Carver said. 'He is kind. He could perhaps arrange extra rations for Joseph.'

'Thank you,' Mother breathed. 'I don't want to deprive any other poor mite but…' She bowed her head to her laundry.

Dorothy too was flagging, badly weakened from seasickness. She was so thin. Even when she wasn't seasick she didn't want to eat. She looked as if she might break in two. 'Here, let me help,' Priscilla said. 'You sit and rest awhile.'

'Oh thank you. I don't seem to have any strength.' Dorothy gave a little laugh, but even on this fresh, invigorating day she seemed listless and despondent. She looked down the beach to where Mr Alden and his crew were working on the shallop, splitting logs, sawing, and planing. 'Looks like a big piece of work. I fear winter coming before…'

'I know Mr Alden will do his best.' Priscilla tried to keep the edge from her voice.

The sun was high overhead when Priscilla and Mother had wrung out the last of their washing. Priscilla was spent. Mercifully, Howland and the other two men put down their muskets to carry the waterlogged linen and help spread it on boulders to dry. Priscilla noticed Howland paid special attention to Lizzie Tilley. *Good. Perhaps now Lizzie will leave Mr Alden alone.* She also had the thought that if the Indians intended to attack, now would be the moment, when the men did not have their muskets to hand.

It wasn't many minutes before every boulder near the pond was draped with dripping washing. Women and children labored through spongy sand to the rock pools by the shore.

'Look at this! Would you believe it? Fresh shellfish!' Digging in the muddy sand they found a multitude of soft shell clams, quahogs, cherrystones. Large fat mussels clung to the rocks. They gathered and ate; gathered and ate. Priscilla smiled to see Dorothy eating her fill.

'First time in weeks my hunger is stopped.' Mother stood and stretched. 'This crisp air and warm sun does feel good.'

The women sat in the sun, leaning back against large boulders, savoring their unexpected feast. Mother and Mistress Carver talked of learning to read, of the fascination and magic in books.

The children played tag, leap-frogged and cartwheeled. The dogs barked and pawed at the surf, venturing in a way and out again. Priscilla spied Mistress Brewster sitting off by herself, praying. She sat with Dorothy listening to the lap and rattle of small waves washing on the pebbled shore, the cawing gulls. She tried to think of things to say to help her friend be more hopeful.

'It will be an adventure, and look, so many trees we'll have big houses and need never… Dorothy, are you ailing?' Dorothy wiped her brow, specked with beads of sweat. She took on a greenish pallor, clutched her stomach and doubled over retching.

'What?' she gasped. 'Am I poisoned?'

Priscilla held Dorothy steady wishing the vomiting would stop. She saw Mother and Mistress Carver double over, and gradually one by one, others succumbing. By now she felt a cold sweat creeping over her; then the nausea, then the retching.

Priscilla retched and retched. She was frightened. Never in her life had she been sick like this. Would it ever end? Her temples throbbed; a sick, harsh taste permeated her mouth and throat and her stomach ached from spasms of heaving. Emptied out at last, she straightened, and holding onto a boulder, wiped the sweat from her brow.

Only a few children were not sick, Joseph amongst them. He ran over. 'Mother, Priscilla, what is the matter?' Francis Billington wasn't sick either and he pointed and mimicked and pulled at his mother's hair and skirts.

'Yah, yah – pox on ye.' Goody Billington tried to cuff him out of the way, but she was too sick.

Mother and Mistress Carver tentatively took a few steps, testing their balance. Dorothy lay in a crumpled heap, little Jasper More, close by her, inert.

'Is he alive?' Priscilla knelt beside the small limp body. She pressed her fingers to his wrist, his neck, feeling for a pulse. 'There. Faint, too faint.'

Mother and Mistress Carver bent over Dorothy, lifting her to stand, but her legs gave way as if they too had been emptied out.

Priscilla cradled Jasper; Mother and Mistress Carver supported Dorothy. The sun was low in the sky and a wind off the sea brought a damp chill.

'May we return? I am spent,' Goody Billington implored Mistress Carver.

'Of course. As soon as these poor dames have recovered.' She gestured toward the half-dozen women still bent over, kneeling, helpless. 'Priscilla, would you go along and ask Mr Alden if he could help us carry the linen?'

'Yes, Mistress Carver.' She handed Jasper to Dorothy.

'I'll ask Howland to help as well,' Mother said.

'Wait.' Mistress Brewster stood before them. 'We do not need Mr Alden's help. Howland and the servants will carry the linen.

Howland will deal with the ferrying.' She took Jasper from Dorothy's arms. 'He is my responsibility. I'll have him walking in a moment. Off with you, Desire. Don't cling to Mistress Carver.' She strode amongst the recovering women. 'Hurry now.' Confronting Mistress Carver and Mother, she said, 'I'll take Dorothy. I know Mr Bradford would want me to care for her.'

Hoisting Jasper over her right shoulder, Mistress Brewster grasped Dorothy's arm with her left hand. 'Come along. I'm sure you can walk if you try. Mr Bradford does not need a weak and feeble wife.'

Priscilla gasped. 'Poor Dorothy. Why is Mistress Brewster so harsh?'

'She's had a hard life,' Mistress Carver said. 'Perhaps the Elder being in hiding so many years...'

Priscilla had noticed how women on board looked to Mistress Carver for advice, even before Deacon Carver was elected governor. And they turned to Mother, just as in Dorking. She watched Mother comforting a poorly child. Tears of love and pride pricked her eyes. A small hand took hold of hers. She bent down and kissed the top of Joseph's head.

Howland and his companions helped gather and fold the dry linen. Then the weak and weary women began the trudge across the broad beach to the shore. Of a sudden, an arrow whistled past, perilously close to Mistress Brewster's head and lodged in the hard packed sand. Women screamed. Howland fired his musket into the air. Shielding her eyes, Priscilla scanned the trees, looking for Indians. No sign.

'Silence,' Mistress Brewster commanded. 'We will await whatever befalls us in orderly quiet. I will assign boatloads.'

As the women's shrieks and moanings subsided, Priscilla admired Mistress Brewster's calm courage, and was relieved to see her putting Dorothy and Jasper in the first boat.

She boarded the *Mayflower* limp with retching, fear and now relief. A day that started in warm sunshine and hope had ended in poison and danger. Her longing to get off the *Mayflower* ended in gratitude that foul as their quarters were, at least they were a safe place.

As Priscilla climbed over the rail onto the ship's deck, one of the ship's mates who had sailed in these parts before, on hearing of their stomach upset laughed and said it was the mussels made them so sick. *If only he had warned us. Jasper nearly died.* She resented him acting as if it were a joke.

As she helped Mother make up their bunk with salt-free linen, Mr Alden brought a jug of ale for Dorothy, another small jug for Jasper and with a slight of hand, he gave Priscilla a small parcel. 'For Joseph,' he whispered, 'extra rations.'

She smiled. The parcel brought hope in the midst of sadness as Jasper's cries 'Doorty, Doorty' filled the living quarters.

Chapter 16

November 1620

Rape

Day after day Alden went ashore to work on the shallop and Mr Martin reigned in the cargo hold.

'Priscilla, would you please go beg Mr Martin for some ale,' Mother said. 'For your father and Joseph.' Priscilla's heart sank.

'Couldn't someone else?'

'You needn't worry,' Mother said. 'Mistress Carver said Captain Standish had words with Deacon Carver about Mr Martin. He's been warned he'll be sent back to England along with a letter of complaint if he misbehaves.'

Priscilla took a deep breath and climbed down the ladder.

'Ah! Mistress Mullins.'

'Mr Prence!' *Why? How is it?*

'There are suspicions about Mr Martin's trustworthiness; Deacon Carver asked if I would take his place while Mr Alden is ashore.' He stood close to Priscilla, his luring brown eyes seeking hers.

She stepped aside. 'Mother sent me. Begs a jug of ale for Mr Mullins and Joseph.'

'Of course. But first, I have something delightful to show you. A surprise. He put his arm around her waist and propelled her through the alley of stacked provisions. Priscilla tried to turn back but he was strong, and besides, what was her excuse? She would humor him, and secure the jug of ale.

'As you know, Mistress Mullins, I have been studying with Elder Brewster, learning the teachings of the Church of Christ. He has been instructing me how to pray, to discern God's will.' Prence spoke softly, almost secretively.

'Yes.'

'The Elder favors me; says I am chosen by God to be one of his own and therefore he trusts that I do right and speak the truth.'

They reached the pile of armaments. Mr Prence pulled aside muskets, corselets, helmets, to reveal the calico cat and her kittens. Without thinking, Priscilla knelt to stroke them. Mr Prence fell on his knees beside her.

'It is God's will you should be mine, Mistress Mullins. We belong together. Mr Alden is not worthy of you. It is God's will I should have you.' His breathing was heavy. He grasped her shoulders pushing her back, fastening his mouth on hers with such strength she couldn't move to scream. *That smell. The same smell, the acrid smell of scent and the sweat of arousal.* He pinioned her arms behind her, put one hand over her mouth and with the other loosed his breeches and drew up her skirts. Priscilla kicked, thrashed, bit. She freed an arm and clawed his face.

'Hie! Anyone here?'

Priscilla bit with all her strength. Still Mr Prence held her mouth shut as he gathered his breeches. 'It is your word against mine,' he whispered. 'The Elder will believe me, not you. So I advise you to say nothing if you don't want to be investigated for a seducing witch. Remember the singing?'

'Hie!'

Arranging himself, Mr Prence stood. 'Captain Standish. What is it you need?'

Shaking, her cheeks wet with unstoppable tears, Priscilla pulled herself upright, hanging onto trunk handles. Unsteadily she made her way to Captain Standish.

'Mistress Mullins, what has happened? Are you injured?'

'I was showing Mistress Mullins... her father's muskets, and she tumbled. Poor lady.'

'May I please have the jug of ale,' Priscilla said.

'A tot of brandy for my Rose,' Standish said.

Priscilla could not stop shaking, nor could she stop her tears, hastily wiping her cheeks.

Captain Standish looked from her to Mr Prence, his flushed face, his breeches unable to disguise his arousal. Standish took the jug of ale, and the brandy. He said one word. 'Scum,' and spat in Mr Prence's face.

Safely in their cabin Priscilla collapsed, curled herself in a ball, shaking and sobbing. Quietly Standish told Mother and Father. 'Trouble is, the man has a hold on the Elder. If Elder Brewster is convinced a pupil of his is chosen by God, then as night follows day, that pupil is trustworthy and no one can convince him otherwise. Not even Governor Carver. He's a cunning ruffian, that Prence. Knows exactly how to curry favor. Best Priscilla doesn't go to the cargo hold unless you know Mr Alden is there.'

'If that weasel touches my daughter again I'll kill him with my bare hands.' Father gathered Priscilla against his breast. 'My lass, my lass.' He rocked her as she sobbed and clung to him.

When he returned at nightfall Mr Alden stopped to pass a few words with the Mullins family. 'We're making good progress, but she won't be ready – two weeks earliest I reckon.'

'Master Jones is teaching me about the tiller and the wind,' Joseph said. 'So I can sail her.'

Alden squeezed the lad's shoulder. Looking fondly at Priscilla he said, 'I'd best go below. Relieve Mr Martin. Any trouble?'

Priscilla blushed and bowed her head. 'I… he…' she choked.

A few moments after Alden descended the ladder, Captain Standish followed.

After that, every morning as he was departing to work on the shallop, Mr Alden left a jug of ale and a parcel of extra rations in the Mullins' cabin.

Chapter 17

November 1620

Indian booty

The days passed, gray and cold with a threat of snow in the air. While taking a short turn on deck, Priscilla and Dorothy overheard some of the crew grumbling. 'We should put all these folk off on the beach so we can sail for home before all the provisions are eaten.'

Dorothy shivered. 'Oh no! Surely Master Jones would not do that!'

'I pray not. I don't think he would be so unkind,' Priscilla said. They went below to huddle near the fire.

That evening, following prayers, Elder Brewster announced, 'Captain Standish will lead another expedition on foot. We cannot wait until the shallop is ready. They will march south to find the river we saw flowing into a harbor as we sailed along the coast.'

Dorothy fairly collapsed with relief when the exploring party returned three days later, all safe, though frozen, exhausted and corselets ripped to shreds. Bradford limped. "Tis nothing…'tis nothing.'

However, they did bring booty, their pockets and pouches full of Indian maize, red, blue, yellow kernels of corn – a welcome addition to their dwindling supplies.

Mending ripped pantaloons and corselets, the women speculated on what could have caused the tears.

'Why do the men refuse to tell us?' Priscilla stabbed her needle into the thick cloth.

'My own husband won't tell me why he limps,' Dorothy sighed.

Priscilla noticed that of an evening, when Mr Alden had returned from shore, Captain Standish often went below. *Does the captain talk to Mr Alden of their adventures?* she wondered.

Frustration mounted. The children, desperate for space, grew ever more troublesome, especially Francis Billington. He wasn't bad, but he was restless and a scamp, peeking up underneath skirts, interrupting other lads' games with pinching and pulling, and worst, getting into parts of the ship where passengers were forbidden. As his mother paid no heed, Priscilla kept an eye on him.

More and more folk were falling sick. Dark circles under Joseph's eyes were the only color in his pale face, and he was growing listless. Sporadic moments of excitement made him cough. His lessons with Master Jones renewed his strength, but the first mate had to half-carry him to and from the captain's cabin.

Father coughed, in rasping, convulsing spasms. Priscilla's spirits faltered as she looked into his gaunt face, eyes disappearing under bushy eyebrows. She could tell he forced himself to appear hearty.

The winter wind and sleet locked passengers below deck with no relief from the sour stink. Time seemed to stop. Priscilla became numb with the repetition of days consumed in odious tasks, tired with telling stories and keeping children occupied.

One evening as the Mullins family was eating their meager rations Mr Alden stopped by, grinning.

'The shallop is ready.'

There was a flurry of activity as Captain Standish organized an expedition. Priscilla's hopes rose. *Almost the end of November, Father said. Surely they must find somewhere to settle. Otherwise…* she dared not think. Whereas the day before Priscilla was trying to pull the children out of lethargic picking and teasing, now they were bouncing and hopping about. As she was settling them for a story at the bow end of their quarters, Mr Prence came to her. He stood close, gently pressing against her and spoke softly. 'Captain Standish has chosen me to be one of his party. I am going into danger. Pray for me, my beloved.'

'Mr Prence.' Priscilla stepped aside as he pressed closer against her. She spoke sharply. 'Please go.'

The next day a large expedition of thirty-three men set out taking the shallop and the ship's boat. Master Jones was in command. Now Joseph joined Dorothy in worry. 'Will Master Jones come back? Will he be harmed? Why did he go?'

'I reckon Master Jones was longing to get off this ship,' Priscilla said. 'As we all are.'

Four days later in the morning, Master Jones' party returned, frozen to the marrow, wet, some with frostbite and bringing strange booty, but not an answer to the only question that mattered: 'Have you found a place to settle?' Father joined the leaders in the great cabin to deliberate whether to settle at the one place the explorers found – Corn Hill.

Needing Dorothy to help entertain the children, Priscilla found her sitting on her bed. 'Look what William brought me!' She held out a small basket, finely woven with an intricate pattern.

'How beautiful. Where did he find it?'

'In an empty Indian hut. There were a number of huts. They took some of the prettiest things, left the rest.'

They shouldn't have. That's stealing. Aloud, Priscilla said, 'The children are restless. Mother is busy tending to the sick. Can you help?'

As the children gathered to hear stories, a girl showed off a bracelet made of colored beads. 'Where did you find that?' Priscilla asked.

'It's from the expedition. From a dead man,' the girl said.

'What? How is that?'

'He had yellow hair. And a little boy with him.'

Priscilla was aghast. 'Where was the dead man?'

'They dug the grave. There are more pretty things from it.'

Priscilla was choking with revulsion and for want of fresh air. Though the clime was freezing and damp, the wind had dropped. In this respite from lashing sleet she wrapped her winter shawl close and went up on deck. She spied Howland and Lizzie Tilley; a few sailors were about, checking the rigging and seeing ropes were properly stowed. She selected a place by the rail halfway between Howland and the sailors, in case. The cape spread before her, ruffled gray waters, austere home to all manner of wild fowl, swooping, diving, coasting on the waves. To Priscilla, accustomed only to the ponds in England, it was a huge body of water spreading from the strip of land that sheltered them from the sea across to the bleak landscape of America. She took deep breaths of salt air, expunging the fetid stink of their living space.

'Mistress Mullins.'

No. Please not Prence. She started to move away.

'Wait, my dear,' he blocked her. 'I have brought you a gift.' From his pouch he pulled a folded silk handkerchief. Unwrapping it he held two exquisite strings of fine white beads.

Priscilla stared. 'Where did you get those?'

'On our expedition. Found them in the grave.'

'The grave you dug?'

'Aye. An Indian grave. 'Tis of no account. How handsome they'll look against your fair bosom.' As he spoke, Prence made to loosen her shawl and drape the beads over her head.

'Get away!' Priscilla raised her voice almost to a scream. Howland hurried over. She pushed past Prence and plummeted down the ladder.

'He won't leave me alone.'

Mother straightened, pulling their trenchers from the trunk. 'Don't go up there unless you have someone with you.'

'It's not right. It shouldn't be thus,' Priscilla fumed. *I know it is wicked to think such thoughts but I wish he had not come back – got lost – or something.*

Mid-afternoon. Still the men deliberated. Mother slumped on to the bed and wiped her brow. 'Some folk are very bad. Hardly know what to do for them. Oh, for some chicken broth!'

Priscilla rested her mending on her lap. 'Would you like me to ask Mr Alden for more ale?'

'Aye, thank you.'

'May I please have some cumin and aniseed for my breath?'

Mother looked at her sideways and raised an eyebrow. She lifted the lid of the trunk and had to tunnel down to the bottom so she was almost on her head when she withdrew the jars of spices. 'Please take these over to poor Rose.' She counted out six cloves onto Priscilla's palm. 'She's got terrible toothache, bleeding gums, making her ill.' She shut the trunk lid with a bang, and stood, hands on hips. 'By God's providence, Father's leg is on the mend. Because he did as I said and rested it.' She whispered, 'If only he'd done as I said and abandoned this foolish voyage. We'd be snug at home.' Her voice caught.

Priscilla put her arm around her mother's shoulders. 'You are brave. And what would we do without your doctoring skills.'

'You're a good daughter. We can only do our best. Would you also ask Mr Alden for a tot of brandy for Rose. Anything to ease the pain.'

Priscilla was relieved Mr Alden was alone. After delivering Mother's request she said, 'Mr Alden, could I ask you about…' she hesitated. 'About the expeditions?'

Alden frowned. 'I wanted to go on this latest one, and Captain Standish requested me. But Deacon Carver said I was needed here.' He lowered his voice and glanced up at the hatch. 'When I was working on the shallop, Mr Prence told the Deacon he caught Mr Martin pilfering brandy.'

Still facing Priscilla, Alden lifted a sack into place. 'Mind, I sometimes doubt the truth of what Mr Prence says. I reckon Mr Martin is a pompous half-wit and I know he likes his drink, but he's not pilfered before.'

Not wanting to recall Mr Prence, Priscilla looked down. She raised her eyes and asked, 'Has Captain Standish… has anyone told you, why the torn corselets? Where did the corn come from? Why is Mr Bradford limping? The pretty things taken from the Indian huts? What is Corn Hill? And the grave! It seems our men dug up a grave and robbed it!' Priscilla's questions tumbled out.

Mr Alden held her eyes for a long minute. 'Can I trust you? If I answer you, you're not to tell **anyone** not your mother, nor father, nor Dorothy. No one. Because Standish has trusted me.'

'I promise. Truly.'

'Come over here.'

Priscilla followed Alden as he threaded his way through barrels and trunks to a hidden place.

'Here are a couple of half-empty sacks we can sit on, and I'll have sight of the hatch.'

Seated, Priscilla sat still and waited.

'On the first expedition…' Alden focused on her face, frowning slightly as if not sure whether to go on. Priscilla said nothing, willing him to trust her.

'On the first major expedition, marching along the beach, Standish and his men spied half a dozen Indians, about five hundred yards distance. On spotting our men the Indians ran off and Standish gave chase. The Indians disappeared, leaving no tracks, not a trace, and the men found themselves in a tangle of huge bramble thickets with thorns like needles. Tore their corselets to shreds before they found their way back to the beach.'

'Merciful heavens!' Priscilla breathed. 'They could have been lost forever.'

'Standish admits he shouldn't have given chase. Says these parts are strange; so much to learn.'

'The corn?' Priscilla said.

'Coming upon an array of hillocks, Standish dug into one. It was a store for Indian seed corn. As our corn is moldering they took as much as they could. Mr Bradford is limping because he disobeyed orders, went wandering off and when called didn't look where he was putting his feet so trod in a deer trap. He is lucky to have got away with a bruise.'

'Bradford? So reckless?'

'Aye. Standish says he cannot believe how ill-disciplined these men are. As if they do not understand about obeying orders.' Alden glanced up at the hatch. He froze. Priscilla looked. Mary Brewster!

'Bend over, stay crouched low. Don't move,' Alden whispered.

'Mistress Brewster, can I help you?'

'I thought 't would be a moment for me to inspect. I've heard you keep the stores in good order. Wanted to see for myself.'

'I am honored, Mistress Brewster, but could we arrange another time? I am about to portion out the rations. Tomorrow morning perhaps?'

'As you wish. Ah. Mr Alden, there is another thing.'

'Mistress?'

'Cloves. Terrible toothache. Any cloves to spare?'

'So many suffer with toothache – not many left.'

'Never mind – I'll manage.'

'Wait, Mistress Brewster. If anyone deserves the last few...'

'Thank you, Mr Alden.'

'May I help you up?'

'I can manage. Good day.'

Priscilla stayed bent double until she felt a hand on her shoulder.

'Well done. That was a near one.' Alden lowered himself onto the sack, keeping his eyes on the hatch. 'We mustn't linger long.'

'No,' Priscilla nodded.

'However, I will answer the other puzzles.' He smiled. 'The Indian huts – not an Indian to be seen, but full of provisions, as if vacated only hours before. Our men stole their belongings.' Alden shook his head and sighed. 'The grave – Standish dug down uncovering two perfectly preserved bodies – a man and boy – looked European. Yes, they stole a few items from the grave.'

Priscilla sat stock-still, trying to take it all in. 'I hope we don't pay for this,' she said. 'We stole the Indians' belongings and their corn. We disturbed a grave! It was wrong.'

'Finally, Corn Hill. A good defensive place, fertile land, harbor large and full of fish but too shallow for ships to anchor. There are no freshwater streams. Every drop of water would have to be carried up the hill from ponds in the meadow, and in summer they might dry up.'

'What is your view, Mr Alden?'

'I agree we should not have stolen the Indians' belongings or desecrated the grave. But we do need the corn.' He kept his voice low. 'I wish we could find a better place to settle.'

'Thank you, Mr Alden; I'll keep my promise.'

Priscilla met his eyes. Her heart full with his trust, she couldn't restrain a slight shiver. He impulsively clasped her hands in his, then, letting go, caressed her cheek. She knew the blush suffusing her bosom and face betrayed her desire. A smile hovering, she lowered her eyes. She followed Alden back to the barrels of ale and brandy. He poured rations of each.

'I'll carry it up.' His voice caught. 'After you.'

Emerging from the cargo hold, which smelled of clean produce, wine and brandy, the stench of the passengers' quarters hit hard. Alden handed Priscilla the tankard of ale and tot of brandy, his hand closing briefly on hers, and disappeared down below.

She lingered, wanting to remember the feel of his touch: warm, gentle, strong, not cloying, or clammy, or hot; not grabbing. A touch that felt delicious, not demanding. Her head reeled.

'Priscilla. I've been searching for you.' Dorothy picked her way through the jumble and mess, holding her skirts close round her ankles. 'I was hoping you would come with me up on deck. This air is so foul I feel nauseous.'

'Of course,' Priscilla said. 'I'll take these liquors to Mother first.'

Standing at the rail, looking toward the shore they breathed in deep draughts of the cold salt air. Priscilla wrapped her shawl tighter. 'I'm glad the wind is at our backs.'

'Aye,' Dorothy shivered.

'If only we could find a good place to build,' Priscilla said. 'I want to get off this ship, away from the stench, the tiny cabins with hardly space to breathe.' Dorothy did not reply. Priscilla looked into her face: pinched, frowning, fearful. 'You must be longing to be on land and building a home with William – are you not feeling impatient?'

Dorothy hesitated. She looked down, but spoke clearly. 'William says we must be patient and willingly endure whatever difficulties come our way, as it is all part of being tested for God's purpose. We must use our difficulties to become stronger.'

'But Dorothy, what do you really feel?'

'I am learning to cultivate patience, Priscilla, and not bother about what I might feel. God's will is what is important, not what I feel.'

'Dorothy, you have told me how desperate it was, to part from your little John. Are you pretending that your feelings don't matter?'

'I am not pretending. It is a fact. My feelings do not matter. Building a new kingdom of God is all that matters.'

'Dorothy. Surely… do you really believe God is so merciless? That your love and longing for your son and his for you is of no account? That is madness. It is love that gives us strength.'

Dorothy stepped back, eyes wide, mouth open. 'Please do not speak that word, *madness.*' She waved her hand in front of her face. 'And do not speak to me of mercy. I have prayed long for mercy. There is none.'

Priscilla was shocked. Dorothy was always so gentle and meek. Here was a strain of bitter anger she'd not seen before. She put her hands on Dorothy's shoulders, drawing her close.

Dorothy crumbled, sobbing. 'I am so unhappy and so afraid. I am not up to this adventure, as you all call it. William needs someone like himself. Full of eagerness, full of God's purpose, strong, striving, someone cheerful and determined, whose only care is to be a good wife. This is God's plan.' She stopped, quenching her tears, standing straight. 'It is as Mistress Brewster says. Our sole purpose in this life is to be good wives for our husbands and good mothers, for God's kingdom.' She looked out to sea and back, twisting her hands. 'I don't think I can do it, Priscilla. I am too weak.'

Priscilla grasped her shoulders. 'You are so kind and loving; so good with the little ones. We need you. William needs you. Please do not listen to Mistress Brewster. When you are stronger and not so thin; when you can eat well, you will feel differently.' Priscilla hugged Dorothy close. 'Come. It is too cold up here. Come below out of the wind.'

Dorothy gathered herself together, adopting an air of patient calm.

That night as she lay in bed, Priscilla thought of Dorothy. *Does William love her? Probably in his way he does, but Dorothy doesn't gain strength from his love.* She thought of Mr Alden and almost sat up, startled, knowing in a flash, she needed John Alden's love. His love would strengthen her. In her bones she knew this to be true.

The deliberations and discussions continued next day. Helping her mother rip another petticoat to use as bandages, Priscilla said, 'Why take so long? What more can they find to discuss? Can they not see how disease is consuming us?'

'Priscilla.' Mother's tone was sharp. She aggressively tore the fabric. 'Your complaints do not help. They only stir bad feeling. It is not our place to question. You must be patient.'

Priscilla said nothing. When she had rolled the final bandage strip she went on deck, desperate for fresh air. She paced up and down, put her hands to her temples, feeling her head would explode with frustration, hating the word *patience*. Then – Bang! Bang! – Gunshot!

'Fire, fire, the ship's on fire.' Shouts and screams came from below deck. She ran to the hatch and down the ladder, followed by men running from the great cabin, and Master Jones. Once below her nose and eyes burned with the stench and smoke. Then there was quiet. Mother whispered to her, 'One of the crew moved like lightning. He grabbed a bucket and quenched the fire.'

'Who did this?' Master Jones demanded.

Priscilla trembled and held Joseph's hand.

A seaman came forward, pulling Francis Billington by the ear. 'It were him, sir. He got 'old 'o some gunpowder, sir, and made squibs and this firearm, and shot squibs int' barrel half-full 'o gunpowder, sir. And there were bits 'o flint and iron pieces lying about, sir. It were a blaze, sir. Wonder th' ship didn't go up in flames, sir...'

'Enough. Where's his father?' The captain's voice was quiet and hard.

John Billington came forward.

'Might have known. Your son's to be whipped. See to it, seaman.'

'Aye, aye, sir.'

'Rascal. Deserves every lash he gets,' Billington muttered.

'And you, Billington. If you don't keep that lad under control; if there's any more mischief, you and he'll be put off this ship, to wander in the wilderness and be scalped by Indians or eaten by wild beasts.' Master Jones turned on his heel and climbed back up on to the deck.

The seaman dragged the whimpering Francis up the ladder.

His mother wept and wrung her hands. 'My poor boy.' She pushed forward and climbed several rungs calling, 'Master Jones, please. He didn't mean no harm... please... '

Billington grabbed his wife by the arm and wrenched her off the ladder. She fell, moaning.

Priscilla covered Joseph's ears and held him close, but she couldn't block out the crack of the whip and the lad's screams as he endured ten lashes. She, together with Mother and Joseph, kept to their cabin. They could hear Francis whimpering and Mr Billington scolding him.

'Mother, if we can't get off this horrid, crowded, stinking ship soon I shall go mad! And please do not tell me to be strong and patient.'

'Priscilla!' Her mother heaved a sigh. 'There's folk worse off than us – who are more crowded and suffering more from sickness. We'll be off the ship before long, I'm sure of it. But it's no good somewhere if it's not fit.'

'Yes, Mother, I'm sorry.'

The men continued with their deliberations all next day. Priscilla grew despondent. *Master Jones can't wait forever. He will eventually lose patience.*

That evening Father brought news. 'The first mate has just told us of a harbor directly across the bay. He recalls it from when he was here before. He says Captain John Smith found it nigh six years ago and named it Plymouth Harbor. It is also called Thievish Harbor because one of the wild men stole a harpoon from the Europeans when they were trading there. We decided we must explore it. Could be good.'

'Why did the ship's mate not speak of this before? Why only now, after all these days lost with discussing?' Priscilla could not contain her frustration.

'Priscilla, hold your tongue.'

Chapter 18

December 1620

Finding Plymouth Harbor

Hour after hour Captain Standish and his troop sailed through lashing sleet with rough seas tossing the shallop and drenching the explorers. This was the second day of their search for Plymouth Harbor and John prayed he could endure. Never had he been so frozen; head and limbs numb, unable to think or move. Longing for oblivion, he felt himself drifting when a wave splashed him awake. Not wanting to disgrace himself he forced his eyes open, scanning a shoreline shrouded in cloud and swirling mists. On they sailed, in silent misery, the only sound the occasional cawing of a seagull piercing the noise of buffeting wind and waves.

'There! A stream running down!' John pointed.

'Freshwater! Put ashore!' Standish commanded.

As on the previous night, John and a small crew put up a barricade. As he hammered logs into the ground, Standish stood beside him. 'Glad I brought you along. There's none quicker putting up a fort and you follow orders.' He clapped John on the shoulder.

'Thank you, sir.'

Sentries posted, prayers and a meager meal completed, John spread his pallet and stretched out, musket at his side. Exhaustion and the comforting blaze of the campfire brought instant sleep.

'My God! What?' John started up, grabbing his musket. A hideous unearthly howling circled the camp.

'At arms,' Standish shouted. John rushed to take his place, resting his musket on top of the barricade.

'Fire! Cease!' Silence.

'Fire! Cease!' Silence.

'Reckon it were wolves, sir,' a sailor said. 'Been in these parts before and heard wolves. Sounds the same. Full moon brings 'em on.'

'At ease, sentries, keep your posts.' As they settled down again Standish sat beside John and spoke quietly. 'So different from the battlefields of Europe.'

'Why did you leave Europe, sir? Your position of command.'

'The hierarchy. Subservience. If a man's superior officer was a good leader – fine. But most often they were idiots, happy to slaughter hundreds upon hundreds of men at a whim. If I had protested...' He drew his finger across his neck. 'Men I had trained, who trusted me, trusted they were fighting for a good cause; in the end I could no longer bear the betrayal.' Standish looked round the sleeping men in his charge, features caught now and again in the flickering firelight, each in his own posture, emitting his own sleeping sounds into the still, moonlit night. Bradford lay semi-curled, softly wheezing, Deacon Carver, flat on his back, his deep breathing interrupted by the occasional snore. 'I am happier with a small band, all of us with the same purpose. Here in the wilderness God knows what dangers lurk unseen, testing, and these men have no idea of discipline. But I am determined to pull them through.'

'Reckon if anyone can, it is you, sir.'

Standish rested his hand on John's shoulder. 'I know you are worried, leaving Priscilla with that rogue Prence lurking about. You can be sure Master and Mistress Mullins will not send her to the cargo hold. They said they'll use Francis Billington to fetch and carry. Keep him out of mischief. Priscilla will be on her guard. She'll not go anywhere on the ship unaccompanied.'

'Thank you, sir. I'll breathe easier now.'

'Sleep. Adventure tomorrow.'

But John lay awake. He thought of Priscilla caring for the sick, little Joseph, poor Rose Standish, her mouth weeping blood. 'Please God,' he prayed. 'Please may Plymouth Harbor be a good place. We **must** build soon.'

He fretted the night through until Standish commanded they rise, just before daybreak.

'Soonest we're off the better.' He detailed John to help prepare breakfast. Sorting portions of hardtack and salt beef, he noticed several men heading to the shallop with their knapsacks, bedrolls and muskets. 'Do not leave your muskets in the shallop,' Standish commanded.

'Please gather for prayers,' Deacon Carver called. Hurrying back from the shallop without their muskets, one of the men mumbled, 'We don't need muskets now, it's daylight. There won't be any trouble.' To John's surprise Standish didn't insist.

Perhaps he didn't hear. Perhaps he didn't want to confront at this moment. Famished he chewed his hardtack, gaining hope from the fair dawn light bringing the promise of sun.

John jolted upright as if he had been shot. Those strange and terrible cries, more fearsome, notes screeching up and down, so loud so near.

'Men! Indians! Indians!' A sentry rushed in ahead of a shower of arrows.

'To arms!'

John threw himself into position and fired at the rapidly shifting targets, half-seen; an arm stretching a bow from behind a tree trunk, tall bare-limbed figures flitting like shadows from tree to tree, so quick, impossible to keep them in his sights. He dodged arrows lopping over the barricade.

'These matchlocks take so long,' Winslow grumbled, struggling to reload. From behind a man called, 'Come, fetch our muskets.' From the corner of his eye John spied several men running from the fort.

'What the hell?' Standish shouted. 'The Indians are after them. Go, John, quick.'

Whooping and screeching, giants of men, tall, muscular, brown-skinned, glistening with bear grease and war paint, danced around the small group of English, closing in, flailing the air with tomahawks and knives.

With three others, John ran out brandishing muskets and cutlasses; shooting, slicing and yelling. With a flourish of tomahawks and departing war-whoops, the Indians ran back into the woods. Only one, a tall, stout, brave stood his ground behind a tree, shooting arrow after arrow whizzing into the barricade. The explorers fired volley after volley but he didn't budge or pause in his shooting. John heard Standish mutter, 'Enough.' The captain took careful aim and fired. His bullet grazed the tree trunk by the brave's ear. Bits of bark splintered and flew about his face. With a huge shriek, the warrior disappeared off into the woods.

'After him,' Standish led a chase. 'Show him we are not afraid.' After a couple of volleys, he commanded, 'Cease fire,' and led the party back to their camp.

'Our coats!' Deacon Carver exclaimed. 'Shot through and through! That could have been one of us! It is truly miraculous none of us was harmed. God be praised.'

'Attention!' Captain Standish waited for his men to be still. 'This was a dreadful huggery. We were caught with muskets left in the shallop and then – the stupidity of running out from the barricade. How many times have I ordered, *you must obey* my commands. This is a military expedition. We could be attacked at any moment. You do not deliberate, discuss or make your own decisions. Deacon Carver is right. It is a miracle none of us were hit, or killed. But we cannot rely on miracles. The success of this expedition relies on sensible care for our safety. I am to be the judge of sensible care. Is that understood?'

'Aye, sir.' The company nodded in assent.

Standish posted sentries.

In hurried silence John helped stow belongings and provisions in the shallop, often glancing round for signs of another attack. He was one of the last to board, easing himself into the space reserved by Standish's side. Officer Clark at the tiller.

'Hoist the sails,' Standish ordered.

John offered a mute *Thank God* as the wind filled the canvas, pushing the shallop from shore. He kept an eye on land until the boat was out of reach of arrows. Heaving a sigh of relief he noticed Standish relax a little, stretching his legs, leaning back against the gunnels. 'Excellent,' he said. 'Wind behind, tide in our favor, day looks set fair.'

'I fear it won't last, sir,' Officer Clark said.

'Looks set fair to me,' Standish scanned the sky. Reveling in the blue skies, sun, purposeful bow wave, John felt inclined to believe Standish.

Judging by the position of the sun he reckoned they'd enjoyed good fortune for about two hours when Clark said, 'Here it comes.'

'Please God no,' John uttered a futile plea as the sky turned purple and gray. The wind whipped up, bringing sleet and snow, churning the seas. The shallop bounced up and down, tossing every which way.

'I can scarcely hold her, sir,' Clark gasped.

The boat shuddered, slithered sideways.

'The rudder's gone!'

'To oars! Alden and Clark. Man the oars together!' Standish shouted above the din of waves and wind. He leaned forward. 'I'm damned if this storm is going to defeat us. Hold on; hold to it, well done, you can do it.' He called again and again. 'Hang on there, Alden… Clark.'

John strained to hold his oar against the buffeting seas. He saw churning foam pour over the gunnels. Waves rose and slapped him. He saw men bailing. He dimly heard Standish's cries, 'Steady, hold her, well done… steady, hold her…' He felt and thought nothing. Not the cold and wet, nor fear. Underneath the shrieking moan of the wind he listened to his oar grinding in its rowlock. Hold steady… hold steady… on and on. The muted dark of the storm was becoming the dark of night.

'Hoorah! Take heart! I see the harbor!' the ship's mate called out. 'Run up the sail, beat the dark.'

John hung onto his oar as men hoisted more sail. The shallop leapt forward, galloping through huge seas. He almost lost his oar.

CRACK!

'The mast is breaking!'

John looked up as the mast splintered and broke in three places, toppling, toppling, smothering the crew in billowing canvas, falling into the rough seas on his side. He struggled to get out from under flapping sails, gripping his oar with both hands. He almost fell overboard as the shallop heeled over, on the brink of capsizing.

'Three hands on starboard to cut her free. All other hands on port. That's it, steady as she goes,' Standish commanded. John and Clark managed to hold her 'til the crew cut the mast free. 'Near miss,' John muttered. The small vessel righted herself and sped forward. 'We're caught in a flood tide,' he yelled. The churning tidal race whooshed them into the harbor entrance.

'To the north, the north,' the ship's mate called. 'Lord have mercy! I've never seen this place before!' In an instant the shallop was swirling in a cauldron of breakers, crashing toward the rocks. 'About, about, or we will perish!' Standish shouted, 'All hands on oars.'

John pitted all his strength and more. 'Forward, down, pull, up… forward, down, pull, up.' He did his best to row in unison with the others. Rowing through whirling eddies, no steady current, impossible to get a rhythm. Then, as if they'd crossed a divide, quiet waters. As his muscles relaxed he began to shake. Sweat poured down his face. The crew rowed to the shelter of a wooded shore, barely discernable in the pitch black. 'Could do with a moon,' John mumbled.

As they rounded up in the lee of the shore Standish said, 'Well done, men, we are still alive. Reckon we'd best sleep in the boat. Can't see a thing and there may be Indians on shore. Cast an anchor.' John curled up; his back against the gunnels, hugging his knees, hoping this would stop his shaking. No sooner had he got settled than the wind changed, bringing howling gusts of sleet and snow.

'Strewth. We're in another gale. We'll freeze,' Officer Clark exclaimed. 'I'd rather risk drowning or being scalped than freeze to death here in this boat.' To John's surprise, Standish didn't protest.

'As you wish. Good luck!'

John joined the few men who chose to go ashore. Over the side of the shallop into icy waters, waist high, squalls of sleet buffeting his head. Stepping on a stone that turned under his foot he lurched and almost fell headlong. He regained his balance and kept his musket dry. Reaching the shore he followed Clark, clambering up the steep slope, hanging onto saplings and bushes. Once he was standing on level ground, he realized he'd stopped shaking. The men quickly gathered wood for a fire. As there wasn't a dry twig to be found, it took several goes striking a flame, but finally, success. A warming blaze. Bradford and Carver volunteered for sentry duty. Asleep on his feet John collapsed onto the frozen wet earth.

'Ahoy, ahoy!' He roused himself to stand. Captain Standish and the remaining crew clambered up the bank. 'We saw you'd got a fire going and couldn't resist.' He trudged wearily to stand by the blaze, next to John. 'You did well. Thank you.'

'You led us well, sir. We must find somewhere soon!'

'Aye.' Standish looked into the distance. 'There are too many sick to the point of…' He abruptly bent to unroll his pallet. 'But now, sleep. Where is your pallet, Alden? You mustn't sleep on the freezing ground.'

'Too tired to bother, sir.' John obediently unrolled his pallet. His last thought as he fell asleep was, *I admire this man, I like him.*

'We are on an island.'

John rubbed his eyes. He'd slept past sunrise!

The captain continued, 'It is thanks to Officer Clark we had a warmer, sheltered night on land. I propose we name this island *Clark's Island* in recognition.'

'Aye, aye, to Officer Clark.' The troop raised their hands in salute.

'So far no sign of Indians. We'll keep sentries posted at all times, but all of you must be alert.' Taking short, quick steps, Standish paced back and forth. 'As we are utterly spent and wet and cold, we will rest today; dry our clothes and clean our firearms. We must also make a new mast for the shallop and dry the spare sail.'

'Tomorrow is the Sabbath,' Bradford said.

'Ah well two days of rest won't go amiss,' Standish said.

'Thank you, sir,' Clark's words of gratitude set off a chorus of 'Thank you'.

On Monday Standish roused his men before dawn. 'Be ready by daybreak to sound the harbor.' Prayers and breakfast were over by first light. 'Have we got the plumb lines and every man his musket?' The captain made sure all was in order and they shoved off in the shallop. One of the sailors lowered a line of twine with a lead weight on the end at many different points as the shallop rowed all over the harbor, back and forth, back and forth whilst Officer Clark recorded the depths and locations of the soundings, using a hand-held compass and landmarks on shore to triangulate.

'Ah this is good news. Plenty of depth for ships to anchor this far out in the lee of the island, and it is sheltered,' Officer Clark said.

'Excellent. We should just have time for a quick reconnoiter on shore before nightfall. Hurry on.' Captain Standish spoke with renewed energy. Clambering ashore he said, 'All keep together. Remember the huggery. We'll survey as much as we can of a square mile before daylight goes.' He led with John beside him, Officer Clark bringing up the rear.

'Indians have cultivated here. Cornfields, and look, a freshwater brook, and that hill there. A good place for a fort.'

Bradford quickened his pace to trudge alongside Standish. 'Thank you, sir, for bringing us here safely.'

Standish rested a hand on the serious young Pilgrim's shoulder. 'We'll make it work and now you'll have good news for your Dorothy; smooth out the worried frown she wears.'

'Aye, praise God.' Almost smiling, Bradford looked to heaven. 'It will be good to greet her with this news.'

Chapter 19

December 1620

Desperation

A pall of silence greeted the returning party as they boarded the *Mayflower*.

'Where is Dorothy?' Bradford asked, his eyes searching the deck.

Elder Brewster took him by the elbow. 'A word in private.'

John greeted Priscilla. 'Mistress Mullins, is something amiss?'

'Aye,' she whispered, head bent, eyes lowered. 'Dorothy fell overboard.' She choked back a sob. 'She drowned.'

John groaned softly. Feeling he shouldn't, he studied Bradford as Elder Brewster delivered the news. His face turned ashen gray. He stumbled to the hatch and down the ladder.

'Poor William, poor Dorothy.' Priscilla couldn't hold back her tears, wiping her cheeks, biting her lip.

'I'm so sorry.' John kept his voice low. He longed to hold her. She seemed so fragile just then, so vulnerable. 'You've lost a dear friend.'

'It happened and no one knew, not 'til the morning. She went on deck in the night… and was gone. And just the night before she held little Jasper More in her arms as he was dying, gasping 'Doorty, Doorty' with his last breath. Dorothy clutched his little body close and wept and wept.' Priscilla wept.

On hearing the news, the returning party removed their hats. 'Damn! Damn! Such a lovely girl.' Captain Standish slammed his fist into his palm.

'What will this do to Bradford?' John wondered aloud.

'Dorothy was frightened she'd not be able to cope. She said she felt too weak, wouldn't be a good enough wife.'

At that moment Bradford came on deck and engaged in earnest conversation with Elder Brewster and Standish and Deacon Carver. John stared. 'Bradford is Dorothy's husband and he's behaving as though nothing had happened.'

'How can he?' Priscilla asked.

'Perhaps it is his way of coping.'

'Like Dorothy. She was so sad and she hid it, just like Mr Bradford. Mr Alden…' For the first time since he'd come on board this day, Priscilla looked at him directly. 'Do you think all this… this misery is part of God's plan? A plan to test a chosen few?'

'I've not thought on it like that. 'Tisn't how I look on it.'

Deacon Carver raised his hand. After a short prayer giving thanks for the safe return of the explorers he said, 'Tomorrow morning there will be a meeting in the great cabin to discuss our options.'

''Tis cold up here in this keen wind, Mistress Mullins. Will you come below?' John escorted Priscilla to the Mullins' cabin.

★ ★ ★

Consumed with restlessness, finding the confines of the cargo hold nigh unbearable after almost a week exploring, John persuaded Mr Martin to oversee the stores while he sought fresh air and light up on deck. He was also disgruntled not to be included in meetings in the great cabin. Standish had tried on his behalf, but Deacon Carver insisted he was needed to safeguard their now scant supplies. John was sure in his own mind Plymouth Harbor was the right choice, with its freshwater brook; superior to Corn Hill, and he judged, with winter upon them there wasn't time to search further. If they didn't build a colony soon, there would be no one left alive to live in it.

Late afternoon, would soon be dusk. The wind whistled, thumped and buffeted. Standing by the rail near the stern, looking toward land, he heard the soft plop of another body being sent to a grave in the sea; prayers of committal an indistinct murmur. He did not look.

But who was that? To his right, he spied a lone woman far along up near the fo'castle. Edging along toward the bow he could see her shoulders shaking, head in her hands. He came closer. It was Mistress Mullins. She stamped her foot. 'It's so stupid.'

'What is stupid, Mistress?'

Priscilla jumped and whirled round, hastily brushing away her tears. 'Mr Alden! I didn't hear you.'

'What troubles you so?'

'Oh it is what happened to Dorothy. I feel I failed her. And… and… I hate Mistress Brewster for what she said. She said to Dorothy that Bradford doesn't want a weak wife and after Dorothy was gone she said perhaps 'twas for the best! Part of God's plan.' Priscilla looked over the rail into the water. 'I'm sure Dorothy wouldn't have purposely jumped overboard; 'tis a mortal sin. But perhaps, I can imagine her leaning, leaning, looking into the sea, longing for her little John and her balance going the wrong way.' Distraught, Priscilla turned her head to and fro; hugged herself round her waist.

'It is heartbreaking.' John did not know what to say. 'Please do not feel you failed her. It was her own who failed her. I could see how she loved you.'

Priscilla took a deep breath, collecting herself. 'Thank you, Mr Alden. Your words are comforting.' She stood quiet, looking out across the cape. Facing John again she said, 'I cannot understand how, when time is so pressing, when we so urgently need to get started building and Master Jones needs to sail back to England – how can it be reasonable to lose so many days in preparing for and keeping the Sabbath. And these endless discussions, going on for days. Folk are desperately sick. If they don't get off this ship soon they'll not live, and winter...'

'I agree, but these Church of Christ folk believe they must keep the Sabbath to earn salvation, and that is more important to them than life here on earth. As to the endless discussions, your father explained to me the hesitation about Plymouth. First, the deep water where ships can anchor is a mile off shore. Second, there is no river flowing inland. A big obstacle to exploration and trade. So there are a number who reckon we should search further.'

'Where?' Priscilla thumped the rail. 'Soon there'll be no one fit enough to build. We are almost out of food.'

'Ssh, I know.' John held her gaze. 'But as your father says, we chose Deacon Carver to be our governor and he and the other leaders are all of the Church of Christ. If we are to survive we must all pull in the same direction, even when we disagree. I know Deacon Carver thinks highly of your father. Wants to include him in the governing council, even though he is not of their church.' He spoke quietly, earnestly, and leaned toward her, inviting. She almost came into his arms, but checked herself. She took half a step back.

'I know you are right,' she smiled. 'Rose says Captain Standish was glad to have you on the expedition. Said you rowed with the strength of Samson and are expert at putting up a barricade faster than that,' she snapped her fingers – 'and a great bonus, you obey his commands.'

The door of the great cabin opened. Deacon Carver and Elder Brewster emerged first, followed by Mr Mullins and Winslow.

'Father,' Priscilla said. 'A decision?'

'Plymouth. We're to settle in Plymouth.'

'Hallelujah!' John punched the air.

The First Winter

Chapter 20

December 1620 – January 1621

John talks with Master Mullins

''Tis worrying to be so low on beer,' Mother said. 'We need the goodness in it. I shouldn't wonder it's the seawater bringing such maladies. Any water is a danger and this itchy seawater is the worst.'

'Aye. We need fresh springs and running brooks for safe water. Mr Alden says there is an area ashore by the big rock, has a good running brook.' She stooped to help Joseph sit up. He was coughing so hard he couldn't get his breath. The coughing eased. 'Here – try to take a sip of this beer.' She continued, 'And there's a high hill. Would be good to mount our cannons on.'

'I… help… with cannons.' Joseph fell back against the pillow.

'There, try to sleep, love.' Priscilla stroked his brow. 'And there is another smaller hill, would be a good place for houses. And we could land smaller boats by the big rock.'

'It does sound like a good spot,' Mother said. 'As good as we'd find any time soon.'

That afternoon Father came down from a meeting in the great cabin. 'It will be the area near the rock, with the high hill. A party of twenty will go ashore and spend the night there, ready to begin building at daybreak.'

Priscilla's heart surged. She hurried down into the cargo hold to ask Mr Alden for some more beer. He was checking the barrels were tight. 'Mr Alden, isn't it good news – the place they've chosen!'

'Aye, and I'll be in the party going ashore.' He left his task and came to greet her. 'High time we started building. Is there something you need, Mistress Mullins?'

'Oh, yes. Please could we have some more beer for Joseph? He is very bad.'

'Ah. Poor little chap. You'd better have a fair amount; Mr Martin will be here in my place.'

'Oh. I'm glad you'll be able to go ashore at last, and I know you are needed, but I wish...'

As Alden handed her the tankard of beer he caressed her hand and kissed her cheek. Priscilla almost dropped the beer. His touch sent tiny shock waves all through her.

'Steady there.' He smiled.

Priscilla put on an air of demure shyness. 'Thank you for the beer, Mr Alden,' she said with a slight curtsy. She almost tripped going back up the ladder with the beer in one hand and no free hand to gather up her skirts. When she handed Mother the beer she was blushing with the effort and with happiness. Mother raised her eyebrows but said nothing.

Mr Alden made several trips up and down the two ladders with bedding and provisions. Father and Priscilla went up on deck to see the party off, Priscilla tightly wrapped in her thick winter shawl.

'Ah, 'tis a cold wind, and I don't like the look of that dark sky. Thunder clouds.' Father's voice was hoarse and rasping and he stifled a cough. They stood at the rail waving to the departing shallop. Mr Alden raised his hand, looking directly at Priscilla.

Father took Priscilla's arm and turned her to face him. 'Last night when I went down to the cargo hold to have a chat, Mr Alden asked my permission to court you.'

Priscilla gasped and put her hands to her coloring cheeks. 'Oh! Oh Father.' Unsteady, she hung onto her father's arms.

'I said yes, if you are willing. He is a good man.'

Priscilla lowered her eyes. 'Yes. I've known in my heart a fair while. I am willing.'

'I thought as much.' Father coughed. The twinkle in his eyes shone through misty tears. 'I reckon you'll do well together. Now. Let us go below, out of this wind.'

In spite of the icy blowing damp, Priscilla felt warm and glowing inside.

That night the winds gathered force into a crescendo of shrieking gales. She heard the command above, 'Cast another anchor,' and the sound of hurrying feet along with further commands. As the *Mayflower* lurched this way and that she thought of the men on shore. They would be freezing cold and drenched, with only enough food for one meal.

Next morning, her head aching from the cloying stench of their quarters, Priscilla climbed the ladder to the upper deck. A ferocious gust almost threw her down. She caught hold of the capstan. Gales churned the harbor. Gasping in the stinging wind she watched as sailors loaded the shallop with provisions and lowered her into the chaotic waters. *Food and dry gear. I pray they reach shore.* She went below.

Mother was holding Rose Standish in her arms. Poor Rose. Priscilla held a cloth to absorb the blood streaming from her nose. Mother was then able to soothe the hot livid spots covering her face and chest and arms. Blood seeped from her gums. The scurvy was very advanced.

'It's no good,' Rose said. 'Please God, may I die quickly.'

'Now, now,' Mother spoke gently. 'Try to sip some beer. 'Twill help you recover.' But Rose was taken in a fit of coughing, heaving up globs of bloody phlegm. Her head fell forward.

'There now.' Mother laid her head back against the blood soaked pillows. 'Can you stay with her, Priscilla, while I go to Mary Allerton. She's gone into labor.' Priscilla did what she could to comfort and soothe Rose, wishing for more linen. There wasn't a piece of cloth to be found.

'Miles, oh Miles.' Rose's longing, pleading call was weak and far away. Priscilla ripped off a strip of her petticoat. 'Rose. You lovely merry woman. You deserve a decent cloth to wipe your face.'

She heard Joseph coughing. He called, 'Priscilla, Priscilla.' Quickly she went to him. He needed to vomit. There hadn't been time to empty the chamber pots. She heaved and gagged, holding Joseph as he retched and retched, bringing up only phlegm. Rose moaned and Mary screamed in pain. Children called, 'Help. I throw up.' Women and men ranted and cursed in their fevered delirium.

'Lie still now, Joseph,' she said. 'I must go to Rose.'

'No, no, don't leave me.' He grabbed her arm as hands behind clutched at her skirt. 'Help me, help me please, for God's pity.' Priscilla hurried to Rose, upsetting a chamber pot as she stumbled past yearning eyes and beseeching hands. She found a filthy sheet and covered the mess, shoving it behind a trunk. ''Til later,' she muttered.

When she had done all she could for Rose, Priscilla hurried from one poor soul to the next.

Mother stumbled through the litter of mess and imploring bodies to Priscilla and Joseph. 'Mistress Brewster said I wasn't needed, that she knows better how to birth.' She wiped her brow. 'Sent Mistress Carver away too.'

'That is wrong. Sit down a moment, Mother. You need a sip of ale.'

Would Mary ever get through this awful birthing? Her wailing and screams continued all through the afternoon and into the evening, dinning into Priscilla's aching head. When at last the baby boy came forth, he was dead. Exhausted and too weak to weep, Mary heaved with silent sobs.

The storm raged on another day. Then, on the morning of December 23rd the ship was still. Priscilla climbed on deck into clear skies and a gentle wind. The shallop set sail across the harbor taking an additional party of men and provisions to shore.

To her relief, Mr Prence was amongst them. He'd continued to try to woo her, saying last eve he'd begged to go ashore, to build a home for his beloved Priscilla. He refused to believe she had accepted John Alden as her suitor.

Although Father and Elder Brewster protected her from Mr Martin's silly cosseting, making sure she never had to go down to the cargo hold for rations or ale, she longed for John Alden, for their brief moments, his reassuring strength. Every minute, even whilst tending the sick, she thought of him, wet, freezing, hungry, working to build a settlement.

Chapter 21

Building in the wilderness

Soaked and shivering, the party on shore roused themselves after a night of fitful sleep as early twitterings of birds announced the approach of dawn. John wished he could set to felling trees immediately. That way at least he could warm himself. However, morning prayers were obligatory. Breakfast was only a piece of hardtack, a biscuit made of baked oats and wheat, sailors' standard fare – welcome, but it did little to assuage his gnawing hunger.

Stomping and slapping themselves the men were eager to get moving.

'Wait,' Standish said. 'We will divide into groups. You to fell trees, you to saw, you to carry, and you to put up temporary shelters.'

John admired the captain's quick efficiency and was pleased when Standish beckoned to him. Axes in hand, they trudged together across the cleared land up the incline toward the forest.

'Look!' John pointed at a bright red, crested bird perched among the branches of a white barked birch tree catching the early morning sun. 'About the size of our blackbird.' Not watching his feet, he tripped. 'What?' He bent over and picked up a half buried whitened skull.

Standish stopped to examine it. 'Reckon there must have been an Indian settlement here, but why they left? Who knows?'

'All these trees! All the trees we will ever need, and a good variety: pine, walnut, beech, ash, hazel, birch and sassafras.' John recognized familiar species. 'We'll make some money with these.'

'Aye, and have plenty to burn,' Standish said. 'No number of King's navies could use up all these forests. Wood to last us forever and it won't cost us a penny.'

The two men swung their axes, one on each side of a tall, straight tree and fell into a good rhythm.

When the shallop crossed the harbor and unloaded twenty more men and a good supply of provisions, John smiled with relief to see Mr Prence among the new arrivals. *Good. Keep him here so he can't bother Priscilla.* During his near sleepless nights he'd fretted to think of Priscilla locked up on the *Mayflower* with that man. He set to storing the provisions in the first shelter they'd erected while Standish deployed the new workforce to various tasks.

John relished his labor. Sounds of chopping, sawing, trees falling and men's voices calling and shouting filled the sharp clear winter air. He and Standish brought down tree after tree and hauled them to the site for the common house. However, come mid-afternoon the skies darkened with large deep gray clouds. The wind picked up, and down came the rain, lashing and soaking.

The men huddled in their shelter, gathered round a small fire, taking care to keep their muskets dry, as they endured hours of listening to the rain and wind threatening to blow down their temporary home. After prayers and food they arranged themselves as best they could on the damp earth to sleep. John dozed off and on in the fatigue of hard work. Late in the night he heard the wind and rain easing, going on their way, then silence. A silence such as he'd never known. No sound at all: only the dying wind in the trees and the grunts and snuffles of his sleeping companions. None of the night-time noises of the town: the town crier calling the hour, the occasional clip clop of horses' hooves and the rattle of the night post coach – nor the sounds of shipboard: wind in the rigging, waves lapping against the hull, the occasional call and footsteps of sailors on watch. This was the silence of wilderness and the sounds of a few exhausted men sleeping. The silence filled him with dread of all that was unseen, unknown, roaming in the dark wilderness.

As John felt himself drifting from reverie into sleep strange eerie cries pierced his brain. Standish was instantly on his feet. 'At arms!' he barked. 'Muskets in hand. Indians.' Clumsy with sleep, John tried to hurry. He grabbed his musket and stumbled out into the black night.

'Aaye!' Bradford tripped over a hummock of turf and fell to his knees. Fortunately the tumble did not discharge his musket and one of the sentries quickly helped him up.

'Quiet,' Standish commanded.

John peered into the dark, wishing he had good night vision. There was no moonlight. Again the cries pierced the still air. 'Where are they?' he wondered aloud. The cries eventually ceased, but all through the remaining hours of darkness the party stood silent, ready to fire, tense, waiting for an attack.

Dawn filtered through the dark into daybreak. No sign of Indians anywhere. Strange. Today was the Sabbath. No work. John tried not to let his frustration show. Thankfully the morning brought sunshine and some warmth. The afternoon was a repeat of yesterday: lashing wind and drenching rain. In the night, the fearsome Indian howls and screeches came again.

Monday dawned bright. Christmas Day!

'Merry Christmas!' Alden and Standish's wishes of Christmas cheer were quickly squashed by Bradford and others of the religious group.

'Christmas has nothing to do with the true word and teachings of Christ,' Bradford pronounced. 'We do not know when our savior was born. Most certainly not on December 25th. We serve our Lord best by working to build His kingdom here in this land.'

No more Christmas greetings. John and Standish worked non-stop, missing the midday meal.

'Please God it doesn't rain,' John said.

'Aye, a dry afternoon would be a good Christmas gift,' Standish replied.

The day stayed fine and by sunset the party could stand and admire their work. The frame of the common house was up. Their first building. Into the exhausted joy of the moment came the Indians' screeching.

John remained on shore, working hard whenever the weather allowed. Mornings were usually fine but afternoons brought wind and rain.

During the wet afternoons and in the evenings, Bradford and Winslow, Governor Carver, Elder Brewster, Standish and John worked on plans for the layout of the colony.

Standish suggested a pattern he'd learned when studying military engineering at the University of Leiden: a main street with parallel streets and a cross street, being the easiest to defend.

'All in favor?' Governor Carver asked.

'Aye,' came the response in unison.

Having a plan infused the men with renewed energy, and over the next week the frames for several more houses went up.

John kept his distance from Prence but noted the man worked hard. Several times he heard him voicing his desire to proceed with building a house for himself and his future wife. Standish advised that could happen as soon as houses were built for passengers waiting on the *Mayflower*, and contrived to keep him ashore.

The shallop sailed to and fro bringing provisions and change-over working parties.

Happily, the weather was kind for a few days and the entire workforce doubled their efforts. One afternoon when John was up on the hill, splitting logs, he heard cries coming from below in the fields. 'Bradford, Bradford.' Looking down he saw a cluster of folk gathered around a body lying on the ground. Dropping his axe he ran down the hill. Even before he got there, he could see Bradford curled and writhing in pain.

'Quick, into the common house,' Winslow said. 'Stand back, everyone.' John bent low, carefully picked up Bradford in his arms and carried him to the common house. He was surprised Bradford weighed so little. Always slender, he had become bone thin, face gaunt, eyes hollow. Now he gritted his teeth, refusing to cry out.

Winslow had run ahead and was laying out a pallet and pillows. John knelt, gently easing him onto the pallet.

'Please stand back.' Winslow spoke firmly to the men gathered round. Bradford was ghostly pale and gasping. Winslow knelt down, placing his hand on his friend's chest. 'His heart is racing. Not good.'

Watching Bradford tossing and moaning, John feared he might not live.

'I'll stay by him,' Carver said. 'Verses from the psalms might calm him. He loves the psalms.'

Last thing before bed, John went to see Bradford. He was still in pain and pale, very sick, but he was breathing more easily and Winslow was caring for him, helping him to take a few sips of beer.

'The hardship of the voyage is taking its toll,' John said, struck by the number of men lying sick on pallets.

Winslow settled Bradford back against his pillow, and joined him. 'Every day a few more collapse. We are fortunate there are more to come from the ship.' He placed a hand on John's shoulder. 'Thank you for carrying him so quickly and carefully. I'll stay here through the night.' John felt warmed by Winslow's words of appreciation.

After breakfast John was preparing to go to the reed beds for thatch when Standish called to him. 'Over here, Alden. You are more use felling trees. Goodman and Browne can go for reeds and with their dogs they might bring home a duck or even a deer.'

Glad to fell trees instead of cutting reeds, John said farewell to the two men as they set off with their muskets, sickles and dogs.

'See you at dusk, hopefully with fowl and venison.'

'We'll do our best.' Off they went, whistling, for the day was fine.

Dusk fell and the two men had not returned. The Indians' cries sent shudders through John's veins. He was on sentry duty and all through the bitter snowy night he peered into the darkness, willing the two men to come stumbling into the settlement. Morning brought a blanket of snow and still no sign of Goodman and Browne. All day the settlers waited anxiously, now and then stopping work to look and listen. The day faded into another snowy dusk, laced with Indian screeches. John and Standish exchanged looks of fear which needed no words. Again it was time for bed and sentries were posted. John was despondent. Thoughts of what tortures the two men might suffer if captured by the Indians plagued his mind.

'Halloo – who goes there?' a sentry called out.

'Help – it is us.'

John recognized the voice and rushed out. Winslow and Carver lit lanterns and followed. The two men were nearly fainting with hunger and cold and Goodman could hardly stand on his frostbitten feet. John took his weight, helping him into the common house, easing him down by the fire. The swelling and pain were so bad John had to cut away his boots.

'Thank God. Thank God you are safe,' he said, near to weeping in his relief. Winslow brought warm beer and blankets.

Next evening after prayers and supper, the settlers gathered round the fire to hear Browne recount their adventure. Goodman was still in the grip of a chill, shivering one minute and hot with a fever the next.

'We cut reeds all the morning. After our midday food we decided to take the dogs for a short ramble. We went into the woods and came upon a pond, and there on the other side stood a large stag, looking straight at us. Magnificent set of antlers on him. The dogs disappeared off pursuing the beast. We chased after but by the time we caught up with the dogs we were hopelessly lost. Then came the rain, sleet and snow. In the dusk we searched for an abandoned wigwam to shelter in and there came a terrible sound, like a wailing screech and a roar all at once. Reckon 'twas lions and they roared all night. Sounded like a poor soul, a woman, being murdered. Have never been so afraid. We found a tree we could climb if the lions came. All night we paced round that tree, holding the mastiff by her collar and keeping tight hold of our sickles. Come dawn the roaring stopped. We set out to find home but we'd lost our bearings and it was almost dusk when we came to a hill. We climbed to the top and thank God there was the harbor in the distance. Now we knew where to go and that gave us strength. Thank God the lions didn't come. Thank God we aren't still lost and freezing and starving to death.'

'Aye. It was a good escape and thanks be to our Lord,' Bradford called from his bed, breaking into the hush.

'Aye, 'tis so.' Rumbling murmurs of assent circled round the fire.

As John and Standish walked to the shelter Standish said, 'If we're not careful the wilderness could defeat us. So easy to lose one's bearings. Those two were lucky to come back alive.'

Chapter 22

January 1621

A fire, a discovery, a death

Deacon Carver raised his hand, bowed his head in silence, looked up again, and said, 'We are gathered together in the name of our Lord Jesus Christ to worship God our Father. We will begin with Psalm 19. "The Heavens declare the glory of God…"'

The Deacon was holding prayers in the open air by the door to the common house so those indoors, too sick to stand, could hear. Hovering at the back, bored and impatient, John looked down at the ground and scuffed his boot. He raised his eyes. What was that gray wispy shape creeping along the roof? A rat? No… it's smoke… then a small red flame… 'FIRE!' he shouted. 'The roof… on fire! Get the gunpowder out quick!' He heard a few seconds of stunned silence as he pushed through the group and ran into the building. Then shouts of panic. Sparks fell on the sick, on clothing and belongings, all round. He heard Standish's commands outside. 'Quiet! Stand back. Winslow, Hopkins, Howland, go in. Get the gunpowder and muskets and all the sick folk out.' John hoisted a barrel and ran for the door, almost colliding with Winslow coming in.

He carried the barrel of gunpowder upwind, well out of reach of blowing sparks. *I need something to beat out the flames on the roof – good – a stack of reeds over there by that tree.* He grabbed a bundle and climbed up the corner of the building where the protruding ends of the logs made a sort of ladder up to the eaves. Clutching the thatch with his free hand and digging the toes of his boots in for footholds, he climbed to the ridge of the steep roof. Levering himself astride he flailed at the flames with the wet reeds, inching along, reaching down, far down on either side, gripping the ridge with his knees. Leaning too far, blinded by the sunlight, he slid, falling. He grabbed the thatch with his left hand, not letting go the bundle of reeds. Using his feet to dig in he slowly climbed back up to the ridge. Gasping breaths of smoke he carried on. The sun shone bright and the wind fanned the flames. Sparks blew up in his face and hair and burned holes in his clothes. His eyes burned with sweat and heat. The wind whistled in his ears, and voices shouting commands below sounded far away. He reached the end of the ridge and then worked his way backwards, checking all the flames were put out. Alden looked down on a tableau of the sick lying prostrate on the cold ground or sitting, leaning against trees. Winslow was moving from one to the next, wrapping them in blankets, covering their bare feet. Now the sky was darkening, bringing a chill to the air. He looked up to see huge purple-black clouds moving in across the harbor.

Slowly, he climbed down, knees wobbly, hands cut and bleeding. Feet on the ground he hobbled over to the array of sick. Goodman lay flat, shivering with fever, Winslow kneeling beside him.

'Is there anything I can do to help?'

'We need to get all these poor folk back inside as soon as possible,' Winslow said.

'Where is Standish?'

'Indoors, checking for sparks.'

John went into the common house. Standish stood, scanning the roof and inspecting the floor.

'Well done, Alden,' he said. 'Now we must wait and watch for unseen smoldering embers.'

'But sir. Have you seen the sky? It has clouded over, full of rain. Those sick folk will be drenched and so cold. And Goodman is shaking with fever.'

'Would you have them burn to death?' Standish shot back.

Windswept rain lashed down.

'Carry the sick back indoors – quickly.' Governor Carver called out an urgent, vehement command. 'No time to lose!'

John ran out to Goodman. Gently lifting him, he could feel the man was burning up inside.

That night Goodman died.

Waiting for dawn John wept silent tears. His first task was to make Goodman's coffin. As he hewed planks from a tree trunk he wondered, *How many more of these will there be?* He shivered. *We are not building the settlement fast enough. Folk still on the Mayflower have nowhere to live. How can the sick hope to recover cooped up in that rat warren?* He was desperate to see Priscilla. *Is she still well?*

After Goodman's burial John spoke to Governor Carver of his concern.

'I agree,' Carver said. 'Too many are sick unto death and I reckon you, Mr Alden, with your building skills, are the man to lead our workers to best advantage.'

Aided by fair weather and infected with John's enthusiasm, the workforce made good progress.

The Billington males, father and two sons, co-operated as never before, helping to saw and mix daub with gusto. However, one day John noticed young Francis Billington was nowhere to be seen. The scamp was usually either mixing clay and reeds for daub or pestering first this person, then that. His father was felling trees with Howland.

'Captain Standish, I cannot see Francis anywhere. I don't like it. I think I'd better have a word with his father.'

'Don't be long.' Standish's response was gruff. 'They're not worth the bother, that lot.'

'Billington,' John called as he trudged across the hummocks of turf, 'do you know where Francis is? He's not to be seen.'

'Fie on him,' Billington replied. 'The rascal. I'll not take time to search now. If he ain't back by the cursed prayers I'll go and seek him.'

'Aye,' John said. 'I thought I'd better tell you.' He resumed felling trees with Standish.

By evening, when folk were gathering in the common house for prayers, there was still no sign of Francis. As he was going in the door John felt a tug at his sleeve. It was Billington.

'I've got to try to find Francis.'

John nodded. 'Of course.' All during prayers he was thinking of what might have happened to the lad. It could be Indians, wolves, getting stuck in the marsh – anything. He wished Billington had gone to search much earlier.

Deacon Carver was preaching, '"For where two or three are gathered together in my name, there am I in the midst of them." So rest assured my brethren that our good Lord, the Christ, is with us always in trials and…'

Exuberant high pitched shouts broke in.

'A sea! I found a sea!' Francis ran lickety-split into their midst.

Never mind about the Lord, thank heavens the child is here. John grinned in his relief. Francis was scratched and gasping for breath.

'I climbed a tall tree – up to the top – and there below I saw a vast sea. Truly.'

'He's telling tales… making up a story to cover his mischief. And now his father's gone off. Will we ever see *him* again?' Disgruntled mutterings circled the room.

'Come here, Francis. You need some food, gone all day.' John ushered the lad over to the hearth and dished him up some pottage.

'Now sit here and tell me where you went.' To John's amazement, Francis could remember the precise details and landmarks of his trek.

'And then, in a clearing, up a hill, there was this tall tree – a perfect climber – so up I went. Oh it were good after so long cooped up in the ship. And when I reached the top I couldn't believe what I saw. A vast sea, only not big waves. And covered with ducks and birds and fish jumping.'

'You've had an adventure, Francis,' John said. 'But we didn't know where you'd gone. You know by now there are dangers away from the settlement and we were all afeared for you. Now your father's gone to search. Pray he comes back alive.'

Francis nodded. 'Yes, sir.' But by now, with food inside him and warmed by the fire, his eyelids fell in drowsiness. John carried him to his pallet, took off his boots and tucked a blanket round him. He then fetched himself a trencher of food and joined Standish.

'That lad remembers all the details of his trek. I think someone should go with him to find out the truth of what he's saying.'

'Perhaps,' Standish replied. 'But we need all fit men to finish building. Look – here's Billington back again.'

'He's here – came back during prayers – said he's found a sea,' John called out.

'That rascal! I'll tan his hide, causing all this trouble. Runnin off, not sayin.' Billington strode over to his sleeping son and grasping him by the ear yanked him awake. 'Up wi' ya – tha's commim wi' me.'

'Poor lad,' John muttered. He flinched, hearing Francis' cries mingled with the Indians' screeches from afar. The thrashing seemed to go on forever until at last the boy was quiet. Billington dragged his whimpering son back into the common house and threw him down on his pallet.

'That'll teach ya to go off.'

I'll not thrash my children, John vowed. *There has to be a better way.*
After the final prayers of the evening, John spoke quietly with

Governor Carver. 'I think we should investigate this "sea" the boy says he found. Could one of the ship's hands go with him to find it?'

'Aye, aye,' the governor nodded thoughtfully. 'Perhaps you are right. Who knows? I'll arrange it when the shallop comes over.'

The governor was true to his word and when the shallop next brought supplies from the *Mayflower*, the First Mate disembarked. He requested Francis take him to where he found a sea.

When they returned late that afternoon the Mate said, 'By gum, the lad was right. It was just as he described. A great expanse of water, two lakes actually, full of fish and fowl. And a freshwater brook.'

'And we found Indian wigwams,' Francis danced about.

'Aye, but not an Indian to be seen. I must be off. The shallop is waiting. But well done, Francis.' The Mate saluted the young explorer.

In the common house, John relayed the news. He saw Captain Standish and Billington both shaking their heads in disbelief. 'Well I never! Who'd have thought it?' They spoke as one.

Agreement between those two. That is a first. John raised an eyebrow.

★ ★ ★

A fine crisp morning. End of January and we are ready to store provisions and then, folk from the ship. Priscilla. John's heart flipped. He clenched his axe handle. The dwellings were now all completed except for Brewster's lean-to and roof. Crossing the clearing he balanced on tuffocks of rough grass so as not to get mired in the sticky mud. Picking his way he did not see Prence coming to meet him.

'Mr Alden.'

John stopped. This was his first encounter with Prence since the man came on shore. 'Mr Prence.'

'I request time and men to erect my own dwelling for my intended.' He stood, legs astride.

'No, Mr Prence. Governor Carver has directed us to continue building houses for the sick folk still on the *Mayflower.*

'You do not understand, Mr Alden.' Prence fixed John with his soft brown eyes and spoke with serious devotion. 'It is God's will I should build a home to keep my beloved safe.'

'Who is your beloved, Mr Prence?'

'You know who – Mistress Mullins.'

'Master Mullins has agreed **I** should court his daughter.'

'It is God's will that **I** should.'

'You do not have my permission to build your own house. If you are not satisfied speak with Governor Carver.' John pushed past Prence, striding the remaining fifty yards to the Brewster house, and hammered a stake into the ground with such force it split.

'Hie! Look – the shallop.' Standish called from the roof. 'So laden her gunnels are nearly in the water. Our provisions!'

As one, they loped down and stood ready to wade into the icy water and unload.

'Elder Brewster and Mistress Brewster. A welcome surprise,' John said as he and Standish helped the Elder and his wife disembark and wade to shore.

'I have come ashore to stay and care for your sick men,' Mistress Brewster announced.

'Good day, Mr Alden.' Brewster did not smile. 'Captain Standish, a word in private if you will.'

John's stomach knotted as the two headed for the shelter. *I know what's coming.*

In a short while Brewster came out and confirmed Rose had died in the night.

Without thinking, John strode into the shelter. The captain knelt, his back to the entrance, head in his hands, rocking, moaning softly.

'Sir.' John knelt beside him and put an arm round his shoulder. 'I am so sorry.'

Standish hugged himself and sobbed, huge wracking sobs. 'Rose, Rose,' he choked. 'She was so dear, so merry, and lively, and pretty.' He shook his head from side to side. 'I wasn't with her. She died without me there. Poor lovely, lonely Rose.'

'Sir.' John held the captain until his sobs were spent. 'You couldn't be there. You are a lynchpin here, organizing, planning, building. We wouldn't have made half the progress without you.'

'Rose couldn't know that, and she was in pain with the scurvy. You know how horrible that is. Oh God! Damn!' He punched the earth. 'How high a price for this new life? I know life is cheap. Folk die all the time of whatever. But she was precious.' He sobbed, head bowed. 'My own. I loved her most in all the world, and I left her to suffer dreadfully, helpless.' He looked up, as if to heaven. 'Is it worth… all this?'

'Sir.' John took Standish's hands in his. 'Rose knew you loved her, and she loved you. It was there for all to see. She also knew it was your place to lead the expeditions and be here now. She did understand. And I know Mistress Mullins and Priscilla loved her too; would have done all in their power to ease her pain. She did not die alone, uncomforted. You can be sure of that.'

The captain nodded. He contemplated John's face through thick red lashes, wet with tears. 'Thank you.' He placed a hand on John's shoulder. 'I'd like to be alone now.'

'Aye, sir.' John stepped out into the bright sunlight.

Chapter 23

February 1621

The Mullins family comes ashore

'The shallop! The shallop!' Francis' high pitched clarion call resounded from his crow's-nest perch in the tall pine tree.

Working together thatching the Brewster house, John and Standish clambered to earth and hurtled down the slope. They caught up with Prence who, in his haste, tripped on a rut in the track, arms flailing to keep his balance. John and Standish reached the landing rock first. As it was high tide the shallop could sail right in alongside the large boulder.

'I'll keep Prence out of the way,' Standish said.

'Thank you, sir.'

The working party gathered round to welcome and assist the passengers. John scanned the small vessel as she sailed nearer. Was that the Mullins family? At the stern?

Yes! He waited while folk gradually, weakly, staggered ashore and were helped on their way across the clearing. The Mullins family were last. Little Joseph came first, hollow eyed, barely able to stand. John gently lifted him over the gunnels. *By God. He's light as a feather. Nothing to him.* Then, 'Mistress Mullins, Master Mullins. How good to see you.' He was aghast at their state, so thin and gray. Master Mullins doubled over in a bone shaking fit of coughing. Safely on shore they stood clutching one another to keep upright. At last, Priscilla. 'Mistress Mullins, you are here, thank God,' he said, taking her hand.

'Mr Alden,' she replied, her head bowed, eyes downcast. 'Thank you.' As she climbed over the gunnels she heaved a sigh, caught her breath and stumbled. John held her. He could feel her thinness, her bones. She had no flesh. Her gown hung so loose. Poor Priscilla, so haggard.

As he steadied her she said, 'Oh, 'tis good… thank you… I must help Father and Mother.' She was shivering.

'Rest easy. I'll help you.' John beckoned to Standish who sent Prence to help Mistress Brewster and hurried over. He took Mistress Mullins on one arm and Master Mullins on the other. John kept hold of Priscilla and Joseph.

'I must be strong, I must be strong,' Priscilla repeated again and again as if in a delirium.

'You need rest. I'll help you now.' It was a raw day, with a northeasterly wind slicing across. 'Ach, 'tis cold. But at least no rain or sleet.' From the corner of his eye John saw Mistress Brewster come from the common house, walking quickly to join them. 'I've laid out pallets,' she said pointing to the nearest small dwelling. She hurried ahead and led them through the door. Pallets were laid out on the earthen floor and a fire burned in the center of the room, giving off some warmth and a lot of smoke.

'Here, come lie down.' Mistress Brewster took Joseph. Standish led Master and Mistress Mullins to two pallets laid side by side. John led Priscilla to the remaining one. Gently he eased her from his arms onto the meager bed, wishing the floor weren't so damp. 'There, Mistress Mullins. Lie quiet now and try to sleep. We'll care for you and your folk,' he murmured.

'Thank you, Mr Alden.' Priscilla could barely speak.

Mistress Brewster hurried over. 'I'll see to her now.'

John lingered while Mistress Brewster knelt and tucked a blanket round Priscilla. Standing up again she led him outside. Prence hovered in the doorway. 'Mr Prence? Why are you here?' The matron's tone was curt.

'I… I must greet my…'

There is no need for you here at present.' Mistress Brewster cut him off. 'These folk need to rest. Surely you would be better employed building.'

'Yes, Mistress.' Head high, Prence marched off.

Mistress Brewster turned to John. 'Elder Brewster and I decided the Mullins family must come ashore with this first group if they're to have any hope of recovering. I think Priscilla is just utterly exhausted, but Joseph and her parents, I fear for them.'

'Thank you, Mistress Brewster. Thank you.'

John half-walked, half-stumbled, head bowed, to find his axe where he'd left it, over by the Brewster house. Standish fell into step beside him.

'They're very poorly,' John said. 'We need to complete this bigger house. The air will circulate better and there will be more light. Those small dwellings are so full of smoke a body can barely breathe, and so dark.'

Two days later the party working on the Brewsters' house stood back and surveyed their labors.

'We've done well,' John said. 'We'll move the sick in the morning.

However, that night the winds rose to a fearful pitch; the pounding and whistling drowning out even the Indians' screeches. The rain came down in torrents. No one slept. A voice outside the men's shelter called, 'Come, come quick! The daub is washed off! The sick are getting drenched and freezing in the wind.'

John was first out. He ran up to the small house, stumbling and tripping in the dark. Entering the wet, wind scoured dwelling, he scooped up Priscilla with her pallet and blanket, holding her close, trying to protect her from the wind and rain. She was so light, so frail, and shivering.

'Mistress Mullins,' he said, 'I **will** help you get well.'

'Thank you, Mr Alden,' she stuttered.

He carried her into the Brewsters' house, up close by the hearth and found a place for her pallet. 'It's warm and dry here. You are wet through.' Over his shoulder he called, 'Has anyone got a dry blanket?'

'I'll take care of that, Mr Alden.' Mistress Brewster came up behind him with Joseph. 'Thank you. There are more sick folk in the other small house need bringing down.'

John turned back toward Priscilla and for an instant her eyes met his.

'Mr Alden. Hurry.' Mistress Brewster's stern command propelled him away.

All next day the storm raged and John fretted. Looking across the harbor, white caps chopping and churning, he could see the *Mayflower* dancing about, blown like flotsam, even with all her anchors down. Emptied of the colonists' provisions she had no ballast to keep her settled in the water.

This is the most vicious, fearsome on-shore storm I have ever known.

★ ★ ★

'Here, lass.'

Priscilla slowly opened her eyes. 'Where am I?'

'You're ashore now. You've been having a good long sleep.'

She recognized Mistress Brewster. Raising her head she struggled to sit and sank back.

'You are still weak,' Mistress Brewster said, putting an arm round her shoulders, helping her to sit. 'Sip as much of this as you can. It will do you good.' She handed Priscilla a beaker.

The warm, bland broth was comforting. Priscilla peered around the dim, smoke clouded room, noisy with the sound of coughing.

'Where are Mother and Father and Joseph? I must . . . '

'You must not worry. Master Winslow and I are caring for them. You need to rest and eat and I wager you'll have your strength back before long.' She gently helped Priscilla lie down again and made sure she was tucked in with blankets to keep out the cold draughts.

Gradually, over the days Priscilla felt her strength coming back. She was awake more of the day and able to sit up without help and then she could stand without fainting. The floor was covered in bodies lying on pallets. Yellow coat-tails peeking from the edge of a blanket identified Mr Martin. Slowly, carefully, she stood up and picked her way to where Mother and Father and Joseph were lying. Happily they were nearby; even so she almost tripped over one of the pallets.

'Ah, Priscilla.' Mother's voice was weak.

'Yes, Mother. I'm feeling better now,' Priscilla said. 'Father.' She knelt and clasped Father's gnarled, worn hands. He was so thin he seemed to be disappearing. His dear face, once so full and hearty, was shrunken, his eyes sunk in the hollow of their sockets, his cheekbones jutting out beneath the thin covering of flesh.

'My lass. I wondered where you'd gone.'

'I was very tired and weak. But I'm better now.' She crawled to Joseph's pallet. 'You must get well soon. Master Jones might need your help.'

'Priscilla! Oh yes!' Joseph's small, weak voice rasped his delight.

As she was gathering her skirts, trying to stand, Mr Alden entered, carrying two brace of duck. He dropped the fowl and strode to her side, offering his hand.

'May I help you?'

'Thank you.' She took his hand and pulled herself upright. Raising her eyes to meet his she swooned and grabbed his arm with both hands.

'Oh – oh, I'm sorry.'

John put both arms round her, holding her steady. 'Priscilla,' he murmured, his face bent to her ear. It was the first time he'd used her own name.

'John.'

'Now. What is the matter?' Mistress Brewster demanded.

'Mistress Mullins had a fainting spell. I couldn't let her fall.'

'Thank you, Mr Alden.' Mistress Brewster's tone was firm. 'I'll see to Mistress Mullins now. I'm sure you have other duties to attend to.'

'Yes, of course, Mistress Brewster. I've brought you four duck.' John promptly left the house.

Priscilla didn't see John again for days. But she could hear his deep voice ringing out as he directed the construction of more dwellings. Her heart felt full, knowing he was there, nearby. Remembering him holding her close helped her to endure the misery of watching as Father drifted ever closer to death.

'Take care of Mother and Joseph,' he drew out the words slowly, one by one, so faint she could barely hear.

'Yes, Father, dear Father.' Her voice caught. 'We will carry on and work out your reason for coming to this land. We'll build a good life, Father.'

He closed his eyes and slept.

'Alarm! Indians!' Captain Standish rushed in, his face flushed red, nearly tripping over his feet. 'We've been hearing their screeching for weeks. Now we've seen some.'

Master Winslow rose from helping Mistress Brewster to change a dressing. 'Where?'

'One of our men was hiding in the reeds to shoot fowl,' Standish said. 'He was crouched down and of a sudden spied a line of Indians going past – not five feet from him – about a dozen. Thank God they didn't see him. All our men, whatever state they're in, are to go out into the clearing armed with a musket. If a body can't stand he must lean against a tree,' Standish commanded. 'The Indians must not know how weak and depleted we are.'

'But Father is far too sick,' Priscilla pleaded.

'Aye, she's right,' Winslow said. 'Master Mullins must be left to rest where he is.'

Turning to Master Winslow, Priscilla bent her knees in a half curtsy. 'Thank you, sir.'

His response was a smile, an open, embracing smile revealing the gap between his teeth, the one flaw in his handsome dignity. When he smiled, Winslow came out from his remote place; his warmth was immediate, comforting.

'Thank you,' Priscilla said again.

'Agreed,' Standish said and went on his way. Priscilla heard him issuing orders to folk in the other dwellings.

All that night she lay awake hearing the terrible Indian screeches and war cries whirling through the air. In terror she prayed they wouldn't attack and wished John Alden was with her, holding her safe.

Next morning as she was kneeling beside Mother, gently wiping her face and crusted mouth, she heard the rustle of a skirt behind; then a woman knelt beside her.

'Alice, my dear Alice.' Catherine Carver's voice was deep and soft.

'Catherine,' Mother whispered. Her eyes kindled.

'May I bide awhile with your mother?'

'Oh. Yes. Please do. I'll see to Joseph,' Priscilla said.

As she was helping Joseph sip some broth, Priscilla watched Mother and Mistress Carver from the corner of her eye. It was as if she'd never really seen Mistress Carver before: her quiet beauty, defined features in proportion, kind eyes and mouth, and thick black hair falling in waves round her clear pale face. She was thin but otherwise appeared unscathed by the ravages of the voyage. *They're like old friends. I never realized, so close, Mother is smiling, almost laughing.* She heard Mistress Carver say, 'I promise, like my own.'

'Mistress Carver. I did not call for you. Your services are not needed here.' Mistress Brewster strode through recumbent bodies to stand by Mother's pallet. Mistress Carver squeezed Mother's hands and kissed her forehead. 'Goodbye, Alice. I'll come again soon.' Slowly she stood to face Mistress Brewster. 'I am acting in our Lord's service when I visit a loved one.'

Mistress Brewster straightened her back. 'May I remind you that Elder Brewster founded our movement and has always been our leader. Our mission is to build God's kingdom in this land and it is **my** sacred duty to tend the sick. Goodbye, Mistress Carver.'

Catherine Carver declined to respond and slowly, gracefully, left the house.

'Tell me a story, please,' Joseph said.

Priscilla embarked upon a story about Sir Francis Drake fighting pirates, when Joseph pointed to the door. She looked up to see Master Jones.

'I'm looking for Mistress Brewster,' he said, stepping into the room. 'Is this Joseph? Sick a bed?' His voice softened. 'Ah, lad. You'd best eat up your victuals – we need you to be strong again.'

Joseph flushed with excitement. 'I be a sea captain.'

Mistress Brewster hurried in. 'Master Jones! What is this by the door?'

'A goose and a duck and a deer, Mistress Brewster,' he said. 'To help these sick folk get well. Shot the fowl yesterday and found the deer being eaten by wolves. Persuaded them to let me have it.'

'Thank you, thank you…' Priscilla joined Mistress Brewster's gratitude and drank in the warmth of Master Jones' kind face.

'But that sack – with wriggling, hissing creatures inside.' Mistress Brewster looked toward the door. 'Whatever?'

'Ah – the sack.' Priscilla could see Master Jones was holding back a chuckle. He went to the door and brought in a thick hemp sack drawn tight at the top. He untied the cord and laid the opened sack on the floor. Out they came, scrambling and pushing, the three kittens! Though by now they were small cats. One was jet black with white paws and a bib and long white whiskers. 'He's a tom,' Master Jones said. He ran his hand down the back of the smallest cat. 'This pretty little thing is a female and the biggest – he's a ginger tom.' Priscilla picked up the female and stroked her.

'Very unusual markings, she has,' Master Jones commented. 'Unusual for a female to be ginger.'

'She is pretty, with her white bib,' Priscilla said.

'Well,' Mistress Brewster said. 'Well, well, well. At least we won't be troubled by mice. They look healthy.'

As the two tom cats set about exploring their new territory, Priscilla handed the female to Joseph. The little cat curled up beside him and responded to his stroking with loud purring.

'Thank you, sir, thank you for keeping them safe and bringing them to us,' Priscilla said. 'They'll be a help to all our spirits. Is their mother well?'

'Aye. She's small but tough. You are welcome, lass,' he replied. 'Now. I hear there's to be a meeting today to establish military orders. Wise. You need to be ready to defend yourselves. I'll go speak with Captain Standish about bringing the cannon ashore.'

'Cannon. I help,' Joseph squeaked and then fell to coughing.

'Goodbye for now, lad.' Master Jones raised his hand to Joseph. 'I'll call in again.'

Priscilla could hear reverberating shouts as men passed the word, summoning all to gather at the fort.

'Mistress Brewster,' she asked, 'if all is in order here may I step outside to watch?'

'Aye,' Mistress Brewster replied. 'But wrap up well. It's a keen wind comes off the harbor. I'll get started plucking these fowl.'

Priscilla walked quickly to a stout oak not far from the house, partway up the hill. Leaning against it she had a good view.

Governor Carver spoke first. 'As you must understand, we urgently need to have organized defense procedures and I motion we officially appoint Captain Standish to be our military commander. Do I have consensus?' There came a chorus of 'Ayes', but Priscilla noticed that Billington looked at the ground and said nothing.

'I defer to you, Captain,' Governor Carver said.

Captain Standish drew himself up to his full height, about five feet, and stood facing the motley group of men. 'We must become a disciplined military force…'

Billington raised his fist. 'I'll take no orders from this podgy pink faced shrimp. He's nowt but a pygmy – 'ad to shorten his sword so's it wouldn't scrape on the ground. 'E's a midget and too big for 'is boots.'

Priscilla was aghast and laughing at the same time. In that instant, two Indians appeared on the top of the hill across the brook. Covered in war paint, fierce and threatening, they beckoned to Standish to come to them. *Oh no.* Priscilla clutched at the rough bark of the tree. *What if there are more, hundreds more?*

Standish beckoned to the Indians. They wouldn't budge. So he and a companion, taking only one musket, advanced slowly and laid down the musket on their side of the brook to show they came in peace. Instantly the braves ran off, down the other side of the hill, and a great noise of cries and screeches rose up. It sounded like hundreds. Priscilla ran back into the Brewsters' house.

The frightened sick folk moaned and wailed. 'What is happening? Are we being attacked?' Some tried to stand. Others covered their heads with blankets. Mistress Brewster went from one to the other, trying to bring calm. 'Our menfolk will defend us if need be, and it is probably just an alarm.' She spoke in a quiet soothing tone.

Priscilla knelt beside Mother and Father and Joseph. 'Don't worry. Captain Standish is very brave and our men are in order and ready.' Stroking Joseph's fevered head she began a story. 'Once upon a time…' She spoke loud enough so the other children lying sick could hear too.

The Indian cries gradually subsided and the room was calm once more. As Priscilla came to the end of her story Joseph fell asleep. She sat wondering, trembling. *The Indians' behavior is strange. Why do they make a fearsome noise, show themselves even, and run away? Are they trying to frighten us into leaving this place? Make us weak with fear?*

Chapter 24

February 1621

The sickness takes its toll

'Priscilla, come in; don't mind your feet.' John answered her hesitation.

Priscilla stepped into the quiet, pleasant smelling storehouse. John pushed the door to, allowing just enough light to see. 'Priscilla.' He took her hands in his, drawing her close. 'How are you? I seldom have a chance to be with you.'

Priscilla longed to lean into his arms. A dizzy spell caused her to sway. He caught her. She stayed.

'You work night and day, I've been told, and there is little to eat.'

'I fare well, except for a few dizzy moments, and the Indians – a body is never safe, always afraid. But Mother, Father, Joseph.' Her voice wavered. 'I fear for them.'

'I'll help however I can.'

Priscilla wanted to rest, held in his arms. 'Thank you, John.' She stepped back. 'I almost forgot. Mistress Brewster begs a little barley, for the pottage.'

As John reached into the barrel they heard a woman's cries; 'Please, please, sir, have mercy.' Male voices joined in. 'Didn't mean no harm, 'e just forgot 'iself.'

'Whatever?'

Pushing the door open, Priscilla and John saw yellow coat-tails disappearing round the corner of the building.

'The pest.' John locked the door.

The pleas for mercy led them to the clearing where Standish, Bradford and Carver were strapping a struggling John Billington to a post, hands and feet tied.

'For insubordination to a commanding officer you will endure a day of public humiliation, hands and feet tied together, on this spot,' Governor Carver pronounced.

'Aye, and that is lenient enough,' Standish said.

'I really didn't mean it, sir,' Billington said, looking first at Governor Carver and then at Captain Standish. 'It were... I were on edge, sir... what with the Indians. I won't ever do such a thing again. I pledge my loyalty. Captain Standish is a fine man and I will follow him, sir.'

'Aye,' Billington's comrade spoke. 'He's a good man, really. Just sometimes his tongue don't know what it's doin. He'll be loyal, true as true.'

Governor Carver motioned silence. Only the sounds of crows cawing and songbirds chirruping broke the stillness. 'As these are peculiar, difficult times, I revoke the punishment.'

'Hoorah! Hoorah!' Billington's friends stamped and punched the air.

'But if there is any further trouble,' Carver raised his voice, 'the punishment will be far worse.'

Standish shook his head. 'Doesn't deserve it, the lout.'

'Look.' John pointed to the harbor. 'The shallop is pulling in with Master Jones and the first cannon. I'll give a hand and then shall I get Joseph settled to watch? Before I help with the hauling and pushing?'

'Yes, yes please. Joseph will be thrilled.'

Under the spell of John's kindness and – love? – *surely it is love,* Priscilla paced slowly toward the Brewster house, savoring her feelings.

'Mistress Mullins, my dearest.'

That voice, a hand on her back. She whirled round, stepping back, away. 'Mr Prence. How dare you?'

'You are unnerved, my dear one, in distress for your family. I understand. But when you are in your right mind you will desire me; desire to be my wife. I am certain.'

His smooth velvety speech sickened her. 'Leave me, Mr Prence, I command you.' She lifted her skirts and ran.

Priscilla knelt beside her mother. 'We're taking Joseph to sit in the sun and watch Master Jones and his men haul the cannon up the hill and onto the platform.'

Mother smiled. 'Good,' she said, raising her head. 'Give the lad a bit o' fun and fresh air.' She gave up talking, breathless and wheezing, and collapsed back onto her pillow. Priscilla mopped her mother's mouth and brow. Her nose was bleeding slightly and her face and hands showed the tell-tale spots of scurvy. Holding back tears she helped her to settle. Then, fetching Joseph's pallet and blankets, she picked her way over to the doorway where John stood holding Joseph as he would a babe in arms.

'We'll go round to the side of the house in the sun,' Priscilla said. 'You'll have a good view down to the harbor where the action is.' She laid the pallet on the ground, and John settled Joseph, wrapped in blankets, leaning back against the sun warmed wall. He raised his thin, pale face to the gentle heat.

'Look,' Priscilla said. 'They're unloading the cannon. I'm going to fetch my pallet, Joseph. I'll be back in an instant.'

Mistress Brewster stood in the doorway. Her face soft she whispered, 'I don't think your father has much longer. I'm sorry.'

Sinking onto her knees beside Father, Priscilla took his hands in her own. 'Dear Father. You have been so good and kind and given us so much. Thank you. God bless you and keep you safe.' She kissed him and mopped his brow. She wished for a priest. It didn't feel right for Father to die without receiving the last rites. She must do her best. Glancing back over her shoulder to be sure Mistress Brewster wasn't looking, she made the sign of the cross and whispered, 'May thy soul rest in peace and rise in glory. Amen.'

Father gained a moment of recognition and looking into Priscilla's eyes mouthed the words, 'Thank you, lass.' She clutched his hands to her heart. When he was still and gone, she gently closed his eyes and pulled the blanket over his face. Mother slept.

Settling herself beside Joseph, Priscilla put an arm round his bony shoulder and hugged him close. 'Now, tell me what's been happening.'

'Master Jones and Captain Standish are telling the men what to do. Who's to push and who's to pull on the ropes, and who's to slide planks under the cannon's wheels.' Joseph's exertion made him cough. Priscilla wiped his face with her handkerchief. 'There, be still a bit,' she said gently.

She leaned back against the wall and closed her eyes. The voices and scene below seemed far away. Slowly she entered a dream, back in their Dorking home; the Christmas Day when Father had bought a specially big load of wood at great expense so they had a blazing fire on the hearth. She felt again Father's pride and pleasure in presenting Mother with a beautiful pair of boots, and her with a smaller pair, just the same, then Joseph with a small 'man's' pair just like his own. In the big kitchen, with cousins, aunts and uncles, they'd sat round the table, and Mother, plump, rosy-cheeked and merry, carried the Christmas goose and pies and stews from the hearth, and John Alden was there too.

But she mustn't. She pulled herself back to where they were now. She must somehow be sure Mother and Joseph recovered.

John Alden carefully placed planks of wood in position for the cannon to ride on and then rushed back to his position as hauler.

Again and again. *And he works all night making coffins and digging graves.*
As the cannon drew level with Priscilla and Joseph, Master Jones
told Captain Standish to take command and strode over to Joseph.

'What do you think, my lad? 'Tis to your liking?' He sat down
beside Joseph and began to explain how the system of ropes and
pulleys worked.

Joseph stared, first at Master Jones' face, then in the direction he
was pointing. He tried to ask questions but choked and coughed.

Master Jones put his arm round Joseph's shoulders. 'Goodbye
for now, lad. Must get on with my work.' He got to his feet, shook
Joseph's hand, saluted and walked slowly back to the working party,
head bowed.

'There. Master Jones saluted you,' Priscilla said. Joseph smiled
and nestled into the crook of his sister's arm. As they were soaking
up the last of the warm sun, Mistress Carver walked up the hill
toward the house. She waved as she entered. *Good. She brings comfort
and peace.*

With the sun gone round behind the house, the air took on a
chill. 'We must go in,' Priscilla said. 'Put your arm round my neck.'
She bent low. 'Up you come.' She helped Joseph shuffle into the
house. Mistress Brewster hurried to fetch his pallet and blankets.

'I'll settle the lad,' she said. Then she whispered, 'I sent Mistress
Carver away and told your mother.'

Why did she do that? It was for me to tell my mother. A spark of anger
burned in the pit of her stomach, which she tried to quench, telling
herself Mistress Brewster thought she was doing the right thing.
She sat on the floor beside Mother.

'I've known for a long time he wouldn't recover,' Mother said.
'Dear William. He was a good man and a good husband and father.
Rare these days.' She stopped to regain her strength. 'He gave us
many good times. I wish I could have been with him at the end, but
I'm too weak to move.'

'I was with him. He knew me.' Priscilla whispered, 'I said our
last rites and he smiled.'

Mother squeezed Priscilla's hand. 'It will be my time soon. I asked Mistress Carver to care for you and Joseph. She is gentle and kind and would love to take you in.' Mother was too weary to say more. Priscilla kissed her and lay down next to her, holding her close.

That night Priscilla lay awake. Mingled with the Indians' cries and wolves' howling was the sound of sawing and hammering; John Alden making coffins. She felt numb with disbelief and fear. If only this were a terrible nightmare and she could wake up out of it. Unable to sleep, she was relieved when dawn broke and she could be busy.

Joseph asked, 'Where is Father?'

'We've taken him to the common house where Master Winslow can care for him. He knows all about remedies,' Priscilla said.

Two days later, when Mother died, she told Joseph the same story. He must be protected from sorrow. He **must** get well.

Priscilla worked tirelessly, helping Mistress Brewster prepare the scarce victuals, especially broth, caring for the sick and boiling soiled linen. She couldn't help giving Joseph special attention.

'Please try to take a little more broth, love,' she pleaded. 'You need it to get well.' She felt afraid for him. He was now having nose bleeds and red spots marked his face. Aware of someone standing behind her, she looked round.

'Mr Alden, John. You've come.'

'Aye, to see how you fare.'

She handed him the beaker and struggled to her feet, catching her skirt under her heel. John held her steady with his free hand.

'He's a brave little soul,' he said, looking down at Joseph.

'He's hanging on, hanging on, wanting to help Master Jones. If only we had some beer. It's the only hope against the scurvy. I hoped and prayed he wouldn't get the scurvy.'

'Mr Alden. Why are you here?' Mistress Brewster hurried from the hearth, frowning. 'Surely you are better employed building.'

'And hunting. I've brought you a brace of duck, Mistress. They're by the door.' John doffed his hat, pressed Priscilla's arm, and took his leave.

Next day Master Jones entered the Brewster house carrying a tankard.

'Mr Alden sent word of your plight with no beer for the scurvy. My men need some if they're to recover. They're most all sick too, but I'm giving you my personal supply. There's a barrel being hauled up to your storehouse.' He handed Priscilla the tankard. 'This is especially for Joseph.'

'Thank you. Thank you so much, sir,' Priscilla exclaimed. She knelt down. 'Joseph – look – Master Jones is here and he's brought you some beer.' She put her arm round his shoulder, raising him from his fevered stupor. Master Jones knelt beside her and took Joseph's weak limp hands in his own. Priscilla willed that strength pass from the captain's large, strong calloused hands into Joseph's. She brought the tankard to his lips.

'Just sip slowly now, so you don't choke.' Joseph swallowed a few times and was then too tired. Priscilla settled him again to sleep. She walked with Master Jones to the door.

'Thank you, sir. It's our only hope.'

'I'll call again soon,' Master Jones said, 'to see how he's doing.'

The battle went on for three more days, but by then Priscilla knew her little brother was slipping away. She knelt down beside him, talking softly, telling him a story, trying to bring him out of his fevered delirium. In the midst of her story, she saw a pair of large black boots beside her. Master Jones knelt down.

'Joseph,' he said. His soft deep voice brought Joseph out of his ravings. His eyes looked into the captain's kind, blue gaze.

'I... be...a... sea... capt...' The frail voice faltered.

'Aye, ye're a fine lad.' The captain laid his hand on Joseph's forehead. The boy's eyes closed, a smile hovered on his lips and he slipped away, his frail little body relaxing into death.

Tears coursed down along grooves in the captain's worn face, falling into his gray beard.

'Farewell, little lad,' he stammered. He laid a hand on Priscilla's shoulder. 'There, there, lass. He was a fine lad. Be proud of him.'

The two got to their feet. Priscilla said a broken 'thank you' and kept her eyes on the strong sturdy back as Master Jones slowly paced toward the door. She knelt again, closed Joseph's eyes and pulled the cover over his head.

'Dear Joseph.' She buried her face in her hands. She felt emptied, gouged out, numb. She lost all sense of time.

'I'm so sorry.'

Priscilla looked up, welcoming John Alden. He helped her to her feet, and looked down at the small body.

'Poor lad. He did put up a fight. If you wish I'll take him and lay him to rest with your mother and father. I've saved a special spot.' Priscilla met John's eyes and stayed.

'Thank you.' She stood by as John stooped and gently lifted Joseph, cradling his head in the crook of his elbow. She pulled the cover back and kissed her brother goodbye. Her gaze remained fastened on his body as John carried him away.

'Now come along, Priscilla.' Mistress Brewster beckoned from the hearth. 'You need some broth and a rest. You haven't eaten for days.'

Priscilla picked her way to the hearth. 'Thank you, Mistress,' she said, 'but I'm not hungry and I'd rather keep busy.'

Priscilla worked as hard as she could, long into the night, caring for the sick with only the light of the fire to see by. She stayed longest with orphan Richard, Joseph's special friend. Although she knew she shouldn't favor him, she gave him extra of Master Jones' beer, and took special care to be sure he drank up all his broth. If only they had some nourishing solid food. But no. The chickens and goat and sow had all perished on the voyage, so they had no milk, no eggs, and of course no bread. Nothing except duck and geese and venison and shellfish. Folk were too sick and frail to digest such rich food. Their stomachs just heaved it up again, especially the children. She must bring Richard back to health. For Joseph's sake.

Finally, a few hours before dawn, when she was too tired to stand Priscilla collapsed onto her pallet and dozed fitfully. All gone. Mother, Father, Joseph – her loves – gone.

With the first birdsong she rose, and still unable to eat, again worked all day. The task of boiling linen was laborious work; what she needed to absorb the pain. As she was laying towels and sheets on tufts of grass to dry in the sun, John Alden left off working on a house and came over to her.

'Priscilla. How are you?' He spoke quietly, his voice full of sympathy. Priscilla couldn't answer. She opened her mouth but no words came out. John continued. 'I laid Joseph to rest with your mother and father. Would you like to come in the late afternoon to bide by the graves?'

'Yes,' she said, her voice a hoarse whisper.

'I'll come for you in time before prayers.'

The sun was easing its way down the western sky when John came. She stood silent as he explained where they were going. Bowing her head as they left the house, she was grateful he took her arm. She felt unsteady. She was also glad he didn't try to make her talk. John led her round the hill where the cannon were mounted. There, between the other side of the hill and the forest, was a tiny graveyard, with three graves, a cross marking each one.

'We'll not be able to leave the crosses, because the Indians mustn't know. But I wanted to put them there for you today.'

'Thank you.' Priscilla stood, staring. Mother, Father, Joseph. Images of their lively loving faces danced in her mind. Father, returned from London, holding out to her the precious book on gardening, his face full of eager anticipation, deep blue eyes shining with excitement. Mother, with her look of astonishment, soft brown eyes laughing, cheeks blushing, as Father held her tight and whirled her round the table. And Joseph; his blond curls dancing, blue eyes wide with amazement and pride as Father handed him a musket, made specially for a nine-year-old lad. She felt herself going dizzy, swaying, falling into blackness.

Part 2

1621–1632

The First Spring

Chapter 25

March 1621

Priscilla grieves

Hands patted her cheeks. Priscilla heard a voice. She opened her eyes; a woman's face. No, it wasn't Mother. She faded back into a comforting gray mist.

'Wake up, wake up. You must wake up.' The hands patted her cheeks and the voice grew louder, more insistent. Then she felt an arm around her, behind her shoulders, supporting her head, pushing her up, forcing her into recognition.

'Priscilla. Thank God you're awake again. My dear, my dear.' That insistent voice. Now she knew. Mistress Brewster.

'Try to take a sip,' she said, holding a beaker to Priscilla's lips. 'We've saved some of Master Jones' beer for you.' Priscilla did as she was bid and then coughed and choked.

'Ah well,' Mistress Brewster said, 'you'd best lie back. We'll try again later.'

In the grip of fever and delirium Priscilla lost touch with time. One minute she was boiling hot, the next, shivering. She lived in a torment of terrifying dreams. Again and again a circle of feet kicked at a small huddled girl. Hands pulled her hair. A pair of kicking feet grew and grew into a giant female, bearing down, clawing at the crying child. She woke screaming, calling for Mother. Coughing fits shook her and she could hear her chest rattle when she drew a deep breath. Faces hovered above her; kind brown eyes and a white cap, a red beard, a dark beard above a broad white collar. Day and night were all one blur.

Then one day she woke from a deep, quiet sleep into the dawn light and birdsong. The spells of hot and shivering had gone. She felt calm.

For days Priscilla did nothing but sleep and take in nourishing broth and beer. Eventually she felt strong enough to eat small portions of food and she was awake more hours of the day.

'Would you like to sit up awhile?' Mistress Brewster asked one morning.

'Yes, please.'

From a sitting position the room felt different. She rested her head back against the pillows, closing her eyes a minute before re-engaging. Memories assembled in her mind, bringing a sense of urgency and fear. 'Where are all the sick folk? Where is orphan Richard? Did he live?'

Mistress Brewster looked down at her hands folded in her lap. 'Sadly, no.'

Priscilla hastily wiped away a tear. *Best not think on it. Joseph's friend. If I hadn't fallen ill I'd have made sure he lived. But don't think on it.* 'Ah. Bibs.' The pretty ginger female ran to her, tail upright, and leapt onto her lap. 'You lovely creature. Where are your brothers?'

'The ginger resides with Captain Standish, and his white pawed black brother with Governor Carver,' Mistress Brewster said.

Priscilla looked round the room. 'That's strange. Why is my pallet raised up off the ground?'

'Your pallet is raised...' Mistress Brewster hesitated. 'Your pallet is raised because Mr Alden thought it would help your recovery to be up off the damp floor. So he built a slatted frame. He's working on some more for the other sick folk. And he's busy building houses.'

Priscilla felt warm all through. *John Alden was caring for me. I* **will** *get better.* She returned to her first question. 'All the sick folk – they were everywhere, all over the floor.' *Peculiar. When the room was littered with bodies it appeared larger. Now it seemed to have shrunk, closing in and dim.* 'Where are the sick folk now?'

'Most have died.' Mistress Brewster bowed her head, twisting her fingers. 'And a few are convalescing in the common house.'

'Is Mistress Carver alive?'

'Yes.'

'I know Mother wished for Joseph and me to live with Mistress Carver, and she promised.'

Mistress Brewster stiffened. 'Elder Brewster and I agreed we are better suited to care for you, to help you grow strong in your soul. Did you know that the Elder and I took in Mr Bradford when he was orphaned as a lad?'

'I did not know.' Priscilla looked down at her hands, clenched tight, closing her eyes against a welling of tears.

'We raised him to be the fine man he now is. Governor Carver could but agree. You know Elder Brewster was a founder...'

'Yes. I've been told many times.'

'In any case,' Mistress Brewster's lips pressed tight, her jaw set rigid, 'Mistress Carver is not fit to care for you. She is too lax, too easy in her ways.'

A wave of sick sadness engulfed Priscilla. 'Thank you for caring for me, Mistress Brewster,' she said, her tone flat, listless. 'I hope I'll soon be up and able to help with the chores.'

'Rest now, my dear. All in good time.' Mistress Brewster adjusted the pillows for Priscilla to lie down again. 'I'll bring some pottage soon.'

Priscilla lay back, turned on her side to face the wall and curled up in a ball. Grief gouged her insides. She shivered, clenched her teeth. *Mother, Father, little Joseph, all gone. It happened so fast, and Mother, Mother, I wasn't there, wasn't with you to say 'goodbye'. I'm sorry, how could I have left you?*

The blurred, damped down memory hit Priscilla with the stark force of clarity. She'd known, but didn't want to know, that Mother was nearing death. She had even welcomed Mistress Brewster's request that she go and beg John Alden to spare a little more barley. Leaving the Brewsters' house she had met Mistress Carver; 'I'm going to call on your mother,' and Priscilla's heart felt a flicker of gladness. Then, in John Alden's company she had lingered, drinking in the comfort of his care, savoring the pleasant smells of dried produce, grain and liquor, savoring John Alden's healthy strength. She did not want to go back to the foul odors of sickness and death.

When she did return, Mistress Brewster met her at the doorway, her face a mask. 'I sent Mistress Carver away and took upon myself the task of ministering to your mother as she drew her last breaths.'

Uttering a hoarse 'No', the only expression of her silent scream, Priscilla had pushed past the matron, tripping over bodies to reach her mother. Kneeling, she pressed her ear against Mother's breast, willing a heartbeat, buried her head in the inert stomach, ignoring the closed eyelids. *No, No, No.* Aware of Mistress Brewster standing behind her, she clasped her mother's hands, kissed her forehead and dry eyed, got to her feet. Pushing her misery down, down, she picked her way to Joseph, resolved to restore him to health. *But I failed, failed you all. How is it I am alive? Please come back. How can I go on? You loved me. There is no one here, no home. Except John Alden. Please God may he come to me soon, come now. I need him now.*

In spite of her held-in grief and battles against sudden onrushes of tears and feeling sick, Priscilla's strength gradually returned. However, as the days passed, she suffered a gnawing bewilderment that John Alden still had not come to see her.

One day in early March the air felt different, unusually warm with a gentle hovering sun. Priscilla sat in the doorway mending, listening to the urgent calling, squawking bird racket proclaiming the time of mating and nest building, competing with the sawing and hammering and calling voices of men building houses. Resting her hands she leaned back against the doorpost. In the past few days two more houses across the track had been completed. Glancing up the slope to her right she saw John Alden up on the roof of a house, thatching. Moving into a patch of shade so the sun wasn't in her eyes, Priscilla craned her neck to see him better. He was balancing on the steep roof almost up at the ridge. What was there for him to hold onto? Only the slats with great gaps in between. She strained to see. He had to use both hands to secure the bundles of reeds to the rafters. Two big black crows flew round his head, cawing and fighting. Priscilla almost cried out. Mouth closed she called to him. *No! Don't fall. Just ignore them.* She felt giddy and almost lost her own balance. Sitting down on a large hummock of grass she said to herself, *Of course he couldn't pay me any heed. Perhaps he'll call in.*

In the evenings the Brewster household gathered around the hearth and sat quietly while Elder Brewster quoted scripture. There wasn't light enough for him to read from the Bible, but it didn't matter. The Elder could recite and extemporize. Priscilla couldn't keep her mind on what he was saying, but the cadence of his calm, deep voice was comforting. When he finished speaking it was time for bed. Mercifully the Indians had ceased their screeching, but in some ways it was just as frightening not knowing what they were up to, or why they had gone quiet. Almost every night she fell asleep to the hateful sound of wolves howling. She dreamed she was in the pretty orderly garden at home, forking rich friable soil, which turned into hummocks of tough grass and sticky clay. She dreamed of being tucked safe in bed in the attic room she shared with Joseph and woke in this harsh, sparse public room.

The Sabbath. For the first time since she fell sick, Priscilla felt strong enough to walk to the common house for prayers. With Elder and Mistress Brewster on either side of her and their two boys behind, she walked slowly but steadily.

As they entered, Governor and Mistress Carver crossed the room to greet her. 'Priscilla, it is so good to see you recovered.' Disregarding Mistress Brewster's hard stare Catherine Carver hugged Priscilla close. 'I'm so sorry,' she whispered.

Priscilla clung to her. 'If only, I wish…'

'That's enough. You'll be delaying prayers,' Mistress Brewster snapped.

Mistress Carver squeezed Priscilla's hands and took her place beside her husband, facing the gathering.

Priscilla was shocked at how few folk were left. To her relief, there was no sign of Mr Prence. Perhaps he had died. John Alden stood with Captain Standish on the edge of the group and paid her no heed.

Elder Brewster took his place and folk fell silent. 'We will begin with Psalm 100. "All people that on earth do dwell".' Beautiful words, drearily chanted. She glanced at John Alden, but he stood looking straight ahead and when prayers were over he quickly left – first out the door, skirting round behind before folk gathered themselves to depart. Captain Standish eased his way through and greeted the Brewster group, giving Priscilla an especially warm 'hello'. She stared at his red beard. That beard – part of her fever – floating before her eyes. Her mind raced. Was Captain Standish caring for her when she was sick? She shuddered. He walked with her and the Brewsters across the clearing, deep in conversation with the Elder. Priscilla was silent, eyes downcast. She felt stung, bewildered, and of a sudden, so tired. They reached the Brewster house.

'Come and join us for our Sabbath meal,' Elder Brewster invited Captain Standish. 'I'm sure our women can provide for one more.'

Priscilla hurried to help with the pottage of venison and fowl. The Brewsters had a fine oak table for dining, brought from

England, and stools. She served trenchers of pottage to the men and the two Brewster lads.

'You sit down too, Priscilla,' Mistress Brewster said. 'I'll join you presently.'

'No thank you,' Priscilla said. 'I'm not hungry. 'Tis best the men and boys have plenty. I'll bide on my pallet awhile.'

Mistress Brewster frowned and shook her head, but said nothing.

As it was forbidden to work on the Sabbath, even to wash the trenchers, there was nothing for Priscilla to do. The settlement was quiet. No chopping or hammering, no calling out from man to man, no noisy children. Overcome with grief she took from her box of belongings the beautiful book Father had brought her from London. Turning the pages, she was transported back to the world she knew; where Mother grew herbs, where she learned how to grow vegetables and fruit trees, and where gardens bloomed with snowdrops, then primroses and cowslips, then hollyhocks and roses, all in their season. A shadow fell over the page. Priscilla looked up. Mistress Brewster spoke, her voice quiet but very firm.

'My child,' she said, 'what is this?' She took the little book from Priscilla's hands. Leafing through the pages, she said, ''Tis the work of the devil – to entice you back to the old world.' Her tone was gentle and kind as if speaking to a child who didn't yet understand. 'We are here to build a new world, a kingdom of God in this land. That is our whole purpose, my dear.' Kneeling down beside Priscilla she continued, 'Now search out your Bible and psalter.'

'But Father gave…'

Mistress Brewster put a finger to her lips and shook her head. 'None of that talk. We must put the past out of our minds. I'll keep the book until you have a husband and home of your own in our **new** kingdom. Think on my words awhile and then come join us by the fire.'

Priscilla thought that if she heard the words 'a new kingdom of God' once more, she would scream. Dutifully taking out her Bible she let it fall open where it would.

'It is good that one should wait quietly for the salvation of the
Lord.
It is good for one to bear the yoke in youth.
To sit alone in silence when the Lord has imposed it,
to put one's mouth to
the dust (there may yet be hope)
To give one's cheek to the smiter, and be filled with insults.'
(Lamentations 3, v 26 – 30)

*Alright. I'll be silent. And I will work hard, bowed down and obedient, to the
dust. I'll work ever harder and that will help me to feel nothing. But I will
not eat that woman's food. She took away my book, my beautiful comforting
book. I'll not give her the satisfaction of giving me food. I wish I were with
Governor and Mistress Carver as Mother wished. I will not become the
person Mistress Brewster wants me to be.*

As if in sympathy, Bibs trotted to her, abandoning her place by
the hearth, and jumped onto her lap. Priscilla stroked the purring cat,
remembering Joseph, comforted by Bibs to the end of his short life.

★ ★ ★

By the third week in March Priscilla had regained enough strength
to help in the rush to prepare the ground for planting: peas, wheat,
rye, barley and corn. She worked alongside Lizzie Tilley, fighting
the hard ground. With her foot she wedged the prongs of the fork
under hummocks of grass and then pulled at them with her hands.
Slowly, painfully, she turned over mats of earth.

'This is terrible hard.' Lizzie straightened up. 'Oooh. 'Twill
break my back. In England we'd never be working in the fields thus.
Man's work. Wish they'd leave off building and help us. Only five
of us women survived and if this labor kills us off – then where will
they be?'

When it came time to stop laboring in the fields Priscilla helped
Mistress Brewster prepare the pottage for the evening meal, while

Elder Brewster sat reading his Bible. He looked up. 'My dear. I've just remembered. Captain Standish will dine with us. Have you enough for the pot?'

'Please fetch a beaker of barley, Priscilla, and one of peas.'

Priscilla was glad to retreat to the lean-to, dim, quiet, strangely peaceful, its only occupants a few sacks of provisions, two pronged forks, a spade, an axe and a mattock.

'Good evening, Captain Standish. Welcome.' She heard the Elder's greeting. They invited Standish almost every evening. She wished they wouldn't. *Why do they not invite John Alden? He is close friends with Standish. They live together. Is it because John is only a cooper? John, John. What has happened? Why do you avoid me? You were so attentive and caring before I fell sick. Now – have you changed your mind? Are you courting Lizzie Tilley? I cannot bear it.* She bit her knuckles.

'Priscilla!' Mistress Brewster called.

After the meal, as she washed the trenchers and beakers, Priscilla listened.

'The rendezvous is finished, thanks to Mr Alden,' Standish said. 'The man is a genius with wood and inspires his crew.'

'So now we have a secure building where women and children can hide in case of an attack,' the Elder said.

'Aye. I wanted to have that completed before assembling the men for another attempt to organize our defense. You remember what happened on the occasion of our previous effort. Men all gathered together, women and children left unprotected; a brief glimpse of two Indians and then howling and whooping behind the hill. Sounded like hundreds.'

'Uncanny how the Indians seem to know what we are doing. 'Tis eerie and worrying.' The Elder stood and paced the floor, hands behind his back. 'We must be prepared for anything. You are doing a grand job, Captain Standish.'

'I'll muster the men tomorrow. If Mistress Brewster could gather the women and children into the rendezvous, I'll assemble the men by the fort.'

'Good plan. Let us know the appointed hour.'

★ ★ ★

Priscilla woke before daybreak. In the cool pre-dawn half-light she fetched four pails of water from the brook. To and fro, to and fro. The silence was soothing: no Indian cries, no hammering, no calling and clatter. Only the sporadic twitter of birds awakening.

She was determined to escape to the fields immediately prayers and breakfast were over. 'If I start early I can achieve more before the sun is hot.' She made her excuses to Mistress Brewster. Thankful for the hour alone she struggled against the earth which needed a man wielding a mattock to penetrate. Feeling dizzy she stood, clinging to the fork handle, breathing in the soft air. Who? She shielded her eyes. Master Jones! He strode across the clearing.

'Priscilla, my dear. How good to see you recovered. I heard you were taken very bad.'

Priscilla hadn't seen Master Jones since Joseph died. She sought comfort in his kind face, now grown haggard. 'Aye, sir. I was bad but I'm well now.'

'But you are far too thin. You look as if a wisp of wind would blow you away, and the hollows of your eyes, so dark. Is Mistress Brewster feeding you enough?'

'Oh, yes, sir. Indeed she tries to make me eat more. But I cannot. I have no hunger for food.'

'You are pining, lass. I know. You've lost all your dearest loved ones. 'Tis a terrible sorrow.' He took her rough, blistered hands in his as if to provide shelter. Priscilla broke down, bowing her head. Tears fell onto his hands. Her shoulders shook. The hardened sea captain took her in his arms.

'Poor lass. So alone. Is there no one in the colony to give you comfort?' He hesitated. 'On the sea voyage I thought Mr Alden seemed fond of you.'

Priscilla moaned, clung to Master Jones and then stepped back, twisting her hands, looking down at the earth. 'I thought as much too. But since my sickness he'll have naught to do with me. So I have no hunger.' She wiped her cheeks and looked into Master Jones' concerned eyes. 'You are so kind... and with Joseph... he loved you, Master Jones.'

'The world can be terrible cruel,' he said.

'I... I am very happy you are still here. How long?'

'Half my crew died but those left, fifteen of us, are almost all recovered. It won't be long now.'

'Priscilla! Hurry! To the rendezvous. You are last!' Mistress Brewster called.

Master Jones placed his hands on her shoulders. 'God bless you.'

Chapter 26

March 1621

Treaty with Massasoit

John's anger

The horn sounded, echoing across the settlement and beyond. John clambered down from thatching a roof, ducked inside the house he shared with Standish to grab his musket and strode quickly to the fort. He remained on the edge of the assembled group.

'Form straight rows. Stop your babbling. You aren't women.' John smiled at the captain's attempts to bring order to this unruly collection of men. A hand on his shoulder. 'Master Jones! Good to see you. Have you come to watch the proceedings?'

'Aye. How goes it, John? Pleased you came here?'

'Plenty of scope for my skills. Relish the challenge. But.'

Master Jones tilted his head and raised his eyebrows. 'But?'

'I'll see how it goes. Come to the end of my contract I might sail back to England.'

'And Mistress Mullins? I thought you were courting…'

'Don't speak of her.' John broke in. His cheeks flushed. He clenched his fists.

'At arms,' Standish commanded. 'Hopeless.' He endeavored to demonstrate the rudiments of military discipline.

Losing interest, John looked beyond the captain toward the hill. 'An Indian!' He pointed.

A single tall, muscular Indian strode purposefully down the hill, across the brook, past the houses, heading straight for the rendezvous. He carried a bow and sling of arrows and was stark naked; not a stitch of clothing apart from a leather string round his waist with a fringe that hung down about nine inches. His jet black hair was long at the back, short in front.

John and Master Jones followed Standish with Bradford and Winslow, chasing after the brave. He had nearly reached the door of the rendezvous when they caught up. He halted, held up his hand and said, 'Welcome, English.'

Captain Standish regained his aura of command, standing very straight as if trying to add inches onto his height for he hardly reached the shoulder of the intruder. Elder Brewster hurried up the path carrying a long red horseman's coat. He draped it round the warrior's shoulders saying, 'There's a chill wind blowing.' With dignified acquiescence the Indian allowed himself to be escorted to the common house.

'For a parley,' Standish said.

John was still facing the door of the rendezvous when Priscilla stepped out. He couldn't avoid her pleading eyes. Wrenching himself away he strode down the slope where Standish and Winslow beckoned him to attend the parley.

Having arranged cushions in a circle on the floor of the common house, Governor Carver and Brewster welcomed their guest. Carver motioned him to sit at the head of the circle. The Indian settled himself and the colonists followed, waiting in silence.

'My name – Samoset. Beer please. English beer – best in the world.'

Winslow knelt before Samoset. 'I am sorry. We have no beer, but we have strong drink.' He nodded to John who hurried to the storehouse. He fetched aqua vitae and biscuits, locking the door behind him.

Samoset graciously received the offerings, along with mallard supplied by Brewster. He relished his feast and told his story.

'I was sachem of a tribe in Maine. English traders came to our shores and shared their beer.' He smiled broadly and smacked his lips. 'I come here – sail with English trader to Cape Cod – then trek across land to here – Patuxet. Find only bones of the dead. Follow trail to camp of Big Chief Massasoit. He said Patuxet tribe – wiped out.' He drew a finger across his neck. 'Terrible mystery disease.'

John admired the Indian's physique: his lean body, clear brown skin glistening with bear grease, strong cheekbones. He sat cross-legged, erect, and, unlike the colonists, was able to hold that posture throughout the afternoon, moving only his head and upper torso as he ate, drank and talked. Winslow offered him a pipe. Samoset and the colony's leaders smoked as he described all the tribes in the area, reciting their histories and customs. As Samoset spoke English passably well, John grasped most of what he recounted.

'The Nauset tribe. Strongest. You stole their corn. They ambushed you. But no worry. Massasoit my friend – Big Chief over all tribes. If he is your friend he will protect you.'

As evening drew in Governor Carver rose, bowed to Samoset and offered a prayer of thanks to God for bringing him here. 'And now,' Carver bowed again, 'Goodbye. It is time for sleep.'

Samoset said, 'I sleep here. I sleep here with you,' he swept his arm to include all the company, 'and your wives.' John smiled at Carver's consternation.

Winslow stepped forward. 'I suggest Samoset stays the night in the Hopkins' household.'

Without a hiccup, Hopkins graciously offered Samoset his arm and escorted him from the common house.

Good choice. Hopkins has dealt with Indians before, when he was in the Caribbean. John stumbled out into the evening air, his head aching from the mingled smells of bear grease and pipe smoke.

Working in the fields next morning, John leaned on his mattock handle and watched as Samoset came out of the Hopkins' house, preparing to depart. His bearing and stature were dignified, yet he was friendly and playful with the children, swinging them in the air and cuffing them about like a mother cat with her kittens. John smiled and hoped he would return soon. His presence was reassuring.

★ ★ ★

'Fie this earth is hard.' John swung his mattock, digging into the clotted, dry turf.

'Praise be Carver decided to stop building. We must get the crops in.' Standish bent double, tugging at a stubborn tuft.

John straightened his back. 'Hie! Samoset – with company.'

Samoset and four braves loped down the hill. Dropping their mattocks, John and Standish hastened to meet them.

'Greetings.' Standish saluted.

'Squanto.' Samoset introduced a handsome brave, lithe with a lively gait. 'Squanto belong to this land,' Samoset said, 'but went captive to Spain. Escaped to England. Speak English well. Better than me.'

'We have brought Big Chief Massasoit and his brother and braves,' Squanto said. 'They are nearby, over the hill.'

'Please come with me.' Standish bowed his invitation. 'I would like to introduce Squanto to our governor. Mr Alden, please stay here and watch for Chief Massasoit. Bring word when he comes.'

Not many minutes had passed before a huge Indian appeared, leading a large company of braves up from the other side of the hill, until they stopped and amassed on the top. A giant of a man, the leader was unmistakably the Big Chief. He resembled a formidable statue, his face painted deep red, his hairless body gleaming in the sunlight.

John ran across the fields toward the common house. In the 'street' he passed Howland carrying an ailing Elizabeth Winslow, and on reaching the door almost collided with Priscilla coming out, carrying a pallet and blankets. He stopped. His heart lurched.

'John,' she whispered.

He bit his tongue to stop his mouth and pushed past her calling, 'The Big Chief and his braves are on the hill.'

Priscilla's obvious distress and mute 'why?' haunted him as he followed orders and formed a small party of musketeers to accompany Standish and Winslow, who donned his steel corselet and sword. Samoset, Squanto and the other three braves joined them.

Halted by the brook, John stared at the gathering on the hill. There must be fifty – sixty braves, he reckoned, three times the colonists' army. They glistened with war paint: red, black, white, yellow, decorated with crosses and other symbols.

Squanto acted as interpreter between Standish and Massasoit, crossing back and forth across the brook several times. Massasoit and Standish both refused to cross the brook. Impasse.

After a few words with Standish, Winslow, renowned for his diplomacy, climbed the hill. John caught his breath at the risk. Massasoit could hold Winslow hostage, abduct him, anything; and with Elizabeth sick unto death.

Winslow presented the chief and his brother with gifts. For the brother, a knife and an earring. He presented Massasoit with a pair of knives, a copper chain with a jewel pendant, biscuits, butter and a pot of strong water. John could see that although Massasoit accepted these offerings, what he really wanted was Winslow's corselet and sword, reaching out to take them from him.

Winslow took a step back and began a speech. John caught, 'King James… peace… friends.' It was a long exchange, and he could see Winslow was working hard to break through the chief's skepticism, portrayed by frequent shaking of the head and thumbs down motions. Eventually, with much bowing and scraping on Winslow's part, there seemed to be agreement. Winslow stayed hostage with Massasoit's brother and the majority of the warriors, whilst Massasoit chose twenty braves to accompany him. Leaving their bows and arrows behind, they advanced with measured pace, walking fully erect, looking straight ahead, their faces inscrutable.

As they crossed the brook Standish stepped forward to greet Massasoit. Seeing the two standing together, John reckoned the captain, some four heads shorter than the powerful Indian, did indeed resemble a 'pygmy shrimp'. Standish appeared not to be fazed as he escorted the chief, a picture of silent, dignified solemnity. His position as sachem was marked only by a weighty chain of white bone beads hung round his neck with a long knife hanging from it in front and a tobacco pouch behind.

John and his small 'guard of honor' followed. *This could be a dream. Feels unreal. Even I am dwarfed by these massive braves.*

Captain Standish led them to an unfinished house where John saw every effort had been made to show hospitality. The earth floor was laid with a green rug and strewn with cushions. Standish invited Massasoit to be seated, and on cue, horns blared, drums rolled and Governor Carver with another armed squad appeared in the doorway. Massasoit rose and kissed the governor's hand. Carver reciprocated, and called for a pot of strong water. John raised his eyebrows as Massasoit took several long swigs. The chief broke into a sweat and a tremble. John wondered, *Is Massasoit not accustomed to alcohol? Hopkins did say Indians cannot hold their drink. Or is there something else causing his tremble? We have no idea what Squanto is really saying.*

In spite, or perhaps because of this, negotiations successfully concluded in a peace treaty which, Massasoit assured them, would apply to all the tribes under his governance. The sachem made his mark on the document; then Governor Carver signed. A procession of musketeers escorted the Indians back to the brook. The governor and sachem embraced; the Indians made their stately way up and over the hill, and Winslow rejoined the colonists.

John felt weak at the knees with relief and admiration; admiration for Standish, Brewster, Carver and especially for Winslow, with gratitude for his diplomatic skills. Keeping in formation, with Standish leading, the musketeers marched back into the town, this time along an avenue of women and children lining their way.

'What news?' Catherine Carver called out, setting off a chorus of excited questions.

Too late, John realized he was to march close by Priscilla who was standing with Mistress Brewster. He saw her blue eyes fasten on his face. Passing by, close enough to touch her, he felt his face redden and stared straight ahead. He sensed her gaze following him and he knew Mistress Brewster too was watching him closely. *Damn! Damn! Damnation!*

Chapter 27

March - April 1621

The Mayflower departs

The household settled for sleep but Priscilla lay awake. A day never to forget. She'd felt swept up in the drama, fear, excitement; amazed, riveted by the fearsome magnificence of the warriors, and happy with relief at the outcome. However, she also felt apart, not belonging with these people, and the pain of John Alden's rejection seared her heart. *If only Mother and Father and Joseph were here. I need you*, she wailed silently. She stuffed her fist into her mouth to stifle her sobs and remembered Dorothy. Perhaps she could sail back to England with Master Jones. He would help her get back to Dorking and find her cousins. But the thought of crossing the ocean again was terrifying. And what of Father's dreams? He'd entrusted them to her. Feeling she would go mad, she lay huddled up, awake all through the night.

In the days and weeks that followed Priscilla worked so hard her feelings were deadened and by nightfall weariness sent her to sleep.

Not only was there pressure to prepare the land for planting, but the treaty with Massasoit brought constant visits from his braves and their wives and children, expecting to receive the same hospitality of strong drink and food given to their chief and his warriors. And the number of visitors increased as news of the treaty spread to other local tribes under Massasoit's 'rule'.

Squanto and Samoset remained in the colony. Priscilla enjoyed Squanto's expressions of delight at being back in his homeland. He often stopped in his tracks and knelt down to touch the earth, sifting the light surface soil through his fingers.

One day, as Priscilla stepped out of the house, her arms full of washing, Squanto came running toward her, his hands full of writhing eels. She dropped the washing as he almost knocked into her, dashing into the house to give his quarry to Mistress Brewster. She followed him in.

'I know a special place, a creek where just in this season they lie half-asleep in the mud. I tread them out like this.' He showed a heel to toe rolling motion with his feet. 'And they all squiggle out, and here is a feast!'

It was indeed a feast. Squanto brought enough eels for each household to have a good number.

'Never have I eaten such fat, sweet eels,' Elder Brewster exclaimed. 'Have another, Priscilla.'

'No thank you, sir,' Priscilla answered. 'One is plenty and there's others need them more.' She looked at the two Brewster lads, Love and Wrestling.

Every day Priscilla woke before daybreak and waited until she heard Mistress Brewster raking the hearth and building the fire. That was the moment for her to rise. With both women bustling about, the men folk rose as one and the household gathered for prayers before breakfast. The fare was a small portion of pottage and a biscuit.

Priscilla's first daily task was to fetch freshwater from the brook for washing and cooking. This was slow and laborious. The full pails were heavy; water splashed out onto her skirts and feet, and as she had no free hand to gather up her skirts, she had to try to kick them out of the way so as not to trip. When she returned with her fourth load of two pails full, Mistress Brewster held out a basket.

'Would you like to go down to the harbor and dig for clams? Tide's out so you might find a good many.'

'Yes, Mistress,' Priscilla said, glad to be relieved for an hour or two from toiling in the fields.

As she stepped out onto the track she saw Master Winslow coming from the common house, carrying a body covered in a white sheet. 'Poor Elizabeth,' she said to herself. 'She's gone. Please God she's the last to die. She did put up a fight.' Saddened with memories of her own small family, she hurried down the track, glancing among folk to the right and left in case Mr Prence should appear and ease his way to walk with her. Reaching the shore she found a spot where she could be alone, away from a cluster of women and children clamming, far to her right. The harbor waters shone ruffled and blue in the sun. The *Mayflower* rode at anchor by Clark's Island. The wind was sharp and fresh these March days, with the sun gaining heat. She took deep breaths, drinking in the invigorating salt air. Birdlife made a lively racket: crows cawing, a woodpecker drilling rat-tat-tat. She looked up into the bare branches but couldn't see him. Gray squirrels chased and leaped from branch to branch, tree to tree. And honking geese! High in the sky a V shaped formation of geese flew in perfect order, headed north. Every day brought something new. If only…

'Mistress Mullins.'

Priscilla jumped. She hadn't heard footsteps. Mr Martin swept in front of her, bowing deeply, brushing the earth with his now crumpled hat.

'May I have the pleasure of your company on this fine morning?' The 'bullyfrog' did a two-step on his bandy legs. Hunger had reduced his swollen belly but his face retained its podgy pudding-like shape, now flecked with broken blood vessels; his hair and beard were straggly and unkempt. 'I'll help you fill your basket. Should be clams aplenty. It would be an honor to be of service. I've seen how hard you work, poor lass. There is no flesh on you.' He surveyed her body.

'No thank you, Mr Martin.' Priscilla swung round turning her back. 'I'm sure you would be better employed building houses or working in the fields.' She walked hurriedly back up the track, eyes on her feet so as not to trip. 'Please leave me,' she said to her persistent pursuer.

'What is this?' Captain Standish stood in front of them.

Mr Martin dodged aside. 'I must see to...'

'No. You come with me.' Standish grasped his arm in a grip that caused Mr Martin to gasp.

'He'll not trouble you now, Mistress. I'll see to that.'

'Thank you, sir. I, I am most grateful.'

Standish sought her eyes with his bright blue intense gaze.

Priscilla looked down.

'Good day, Mistress Mullins. Until this eve perchance.'

'Aye, Captain Standish.' She faced back toward the harbor and let tears fall. If only John Alden had rescued her. The incident spoiled any goodness the morning had held. She looked across the harbor to the *Mayflower*. How long before Master Jones sailed back to England?

Priscilla never spared herself, knowing if they didn't plant and reap a good harvest, they would starve. Although she was becoming weaker she stubbornly carried on. *We must be strong. We must be strong.* Mother's words sounded in her mind. Head down, hacking at the turf, she felt a tap on her shoulder. Startled, she stood up quickly, swaying with dizziness.

'Master Jones! Good day.'

'Good day, lass.' He put his hands on her shoulders to steady her. His eyes grew misty. 'I've come to say goodbye. We set sail for England in the morning.'

Stunned, Priscilla averted her face, swallowing her sobs and tears. 'Oh,' she said. 'Oh, I wish.' She longed to ask 'May I come with you back to England?' but the words wouldn't come.

He continued, as if answering her unspoken plea. 'Your father would be proud of you, surviving and carrying on. And your mother and little Joseph.' He put a hand on her arm. 'You're a good lass. In time things will come right for you – give it time – and try to plump out a bit.' He managed a smile and chucked her under the chin.

'Goodbye, sir,' she said. 'And thank you, thank you.' She struggled to speak. 'Please send word.' She choked. 'Please send word when you are safely back.'

'Aye, I shall.' Master Jones bent and kissed her cheek, giving her shoulders a comforting squeeze. 'Goodbye, Priscilla.' He turned and strode down to the harbor.

Looking after him, Priscilla had a vision of Joseph, trotting along at his side, blond curls bouncing, his small hand held in the captain's kind grasp. She watched as they boarded the ship's boat and set sail to cross the harbor. She hung onto her fork, fearing she might collapse.

Next morning, shortly after daybreak, the colonists all gathered at the harbor's shore. A gentle insistent wind ruffled the water. Silently the small band of settlers watched as the *Mayflower*'s sails filled and pulled. They waved. Elder Brewster said, 'God bless her.' Slowly, the ship which had brought them across the ocean through fierce storms, and had been their home in the care of her big-hearted captain, disappeared round the sand spit. Priscilla struggled to keep her grief under control. It helped to see all heads bowed in sorrow, as folk turned and slowly walked across the clearing to begin the day's work. They were now truly alone, and only thirty adults alive after the terrible winter.

On reaching the house, Mistress Brewster put an arm round Priscilla. 'You look unwell, child,' she said. 'Come in and do sitting down jobs today. There's the ducks to pluck and two geese, and the mending piles up and up.'

Priscilla did as she was bid, but having to chat with Mistress Brewster and hide her grief was more exhausting than working in the fields. In addition, Mr Prence called in for tuition with the Elder. His visits were becoming ever more frequent and he hovered over Priscilla, murmuring words of endearment and obsequiously praising Mistress Brewster for her care of this precious orphan. Joining the pain of grief, the acid of bilious anger and disgust ate away at Priscilla's insides.

On the morrow, Governor Carver called for the men to leave off building for a day or two. 'Squanto says the time has come for the herring to return to the brook. He says we need the fish to fertilize this poor soil, so we must get the fields prepared for planting corn.'

Priscilla wasn't entirely sure she understood, but she was prepared to work as hard as she could. Looking across the field she spied John Alden, working on the far side. Her insides heaved.

When the sun was high, a trail of loud whooping shouts preceded Squanto running up from the brook. 'They've arrived! The brook is bursting with herring.' Priscilla dropped her fork and joined a group hurrying after Squanto. He was right. The brook teemed with flashing, sparkling, jumping herring. Squanto was so pleased and proud, as if he himself had caused the fish to come to this very spot.

'Now – hurry to work the land,' Squanto said. 'I catch the fish and you make the land ready.' The workforce obediently trudged back to carry on with their labor. With the men wielding large mattocks, progress was much quicker.

By late afternoon Priscilla was flagging. She stopped a moment to lean on her fork. Absently, she let her gaze drift across the fields and she saw John Alden had paused and was looking her way. Her heart thumped. But he looked away and carried on mauling the ground. So strange. Thwack, heave… thwack, heave… The clods of earth flew up. Priscilla listlessly resumed forking the ground. The day was especially hot; a yellow sun set in a blazing blue sky;

no clouds except for a few white wisps high up. In England the skies would be gentle dove gray, the sun filtering through, warm on some days, others cool and windy. The snowdrops would be over; primroses, violets, cowslips decking hedgerow banks; blackthorn blossom full out, delicate white, tiny petals shading inwards to pale pink and a green center. Some years it was so thick one could mistake it for the may. Gentle March rains. She shook herself. She must not remember.

Dusk encroached. The fields were ready. Squanto had hauled up baskets and baskets of herring and tomorrow he would show them the Indian way of planting.

Chapter 28

March - April 1621

Planting the corn

Governor Carver dies

At sunrise, Squanto stood in the nearest field, feet astride, surrounded by baskets of herring. John Alden went to the storehouse and brought the corn they'd stolen from the Nauset tribe.

Imitating Governor Carver, Squanto raised his hand for attention. 'We must plant fish in the soil to make the crops grow. I show you.'

'Very strange,' Mistress Brewster muttered. 'Who ever heard of such a thing? I pray this is not a foolish waste – heathen practice.'

When all eyes were focused on him, Squanto demonstrated how to use the mattock to mound heaps of earth about a yard wide. He placed several fish in each heap. Then he flattened the top of the heap with his hand. He planted seven kernels of corn; six round the outside of the circle and the seventh in the middle, covering the kernels with soil. He explained, 'When the corn sprouts you must add seeds of beans and squash to each mound. These plants produce creepers which will grow up the cornstalks and give shade to protect the roots from the **very** hot sun. The sun in summer here is much hotter than it ever was in England. You will see.' He held his hands over his head and pretended to wilt and crumble. The children laughed and clapped. The solemn adults smiled. Some even chuckled.

Governor Carver organized men and woman into groups; the men to mound heaps of earth, inserting the herring; the women to follow, planting the corn. Squanto leapt from one to the other, checking they were doing it correctly. He also instructed they must stand guard, especially at night, to stop wild animals from digging out the fish before it was rotted into the soil.

As they did most days, visiting Indians began to arrive, hovering on the edge of the clearing. Squanto beckoned to them to come and help. Braves, squaws, some with papooses on their backs, and children, loped across to the fields, pleased to be summoned.

'Ah. Those beautiful little ones,' Priscilla said softly. Shyly she approached a young Indian woman who had a papoose strapped to her back. She wore a deerskin skirt and nothing else except for a bead necklace. Like the braves, she stood straight, lithe and graceful. She smiled as Priscilla gestured to the papoose, and took the bundle from her back. She laid the babe in Priscilla's arms and pointed to one of the boys, indicating the sex. So tightly bound he couldn't move, the infant was content and smiling. He gurgled as babies do and his black eyes sparkled.

'Oh – he is beautiful.' Priscilla held the baby close, smiling with her eyes full of tears. She felt a kind hand on her shoulder and looked up into the mother's face – a face who knew. There was no need of words.

'Priscilla.' Mistress Brewster called.

'I must go, but thank you,' Priscilla said, taking the squaw's hands in her own. The Indian woman nodded.

Priscilla joined Mistress Brewster with a lighter heart. Whenever she dared she paused to watch the Indian children. They dashed about, knowing exactly how to place the fish, just so. Their silky nut-brown skin and jet black hair glistened in the sun. They were agile and healthy.

On they toiled as Squanto brought basket upon basket of fish. The men mounded and fertilized the field and then worked to clear more land. The women followed with the corn. As there was no more beer, the children were sent with pails to bring fresh drinking water from the springs above the brook. Folk ate their midday rations of hardtack sitting in the fields.

As the adults sat idle a moment to eat and rest, the children, Indian and English, played games together: dancing, chasing, leaping, and then several of the older Indian boys who carried bows and quivers of arrows, obliged the English boys' entreaties to show them how to shoot.

Priscilla was the first to spot impending disaster; Francis Billington armed with a bow and arrow. She jumped up and rushed over, holding up her skirts, trying not to trip on the rough ground. 'Francis! No! You cannot aim. You might shoot someone!' Startled, Francis hesitated and in that instant Squanto was there. He spoke severely to Francis.

'If you shoot an arrow and it hits someone you will be hanged,' came the dire threat. John Billington charged over, ready to give his son a thrashing. Squanto held him back, saying, 'No need.' Billington skulked off and Squanto turned to the Indian lads, no doubt explaining that these English don't have the skills of Indians. There were no more efforts to teach the English youths how to use a bow and arrow.

Priscilla smiled to herself as she resumed work with Mistress Brewster.

'I'm not sure it is wise, our children and the Indian children playing together. The Indians are heathens. They aren't Christians and don't have our knowledge of God and virtue. But we must be friends,' Mistress Brewster said. 'Please God this planting is successful. It is truly a strange way to plant. And we have only a few rows of peas and barley to rely on if it doesn't work. Ah well. We must trust in the Lord.'

'Squanto knows this land,' Priscilla said. 'It is different from the soil in England. I'm sure his ways are tried and tested.'

'The Elder and Mr Bradford say 'twas God's will disease wiped out the Indians who lived here; part of His design that we Pilgrims should settle here. Perhaps Squanto is part of His purpose for us.'

In her mind Priscilla questioned this presumption but she said nothing.

★ ★ ★

Planting continued day after day and the sun grew hotter and hotter.

'This is a heat such as we never had in England, even at the height of summer,' Mistress Brewster said.

'Aye. It makes for hard work.' Priscilla mopped her face with her handkerchief.

'I'll tell the children to fetch more water.' Mistress Brewster went off to gather the children and distribute pails.

Priscilla bent to pick up a basket of corn and jerked up again, hearing a man cry out, 'Governor Carver!' John Carver lay on the ground. He didn't move. Master Winslow hurried to him, knelt down, bending his ear close to his chest and mouth, fingers on his wrist. 'He is alive. Lift him carefully. To the common house.' John Alden and John Howland carefully lifted the governor and carried him from the field. Catherine Carver followed close behind, crying softly, 'John, Oh John...'

Folk all stood silent, in a daze.

'We must carry on.' William Bradford's strong voice broke into the stunned stillness. The workers resumed planting and clearing more land.

Two days later Governor Carver died. Winslow reckoned it was heart failure, working in the hot sun. The colony came together as never before in their grief and regret. Even the hard, coarse Billingtons softened in sorrow.

'He were a fair man,' John Billington said. 'A fair man wi' a kind heart.'

Aye, Priscilla thought. She remembered the tall handsome man standing on the warf in London, supervising the loading of supplies onto the *Mayflower*, kindly, firmly, keeping the passengers in order. 'I shall miss him,' she murmured.

Although the day of Governor Carver's death was not the Sabbath, work ceased and folk gathered in the common house for a time of prayer and remembrance. Catherine, overwhelmed with shock and grief, hunched over shaking with sobs, trying to keep silent. Priscilla saw her trying to struggle out from Mistress Brewster's embrace. *She wants to get free. She wants to run out of here and scream and I don't blame her.* She cast a quick glance round, searching to locate John Alden but couldn't see him. *He must be at the back so he can make a quick exit.* She too wanted to flee and scream out her sad bitterness. Mr Prence hovered near. Priscilla squirmed, repelled by his adoring scrutiny.

On the morrow the colonists gathered again to lay their governor to rest. As the coffin was lowered into the grave, Elder Brewster offered up prayers of committal. Accompanying the thuds of earth shoveled onto wood, volleys of shot rang out from every man who had a musket – orchestrated by Captain Standish.

Catherine Carver could barely stand for weeping. After the burial, Mistress Brewster brought her to stay in the Brewster house while the men met in the common house to elect a new governor. She sat Catherine at the table and read to her from the Bible.

Priscilla sat in the doorway, plucking a brace of mallard ducks. Beautiful birds; vibrant greens and purples, black, white against mottled brown; she mused looking out over the fields of corn heaps and down toward the harbor. Tight spring green leaves unfurled. Blossom petals dropped. Birds warbled, chattered, screeched. An air battle between a crow and a bright red bird was holding her attention when the men of the colony came from the common house with an air of business accomplished. In twos and threes they walked purposefully past, John Alden and Captain Standish together. Standish looked in her direction and raised a hand. John kept his gaze fixed straight ahead.

Priscilla bowed her head. Tears fell on the vivid plumage. She mustn't. Wiping her eyes with the back of her hand, she saw, on the stump by her knee, a butterfly unfolding its wings. Was it newly hatched? Red and black. The upper wings were red with black markings on the tips; the lower wings black with flecks of red. As she studied the delicate creature she became aware of a change in the light, the sky now strangely opaque. Birds abandoned their flight and song and perched in the trees. Big dark purple-gray clouds rolled in from the west obscuring the sun. A streak of lightning shot through the sky followed by several cracks of thunder, tapering off into a distant rumble. Priscilla marveled. There was never any such thing in the sky in England. Folk working in the street and fields looked up. Another clap of thunder let loose pouring drenching rain. Priscilla didn't move from her seat, staring at the soaked butterfly. She willed it to survive. The storm clouds blew east opening the sky to hot sun. The butterfly fluttered its wings too sodden to fly. Priscilla sat still as it slowly, falteringly, died. She carefully picked it up and placed it in the midst of a clump of thistles growing against the wall of the house; the only protective plants in sight. Heavy with sadness, she gathered up the ducks and her stool and went indoors. Time to stir up the pottage, add a few bits of fowl, and lay the table.

'We have unanimously elected William Bradford to be our governor,' Elder Brewster announced as he ushered Winslow across the threshold. 'I have invited Master Winslow to sup.'

Mistress Brewster insisted Catherine Carver stay as well. 'You need food.'

Priscilla looked into Catherine's drawn, pinched face. Her deep brown eyes seemed sunk back under her brow as if trying to escape. She sat at table but as she lifted a morsel to her mouth she heaved. 'It's no use,' she said. 'I am sorry, Mistress Brewster, I know 'tis excellent fare.' She swooned and grabbed hold of the table. Master Winslow caught her. 'Please take me to my bed,' she pleaded, her voice fainting away.

Priscilla could not eat either, so bitterly did she feel for Catherine's suffering. *No. Of course she cannot eat and doesn't want to stay here. She wants to be where she and Governor Carver lived together, amongst their belongings. And she would probably rather you were not with her, insisting that she be comforted by your words, Mistress Brewster.*

When Master Winslow had left, escorting Catherine Carver, Mistress Brewster turned on Priscilla. 'You *must* eat.' She was quietly vehement, her voice hard, the broken veins in her face flushed. 'God has pleased to see you recovered. I told your mother I would care for you as I am more capable than Mistress Carver. But you make it impossible.' She sat ramrod straight, hands clasped on the table, her ash gray bug eyes boring into Priscilla. 'We are here to fulfill God's purpose, His plan.' Her voice raised in pitch. 'This is Satan working in you. God needs us to be as strong and robust as our meager supplies will allow, and you refuse all you are given. It is a sin, Priscilla, a sin.'

Priscilla sat staring, stunned.

Mistress Brewster's pinched mouth opened again. 'You wouldn't want folk to think you are possessed by the devil – that you are a witch!'

The ultimate threat. 'No, Mistress Brewster,' Priscilla said meekly, eyes on her plate. Dutifully she ate. Feeling sick, her head spinning, she stumbled to help clear away in preparation for prayers.

As the Elder prayed, Priscilla sat, hands folded on her lap, head bowed, seeing the faces of her dear family, with her no more, remembering. The Elder's voice ceased. She raised her eyes. He was looking directly at her.

'As St Paul says, "...let us also lay aside every weight and sin that clings so closely, and let us run with perseverance the race that is set before us..."' He closed the Bible. 'Amen.'

Priscilla went to her pallet. She lay awake, curled on her side, knees drawn up, clutching her stomach. No tears came, no sobs.

Chapter 29

May 1621

Priscilla makes a decision

Catherine Carver dies

On the last Sabbath of April, at the close of prayers, Governor Bradford announced that Master Winslow and Susanna White were betrothed. They would be wed on the 12th of May.

When the day came Priscilla wished she could stay away. Attending a wedding would only inflame her misery. Also, she wondered, how could Susanna marry so soon after her husband's death – only months, and Elizabeth Winslow's – even more recent? *Does she want to marry Master Winslow? Or is she simply doing what is expected; marry and produce children?* Priscilla felt uneasy, knowing there would be increased pressure on herself. John Alden seemed to have disappeared. She never saw him or heard his deep ringing voice. Instead she was constantly fending off the attentions of odious Mr Prence, eager Captain Standish, and pesky Mr Martin. She offered to work in the fields but Elder Brewster said her presence at the marriage was required, as a witness.

With Mistress Brewster on her left and Elder Brewster on her right, she walked to the common house in the still heat, punctuated by the usual sounds of sawing and hammering, men calling to one another, women in clusters, gossiping and scolding idle children.

When they entered the common house Governor Bradford and the wedding couple were already there. *Oh! She looks lovely.* Priscilla caught her breath. The bride wore a simply cut ruby red gown, her blond hair shining and blue eyes sparkling, inviting her handsome, dark haired fiancé.

Governor Bradford spoke. 'As there is no instance in the Holy Bible where a priest performs the ceremony of marriage, we will follow the custom of our brethren in Leiden and conduct a civil ceremony.'

How different it is. No church with communion, no wedding feast, no dancing. Would there be any celebration at all? It seemed not. Governor Bradford followed the procedure for a civil wedding and proclaimed the couple man and wife.

Master Winslow and Susanna walked arm in arm to their newly finished house. A few well-wishers called out congratulations from the fields.

Walking back to the Brewster house, Mistress Brewster said, 'This is a happy event. The first wedding in our new colony.'

'Aye,' Elder Brewster replied. 'Mr Alden has built them a good sized house – Susanna with her two boys, and then they'll have little ones of their own.'

Priscilla was silent. Her heart writhed. She knew that as a young woman of childbearing age she would be expected to marry soon. But there was only one man she wanted to marry and he paid her no heed. She looked down at her feet. A few paces on she became aware of someone walking beside her. It was Captain Standish.

'Good day, Captain,' she said.

'Good day, Mistress Mullins.' His greeting was hearty. ''Tis a fine moment, is it not, when a man and woman decide to wed.'

'Aye,' she said, looking down at her feet again.

'Ah, Captain Standish,' Elder Brewster said. 'Mary, I've invited the captain to join us for our midday meal.'

'We'll be glad of your company, I'm sure,' Mistress Brewster said.

On entering his house, Elder Brewster opened his Bible for prayers.

> "I will indeed bless you, and I will make your offspring
>   As numerous as the stars of heaven
>   And the sand that is on the seashore.
> And your offspring shall possess the gates of their enemies,
>   and by your offspring shall all the nations of the earth
>   gain blessing for themselves,
>   because you have obeyed my voice."
>
> (Genesis 22 v. 17 – 18)

'This is our purpose too, my children,' the Elder said. 'We must do right and obey God's commandments and multiply. Amen.'

All through the meal Priscilla kept her eyes on her plate. Captain Standish sat opposite her and she did not want to meet his gaze. Eating was a torment. She hated the food. She hated the thought of marrying just to supply children. The thought of being in bed with Captain Standish made her shudder. He may be a good, fine man, but he was not for her.

After a wakeful night, Priscilla stepped out in the misty pre-dawn light to fetch water needed for the day.

On reaching the brook, she made sure no one was about and sat by the water's edge. She needed to think. She tried to weigh up her predicament. John Alden, for whatever reason, no longer cared for her. She was not happy living with the Brewsters. She could not fall in with their way of seeing things. They were too harsh. The only person with whom she felt 'at home' was Catherine Carver and she was sick, nigh unto dying. She could not bear the thought of marrying any man in this colony other than John Alden. If only she had returned to England with Master Jones, but she hadn't dared ask. What to do? Sooner or later another ship would come from England bringing more settlers and supplies, to return with beaver pelts and clapboard. She knew this from listening to Elder Brewster. She would somehow hang on. Refuse to be married. And when the next ship arrived she would take passage and sail back to her home. She could go back and if they prevented her she would bide her time. She would not be forced into marriage in this settlement. She remembered the young Indian squaw. For all their screeching, the Indians had not attacked and now there was a peace treaty. If she had to, she would run away, seek refuge with the Indians. At least they were merry. The Pilgrims seemed to think it was a sin to be merry. *I'll not be cowed*, she decided.

Having formed a plan Priscilla felt stronger. She filled two pails with water. It was a beautiful sparkling brook, still churning with squiggling, thrashing herring. Spring vegetation covered the banks. Some must be edible. She would ask Squanto. The brook cascaded in waterfalls, glinting in the sunlight, spilling down over large moss covered rocks with a loud rushing sound such as she'd never heard before; insistent, merry. Between the rocks and spills of water were hidden shadowy pools. It was enchanting. She would have liked to stay awhile longer, but there was so much to do. She lifted the heavy pails, straightening her back.

Pressure mounted to prepare the land for sowing peas. They were late. To Priscilla's relief, a decision had been taken to abandon sowing flax this first year. Not enough time or labor to process the crop. She struggled with her fork. Dig, heave, twist and then pull at the tufts with her hands. By noon sweat soaked her gown and ran down her forehead into her eyes. It stung. Her sweaty hands slipped on the fork handle and she had difficulty getting a grip on the grassy tufts. '*I must be strong… I must be strong…*' she repeated to herself over and over. Her back was always sore, twinging and aching. When she stood straight to rest a moment she saw the blisters on her hands had burst. Blood joined the sweat marks on her gown and tears joined the sweat in her eyes. She wiped them away with the back of her hand, not wanting to mark her face with blood.

'Oh, my dear, just look at you.' Priscilla knew the voice well. At this moment it was kind and sympathetic. Mistress Brewster came to her side. 'This is such hard work,' the older woman said, 'and you've been laboring since dawn. I'll take a turn. Go and sit with Mistress Carver awhile.'

'Thank you, Mistress Brewster. Thank you.'

Fighting her dizziness, she stumbled across the field and clearing to the common house, and into the cool, dim room. Only Catherine Carver was there. Shafts of sunlight filtered through the small windows, penetrating the gloom, glinting on the orange coat of Bibs, curled up close beside the frail, fading woman. Her beautiful tired lined face lay in a mass of luxuriant long, black hair, vivid against the white pillows. She had high cheekbones, large oval eyes, closed under gently arched eyebrows, and a strong nose, not large, but defined. Though not old, Catherine wore the face of a woman who has lived a long life.

Priscilla quietly drew up a stool.

Catherine opened her eyes. 'Priscilla, good. I'm glad it's you. Always better when you come.'

'Thankfully I've been released from working in the fields to be with you.' Priscilla took a small linen towel that lay folded on the stool which served as a bedside table and dipped it in the bowl of water. She wiped Catherine's face and parched lips. 'Would you like a drink?'

'Yes… please… I want… to sit up.'

Cradling Catherine's frail body, Priscilla raised her to a sitting position and arranged the pillows so she could lean back in comfort. She draped a soft gray shawl round her shoulders. Then she helped Catherine take a few sips of water from her beaker.

'Thank you,' Catherine said and rested her head back against the pillows. Her voice lowered so Priscilla could barely hear, she said, 'Priscilla, I need to tell you, I do not have the will to go on.' She clutched Priscilla's hand. 'God's purpose or no, it is not worth living without John. Pray, don't tell a soul.' Her lips tightened. ''Tis considered sinful, but no merciful God, nor John, would want me to go on in misery.' Haltingly, she talked of their shared dream, of a society where folk were true, just and kind; where children were taught to read and write and think for themselves.

Priscilla confided her dream of having a little school where girls as well as boys learned to read and write.

Catherine Carver sat quiet, conserving her strength. 'Your mother was a good person. We had many happy moments. I am sorry you are in Mistress Brewster's hands. I can see you are suffering. Their way to salvation is so hard – scourging the soul. John and I believe the soul is like... like a newborn babe.' She smiled. 'Needs good food and gentle care to flourish.'

'That is a wonderful way of seeing it. I wish, how I wish.' Priscilla wiped her cheeks.

Catherine twisted the ends of her shawl. 'John felt he had to defer to the Elder, and I fear the Elder bows to his wife, at least on social matters. I pray you get free.' She held Priscilla's eyes. 'You'll say nothing of these things?'

'Of course not, Mistress Carver. I'll say nothing.' Priscilla squeezed her friend's hand.

'Thank you. I needed to confess.' Catherine closed her eyes. Bibs stood and stretched, arching her back; she rearranged herself at her lady's feet. Catherine smiled. 'She's a comfort, her soothing purring.' Leaning forward she said, 'Now, would you fetch my box... there at the foot.' She gestured.

Priscilla found a large box covered with a blanket. She ran her hand over the gleaming polished elm, a wreath of roses and ivy carved on the lid. She laid it gently on Catherine's lap.

'The key... I can't untie it.' Catherine struggled, fingering her waistband.

'I'll help,' Priscilla said. 'It's a tight knot.' She handed Catherine the key.

'Pull your stool closer so you can see.' Catherine unlocked the box and raised the lid. There was a Bible and a psalter. She struggled to lift the heavy books, but defeated, sank back into her pillows. 'Please.'

Priscilla lifted them from the box. Hidden underneath was a leather bound folio and a small purple velvet bag closed with a drawstring of corded black silk. Catherine unloosed the string and pulled out a small oval mirror with a beveled edge, set in a handled elm frame.

Priscilla gasped. 'How beautiful!' Only the nobility possessed objects like this made of glass.

'A fine good lady gave me these.' Catherine stroked the soft leather cover of the folio. 'Shakespeare's *Hamlet*.' She leaned back and closed her eyes. 'John and I worked in the household of the Duke and Duchess of Norfolk; John was retainer; I was companion to the Duchess. Like sisters we were.' Catherine paused and Priscilla stayed quiet. 'As I could read and write we shared books; read aloud. My lady used to send to London for Shakespeare's latest. She especially loved *Hamlet*. "To thine own self be true, And it must follow, as the night the day, Thou canst not be false to any man." Those lines... I've always remembered... and think of my lady. My poor lady. The Duke was always away... mistresses... no children. So sad.' There followed a long silence. Wondering whether Catherine needed to lie down again, Priscilla said softly, 'Mistress?'

'Ah.' Catherine opened her eyes. 'When the time came for John and me to leave, to join the Brewsters' group, my lady gave me this box and all that's in it.'

'And you've kept it with you always!' Priscilla exclaimed. 'On the escape to Holland, then across the North Sea to Southampton, and then across the vast ocean.'

'Aye,' Catherine said. 'And now I'll be on another journey. To life everlasting with John, I pray.'

'Mistress.' Priscilla laid her hand on Catherine's arm and looked into her deep brown eyes, silently pleading with her not to go. *I need you. I need you to live. You are the only person I have who understands.*

'And now,' Catherine said, rousing herself. 'To the point. I would like you to have this, Priscilla, when I'm gone. The box and the holy books, the mirror and this folio.'

'But Mistress Carver, it is all too lovely and valuable to belong to me.'

'Nonsense,' Catherine's voice became stronger. 'Look into the mirror, Priscilla, and see you are a beautiful part of God's creation. Look into your eyes and ponder who you are. 'Tis not a vain sin… not if you remember, "It is He who hath made us and not we ourselves".'

Priscilla thought she saw in Catherine's eye the ghost of a sparkle. She felt shaken, in a tumult of gratitude, love and fear.

'I know, 'tis a dangerous gift,' Catherine said. 'I know this colony. They'd say it's blasphemous. If you think it is too dangerous, I understand. I can ask Master Winslow to send it back to the Duchess.' A coughing fit caught Catherine. Priscilla supported her head until it was over; then she gently wiped her friend's lips and settled her back into the pillows. Holding Catherine's hand, Priscilla struggled within herself. This precious gift, full of love and memories; Mistress Carver wanted her to have it, and she longed to keep it. But if the box were found… God knows what they would do. Smash it all up, probably, and punish her severely. She looked at the mirror resting on Catherine's lap, and rested her gaze on the tired, kind face.

'Thank you, Mistress. This will be more precious to me than anything else I own. And when I look into the mirror I will see you there.' Her voice shook and broke and tears fell onto Catherine's hand.

'Thank you,' Catherine whispered. 'You are a good, brave lass. And now, I'm tired.' She put the mirror back into the velvet bag and placed it and the folio in the box. Priscilla laid the holy books on top. Catherine locked the box and asked Priscilla to retie the key onto her waistband. Priscilla replaced the box at the foot of the pallet and then helped Catherine to lie down.

'Bide with me awhile please.'

'Aye, Mistress Carver. I'll be pleased to.'

'I'm so tired.' Catherine's long-fingered elegant hand searched for Priscilla's.

'I'm with you, I'll not leave you.'

Priscilla remained with Catherine in the cool quiet. Bibs changed position, curling up close to her patient's waist. Mistress Carver's face relaxed into repose. Priscilla's head throbbed. For Catherine's sake she wanted what Catherine wanted; her release from this tortured life; to join her beloved. But for her own sake she could not bear the loss of her only friend. If Catherine Carver died she would be utterly alone among folk who, to her, felt hostile, and with no one to love.

Mistress Carver gripped Priscilla's hand. Her breathing grew labored, fighting for air. *Oh please, God, don't let her suffer anymore*, Priscilla prayed. Catherine heaved a deep rattling breath and let go. Priscilla sat holding her hand for a long time. *She's going to her dear John.* Priscilla too let go and wept, strong, wracking weeping, willing her tears to wash away the grief and loneliness, to carry her away, like Catherine, to the man she loved. *Please, please, God. Don't make me go on like this.* Gradually her sobbing subsided and she sat quiet. She studied Catherine's hand, the slender fingers, longing for them to come alive and press her own hand. All sense of time left her as her spirit strained to join Catherine Carver's.

When she roused herself the shafts of sunlight had gone. She closed Mistress Carver's eyes and kissed her forehead before pulling the cover over her face. 'Goodbye,' she whispered.

Emerging from the common house, Priscilla was unnerved to see folk coming in from the fields, the day's work done. *I'd no idea I'd stayed so long.* Meeting Mistress Brewster, she said, 'Mistress Carver has died – a short while ago.'

'I thought it wouldn't be long. I'll tell Elder Brewster and he'll arrange the burial. 'Tis as Governor Bradford said. She was a weak woman to take to her bed so soon when there was nothing wrong with her. She lacked will.'

Swallowing her anger, Priscilla said nothing.

★ ★ ★

The morrow dawned fair, heralding another hot day. Sick with grief and rage, Priscilla hacked at the harsh turf. How would they ever clear enough land to sow the peas? Feeling a tap on her shoulder, she jumped and turned, scowling. 'Oh! Master Winslow!' she exclaimed, now embarrassed as well as bad tempered.

'Would you come with me a moment, Mistress Mullins,' he said.

'Yes, yes, sir.' Priscilla saw Mistress Brewster staring at her with an inquisitive frown.

Priscilla walked beside Master Winslow to the common house. He pushed open the door. Where Mistress Carver had lain there was only Bibs, mewing and prowling, trying to find her poorly companion. Priscilla swallowed hard. She mustn't weep now. She mustn't.

Master Winslow walked to his writing desk. Slowly, respectfully, he laid his hands on a large sack-encased object. He looked down at it and then at Priscilla, kind searching in his brown eyes; the beginnings of a smile on his lips.

'Mistress Carver requested this box and its contents be left to you on her death.' He handed her the small key. 'A sad moment, losing Master and Mistress Carver.'

'Aye. Thank you, sir.' Priscilla bowed her head. She tied the key onto her waistband and reached across the desk as he lifted the box into her arms. Master Winslow sat down.

'I'll bide here. I've some papers to see to.'

'Aye, sir,' Priscilla replied. She turned and calling Bibs in a faltering voice, left the shadowy peace of the common house, stepping back into the hot bright sunlight. She hurried up the track to the Brewsters' house, fearing the eyes that followed her. Placing her treasure beside her own box at the foot of her pallet, she covered them both with a blanket. She then returned to her work in the fields.

All that day, and while they were preparing the evening meal, Mistress Brewster said nothing. Priscilla was beginning to hope there wouldn't be an inquiry. However, when the Elder came in to hold prayers, the Mistress said, 'Priscilla, I think you should show us what you have acquired.'

'But Mistress Brewster, it is private.'

'We do not keep secrets here. There should be nothing hidden. Anything that is part of God's truth is fit for all to see.' Mistress Brewster looked to her husband. 'Am I not right?'

'Aye. 'Tis right you should share what you've been given.'

Priscilla felt her face grow hot with fury and fear. *Keep your head. Please God, not this betrayal.* She went to her pallet, slowly untying the key from her waistband. She removed the box from the sack and held it close to her waist.

Mistress Brewster gasped. ''Tis fine! Too fine!'

Priscilla unlocked the box and opened the lid, ensuring Elder and Mistress Brewster could not see over the top. She handed them the Bible and psalter and closed the lid. They hadn't seen the purple bag or the small folio.

'These are the Lord's holy books,' Mistress Brewster pronounced. 'They should rightfully belong to us all. Part of a community collection of holy texts.' She and the Elder opened the front covers.

'They are inscribed! "To my dear friend Priscilla".' Hoarse with indignation, Mistress Brewster rasped, 'You were with her only a little time. She did nothing to care for you. And what did you ever do to earn such gifts and gratitude? I'm the one who cared for you.

I nursed you back to health. I've guarded your soul. You shouldn't even want these gifts. You should care for *me*. I'm the one who gave most hours to caring for Mistress Carver. She should be rewarding me, not you. Besides, this Bible and the psalter are in the language of the Church of England, of the dastardly King James. They should be burned!' She thrust the Bible at her husband.

'No, no.' Priscilla entreated Elder Brewster, pleading with her eyes.

The Elder stood thinking. He handed Priscilla the Bible and the psalter and put an arm round his wife.

'My dear, your view is right in its way. But Governor Carver was loved by us all, and he was devoted to Catherine. It would be wrong to burn her holy books.' Solemnly he said to Priscilla, 'You may keep them, but only as objects in memory of Mistress Carver. You must promise to read only *our* Bible and psalter.'

'I promise.'

Mistress Brewster fixed Priscilla with a stare of tormented fury.

Chapter 30

May 1621

Captain Standish calls on Priscilla

The day came to sow the peas. Hour on hour, Priscilla bent double to plant the precious peas in roughly tilled rows. When the job was finished she eased herself upright. *Now we need a good two weeks of sun and gentle rain and no strong winds.*

As if the heavens had heard her request, a soft rain fell in the night and continued day after day, alternating with bouts of hot sun. Blessed relief, she could now attend to cooking, washing and mending; tasks which allowed her blisters to heal and her back and legs to rest.

One steamy afternoon, just past midday, Priscilla sat in the cool of the house mending. Mistress Brewster was out, checking on the goodwives and the Brewster lads were digging for clams. The Elder was probably in consultation with Governor Bradford, as ever, so she was enjoying a few longed for moments of solitude.

The pile of mending reached from her foot to her knee. Mostly breeches, torn and ripped on brambles and sharp twigs when men were out hunting, and building. Building was terrible for producing torn breeches and shirts and stockings: constant snagging on rough ends of timber and sharp thatching reeds. Priscilla took a pair of breeches from the top of the pile and found her packet of needles and a spool of tough brown thread in her sewing bag. The thread was so thick it was a job to push it through the eye of her needle. In her efforts she pricked a blister. Blood and puss oozed out. 'Oh bother.' Dropping the breeches she hastily drew her handkerchief from her pouch. The bleeding stopped and she retrieved the breeches, finally threaded the needle and settled to repairing a tear across the knee. *I wonder whose breeches these are? John Alden's?* Priscilla slipped into a daydream of sitting by the hearth, with John Alden in his chair across from her. She was mending his breeches, and then would sew patches on their small son's breeches, and mend a tiny tear in their little girl's smock.

'Mistress Mullins, may I come in?' Without waiting for a reply, Captain Standish stepped briskly across the room to stand in front of her. He was dressed in his military uniform, sword at his side, buttons polished, boots shining, helmet resting in the crook of his right arm.

'Good day, Captain.' Priscilla did not stand. Her stomach knotted. She stared at the breeches in her lap and waited, counting the seconds. On reaching sixty she raised her eyes. The captain stood, rigid, legs slightly apart. Beads of sweat trickled from his hairline down the side of his face. He clenched and unclenched his left fist, opened and closed his mouth. His red, polished figure had a certain glow in the dim room where the only sounds were those of folk outside going about the tasks of the day. In spite of her dread, Priscilla struggled to suppress a giggle.

The captain cleared his throat. 'Mistress Mullins.' The words emerged hoarse, choking. He coughed, politely covering his mouth with his hand. 'Mistress Mullins, I have admired you from... for a long time... your beauty, how you care for the sick, and work hard, never sparing yourself.' Standish looked to the side of Priscilla, past her gaze. 'I... perhaps you don't know... I helped tend you in your illness.'

Priscilla lowered her eyes, stifling a shudder.

Standish dropped onto one knee, maneuvering his sword to rest on the floor. 'Mistress, I have come to ask for your hand in marriage.'

'Please stand,' Priscilla commanded. When Standish was on his feet, she rose. 'You are a fine man, Captain Standish, but my answer is no.'

Standish lurched back as if he'd been hit.

'There is one man I love. John Alden. I thought he cared for me but... therefore I have decided I will return to England on the next ship.'

The captain reached toward her, entreating. 'But you do not understand. Mistress Brewster and the Elder look on you as their own. The colony needs you. They will not allow you to return to England.'

Unmoving and mute, Priscilla stared at Standish in disbelief. She saw it all; one of their own; a part of God's plan for a new kingdom.

'I... I am best suited,' Standish declared. 'I have a good estate.' He paced a few steps to and fro. Priscilla watched his face set in flushed determination. 'I can provide for you. I would love and cherish you.'

Priscilla clenched her fists. 'No, No, No.' She ran from the house. Holding up her skirts so as not to trip she ran along the path to the brook. Thankful for the protective cover of the foliage she stopped an instant to catch her breath. She ran along the brook up to its source on the edge of the forest. She glanced behind. Good. No one following. Hurrying, she half ran under the canopy of leaves, slowed by the scrub of saplings and bushes. Further and further she pressed on, not thinking, not bothered that sharp twigs snagged her skirts and cut her ankles. Her coif slid down her back releasing her hair to fall in her eyes. Sweat trickled down her face; mosquitoes whined and bit and stuck to her skin. Her head throbbed so she was only dimly aware of birdsong and the cawing of crows overhead. As the minutes passed Priscilla slowed to a walk. She wiped the sweat from her face and stinging eyes. The sun was low enough in the sky to blind her. Her initial spurt of energy gone she felt her strength draining, her legs growing heavy. When eventually she saw a clearing ahead, graced with a few boulders, she allowed herself to stop. She selected a flat, moss covered rock and sat gazing up through the leaves spreading high above, allowing shafts of sunlight to filter through, home to dancing particles of dust and tiny insects. Her head felt fuzzy; there was a humming sound in her ears; she knew she was fainting and didn't care. She slumped and fell onto the ground.

On waking, Priscilla choked from the stench. She was held tight in the grasp of an Indian brave, carried as if a babe. She knew it was useless to struggle. She was too weak and if she did break free she would be caught again. But the smell of bear grease made her want to retch. What would he do with her? Torture? Rape? Slavery? It was dark. Where was she? How far had he carried her? Would she be scalped? This brave's trophy? He loped along. The moon shone bright. Wolves howled. An owl hooted. She saw glowing green eyes in the scrub. With one swift movement the brave put her down, and standing on her skirt, drew his bow and shot an arrow. The green eyes were no more. He picked her up again and loped on, smoothly, silently.

When he stopped they were in a large clearing dotted with round, domed huts shaped rather like the beehives Priscilla remembered from England. He carried her to the entrance of one of these and called softly. An Indian woman came out; she and the brave spoke. The woman took Priscilla's hand and led her inside. She bade her sit by the fire in the center of the room where smoke spiraled up through a hole in the roof. Clay pots sat amongst the ashes and hanging from the roof were bundles of dried plants. Priscilla sat on rushes that covered the earth floor. The air was fetid, rank. Try as she might, she could not stop herself from choking and coughing. The Indian woman handed her a gourd of water and smiled. Slowly, Priscilla recognized her. She was the squaw with the papoose – in the settlement when Squanto had shown them how to plant the corn. She almost wept with relief. The Indian pointed to herself, 'Aijana'. Priscilla did the same. They practiced saying each other's names as Aijana took one of the clay pots from the ashes and dished a serving of cornmush onto a wooden plate, indicating Priscilla should eat. She then gave her a clay cup containing a warm herbal liquid. Priscilla drank, and dizzy with exhaustion, let herself be led to a pallet by the wall of the hut. Aijana covered her with a bearskin. She fell into a deep dreamless sleep.

A throbbing in her ears roused her. She tried to sit up but collapsed, unable to combat her wooziness. She lay still. The throbbing sound intensified. She realized it wasn't in her head; it was soft drumming outside. Aijana came to her bringing another dish of cornmush. She helped Priscilla to sit up and eat and handed her the gourd of spring water. She then pulled Priscilla to her feet and led her outside to join the many women and children sitting in a large circle round a fire where warriors, painted and glistening, began to dance, circling the fire. As the drumbeat grew louder and more rapid, the warriors shrieked and wailed, reaching their arms to the sky, bowing, raising their knees. Faster and faster, increasingly frenzied, they sliced the air and the flames with their knives. The blades sparkled.

Priscilla's fear grew to terror. Had Aijana drugged her? Were they preparing to kill her? Was Aijana's kindness a trick? She couldn't breathe. She gasped and vomited. She moaned and wept, bowed over, clutching her stomach. 'Mother, Mother.'

A warrior shouted. Silence. Priscilla looked up. The warriors stood, bows and arrows poised, pointing – not at her. She followed their aim. John Alden! Like a tall blond statue, he stood on the edge of the clearing. At a command a number of the warriors dispersed into the forest; *to search for more white men?* Keeping his bow and arrow poised, the lead Indian who had carried Priscilla here strode to John. John pointed to Priscilla and took a step toward her. The Indian grunted and barred his way.

Weakened by terror and the potion, Priscilla could only reach out to John beseeching, 'Please… please.' She tried to stand, stumbled toward him and fell. With a questioning frown the Indian stepped one step back. Ignoring the arrow aimed at him, John leapt to kneel beside Priscilla, taking her in his arms, murmuring, soothing as she wept.

Aijana bade the clustering, jabbering women be gone. She beckoned John to carry Priscilla to her hut. Priscilla could not stop shaking. Aijana offered her another potion but she refused and would not release her grasp locked round John's neck.

In the morning Priscilla woke to a vision of sunlight streaming through the door of the hut. Her back was pressed against a body and arms held her, John Alden's arms. Was this a dream? She took a deep breath; pinched her cheek, and knowing she was safe, drifted away into a contented sleep.

Later that morning the lead warrior introduced himself. 'Tinsin.' He indicated that Aijana was his squaw. Priscilla took Aijana's hands in hers. Aijana smiled, kissed her cheek and gave her a small basket woven from slender stalks. Priscilla marveled at the intricate many-colored patterns. 'Thank you, thank you.' She bowed.

Tinsin led Priscilla and John to an Indian trail which would take them back to their settlement. He saluted, gestured 'goodbye' and disappeared into the forest.

As they followed the trail hand in hand, John talked about the previous day. 'When Standish returned from proposing to you he was puce red with rage and hurt pride. He said you had run off – to the brook, he thought. When evening came and you hadn't returned I slipped away unseen to find you. You'd left a trail a blind person could follow – until the clearing. Then nothing.'

'That was where Tinsin found me.'

'I guessed. The Indians know how to navigate the forest leaving no trace. When I heard drumming and shrieking I followed the sound.'

'I was so frightened. Aijana was kind, but the warriors; I thought they were preparing to torture me, kill me.'

'Reckon they supposed you had reason to flee the colony; perhaps were invoking the spirits for guidance what to do with you. When Tinsin saw you try to come to me, he decided to let you go.'

Priscilla pulled him to a stop. 'Why, John? Why have you ignored me so long? What happened?'

'I am sorry, very sorry. I could see you were suffering. Mistress Brewster said I was to leave you alone while you recovered from your illness. As you may know, Captain Standish is my truest friend. He often confided how much he desired you and on the day of the Winslow wedding he told me Mistress and Elder Brewster indicated he should ask for your hand.'

'Why did you not protest? Why did you not tell the Brewsters of my father's consent you should court me?'

'I am only a cooper.' John looked at the ground. 'Do you remember when we were on the *Mayflower* and I said that in this new land status wouldn't matter? I thought I would be valued solely for my ability. I was wrong. There are no lords and ladies among us, but men who own lands and have had positions in court are more highly esteemed.' He took Priscilla's hands. 'I have no estate. Captain Standish can provide so much more than I. He was hopeful you would say "yes"; said there were signs you cared for him. Also, I knew from when we first met, position is important to you.'

Priscilla squeezed his hands. 'I never gave Captain Standish cause to hope.' She bowed her head. 'But you are right; at the beginning of the voyage I was seeking to wed into a high position. But now I see.'

'I had no way of knowing that, as I hadn't so much as set eyes on you for weeks. I couldn't bring myself to betray Standish. But now I have. He may never forgive me.' He put his hands on Priscilla's shoulders, looked into her eyes. She waited, searching his face.

'Priscilla, it is you I desire, more than all else. Will you have me to wed?'

'Yes, John, I will.'

'Are you sure, Priscilla? God knows how we'll be greeted. They may turn us out.'

'I'm sure. I'll be true to you always.'

He held her close.

Several minutes passed before they walked on. 'Do you want to stay in this settlement ruled by the Pilgrims?' Priscilla asked. 'I'd vowed to return to England if I couldn't have you to wed.'

John said nothing, considering. Then, 'Reckon we should stay. It is a land full of fishes, fowl, game, fruits and endless trees. A vast land. Remember your father's dream; to prosper and build a good life for our children. You and I together can do that. Without you, I'd have returned to England.'

Priscilla laughed, and was startled by the sound of her own laughter. It was a sound she'd not heard for months. She gazed up through the forest canopy, sunlight filtering through, birds singing. ''Tis beautiful now.' She pondered a moment. 'Promise me, if we stay in this settlement, we'll not be cowed by the likes of Mistress Brewster.'

'I promise.' John hugged her.

It was late afternoon when John and Priscilla emerged from the forest to descend the hill to the cluster of houses that made up the colony. There weren't many folk about: a party working in the fields and a squad building a house on the far side of the clearing. It was the time of day when women were indoors bent over the hearth, so the couple passed unnoticed as John escorted Priscilla to the Brewster house. The door was open.

'Good day, Mistress Brewster,' John said and led Priscilla across the room to the hearth. Mistress Brewster, startled, looked up from stirring the pot.

'So you've decided to return have you? Wretched lass, causing us all to fret.' She scowled. 'Suppose now you expect welcome and forgiving.'

A tightly coiled rage rose up inside Priscilla. 'No, Mistress Brewster. It is you who should ask **my** forgiveness.' Her tone was calm and measured. 'All these months I have been ill with pining, no hunger and confused, weakened – all because of your meddling.' She fixed the older woman with her stare. 'I will **not** marry Captain Standish, **ever**, or any other man in this colony except for Mr Alden. I love him and he says he loves me. We are betrothed.'

'She speaks true,' John said. 'I love her and she says she'll have me.'

Mistress Brewster pushed past them, hurrying out the door. Some minutes later she returned with the Elder. He addressed John.

'Mr Alden. You have caused serious upset. Captain Standish was most distressed and angry. Said he'd not stand to be made a fool and betrayed as you have done. He has taken a small party and gone exploring.'

'I am truly sorry for that, sir.'

'I have been conversing with Master Winslow. He offers you victuals this evening. Mistress Mullins will stay with us of course. Master Winslow and Governor Bradford and I will consult on this matter in the morning.'

'Yes, sir. However, please understand, Mistress Mullins and I **will** marry.'

That evening Priscilla sat at table with the Brewster family. Except for prayers the Elder and Mistress Brewster remained silent. Priscilla did not care. Her heart was full; she ate with relish, and asked for more, complimenting Mistress Brewster on her excellent fare, enjoying her scowl.

The sun was high in the sky when Master Winslow summoned Priscilla from her labor, boiling linen, and John from his work building another house. Governor Bradford answered Winslow's knock. They entered the dim room and sat where Bradford indicated, on one side of a large table, facing Winslow, Bradford and Elder Brewster. The Elder spoke.

'We understand that you intend to marry. Whilst we regret your unseemly behavior, we have agreed to your union on condition you have a year's supervised courtship. Unlike the Winslows you are young and 'tis the custom. During this year Mr Alden will reside with Governor Bradford and receive tuition in the way of the Church of Christ. Mistress Mullins will continue to reside with us. The two of you may meet on Sabbath evenings in the company of Mistress Brewster and myself.'

'Thank you, sir, for your proposal,' John said. 'I will consult with Mistress Mullins and we will decide whether to accept your terms.'

'What?' the Elder stammered. 'Consult... decide?'

Priscilla wanted to laugh. She caught a twinkle in Winslow's eye and a smile twitching his lips.

Priscilla agreed with John that if they chose to make their way in this colony, they should, for the sake of goodwill, accept the leaders' terms. However, she wilted knowing she would have to wait a whole long year before she could lie in John Alden's arms again.

Chapter 31

May 1621

Hobbamock

Heavy with remorse, John entered Standish's house to collect his belongings. He stopped still a moment in the familiar quiet room. The captain's writing table stood against the opposite wall and above it was the shelf John had put up to hold his selection of books. He stepped over to the shelf and took down *The Iliad*, letting it fall open at random. He could pick out only a few words here and there, but he remembered pleasurable evenings when, by the light of a pine knot and the flames on the hearth, Standish read aloud passages of Homer's heroic verse. The captain became a different person then, his voice melodious and full as he read of Hector and Achilles. *He said he'd teach me to read.* John wistfully returned the book to its place. *I pray he forgives me. He has been a good and loyal friend.* Slowly, he packed his clothes into his knapsack, reflecting that a shirt and breeches were in Priscilla's pile of mending. He took his musket down from the wall and with a last fond look round the room, stepped out into the bright day, closing the door behind him.

He walked slowly down the slope toward Bradford's house. *A whole year lodging with Bradford. An entire year of religious instruction. Fie on Mistress Brewster for insisting and on the Elder for agreeing. It is too long. Priscilla agrees. How is it? There are more folk here who do not belong willingly to the Church of Christ than those who embrace it. And yet we are all expected to follow, without question, the rules laid down by the leaders of this new church. Doesn't seem right.* Then he recalled Master Mullins' advice. 'We must all pull together or we'll perish. The Pilgrims have led us from the start. They are strong leaders. If pulling together means following them, so be it.'

Aye. He was a wise man. And I am betrothed to his daughter. This long year will be a torment, but a sweet torment compared with what we've been through. Poor Priscilla, a brave woman, **my** *woman.*

Two weeks passed with no sign of Captain Standish. The entire colony was tense with waiting. Without him who would organize defense? Who would command should there be wars with the Indians, or other European settlers?

John could not sleep for fretting. Had the captain and his men got hopelessly lost? Been killed? If so, their lives lay at his feet. *Please God, let them return safe. I don't expect forgiveness, but let them be alive.* This was his prayer every hour.

Today a search party would set out. John wanted to go but was advised 'no' as the state of Standish's temper was unknown. When he left, the captain was in a mood to shoot John dead. With the Brewsters and Priscilla, John walked up the hill to the edge of the forest to bid the search party goodbye. Led by Winslow, they would follow the trail Tinsin had shown John and Priscilla. The cool forest beckoned. He longed to disappear among the trees and give his all to searching.

'Halloo… Halloo…'

'It's Standish!' John whirled round.

Winslow held him back. 'You stay here.'

With Priscilla's hand in his, and Mistress Brewster standing on his other side, John watched as Brewster, Winslow and Bradford led their troop down the hill to meet Captain Standish and his small group as they entered the colony from the direction of the brook.

'Praise God he's safely returned,' Mistress Brewster said. 'A fine man and captain he is. His loss would be a severe blow to our colony, unlike some I could mention.'

John felt Priscilla stiffen as she tightened her grasp on his hand. For himself, he was too relieved to care, and in this instance he rather agreed with Mistress Brewster. The thought flitted through his mind, *I would like to be valued as Standish is, one day.*

He was the same proud Standish, half-strutting as he walked toward the welcoming group which was increasing in number as folk came running from dwellings and fields to greet their captain. He and his small band carried the fruits of their hunting: deer, water fowl, a turkey and even a wolf. In addition, beside Captain Standish strode an Indian warrior of extraordinary stature and dignity, even surpassing Massasoit. Folk stared, silent.

'What?' John exclaimed, wishing they could hear what was said. Captain Standish introduced the Indian and in response Bradford, Winslow and Brewster bowed deeply, as they would to royalty. The Indian nodded, receiving their obeisance. He stood quietly, staring straight ahead while Standish conversed earnestly with the colony's leaders, gesturing and smiling.

Governor Bradford looked up the hill and beckoned to John. He squeezed Priscilla's hand and strode toward the group. He hadn't taken many steps before he saw Standish grinning in his direction. He broke into a run, and happily, eagerly, grasped his friend's outstretched hands.

'Standish – you're back. Thank God.'

'Aye. Congratulations, John. 'Tis for the best.' Standish turned to face the Indian. 'Meet Hobbamock.' John bowed deeply as he had seen the others do.

Elder Brewster spoke. 'You must all come to my house and eat. I'm sure the womenfolk will cook up enough pottage. Come with me.'

John walked alongside Standish, Hobbamock on the other side. He took the chance to speak quietly in his friend's ear. 'Thank God you are safely back and thank you for forgiving me. Bradford said I should move in with him, to receive religious instruction, so that's where I am.'

'It works out,' Standish said. 'Hobbamock will live with me.'

They entered the Brewster house following Bradford and Winslow. Elder Brewster indicated that Standish, Hobbamock, Winslow, Bradford and Squanto should sit with him at the table. Everyone else to sit on the cushions strewn on the floor.

John lowered himself onto a cushion beside John Howland and reveled in watching Priscilla as she hurried to greet Susanna Winslow and Lizzie Tilley, helping them through the door with their large pots of pottage which they hung over the fire. Priscilla was flushed, her deep blue eyes sparkling. Susanna and Lizzie left to return to their own homes.

Raising his hand for silence, Elder Brewster offered a short prayer of thanksgiving for Captain Standish's safe return. 'And now we will eat.'

Mistress Brewster served the men seated at the table; Priscilla served those seated on cushions. She brought a trencher full of pottage for John to share with John Howland. John looked up into her face. Everything about her was dancing and merry.

'I'll bring your tankards in a trice,' she said gaily.

'Congratulations,' Howland said. 'She's a pretty, merry lass of a sudden. Never seen such a change from misery to joy. You've perked up a fair amount too.'

'Aye,' John said. 'It was a near run thing. Word goes round you and Lizzie Tilley are courting.'

'Aye. I'd fancy to have her to wife, and she shows she loves me, but I'm only a servant, and her father was a silk worker, member of a London guild.' He eyed the table. 'I know there's some think I'm setting myself too high to be wanting Lizzie.'

Priscilla swooped over bearing two tankards of beer. 'Would you like some more pottage?' she asked, tilting her head to one side and smiling. 'I'm sure I could find some in the bottom of the pot.'

'Oh, yes. Thank ye, ma'am,' Howland said.

Priscilla gave him a wink and took the trencher, brushing her leg against John. He looked up at her and grinned, blushing.

'You will be a pair, you two,' Howland said.

When the company had all eaten and filled their pipes, Captain Standish stood and formally introduced his Indian companion. 'Meet Hobbamock, a special envoy from Massasoit.' He motioned for the Indian to stand and bowed in respect. He then addressed Squanto. 'Would you please explain Hobbamock's position?'

John thought Squanto looked rather discomfited. He stood and spoke; 'Hobbamock is a "pinese", that is, a priest, warrior and statesman to the chief. The training for this position is long and hard. Only a few ever achieve it and they are under special protection of the gods.' Squanto bowed to Hobbamock and then added, 'But Hobbamock has not been to England. He does not speak English as I do. He does not know the ways of the white man as I do. I am more valuable to you than Hobbamock.' Squanto cast a look of dislike at the pinese and sat down. Captain Standish and Hobbamock remained standing.

Standish said, 'I had lost my way. It is easy to lose one's bearings in the forest and we had been wandering for several days. Hobbamock appeared. He said he belongs with Massasoit and he led us home. He will stay with me in my house for Massasoit has commanded him to stay in our colony.'

John saw Squanto scowl. *He is jealous. I wonder if Massasoit sent Hobbamock to keep an eye on us and Squanto, and report back. I like the look of him. He seems true.* His thoughts ran on. *I'll be able to ask Priscilla what she thinks.* He felt an excited happiness, going forward in this new land, with all its adventures, with Priscilla at his side; lovely, clever, spirited Priscilla, and with Standish, his friend.

The First Summer

Chapter 32

June 1621

Expedition to Massasoit's camp

In the cool misty blue-gray light of a summer's dawn, one by one the expedition party left their dwellings to gather by the fort. John stood quiet, gazing eastwards toward the harbor as the sun rose over the horizon spreading flame red streaks across the glassy water. This morning, still and gentle, he thought of the *Mayflower*, the storms, the deaths. How far they had come, only five women and twenty-plus men surviving. Lots of children. John reckoned there must be upwards of fifteen. Especially he thought of Priscilla. He had come so close to losing her. Although honored and eager to go on this expedition, he was almost afraid to leave her lest she come to harm, especially from Mr Prence. The wretched man continued to pursue Priscilla as if he were betrothed to her himself. He lurked everywhere and was a constant caller for studies with Elder Brewster.

Ah, there. With Susanna Winslow and the Brewsters, leaning forward, holding her skirts in her hands, with short quick steps she hurried to him. He longed to take her and hold her close, but such a display would not be tolerated. So he made do with clasping her hands in his, holding her with his eyes, and whispering, 'I love you.' She nodded and tried to smile, her eyes brimming with tears.

'Mr Alden,' Winslow called.

Letting go Priscilla's hands, John strode through the fields, joining the others as they entered the forest. Knowing the day would be hot, with a long trek ahead, he was glad of the green canopy above. He had been surprised when Winslow chose him along with Squanto and Hopkins to come on this expedition. They reckoned to be gone about four days and Winslow had said he wanted an accomplished woodsman, efficient at putting up a shelter and a good marksman, and someone who could be relied upon to behave appropriately in Massasoit's camp. The colony's leaders had decided it would be wise to pay a courtesy visit to the big chief to cement the Indians' commitment to trade exclusively with Plymouth, and to beg him to rein back the numerous Indians who, with their wives and children, repeatedly came to Plymouth demanding food and drink as had been served to the big chief when the treaty was signed.

Squanto found the trail. The earth was packed hard. John looked round, enchanted. Sunlight filtered down through the treetops onto the forest floor. There was little undergrowth.

'One could easily ride a horse along here.'

'Aye,' Winslow agreed. 'One day. When the colony is well established.'

'The birds are making a racket,' Hopkins said.

'They don't like us being here,' Squanto replied.

The four walked briskly, single file.

'What is this?' John asked. At the front, he was the first to come upon a circle cut into the forest floor, about a foot wide and a foot deep. The four men gathered round and Squanto explained, 'This is a memory hole. There are many. They mark places where an important event happened, going back, way far back to the beginning of our time. It is our duty to maintain the holes and to remember and repeat the stories to our companions and children so that our history is not lost. We remember from the beginning. Our stories are in us, in our being.'

John stood in silent respect, as did Winslow and Hopkins. They walked on, through lands that had clearly once been inhabited and cultivated – now empty. Squanto swept his arm in a wide arc. 'All our people… wiped out by the plague.' *The plague brought by us Europeans*, John frowned. *The tribe is hanging by a thread. The memory holes keep them going.*

Chattering, laughing voices carried unseen from behind. About a dozen Indian men, women and children, carrying baskets full of lobsters, came running to join them. The children were fascinated by John, pointing in delighted amazement at his blond hair. They danced about him, brown eyes merry and sparkling, pulling at his breeches and jerkin, jumping up wanting to touch the blond curls. John wished he could linger and play with them. He remembered Priscilla asking the Indian squaw if she could hold her papoose that day in the fields. Then when she ran, shouting 'Stop' as Francis Billington was about to shoot a bow and arrow. *She didn't know I couldn't keep my eyes off her.* He smiled to himself.

'Where have these Indians come from?' Winslow asked Squanto.

'From Plymouth Harbor,' Squanto replied. 'This is the season when lobster is plentiful so we go to harvest as much as we can. We fish and hunt wherever there is a good supply of food in season. These Indians are on their way home to Nemasket.'

''Tis good fortune we have peaceful relations with these Indians,' Winslow mused. Pausing in his stride, placing his hand on John's arm, he said, 'Otherwise your blond scalp would be a highly prized possession.'

John shuddered. 'Aye. It is vital we have good understanding and trust with Massasoit. But that depends on Squanto and now on Hobbamock as well.'

Winslow nodded. 'Could be tricky.'

Eventually, the trail joined a river. Squanto stopped. Sweeping his arm in an open palmed gesture of welcome, he said, 'The Titicut.

Our highway. It carries goods and gives us many fish.' As if to prove the truth of his words, at sunset they came upon another group of Nemasket Indians who had made a weir to catch striped bass and herring. In startled response to Squanto's 'Hail' they secured their fish and hurried over, clustering round the group of weary English much as the Indian children had earlier. Gesturing toward their open-air camp in the adjoining fields, they invited the travelers to stay the night.

'We provide you with fish to eat,' Squanto interpreted.

'And we provide a partridge,' Winslow said.

These Indians are so hospitable and affectionate, John mused. *It isn't surprising they expect similar hospitality from us.*

Despite the stony ground, and the Indians' snoring and sing-song sleeping moaning, John slept soundly, under the stars.

They were up and off at daybreak with six of the Nemasket braves who had decided to come with them. Breakfast was a few pieces of hardtack, shared as they walked. Their trail continued to follow the river. The forest was quiet in the cool early morning; rays of hazy sunlight filtering through the trees and sparkling water. As if reluctant to disturb the early morning peace, the group walked in silence – even the Indians.

Judging by the place of the sun in the sky, John reckoned it was mid-morning when the Indians stopped and pointed at the river. Squanto explained it was necessary to cross and the water was shallow enough here to wade, so they should take off their boots and breeches.

John removed his boots and tying the laces, hung them round his neck. When he, Winslow and Hopkins were all bootless and without their breeches, muskets and belongings held high, the crossing began. Near the bank the river bottom was thick squidgy mud and the water warm. But a few feet further out, they stumbled on stones, some of them sharp, and the water was waist high and cold, with a strong current pulling. No one uttered a sound, but John could see that like himself, Winslow and Hopkins both stumbled and winced. The Indians, whose feet were tough as leather from going barefoot, had no trouble. They kindly offered to carry the white men's belongings so they could use their arms to balance – an offer gratefully accepted. However, each kept hold of his musket.

Halfway across, piercing, shrill cries froze Indians and settlers alike. John stopped and peered into the riverbank grasses, musket ready. He spied two Indians crouched low, running through the tall grasses and reeds, bows drawn, ready to shoot. The Nemasket Indians called out. John held his breath. The two strangers relaxed, put their arrows back in their quivers and beckoned in welcome.

Relieved to reach the other side without falling over, John flopped down in the long rough grass, grateful for the hot sun to warm his torso and dry his shirt. He checked his feet for cuts. He was lucky but Hopkins' feet were bleeding. As Winslow wrapped linen strips round Hopkins' feet the Indians shook their heads and pointed. *They can't believe our feet are so soft, the skin so thin.*

Re-clothed with breeches and boots, the party set out again. Squanto explained that the two strange Indians, both elderly, over sixty, were the only survivors from a village wiped out by the plague. They feared attack by the Narragansetts who often raided plague-weakened villages in this area.

The midday sun beat down and John wiped the sweat from his brow. There was no breeze this far inland and the weeds and thistles, head high, scratched his face. The Indians took pity on the suffering English and offered to carry their corselets and jackets, and their bags of possessions. All three gratefully accepted, once again keeping only their muskets in hand.

'This is a fine stretch,' Winslow said. 'The undulating hills remind me of England, and just look at those magnificent trees! Oak, beech, fir, walnut – and the chestnuts are massive!'

It was a long, hot trek, and several more times they encountered small groups of Indians carrying their seashore harvest of roasted crab, fish and shellfish. As the afternoon wore on the sun lessened its heat, casting long shadows. By the time they reached Massasoit's village, the English were tired and very hungry.

Squaws, children and braves greeted them in great excitement, chattering and running about. Big Chief Massasoit wasn't there, but hopefully wasn't far away. Two braves departed to find him. Squanto told the English they should greet Massasoit with a discharge from their muskets. John was the first to lift his firearm in readiness. But his action sent the women and children running away screaming in terror.

'You'd best find them and explain we mean no harm,' Winslow said to Squanto. Squanto did as he was bid and brought the women and children back. Massasoit strode into his domain not many minutes later. The military salute pleased him greatly. He grinned and held up both hands in greeting. Winslow stepped forward with a copper chain and the red horseman's coat which had covered Samoset's nakedness, now embellished with a white lace collar and cuffs, sewn on by Mary Brewster. Squanto stood with him to interpret.

'Your Highness,' Winslow said. 'We present you with this coat and chain as a token of our continuing desire always to be at peace with you, our nearest neighbors. Your people come visiting very often, with wives and children, and they are welcome, but we, still being strangers in this land, do not yet know how our corn will grow, and much as we desire to give them entertainment, we fear lest we be lacking in food. We are always happy to provide a meal if you yourself wish to visit us, or any special friend of yours, and we would know him if he brought the copper chain.'

Massasoit smiled and vehemently nodded in agreement. 'Yah, Yah.' He motioned for one of his braves to drape the coat round his shoulders like a cape. The attendant then lifted the copper chain over the chief's head. With a flourish, displaying his lace cuffs, Massasoit walked in a large circle, proclaiming, 'I am King James' man.' The circle completed, he beckoned his guests to come into his wigwam.

Good! Food at last. John was eager.

Massasoit motioned for all his braves to gather round. The chief sat cross-legged on the ground, and his braves and the English followed suit, forming a large circle. John cast a quick glance round, hoping to see a fire and a cooking pot. *Nothing. Perhaps the women are cooking in another wigwam.*

Massasoit asked Winslow if he had any further messages.

Winslow said, 'Yes, Your Honor. In the course of our early explorations, when we first anchored, we took some corn which we found buried in the ground. We would like to repay whoever owned the corn with whatever commodities they desire.' He paused as Massasoit nodded his approval. The chief then looked at Winslow as if to say, 'Anything else?'

'There is one further matter,' Winslow continued. 'We desire exceedingly to trade beaver skins with you and your people; that you and your people bring skins to us and not to other Europeans who may come to these shores.'

Massasoit nodded again. *He understands, he understands completely.* John was admiring. *But I am* **so** *hungry.*

The chief then embarked on a discourse, enumerating by name at least thirty different tribes, pledging their adherence to Winslow's requests. When he came to the end of this seemingly endless speech, he slowly lit his pipe. Then he frowned and shifted himself. *What next?* John wondered. Massasoit turned and murmured in Squanto's ear.

'The chief is delighted to see you,' Squanto said. 'But he greatly regrets he has no food to offer you. They have eaten up everything from their last hunting expedition and need to hunt again to replenish their stores.'

'Ah – we understand,' Winslow said.

Now Massasoit's face was wreathed in smiles of relief. He took a long, leisurely pull on his pipe and embarked on a discourse about the good land called England. 'My allegiance is with King James,' Squanto interpreted. 'The French traders will no longer be welcome in Narragansett Bay.'

As the hour was late, Winslow asked if they might settle for the night. Eager to give what hospitality he could, the sachem directed the three English to sleep with him and his wife on their platform; they at one end, the English at the other. John and Winslow and Hopkins arranged themselves head to toe.

'Should we keep our muskets by us?' John asked Winslow. Winslow thought a moment. 'We don't want to appear untrusting. We'll put them on the floor at the end. I'll lie at the foot where I can grab them if need be.'

At last. John settled himself between Winslow and Hopkins. *An empty belly, but sleep will be welcome.* He was closing his eyes when two more bodies descended onto the platform: two of Massasoit's braves. *How would they all fit?* Up for a rearrangement. Settled again, there were no more moving bodies. But...'What is that?' John whispered to Hopkins.

'Damned if they aren't singing, if you can call it that,' Hopkins whispered back.

'Why?' John asked. 'Are they singing themselves to sleep?'

'Guess so,' Hopkins answered. 'Damn these mosquitoes – they're eating my ears. And the whining is as bad as the singing.'

'Oh, Lord have mercy!' John's attempts to whisper nearly failed. 'This place is full of fleas jumping and lice crawling. I wish we could sleep outside.'

'Forbearance, men forbearance,' Winslow whispered.

Morning dawned at last and they could escape from the wigwam, the cool, fresh air soothing their bitten faces. John wished he could go and bathe in the river to get rid of the lice and fleas. However, the day was given to entertainment; games of chance and demonstrations of prowess. The village swelled in numbers as several minor sachems arrived, eager to set eyes on the Englishmen and witness their renowned shooting skills.

'Ooh, ooh, aah,' came the awed moans as John fired a round of small shot, filling his target with holes.

The sun was past midday when two braves walked into the camp bearing two large striped bass. The women quickly got a fire going, with a tripod over it to roast the fish. But two fish didn't go far amongst nearly fifty people and the English were careful not to take more than a bite.

'How do they keep going, not eating for days at a time?' John asked Winslow.

'I don't know,' Winslow said. ''Tis strange. I wonder whether our visit is preventing them from going hunting.'

The second night was just as bad as the first, and next morning, to John's relief, Winslow decided they must make for home or they would have no strength left.

Massasoit again said how sorry and ashamed he was that they had no food for his visitors. But he was eager to pledge his support and help. He decided Squanto should remain with him, and travel to all the villages, to explain they must trade with the English and not the French. He appointed a trusted brave, Tokamahamon, to guide his visitors back to Plymouth and remain there, at least until Squanto returned.

'Thank you, Winslow,' John said as they set off. 'I am about ready to faint from hunger and no sleep.'

'Likewise,' Hopkins agreed. 'But we did well. Massasoit seems pleased and you secured an excellent trade agreement, Winslow.'

The four men settled into an even pace, John falling into step beside Winslow. 'Thank you, sir, for bringing me along... seeing first-hand how the Indians live... and your skill in parley... I fully understand how we depend on their goodwill and knowledge, or we could perish.'

'Aye. You understand rightly. We *must* live peaceably with Massasoit's tribes – and amongst ourselves.'

After this brief conversation the day's trek passed in silence, the exhausted walkers giving all their concentration to placing one foot in front of the other. As before, they met with several groups of traveling Indians, who gave them a few of their harvest of fish.

As dusk closed round them, Tokamahamon sniffed the air and looked up at the sky. 'Rain,' he said. He motioned for them to stay where they were and dashed off disappearing into the shadows.

Long minutes passed.

'What can he be doing?' Winslow fretted.

'I need to pass water,' Hopkins said and pushed his way through the undergrowth into the forest. John scanned the blurring outlines of the trees, merging in the shadowy gray dusk.

'Aah,' a scream. Silence.

John leapt into the shrubs where Hopkins had gone. About fifty yards into the forest, Hopkins lay flat, his leg caught in a trap. John followed the direction of his paralyzed gaze. Lurking in the shadows, shaking its head, pawing the ground, a black bear sniffed and slowly padded toward the detected scent. John cocked his musket and waited, the bear's head in his sights. When the beast was within close enough range, it rose on its hind legs. John aimed at the side of its head and fired. The bear growled, began to charge. John fired, again, again, and again. Confused, in pain the beast lumbered about, this way and that. John had to reload. From behind, an arrow whistled past his head, lodging in the bear's eye. It lunged and pawed. Another arrow and another, arrow on arrow until the bear lay still. Tokamahamon strode silently to collect his arrows. He prodded the black fur with his foot and leapt aside as the beast raised its paw in a dying swipe.

John knelt beside Hopkins and loosed the trap – a deer trap. With John taking his weight Hopkins got to his feet and gingerly tested his leg. He couldn't put all his weight on it but it wasn't broken. With John's support he hobbled to join Winslow.

Winslow pronounced a bad sprain and bound it tightly.

Tokamahamon led them to a small clearing, a good place to camp.

The sound of rain roused the party just before daybreak. Sustained only by sleep and a few bites of fish, the four set off. Hour after hour they labored in the pouring rain, stopping only once to exchange greetings with some passing Indians. Their clothes were so drenched they didn't bother taking off breeches and boots to cross the river. Every footstep squelched and the water added weight to their load. With Hopkins restricted to a hobble, progress was slow. John's feet were very sore; it was becoming ever harder work to put one foot in front of the other. Tokamahamon, unencumbered and fit, could have walked at least twice as fast, but he patiently kept pace with the English.

'It feels like late afternoon,' Winslow said. 'But with no sun it is difficult to tell.' Tokamahamon gestured and pointed up the trail and made a picture of a wigwam with his hands. He ran off ahead.

'I hope we don't have another night in the forest,' Hopkins said. 'Surely we must be nearly there.'

They plodded on. Another half-mile went by when Tokamahamon came running back, smiling, beckoning them to hurry.

John could have whooped for joy as they emerged from the trail into the edge of the settlement and saw a group of folk hurrying to meet them. 'Yes! Priscilla! Light-headed and shaking, John half ran, half stumbled to meet her and clasped her tight in his arms. He didn't hear the disapproving *Harrumphs* and he knew she didn't either.

'Priscilla!' Mary Brewster's sharp tone pulled her out of John's embrace. 'Hurry along with me now to prepare the victuals. The men need to get into dry clothes.'

'Oh John,' Priscilla murmured. 'You're back, alive and well, oh, thank the Lord.'

Chapter 33

June 1621

Mr Prence's first ruse against John

Pigeons

By Bradford's hearth John rubbed down with linen towels and donned dry clothes. He reckoned he'd have to endure wet feet for days as his only pair of boots squelched with water. No matter. All he wanted now was to see Priscilla and to eat.

With Bradford he hurried to the Brewster house.

'Come in, come in,' Elder Brewster opened the door wide to Bradford's knock. 'Welcome,' he ushered John and Bradford to the hearth. Priscilla looked up from stirring the pot, smiling and flushed from running ahead of the men.

'Take off those wet boots, Mr Alden, and your hosen. They can begin to dry by the hearth.'

John gratefully did as the Elder bade, and took his place at table.

The Elder bowed his head to say grace. 'Amen.' Sitting up straight, he said, 'Now, ladies, may we have some food?'

John ate with gusto and basked in Priscilla's adoring delight. After the third trencherful he said, 'Thank you, Mistress Brewster. That was delicious. I should sleep well tonight.'

When the trenchers and tankards were cleared, Elder Brewster lit his pipe. 'Now, Mr Alden,' he said. 'Tell us all that happened.'

John told them about the Indian trail, and the memory holes, and the Nemasket Indians, and crossing the river, and the Indians' bedtime customs. 'It will be good to sleep in a quiet room again,' he said. Priscilla sat entranced. When he told of Hopkins' mishap and the encounter with the bear, Priscilla clapped her hands on her cheeks, eyes wide.

Seeing her thus, John was overwhelmed with longing to be with her, in their own bed, in their own home. As he resumed his story his eyelids drooped; his speech slurred. He was fighting to stay awake.

'I think I'd better put him to bed.' Bradford roused John, helped him put his wet boots back on and led him to the door.

Someone shaking his shoulder woke John from a deep sleep. 'I'm sorry... I've already let you sleep late,' Bradford said.

'Aye, sir,' John mumbled as he pulled on his breeches and damp boots.

Bradford motioned him to sit by the hearth, offering him a meager portion of hardtack and salt beef. 'There is a matter I need to mention.' The governor drew up a stool and leaned toward John, elbows resting on his thighs, hands clasped. 'I asked Mr Prence to take charge of the stores in your absence.'

'But sir, I had already given that responsibility to Mr Howland.'

'Elder Brewster is favorably impressed with Mr Prence, his eagerness to adopt the ways of our church. He and I agreed Mr Prence would be better suited, more mature and trustworthy.'

John looked at the ceiling, then at the floor. He felt a flush creeping up his neck.

'The point is,' Bradford continued. 'Mr Prence found a hole in the barrel of barley. He said it was gnawed through by rats.'

'No. That cannot be true.'

Bradford held up his hand. 'Mr Prence has plugged the hole, cleaned up the mess; but he reports, well, negligence.'

John stood and paced. 'I do not understand.'

'It is not entirely surprising that in your adventures with Mistress Mullins you have been less attentive, and we will let this go as a momentary lapse.'

'Mr Bradford, you know I store the barrels on top of tall plinths I have made in the fashion of staddle stones. Precisely to keep the rats at bay.'

'Mr Prence is an honorable man. He would not...'

'Honorable? You say *honorable* after what happened on the *Mayflower*?'

'That was a mishap. Mr Prence has shown remorse and repented of the incident, and we have no way of knowing; Satan's wiles do inhabit women.'

'Sir! If you are implying...'

'We will leave it there. Mr Winslow is coming to call presently. Good day.' Bradford held the door open.

'Good day, sir.' John strode to the storehouse. *I'm not sure I can survive a year living with that sanctimonious*— He unlocked the door and stepped into his quiet, orderly domain. Checking that barrels of provisions were all as he had left them, he examined the plugged hole in the barrel of barley. *Rather a shoddy job for a first class carriage-maker.* He removed the plug. *This hole was not gnawed by a rat. It was whittled with a knife.* John replaced the plug. *I'll make a proper one later.* He checked all was in order. *No other traps set by that weasel. Right, I see what he's up to. I'll not let on, behave as I should, always polite. I won't give any of these misguided fools cause for complaint. And I have my Priscilla.*

A week passed with no further disturbances. Squanto returned from his tour of the tribes and Tokamahamon stayed on to help in the fields. John took special care to keep a watch on the storehouse, checking often to be sure all was in order. Having completed an early morning inspection, he locked the door and stepped out onto the track.

'Corn... the corn... sprouting...' Her voice, clear as a bell. He ran. As he crossed the clearing, Standish and Hopkins dropped their axes by a half-split log. Winslow and Bradford hurried from Bradford's house. A small Billington child tripped and fell. 'Up wi'ye... oh look, y've gone and cut that knee... breeches stained wi' blood... Fie!'

'Praise be to God. Praise be to God.' Bradford heralded the good news.

'Priscilla, you were the first to see!' John panted, stopping close by her. She beamed.

Squanto stood facing them all and raised his hand for silence. 'Praise to Squanto!' he proclaimed. *Yes Squanto*, John thought. *Praise to you.*

Bradford stepped forward beside Squanto. 'Praise God for Squanto,' he called out.

'Aye, aye, Praise God for Squanto... Praise God for Squanto...' The chant became a chorus. Children danced about and yelled in their high pitched voices, 'Praise God for Squanto...'

Holding down her laughter, Priscilla turned to John. 'Hopefully, everyone will be satisfied – even God,' and clapped her hand over her mouth. John chuckled and whispered, 'Be careful.'

Squanto raised his hand again. Silence. 'Now, today we plant beans and squash and pumpkins on each mound. Before it rains. It will rain soon – be quick! I have the seeds. Fetch your hoes.'

Priscilla looked up at John. 'But I haven't fetched the water yet.'

'I'm sure Squanto will understand about the water. Quick, I'll help you. It's too heavy for you to be lugging anyway.'

As they half-walked, half-ran to the brook, Priscilla panted, 'Thank goodness today isn't the Sabbath, nor the morrow.'

'Aye,' John replied. 'We wouldn't want a disagreement between Governor Bradford and Squanto!'

Trying to hurry, but not splash out too much water, John and Priscilla made two trips.

'I'm all flushed and breathless,' Priscilla exclaimed. 'And I've not even started work in the fields.'

'Aye.' John caressed her cheek. 'And all the prettier for it.'

'Priscilla! Where are you?' Mistress Brewster's shrill call came from within the house.

'Oh, dear,' Priscilla whispered.

'She's here, Mistress,' John called. 'We've fetched your water.' He put his hand on Priscilla's shoulder. 'I'll carry it to the house and fetch two hoes.'

As John bent to pick up the pails of water, a sudden dark cloud and whirring sound stopped him still. Clouds of birds rolled above, silent except for soft beating wings. The sky grew ever darker until there was no sunlight, no blue. The birds dropped out of the sky, all around them.

'Pigeons!' John exclaimed.

'Muskets! All men – muskets!' Standish boomed. 'Women and children to the rendezvous!'

John dropped the pails and ran to fetch his musket, as Priscilla joined the shrieking, crying women and children. Bowed over against pigeons flying round his head, he tripped over birds scouring the ground. Pigeons flew up in his face. Their droppings fell on his head and back and down his neck. He heard the crack of branches breaking under the massive pests, bigger even than the ravens of home.

He stumbled through Bradford's door, grabbed his firearm and stepping out, tripping over pigeons, made his way toward the fields. They must save the corn. It was so dark the other men were anonymous shapes, running through the gloom, shooting. *Please God we don't shoot one another.* He shouted as yellow coat-tails flapped in his line of fire. 'Out of the way – where is your musket?'

'I'll frighten them with my coat-tails,' the high pitched voice squawked.

'You idiot. Begone or you'll be shot.'

In the fields John fired, reloaded, fired, reloaded… hour after hour. *Would he run out of shot?* He spied Squanto and Hobbamock, two blurs, shooting arrows, spearing bird after bird, and with what speed. They chased away one flock and another arrived. How could they save the corn… and without it… nausea from the stench and from fear cramped his belly. Even in his nausea he was hungry.

How many hours passed until no more flocks swooped in, until the evening sun sent rays slanting from the west illuminating a scene of devastation and stink. The ground was covered in pigeon droppings and dead pigeons.

Captain Standish organized men, women and children to clear up. Sacks full of pigeons for food and sacks of droppings for fertilizer.

John shoveled pigeon dung into sacks. He spied Priscilla across the field picking up dead birds. Sack upon sack. Hour after hour until the moon was high. He worked his way across the field to be alongside her. She could not speak for exhaustion. He feared she might collapse, but she kept on, and on. He was proud. When the job was done, John put his arm round her shoulder. He did not care that this wasn't allowed. She leaned against him.

'Squanto says we saved about half the crop,' John said.

'Amazing,' Priscilla heaved a deep sigh. 'Not all is lost.'

'He also said there won't be another deluge of pigeons again this year, but warned that every year at this time we must be prepared.'

Daybreak. 'All souls to the fields! With hoes!' Captain Standish's reverberating command was followed by three long blasts on a horn. Not a moment to lose.

Armed with a hoe, John hurried to the fields. In the melee of gathering folk he found a place beside Priscilla. 'We'll work together,' he whispered in her ear.

Squanto held up his hand. Silence. 'Now see,' he demonstrated with his own antler hoe. 'Indent holes, this deep, so far apart, all round the mound – and another row below round the foot. Then plant the seeds so; bean, squash, pumpkin... bean, squash, pumpkin... and cover over – and then we want gentle rain and hot sun.'

John and Priscilla worked together all that day. John told her more about the trip to visit Massasoit... how kind the Indians were, and how different their way of living.

'Aye,' Priscilla said. 'They are so different, but their eyes sparkle with fun. Their life is rough and cruel, as is ours, but they seem much happier.'

'Priscilla, my love,' John said, straightening his back and taking her hand, 'There isn't a happier soul anywhere, man, woman or child, Indian or English, than I, now that we are betrothed.' Priscilla blushed and smiled and tilted her head just so, flashing her eyes beneath their long dark lashes. John reveled in her lithe energy, her coquettish smile and tilt of her head.

By the end of the day all the fields of corn had been planted with beans, squash and pumpkin. Squanto promised it would rain tomorrow.

John woke to the sound of gentle rain. Delighted, amazed, he sat up. Bradford was bent over the hearth, stirring up the embers.

'It is raining,' John said. 'Just as Squanto said it would.'

'God be praised.'

'Squanto be praised.' The Indian rose from his pallet in the corner.

'Aye, Squanto,' Bradford said. 'You are a wonderful help to us. But it is *our* God who sends the rain. Our God rules over all the earth and heavens.'

Squanto looked quizzically at Bradford, but he did not argue.

A loud urgent rapping at the door; Bradford opened to Winslow. 'John Billington – the son is missing. Has gone missing these past two days. We were so busy with the pigeons and planting we didn't remark he wasn't there. Goody Billington is frantic.'

'Reckon we should send Hobbamock to search,' Bradford said. 'As a pinese he is most respected amongst the tribes and we need their goodwill.'

John perceived a scowl briefly pass over Squanto's face.

Chapter 34

July 1621

Mistress Brewster attempts to impose her will

Slipping out the door before another soul was awake, Priscilla ambled along the path to the brook, taking deep breaths of the warm air, bringing a soothing joy of refreshment. She'd grown to love the pretty, merry brook, tumbling over moss covered rocks. Not sparkling in morning sunlight now, rather absorbing the soft gray rainfall. *If only I could sit here awhile.*

As she made her way back from her second trip, Priscilla met John walking quickly up from Bradford's house, tools in hand. There was no one else about.

'Let me take these,' he said, dropping his tools and taking the pails of water from her. 'You should not be carrying this heavy load. When we're wed, I'll fetch the water of a morning.'

'Oh, thank you. Thank you, John.'

He put down the pails, took her in his arms, and held her close. She lifted her face to receive his kiss, his lips pressing into hers. Priscilla sank into a luscious place, his strong arms holding her. Her rain drenched body arched in desire as she felt his longing, strong, urgent.

'Ah, Priscilla,' John whispered. 'I want you. I want you now.'

'Aye,' Priscilla murmured. ''Tis terrible harsh to make us wait so long.' They joined again. Dizzy with desire, she fell into him, losing all sense of where she was. Dimly, she became aware the rain had stopped. It was as if a protective cloak had been withdrawn, leaving them uncovered. A voice inside her said, *Be careful – folk watching.* Slowly, she pulled back. She must recover herself. They stood quiet for a few moments. John stooped to pick up the pails. Musing, Priscilla said, 'I wish these church folk weren't so strict and harsh, though some are kind: the Carvers and Winslows.'

John put the pails down again. 'When we're wed, we'll build a good life as we see fit.' He went on, 'A life such as your father intended.'

Priscilla looked up into his eyes. 'John, dear John.' She held his face in her hands. Dropping her hands round the back of his neck, she said, 'I love you more than I can say.'

The hour was still early when Priscilla crept back into the house. Mary Brewster was building up the fire, and the children were just beginning to stir. Elder Brewster was seated in his chair, engaged in his prayers.

'Good lass,' Mary Brewster said. 'You were early this morning.' She continued, 'Now the weeding is done I reckon we'd best be seeing to the mending – just look at that pile!' She nodded toward the big pile of clothes over in the corner. Priscilla shuddered. Hour upon hour of sitting still, sewing, and listening to Mary Brewster's religious instructions and admonitions. It was like a day-long sermon. She wished she could be working outdoors like John.

Breakfast over, pallets put to one side and the room swept, Priscilla and Mary Brewster sat by the hearth, needles and thread in hand.

'This pile of mending grows faster than we can keep up with,' Mary Brewster said.

'Aye,' Priscilla replied. 'Do the other women have as much as we?'

'Now there's a question. As you know, like our food, the

mending should be distributed evenly. But Goody Billington n'ere lifts a needle, and that lass Lizzie Tilley is so slow and clumsy with her needle, she is fairly useless. In the end it works out most goodwives just do for their own men and all the rest gets left for we two and Mistress Winslow.' She went on, 'Look – here's for Mr Alden, Governor Bradford, Captain Standish, Mr Allerton, Mr Warren, Mr Fuller and how many others whose wives have died. And with all this building work and hunting in the woods there's rips and tears collected every day.'

They sewed for a time in silence. Priscilla glanced at Mary Brewster. Her lips twitched and a frown formed a deep crease down her forehead ending in a knot just above the bridge of her nose. With a pinched voice she said, 'But I must not complain. We are following the example of the first apostles. This is all part of God's test. We must have patience and show charity, and humility, and complete the tasks before us with a willing heart.'

'Ow!' Priscilla pricked her finger and the word escaped before she could stop it. 'Oh, I'm sorry Mistress Brewster. Yes. I have attended to all you said.' She put her finger in her mouth to stop the bleeding. *And I've heard it all so many times before.*

A hesitant, polite knock at the door drew Elder Brewster from his book. 'Come in, Mr Prence. Welcome.'

Priscilla kept her eyes lowered, and did not respond to Mr Prence's greeting.

'Good day, Mistress Brewster, Mistress Mullins. Fair ladies, serving us menfolk well with your needles. We could not survive without you.' His voice softened as he bent toward Priscilla. She could not stop herself shuddering.

The Elder cleared his throat. Mr Prence turned away and sat on a stool opposite him.

'This morning we will study St Paul's first epistle to the Corinthians,' the Elder said.

All morning Mary Brewster and Priscilla sewed to the background quiet of men's voices droning on. In her mind Priscilla returned to John's arms, resavoring the luscious desire, wanting to flee this house and run to him.

'Midday.' Mary Brewster pronounced.

'Will you stay and dine with us?' the Elder asked Mr Prence as he rose from his stool.

'Nothing would please me more,' Prence fastened his gaze on Priscilla. 'But Mr Bradford has asked me to dine with him, to discuss matters of governance.' He bowed.

The door had barely closed behind him when Mary Brewster said, 'A fine man. Established and eager to learn our ways. He'll make someone an excellent husband.'

Priscilla looked into the cooking pot avoiding the Mistress's pointed stare.

'If you won't have Captain Standish, why not Mr Prence? He clearly favors you, has an estate. Governor Bradford thinks highly of his ideas.' She put the mending into piles. 'Mr Alden is so rough and far too lax in his devotions.'

Priscilla felt her cheeks and neck redden.

'Now, wife,' the Elder interrupted. 'As we have been learning this morning, we are all one body in Christ, each with his own gifts. Mr Alden is strong, and has many practical gifts we need to build our kingdom, not least he is a good shot.'

Mary Brewster joined Priscilla at the hearth. 'Fortunately we have given you a year, and if you should see your error...'

Raging inside Priscilla knew she must behave. If she was rude she would make John's path harder. She said calmly, 'I have chosen the man I love,' and watched with interest as Mary Brewster's cheeks and neck reddened.

'Prayers,' the Elder said.

'Hallo, hallo.' Governor Bradford ran into the house without knocking. 'Hobbamock has returned... found the Billington lad... held captive by the Nausets of Cape Cod... we stole their corn... they ambushed us.'

Chapter 35

July 1621

Mr Prence's second ruse against John

Indian threats

A day later, John stood with Standish on the harbor shore. The expedition party were all aboard the shallop, anchored two hundred yards out, their mission to rescue young John Billington from the Nauset tribe.

The captain stroked his beard. 'It would be the Nausets we have to reckon with. Remember the huggery?'

'Aye. They're a fearsome lot. I wish you good fortune, sir.'

'Thank you, John. I told Bradford I need you on this expedition but he said he needs you more here. We were having a right tussle over you, we were.' Standish looked out across the harbor and then directly at John. 'Please call me Miles. No more sir.'

'I – I'm honored. I might have trouble remembering, at first.' John grinned his delight and pride.

The two men waded out to the shallop. Standish boarded and John gave her a shove.

'Hoist the sails,' the captain ordered.

John stayed, watching as the shallop, sails filled with a fresh breeze, sailed out of sight. *He is our captain, superior to me in every way: age, position, education, and he has asked me to use his familiar name. Pray he returns safely, and I will greet him 'Miles. Welcome home'. Wonder what Bradford, Brewster and Winslow will make of it.*

As John splashed his way back to dry land he wished Standish would consent to building a landing stage but the captain insisted that would make it too easy for marauders to invade. He noted billowing thunder clouds on the horizon coasting slowly inland. *They'll be caught in a squall for sure.* Head down, he trudged up the track to Bradford's house to collect his tools. If they achieved their goal of eleven houses built before the year's end he would start on the Alden house, for he and Priscilla would marry in the spring.

John found Bradford pacing. 'That Billington family is always causing trouble. They're the profanest lot I've ever beheld, and the irony is, not one of them perished from the sickness, nor the Hopkins who are also profane.' He stood still. 'Nor, praise be to God, any from the Brewster family. Here we are, sending two thirds of our able-bodied men to go chasing after that lad because he's held captive with the Nausets! Only the Narragansetts would be worse!' He heaved an exasperated sigh and shook his head.

''Tis worrisome, sir. But what else could you do? Confronting the Nausets requires a show of strength. And our men should return in three to four days.'

'Aye. Thank you, Mr Alden.'

'I'll press on with building, sir. Thunder clouds in the distance.' Although he wished he could have been one of Standish's party, John was proud Bradford wanted his presence in the colony. Precious Mr Prence would not suffice.

Midday. Hot. Thankfully a strong sea breeze kept the mosquitoes at bay. Astride a roof, John heard high pitched shouts and laughter. 'Gotcha!' Below, Francis Billington and several other boys were chasing Mr Martin, grabbing at his yellow coat-tails. Looking back over his shoulder at his pursuers the unfortunate man fell into a sawpit. Arms reaching up, his flamboyant hat all askew, he struggled to get out. 'Help!' The miscreants disappeared behind a house. *I fear they'll drive Mr Martin out of his wits*, John mused.

Then, shrieks of 'Fire... Fire!'

John clambered down, jumping from the eaves, and followed the beckoning boys to the second house beyond. Flames licked the thatch. 'Go to all the houses and tell them... water... fetch water... and blankets. Quick!'

They ran off shouting, 'Fire, fire!'

For hours the colonists battled. The wind pounded and buffeted, blowing in gusts every which way, carrying flames from one spot to the next, feeding on the infill of daub and lathe.

By the time the fire was extinguished the house was a ruin. It would have to be rebuilt.

Sad and weary, John stood looking at the charred remains of the small house – the home of three single young men, all away on the expedition. He felt a hand on his arm and started. 'Priscilla! I did not hear a footstep.'

'You did well, John. 'Tis terrible hard, the house gone, but the fire didn't spread in spite of this vicious wind. Elder Brewster says come for a bite of pottage.'

'Ah, thank you,' John managed a smile. 'I'd best have a wash and change first.' He pointed to his blackened arms and shirt. 'You've collected a few smudges on your pretty face.' He drew a finger across her forehead.

Priscilla smiled. 'I must be off helping. Mustn't tarry.'

John caught up with Bradford. 'Ah. Mr Alden. I thank the Lord I didn't send you on the expedition. With both you and Standish away I dread to think what might have happened. I now regret sending so many of our men. We need more hands here.'

'You weren't to know, Mr Bradford, and we can be thankful it is only one house gone.' John frowned. 'But I'm puzzled to know what caused it with no one there, and no fire on the hearth.'

''Tis worrying,' Bradford replied.

Soothed by the dim cool of Bradford's room, John stripped off his shirt and pouch. He raised an eyebrow to see Prence seated by the hearth, reading.

'I've already washed – and I rescued Mr Martin from the sawpit,' he said.

John and Bradford stepped outside to wash.

'Good of Elder and Mistress Brewster to feed us – especially as they both worked like demons,' John said.

'Aye, and your Priscilla. She worked as hard as any of us.' John reveled in the governor's admiring affection for his betrothed.

Bradford shuffled into the main room. 'Are you joining us, Mr Prence?'

John grimaced. He waited, listening.

'I have to decline. I've accepted to eat with Goody Hopkins. I'll be taking Mr Martin with me, poor man.'

'You are kind, Mr Prence. We'll resume our studies in the morning.'

'Good day, sir.'

John's stomach turned. Mr Prence's smooth ingratiating tone… thank God the wretched man would not be dining at the Brewsters'.

The morrow was ration day; a fine fresh morning, leaves and grass glistening in the sunlight after rain in the night. Striding along the track, John sucked in deep breaths of early morning cool air, hoping Mistress Brewster would send Priscilla for their rations. He reached into his pouch for the key to the storehouse. He stopped. Not there. The only key. John kept it always on his person. Breaking into a run he lurched amongst the ruts. The door of the storehouse stood open. He hurtled into a scene of devastation. Barrels on the floor, overturned, grain spilling out, stacks of farm tools and domestic furniture scattered. In the midst lay Mr Martin clasping a barrel of strong water, spigot held to his mouth. Beside him on the floor lay the key.

John roared. 'How did you get this?' He seized the barrel and shook the key in Mr Martin's face.

'Mustn't tell… if tell,' …he hiccupped. '…kill me… our secret.' Hiccupping again Mr Martin turned on his side and tried to stand. He fell down.

'If you don't tell me, I'll kill you.' John held Mr Martin down with his knee, drew his knife and pressed the blade against the drunken man's throat.

Wide-eyed, ashen faced, Mr Martin whispered, 'P… P… Prence.'

'Damn him.' John heaved Mr Martin to his feet and threw him out the door. He worked like a madman to restore order before the colony's few women called in for their weekly allowance of grain, hardtack, dried peas and beans. Naught else left and precious little of that.

Summoned, John sat at Bradford's table across from Bradford and Brewster.

'Did you give Mr Martin the key?' Bradford asked.

'Of course not.'

'So you must have left it lying around – negligence.'

'I keep the key on my person always. Mr Martin said 'twas Mr Prence gave it to him. I can only think Mr Prence took the key from my pouch whilst we were outside washing after the fire.'

'Ridiculous!' Brewster and Bradford raised their voices in unison. Brewster leaned toward John. 'Mr Prence would never do such a thing.'

'With a knife at his throat, Mr Martin would lie.' Bradford stood. 'We'll give you one more chance, Mr Alden. Any further negligence and the care of the stores will pass to someone more responsible.'

Hammering stakes to mark out a house, John fumed. *I'm giving my all to this colony. I want to hold a position of responsibility. I am worthy and this rat is discrediting me; has stooped so low as to exploit Mr Martin's longing for drink. Bradford and Brewster are blind.*

★ ★ ★

Squidging her feet in the mud Priscilla let her tears fall. *Vile Mr Prence, calling in yesterday, saying what a pity Mr Alden is failing in his storehouse duties; allowed Mr Martin to have the key. Cannot be true. Cannot.* Absentmindedly she filled her pail with clams, and gave a passing glance at the ruffled harbor, billowing white clouds. She was grateful for the soft breeze. The sun was high when she put her shoes back on. She trudged along the dry, rutted track, watching where she placed her feet. Shouts drifted from the clearing: children's voices and a man's moaning. She stopped; a sight not yet seen in the colony, a man in the stocks. Mr Martin. A group of lads, Francis among them, pulled at his hair, kicked his legs, poked his torso and arms, as he sat trapped, helpless. Priscilla's head swam. She put down her pail and ran at the boys. 'Get away. Go home and be useful. You are bad, cruel.' She shouted, scolded, pulled Francis by the scruff of his neck. 'I'd have thought better of you.'

Francis stood, contrite. 'Sorry, Mistress Mullins.'

'Say sorry to Mr Martin and be gone. All of you.' She shooed them off. Putting a hand on Mr Martin's shoulder she said, 'I'm sorry this has happened. I truly am sorry.'

'Priscilla.'

She twisted round. 'John.'

'Come with me. There's a log behind the house yonder where we can sit. Hurry before we're seen.'

Sitting beside John, Priscilla listened and bristled as he told her of his suspicions. 'I cannot bear the sight of that man,' she said. 'It is wicked to take advantage of Mr Martin, his mind frazzled.'

'Aye, and the stocks.' John bowed his head.

'Every day Mr Prence comes for religious instruction with the Elder, all righteous and holy. Mistress Brewster fawns over him and the Elder's completely taken in.'

'I'm determined Prence will not get the better of me,' John said.

'I'm with you.' Priscilla grasped his hand.

Days passed and the expedition did not return. Bradford clenched his jaw, his bearing pinched with tension. John managed a smile for Priscilla but a frown creased his forehead. He confided to her his longing for Standish to return. Elder Brewster prayed all the day long, even dismissing Mr Prence, the only person seemingly untouched.

Released from the stocks after twenty-four hours, Mr Martin, now almost entirely out of his wits, found refuge with Susanna Winslow who fed him and kept him out of harm's way.

Mary Brewster fretted, voicing the unspoken fears of all. 'They've been massacred, sure, every one and what will we do? Only a few of us left.'

The Elder reprimanded her. ''Tis best to pray for God's goodness, not get caught up in fears and moaning.'

Numb with worry Priscilla wrung the washing and carried it out to spread over scrub grass and bushes. *Should dry soon in this hot sun.* Across the way Susanna Winslow was doing the same. She straightened and waved. Priscilla waved back but felt it would be disrespectful to initiate a conversation with a woman almost her mother's age.

Susanna never called in on Mary Brewster, nor did she attend the hateful women's prayer meetings held for the purpose of confessing sins and scouring one's soul.

Mistress Winslow disappeared indoors. Priscilla stayed out to watch John and Bradford raising another house. *Would it be needed?* John said that Bradford could not sleep at night, pacing, pacing. Nor could he hold still by day, so he chopped, sawed, hammered, all Bible study abandoned. Priscilla tried to keep her own mind averted from fears by imagining the pleasures of living with John in their own home; the delirious freedom from watchful eyes.

A shrieking carried up the hill, followed by Francis, running, hopping, tripping, waving his arms in the opposite direction.

'I... to... harbor... the shallop...' he yelled. 'Mr Bradford, I seen her sail, way out!'

Bradford and John dropped tools. John beckoned. Priscilla ran with them, followed by every living soul in the colony, all shouting their excitement.

Priscilla stood beside John on the shore.

'They're hardly moving,' he said. 'Sail's luffing. They should tack to catch what little breeze there is.'

Goody Billington stamped, twisted her hands, knotted her apron, paced back and forth. Bit by bit the shallop sailed close. John Billington waved. His mother lost all restraint in her display of joy. She shrieked and laughed and danced in circles and clapped her hands and hugged herself.

'Quiet, woman,' her husband growled. 'Or you'll get a beating after I've given that lad the thrashing of his life – running off and causing all this trouble.'

'Oh no, please no,' his wife implored.

The shallop drew up as near to the shore as possible. John waded out to take the mooring lines.

The weary party climbed out. In response to the clamoring questions, Standish called out, 'All safe. And success with the Indians.'

Priscilla watched as John greeted Standish, clasping his hand. She heard, 'Welcome home, Miles.' The captain grinned and clapped John on the shoulder. *Good. That is good.* She smiled.

As they waded ashore, Standish greeted Priscilla with a slight bow.

Bradford grabbed Standish by his shoulders. 'Thank God, thank God.' Priscilla saw him hastily wipe away a tear as he turned to greet Winslow, one of the last to wade ashore.

'What a commotion,' Standish said, looking toward the chattering, welcoming inspection of John Billington, a small throng round him looking for signs of maltreatment.

'Looks well enough – not a scratch – and fancy – he's wearing a necklace of shell beads! T'Indians must've liked 'im well 'nough.'

Striding forward, Elder Brewster shouted his joy. 'Welcome back. God be praised. Standish, Winslow, please dine with us and recount your adventures.' He looked at Priscilla. 'I reckon Mistress Brewster will be needing you now.'

'Aye, sir.' Priscilla hurried off.

Priscilla's relief and excited longing to hear the men's story gave her renewed vigor. She skinned and de-boned fowl, butchered and chopped venison. The entire week's ration of barley and peas went into the pot as well.

Came time to sup, Brewster welcomed his guests. Priscilla was thrilled to see John had been invited. But she felt sorry for Susanna Winslow, deprived of a welcoming evening with her husband.

Thankfully, Elder Brewster shortened his 'before dinner prayers'. After the 'amen' he said, 'I understand there is good news and news of trouble. Winslow, would you please relate the good news before we eat and save the other for after.'

'Aye,' Winslow said. 'As you have all seen, young John Billington is none the worse for his period of captivity. In fact he said he preferred living with the Indians to his own family. They were much kinder he said.'

'Well I never!' Mary Brewster exclaimed.

'Hush, my dear,' the Elder said.

Winslow went on. 'We came into the Nausets' territory fearing they would be hostile, though they are part of Massasoit's domain. We found that they are a very strong force with more men than Massasoit's own tribe. Squanto says it is because they were not so badly hit by the plague.'

'Why did they keep the lad captive?' Bradford asked.

'We stole their corn,' Winslow said. 'And we tramped all through their land and stole from their huts and looked into their graves. We didn't know it, but they were watching. Small wonder they attacked us in the huggery when we were searching for Plymouth Harbor. By keeping John Billington they were forcing a reckoning.'

Standish broke in. 'Before they brought John Billington to us, we met the very warrior whose corn we took. We apologized and promised that whenever he wants to come to Plymouth we will make good.'

'Aye,' Winslow said. 'When their chief, Aspinet, finally appeared bringing our lad, I presented him with a knife which pleased him greatly and we pledged peace.'

'Good work. Well done,' Bradford said.

'Now – for some food.' The Elder beckoned to Mistress Brewster and Priscilla.

Priscilla tingled with pleasure, serving John, watching him eat hungrily. She was happy to see the beginnings of a smile hovering on Bradford's lips, the tension loosening its hold on his body. If only there was no bad news to mar the happiness.

Trenchers collected, tankards replenished, the Elder invited Winslow to continue.

'By now it was nearly dark. As Aspinet and I were bidding farewell, the chief said, "I have bad news. Our big chief, Massasoit, has been captured by the Narragansetts and several of his warriors killed".'

'God have mercy,' Bradford interrupted. 'In our treaty with Massasoit we promised to defend one another in war. We could be at war with the most powerful, warlike tribe in all the area!' Bradford put his head in his hands.

'You can imagine,' Winslow said, 'we were hard pressed to return with all haste, knowing there were so few of you here to defend Plymouth. But night had fallen so we had to wait for the morrow, and our return was beset with a contrary wind and the need to foray inland to find fresh drinking water.'

'I can tell you,' Standish said, 'we were not a little relieved to find you all here, alive and safe.' He looked at John and Bradford. 'All we can do now is wait and be alert for signs of danger.'

'I'll send Squanto and Tokamahamon on a reconnoiter,' Bradford said. 'I don't know where Hobbamock has gone.'

Priscilla's stomach knotted. They could all be massacred. There was no safe place. She felt a surge of longing to return to England with John.

Chapter 36

July 1621

Trouble with Corbitant

Only the sounds of chopping and sawing and the incessant buzzing of flies and whine of mosquitoes disturbed the air. Drawn into a cocoon of heat and labor where time seemed to stop, John and Miles suddenly jolted up, hearing gasping, scratching efforts at speech. There stood Hobbamock. They'd not heard a footstep. He was lathered in sweat, heaving to get his breath.

'Squanto... dead!'

'What?' Standish exclaimed. 'How? What happened?' It was some moments before Hobbamock could speak and his broken English was difficult to follow.

'I run – from Nemasket – no stop.'

'But that is more than twenty miles,' John said.

Hobbamock nodded. 'Little sachem Corbitant want spoil treaty with Massasoit. He no like English. He like Narragansetts. So he think, "I kill Squanto – then English are helpless – no understand

– we trick them." He took Squanto and Tokamahamon in his wigwam. He hold knife at Squanto like…' Hobbamock thrust his finger at John's chest to demonstrate.

Standish put his hand on the warrior's shoulder. 'Thank God you are safe, Hobbamock.'

'Just when I was thinking we might have a time of relief from rumors and troubles, knowing Massasoit is free and hearty and the Narragansetts are not planning to attack. And now this happens.' John hacked his axe into a log.

On hearing Hobbamock's story, Bradford called a meeting. Standish insisted John be included, along with Elder Brewster and Winslow. All afternoon they discussed the situation. Finally there was agreement that Corbitant had to be stopped and hit hard.

'Even as the Israelites, with God's help, vanquished their enemies, so shall we,' Elder Brewster said.

'Aye,' Bradford said. 'The Israelites were merciless against their enemies. An enemy of God's chosen people was an enemy of God.' Bradford raised his eyes heavenward. 'It is right we show no mercy toward those who show they are our foes.'

Standish rose from his seat and paced rapidly. 'I'll hit 'em hard.' He punched the air. 'Teach Corbitant a lesson he won't forget. I'll take a party of ten men. Hobbamock will take us to this petty chief's wigwam and we'll ambush him. Surprise him in the dead of night.'

'Thank you, Captain,' Bradford said. 'The man is a traitor. If he has killed Squanto bring back his head on a pike. He can receive the English punishment for traitors.'

John inwardly recoiled, hearing the venom and bitterness in the governor's voice, and Standish's excited eagerness made him nervous.

'If everyone agrees with this plan,' Bradford said, 'I'll leave it to Captain Standish to select the men he wants to take – with my agreement of course.'

John walked with Standish and Hobbamock back up to the houses to collect his tools. Evening sun rays slanted across the settlement. A slight breeze stirred. Birds sang out in the gentle air. *Strange how peaceful it feels.*

'I want you to come on this expedition, John,' Standish said. 'I need men who will keep their heads and follow orders, not do any fool thing that takes their fancy.'

'Thank you, Miles. I'm honored.' John went on, 'I've missed your company, lodging with Bradford.'

'Likewise.'

John looked at the ground. 'There is just one thing. Mr Prence.' He recounted all that had happened while Standish was away: the storehouse incidents, Mr Martin in the stocks. 'Trouble is, if I don't keep watch on the man he'll find another way to put me in the wrong.'

'We'll take him along. He won't be able to cause mischief and we can see what he's made of.'

John grinned. 'Thank you, Miles.'

Came the morning for Standish's party to set out, the weather broke and a soft summer rain showered the marching group all day.

'This is better than hot scorching sun.' John walked alongside Standish, neither saying much, but he felt a shared sense that it was good to be comrades together again. Behind him he heard Winslow's voice. 'Hurry on, Mr Prence. You're slowing us.' John smiled.

Late in the afternoon, Hobbamock led them off the trail.

'Nemasket three miles.' He pointed in the direction of the Indian village. 'Corbitant's wigwam, one mile outside the village.'

'We'll wait here well into the night. Now listen carefully, I will say this only once.' Standish spoke in a hushed voice. 'At midnight Hobbamock will lead us to Corbitant's wigwam. Position yourselves all around it, Winslow to be in command. Do not shoot unless he gives the order. I will enter the wigwam to take Corbitant by surprise.

Alden, I want you and Hobbamock to come inside with me. Above all keep silent. We must not be discovered.'

John was taken aback Standish wanted him to go into the wigwam. *Why not Winslow? Perhaps because I'm a better shot.* He shuddered. Weary and weighed down by wet garments, he found a stump to sit on and ate the last bits of hardtack and fowl in his knapsack. The hours passed. Hours of persistent rain falling from a black sky. No moon. So dark a man could scarcely see his own feet. No one spoke. John mused. *Pray Standish does nothing rash. Not sure about this 'hit 'em hard' approach; surprise attack. We could stir up a hornets' nest and suffer unspeakable revenge.* He abruptly stood and stretched to chase away thoughts of Priscilla at the mercy of attacking Indians. *But Winslow hasn't opposed. Perhaps our only option is to cow them, show them our strength. In any case, we're here now. Just want to get on with it.*

At last Hobbamock judged the hour had come. Standish whispered last minute words of encouragement. 'Be of good heart, men,' he said. 'Stay quietly at your posts and do not fire unless Winslow gives the command.'

Hobbamock led them forward. After half an hour's hike the wigwam loomed in the dark. *Strewth! It is huge! The rain falling on the matting should muffle our footsteps.* Silently Winslow and Standish positioned the men to surround the wigwam. Then Standish whispered, 'Ready?' John nodded. He tightened his grip on his musket. Standish gave the signal to Hobbamock and they burst in, Standish shouting and Hobbamock shrieking. 'Don't move! Corbitant – where is Corbitant?' It was dark as pitch. Only a few embers smoldered on the hearth.

John reeled, hit by an avalanche of rank Indian smells: bear grease, closely confined bodies, pungent herbal concoctions, and dead animals. He gasped, swallowed hard. Smoke stung his eyes.

The Indians, asleep on their low platforms jumped up, so terrified they could not utter a sound. Then there was mayhem. Screaming, screeching, women throwing themselves on Hobbamock; arms around his waist, clinging to his legs and arms.

In their panic some Indians broke through the walls and guns fired outside.

Hobbamock calmed the Indians enough to learn that Corbitant was not there, and no one knew where he was. They said Squanto and Tokamahamon were still alive.

Hobbamock hoisted himself up through the smoke hole onto the top of the roof. John heard Winslow shout, 'Don't shoot!'

'Go out quick, and help keep order,' Standish said. John groped for the entrance to the wigwam and stumbled out into the black, wet night. He could see the shadowy shape of Hobbamock standing on the roof, and musket barrels trained on him. 'Don't shoot! Lower your muskets. It is Hobbamock,' he shouted. One man disobeyed, preparing to fire. It was Prence. John whacked him across his shoulders with the butt of his firearm. Prence fell. His musket went off.

'You idiot.' John yanked his adversary to his feet. 'I ordered don't shoot. Hobbamock is our friend and Massasoit's most trusted warrior.'

'Only good Indian is a dead one,' Prence muttered.

'Go on. Get back over there out of the way. No, you leave this with me.' John stood on Prence's musket.

Hobbamock called out for Squanto and Tokamahamon, who then emerged from the forest. Standish's troop clustered round their Indian friends. 'Praise be... you are alive... welcome... welcome.'

'That stupid little sachem Corbitant tried to kill me but Tokamahamon helped me fight him off and we escaped,' Squanto said.

It became clear that Corbitant and his braves had fled.

'Do you think he found out we were coming?' John asked Standish.

Standish shook his head. 'Damned if I know.'

In the first light of dawn Standish led his party into the center of Nemasket, and with all the Indians gathered round, delivered a strong message. 'If Corbitant continues to threaten the English, or provokes others against us, or ever causes any other violence to

Massasoit or his subjects, most especially to Squanto, Hobbamock and Tokamahamon, the English will see him revenged.'

Wet but relieved, their hunger assuaged by the Indians' generous breakfast, Standish and his men set off. The trek back was much less arduous. Their mission was completed and no one had been killed or badly wounded. The sun shone.

Again, John and Standish marched together.

'Why did Hobbamock lift himself up through the smoke hole and stand on the top of the wigwam?' John asked. 'Prence very nearly shot him.'

'Remember, Hobbamock is a pinese, a warrior possessing the highest spiritual and physical powers. The Indians believe a pinese cannot be killed by arrows or bullets. Hobbamock was showing his supreme power.' They walked on a few paces. 'You say Prence nearly shot him?'

John told the captain what had happened.

'Insubordination, disobedience in line of duty. An offense that will have to be reported – and to my thinking – punished.' Standish shook his head. 'The stupid fool. Dangerous fool.'

Next morning at first light as John closed Bradford's door behind him, he scanned the track up and down hoping to see Priscilla. Then stepping out across the clearing he spied her in the distance, across the fields, carrying two pails full of water. He leant his axe against a tree and loped along the path to greet her. 'I'll carry those. Come here.' He held her close, reveling in her quickening breath and flushed cheeks.

'The delight you're here. I've missed you and been so afeared for your safety – and I long to hear all about the raid, every detail.' Priscilla skipped a few steps to keep up with John's long stride. She clutched his sleeve. John faced her and concerned by her sad, serious look, put the pails down.

'Has Bradford told you what happened while you were gone – of Mr Martin's death?'

'No. What?'

'Mr Martin was playing tag with some of the lads. They were chasing him, grabbing at his yellow coat-tails, taunting him, but he was so addled he just kept on running and ducking, and then he tried to shinny up a tree and fell, and hit his head on a sharp stone.'

'Lord.' John wiped his brow.

'Mistress Winslow did all she could to staunch the wound and bring him round, but he died.'

'Poor blighter. Came on the *Mayflower* a pompous fool and died a witless idiot. Prence's stooge and the colony's laughing stock.' John kicked a tuft of grass.

'He was a frightful pest, but he wasn't a bad person. I reckon it was when they put him in the stocks tipped him over into madness.' Priscilla searched John's face. 'Why do folk have to be so cruel?'

'I wish it weren't so.' John stooped to pick up the pails.

Later that day, John sat at Bradford's table with Standish and Winslow to give an account of their expedition. Bradford and Elder Brewster were seated opposite.

'A success I believe,' Bradford said.

'Aye, sir.' Standish did most of the talking, and his recitation received expressions of amazement and approval.

'We are vindicated. The power of the Lord has won,' Bradford exulted.

'However,' Standish said, 'our careful planning and execution were very nearly undone.' He recounted Mr Prence's disobedient behavior. 'If Mr Alden hadn't acted quickly and decisively I dread to think what might have happened. Rightfully, according to military practice, Mr Prence should be punished.'

During a long silence John studied his hands folded on the tabletop. *Now will they see Prence's true colors? Will they cease their cosseting and fawning over this devious, conniving man?* A mosquito whined and landed on his cheek. He swiped at it. Brewster spoke.

'In my judgment we should not punish Mr Prence. I am sure his behavior was caused by the heat and anxiety of the moment. Although he is evidently not suited to participate in military excursions, he takes great pains to understand our ways and convictions. With Governor Bradford he is studying Hebrew to better interpret the Bible. I fear the humiliation of punishment would harm his sensitive nature, throw him off course. His gifts lie in the area of governance and I believe it is our duty before God to nurture him to that purpose.'

Bradford rose, saying, 'I agree with Elder Brewster. Thank you, gentlemen.'

With Standish on his left and Winslow on his right John plodded up the track. The sun beat down. Raging inside he gritted his teeth.

Winslow spoke. 'I fear the Elder and Governor Bradford place too much confidence in Mr Prence. Hopefully one day they will see. You did well, Mr Alden.' He placed a hand on John's shoulder.

'If stupid Mr Prence had shot at a lesser Indian it wouldn't have mattered so much,' Standish said. 'But Hobbamock!'

'In my view, it would be wrong to shoot any Indian without justifiable provocation,' Winslow said.

He is a wise man. John sighed, realizing he was in for a long struggle against Mr Prence.

Chapter 37

August 1621

A duel

The sun was high. Priscilla felt faint under the blanket of hot air, so humid a body could hardly draw breath without sweating. Stoop, gather a bundle of barley, tie it with a stalk and leave it to lie 'til all the field was cut, bundled into sheaves and ready to be stood on end in groups to dry. Again and again, bundle after bundle.

'Aah. My back,' she straightened. 'Stop a minute, Lizzie.' Lizzie Tilley and Priscilla looked across the field watching John and Howland rhythmically swinging their scythes, laying the barley flat.

'Pity 'tis such a poor crop,' Priscilla said, 'after all our hard work clearing the land.'

'Hope… hope we can… get a brew of small beer.' Lizzie's voice shook.

Priscilla turned to her. 'Lizzie, what is wrong?'

Lizzie wiped tears from her cheeks. 'It's John. My John.' She sobbed. 'But I do not know if he will ever be my John. He says he loves me, and often I've thought he was about to ask for my hand, and then he doesn't.'

'Strange.' Priscilla put her arms round Lizzie.

Stepping out of Priscilla's embrace, sniffing, wiping her nose, Lizzie said, 'Mistress Brewster called in yesterday. Said I should stop seeing him. She said as my parents left me a good estate he is surely after my wealth, being as he is only a servant.'

'That dreadful meddling woman.' Priscilla put her hands on her hips. 'She's probably been working on John, or the Elder has, telling him he isn't good enough for you. You leave this to me. And don't stop seeing him.'

'Thank you,' Lizzie said, managing a smile and heaving a deep sigh. 'We'd better get back to it. Oh how I itch. The heat... the mosquitoes and flies. Drive a body mad.'

They stooped to their work. It was the first day of harvest; Indian corn, beans, squash, pumpkins all looked to be coming on well. Priscilla mused. *Thanks be for Squanto.*

What was that? The bellowing cry of a man? Priscilla stopped and listened. She saw Bradford standing still, looking toward the marsh.

'Alden... Howland. Go quickly.'

Dear Lord, please don't let them be attacked. Priscilla prayed silently.

'What can it be?' Lizzie asked in a strangled voice. 'So strange, eerie, surely not Indians?'

Priscilla tried to carry on working but as she was tying a sheaf her hands shook and the barley scattered on the ground. Lizzie came beside her. 'I'm having the same trouble. You gather and I'll tie,' she suggested.

After some minutes the bellowing ceased. 'Why don't they return?' Priscilla asked.

'If they don't come soon surely Governor Bradford will send others to find them,' Lizzie said. 'It seems hardly two days go by and something dangerous happens.'

'Hie! Hie!' Bradford shouted. Priscilla looked toward the marsh.

John and Howland each had hold of a man by the scruff of the neck. She squinted and shaded her eyes.

'It's Doty and Leicester!' Lizzie exclaimed. 'Hopkins' servants!'

'Aren't they strong, our two men?' Priscilla said. 'Look – look – a sword and a dagger!'

Priscilla and Lizzie followed behind as John and Howland brought the two men to Governor Bradford. Doty dripped blood from his hand and Leicester from his thigh.

'They were fighting a duel, sir,' John said. 'Bellowing like bulls.'

'What?' Bradford stared. 'Whatever is this about?'

Doty spoke first. 'I see'd 'im fornicating, in the reeds with Desire Minter – had her he did – and she was to be mine. He dishonored her, sir. So I fought for her honor.'

'He lies,' Leicester bellowed. 'He accuses falsely because Desire Minter really favors me.'

'Enough,' Bradford slammed the word. 'Take them and tie them head to head, feet to feet, to lie twenty-four hours without meat or drink.'

'Oh,' Priscilla gasped. She turned away, head bowed. She could not join the gathering eager to see the punishment inflicted. 'They're wounded. It is so hot. The flies and mosquitoes.'

'Aye, 'tis too harsh,' Lizzie agreed.

Folk resumed harvesting. The pitiful cries of the two men joined the torment of the heat. Near to fainting, Priscilla straightened up for a moment to get her balance. She saw Mr Hopkins conversing with Governor Bradford. The governor nodded. Mr Hopkins hurried off. It wasn't many minutes before the cries ceased.

Thank you, God. Mercy has prevailed. Priscilla remembered Mistress Carver. 'John and I believe in a merciful God.'

Next day, harvesting began at daybreak. Leaving the house, Priscilla looked to the left toward Bradford's house, hoping to meet John on his way to the fields. But this morning he and Bradford emerged together with Doty, his hand wrapped in bandages. As they drew close, John pointed up toward Standish's house. The red-headed captain had Leicester in tow. The tall, dark, swarthy young man scowled, limping with a bandaged thigh.

It wasn't fit for Priscilla to walk with John and his companions, and working in the fields he was scything so far ahead it was impossible to catch a moment with him, so she was glad Lizzie hurried to work alongside her. Scanning the fields, she said, 'Desire Minter isn't here.'

Priscilla looked about. 'You're right.'

'Did you see her face when they brought Doty and Leicester before Bradford? She was right terrified,' Lizzie said. ''Tis a grim reminder,' she went on, 'of what lies in store if you're caught. In England folks'd turn a blind eye – unless a body had a grudge and wanted to make trouble. And if you got with child, well then you wed.'

'Aye. It was kinder.' Priscilla felt a pit of sadness opening up inside her.

They labored on, drugged by the repetition of their work and the heat. It was too hot to talk. Even the birds hadn't the heart to sing.

At last, when it came time to stop for evening prayers, Priscilla saw John leave Bradford to escort Doty and walk toward her. She stepped apart, away from Lizzie to meet him, raising her eyebrows in question as he took her hand.

'Bradford decided the two cads should be taken out of Hopkins' home and separated. I'm to keep an eye on Doty and Standish has Leicester to look after. As much a punishment for us as them. Makes it even harder to snatch moments with you. Oh, this damned supervision,' John moaned.

'I hate it too. If only we could even labor side by side.' They walked slowly together, hand in hand. 'After this harvest is done you'll be able to start a brew of beer. We've harvested and dried the peas, and I've been picking wild strawberries. They're sweet!

There's lots between the brook and the marsh. And the plum trees! And grapes! Grape vines twining in the shrubs and trees; laden with plump grapes, not quite ripe yet. Everything is thriving.'

'You're a busy hard-working lass. Accomplished all that whilst I was off on an expedition – or building houses – which then mysteriously catch fire.'

Priscilla stopped. 'John, Lizzie Tilley was in tears, terrible upset. Mistress Brewster has told her she must stop seeing John Howland as he is only a servant, not good enough for her. Says he is after her estate.'

John's face darkened. 'Howland's been afraid of this. Damn. It is not right. He is a good man. Deacon Carver loved him like a son. First us, now them.' He squeezed Priscilla's hand. 'I'll try to persuade Governor Bradford.'

They had reached the Brewster house. John kissed Priscilla's forehead and strode down the slope.

Pushing the door open, she started back. By the hearth stood Edward and Susanna Winslow. In front of them, hunched on a stool, sobbing, was Desire Minter. And facing Desire, Mistress and Elder Brewster; the Mistress seated on a stool, the Elder standing. Priscilla didn't move. Mistress Brewster was leaning forward, her intent, ferreting face within inches of Desire's bowed head.

'You must tell us, child. The truth must be known – or God's wrath will fall on us all. Did you... fornicate?' The word came out in a hoarse whisper. Mistress Brewster wiped her mouth with the back of her hand as if to cleanse herself from the utterance.

'No... no... no... I never...' Desire wailed.

The First Autumn

Chapter 38

September 1621

Priscilla and Susanna Winslow become friends

At dawn, nearing the brook, Priscilla came upon Mistress Winslow standing still, looking down at the water. 'Mistress Winslow!' she kept her voice low. 'You are about at this early hour?'

'Aye, Priscilla, I could not sleep; none of us could, with Desire moaning and sobbing, curled up face to the wall – all night long. I tried and tried to comfort her, but it was as if I wasn't there.'

'Terrible for her, being questioned so harshly. I couldn't sleep for remembering.'

'Desire was very attached to Catherine Carver. There was a loving woman. When Catherine fell ill the lass came to us, to be my servant, but she couldn't settle; appeared distracted, would suddenly disappear. That was bad enough but this…' Susanna looked up into the boughs of the trees beginning to stir with the dawn breeze. 'Such peace, and such torment.'

Priscilla looked into Susanna's troubled cornflower blue eyes. 'Perhaps I could sit with her awhile, give you some time to see to your own work and care for little Peregrine.'

Impulsively Susanna clasped Priscilla's hands. Her smile dimpled her honey cheeks. 'Thank you so much. I'll find some way to persuade Mistress Brewster to let me have you an hour or two.'

As she entered the Winslow house Priscilla spied Desire, huddled on her pallet, face to the wall, thumb in her mouth, moaning. A shrill wail punctuated the monotone misery.

Priscilla knelt beside the young woman. 'Don't fear, I'll not be harsh, nor judge you. I'm sorry you are so distressed. I know you loved Mistress Carver.' The moaning stopped. Desire sat up suddenly, so quickly that Priscilla almost fell backward.

'Mistress Carver, Mistress Carver.' Her speech was rapid, her eyes glazed.

For nigh on an hour Priscilla talked with Desire about Catherine Carver; drew out happy memories and assured the girl that Mistress Carver would not want her to be so unhappy. 'She knew all about the misery of losing someone we love. Misery can cause us to do things we wouldn't usually do. I promise you she wouldn't want you to go on feeling so bad.'

Desire caught her breath as she quietened down. 'Do you really think so?'

'I'm sure of it.'

Desire smiled weakly.

'I must go now because we're making soap today, but I'll come and see you again tomorrow. You stay quiet and rest.' She squeezed Desire's hands and smiled, returning the girl's hopeful gaze.

As Priscilla was saying goodbye, Susanna, with little Peregrine in her arms, stepped outside with her. 'He's trying to walk,' she said, setting him down. 'Thank you so much, Priscilla. This is the first time Desire's called out for Mistress Carver by name. Seems to have brought her wits back. Whoops, that was a tumble.' Susanna picked up her crying babe. 'I do hope you'll come again tomorrow. I'll ask Mary Brewster for some more of your time.'

'Please God she says yes,' Priscilla said. 'Oh, look – all the women are gathering, bringing pails, must be ashes and grease for the soap-making. I'd best make haste.'

With a hop and a jig of happiness Priscilla hurried to the gathering. She was happy she'd helped Desire and happy Susanna seemed to like her. She wanted to spend more time with Susanna. To her delight she spied John Alden, her John, laboring up the slope carrying a large barrel. Disregarding Mary Brewster she skipped to meet him and dropped a curtsy. He put down the barrel and looked only at her. It was as if all the rest of the world had disappeared.

When John had placed the barrel on three stumps he set off to the brook to fetch pails of water. Priscilla poured the pails of ash into the barrel. She squinted to keep it out of her eyes and wished she weren't being covered in gray dust. It stuck to her sweaty skin and itched. Under Mary Brewster's watchful eye John poured pails of water onto the ash. As the water soaked through the ash, lye dripped out through the spigot into a pail placed underneath.

'That will be all, Mr Alden. Thank you. Reckon the lye will be ready midday,' Mary Brewster commanded.

With a wink for Priscilla, John made a slight bow of obeisance to Mary Brewster. 'Yes, Mistress. Until midday.'

Priscilla bent over the barrel with her stirring stick, stifling a giggle. She had to recycle the lye through the ash until it was just the right strength, so a turnip slice would float on the surface, Mother always said. But they had no turnips to test with.

The other women and children gathered baskets of brushwood and as predicted, around midday the lye was ready.

Elder Brewster heaved his way out of the house half-carrying, half-dragging a big cast iron cauldron. 'I must be getting old,' he gasped as he let his burden fall to the ground. 'That pot is heavier than I remembered. Look, there – the hook is inside.'

'Thank you, sir,' his wife said.

John clambered down from thatching a roof and set to clearing a patch for the soap-making fire. He erected a sturdy tripod over it, hung the cauldron on the tripod and poured in the buckets of cooking grease collected during the year. Then he lit the fire underneath. When the grease had melted he poured in the lye.

'Thank you,' Mary Brewster said. 'Now you may get on with your work.'

John didn't move. 'I see you haven't much brushwood. That lot won't last long. I know of a good supply amongst those trees over yonder.' He pointed to a copse up behind Standish's house. 'If you could spare Mistress Mullins a minute we could fetch you a good supply.'

Mary Brewster pursed her lips. 'Aye, aye. I suppose so but ye're not to tarry.'

John picked up a large empty basket.

Joyously, Priscilla half-ran, half-walked, and skipped alongside John, taking three steps to each of his strides.

John was right. The copse floor was covered in dead branches and twigs. They'd filled the basket in a trice. He stood up, facing Priscilla, and grinned. 'Come here, my ash lady.' He pulled her into a dense clump of birch trees. Taking a large, as yet unused, handkerchief from his breeches, he carefully wiped the ash from her forehead, eyelids, cheeks, nose and lips. 'There.' He gathered her into him.

'Priscilla… John… where are you?' Reedy, piping voices roused them.

'Damn,' John said. They stepped out from the birch trees.

A party of lads greeted them, led by Francis carrying another basket. 'Mistress Brewster sent us to help.'

'Did she now? Very well. Let's to it; see how fast we can fill your basket. There. Full to overflowing. Off you go.' He sent the lads ahead struggling with their substantial load.

Following several paces behind with John, Priscilla said, 'You tried, John. Why can't that woman allow us a few moments alone together?'

As they slowly walked on John said, 'I've had a word with Bradford about Howland, reminding him that Deacon Carver spoke highly of his servant, saying he loved him like a son. Our governor said he'd think on it.'

'I hope his thoughts go the right way,' Priscilla said.

All the long hot afternoon Priscilla took turns with Mary Brewster, feeding the fire and stirring the boiling grease and lye. The stirring became harder and harder work as the mixture thickened. It was a sleepy afternoon and through her lassitude Priscilla could hear shouts and laughter as a crew of men chopped and sawed, building houses. *When will they begin on a house for John and me*, she mused smiling. *This time next year we'll be wed.*

'Priscilla!' Marry Brewster's sharp tone jolted Priscilla out of her reverie. *Oh dear, I've stopped stirring.*

'I'm sorry, Mistress.' She stirred extra hard.

By early evening the soap was made – clear and soft.

'One would not believe it was made with wood ash and grease,' Priscilla said. 'As Mother used to say, "We had good luck with our soap".'

'Aye, 'tis a good batch,' Mistress Brewster agreed. 'Ah… a breeze. Praise God. These strange climes, all part of His testing.'

Priscilla remained silent.

'I near forgot,' Mary jabbed at the soap. 'Mistress Winslow has asked if you might help with her mending for the next few days until the backlog is cleared. I agreed. But if that miserable wretch of a girl Desire would help… reckon Satan's got into her. If she doesn't work as she should soon I'll have to question her again, empty out her bad insides and teach her God's ways. We can't have Satan in our midst.'

Priscilla stifled a gasp. 'Yes, Mistress.'

The following day on her way to the Winslows' home, Priscilla met Susanna on the track, helping Peregrine learn to walk. She greeted Priscilla with a beaming smile. 'Desire is so much better

– you've done wonders with her – and what a difference it's made to me!'

'That is good news. Especially as Mistress Brewster is threatening another examination.' Priscilla recounted what Mary Brewster had said.

'We'll not let that happen. With Edward's help it won't happen. Come in.'

Priscilla crossed the room to Desire who was seated on a stool near her pallet. 'You are helping with the mending?' Desire nodded.

'The lass is quick and deft with her needle,' Susanna said. 'And she helped with breakfast.'

Priscilla drew up a stool beside Desire. 'May I help?' Desire smiled and searched out the packet of needles and a spool of thread.

'Did Mistress Carver teach you to sew?' Priscilla asked. Desire nodded and a tear spilled onto the shirt she was patching. She hastily wiped her eyes.

'What is it, Desire?'

''T'were just before Deacon Carver fell in the field – she'd begun teaching me to read. I was so thrilled!' She hid her face in her hands weeping.

Priscilla put an arm round Desire's shoulder. 'Perhaps if Mistress Brewster can spare me the time…'

At the mention of Mistress Brewster Desire cowered and wept.

Susanna knelt beside her. 'Desire, listen. Priscilla and I will protect you. We won't allow Mistress Brewster to hurt you and Master Winslow will back us up if need be. But you must show you are willing to work for the colony – so she'll have no cause to complain.'

'We're all to go to the fields tomorrow, to weed the mounds of squash, pumpkins and beans. It is a chance for you to show Mistress Brewster you're a good hardworking lass,' Priscilla said.

Desire looked from Priscilla to Susanna, studying their faces. 'You promise she won't hurt me?'

'We promise.'

Susanna stepped outside the door with Priscilla. 'I can't thank you enough – Edward too. You've worked a miracle. Only problem is, I no longer have an excuse to "borrow" you from Mistress Brewster.'

'Mistress Winslow, I wish… I would so like…'

'We'll contrive it somehow.' Susanna smiled and winked. 'And please call me Susanna. See you in the fields tomorrow.'

Chapter 39

October 1621

John moves in with Standish

'Goodbye, sir.' John hovered in the doorway shaking Bradford's hand. 'Thank you for my stay and tuition.'

'You've done well,' Bradford smiled, a small smile that did not disturb his serious demeanor. 'Now to prepare for Howland.'

The two men saluted as Bradford stepped backwards into his house.

Knapsack on his back and musket in hand, John walked briskly up the slope toward Standish's house, drinking in the crisp early morning autumn air. Reaching the captain's dwelling, he stood a moment, looking out over the little colony, still all quiet indoors. Almost a year gone and not yet a dozen houses, clustered together on this piece of cleared land, leading down to the harbor; dwellings that hardly merited to be called 'house'; hovels rather, exceedingly small with packed earth floors. However, with so few able-bodied men survived from the sickness, labor had to be rationed. When one stopped to think about it, they hadn't done badly. John felt a surge of affection for this small collection of homes huddled together, the only settlement of folk from across the ocean in this vast wilderness. Tendrils of smoke curled from chimneys; evidence of embers kept burning through the night. A stronger plume rose from the Brewsters' house, a sign that Mary Brewster was up, stoking the fire. The household would now be stirring. Priscilla. Would she be sweeping the floor? Setting out soon to fetch water from the brook? When he built a house for Mr and Mistress Alden, he would lay a floor, keep the damp at bay. The sun peered above the horizon, chasing the faint pearly mist. The ruffled harbor sparkled and a breeze stirred the rich autumn foliage, decorating the blue sky with yellow, orange, deep red, russet. *Aach. 'Tis a beautiful land and full of riches. Give us time without sickness or war, with more settlers to swell our number, and we will prosper.* John shook himself and rapped on the door. It opened slightly, revealing a portion of the captain's half-dressed body.

'John! Ye're here – with belongings I see! Come in, come in.' Standish stepped back, opening his door wide and hoicking his braces over his shoulders. 'Has Bradford released you? There's your pallet just the same. I'll rake up the hearth and put some meal on to heat.' The captain was in a flurry of welcome.

'Yes,' John said. 'I'm released. Howland is taking my place.'

'How is that?'

'Howland wants to wed Lizzie Tilley. But he sensed the leaders' disapproval. They suspected he was after Lizzie's inheritance. I spoke to the governor on his behalf and the upshot is they may wed after a year's religious instruction – and observation – so here I am, if you'll have me.'

Standish, bent over the hearth stirring the cornmeal, straightened up, clapped his hands and threw back his head in a guffaw.

'So! Now it's poor Howland's turn! Cleverly done, John. I'll wager he loves you for it.'

John lifted his musket into its old place on the empty pegs. 'He's not best pleased – but prepared to suffer for Lizzie's hand.'

'This is very good news. Welcome, John. Welcome. Now, pull up that stool and we'll have a portion of meal and spring water. Have you got a brew of ale started?'

'Should be ready in a few weeks. Wonder if we'll ever make as good a brew as in England. But your expedition, a success?'

'Aye, it was. And this eve, when our day's work is done, I'll tell you of it. Forsooth! 'Tis good to have your company again!' The captain slapped his knee.

Now the harvest was in, the two men labored all day, planking logs and working to build more houses, stopping only for a piece of cornbread and a drink of water at midday. They sat side by side on a fallen tree trunk in the warm sun.

Standish's eyes took on a faraway look as he gazed over the harbor. 'The old country seems a lifetime ago.' Then he shook his head. 'But we're no doubt better out of it. Wars and recession and the plague. Headed for hard times over there.' He stood up and faced John, his back to the harbor. 'Speaking of the plague,' he said, 'a couple of days ago, out on the trail, Squanto let slip he'd told Massasoit we have barrels full of the plague buried under the common house – and if he displeases us, we'll unleash it.'

'No!' John said. 'The devil. Does Bradford know this?'

'I don't know,' the captain replied. 'I'm thinking perhaps that's why Corbitant and all the local sachems were so eager to sign a peace treaty.'

'Will you tell him?'

'I don't know whether to or not.' Standish paced a few steps. 'Perhaps 'twould just complicate matters. What do you think?'

John was quiet, studying his boots. 'I think maybe say nothing for the time being. Bradford is so… well… enamored of Squanto. Perhaps we shouldn't upset his trust.'

'Good point,' Standish nodded.

By the end of the afternoon one of the houses was completed and ready for habitation.

'I'm parched thirsty and clogged with sawdust,' Standish said as they surveyed their work. 'We've done well. Hark!'

They turned in the direction of merry feminine voices. Susanna Winslow, Priscilla and Lizzie Tilley came staggering up the slope lugging a large, heavy pot. The two men ran to meet them.

'Your supper,' Susanna said, 'for tonight and the morrow and the next.' They put the pot down.

Lizzie danced round to John and planted a kiss on his cheek. 'Thank you, thank you. I'm so happy. We're betrothed!'

'She's been dancing and useless all day.' Susanna put her arm round Lizzie's waist.

'It's this lass you want to thank,' John said, catching Priscilla by the hand and drawing her close. 'She worked out the problem and sounded the alarm.'

Standish stepped to face Susanna. 'How's my favorite goodwife? Carer of all.'

Susanna curtsied. 'Good sir, you do me proud.'

'This good woman has brought me excellent sup day after day. If it weren't for her I'd have surely starved.'

'And that would have been a disaster,' Susanna winked. 'Come, girls – we mustn't tarry.'

Later that evening, as dark closed in around the settlement, John and Standish sat by the hearth smoking their pipes. They rested quiet for a time, listening to the wolves howling in the distance. Then Standish leaned forward, turning toward John. 'I've been intending to say, blessings on you and Priscilla. You're a good pair.'

'Thank you, Miles.' John hesitated. 'You are gallant.'

'Not so much gallant. I could tell she didn't take to me. 'Twas the Brewsters pushed me to pursue her. Reckon they thought if I was wed to the fair Priscilla I'd not be tempted to return to England. And I persuaded myself she would be happy with me in time.'

'Well, I'll be!'

'My pride was hurt awhile, but 'tis good you two are together.' Standish took a long pull on his pipe. 'Now – about my expedition.'

'Aye. What did you discover?'

'We followed an Indian trail north. Must have been about forty miles – four days trekking. It led to a fabulous big harbor, deep enough for ships to anchor right up to land. Surrounded by fields; rich fertile soil, not spent like here, and rivers leading inland. I tell you, John, 'tis where we should be – a place to prosper.'

John groaned. ''Tis too late. More's the pity for I'm of a mind to prosper. And with so few of us left from the sickness we need rich fields, good harvests. We need food, Miles, and lots of it. Thank God for Squanto teaching us how to plant.'

'Yes. Will we ever have full bellies? But take heart.' Standish blew a smoke ring. 'The Indians of those parts, the Massachusetts, have promised to keep beaver pelts for us to trade.' He chuckled. 'Just as we were departing, a group of Massachusetts women, all clad in beaver coats, followed us. So taken with our trinkets were they, they stripped off, giving us the beaver for a few baubles, and then, ashamed at being seen naked, tried to cover themselves with branches.'

John laughed. 'Praise to their modesty... more modest than many an English damsel. Our good fortune they are so keen to have our worthless trinkets.'

'True enough,' Standish said. 'But a curious thing... Squanto... he said the Massachusetts were hostile to us. That we should strip the women by force and take their coats – to show our power. What is he up to? We'd have stirred up a hornets' nest for sure if we'd done that.'

''Tis odd,' John said. 'I know we owe Squanto. Without his help we would surely have starved. And he alone speaks English so well. But I'm reckoning Hobbamock is more trustworthy.'

'I agree. Time will tell. But above all, we need to keep the peace with Massasoit. We'll need our wits, John.'

John stood up, and tapped the ash from his pipe bowl onto the hearth.

'Perhaps we should invite Massasoit to a feast, soon.'

'Good thinking,' Standish said. 'I'll have a word with Bradford.'

Chapter 40

October 1621

The first Thanksgiving

Priscilla skipped down the slope toward the harbor, an empty pail in each hand. Clams needed for supper. She felt light of heart, intoxicated with love and the tang in the air. Inhaling deep breaths of salt and pine she thought how different this was from the smells of Dorking; the acrid stink of tanning vats and animal dung. Nearing the harbor's edge she took off her shoes. The tide was far out and she relished squidging her toes in the firm mud. A flock of geese honked overhead. She looked up at the V of birds, black shapes winging across the blue sky. Amazing how they never veered out of formation, not one; in the spring headed north, in the autumn, south. Finding a large, flat boulder, she sat and looked out across the harbor. In her mind's eye she saw the *Mayflower*, sailing away, out through the sand spits. *I wonder where Master Jones is now. He was so kind when I was desperate in grief, and so, so good with Joseph.* She remembered her despair, the foul-tasting, bitter need and loneliness. Now her sadness was softer; wishing her family could be here to share this new life. They would be happy for her. Father proud. Mother educating her in women's ways and housewifery, Joseph being a delightful pest.

She squiggled as if snuggling into a blanket of warm sunshine. *Ah well – mustn't sit here too long – busy days ahead.*

Last Sabbath, the governor had announced a three-day holiday, to celebrate and thank God for their blessings: no sickness since March, seven buildings raised, a good harvest of corn, and peace with the Indians. He would invite Massasoit to join in the festivities. The colony was abuzz with excited anticipation. Only three days left to finish preparing.

The sun was halfway to its noon place in the sky when Priscilla, pails full, found a rock pool to wash her feet and put her shoes on. *Only mid-morning and I'm starving hungry. Will we ever not be hungry? Never mind – this air is nearly as good as food. I'm sure it makes me livelier.* She didn't hurry up the slope, wanting to delay going back into the dim severe atmosphere of the Brewster house and the inevitable encounter with Mr Prence. Sauntering, she looked up into the trees, the vivid foliage stirred by the breeze; the highly colored birds, gold-green, red, large blue and gray – flitting from branch to branch.

Suddenly she felt two hands grasping her waist from behind. 'Aiee!' She whirled round. 'John! I never heard you! How could you be so silent? I nearly spilt all the clams!'

'Hobbamock has been teaching me to run like an Indian. Even with these heavy boots.' He took the pails from her.

'Come with me. Help me taste the wine, to see if it's matured enough for the celebrations.'

Glancing round as they went, to check for supervising elders, John led Priscilla to the storehouse. He unlocked the door and drew her inside; leaving just a crack of opening so they weren't in total darkness. He took down a tankard, placed on the top of a wine barrel.

'For tasting,' he said. 'Our reward for picking all those baskets and baskets of grapes.' He filled the tankard from the spigot. 'For us.'

Priscilla sipped. 'Oh, 'tis sweet and strong!'

John sipped. Priscilla sipped. John sipped again. When the tankard was empty John replaced it on the barrel and gathered Priscilla into his arms, clasping her hard against him. Desire pulsing through them, they stayed, loving, caressing, murmuring, delirious with longing. The sound of approaching voices penetrated. Gasping, John pulled the door tight shut. The voices, recognizable now as Bradford and Brewster, came closer.

'I hope the wine is ready,' Brewster said. 'Mr Alden's kept it locked away.'

'Good man he is,' Bradford said. 'I'll send him with some others to shoot game – only three days left.'

Holding their breath, John and Priscilla waited for the footsteps to die away.

'Well,' John sighed, 'reckon I'd better be a good man.'

Priscilla giggled and held him close. 'The wine is good,' she whispered, and kissed his ear.

She left the storehouse first, carrying her pails of clams, warily checking to see who was about. She spied Lizzie Tilley across the way – no sign of Bradford or Brewster. But – behind that tree? A woman darted out, hunched and hurrying up the slope, to enter the Brewster house. *Oh no!* Priscilla wailed inwardly. *She was there – saw us go in – who knows how long. Oh no, no, no, she's bound to punish us.*

Heavy with fear, Priscilla trudged up the track, head down. As she approached the Brewster house she saw the door was ajar. She stopped and stood straight, bracing herself. *I'll behave as if I've done nothing wrong – and I haven't, not really.*

'Ah, my dear,' Mistress Brewster said cheerily. 'That is a good haul. Plenty for our supper and some left to take to Mr Alden and Captain Standish. They've been working hard all morning – rebuilding the damaged house. It is a marvel how hard they work, giving everything they've got to build God's kingdom.' She spoke rapidly in a high pitched voice, going on and on about God's favor falling on His elect who work to build His kingdom, repeating herself, rambling hurriedly.

She's hiding it. Is she holding back, waiting to stage a confrontation to cause us the most shame?

The day passed, and the next, with no indication from Mary she'd seen them. *Am I imagining this? No.* The worst was she had no chance to talk with John as he and Standish were out hunting all the day long.

Piles of pumpkins and squash and baskets of dried beans gave the common house the air of a well-stocked barn. Fowl and deer lay deposited at the Brewster doorway, to be plucked and butchered. And there was the endless task of grinding Indian corn in the pestles and mortars brought from England. The children were sent out berrying. Sitting in the doorway, plucking fowl, Priscilla smiled at the sight of Francis and his friend scampering off, knocking their empty berrying pails together. Folk were merry as they worked to prepare, all except for Mary Brewster earnestly stern as ever, and Priscilla, whose fear mounted as time went on and nothing happened.

★ ★ ★

On the morning set for the first day of festivities Priscilla stood outside the doorway of the Brewster house, taking deep breaths, trying to calm her nerves. Already the colony was in action. Guffaws and whistling echoed up the slope as Alden, Howland and Standish dug pits down by the common house and erected spits for roasting the deer and turkey. Brewster and Bradford were setting up trestle tables, carefully maneuvering and placing so they would be level and not topple over under the weight of heavy pots of victuals.

How festive it is, if only…

'Priscilla!' Mary Brewster called, her tone sharp.

'Yes, Mistress.' Priscilla re-entered the house.

'Here, take this basket and fetch a good lot of sallet. Massasoit is due to arrive mid-afternoon and we want to have everything ready.' Mary's brow furrowed in concentration.

'Yes, Mistress,' Priscilla said, and tried not to show her eagerness to depart. She hurried across the clearing toward the brook, hoping she could get there without having to talk to anyone. *Made it. How good to be here alone.* She balanced on the stepping stones to cross over. *The beauty and peace of this place.* The burbling, rushing water sang to her as she stooped to gather salad greens growing wild along the bank. Stroking moss covered rocks and kneeling to let the cool water run through her fingers, she lingered, slowly following the brook up to the waterfall. Just a few handfuls more and her basket would be full. Priscilla straightened her back. Silence; only the music of cascades falling, running over the rocks, mingling with birdsong. She was standing amongst silver birches and large hazel shrubs, boulders large enough to sit on strewn here and there. Choosing a flat boulder, she sat gazing up through the trees, watching tiny insects, no bigger than motes of dust, reeling and dancing in streamers of sunlight. Time passed until the sun was not far off midday. *I must get back. But I'll do a short detour to check the berry brambles over by the marsh. The children may not have picked there. It won't take long.*

Priscilla followed a deer track which led to the furthest stretch of brambles next to the swamp. As she approached she heard a strange sound, a soft moaning – a human voice? She slowed her pace, cautiously stepping forward and peered through the briars. There was a huddled form, a woman, kneeling, head bowed, rocking, hands clasped in prayer. It was Mary Brewster! Her empty pail by her side.

'Please God, cleanse me, my soul is rotten... will go to hell...'

I shouldn't listen. She is praying. I wouldn't want my prayers to be overheard, and she thinks she is alone... but...

'Satan has filled my heart with evil feelings, bitterness tasting like bile. Why? Why can't I rejoice? I cannot bear to see them so happy. I gave up love, always alone… William away… persecuted… for the sake of…'

Mary heaved with sobs and Priscilla couldn't move.

'For the sake of your will. I feel so dried out. They are together, happy together. Priscilla is not left. She has love. Oh God! I… can't… bear it.' Mary beat her fist against her head and clasping her hand against her mouth, fell forward, face down on the earth.

Priscilla held her breath. *She mustn't see me.* Looking back over her shoulder, she crept away, hastening her steps as she gained distance. She tried to lift her skirts whilst holding her basket steady. *Mustn't leave a trail of sallet.* Finding the deer track she hurried, almost running. Briars tore at her skirts, crows cawed and flapped overhead. Afraid of tripping on a root or stone, she kept her eyes on the ground. Minutes felt like hours. Nearing the settlement at last, she stopped to pick the burrs and thistles from her skirts. *I should not have spied on her but at least now I know why she is so harsh. I promise before God I'll not tell anyone of this, not John, not Susanna, no one, ever. Perhaps as she is trying to redeem her soul she won't punish us.*

Approaching the outskirts of the clearing, Priscilla smelled roasting venison and heard an excited babble of voices. She hurried, and skirting round the Winslows' house, saw the colony all gathered by the brook at the foot of the hill. Thanks be, there's John's blond head, taller than the others. She wriggled through the crowd to stand beside him.

'Priscilla! Where have you been?'

She showed him her basket of sallet.

'I see.' He put his arm round her waist and she leaned against him.

'Look! The Chief! Massasoit!'

Priscilla jumped and stood on tiptoe. There he stood on the top of the hill, dressed in full kingly regalia of war paint, a single feather in his long hair, a wide shell necklace and a small leather apron hanging from a thong round his waist.

Winslow, Bradford and Standish stepped forward to meet him; Standish in full military dress, Winslow and Bradford in their Sabbath best. Massasoit, erect and proud, marched slowly down the hill. Then appeared a brave, and another, and another. On and on they came, spaced apart, pacing slowly to form a dignified and impressive column. However many were there?

'What is this about?' Priscilla asked.

'I don't know. We didn't expect it for sure,' John replied. 'Standish would have told me if he'd had an inkling.'

Priscilla saw Mary Brewster standing beside the Elder; her usual composed self. 'How will we ever feed them all?' she muttered.

Anxious mothers gathered their children close and Susanna Winslow came alongside Priscilla.

The welcoming trio greeted Massasoit, while Elder Brewster raised his hand for silence and spoke reassuring words to the colonists.

Still they came. Brave after brave.

'I've counted ninety!' John whispered.

Bradford turned and beckoned to Squanto who stood hovering, ready. He translated Bradford's words to Massasoit. The Big Chief beamed and spread his arms in the direction of the forest. A dozen braves loped off as directed.

Bradford addressed the colonists. 'They will bring more meat.'

Alden and Howland hurried off to prepare more roasting spits. Priscilla followed Mary Brewster.

'Quick now,' Mary said, 'we'll be needing more cornbread. But first, run round the womenfolk and tell them each to set another pot of pottage to cooking.'

Priscilla did as she was bid. Even while she was running from house to house, two braves returned from the forest bearing deer. While Mary and Elder Brewster and their sons skinned and butchered the deer, Priscilla started a pot of pottage to cook and stirred up a batch of cornbread.

By evening, five more deer and wild turkey were roasting. The deer set to roast earlier were ready to eat and the tables were laden with pots of pottage, pots of cooked pumpkin and squash, and baskets of cornbread and berries and sallet.

Priscilla watched as her John and Howland set two barrels of wine on stands. They each filled a tankard. John brought his to Priscilla.

'For you to taste.' He winked.

Priscilla sipped and smiled into his eyes. ''Tis sweet and strong,' she said, and winked. They stood together and slowly, in turns, drank the wine.

''Tis fine to see folk so merry,' John said. 'We need seasons of merriment.'

'Aye.' Priscilla took his hand. 'And you and I and our children, we will be merry, through good times and bad.' She looked up at him.

He cupped her face in his hand. 'We will.'

The sound of a reveille played on a horn pierced their moment.

Standish, splendid in his uniform, sounded the reveille again, his horn polished and glistening. The excited hum and babble fell silent and Bradford stepped forward to speak, with Squanto translating. He delivered many words in praise of Massasoit, expressing trust and hopes for enduring peace. Massasoit beamed and bowed repeatedly in the manner of an English courtier.

'Squanto's taught him how to bow like that,' John whispered in Priscilla's ear.

When Bradford had made his final salutary remarks, Massasoit delivered his reply, which, according to Squanto's translation, was equally appreciative and complimentary, and as if to emphasize his goodwill, he went on and on, extending his speech to at least twice the length of Bradford's. At the close, Bradford bowed to Massasoit, also in the manner of an English courtier.

'At last!' John said. 'We can eat.'

'I'm very, very hungry,' Priscilla said.

'Howland and I are delegated to carve the venison and turkey. Come with me and I'll cut you a good big portion.'

As they made their way down toward the roasting spits, Priscilla saw cushions had been laid on the ground for Massasoit, Elder Brewster, Winslow, Bradford and Squanto, and Standish with Hobbamock. Everyone else sat in groups on the bare earth or ate standing up. It didn't matter. Folk relished the fun of it.

With her large slice of venison and a helping of cornbread she sat with Susanna Winslow, Lizzie Tilley and Desire with Peregrine. The little lad longed to join the older children who ran and cavorted and shouted and whooped. Desire followed after him, ready to pick him up after his tumbles.

'Oh, Susanna! Is this not good?' Priscilla said. 'To be merry and eat and drink wine.'

Susanna's mouth was full so she couldn't speak. She nodded vigorously, took a swig of wine and leaned happily against Priscilla.

Lizzie, engrossed in her meat, didn't notice John Howland beckoning. Priscilla nudged her and pointed.

'Here, have my bit.' Handing Priscilla her piece of venison, Lizzie jumped up and hurried off to join her man.

''Tis good to see them so happy,' Susanna said. 'Like you and John.' She put an arm around Priscilla's waist and hugged her. 'And I gather your John had a part to play.'

'Yes, he did speak to Governor Bradford on Howland's behalf.'

'You must be proud.'

'I truly am. Very proud.'

Priscilla was quiet a moment. The haunting vision of Mary Brewster on her knees in despair hovered over the festivities. Fires glowing under the roasting spits, Indian braves and colonists tending to keep to their own kind, all eating as if they'd not had a meal in days and becoming merry with drink. Some growing noisy. There was Hopkins, surrounded by a group of lads, loudly holding forth.

''Twas the worst storm in naval history – far worse than the *Mayflower*'s – we were near to drowning.'

'How many times has he told that story?' Susanna laughed. 'I'm surprised he can still find willing listeners.'

'This isn't so different from harvest celebrations in England,' Priscilla mused. 'Except for the Indians being here, of course. But we'd be in a barn, sitting on stooks, getting merry on good English ale.'

'And how much we had to eat would depend on the generosity of the farmer,' Susanna said. 'And like as not it would be raining!'

Priscilla laughed leaning back on her elbows. 'Yes, just look at that moon – full – almost golden, hanging low, and the air so clear.'

'I've not had so full a belly since we left England,' Susanna said. 'We should be careful, mind. With our bellies used to being empty, too much victuals could make us sick.'

'Look,' Priscilla pointed. 'Young John Billington and that brave, both looking green. The brave can hardly stand. They're off to vomit in the wood. Friends in misery.'

'Hmm,' Susanna sighed. 'Edward says the Indians get drunk on very little liquor – not used to it.' She chuckled. 'And look, they all seem rather tipsy.'

Lizzie Tilley rejoined them looking downcast.

'Is something amiss?' Priscilla asked.

'John and I were about to... well... go off by ourselves a bit. Only a little while, mind, but Governor Bradford summoned John to carry on serving up venison. He said the Indians keep coming again and again for more, and John Alden can't keep up.' She kicked the ground. 'I think the governor was watching us. Keeping a rein on John. He could have found someone else to help Alden. If we were in England...'

'I know 'tis hard,' Susanna reached up and took Lizzie's hand pulling her to sit down. 'Try to be patient. When you have your own house it will be different.' She put an arm round the sulking young woman and hugged her. 'I'm getting stiff, and I fancy some berries.' Susanna stretched out her arms. 'Help me up, Lizzie.'

As Susanna struggled to her feet, a hush descended on the gathering. Priscilla hastily scrambled upright.

On the track to the harbor, where it went past the common house, Hobbamock and Squanto squared up to each other. Their voices echoed up the slope, loud and angry. Squanto staggered, no doubt the effect of the wine. Perhaps Hobbamock had refused wine, as he stood tall and steady. Squanto was hurling insults, poking his finger into Hobbamock's chest, his tone derisory. Then he began speaking English, but so fast and garbled Priscilla couldn't catch what he was saying. Hobbamock stood, silent, while Squanto embarked on a chant and danced round the supreme brave, poking at him. Still Hobbamock didn't move, silent as a rock. Squanto took to dancing on one foot, then the other. And all of a sudden was flat on the ground.

'So quick!' Priscilla grasped Susanna's arm.

Now Massasoit rose to his feet. Slowly, he walked over to the two braves. He addressed Squanto, now standing again. Squanto said nothing and skulked off to take his place beside Bradford. Hobbamock resumed his seat beside Standish.

'Whatever was that all about?' Priscilla asked.

'I don't know,' Susanna replied. 'But listening to Edward, I get the impression the Indians are just as likely to form alliances and fight each other as we Europeans.'

'Yes,' Priscilla mused. 'Remember the trouble we had with Corbitant back in the summer – wanting to join the Narragansetts and destroy Massasoit's empire.'

''Tis worrying,' Susanna said. 'Why should Squanto want to provoke Hobbamock? Bradford and Edward and Standish have worked so hard to keep a peaceful balance.'

As if nothing untoward had happened, the circle of dignitaries all took out their pipes and the braves stood to the sound of a drum beat, making ready to dance.

'I wager the men will be out a long while yet,' Susanna said. 'Edward said they'll smoke their pipes and drink more wine, and the braves will dance long into the night.'

Mary Brewster's shrill voice rose above the surrounding din. "'Tis time for women and children to be indoors. Please help carry the pots and baskets. Make haste. This pagan dancing will conjure up devils and witches for sure.'

Priscilla bade Susanna and Lizzie goodnight. Susanna hugged her.

Following orders, Priscilla heaved Mary Brewster's big iron pot from the table. Though empty, it was very heavy and she labored under its weight. Not a man in sight to help. They were all watching the Indians dance. By the time she reached the hearth and set it down, she was gasping for breath.

'Thank you, my dear,' Mistress Brewster said. 'We'll be saying prayers, just the two of us together. My lads are staying out with the men.'

'I'll... go stand... in the doorway... just for a minute, to get... my breath back.' *This house feels like a prison.*

The fevered beating of the drums throbbed in her ears, and the circling shrieking braves, decked in war paint reminded her of her hours of terror in Tinsin's camp. Now she had to spend an evening alone indoors with this strange frightening woman. Gazing at the moon hovering behind the branches of the tall pine tree, she imagined John standing beside her, his protecting arm holding her close. *If only.*

'Come, my dear.'

Reluctantly, Priscilla went back in and dutifully knelt with Mary Brewster by the hearth.

'Oh, Lord God, maker of all, we beseech thee, cleanse our souls, help us to know thy will, and please God, protect us from the pagan Indians.'

Kneeling beside the woman praying now, composed and sure, Priscilla saw the woman she'd seen that morning: distraught, tormented, frightened she would go to hell. She shuddered.

Chapter 41

November 1621

The Fortune

'A ship… a ship…'

Muskets on their shoulders, as they tramped across the corn fields to shoot fowl in the marsh, John and Standish stopped in their tracks, shielding their eyes to find the source of the cry. Francis came scrambling down from the tall pine tree, shrieking, 'A ship… a ship…'

Running, stumbling, they retraced their steps. As they reached the cluster of houses, Bradford yanked open his door. 'What? Where?'

'Sails… out beyond the sand spits.'

Folk emerged from their houses, Priscilla carrying a large pile of wet laundry.

'Alden, tell Winslow to bring his telescope and come to the top of Fort Hill,' Bradford ordered.

'Leave the washing.' John took Priscilla's hand. Together they ran to the Winslow house and then with Winslow, telescope in hand, up to Fort Hill. Bradford and Winslow focused their lenses on the narrow harbor entrance. Is it the French? Come to rout and raid? Had they found out how small and weak the colony was? Alarm spread through the crowd gathering on the hill.

Standish mustered men to fight, trained the cannon on the harbor and fired a warning shot.

Priscilla tightened her grip on John's hand.

'Don't fear. We may be few, but we're ferocious, and Hobbamock has run off to alert Massasoit. The Indians will come to our aid if need be, I'm sure.'

'How is it,' Priscilla said, 'you always help me to feel things will come out all right?'

For an hour they waited, eyes straining, under gray skies, a chill wind in their faces. The ship hove into view. A tense silence hung over the small crowd as she raised her colors: a white ensign with the red cross of St George – England.

'God be praised!' Bradford exclaimed and led the noisy charge down to the shore.

John and Priscilla ran hand in hand, laughing as they stumbled over hummocks of rough grass.

'Wonder who's on board,' Priscilla gasped.

'Hoorah! Provisions at last,' Howland called out.

'Fishing gear… flour… grain… livestock…' Loud and exuberant, folk shouted their hopes.

'Look. She's anchored in the same protected spot as the *Mayflower*,' John pointed.

'I wonder how Master Jones fares,' Priscilla said.

They watched the ship's boat being lowered, passengers disembarking.

Standish caught up with them. Puffing, he asked John to take the shallop across to help with the ferrying.

With the wind behind her the shallop sailed at a fair clip and soon passed the ship's boat. John assessed the passengers. *Mostly men. Hope it's a hearty workforce with plenty of supplies.* As he drew nearer he made out the name of the ship, a small vessel, only about half the size of the *Mayflower*; *Fortune. We could do with a good dose of that.*

The first passenger to climb down the ladder was a heavily pregnant woman. John took her weight, easing her from the ladder, helping her to sit midships. Next was a young man and two young women. 'Jonathan Brewster,' he introduced himself. 'And my sisters, Patience and Fear.' Following the trio, a dozen young men hurtled down, not caring who they tripped over or accidentally sat on.

'Have a care!' John shouted. He called up to the ship's mate, 'No trunks, sacks, barrels?'

'Nah. None but what's already gone. A few livestock still to come.'

Something is wrong. This doesn't feel right.

Sailing back across the harbor into the wind, John had to tack which resulted in a longer trip.

'Aiee.' The pregnant woman clutched her belly. 'It's started.'

Please God. Not in the shallop. John used every skill he knew to hurry, as the woman's cries became more frequent. As he lowered the sail and pulled round to the large docking rock, Standish and Howland took his lines. The woman screamed, 'Help, please God. Aiee.' Susanna and Priscilla ran forward onto the rock and when the shallop was steady, John lifted the woman over the gunnels into their arms. 'Thank you.' He was sweating as if he'd chopped down a tree, and weak at the knees.

Now the ship's boat returned and unloaded a hog and sow, goats and a dozen chickens.

Bradford stood a few feet away, conversing with the ship's captain. 'Is that it? No more provisions?'

'None. Only what's ashore now,' the captain replied.

'I cannot believe it.' Bradford slammed his fist into his open palm. 'What does this mean? Why? We are desperate for provisions and with nigh thirty young men to feed – no provisions? They've brought nothing with them – no cooking or farming utensils, nothing of any use whatsoever – only a few suits of clothes?'

John had never seen Bradford so angry. But in an instant he'd calmed himself.

'Standish, Alden – would you allocate these men to different households? Put as many as you can in the common buildings. We are invited to the Brewster house to sup.

Answering Standish's rap on the door, the Elder opened. 'Welcome. Come in.'

Standish swept over to the hearth and bowed. 'Fare you well, lovely ladies? Patience, Fear… beautiful as ever.'

Praise be! Mary looks at least ten years younger. All soft and melting. John caught Priscilla's eye and winked. Grasping his arms, Mary Brewster gazed at her son, who whilst patting her arm, shifted from one foot to the other as if wishing to disengage from his mother's rapt adoration.

Patience and Fear welcomed Standish's courtly flirtations. Priscilla tended to the cooking pots.

'A great pleasure to have you fair lasses with us,' Standish was saying. ''Twill liven our spirits, and Jonathan, so glad you've come. Another fit male and a comfort to your parents.'

'To be sure,' Jonathan said. 'But 'tis a shock seeing how thin and ragged you all are. Do you not have enough to eat?'

John surveyed Brewster's son. *Reckon he's accustomed to a hearty repast.*

Standish cleared his throat. 'Times have been hard. Your father will explain.' He addressed Priscilla. 'Mistress Mullins, is the goodwife safely delivered?'

'Aye, sir. She and the babe, a son, are well. But her husband died at sea.'

Governor Bradford stayed silent, standing beside the Elder. The Brewster's two young lads sat at the table, fidgeting, waiting for food.

Elder Brewster spoke. 'As we are all present may we please say prayers… Oh Lord, we give thanks and praise for the safe arrival of *Fortune* and those who sailed in her, our son and daughters, here with us on these shores.'

As the gathering sat to eat, John could see Bradford was still angry; his jaw set rigid, a frown creased his forehead, his entire body was tight with tension. He carried a letter.

The governor spoke. 'This letter from Weston – 'tis unjust, iniquitous! Listen. "That you sent no lading back with the ship (the *Mayflower*) is strange, and very properly resented. I know your weakness was the cause of it; and I believe more weakness of judgment than weakness of hands. A quarter of the time you spent in discoursing, arguing, and consulting would have done much more... if you mean... to perform the conditions agreed upon, do us the favour to copy them out fair, and subscribe them with the names of your principal members and likewise give account... of how our money was laid out... And consider that the life of this business depends on the lading of this ship".' Bradford raised his head and shook his fist. 'How dare he make such accusations, knowing nothing of all we've suffered, and our depleted state, and how we've managed to survive and dealt successfully with the Indians, and begin to build our colony... sees fit to punish us, sending a shipload of ruffians with no provisions, no fishing or farming gear, only a few animals... how does he expect us to survive, never mind prosper?'

After his explosion, Bradford was speechless. He received sympathy and support from his companions. When he was calmed, they began the business of how to respond.

John tried to focus. He'd seen Priscilla listening carefully to every word. However, after the day's exertions it was more than he could do to think how to respond to such a weasel as Weston. *Why did they ever place their trust in the man?* He was forming the opinion that judgment of a man's character was not their leaders' strongpoint, except perhaps for Winslow. It seemed they'd been duped by Weston, and how could they be so easily trusting in Prence?

'So; rations to be halved again – agreed, Mr Alden?'

John started. 'Yes, yes of course. Beginning tomorrow.'

★ ★ ★

'Surely you can spare a mite more. I've four extra mouths to feed with these newcomers lodging,' Goodwife Hopkins pleaded.

'I'm sorry, but no.' John poured an exact pint measure of corn into her bowl. *'Tis terrible hard. I'd expect begging and wheedling from Goody Billington, but Goody Hopkins, 'tisn't like her. I hate giving so little to folk who are always hungry. The only good in ration days is when Priscilla comes. There she is, making sure she is last.* He held Priscilla close and pushed the door almost shut. He pulled her coif down, buried his face in her hair and felt the beating of her heart. Voices. They drew apart. Priscilla hastily retied her coif and held out her ration bowl. John peered out the door; Brewster, Bradford, and Winslow in deep conversation. They waited while the men passed.

''Tis hard,' Priscilla said. 'Seems we're being persecuted by the very folk in London who should be supporting us.'

'Poor Bradford, 'tis a rough road.' John began putting the barrels back in place, preparing to lock up. 'Still, I wager for all the dangers and troubles, we're better off over here. Bradford came to visit with Standish. He brought a letter from Cushman in Holland. He says over there the recession is getting worse by the day, the plague spreads horrible quick, and Holland and Spain are at war – as well as a Protestant rebellion in France. Sounds dire.'

'I love you, John,' Priscilla said impulsively. 'You talk to me and tell me things as if – as if I were a man!' She hugged herself and swished her skirts. 'Yes, I'd rather be here with you and work and starve than anywhere else in the world.'

'I'm coming to think that in this new world we need every person's good thinking,' John said. 'It goes against the order of things – but why shouldn't a man discuss matters with his love – and even do as she says?' He kept his voice low, drawing her close.

Priscilla clasped her hands round the back of his neck. ''Tis sacrilege to think thus, but it's wonderful – our secret. Promise me, John, we will always be thus, discuss and decide matters together and do what **we** think is right, follow our own rules.'

John stepped back and looked at the floor. 'Aye. But if we want to be part of this colony we must follow the customs of our leaders. All pull together. Sadly these religious folk insist their way is the only right way.'

Priscilla frowned and tightened her lips. 'Captain Standish remains Anglican. 'Tis accepted.'

'Captain Standish is special. He is the only man in the colony fit to be our military commander. He is needed in a way we are not. And Standish does keep the Sabbath. If we want to make our way here, we must publicly conform. But I promise we will share our thoughts and be kind and merry in our own home.' John drew Priscilla into his arms. 'My love, I long for you to be merry. Plump and merry.'

Chapter 42

November 1621

Captain Standish's letter

Desire departs

One evening, in the last week of November, Standish and John sat by their hearth, pipes in hand. Driven by a freezing wind, sleety snow pricked against the parchment windows.

'We're almost there,' John said. 'A few more loads of planking and beaver pelts should do it.'

'A great achievement, to get her laden to capacity in two weeks! By God, but we've worked hard,' Standish said, 'and hungry all the while. Never mind. We're sending her back with five hundred pounds worth of cargo. Half what we owe Weston and his lot.'

'Should keep him quiet awhile,' John said. ''Twill be good to be providing for ourselves again.'

Standish was quiet. He crossed and uncrossed his legs. 'Will you excuse me, John? I've some writing business to do before the

Fortune sails.' He picked up a pine knot from its place on the hearth, lighted it, and carried it carefully to his desk. He took several sheets of parchment from the drawer and a small knife with which he began to sharpen the tip of his quill pen.

John sat quiet, adjusting his legs to avoid the chill draught curling across the floor. He looked across now and again to watch his friend scribbling, crossing out, starting again. Occasionally Standish paused to stroke his beard or put his head in his hands.

I wonder what he is writing? Who is this for? To go with the Fortune – why? It must be important. John focused his gaze on the fire, finding changing colors and rhythms in the flames.

'There.'

John started.

Script in hand, Standish resumed his seat by the fire. 'May I read this to you? I've written to Rose's sister asking for her hand.'

'Miles! You never said. Yes, read it out, though I doubt my opinion will be much use.'

'To my dear friend, Mistress Barbara.

'I write to you from our newly built colony in Plymouth. When I last wrote it was with the sad news of the death of your dear sister. Her loss is a grief we share. Praise God we have had no return of the sickness that took poor Rose. In fact, our little colony is becoming well established. We've signed a peace treaty with the Indians and are set to trade with them for beaver pelts.

'This autumn we reaped a good harvest of corn and squash, beans and pumpkin and there is a plenitude of wild berries and fruit, fish, fowl and deer. Every daylight hour is taken up with building, and providing food. But of an evening, seated by the hearth, my thoughts travel to the old country, and especially to you, my dear. I think of your pretty face, blond curls, and lively merry nature. You always brought happiness and laughter with you.

'I am lonely, and I write to ask if you would consent to join me here – to share this promising life. My dear Barbara, I offer my hand in marriage, humbly hoping you are not already taken, and that you will say yes. I shall eagerly await the arrival of the next ship, daring to hope that you will be aboard.

'Your loving friend, Captain Miles Standish.'

'It's a fine letter,' John said. 'Sure to win her heart if she's not already wed. Miles, I hope so much she'll come to you.'

'She's a fine, feisty woman. I do believe she would do me good – and be an excellent addition to our people.' Standish slapped his knee. 'Thank you, John. I'll write out a fair copy and entrust it to the captain's safekeeping.'

'Miles,' John said, 'seeing you writing and thinking of the hours you've read to me – passages from the *Iliad*,' he paused, looking at the floor. 'I hesitate to ask, but do you think… would you…'

'Would I what, John? Come on, out with it.'

'Would you teach me to read and write? I'm terribly keen to learn before I'm wed – to surprise Priscilla.'

'With pleasure!' Standish stood and clapped John's shoulder. 'We'll devote every spare moment – and have you polished and ready. Good on you, John, good on you.'

★ ★ ★

'Priscilla, Priscilla! Up with you. Are you ailing?'

'I'm sorry, Mistress Brewster. I'll hurry.'

'Fine morning to lay a-bed. With the *Fortune* set to sail in an hour,' Mary Brewster grumbled and scolded.

When the Brewster household was collected and ready, Priscilla stepped out into a cold, gray, swirling mist. Bare tree branches swayed to breaking point; the wind came up under her skirts. Huddled and solemn, the Winslow household joined them, a tearful Desire holding Peregrine tight in her arms. Susanna nodded a silent greeting, subdued, her face set.

How sad, so sad. Desire going back to England just because she's with child. She would be horribly shamed and humiliated if the Brewsters and Bradford and that horrid Mr Prence knew. He is well nigh the harshest of them all. Desire would be dragged, whipped and shunned, except for a ritual

330

examination of her soul. If we were in England, she and the father would wed. And if he ran off, well she'd have a hard time but not as hard as here. Why are we here if we make life more cruel than in England?

They joined the small crowd gathered on the shore to wave *Fortune* God speed and safe arrival.

'The shallop is waiting,' Bradford called, holding the bowline.

Desire hugged Peregrine, kissed and whispered to him, and handed him to Susanna, who put the little lad down and clasped Desire close. 'My dear, my dear,' she sobbed. 'Take care, the captain has promised to take care of you. We'll not forget you. You're a good lass. Good as they come.'

Priscilla grasped Desire's shoulders. 'I'll not forget you. I wish you could stay – but I don't blame you. I'd do the same. We'll miss you terrible.' She wiped her eyes and hugged her friend. 'Stay safe.'

Mute with suppressed sobs, Desire clutched Priscilla's arms, let go and hurried to board the shallop. John Alden was at the tiller. Priscilla stood beside Susanna; they waved.

'Poor girl,' Susanna said as their eyes followed the shallop, battling choppy waves. 'Edward and I would gladly have kept her and her little one as part of the family.'

'It's cruel,' Priscilla said. 'So cruel. If only other folk were as kind as you and Master Winslow. I pray she'll be all right.'

They stayed watching as John sailed the shallop across the harbor, and pulled up alongside the ship. Desire climbed the ladder up onto the deck. Then she was gone.

Priscilla put a hand on Susanna's arm. 'You've been a good mother to her.'

'She's been a good lass – so helpful and kind – after you helped her out of the black state.' Susanna shook herself. 'But how are you, my dear? I've not seen you for days. Mary's been keeping you busy?'

'Yes! Spinning, and mending, and cooking, and grinding cornmeal – dawn to evening prayers. I can hardly stay awake during prayers.'

Susanna set Peregrine between them, each holding one of his little hands. Slowly they made their way amongst other folk returning to their labors.

Of a sudden, everyone stopped still. Priscilla looked up. All eyes were fixed on an Indian they'd never seen before, loping down the hill. Bradford and Standish stepped forward to meet him.

'Squanto? Squanto,' the brave demanded.

'Not here. Away.' Bradford gestured.

The Indian handed Bradford a sheaf of arrows bound with a large snakeskin.

Susanna looked round. 'Where's Edward?'

He was striding forward to join Bradford and Standish. The three endeavored to understand the meaning of this 'gift', using gestures to ask questions. But the Indian merely shrugged, not comprehending, or unwilling to respond. The only word he uttered was 'Squanto'.

Bradford gave up and bade him farewell.

Winslow came to Susanna's side. 'All we know is the sheaf was sent by the chief of the Narragansetts – staunch enemies of Massasoit's people.'

'Sounds worrying,' Susanna said.

'We'll have to wait for Squanto's return. But that snakeskin – it's a rattlesnake. Ominous, I fear.'

Chapter 43

December 1621

Defense

Gently falling snow had blanketed the ground by the time Squanto returned, late in the afternoon. Standish and John, Winslow and Brewster all gathered in Bradford's house to hear the Indian's opinion.

'Bad. A challenge,' Squanto said.

The five English looked at one another.

'A challenge, is it?' Bradford broke the silence. 'I propose we send *our* challenge. We'll replace the arrows with bullets and gunpowder and return their parcel. Give them something to think about.'

'Agreed. Good idea,' Standish said. The others nodded. That hour, Squanto was dispatched with the refilled snakeskin.

In the evening, Miles paced the floor in front of his hearth. 'The Narragansetts are far more powerful than Massasoit's people. This chief could muster several *thousand* braves with a snap of his finger.'

He demonstrated. 'We are hopelessly vulnerable. Our cannon are meant for enemy ships. They're useless against Indians firing arrows from behind trees, or worse still, attacking at night and scalping us in our beds.'

John nodded. 'And I wager Squanto hasn't told the Narragansett chief we've got barrels of the plague ready to unleash.'

'Squanto is, what is the word? Mercurial,' Standish said. 'Shifting loyalties?' He stopped pacing and stood, hands on hips, looking at John. 'There's nothing for it. We must impale the entire settlement.'

'What? That is a mammoth task. 'Twould be nearly a mile of joined planks – and would have to be high.'

'Yes. Almost eight feet I reckon.'

'But that would require an army of men! How would we have any time to hunt or fish?'

'All the food and provisions in God's kingdom won't do us any good if we're massacred,' Standish said. 'I'll ask Bradford to hold a meeting.'

At the meeting next morning, Standish met stiff opposition. Winslow argued that getting food should take priority; hunting, fishing, and trading expeditions to barter for the Indians' corn. Bradford pointed out that already on halved rations, the new influx of men might mutiny if required to work harder on so little food. John interceded, reiterating Standish's argument that more food would be of no use if they were all massacred.

No one spoke. The memory of Corbitant's plotting and the threat of a surprise Indian attack hung heavy. John glanced round the bowed heads and wondered whether each was reasoning, or praying.

Bradford lifted his head, raised his eyes to heaven and said, 'We must build the wall.'

'It must be at least eight feet high made of tree trunks, bark stripped off, set deep in the ground, tight together – no gaps a body could fit through. To run up alongside the brook, around behind

Fort Hill, then down the far side of the clearing and along the bank above the beach back to the brook.' Standish spoke with boyish eagerness.

'Strewth!' Winslow exclaimed. 'That's nearly a mile!'

'We also should have four gates which stand out from the wall with flat roofs we can shoot from.'

Brewster nodded his head and murmured approval.

'I'll muster the men now,' Standish said. 'And I mean to reorganize our men into an effective army. We are not a strong fighting unit.' He shook his head. 'Not at all. And we need to be.' He looked at Bradford. 'May I appoint you, sir, Winslow, Hopkins and Alden to be captains of four units?'

'Yes. Yes, of course.'

'One of these units to serve as a special fire service. We don't want a repeat of the summer fires.'

'Thank you, Standish,' Brewster said. 'It is well advised.'

★ ★ ★

Christmas Day. Priscilla woke into a cold, dark morning, her belly aching with hunger. As she set out with the water pails, lazy, fat snowflakes settled on her face and shawl. *At least the vicious wind is quiet.* Walking along the path behind the Billingtons' house, she spied John, running down the hill, a fowl in each hand, his blond curls blown back.

Dropping the birds, he caught her in his arms. 'Happy Christmas, my love.'

'Happy Christmas,' she replied. 'But I wish we weren't all so hungry.'

'It is hard. And 'tis hard to have to work and behave as if... as if Christmas doesn't exist, is simply the same as any other day.'

'When we've our own home, I want us to celebrate Christmas. In the evening time, after the day's work is done – make it special.'

'Yes. We will.' John held her tight again. 'I love you.' He swayed her back and forth.

'Now it is a happy Christmas Day,' Priscilla whispered. 'Being with you now.' She closed her eyes, relaxing into his rocking.

'John!' a man's voice called.

They stood apart. 'It's Howland,' John said.

'There's been some trouble,' Howland panted, running. 'Sorry to interrupt.'

'What trouble?'

'The men who came on the *Fortune*, and some others not in the Brewster fold have refused to work today. They say it is against their consciences.' Howland raised his eyebrows. 'Bradford has given permission for conscience sake for them to have the day off.' He kicked the earth and twirled his axe. 'No such luck for us. See you up yonder.' He trudged up the hill.

'I'm coming to help you fetch the water and give Mary Brewster these fowl. And wish her Happy Christmas whether she likes it or no,' John said. 'Standish and I are invited to sup in the Brewster house tonight. Standish put in a request for the Elder's advice on leadership – and religious guidance for me.' He winked. 'We didn't want you to be on your own in that grim house, not on Christmas night.'

'Thank you, oh, thank you – and thank the captain too.'

Back from fetching the water, Priscilla sat by the hearth with Mary Brewster and Fear and Patience, plucking the fowl, Mary lecturing on the importance of keeping a constant watch on one's soul.

Oh, I wish she'd be quiet. She just makes life harder than it already is. I wish our wedding could be tomorrow. But with building the wall, how will John ever have time to build our house? She remembered walking along the broad London street with fine houses, well spaced; houses of prosperous merchants. *Father promised Joseph we'd have a house like that one day. Not likely. Will I ever wear a fine gown and the gorgeous sash? Bother this poor place. We live in squalid hovels.*

'Priscilla! Are you listening? Repeat back to me what I just said,' Mary reprimanded.

'About the soul, that we must – hark! Men's voices outside.'

The women listened. Laughter, shouts of triumph. 'I won – ha!'

Mary dropped her fowl and hurried to open the door, just a crack. Priscilla followed, peering round the gray head. Fear and Patience stretched on tiptoe.

The men Bradford had let off work were playing games – stool ball and pitching the bar – having merry fun.

Not thinking, Priscilla clapped her hands. 'Just the same as in England.'

'Pagans!' Mary spat. 'And not a man here to punish them, all working hard to make us safe from pagan Indians. Conscience indeed! The Elder said Bradford was too soft.' She turned on her heel, almost knocking into Priscilla. 'Come. In with you.'

It was noon when the laughter and shouts suddenly ceased. Curious, Mary and Priscilla opened the door. Bradford and Brewster stood silent, facing the men.

Bradford spoke, his voice quiet and hard. 'So this is what your conscience dictates? Very well. It goes against my conscience that you should play while others work.' He took away their balls and bats. 'If you wish to spend the day in quiet devotion, so be it – go into your dwellings. But there will be no gaming or reveling in the street. Ever.'

The men shuffled off, kicking at ruts in the track. No more cheer.

Brewster came to the hearth for his ale and cornbread. 'It is a fine line he has to draw,' the Elder said. 'Too harsh and they'll likely rebel, but they must follow our ways.'

1622

Chapter 44

April 1622

John confronts Bradford

A long hard winter had, in the space of two weeks, given way to a hot spring, bringing a rush to plant. John leaned on his mattock, taking a short breather from hours of pick-axing. He recalled the winter; cruel months of indescribable cold, topsoil already frozen solid in December, and an incessant northeast wind whipping faces with sleeting snow, congealing strands of hair and covering jackets with an icy sheen. John reckoned if it had been so cold the winter of their arrival, no one would have survived, and during this freezing winter, the men of the colony worked to build the wall. They dug the trench, felled trees, stripped off the bark and lugged the heavy trunks down to the trench. Day after day they labored, often swooning from hunger, fatigue and the bitter cold.

John felt himself partly to blame for the measly rations. He'd overestimated the abundance of the harvest and used up too much corn for the Thanksgiving feast. He wished he'd shortened rations sooner. However, no one perished and the wall was completed by mid-March. But no thaw. The land stayed frozen hard until the beginning of April with no hope of planting the crops they so desperately needed.

Bringing his mind back to the present, John wielded his mattock, forcing himself not to swoon, from hunger and a surge of anger against Squanto. On the first of April, the eve before Standish was to set out on a vital trading expedition, Hobbamock arrived in the settlement bringing rumors that Squanto had been secretly circulating among all the tribes in the region, fermenting a plot for the Massachusetts and Narragansett tribes to join in an attack on the trading party, killing Standish and then attacking Plymouth Colony. Bradford refused to believe that Squanto, their loyal friend, would do such a thing. So Hobbamock sent his wife to visit Massasoit to confirm the strength of the peace treaty between the chief and Plymouth, whilst Hobbamock set out on a tour of all the tribes to find out the truth of the rumors.

By now, well into April with no sign of Hobbamock, John and all the settlers were becoming increasingly on edge, fearing the Indians might attack at any moment.

'How goes it, John?' Standish called as he traipsed across the field to pick-axe alongside. Sweat dripped down the captain's face, now bright pink from the burning sun.

John started as a child's screams echoed across the fields; a sound that always tore at his insides. He'd noticed that in this period of tense waiting and severe hunger the beatings had increased. *'Tis wrong to beat children thus. They feel the worry too; makes them misbehave.* He steadied himself. Scanning the fields, he said, 'Not enough men working. Always the same. Where are Billington, Prence and those louts from the *Fortune*? All pull together. Pah. All labor for all to have an equal share.' He spat on the ground. 'A few of us work to feed everyone.'

'I agree,' Standish said. 'Stands to reason. A man will work harder if he reaps the rewards of his labor.' He placed a hand on John's shoulder. 'But for the moment we just have to get on with it. Could do with a drink.' He reached down for his jug and on straightening said, 'Hie! There's Hobbamock!' Thrusting the jug into John's hands, calling out, 'Hobbamock's returned!' he strode to meet the brave.

Bradford, Winslow and John followed.

By now, almost fluent in English, the pinese spoke. 'Massasoit sends greetings and good wishes with fondness for Bradford and the people of Plymouth. He reaffirms the peace treaty between us and promises he'll give warning if he hears of any plots against his Plymouth brothers.' Hobbamock fastened his gaze on Bradford. 'But our chief exploded with anger on hearing of Squanto's plotting. All the winter long Squanto has been circulating among the tribes, telling them that Plymouth has the plague buried under the common house, ready to unleash on any tribe as directed, of course, by Squanto. He's been making each tribe pay him tribute so you won't set the plague on them. They are so in fear they'll do anything he says and are inclined to follow his command rather than Massasoit. Massasoit says Squanto is a traitor and – according to the peace treaty – must suffer a traitor's fate. He demands you hand him over.'

Bradford's face set rigid and gray. 'Thank you, Hobbamock. Thank you. You may go.' The Indian inclined his head and departed.

'I'll not hand Squanto over,' Bradford said. 'He has shown remorse and pledged his loyalty.'

'But sir,' Standish said, 'that violates the peace treaty. You will anger Massasoit.'

'Nevertheless I won't do it. I'll take the risk. That is final.' Bradford looked up to heaven. 'Now – the trading expedition. We need corn, and it seems the Indians are not planning to attack us. I say the expedition should go ahead. Forthwith.'

Standish departed on his trading expedition. Bradford insisted Squanto stay within the confines of the settlement for his own safety. John would have liked to go with Standish but was pleased Bradford wanted his support in Plymouth. Was Prence falling from favor at last?

★ ★ ★

Two weeks, three weeks, John waited impatiently for Standish to return. Fields almost ready to plant the corn, squash, beans and pumpkin. Wed in May. He paused for a swig from his jug. Looking across the fields he spied Priscilla wielding her hoe and dreamed of their wedding night.

'Hie, hie! The shallop!' Francis danced, ran and hopped up the track.

John shielded his eyes searching the harbor. Francis was right; there – in the distance, white sails. He strode fast across the field and grabbing Priscilla's hand before Mary Brewster could protest, pulled her with him, breaking into a stumbling run.

As the tide was in, John and Bradford moored the shallop alongside the landing rock and helped Standish unload a modest haul of corn, beaver and other pelts.

"Tis a good sight,' Priscilla said.

'Also good, Standish says no sign of hostility from the Indians.' John heaved a sack of corn over his shoulder, turned and froze, staring at the track.

There stood Massasoit, in full war paint, his face furrowed in rage. 'Squanto. I demand him. Traitor. Peace treaty say traitor die.'

Bradford stepped forward. He acknowledged Squanto's betrayal but pleaded he was vital to the survival of the colony. 'He is our tongue.'

Winslow came to Bradford's side and joined in his plea, reminding the chief of Squanto's good help in bringing understanding and peace.

Massasoit's demeanor took on a more reflective cast. He said no more, turned his back and sedately walked off, standing tall.

John, Bradford and Standish carried load after load to the storehouse. They were stacking the last of the pelts when they heard a shrill cry.

'Governor Bradford!'

'That's Priscilla!' John rushed out.

Priscilla pointed. 'Indian warriors.'

'Every time we turn around there's another Indian,' Standish grumbled, as the three men hurried to greet the braves.

There stood a warrior carrying a fearful large knife. A small group of warriors stood behind him.

'Squanto,' the warrior said. 'Massasoit.' His gestures left no doubt about Massasoit's demands: the warrior must bring back Squanto's head and hands. The accompanying warriors then produced furs, evidently offering them as payment.

'No,' Bradford said to the offer of the furs. He then spoke a few words in John's ear. John left and returned minutes later with Squanto.

'It wasn't me. This is all Hobbamock's doing.' Squanto spoke with indignation. 'Not my fault.'

Bradford bowed his head in despair. He put a hand on Squanto's shoulder. 'Squanto, how could you?' He stepped back and held out his arm as if inviting the braves to take him.

John shouted, 'A boat. A strange boat – look.'

Bradford addressed the warrior. 'We keep Squanto until we know if the ship be enemy or friend.'

The braves all stamped in rage, briefly mimicked a war dance, turned on their heel and departed.

As the boat sailed closer she raised her ensign. 'English! Hooray! Thank the Lord! But she's only a shallop. Why?'

''Tis a sign,' Bradford said under his breath, 'a sign 'tis God's will Squanto should live.'

Seven men climbed out of the shallop. A rough looking lot, John thought.

The 'captain' stepped forward. 'Governor Bradford.' He held out a packet.

'Who are you?'

'We are from Weston's ship up north. He requests you house and feed us until a place is found for us to settle.'

Bradford blanched. No one spoke. Taking a deep weary breath, he said, 'Standish, please allocate these men to houses. Then I request a meeting at my house, Winslow, Elder Brewster, Alden, Standish.'

Seated at Bradford's table, John knew from the governor's clenched jaw and tight grim mouth that the packet of letters contained bad news.

'Three letters from Thomas Weston and a letter from a sea captain at a trading port in Maine.' Bradford drew a breath. 'From Weston, trouble. First, the *Fortune* was captured by French pirates and all our lading stolen. The captain kept prisoner for some weeks, then released.'

John groaned. 'All that work – five hundred pounds worth – gone.'

Standish, Winslow and Brewster maintained a stoic silence, but John saw a flinch cross Winslow's pale, worried face. *He's afeared for Susanna, with child and poorly, and now this.*

'In another letter,' Bradford continued, 'Weston says that he and a friend have contracted to build their own settlement north of here. He requests we house and feed the lot who've just arrived, until the leaders find a place to build.'

'That is barbarous!' the Elder exploded. 'The effrontery! He refuses to support us and sets up as a competitor – and reckons we should help?!'

'There is worse than that,' Bradford said, 'and I ask you to please not speak of this next to anyone.' He unfolded another letter. 'Weston reports that the venture company, due to quarrels and disagreements, could unravel. We cannot count on any more support from the joint stock company. He closes, "I fear you must stand on your own legs and trust (as they say) to God and yourselves".'

Brewster, Winslow, Standish and John stared into space, stunned.

Bradford went on, 'And this letter from the captain in Maine. He reports that early in the spring, in Virginia, three or four hundred settlers were killed in an Indian massacre. He hopes his warning will serve us well.'

Winslow broke the silence. 'We are hungry to desperation. Folk are emaciated, hardly able to stand even to carry out daily chores. Little Peregrine and Francis with swollen bellies, all puffed out. And Susanna.' His voice broke. 'And now more mouths to feed.'

'Yes,' Bradford said. 'But we cannot in good conscience refuse hospitality to Weston's men. To do so would be to send them off to die.'

'We will all die if we don't get more food. Standish did well but the corn he brought isn't nearly enough. I propose to take the shallop to Maine to thank the captain for his warning and beg for any victuals he can spare,' Winslow said. He twisted his hands and looked at the floor. 'Though I am very reluctant to leave, Susanna is so unwell.'

'I know Priscilla will go to her as often,' John glanced at the Elder – 'as often as she can.'

'Thank you, Winslow,' Bradford said, and the others murmured their appreciation.

'About the massacre,' Standish stood and paced as he spoke. 'Hobbamock has been gathering information about the Indians' doings.'

Bradford started and sat up straight.

Standish continued, frowning. 'Hobbamock says, and it is only to be expected, that because we've broken the peace treaty by not handing over Squanto, we cannot rely on Massasoit's support against an Indian attack.' He looked at Bradford. 'And there are rumors that, knowing we are vulnerable, the Massachusetts and Narragansetts are now planning an attack on our colony.'

All eyes were on Bradford. He stood, resting his knuckles on the table. Only half a minute passed before he presented his solution. 'We will build a fort, atop Fort Hill. Strong enough to withstand attack and large enough to house us all, where we would be safe. Just the sight of it would give the Indians pause.'

'You still refuse to hand over Squanto?' Standish confronted the governor.

'I refuse.'

Silence.

'A fort then,' Standish said.

'Thank you, gentlemen.' Bradford left his place and opened the door.

Smoldering, fists and teeth clenched, John strode quickly with Standish to the captain's house. Once inside, door closed, he raged. 'Bradford is putting us all, this entire colony, at risk, just for that devious, double-crossing Indian. It isn't right. Why is he allowed?'

'Bradford loves Squanto,' Standish said. 'Remember, Squanto appeared at the time Bradford became governor. Bradford is a lonely man in a lonely job. Yes, he has assistants, but Squanto served us well with Massasoit. He showed us how to plant, and he has an endearing childlike way. I suppose we defer because we – perhaps we fear how it might affect Bradford to... to hand the brave over to be executed.' He went on, 'And in so many ways, Bradford governs well. He is brave, devoted, honest, with a firm sense of direction. We need him to stay strong.'

'Damn shame Dorothy died.' Overcome with sadness for all the deaths: Rose, Master and Mistress Mullins, Joseph and the Carvers, John passed his hand over his eyes.

'Listen. That bird.'

Miles and John stood in silence, lost for a time in the full throated rippling notes.

'Sounds like the spring song of our English thrush,' Standish said.

John was quiet a moment. He sat down and bent forward, elbows on his knees. He stared at his finger-locked hands. Then he looked up at Standish and spoke quietly. 'I don't like to say it, but when you put it all together, the rumors of tribes wanting to attack us, the information Hobbamock has gathered; it does seem Squanto wants to replace Massasoit as Big Chief and is using us to achieve his goal. And that **is** treachery.'

'Squanto doesn't think so,' Standish said. 'He has said this is his homeland. I imagine he feels that he and the few of his family left should rule. He doesn't seem to see, or doesn't care that his dealings could harm us.'

'So if Bradford is trying to teach Squanto to see things the way we do, he is wasting his time.'

'Sadly, yes.'

John sighed and stood, gazing at the embers on the hearth. 'Thanks be for Winslow, going for food. The irony; the sea is teeming with beautiful fat fish and we haven't the nets or gear to catch them. Thank God for the shellfish, though they haven't much meat.'

'Pray he gets to Maine and back safely,' Standish said.

'And, Miles,' John ran his hand through his hair, 'I know this sounds selfish, but how will I ever build an Alden house? At this rate months will go by afore…'

Standish broke in with a hand on John's shoulder. 'It isn't selfish. You and Priscilla have been waiting and waiting.' He stood, thumbs tucked into his breeches, rocking back on his heels. 'Tell you what we'll do. I'll get Howland and a group of other good builders and we'll have your house up within a week or two. I'll put the other men to felling trees for the fort.'

John grinned. 'Thank you, Miles! Thank you.' He thumped the table. 'Wait 'til Priscilla hears this!'

The more John thought about Bradford's refusal to hand over Squanto, the more worried and angry he became. *Is the man blind?* He shied away from confronting the governor but felt he couldn't live with himself if he didn't at least try to make Bradford see sense. *I reckon he's grown to trust me. He might listen.*

That evening, about an hour before prayers, John rapped on Bradford's door.

'Come in, Mr Alden. What brings you?'

John glanced round the room to be sure no one else was present. 'There is a matter I wish to discuss, sir.'

Bradford gestured to a chair by the hearth and sat in his own rocker. Fine English oak, John noted. He began. 'It is the matter of the Indians.'

'How is that?'

'Sir, I beg of you. Our future as a colony is at risk without Massasoit as an ally. The massacre in Virginia...'

'Mr Alden. Without doubt the settlement in Virginia had sinned in the sight of God and was receiving their reward.'

'Whether or no, clearly Massasoit is extremely angry. Without him as an ally we are utterly vulnerable. What good a fort? What good a wall? The Indians could torch everything we have built. The colony we have struggled and died for could go up in flames – all because—'

'Mr Alden.' Bradford stood. 'I will not betray Squanto. Furthermore, you are speaking above yourself. I have valued your support but it is not for you to advise me on matters of God's will.' He stepped rapidly to the door and held it open. 'If you wish to attain a position of responsible status in this colony you will remember my words. Good day.'

Shakily, John walked to the door. He looked into the pale blue eyes. 'Good day, sir.' The door closed behind him. Feeling thrashed, winded, he plodded, staring at the ground, lumps of clay sprouting tufts of grass. A small lizard slithered across his path. He shook his head and swatted as if brushing away flies or mosquitoes. Buzzards circled overhead. The early evening air hung onto the acrid smell of heat. He paid no heed to where his leaden feet were taking him. Across a field, through a grove of trees – ah – the sound of rushing water. He sank onto the mossy bank and stared mindlessly at the tumbling cascades. Gradually thoughts began to take shape. *I'll tell no one: not Standish nor Priscilla. I'll behave as if nothing had happened and with deference. Perhaps Bradford won't always be such a dictator. Perhaps it is the strain. Whatever. I know now. I conform – or else. I'll never again challenge authority in this place. If that is the price I have to pay to achieve a prosperous life for Priscilla and our children – so be it.* Even as he made his decision John felt something inside himself shrivel into a knot of fury. *So be it.*

Chapter 45

May – June 1622

The marriage

Priscilla stepped out from the Winslow house, closing the door on the babe's plaintive wailing and Susanna's tears. Goodwife Hopkins was with them; Priscilla must get on and weed the corn.

John ran to her, beaming. 'Our house is to be built – soon now. Standish is collecting…' He stopped. 'Why are you weeping?'

'I'm so afeared for Susanna and the babe, Edward, they're calling him. He is always crying. Hungry and can't suck hard enough, and she hasn't enough milk. Oh 'tis pitiable. We are all so helpless – not a woman in this place could stand as a wet nurse. That's what they need.' She tried to steady herself and wiped the tears away. 'But you are full of cheer.'

'Yes. Good news for us. Standish is collecting a crew of men – to make sure we have a house before we start work building a fort.

'A fort? Why?'

'I'll explain later,' John said. 'Susanna needs food. I'll get my musket and go see what I can find. Not many fowl about 'til autumn. But I might light on a turkey or two.'

'Thank you, thank you. You are a good man.' Priscilla grasped his arms. 'All the women are putting by a bit of food each day for her, even if 'tis only a crumb, and all these extra men wanting food, and some of them so rough.'

'Yes,' John agreed. ''Tis a rogue deal.'

★ ★ ★

The last week in May, Winslow returned from his expedition to Maine. The generous captain had given baskets and baskets of corn, dried peas and beans, dried fruit and dried meat. Nevertheless, with so many mouths to feed they'd have to keep everyone on short rations, at least 'til the harvest.

Late one afternoon as Priscilla was laboring from the brook with replenished water pails, she heard John call. She stopped. He strode across the clearing, head high, bootlace untied again. She smiled. *How does he never trip?*

'Let me have those.' He took the pails from her; set them down. Holding her hands he said, 'Good news. I reckon three days and our house will be ready.'

Priscilla gasped with delight.

'Aye. I'll ask Bradford to marry us three days hence. First of June. Then you will be Mistress Alden.' He held her close. She buried her head in his neck, inhaling the clean smell of his sweat; her mind clouded in a haze of joy.

Priscilla woke. She lay a moment, listening to the swelling dawn chorus. *The first day of June. Today. The day has come. We're to be wed. Susanna and her babe look set to recover and Master Winslow has returned with a good load of provisions and the Alden house is built. Are we entering a time of good fortune at last? We're to be wed, we're to be wed.* She snuggled into the bedclothes and sang the phrases to herself, making them into a chant. *There are still chores to be done, the water to fetch.* She rose and dressed. As she was bending over to pick up the water pails Mary Brewster came to her side.

'Priscilla, 'tis time to return this to you.' She held out Priscilla's gardening book.

'Thank you, Mistress Brewster.' Priscilla took the book, savoring the feel of the soft leather binding. *Oh, how good to have you back.*

'But I've some bad news. The Winslow babe died in the night.'

'No! No, no.' Priscilla clutched her book. 'But he wasn't crying so much, he'd grown quiet.'

'Yes. He was slipping away.'

'We shan't wed. Not today. I'm sure John would agree. Poor Susanna and Edward. I'll go fetch the water.'

She put the treasured book into her private box and then set out for the brook, wailing inside with sadness and rage. 'If only a wet nurse.'

She heard John call her name and turned to meet him. He took the pails, put them down and held her close. ''Tis terrible sad. I'll fetch the water with you – and then…'

Priscilla heard his breath catch and break.

'Then I'll make a little coffin.'

'We must not marry today,' Priscilla said.

'No. We'll be having a burial instead.'

'Shall we wait – until Susanna and Edward have had time? We want them to be with us – and it doesn't feel right to wed while they are fresh in their sadness.'

'I agree. We've waited so long we can wait a while longer. 'Til it feels right.'

A heavy sorrow wrapped round Priscilla and hung in the air. Folk went about their work heads bowed, silent, necessary exchanges subdued. There was an unspoken agreement that no one should intrude on Edward and Susanna's private grieving.

It was a week to the day after the babe died. Setting out for the brook to gather sallet and early strawberries, Priscilla was surprised to see Master Winslow striding up the hill to the forest, his axe over his shoulder.

Approaching the brook she slowed, lingering in the soft sunlight, birdsong, rustling leaves and distant burbling waters. She stood awhile. *Mustn't tarry.* She pushed through a copse of birches and spied a female form bent, picking berries.

'Susanna?' she cried in a hoarse whisper.

Susanna stood, dropping her basket. Arms outstretched she welcomed Priscilla into her warm embrace.

Priscilla clung to her. 'Thank God you have survived. You are here, and well?' She stepped back, wiping tears from her cheeks. 'You look well.'

'Aye. I am well, thanks to your care and Goody Hopkins'. I... I'm sorry about your wedding; you've delayed.'

'You must not be sorry. John and I want you and Master Winslow and Captain Standish to witness more than anyone. We wanted to wait until you feel ready.'

Susanna was silent a moment. Then she spoke quietly, steadily. 'We had so many deaths in the sickness. You've lost all your family. And infants die and mothers die in childbirth as night follows day. But however many die, the pain is just as bad. Edward and I will grieve and feel a dark hole where little Edward should be for a long time to come. But we both know only time and living will ease the pain. And heaven knows – none of us can afford not to work if we're bodily capable. And I am now. I am strong again.' She laughed and raised her arms, stretching to the trees. Resting her hands on Priscilla's shoulders, she said, 'Come to the house as soon as you can for a final fitting of your gown. You are so thin now. When I've had time to alter it, set a date with Bradford. It will give us joy to see you and John wed at last!'

Exactly a week later, an hour before evening prayers, Priscilla stepped out from the Winslow house wearing her mother's deep blue gown; folds of silk and satin falling from the waist, bodice cut low, sleeves off her shoulders, her skin unblemished white. Auburn locks escaped from her coif, curling round the nape of her neck. Father's gift, the sumptuous black sash, set off her tiny waist, tied in a big bow at the back.

John stepped out from Standish's house across the way dressed in what finery he and Standish could muster between them: a military dress shirt, fine velvet black jacket and breeches, and highly polished black boots, his black hat, shaped and brushed, unable to restrain blond curls stirring in the breeze.

Priscilla swayed a bit, from hunger and excitement. The moment was here. *We are to be wed.* She put her arm through John's. They walked down the track accompanied by Standish and the Winslows. It was a quiet walk. Folk were indoors preparing for prayers and supper. All chopping, sawing and banging had ceased. Only the sounds of early evening were to be their wedding music; a light rustling of leaves, birds softly chirruping their pre-roosting tunes. The setting sun cast shadows and warm air.

Mary and Elder Brewster with John Howland and Lizzie Tilley greeted them at the common house. Bradford welcomed them, the documents for a civil ceremony spread on a table. After his words of advice on the importance of mutual respect between husband and wife, accepting that ultimately the wife should defer to the husband, Bradford proclaimed, 'By the civil law of this land, I pronounce you man and wife.'

That was it; no wedding breakfast, no church bells, no taking of holy bread and wine, no priest's blessing, no dancing and feasting long into the night. Priscilla's fullness of heart rested in John. The longed-for moment had come. *If only Mother and Father, and Joseph... and if we were in Dorking I would show Cousin Eliza what a good, handsome man I have, and how beautiful I am. She'd be jealous, I wager! But I mustn't allow these thoughts...* She gave her head a little shake as if to send them far away over the sea.

The little wedding party escorted the pair to the Alden house. The men shook John's hand and slapped his back. The women kissed Priscilla. They all took their leave.

John opened the door and Priscilla stepped into her home.

'This is even bigger than the Brewsters'! And, John!' She looked down in disbelief. 'A wooden floor! Oh John.' Priscilla threw her arms round her husband and drew him into a deep kiss.

'A floor will keep us warmer; keep away the ague, I hope,' he said. 'And when I've time I'll build a porch over the door. That'll help too.'

Priscilla walked slowly across the planks, relishing the solid even surface beneath her feet. She walked to the massive fireplace. There was a fire lit, and a pot of pottage hung cooking. In a daze she touched the two spinning wheels standing at the side of the hearth, her mother's: one for flax, the other for wool. On the other side of the fireplace a stout ladder led up to the loft.

In front of the hearth stood a small table and two stools, the table laid with a trencher, two spoons, two tankards and a jug of ale. And against one wall, all the Mullins' trunks were lined up side by side, dusted and ready for her to unpack.

'John, 'tis…'tis…' Priscilla hugged herself. She hugged John, too amazed and happy to speak.

'But you've not seen the best,' John said. 'Look.'

Priscilla had been so entranced with the floor, the fireplace, the family's belongings; she hadn't noticed the wooden paneling at the other end of the room. It was a wall, an inner wall with a door. John opened the door into a small space and there stood – a bed!

'A bed! For us – a bed! Only the Winslows and Brewsters have a bed.' She clapped her hands. 'And it's all made up.' She stepped forward to touch the bedding. 'Linen, pillows, a mattress.' She turned to her beaming husband. 'But who?' Overwhelmed, she gave way, sinking onto the soft, welcoming covers. 'Now I see why you and Standish have stopped coming to sup with the Brewsters of late. Oh John, 'tis too wonderful. And the bedding, and the pot over the fire?'

'All Susanna.' John came and sat beside her. 'I reckon preparing for our wedding day helped her get better. Edward reckons so.'

Priscilla laid her head on his shoulder.

'Now come and sup, and we'll drink our ale. And later...' He kissed her. 'You are beautiful.'

They supped and drank, and when Priscilla had cleared the trencher and spoons John took her on his knee. 'I've something for you.' He handed her a folded sheet of parchment.

Priscilla opened it out. 'I love you with all my heart. John,' was written in fine script.

'I thought you couldn't write! This is beautiful.' Priscilla's eyes shone with tears.

'And now.' John drew a book from his pocket. He opened to a marked place in Homer's *Iliad* and read.

'"So you, Hector, are father and mother and brother to me, as well as my beloved husband. Have pity on me now; stay here on the tower..."'

Priscilla put a finger to his lips. 'You, John, are father and mother and brother to me, as well as my beloved husband.' They sat quiet a moment. Then she said, 'When did you learn to read? How did you ever have a chance?'

'Standish taught me. These past few months.'

'But that's so quick!'

'I was keen.'

Priscilla nestled her head into John's neck, drifting with the sound of his voice, the rhythm of the lines.

He closed the volume and placed it on the table. 'Now is the month of Maying, when merry lads are playing...' He sang and she sang. John put her from his knee, took her hand and still singing, they danced. They laughed and sang and danced all the tunes and dance steps they knew, until John danced her into their bed.

Chapter 46

June 1622

A ship - the Charity

Even through the parchment window, the sun shone insistently bright.

'Oh, curse the sun,' John said. 'Can it not bide in bed a while longer? Give us a further hour of dark bliss?'

'If only.' Priscilla sighed and snuggled into his arms.

But the sound of shouts, chopping, crashing trees and sawing hammered into Priscilla's soft comfort.

John groaned. 'We'd best be up and about or someone will come knocking on the door.'

'Surely not!' Priscilla exclaimed, hurrying into her clothes.

'I'll fetch the water,' John said. 'I promised when we were wed that would be my task.'

'And I'll have the cornbread cooked when you return.' Priscilla twirled and flung her arms in the air. 'This is our first day wedded, in our own home! Now it's come I can scarcely believe it.'

John took her in his arms and kissed her heartily.

After their meager ration of cornbread and ale, John set off to work on the fort. Priscilla hurried across to the Winslows' house. Susanna answered her knock.

'Susanna! Thank you. Thank you so much for the pottage, all ready – and the fire lit – and the bed! All made up with lovely linen.'

Susanna looked at her sideways, one eyebrow arched in a question.

'Yes, it was a wonderful night.' Priscilla spoke tenderly. 'Did you know he's learned to write and to read? And he made the bed and table and stools. He read to me from Miles' copy of the *Iliad* – about Hector and Andromache – and then we sang and danced until…'

Susanna smiled. 'We always knew whether it was a night for making furniture – we could hear the sawing and banging – or a night for reading and writing, all quiet.' She put her hands on Priscilla's shoulders. 'We women have all agreed, even Mary Brewster, that you should have this day free from common duties to unpack and put your house in order. And I've been assigned to help you.'

'Oh joy!' Priscilla hugged Susanna. Peregrine protested, tugging at both their skirts.

All morning, as Priscilla and Susanna unpacked the trunks and chatted, Priscilla felt her mother's presence, a shadowy figure hovering at her shoulder.

'You've some fine pewter here.' Susanna lifted out plates and candlesticks and beakers.

'For special occasions,' Priscilla said. 'Like Christmas.'

'And here's some earthenware, all carefully wrapped in rags.' Susanna placed bottles and bowls among the array of items covering the floor. 'We'll need to be starting a bottle or two of vinegar soon,' she said.

There was a crash and wailing. Priscilla hurried to Peregrine, sitting amongst a fallen pile of cooking utensils. 'There, there.' She picked him up. 'No harm done. You need something to do.'

She found a basket. 'Those rags, Susanna. Could he have the rags?'

'There's a treasure trove of rags here,' Susanna handed Priscilla a bundle. 'For mattress filling.'

Priscilla settled Peregrine taking rags out of the basket and putting them back in and came to look. She dug her hands down into the soft fabric. 'What's this?' She pulled out a hessian doll. 'Look – a doll I made for the girls on the *Mayflower*. There should be two more. Here.' She took the dolls to Peregrine, who grinned and chortled in delight.

Susanna continued on the subject of mattresses. 'With all the fowl here we should have feather beds soon. I despaired, throwing away all those plucked feathers. But we'd no time to wash and dry them properly.'

'Perhaps this autumn,' Priscilla said. 'Ah, Mother's recipe book. Father brought it from London, when he returned from paying our passage on the *Mayflower*.' Priscilla gently stroked the soft leather cover. Tears pricked her eyes and her head felt fuzzy. She sat on a stool and turned the pages slowly, hardly seeing the words.

Susanna stood quiet. 'I'll go fetch a bite of cornbread and sip of ale.' She gathered up Peregrine.

Alone, Priscilla let her mind wander into memories of Mother at home in England: proudly carrying her tasty pies from bake oven to table, churning butter with such vigor, red-cheeked and plump, bending over the hearth to skim the fat off the juices in the roasting pan. And so long ago, when Priscilla was little, Mother tucking her into bed, soft brown eyes, soft kiss on her cheek. *But I mustn't dwell like this.* She wiped her cheeks dry.

Susanna knocked and came through the open doorway. 'Here,' she said, drawing up a stool beside Priscilla's. 'It's not much, but it'll help us to keep going. Peregrine, you've already had your bit.' She turned to her clamoring toddler and gave him a mouthful. 'Now, that's all.'

'He could have my bit,' Priscilla said.

'No.' Susanna was firm.

Priscilla gratefully bit into her slice and sipped her ale. 'Susanna,' she said, 'I hardly dare ask this, especially as I'm so happy with John... but... do you ever... have wistful feelings for England?'

Susanna stared across the room. 'William and I escaped from England to Holland to get away from persecution. We worshipped in constant fear of the banging on the door, men crashing in and arresting us. William, especially, was devoted to the new Church of Christ. We were outlaws.'

'Always watched and preyed on?'

'Aye.' Susanna went on. 'And in Leiden we could worship free of fear. But the way some of us had to live! In tiny, crowded cottages, all packed together in a stinking part of the city by the Back Canal, a stagnant sewer.'

'Sounds worse even than the Thames – and that was bad,' Priscilla said.

'We had to earn our crust working flax and wool and weaving. All day we worked, even on the Sabbath – the merchants were so greedy. The flax dust ate at our lungs. My best friend died of it. Couldn't have been thirty years old.' She put her hand on her chest. 'It hurt to breathe.'

'That is terrible!' Priscilla exclaimed, thinking of her comfortable home in Dorking.

'I'm sure William had no idea how bad it would be.' Susanna looked at Priscilla. 'He, too, hated it; hated to see our young lad knitting and weaving dawn to dusk, fetching and carrying in those filthy streets, rats running everywhere. No schools.'

'No schools? No grammar schools? No fields to run in? Trees to climb? Pity the children.'

'What's more, we hardly had enough to eat. We were afraid our lads, as soon as they were old enough, would join up with the East India Company and we'd never see them again. Then, while we were deliberating whether to sail to this land, the twelve-year peace treaty with Spain ended. That was the final spur. We knew war would come.'

'And it has.' Priscilla looked down at her hands. 'I've heard a bit about Holland, from Mary Brewster, but I had no idea it was so hard.'

'Do I miss England?' Susanna gazed at the hearth. 'I don't know. There's a lot to fear in England: persecution, the plague, wars. But I do know I'd like a full belly! And proper eating: main meal at noontime and a chance to get indoors out of the hot sun or freezing wind.'

'A proper routine to our days, as it should be.' Priscilla knelt to soothe fretting Peregrine. 'You'd like a full belly, wouldn't you, little one?' She paused, looking up at Susanna. 'Is it wrong, do you think, to look back to the old times? Is it harmful to my soul? Mary Brewster says it is – that the devil might get in. Susanna, I'm afraid about my soul. I think of the old times and… and…' Priscilla blushed.

'What is it, Priscilla? What's troubling you?'

'It's just that… last night was such bliss. Such…' Priscilla hugged herself. 'And we're preached it is of the devil to love carnal pleasure. But I do love it.' She frowned, studying the floor. 'We're also preached God created us as we are, so surely it can't be wrong to love being the way he created us.'

'My dear.' Susanna leaned toward Priscilla. 'Look at me.' Smiling, touching Priscilla's nose with hers, she said, 'I love it too.'

Priscilla laughed a shivery, happy laugh.

'Mary Brewster has suffered much,' Susanna said. 'And I fear her suffering is getting the better of her. Don't pay too much heed to what she says.'

'But you have suffered much too and you stay merry.'

Susanna tilted her head to one side. 'We're all different. Now come on with you or we'll not be in order when your man comes in for his supper.'

By mid-afternoon the hearth was decked: on one side, cooking pots, kettles, skillets, ladles, skimmers and trivets; on the other, fire utensils: bellows, shovels, forks and tongs, brooms. Priscilla placed Father's pipe box on the right outside corner with John's pipes in it, and on the left a basket of pine knots. John had already fitted the hearth with a lugpole and andirons.

'That's a fine-looking hearth,' Susanna pronounced. 'I suggest we take the butter churn and cheese press into the lean-to, out of the way. And the big pickling crocks.'

'Yes. I'd like this room to be as uncluttered as possible.'

Finally, Susanna helped Priscilla push and heave the trunks into place along the walls to store clothes, bed linen, and table linen. They arranged the pewter ware on top of one, and the earthenware on another. On a third, a selection of small boxes for thread, buttons and nails, odds and ends; on the fourth, Priscilla arranged their precious books on either side of a small cabinet with individual drawers for spices.

'Spices!' Priscilla said. 'A splendid day if a ship arrives with spices.'

'A splendid day if a ship arrives with a cow and a bull so we can make cheese and butter,' Susanna said. 'And sheep! Oh, to have wool to spin.'

Priscilla sighed. 'Aye, if only – and soon.'

'I've worked up a sweat.' Susanna wiped her brow. 'But this is a fine room, Priscilla. John should be pleased and proud. And your mother's cloth on the table – a lovely touch!' She put an arm round Priscilla's shoulder. 'You realize your husband has built you the finest house in our settlement. Come the day when we all can live in decent dwellings; not the earthen floored hovels we're in now. I'll be off. Keep what's left of the pottage and the bed linen. It'll be laundry day soon anyway.'

'Thank you so much.' Priscilla kissed Susanna on the cheek and bent to kiss Peregrine's head, ruffling his hair. 'Good little lad.'

'Priscilla, this is splendid!' John came bounding into the room, threw down his musket, axe and saw, and pulled Priscilla away from the hearth into his arms. Cradling her, he said, 'What man could wish for more? His own beautiful wife stirring his supper in this welcoming, fetching home. You have done well.'

'With Susanna's help.' She laughed and pulled him to her for a kiss.

'I'll put my tools away and wash.' John hung his musket on pegs over the door and carried his axe and saw into the lean-to. Priscilla could hear him splashing and singing outside.

'That's better. Got rid of some of the sawdust.' He crossed to the trunk with the spice cabinet and the books. 'These are precious volumes.' He fingered the recipe book and the gardening book, passed his hand over the Mullins' family Bible, psalter and almanac. 'But this Bible – King James? And *Hamlet*? How did you come by these?'

'Catherine Carver gave them to me, when she was dying. We became close.'

'I'll make a special box to hold all these books. It's fine to see them displayed, but they are too precious to leave out in the dust.'

'That would be perfect,' Priscilla exclaimed. She put her hand in his and snuggled against his arm.

'When Howland can give me a hand, we'll bring your father's trunks of shoes and cobbling tools and put them in the loft.'

'And now we're a respectable wedded pair, we can invite him and Lizzie to sup and have an evening with us. And Captain Standish,' Priscilla said.

'This is fine pewter.' John stroked a candlestick. He turned to Priscilla. 'I want to give you the very best I possibly can. Already you have made this a lovely home.'

Priscilla squeezed his hand. 'Already you have made us a bed and table and a wooden floor as well as learning to read and write.'

John hugged her again tight. 'Shall we say our prayers and then sup? I'm hungry.'

Sitting side by side, Priscilla and John held their large Bible open across both their laps.

'Ships! Ships in the harbor!' Francis came running through the open door, shrieking.

'How many?' John asked.

'Two – they're English!'

John and Priscilla ran after Francis. All the colony were running to the shore.

'Provisions – I hope they're bringing provisions,' Priscilla gasped as she ran.

They waited while the ships anchored and the first boatload of passengers sailed across the harbor. John and Winslow joined Standish and Bradford to welcome them and help with the ropes. Priscilla stood with Susanna and watched as the passengers waded to the shore.

'They're all men,' Priscilla said. 'Look as if they've been hauled from a dockside tavern.'

'Perhaps they're leaving women and children 'til last.'

Bradford and Standish, talking with the men, shook their heads, looked to heaven, and threw their arms out, shrugging their shoulders.

John hurried to Priscilla and Susanna. 'Bad news. Sixty men, all Weston's. He demands we house and feed them while the larger vessel, the *Charity*, heads on down to Virginia to discharge some passengers and cargo. No supplies for us.'

'Oh…' Priscilla's one word rose and fell in a long crescendo.

'Standish and Bradford will work out how to allocate them amongst us.'

'I must go,' Priscilla said, 'to put away our books – and pewter.' Abruptly she turned; lifting her skirts, and ran back up the track. Her face was hot and her heart pounded in fury. *This is too much, too much… impossible! Not right… not right.* She ran to their home. *I'll not have these rogues in my house. I won't.* Fumbling with the key she unlocked the trunks and hid away the books, the pewter and the spice cabinet.

As she was re-locking the trunks, John came in. 'We've been given seven to lodge here. Weston has sent some bread, but we'll need to halve rations again.'

'I'll not do it!' Priscilla stamped her foot, hands on hips, cheeks aflame. 'Those wretched men can build their own shelters. You did, in all that terrible weather the first winter. They can go shoot their own game. Why does Bradford do everything Weston wants – even when he's dumped us?'

'Priscilla, hush,' John said. He smiled. 'At least we have our own bedroom.' He moved to hold her.

Priscilla stepped back. 'It makes no difference. Through that thin panel they can hear everything. No, I'll not.' Her voice rose to a shriek.

'Priscilla! Be quiet.' John's face darkened; his tone grew quiet, stern. 'All the colony will be pouring in here to see what is wrong. We *will* house these men, and you *will* behave whether you like it or no.' He turned on his heel and left.

Dizzy and choking with sobs, Priscilla collapsed on a stool, her head in her hands. Her stomach felt full of lead. *Control yourself; you know you have to do it.* She swallowed her rage; a helpful numbness took its place. She fetched her pestle and mortar and ground their ration of corn. *I suppose we'll have to give them Susanna's pottage.*

When John returned with the men, Priscilla had the first batch of cornbread cooking in a skillet over the fire. She dutifully welcomed them to sit on the floor, and handed a trencher of pottage to John first. He put his hand over hers, eyes moist with kindness. 'Thank you.'

At sunrise, when she'd swept and tidied, Priscilla took up the water pails. In his hurry to get the men out of the house and working on the fort, John had forgotten his task. As she stepped out, she met Susanna, hoe in one hand, Peregrine in the other. 'As soon as I've been to the brook I'll join you.'

'Is everything all right?' Susanna asked. 'We heard.'

'No. It is not all right. Why can't those horrid men build their own shelters – or sleep outside? It is summer. Warm enough.'

'I know it's hard – and I sort of agree – but, well, you know how the governors are about everyone working together and especially couples and families. Any sign of discord between you and John and you'll have the Brewsters questioning you. Just take care.'

'Thank you, Susanna.' Priscilla looked at the ground. 'I'll mend my ways. Be with you shortly.' Priscilla hurried along the path to the brook. She mustn't tarry. She must show willing in the fields. *I love John so much, but this is a dreadful hard place to live.*

Pails full, Priscilla lumbered back along the path, water sloshing, flies and mosquitoes whining and biting, fie. She shook her head, trying to unstick them and silently fumed. *I thought when we were wed we could lead our own lives – not be watched and assessed! These religious folk don't believe in the divine right of kings, but they seem to believe in the divine right of William Bradford! Why does he have advisers if they don't question his decisions? Why must we, just newlywed, have these louts in our home? We've had only one night. Unbelievably wonderful. And now… it feels like a dark pit. John commanding me to obey. Oh God, please don't let him be like other husbands, always right. He promised he would be different.*

Setting the heavy pails down in their lean-to, and grasping her hoe, Priscilla headed for the cornfields. She glanced up toward the partially built fort. *Weston's men aren't doing much, just milling about. Pray God we have a good harvest.* As she walked across the field she spied Goodwife Hopkins stumbling away, leaning on her hoe, wiping tears from her eyes.

'What is wrong?' she asked as she joined Susanna.

'Her babe is dying.'

Priscilla stood quiet a moment. 'Susanna, I am ashamed I made such a fuss about housing Weston's men when Goody Hopkins – she's about to lose her babe. As you did. I'm sorry.'

Susanna gave Priscilla's arm a squeeze. 'Your hurt is real too. A high-spirited lass like you, so constrained. Come, this corn crop is in a tangle of weeds. Can't see the beans and pumpkins for weeds.'

Priscilla hoed with all the strength she had. But the ground was hard and she often nearly dug out a precious plant instead of the weeds. It was hot and still. She stopped to wipe her face with her handkerchief and watched little Peregrine as he crawled about, playing with the hoed weeds, feeding them to his hessian doll. *Pray God he stays well.*

That evening, John Alden made a little coffin for the Hopkins babe and dug a grave.

When they were in bed, John with his back to her, Priscilla put a hand on his shoulder. 'I'm sorry I was so angry about that lot.' She thumbed toward where the men slept the other side of the partition wall.

John turned to her and held her face in his hands. 'Do you know, secretly, I'm proud you were so angry. Shows how much you care. If only you'd been quieter.' He kissed her nose.

'Susanna said if I wasn't careful, we'd be investigated by the Brewsters.'

'Lord help us,' John replied. 'Seriously, as your father said, we **must** all pull together.'

'But it seems as if Bradford rules.'

'Sssh, not now – later. When this rabble is gone. Useless, they are.'

Chapter 47

July 1622

Why the fort?

Priscilla lay awake, sweltering through the long hours of a hot sticky night. The place beside her in bed was empty as John had gone with Standish, Bradford and Winslow to keep watch over the cornfields. They meant to discover what creature, during the past week, had been pulling out young shoots of their precious corn. Owls hooted in the distance, calling back and forth. She dozed fitfully, until dimly aware of patchy birdsong announcing the coming dawn. Half-awake she felt the bed dip as John lay down beside her, fully clothed.

'Weston's men – and some of our own – stealing the shoots and eating them raw on the spot.'

'Our own?'

'Yes. We nabbed John Billington. You'd expect him. Glad it wasn't his son. He's a good young man. Does his best. And Jonathan Brewster.'

'No!'

'Lunatic, he was. Babbling and blubbering and thrashing about, shrieking, "The devil's in her, she's a fiend, won't let me eat." Bradford's going to try to bring him to his senses. We only got half a dozen, most ran off. Could have sworn Prence was among those that got away. Standish and Bradford are keeping the men we caught. Whipping tomorrow.'

'Do you have to?'

'No. Standish and Bradford. I'll go out hunting – out of earshot. Wish I could take you with me. But it isn't safe.'

'I'll go as far away as I can the other side of the brook, with Susanna and Peregrine. She won't want the little one to hear it.'

In spite of the whipping, the pilfering continued. By the time the *Charity* returned and collected Weston's men, end of August, the corn crop was sorely depleted.

'Oh, it is good to wave them goodbye,' Priscilla said as John set sail across the harbor ferrying the last of Weston's men.

'Here! Here!' Susanna hoisted Peregrine to wave. She turned to Priscilla. 'Now you can take your pewter and books out of hiding.'

The departure of Weston's men was as good as a meal. Priscilla felt lighter, not so heavy with tiredness, and John was less downcast.

'The bliss, having our house just for us again,' Priscilla said, as they sat by their hearth that evening.

John drew on his pipe. 'Aye. 'Tis as it should be. Another week or two should see the fort completed and we'll be free to hunt fowl and deer.'

Priscilla knew he was trying to be positive in spite of the poor harvest. 'Do we have any trinkets and beads left to trade for corn?'

John shook his head. 'Sadly, no. But we'll manage – we will. And you've got in a good supply of dried berries, and the beans and squash and pumpkins. Come. We'll make merry in bed.'

Priscilla smiled and gave him her hand.

A day of celebration. The moment had come to mount the cannon on the flat roof of the new fort. Standing with Susanna, Priscilla watched rapt as John and Standish led a crew pushing and pulling the huge guns up the ramp. With grunts and shouts of 'heave... look now' the men eased the heavy armaments up onto the roof and maneuvered them into place.

A loud cheer went up. Men punched the air with their fists.

'That'll show the Indians,' Billington called out.

Francis wriggled free from restraining hands, ran up the ramp and pretended to fire the cannon, trained on the harbor. Suddenly he jumped up and down, pointing, yelling. 'A ship... a ship! White sails!'

As always, there was a rush to the harbor's shore. The ship proved to be a trading vessel, offering trinkets in exchange for beaver pelts. Surmising Plymouth's overwhelming need for trinkets to trade with the Indians for corn, the captain struck a hard bargain. He also brought news of Master Christopher Jones' death. 'The *Mayflower* returned safely to England,' he said, 'but Master Jones died the following March. He is buried in his home town, Harwich.'

'Buried in the home town we shared.' John squeezed Priscilla's hand. 'Our friend. A good man.'

When they were seated at table for supper, Priscilla said, 'John, could we put up a cross, in memory of Master Jones?' She caught her breath. 'He was so kind to Joseph – to me – to us all.'

'Aye, we must. That first winter took its toll on him, too.'

Next morning, before he went hunting, John made a cross and carved 'Master & Commander C. Jones' on the cross-piece. Together, he and Priscilla took it to the special plot where John had laid Priscilla's father and mother and Joseph: a quiet space up beyond the fort, a grove of birch trees, three crosses set in the stubby grass. Because of the peace treaty with Massasoit, it was no longer necessary to leave the graves unmarked.

'Let it be beside Joseph, please,' Priscilla said.

John hammered in the cross and stood back beside Priscilla. She took his hand. 'May we bide here quiet a moment?'

Leaving the graves, John and Priscilla walked past the newly completed fort.

'A huge achievement,' Priscilla said. Stopping, she looked up at the cannon. 'Do you think it was right to build it now?'

John turned her to face him. 'You question Bradford's decision. So do I.'

'Susanna says Winslow thinks we should have been building up our crops and hunting and trapping to trade.'

'I agree,' John said.

'Then why?'

John looked up into the sky and back meeting Priscilla's gaze. 'Bradford has felt uneasy about our situation with the Indians. He knows he made Massasoit angry over Squanto. I think hearing about the massacre in Virginia unnerved him – and us.'

'I wish Master Winslow was governor.'

'So do I,' John said.

'If only Deacon Carver had lived, and Catherine.'

'Aye, our lives might have been very different. But, Priscilla,' John put his hand round her shoulder, 'you must not breathe a word of these thoughts. Not even to Susanna, nor I to Standish.'

Priscilla looked into his earnest face. 'I promise.'

'John.' Priscilla hesitated, and looked at the ground.

'Yes?'

'Before we were wed, you said you would listen to me, and even sometimes follow my reason. Is that still true?' She daren't look at him.

John tilted her chin. 'It goes against the way of things,' he said. 'But yes. It's just that in these strange and troubling times, we must all pull together, as your father said. We've appointed Bradford governor. In many ways, he is a good leader. If pulling together means following his lead, we must – at least 'til things are more stable.' He put his hands on her shoulders. 'Do you see?'

'I guess so.' Priscilla laughed a little. 'But I'll hold you to it – to pay heed to what I say.' She twirled her skirt, hands on hips.

'Vixen!'

Chapter 48

November – December 1622

Brewster's blindness

In late October the Plymouth leaders agreed to a joint trading expedition with Weston's men, now settling at Wessagussett, on the shores of the harbor Standish found, near the Massachusetts tribe. Weston's men offered a thirty-ton vessel, the *Swan*, and Plymouth had trinkets to trade. On the very day the *Swan* sailed into Plymouth harbor, Standish fell sick with a high fever, shaking fits and shivering. So Bradford led the expedition, taking Squanto with him. John was appointed to assist Elder Brewster in governing the colony.

Two weeks since the *Swan* sailed; she should be back by now. Standish still not recovered. A swelling tide of fear was seeping through the colony. The wall in fact gave little protection against the Indians, but it kept the wolves out and gave an illusion of safety.

When the vessel did at last sail into Plymouth Harbor, only two of Weston's men sailed to shore in the ship's boat.

'Where are Bradford and Winslow?' John asked. 'And the others?'

'Bradford and your men are trekking inland. We were doing well, successful trading, when a gale wrecked your shallop. Nearly wrecked the *Swan*.' He gestured toward the pinace anchored out. 'So we couldn't bring the goods from shore out to the pinace. The Indians promised to keep them safe until we come and fetch them – which we will soon. Rest assured. Your men are all safe. Set on trying their luck with the inland tribes.'

Elder Brewster joined the welcoming party.

'Just one trouble,' Weston's man went on. 'Squanto died.'

'Died?'

'It was when we were trading with the tribe inland from the shoals and breakers – the rip tide. He suddenly was struck with a red-hot fever and bled from his nose like a water spout. Begged Bradford to pray for him so he could go to the Englishman's God in heaven.'

'Poor Bradford.' Elder Brewster shook his head, staring at the ground.

'Do you know what caused it?' John asked.

'No. The Indians couldn't save him – they had to give up. He died quick. But I've four hogshead of corn and beans – your share – two more on the ship. Let's get these unloaded.'

'Poor dues for all that time in dangerous waters and vicious November storms.' John kicked a barrel.

When he had stored the large casks and locked the storehouse door, he trudged up the track. Mud clogged his boots. The sky hung pregnant with snow. A hollowness ate at his stomach; a cavity of hunger and fear. *Where were Bradford, Winslow, Hopkins, Howland and the young John Billington? What if they were killed?*

He knocked on Standish's door and entered. 'Don't get up. I'll pull up a stool.'

'Good to see you, John,' Standish said, obediently remaining on his pallet. 'Priscilla and Susanna called in. Beefed up the hearth, fed me, told me the news.'

'Miles, I am as afraid as I have ever been. Bradford and Winslow both gone. What if...? Praise God you are here.'

'Would be a terrible loss. But we would cope, John. You have the makings of a fine leader and I can handle the military side, and we have Hobbamock.'

'What do you make of Squanto suddenly taking sick and dying?'

'Reckon Massasoit decided to take matters into his own hands. Bradford need never know and Squanto can't get up to any more of his knaverish dealings. Smart move.'

'Aye. Perhaps life will be more peaceful without him. But I feel sorry for Bradford. He'll probably behave as if nothing had happened, as he did when Dorothy died.' John stood. 'Strange man.' He put a hand on Standish's shoulder. 'Please do as Susanna says. We need you well, Miles.'

'Aye.' From his prone position, the captain saluted.

Every evening, his final task before bed, John did a circuit of the settlement to be sure all was well, with the colonists secure indoors and the animals secure in their pens.

This evening, his round completed, John walked up the track to his own home. Some hundred yards away he spied a man standing, his face pressed to the window of the Alden house. John waited. The man didn't move. Making a slight detour behind the Winslows' house John crept up from behind and grabbed the man's shoulders.

'Aahh.'

'Prence. I might have known. Spying on my wife. Be gone, you sniveling wretch. I've a mind to report you.' John drew back his staff and swung it whistling, stopping his blow within a hair's breadth of Prence's ear. Terrified, Prence ran.

Next evening, John was summoned to the Brewster household.

The Elder bade him be seated, fastening him with agitated eyes. Prence was seated on a stool beside the Elder.

'Mr Alden,' the Elder coughed. 'I am led to believe you visited a violent fright upon Mr Prence last eve.'

'My head swam and I saw stars as if he had delivered a monstrous blow. Terror gripped my insides causing my bowels to...'

'That is enough, Mr Prence.' The Elder held up his hand. 'It seems, Mr Alden, that you accused Mr Prence of spying on your wife when he was only carrying out the duties I and Governor Bradford bestowed on him. Mr Prence leads me to understand you are prone to violent outbursts and I know times are fraught.'

John glanced sideways and caught Prence's triumphant smirk and Mary Brewster's expression of self-satisfied consternation.

'You understand,' the Elder continued, 'I will in due course have to report this to the governor.'

John stood. 'In that case, I too shall make a report. If Mr Prence wanted to check on our religious devotions, he had only to knock on the door when we were both there to see us reading our Bible. But he chose, when I was out, to stand with his face pressed to our window for upwards of ten minutes. I saw him.' John gestured toward Patience and Fear and Mary Brewster. 'How would you feel, sir, if a man persisted in leching your daughters or your wife?'

A flush crept up Elder Brewster's neck. He blanched and John knew he'd struck a nerve. He'd heard stories that Brewster's father was renowned for his lecherous ways. 'If there is nothing else, sir, I'll bid you good night.'

At home, sitting by his hearth with Priscilla, John recounted his meeting with the Elder. He stared at the flaming logs. 'Elder Brewster is wise on so many matters. How can he be duped by such an onerous man as Prence? Is he blind? And Winslow never takes a stand against Brewster. I can see why Bradford wouldn't want to disagree with the man who is like a father to him – but Winslow?'

Priscilla put down her mending and looked John in the eye. 'Some men, as they grow older, become entrenched in their views and insist they are right. I fear Elder Brewster is such a man and I suppose Winslow wants to stay loyal and doesn't want to cause disturbance.'

John reached across the space between their rockers and took her hand. 'My wise wife.'

'I pray, Mr Alden, that as you grow older you will not become so intransigent.' She arched her right eyebrow.

John pulled his wife from her chair. 'To bed.'

Apart from Priscilla 'twas only seeing Standish on the mend gladdened John's heart. Mid-December and still no sign of Bradford and his party. Elder Brewster prayed constantly, all day long. John wondered whether he prayed all night too, he was so haggard, eyes sunk back under bushy brows.

Returning from his day's hunting, John dragged his feet across the fields. He lifted his face to the first snow falling from a quiet gray sky. Owls hooted in the dusk, close by he reckoned; perhaps in the clump of birches surrounding the Mullins' graveyard. He stopped. He wished he could stop and not start. He wished he could fall asleep and not wake until this time of waiting, not knowing, was over. Better to know the worst. A white phantom whooshed by his head, soft feathers brushing his cheek as a large snowy owl bulleted onto its prey – a luckless weasel, carried aloft squealing to its death.

'Halloo, halloo...' a faint distant call. John turned and ran, retracing his steps, past his house and out through the gate up by the fort. 'Halloo, halloo...' Is it? As if he had the hounds of hell chasing him John ran, some superhuman strength carrying him over tufts and ruts, toward the figures, indistinct in the misty gray. 'Bradford, Winslow,' he gasped. 'Praise God... are you all here?' He clutched Bradford's hands, hugged Winslow, slapped Howland's shoulder. 'Come. Come. Come home to a warm hearth and food.' Tears poured down his cheeks and he was thankful for the dimming light. As they walked Bradford gave a brief exhausted account.

'Successful trading… Indians friendly… but no way to bring goods back… collect later.'

It would be a hungry winter, but thank God all the party were safe and well.

★ ★ ★

Christmas Day; a working day. *At least it isn't the Sabbath.* Priscilla plucked a plump goose and a brace of duck, and a turkey. She'd roast the goose and turkey on the spit and cook up a pottage of venison and duck, pumpkin and squash. The corn was ground for cornbread, and she would put out a dish of dried berries. Yes, it was just another working day; hunting, repairing buildings, and John building a new shallop. For the women, cleaning, mending, cooking. But Standish was joining them for Christmas celebrations that eve. She'd have liked the Winslows to come as well, but it would be against their conscience – even Susanna's. And Howland and Lizzie – but Howland couldn't possibly escape Bradford's watchful eye. Yesterday afternoon she'd searched the edge of the woodland for holly. None. So she'd gathered sweet-smelling juniper and pine boughs and after dark she would hang them from the beams.

Dusk came. Folk withdrew indoors. Then it was dark, a full moon in a clear black sky; starlight glistening on a fresh snowfall. In spite of the wolves' howling Priscilla felt a tingle. She changed into her Lincoln green gown and brushed her hair arranging curls to escape her coif, adorning her neck and ears. It was Christmas night and they would be merry.

John staggered in with another turkey and a brace of duck. 'My beauty! I'm not fit to be near you.' He deposited the game in the lean-to and disappeared to splash and change his clothes. Dressed in Sunday finery, he joined his wife by the hearth. 'Our first Christmas together. And you have made it beautiful.' He tilted her chin and kissed her lips.

There was a knock on the door. John opened, letting in a shaft of moonlight and Standish, dressed in full military regalia, buttons and boots and buckles polished, his red hair gleaming as if it had been polished too.

Priscilla smiled; she greeted him French-style – a kiss on each cheek. Blushing, the captain took from inside his coat a silver flute. Having checked the door was closed, he played softly.

'Oh the holly and the ivy…' John and Priscilla sang in muted tones. They all knew if Bradford found out; there would be a knock on the door, a very stern, shocked reprimand and a fine. Every so often John went outside to see if Mr Prence was near, lurking, spying.

The evening passed in gaiety, singing, dancing, and thanks to John's hunting, their hunger was eased.

The next day, Hobbamock returned from a reconnoiter with news from Wessagussett. 'Those Weston men are starving. They're stealing from the Indians. Trouble afoot. Indians very angry.' He drew his forefinger across his neck in a slicing motion. 'Bad trouble for you English.'

1623

Chapter 49

January 1623

Indian trouble

It was in a spirit of keen anticipation that John had set out with Standish's party to collect the goods left in the Indians' safekeeping last November when a storm wrecked Bradford's shallop. Now, sailing home, entering Plymouth Harbor, his mood was markedly different; relief to be returning with men and goods all safely on board, mixed with heavy misgivings about the recent behavior of his friend, Captain Standish.

A strong easterly wind buffeted the shallop through gray white-capped waters under a sullen sky. Noisy hopeful gulls were tossed about in gusts of wind.

Bradford's greeting was warm but subdued. 'Massasoit is sick unto death. Winslow has gone with Hobbamock to try to save him.'

'Pray he succeeds,' John said. His eyes searched for Priscilla. There. Running down the track. He strode to take her in his arms.

That evening in the warmth and comfort of their home, John answered Priscilla's eager questions. She wanted to know every detail of their expedition. John did not hide his concern about Standish's attitude toward the Indians.

'True to their word, the tribes stored our goods. We found all our produce safe, untouched, well preserved. No rot or spoiling. But instead of showing gratitude, Standish accused each tribe of stealing from our supply of trinkets. The Indians didn't know what to make of it – nor did I. It was obvious to me the accusations were false, but when I questioned him he became furious and told me to keep my place.'

'How strange.' Priscilla looked up from her mending as John, agitated with the memory, stood and paced in front of the hearth.

'Most worrying was an incident when we were visiting the last tribe on our list. The chief invited us to a feast and to bed down for the night in his lodge. While we were eating, a lusty, proud brave and his companion entered the lodge. He announced himself – Wituwamat, saying he was from Wessagussett. He then brandished an ornately carved knife which he presented to the chief, who was clearly impressed. Wituwamat then proceeded to mock Standish, mercilessly. Standish turned purple with rage, beckoned us all and stormed out. We put up a shelter and slept there, freezing.'

Priscilla put her mending aside. 'It is frightening. Does Captain Standish not see the damage he does? Can he not see beyond his own pride?'

John groaned. 'I don't know. I pray Standish and Wituwamat do not meet again. Blood is sure to flow if they do.'

★ ★ ★

Days passed in fretful tension, waiting for Winslow and Hobbamock to return. John frequently glanced up toward the forest, willing the two men to emerge from the trees. *We'd be lost without Massasoit. Who else would negotiate with the Indian tribes, advise us how to respond?*

Elder Brewster prayed, Bradford maintained his stoic trust in God's will, and Standish grew more bad tempered with every passing day. John and Standish hunted together as ever, but John contrived to bring Howland along as often as possible.

It was a frosty morning; the world gleamed under a bright winter's sun. Setting out to shoot fowl in the marsh, John stopped a moment, savoring the season's beauty, harsh as it was. Birds, a myriad of colors, flitted and called from tree to tree. Discordant screaming preceded a large blue-gray and white bird with a small crest and black markings. Flying fast, it swooped low to pick up a kernel that squirrels must have dropped, John supposed. Too big for the bird's throat, the kernel got stuck. Choking and stretching its neck this way and that, the bird finally disgorged its quarry; then set to hammering the nut with its bill to crack it. John laughed. The bird flew off. *It feels strange; we have no names for these birds, nor for any of the wild creatures different from our own.* He stooped to tie his bootlace. Straightening up he faced a beaming Hobbamock.

'My beloved sachem lives.'

Winslow loped and stumbled across the lumpy ground.

'Winslow! Praise God you've returned. Massasoit lives?'

'Aye. Alive and well. Just needed some common sense treatment. I'll say hello to Susanna and then report to Bradford. All well with you, John?'

'Aye, thank you. By God it's good to see you safely here again.'

Returning from Massasoit, Winslow brought a report that the Massachusetts tribe had gathered the allegiance of seven other tribes in every direction with a plan to attack the Wessagussett settlement and Plymouth, and kill all the English. John waited to see whether their leaders would take the report to be true and launch their own attack, or try to find further evidence. He reckoned they should not attack in haste.

Whilst Priscilla was helping Mary Brewster he set to work on an oak chest he was making to replace one of the trunks. This was what he loved doing best; making furniture for their home. *Two rockers completed and after this I'll make a settle – keep the draughts from our backs.*

A knock, followed by Standish, interrupted his reverie.

'Sit down, Miles.' John saw the captain was flushed and eager. He drew up a stool facing him.

'We're to do it,' Standish said. 'Send the Massachusetts into disarray. Show them who's boss.' He banged the table with his fist. 'And you're to come! I persuaded Bradford. He and a few other trustworthies can look after the stores.'

'Thank you, Miles.' John forced himself to sound keen.

'There'll be six more besides you and Hobbamock. I've got to decide who. But I wanted to tell you first.' He stood. 'We don't want too many, so they'll think we're only intending to trade.'

'When?'

'Day after tomorrow we sail.' The captain saluted John. 'Assemble by the harbor at dawn.'

'Yes, sir.' With a forced grin, John returned the salute.

'And if I should chance upon that Wituwamat, I'll see he pays. Insolent, villainous, puffed-up Indian.' Standish delivered his parting remarks as John opened the door. 'Ah, Priscilla.' The captain performed a deep, elaborate bow, as if to royalty.

'Come in, love,' John said and closed the door, any trace of a smile gone.

'The captain seems very… bouncy. Full of something,' Priscilla remarked.

'That he is. The scent of battle.'

'War?'

'Sit down. Is there a chunk of cornbread?'

They sat, taking small bites slowly to make it last longer.

'It seems Bradford, Standish and Winslow have decided we should attack the Massachusetts before they can summon the other tribes to attack us.' John put his hand on Priscilla's. 'And Bradford has agreed I should be one of the party.'

'Oh!' Priscilla clapped her hand over her mouth. 'War. You might… Oh John.' She dropped her head onto her arms.

'Don't fear.' John spoke quietly. 'Remember, I'm a crack shot. And I'll keep my wits. This business shouldn't take long.'

Priscilla raised her head and sat straight. 'I know I must be brave, and… accepting. But I shall be praying every minute you are gone.'

'You are brave, as brave as they come.' John stroked her cheek. 'We leave day after tomorrow, so I'll go hunting and get in plenty of game for you.'

'Could, could you shoot some for the Brewsters? The Elder is a hopeless shot and I fear Jonathan isn't much better. I think they don't have enough to eat, but won't say.'

'Of course I will,' John looked at her quizzically. 'Now I know why you've been grinding corn day and night – it's for Mary. You are a good woman!'

Next evening at dusk, John and Howland trudged from the forest laden with game.

'Look!' Howland pointed. About two hundred yards to their left a man with a pack on his back staggered into the fields and collapsed onto a felled tree trunk.

John and Howland hurried over. 'Who are you?'

'From Wessagussett,' the man gasped, shivering with cold.

'I'll leave my game and come back for it.' John laid his deer and fowl beside the tree trunk. He helped the man to stand and half-carried him down the hill. 'Reckon Winslow's is about as far as he can manage. Could you fetch Bradford and Standish?'

Winslow opened to John's knock and stepped back in alarm. 'Come in, John. Who is this?'

They entered a scene of quiet warmth: the room gave evidence of Master Winslow's good estate; a finely carved oak chest was spread with a richly colored, patterned rug, from the Orient, John surmised. Susanna stirred the cooking pot, Winslow's Bible lay open on the table, and there was Priscilla looking after little Peregrine.

John briefly explained and Winslow brought a stool so the man could sit near the fire.

Restored with a beaker of broth and a chunk of cornbread, he introduced himself.

'Phineas Pratt. I had to escape that hell-hole.' By now Bradford and Standish had arrived.

'I must retrieve my game,' John said, 'before the wolves or raccoons carry it off.'

When he returned, Phineas was telling how he'd escaped and was describing the trials of his journey.

'Why did you run away?' Bradford asked.

'It is a terrible plight they're in. Indians threatening, taunting, calling names, making to attack our fort. Our men are starving to death. One night I reported for guard duty, found three men lying dead at their posts for lack of food.' He shuddered at the memory. 'A man was found dead in the mud, too weak to pull himself out, digging for clams. Men are selling the clothes off their backs, their blankets to the Indians, even becoming their slaves. Anything for food.' He stopped to sip from the beaker of broth. 'An Englishman living with the Indians sent word that the Massachusetts' sachem was only waiting for the snow to melt, so they would leave no footprints, before they attacked Wessagussett and Plymouth. They would kill all the English people in one day!'

'Praise God you came to warn us,' Bradford said.

'I knew if you were not told of this plot, we and you would all be dead men. But please may I hide here? The Indians are hunting me.'

'Yes, you may stay with me,' Bradford said.

'Confirms our intentions,' Standish said. 'We sail on the morrow as planned.'

Bradford and Standish, escorting Phineas, took their leave.

Susanna stood, looking at the closed door. 'Weston's men. How pitiful. But I'm sure they've only themselves to blame. We managed.'

'Yes, because we have a strong leader. We may sometimes disagree with his dictatorial ways, but we have held together,' Winslow said. 'And discipline prevails.'

Priscilla kissed Peregrine goodnight.

Susanna took John's hands in hers. 'We'll look after her for you.'

Back in their own home, John maintained a confident air. 'Phineas' story seems to prove the point. We'll get the job done and be back.' He didn't want Priscilla to worry.

'I know you don't really feel so sure about it,' Priscilla said. 'I can tell.'

John looked into her face, her eyes. 'I cannot shake a sense of foreboding.' He paced. ' At the same time, I can't see we have any choice. The Wessagussett situation is intolerable. But damn it, Priscilla,' he stopped pacing. 'Don't breathe a word I said this. It's Weston's men should be got rid of, not attack the Indians! We need their goodwill.' He sat down again. 'And I don't like Standish's mood. He's too eager, I fear... I don't know.'

'I just want you to come back safe. Promise you'll take care. I swear I couldn't live without you, and the colony needs you.'

John lay awake all night, holding Priscilla close.

Chapter 50

February 1623

Wessagussett

The morning dawned clear. Standish's party set off with a fresh breeze filling the sails, John at the tiller. For a time his spirits lifted. The waves sparkled in the sun; he drank in the sharp invigorating winter air, relishing the tug of the tide on the rudder.

On reaching Wessagussett Standish and his party marched into the settlement, encountering a scene of disarray even worse than predicted. Men posted on guard duty slouched in an apathetic stupor of starvation. Some men were publicly consorting with Indian women. As the settlement's governor was absent, Standish demanded to see the assistant governor. Taken by surprise, this gentleman answered the captain's knock buttoning his breeches. An Indian woman sitting on a pallet in the corner of the room pulled a tunic over her head.

Standish briefly presented his plan. 'We will make as if to trade with the Indians, cordial and admiring, and when we are sure they suspect nothing, we'll kill as many as we can. Now call all your men who are whoring themselves to the Indians to return to this fort immediately. Please find us a house where we can lodge.'

They marched out into cold windblown rain hitting them from the east.

'That was a quick change in the elements.' John drew his neck down into his collar and saw Howland flinch.

No one spoke as their guide led them to a small dwelling. The room smelled dank; it was dark.

'A fire, John, please,' Standish said.

Over the next couple of days, Indians came into the fort to trade, bringing furs, wanting trinkets and wampum. Standish had a good supply and, in John's view, was overly courteous, overly smooth. He could see a particular brave looked at him askance, not convinced.

On the third day, as Standish and John were eating their midday cornbread, an extremely tall, powerful warrior came to call on Hobbamock. He measured up to the pinese, his demeanor proud and stern. His message was short, and having delivered it he left.

Hobbamock relayed his words to Standish. 'He is a pinese, like me. He says he and Wituwamat know of our plans and are not afraid. He says, let him begin when he dares, he shall not take us unawares.'

John's sense of foreboding now returned in full force. Later in the afternoon, the pinese returned with Wituwamat. They swaggered up to Standish, looking down on him as if from a great height. His voice full of disdain, the pinese said, 'You are a great captain, yet you are but a little man.' He spat. 'Though I be no sachem, yet I am of great strength and courage.'

Wituwamat brandished a knife in front of Standish's face. He pointed to a woman's face carved into the handle. 'I have another at home, wherewith I have killed both French and English, and that has a man's face on it; by and by these two must marry.'

John shuddered inwardly, keeping his expression fixed. He noted that, whatever Standish felt, the captain gave nothing away; only a slight flush creeping up his cheeks betrayed him.

That evening, when the party were gathered in their lodging, Standish spoke his mind.

'I've had enough of these wretched Indians and their swaggering insolence.' He stood, his back to the fire, legs slightly astride, hands behind his back. 'Hobbamock, I want you to go at first light to Wituwamat and the pinese and invite them to a feast. Say we'll serve them pork. I know the Indians are very fond of pork. To them, a delicacy.'

'Pork?' Winslow said. 'Where?'

'I've brought two suckling pigs, butchered, ready for roasting,' the captain said. 'But Hobbamock, try to discern how many braves will be coming. So we have enough food and drink.'

'Drink?' Winslow questioned again. 'Plymouth ran dry in the autumn.'

Standish ran a hand through his hair. 'Aye. But I've kept my own bottles, in case of emergency.'

John looked at the floor. I never suspected. Well, I suppose he had a right. Good thing Bradford didn't know, believing in sharing everything. 'Depending on how many come, we'll use knives or muskets. More than four it'll have to be muskets. I'd like to kill that Wituwamat with his own knife.' Standish stroked his beard, eyes far away as if imagining the act. Then, abruptly, he went on: 'I want three of you with myself and Hobbamock in here – Alden, Allerton and Howland. Winslow and you others, take care of any Indians within the settlement. Use your muskets. John, fetch a coil of good stout rope.'

The fire dwindled, but no man stirred to put on more wood.

'My plan is to give them plenty of strong water. We all are not to touch a drop, just pretend to drink. We must be absolutely clear-headed. When I judge they are tipsy enough...'

'Shouldn't take long,' Allerton interrupted. 'Indians can't hold their drink, but they do love it.'

'As I was saying,' Standish continued, 'when I judge the moment is right, I'll signal you, John, to secure the door. I'll be sure I'm seated beside either the pinese or Wituwamat and turn his knife on him. Howland, you and Allerton take on the other; Alden, the third. If there is a fourth, bind him fast in the instant you secure the door. All keep alert and take your cue from me. Is the plan clear?'

Silence. John felt sick. Sick at heart and in his stomach. *Well, nothing for it – I'm to fight for my life.*

★ ★ ★

As directed, Hobbamock departed at daybreak. He soon returned. 'Your invitation is accepted. Wituwamat, the pinese, another brave and Wituwamat's younger brother in his teens, and perhaps a few women.'

'Women?' Standish asked.

'For your pleasure, sir.'

'Filthy scum.' Standish scowled. He beckoned to John, who was preparing a roasting spit.

'When you secure the door, bind the brother fast. He's a lad. We won't hack him to pieces. Hang him instead.'

'Yes, sir,' John said. *I mustn't let the horror of this overwhelm me. I can't dissuade Standish. Have to see it out and keep my own skin. But my God! It is atrocious.* He returned to his post at the spit.

By mid-afternoon all was ready: pallets and cushions arranged in a circle on the floor; muskets and a coil of rope hidden under two pallets laid side by side length-wise against the wall by the door; two more pallets laid against the end wall for the women. The bottles of strong water stood by the hearth. Two trenchers full of sliced pork kept warm by the fire, enticing odors wafting in the fetid, smoky air.

John's stomach was churning. Howland paced, clenching and unclenching his fists. They exchanged a knowing look.

A knock on the door. Standish opened and greeted Wituwamat with a deep bow.

'Welcome.'

The other three Indians followed as Hobbamock had said, and three giggling women. They made eyes at Standish, recognizing him as the Englishman to whom they'd given their beaver coats. Allerton showed them to their pallets.

Wituwamat didn't wait to be seated. He chose a cushion near the hearth, by the bottles of strong water. Allerton sat beside him, then the pinese and Standish beside him. Howland sat opposite Wituwamat and Alden sat, back to the door, between the third brave and Wituwamat's brother.

Standish made a brief speech of welcome and hopes for comradeship in the future. Hobbamock translated. Wituwamat returned the compliment. Again, Hobbamock translated. Standish gestured to the bottle at Wituwamat's left hand, inviting him to drink. The bottle did the rounds several times, Standish keeping it going as long as possible before serving any food.

John could see the braves' eyes weren't focusing and they swayed a little, even sitting. The bottle did another round. Wituwamat looked longingly and gestured at the pork. Howland picked up the trencher and handed it to him.

Allerton looked at Standish, who nodded even as he ripped the pinese's knife from its string and plunged the sharp point into the Indian's chest. Allerton did the same to Wituwamat, whose hands were both on the trencher. Howland leapt to hold the pinese's arms. John kicked 'his' tipsy brave sprawling and quickly secured the door. He bound the lad, already knocked senseless by the liquor, hand and foot. By now his adrenalin was pumping, and the blood lust carried him. All fear was replaced by a frenzied urge to kill, along with a curious detachment of mind. He saw clearly what he had to do. Kneeling astride the brave's naked chest, knees on his arms, John seized the top-knot with his left hand, holding the head back, neck stretched taut. He looked into wide open, brown, glazed eyes, curled nostrils and upper lip. With his right hand, John ripped the brave's knife from its string. Ignoring the feebly thrashing legs and buttocks, with deliberate precision he drew the blade deep into and across the waiting throat. He saw his uncle's face, curled upper lip, the Indian's throat became his uncle's throat. The top knot was his uncle's thick mane of dark hair. John gave it a tug. Blood gushed: limbs shuddered and were still. So quick.

Now he helped Standish battle the pinese, while Howland did the same for Allerton. The Indians fought on and on, stabbed again and again in the back, chest, groin. A scene of blood, sliced limbs and faces. Hobbamock stood, overseeing the carnage. In the end, only the lad was alive. And through it all, no one uttered a sound. Only the women whimpered, covering their heads in their arms.

'Come on, out,' commanded Standish. 'With muskets.' On the way, he said, 'Hang the lad. Allerton, you do it. Make it a quick one.'

John ran stumbling, with Standish, to join Winslow and his men. He began to feel weak and giddy, wanting to vomit.

As if anticipating this reaction, Standish continued issuing orders. 'On with you – job not done, not half done! No lagging. John, get that Indian!' The captain pointed.

Knocked into action by the harsh words, John found the Indian in his sights and shot. The man fell. Another. Winslow shot a third. Some of Weston's men joined Standish's party as the captain marched them out of the settlement in pursuit of more Massachusetts. Arrows flew from behind trees, aimed at Standish and Hobbamock. John, trying to cover for Standish, was amazed at how fearless the captain was, almost as if he'd taken on the mantle of invulnerability worn by Hobbamock as pinese.

Eventually Hobbamock said he'd had enough. He threw off his coat in scorn and gave chase. The foe ran, and Hobbamock ran so swiftly after them the English couldn't keep up. John took his chance to lean against a tree and vomit.

A hand fell on his shoulder. 'First time?' Winslow said.

John nodded.

'Nasty business.'

By now there was just one Indian, a shaman, who stood his ground and aimed arrow after arrow at Standish. The captain and

Howland both fired at him and broke his arm. He and the remaining Massachusetts warriors ran off to the safety of a swamp.

Standish's party returned to the scene of carnage. The captain severed Wituwamat's head from his body, holding it aloft in triumph, and then wrapped it in a white linen cloth he'd brought for the purpose.

He had this planned exactly, down to the last detail. Did Bradford know? Agree? John felt dizzy from the stench of blood and mutilation of limbs. He had to step outside to retch again. *I must stop it. They'll think I'm a milksop.* Re-entering, he picked up 'his' brave and followed the others to a place where the bodies were left in a heap outside the settlement.

Standish released all the Indian women. Then he asked one of Weston's men to find them a different lodging for the night. John got a fire going in the hearth. The party of eight sat on pallets and cushions, now a somber group. They passed the trenchers of pork, cold by now. John declined.

'Cornbread?' Standish asked.

'Yes, please.'

'Well, we did it. Job done,' Standish said. 'Thank you all.'

Apart from a murmur of acknowledgment no one spoke.

'They were brave,' the captain said, 'courageous. No screams or moans. And they took so many fearful wounds before they died, striving to the end.'

★ ★ ★

Priscilla held Peregrine's hand as the little lad jumped up and down, pointing, shouting, 'Boat. Boat.' She and Susanna, eager and tense, waited and watched as the small vessel sailed nearer. Bradford and Brewster stood a few paces off.

'Pray they all return safe.' Brewster spoke for all the waiting wives and friends.

The shallop drew up to the landing rock, and one by one all eight stepped ashore. A cheer went up. Standish strode to Bradford and unwrapped his bloody bundle.

Priscilla gasped and covered her eyes as John wrapped her in his arms. He held her tight. So tight she could hardly breathe. When he released her enough to kiss her in greeting, she saw he was not smiling. All round them cheers continued. 'Hoorah for Standish! Showed them... hoorah! Now they know.'

'Find us a pike, John,' Bradford called. 'Good job, Standish. This trophy will go on permanent display.'

Head bowed, John squeezed Priscilla's hand before he resolutely put one foot in front of the other in the direction of the stores.

Brewster came to Priscilla, his face somber.

'How is Mistress Brewster?' Priscilla asked, not knowing what to say.

'Didn't feel up to being with us.' The Elder sighed. 'Just as well. She is very grateful for your help, and so am I.' He watched as John brought the pike, and Bradford and Standish stuck Wituwamat's head on the spiked end.

'Ready! March.' A jubilant Standish cried out his order. He and Bradford headed a procession of colonists, Bradford carrying the adorned pike. They marched up the hill to the fort and mounted the pike with its severed head on the flat roof.

'Let this be a lesson to them,' Bradford announced to the watching settlers. 'Any Indian sees this will remember not to challenge us.'

'Hoorah, hoorah! Victory. Victory.'

Priscilla hated it. *They are all infected with blood lust. Disgusting. Horrible.* She took John's hand and he turned to her, answering her tug. 'I'll go stir up the pot. You must be terrible hungry,' she said.

'I'll be along soon. Wouldn't look good if I didn't stay awhile.'

John dropped his knapsack and hung his musket in place over the door. 'So good to be back with you.' He sat heavily on a stool.

Priscilla served up their trencherful of pottage. 'I prayed every day for your safe return; all the while wondering what was happening, what were your orders.'

'It was appalling, barbaric,' John said. 'Standish turned into a different person: treacherous, butchering. He tricked his selected group, got them drunk and then... knives.' John shuddered, stood and paced. 'And I did it. I murdered in cold blood.' He drew his hand across his brow. 'He became a monster. Why? Yes, Wituwamat insulted him, and he hates to be insulted. But he seems so quick to get up a blood lust against any Indians – except Hobbamock.' John held his hands out, looking at them. 'I never...' He covered his eyes. 'It was wrong. Not even a clean fight. And Hobbamock seemed quite prepared to agree to the treachery. I don't understand.'

'It is hard to believe,' Priscilla said. 'Miles was so caring when we were in the sickness. Never spared himself, did all the filthy tasks.'

'And when Rose died,' John said, 'he was truly full of grief, and wishing, feeling, he should have been with her.' He looked imploringly at Priscilla. 'How can I still be his friend? How can I live with myself? It was a sin, Priscilla. A grievous sin.'

'But John, what could you have done? Disobeyed orders? That would have been treason.'

'True. And I could see Winslow wasn't happy about it. Though he said nothing.'

'Why don't you ask Elder Brewster his views? He didn't look at all pleased.' Priscilla paused. 'But Bradford – he was jubilant. As exhilarated as Standish.'

'He probably agreed Standish should bring back Wituwamat's head. I hope he didn't know of the planned treachery.' John came round to stand behind Priscilla and put his hands on her shoulders. 'Good advice. I'll try to talk with the Elder this evening.'

The hour was late. Priscilla sat by the hearth trying to mend by the light of the smoldering embers. *I hope the Elder has given him some comfort. I've never seen him so upset and turned inward, so full of contrition.*

She heard the latch lift, and swiveled round, standing in greeting. John slumped down in his rocker. They sat facing the fire.

'It was good to talk with Brewster. When I told him the details of the massacre he was horrified. Said if he'd known of the plan he'd have forbidden it. He can't think what has gotten into Bradford to condone such a thing.'

'And your part? Did he say you are stained?'

'He said much the same as you – I didn't have a choice. And as I feel so bad about it God will probably forgive me. The Elder doesn't think I'm a fiend. He said Standish is, as we know, a good man and valuable to us in many ways. It's just that he has this other side to him and someone has to keep him in check. That is where Bradford failed. He, too, lost his wider view.'

'So we shouldn't turn our backs on Standish – as a friend?'

'No. But it is a hard divide to straddle. I'll never have that – what is it? – carefree trust and enjoyment of him as before.' John looked into the fire and put his hand on Priscilla's.

'The Elder said that once blood has been shed, and in so perfidious a manner, the wounds are seldom healed; not for a very long time. He fears what unstoppable currents of mistrust and disturbance have been set in motion. He cautioned me to try always to keep a broad view, with foresight.'

In the middle of the night, screams – 'No! No, don't!' startled Priscilla awake. John sat up, his face pouring with sweat. He swung his legs over the side of the bed, hid his face in his hands. 'They'd lost their strength; their limbs were twitchy and feeble… the liquor. They couldn't fight us off.' He swung around again to face Priscilla. 'If they'd not been drunk we would all have been scalped. Those Indians are so strong and quick – they could have flicked us off as if we were flies, and yanked the door off its hinges. Standish knew that, and they never uttered a sound. Just took it.' He stared into space. 'I tell you, Priscilla,' his voice rose, 'Satan was in that room. Oh God.'

Priscilla put her arms around him and held him close.

John choked back sobs with moans. 'If only I'd said no.'

Chapter 51

April 1623

A drought and hope

'I'll bring you the news.' Standish hacked his axe head into a tree stump and marched to Bradford's house. John hoped the meeting would be a long one. He still found it difficult to look at his friend. Images of the massacre haunted his mind and the sight of Wituwamat's head on the pike sickened him. Every night bad dreams invaded his sleep. He saw his hand drawing the knife blade across the Indian's throat, the Indian's head transforming into the face of his uncle.

For the moment he would seek solace in working with Howland, raising a house for him and Lizzie, sharing his happy anticipation of being wed.

'She's hopeless with a needle,' Howland said. 'But I don't mind if my patches aren't straight and by Jove can she cook.'

'Your Lizzie is a fair lass, and merry.' John slotted a plank into place. 'Reckon she'll make you a warm, happy home.'

'And a warm, happy bed,' Howland grinned.

The morning passed. The sun shone from its noon position. Time for the midday meal. As John and Howland were shouldering their axes, Standish clumsily ran across the clearing. 'Good news,' he panted. 'Communal planting abandoned. John, you and I each have four acres, north of Town Brook. Bradford has drawn a map showing the allocation of land.'

Ducking his head as he stepped through the doorway into his home, John swooned slightly and lowered himself onto a stool by the table. Priscilla slowly left the hearth to sit with him. She was growing listless from lack of food and it pleased him to see her brighten a little as he told her the news.

'I hope we can keep going somehow 'til the next harvest. I'm afraid… afraid we've no beer. I pray the sickness doesn't come again. God have mercy.' In spite of the good news, Priscilla was almost weeping with hunger, fatigue and fear. 'I remember those first days after Father came back from London. He was so full of promise and hopes.'

'What would he have thought?' John pondered aloud. 'Your father was wise. He understood about working together. I reckon he'd have been a leveler. Perhaps he'd have restrained Standish. If he and Deacon Carver… we'll never know.' John took Priscilla's hands in his. 'Don't lose hope. We have our own plot. It's our chance to turn the corner. I'll start mattocking tomorrow.'

'I'll follow with the fork,' Priscilla gave a wavering smile.

★ ★ ★

Six weeks later, John leaned on his hoe, surveying their acres of sprouting corn heaps. 'Bless Hobbamock.' Hobbamock had taken Squanto's place, catching herring to fertilize the soil, and he'd taught Francis and the other lads how to scoop up the fish in baskets. They loved standing in the brook, reaping their haul. They especially relished squiggling their feet in the mud and scooping up the surfacing eels. He smiled, remembering the day Squanto came proudly bearing his catch of big fat eels, delivered to Mary Brewster.

Even the barley and peas were healthily green and strong, unlike the past two years. Their third spring. *Howland and Lizzie are wed and happy.* He chuckled. He looked up at the sky. Clear blue. Bright hot sun. *Now all we need is rain. Gentle English rain.*

Week after week of hot dry days: a month, two months. The crops were wilting, turning brown, beginning to shrivel. Standish organized the men into fishing and hunting parties, alternating rosters, while the women harvested shellfish and searched for groundnuts. But game was scarce this time of year, and not having enough suitable gear, the catch of fish was scant. The brook ran low and sluggish; no water for laundry, barely enough for cooking and drinking. The ground was hard and cracked.

John worried, seeing Priscilla drag herself from chore to chore, unable to muster a smile, performing her duties with mechanical listlessness, and most disheartening, she could not respond to his efforts to bring comfort and hope.

Early that morning, John and Howland had taken a boat out fishing, but their catch was meager and his share only one small cod. He could see Priscilla trying to hide her disappointment, forcing the beginning of a smile, then lowering her gaze.

'Hand me a knife. I'll gut and descale it,' he said.

'Thank you.'

'Coming up the track I met the Elder. He is declaring a day of prayer tomorrow.'

'But it isn't the Sabbath.'

'He reckons drastic measures are needed. All of us, women and children too are to gather at dawn, in the fields by the brook.'

Just before sunrise next day, John and Priscilla stepped out of their home. Joining the Winslows and Standish they walked slowly with the crowd assembling in the fields.

'Bradford and Prence are going from house to house,' Winslow said, 'to be sure no one stays away.'

Already the morning was warm, and the sun mounted the sky, turning from red to orange to yellow, sending a punishing heat and glare. The air was still. When Bradford had ushered in the stragglers, Elder Brewster stood facing the gathering, his lean form straight and solid. He began to pray, his deep voice rolling through his flock and beyond.

John noticed Hobbamock and a small group of Indians standing apart, behind and to the right of the Elder, watching. Hour on hour, Elder Brewster prayed. At first John tried to concentrate on his words, but distracted by the heat and glare, could only hear the sonorous cadences, enveloping, sometimes soothing, and then startling when his prayer reached a pitch of pleading fervor.

Apart from swiping at flies, he and Priscilla stood still, heads bowed. He saw his bootlace was untied and studied the small beetles and grasshoppers scurrying and hopping over his boot and through the rough grass. As the sun reached its zenith sweat trickled down their faces and they swallowed to ease their dry throats. Of a sudden, Priscilla clutched his arm. John caught her as her knees gave way. 'This is madness. 'Tis too hot,' he muttered as he carried her across the field to a grove of birch trees. He knelt, cradling her gently until she came out of her faint.

'My head is fuzzy. I feel sick.'

John helped Priscilla settle with her back against a tree trunk, sheltered in the shade.

'Look.' She pointed feebly. 'Goody Hopkins leaning against that tree, nursing her babe only a month old and out in this heat.' She moaned and leaned her head back, closing her eyes.

'You bide here and rest.' John spoke softly. 'I'll go back to my place.' He threaded his way through collapsed sleeping children. He judged about two hours had passed when Priscilla put her hand through his right arm. He placed his left hand over hers and they stood thus, waiting for the hours to pass.

As the afternoon wore on, a slight breeze from the west soothed their sweat-soaked bodies. John longed for water. When the sun began to set, sending a glory of red and gold rays into the blue, Elder Brewster brought his prayers to a close. Slowly, in silence, the colonists trudged through the fields, heads bowed. John noticed the air begin to cool. He turned his face to the freshening breeze and clutched Priscilla's arm. 'Can it be? Clouds!' Beautiful gray clouds, overshadowing the sun's rays, moving ever closer and then, a spot of rain on his face. *Please God, let there be more, please,* he prayed silently. Every face looked up in wordless hope. And then it came, a cool, gentle rain, running down faces, joining tears of relief. Breaking into the hushed joy came a solitary shout. 'Hoorah! Hoorah! God be praised!' Exhilaration, shouting, jigging, hugging.

In their home, John and Priscilla offered their own prayers of thanks and entreaty that the rain should continue. Then they sat quiet, eating their fish gruel and enjoying the music of soft rain falling onto tree leaves and the parched earth. When they undressed for bed, Priscilla put their clothes out in the rain. They stood together, naked in the dark, bathing in the gentle English rain.

The rain continued to fall, day after day. Soon the ground softened enough so they could hoe round the plants, loosening the soil so the rainwater would seep down to the roots, not run off the surface. It was a joy to see Priscilla's spirits revive, to see her hold out her bodice to let the rain run down her breasts; take off her coif to let the rain wash her auburn hair; to be working together in the rain.

Walking home with Standish after a day's shooting in the swamp, John said, 'This beautiful rain continues day after day as if sent purposely by God to compensate for the drought.'

'Hobbamock and his friends are in awe that our God answered our prayers so promptly, and with a perfect soft rain. He said the Indians' rain dances and ceremonies usually produce lashing, battering tempests,' Standish said.

'It does feel miraculous. I can scarce believe that God should give his mercy and blessing so soon.' *Especially after our cruel, deceitful attack on the Indians.*

When John entered with two brace of duck, he found Priscilla sitting by the fire, studying her gardening book. She looked up, smiled and rose to greet him.

'A grand haul. You are a good shot, husband,' she said, taking the fowl and laying them on the table. 'I'll take a brace to the Brewsters tomorrow.'

'Come here, wife.' John took her in his arms, loosed her coif and stroked her rain-softened hair. 'You are the scent of rain and earth. Delicious. When I return from hunting tomorrow, I'll mattock our garden here by the house. Do you still have your primrose seeds?'

'You remembered!' Priscilla clutched his hand. 'Yes, I have them and the columbine. And I thought I might bring up some ferns and violets from the wood, and sallet roots and mint, and plant our own garden of herbs and flowers.'

'You'll work magic,' John said. 'And you are happy again. We **will** make it, my Priscilla.'

Still relishing the soft, misty rain, musket on his shoulder, John strode up past the fort toward the forest. *The horn.* He dashed back to the settlement. Folk hastened from their houses, fields, garden plots. 'A ship! A ship!' Seagulls wheeled and cawed overhead, apron strings flapped, children tripped over their feet or a root, arms churning to regain balance.

Priscilla called, beckoning. She and Susanna were in the thick of the rush, clutching and dragging Peregrine, now too big to carry. John caught up with them and lifted the little lad in his arms.

Elder Brewster and Jonathan supported Mary, trying to match her weakened pace, but half sweeping her down the track. 'She's English. I can see her flag,' the Elder called out.

'Strange,' Priscilla said. 'Standish is rushing to his house.'

'Look!' Susanna pointed. 'So is the governor.'

When the shallop carrying the first lot of passengers was about two-thirds of the way across the harbor Standish and Bradford joined the crowd gathered on the shore.

'I reckon Standish is expecting someone,' John said.

The captain was dressed for parade: polished helmet and breastplate, combed, glowing red beard, and scarlet breeches. Bradford stood alongside him wearing his very best blue suit, broad collar brilliant white, shoes polished and hat brushed.

'And the governor?' Priscilla asked.

'I reckon.'

Bradford and Winslow greeted the newcomers.

'They are all so healthy and filled out and wearing nice clothes,' Priscilla said. 'And they look at us in horror.'

When the ship's boat from the *Anne* had started back for another lot of passengers, Bradford came over to John. 'Could you take our shallop and help with the ferrying? I'm told there are sixty altogether.' He looked out across the harbor to the sand spits. 'This ship started out with a pinnace, the *James*, sailing in tandem. But a storm hit and since then there's been no trace. Pray God she's safe.'

Amongst the passengers John ferried was a stately woman, firm of figure, wearing a fine soft blue gown. As John helped her onto the landing rock Bradford stepped forward, taking her hands in his. 'Mistress Southworth. Welcome.' He escorted her to his house.

As the ship's boat was bringing its final lot of newcomers John took his place again with Priscilla and Susanna. Standish stood, still waiting, watching as the last ferryload drew near. A woman leaned forward in the bow; she could have been taken for a figurehead. She held her coif in place, blond curls unfurling in the wind. Her eyes searched the waiting group on shore, her mouth an expectant smile.

Winslow offered his hand as she stepped out of the boat. She hardly acknowledged his presence. Eyes fixed on the brass helmet and red beard, she hitched up her skirts and strode straight to Standish.

'Barbara!' The captain took her hands, clearly admiring her plump curves.

'What a beautiful gown. A glorious shade of green. Isn't she like Rose?' Priscilla turned to John. 'Only rounder, more robust – and strong minded I reckon.'

Standish put his arm through Barbara's and they walked together up the track chatting excitedly like old friends.

Winslow took on the task of assigning newcomers to lodgings. John and Priscilla were allocated a young couple from Leiden and their three children: a lad and two younger girls.

At table that eve the woman said, 'You all look in a sorry state. Not what we expected from reading the pamphlet you sent. What a picture of plenitude and well-being was painted. And here you are, thin as poles, your clothes all patched.'

'I hope you have a good crop of barley,' the man said. 'I'm a brewer and miller. When the new houses are raised I'll build you a corn mill.' He shook his head. 'All this time you've been grinding with a pestle and mortar.' He looked at Priscilla and tutted.

'Aye, we've had a hard time of it,' John said. 'I reckon life in these parts will never be easy but it can be good. Needs folk like yourselves to work hard. Then I'm sure we'll prosper.'

When the colony all marched to the fort to keep the Sabbath, Bradford announced that the new arrivals would be given all the supplies on the *Anne* to sustain them until they could reap their harvests. Folk who had come on the *Mayflower* and the *Fortune* would have the benefit of their own crops. Looking across the aisle, John caught Priscilla's eye and smiled. *Good. Our pumpkins and squash are fat. All we've sown looks healthy. We'll reap the fruits of our work.*

Chapter 52

June - December 1623

Charles Prence

A few days later the *James* sailed into the harbor bringing thirty more passengers, storm worn and weary.

John and Priscilla were amongst the welcoming party, standing under overcast skies with a chill wind blowing from the northeast. Rare in June. As it was low tide the beleaguered passengers had to wade from the ship's boat to the shore. John and Priscilla waded out several yards to help women and children as they staggered in the pebbled shallow water. The last few to disembark were a small group of men. John stared. He sensed Priscilla freeze. Prence. The man approaching them looked exactly like Prence, without the mole. John held out a hand. 'Sir.'

'Charles Prence. In search of my brother Thomas.'

'He is most likely in Elder Brewster's house. I'll take you there.'

On opening the door the Elder took a step back. His gaze ossified. He looked over his shoulder to where Prence sat beside Patience.

'I… I am sorry. Do come in. The resemblance is surprising.'

Charles Prence stepped into the room. 'Found you at last, Thomas.'

His face pale, hands trembling, Prence said, 'Charles. What a surprise.' Then rapidly collecting himself he stood and extended a hand. 'My dear brother, welcome. What brings you to these parts?'

Charles spat on Prence's hand. Patience gasped, uttering a tiny cry. Mary Brewster stood as if turned to stone. The Elder harrumphed.

'Don't play the innocent. I am here to reclaim my money, you embezzler. And if you have squandered what is rightfully mine, you'll come back to England with me to stand trial.' He turned to the Elder and John. 'We are twins. Thomas here, unable to make his way as an honest craftsman, used our similitude to persuade my clients to give him an advance on contracts. He discredited me with his shoddy craftsmanship and when he was about to be exposed, disappeared with the money owed me, having ruined my name.'

'He lies,' Prence said.

'This cannot be resolved now.' The Elder stepped between the two men. 'Pray desist from accusations.' He looked at Charles. 'It would not be wise for you both to reside under the same roof. As Mr Prence spends many hours here, and both Bradford and Standish are occupied with newly arrived ladies, could I ask you, Mr Alden, to give our guest hospitality – for this eve at least.'

John and Priscilla welcomed Charles Prence along with the small family already lodging with them. They heard his story in greater detail. Priscilla clapped her hands on her cheeks. 'But that is precisely the tale of woe Mr Prence told me when, when he was seeking to woo me.' She lowered her eyes as if ashamed.

'Thanks be he didn't succeed, the scoundrel. You are too fine a woman to be tarnished with that…' Charles' cheeks flushed in anger.

Now days were a flurry and tumult of house building. John organized teams, with every man put to work. Only one hunting party and one fishing party every two days. Happily at this time of year there was lobster aplenty.

The women all dug for clams, mussels and oysters, and set to grinding corn brought on the *Anne* and the *James*.

Charles Prence worked dawn to dusk as directed by John who became convinced of his sincerity and goodwill. No airs and graces, forthright in his views whilst willing to listen, interested in the colony's origins and welfare.

'Charles would be a good addition to our colony,' he murmured to Priscilla as she stirred the pottage.

'Aye, I can see that. If only…'

The day came for the two brothers to present their cases before the governor and a specially selected council. John and Winslow accompanied Charles Prence to the common house. The morning was fine, the sun gaining heat but not yet punishing. Charles glanced up at the spring green filled with industrious birds, and out over the harbor, still and blue. 'This place has a beauty about it,' he said. 'Could be a good place to live.'

When all the council were assembled, seated round the rectangular table, Bradford invited Charles to state his case.

'Thank you, sir.' Prence's brother stood and spoke calmly, sticking to facts that could be verified. He cited the names of clients he'd lost and the dates of the contracts. He said Prence's actions had cost him his livelihood and his betrothed, but he avoided salacious, slanderous comments. He did not look at his brother but made eye contact with every man seated round the table.

In his turn, Prence put on a performance empty of facts but calculated to win the sympathy of the hardest of hearts, constantly reiterating his indebtedness to Elder Brewster and Bradford, his gratitude to them for ushering him into their church, the one true church. He missed no opportunity to defame his brother's character.

John fidgeted in his seat, cringing. He could barely restrain himself from interrupting, protesting.

When the brothers had finished they were escorted from the room; Thomas to the Brewster house and Charles to the Aldens'.

Only a minute or two into the deliberations it was clear to John that the colony's leaders were not about to turn against Prence; betrothed to Patience Brewster, a true convert to the Church of Christ, devoted to upholding and enforcing its beliefs, always eager to study scripture and interested to learn the rules of governance. John uttered a lone plea. 'Why would Charles Prence, or any man, sail across the ocean at great risk if his story were not true? He wants to see justice done.'

'There is no limit to the lengths some men will go to if they want vengeance,' Brewster said. 'In my view Charles Prence is seeking baseless vengeance on his innocent brother.'

John looked across the table at Winslow. *I know you don't agree with this. Please support me.* But Winslow studied his hands folded on the table, refusing to make eye contact.

Bradford stood. 'Is there consensus that our Mr Prence is innocent? Agreement that we will not take the matter further and will ensure that Charles Prence returns to England when the *Anne* sails?'

'Aye' was the unanimous response apart from John who remained silent.

On leaving the common house John avoided the company of his fellows. He walked quickly out the north gate and up to the Mullins' graveyard behind the fort. He kicked hummocks of earth. His chest ached, as if weighed with a lump of lead, a lump of leaden shame. He'd betrayed Charles, gone with the pack as he knew he would, and in so doing had betrayed himself, again. He thought of his friend Will, left rotting in prison because there was no justice, only luck and favoritism. He'd been so sure that in this new land it would be different. A new world of equal justice for all. What a mockery. *Wessagussett and now this. How many more deceitful, cruel deeds – and in the name of God?* Pain seared his head. *It isn't right. It is the way it is. If I want to build a good home for Priscilla and our children… So be it.*

Heavy with resolution, his head still throbbing, John walked slowly back along the outside of the wall and into the settlement. When he entered his home he found Charles and Priscilla alone, sitting on either side of the table, waiting for him. He slumped onto a stool. 'I'm sorry, Charles.' Charles looked at him, eyebrow raised in question.

'They're protecting your brother. They wouldn't listen to me.'

Charles shrugged his shoulders. 'I expected as much. And, John, praise be you didn't wave a banner on my behalf. You'd have only got yourself into trouble, and for what? Mark. I don't envy you having to toe the line with Elder Brewster and Governor Bradford. Very set in their views.'

Priscilla stood and fetched trenchers of pottage.

Despite the verdict against him Charles continued to work hard as ever. John noticed that sometimes he pounded a stake into the ground with such vehemence he nearly cracked it. Clearly the man had enormous strength. One day when they stopped for their midday corn bread, sitting on two stumps side by side, Charles said, 'Don't let me near my brother. I could easily kill him with my bare hands and I would.'

John looked at Charles' hands; capable of the finest craftsmanship in wood, and capable of squeezing the life out of a man in seconds. 'We'll keep you busy,' he said. 'Don't see your brother about these days. Expect he's hiding in the protection of the Brewster household.'

'Thomas always was a devious, sniveling wretch from a lad. Mind, our father treated him badly; was always beating him; made no secret he couldn't bear the sight of that mole. I found my brother one day – we'd have been about eight years – trying to cut out the mole with our father's razor. Blood everywhere. Father gave him the thrashing of his life and he never tried it again. The mole grew even bigger.'

John shuddered. 'What will you do back in England? Times are hard there we hear.'

'Don't know. Perhaps I'll try my fortunes in Virginia.'

A fresh, cooling sea breeze dried the sweat on their faces. The harbor glittered blue under the hot sun.

'Goodbye, Charles.' John held out his hand. 'Sorry to see you go.' He felt a pit in his belly.

'You've been good to me. Thank you.' Charles' voice cracked. He pumped John's hand and waded out to the ship's boat, not looking back.

''Tis sad,' Priscilla said. 'I shall miss him too. Look. There's Winslow bidding Susanna farewell.'

Susanna wiped tears from her cheeks and tried to smile. Her husband gave her a final hug and turned abruptly to wade out into the shallow water.

John and Priscilla waited and watched with Susanna until the ship's boat had crossed the harbor and Charles Prence and Winslow had climbed the rope ladder and disappeared onto the deck of the *Anne*.

'Come and sup with us this evening,' Priscilla said.

Susanna put a hand on Priscilla's arm, giving a squeeze. 'Thank you – very much. It is lonely without him, especially at first.' Her voice wavered. 'I'll bring my lobster stew.'

★ ★ ★

'You should be proud, husband.' Priscilla and John sat by their hearth, Priscilla mending, John sitting in his rocker legs stretched out, smoking his pipe. Bibs joined them, curling up in her customary spot by John's pipe box. 'All the newcomers have houses – an amazing achievement. How this colony has grown.'

'Aye. Nearly trebled. Best is, we have our own home back, just for us.'

Priscilla looked up at John. 'Do you know if anyone has left us to return to England? The newcomers seemed horrified to find us in such a bad way. Wonder if the sight of us has scared any off.'

'Not that I've heard of. But I reckon Bradford is going to have a job keeping order. Only about a third of the newcomers are Church of Christ. I think Winslow is going to try to negotiate for more folk from Holland to come, and get fishing gear and more animals. He's taking a manuscript he's written defending our massacre at Wessagussett.' John pulled his hand across his eyes. 'Those poor Indians.' He sank onto a stool. 'Hobbamock brought word today that the tribes down the cape – our friends – have all run away into the swamps, they're so scared of us. We've lost our source of trade.'

''Tis frightening,' Priscilla said. 'We are now entirely dependent on what we grow and on Massasoit. How long must we carry on suffering hunger?' She looked into the embers flickering on the hearth. 'Does Standish realize the havoc the massacre has caused? What must Hobbamock think?'

'Puzzles me. Hobbamock is as devoted to Standish as ever. And we know he is absolutely committed to Massasoit.' John stood with his back to the hearth. 'You've just said it. We are entirely dependent on Massasoit for trade.' He struck his forehead with the heel of his palm. 'I've just thought. Perhaps we've been pawns in Massasoit's game. Squanto wanted to dethrone Massasoit, to replace him as big chief. Now Massasoit is not only rid of Squanto; because of Wessagussett all the other sachems who might have rivalled him have run away. He is now in a position of well nigh supreme power. Would explain why Hobbamock was so accepting of the treacherous massacre.'

On the Sabbath at the close of prayers, Bradford announced there would be a double wedding. 'I solemnly do announce the betrothal of William Bradford to Alice Southworth and the betrothal of Captain Miles Standish to Barbara, Rose's sister.' Clapping, cheers, stamping feet; the governor held up his hands for silence. 'Thank you,' he said. 'I have invited Massasoit to be present at our celebrations.'

'Good show. Excellent. Good to know the big chief is our friend.' Howland punched the air.

The wedding day dawned fair. By now summer rains had given way to clear, crisp days of early autumn, the trees showing inklings of the vibrant reds, oranges and yellows to come. Roasting spits were erected, tables laid with pots of pottage and fish stew, berries, sallet, nuts and cornbread. The harvest was rich with plentiful corn, beans and peas.

Just one thing saddened John and Priscilla. Wituwamat's head was still on its pike and in place of the flag of St George, Bradford and Standish had raised the blood stained linen cloth used to wrap the severed head – to please Massasoit.

Shortly past noon, the big chief appeared on the crest of the hill, a black wolf skin draped over his shoulder, and by his side, one of his wives. He'd brought a host of warriors. John counted over a hundred. 'A clear display of power,' he said. 'And he's our only ally.'

★ ★ ★

Christmas night. Merrily, John and Priscilla bade goodbye to Miles and Barbara Standish as they stepped out into the snowy, starlit night.

'Goodnight. Merry Christmas!' They kept salutations to a whisper lest their revelries be discovered.

Closing the door, John said, 'It has been a merry party. Miles with his flute, Barbara full of fun. Singing our English songs, dancing.'

'You seemed a bit distant, slightly strained with Miles,' Priscilla said.

'I cannot be rid of what he did – the treachery. I cannot forget it.'

'You must put it behind you. With Prence constantly snooping, well in the Brewster fold and currying favor with Bradford, you need Captain Standish as ally and friend. Barbara is lovely. Miles does such a lot for the colony. I find him charming and endearing. Try to stay loyal. I hope he didn't notice.'

'I know. You are right. Trouble is I love the man. The bond goes deep. Makes it harder. We'll not talk of it now. 'Twas a splendid evening. What a feast.' John looked at the two turkey carcasses, all that remained of their Christmas fare.

'And a blazing fire to keep us warm.' Priscilla breathed in the scent of juniper boughs; gazed up at the bedecked rafters. 'With our roof space full of pumpkins, squash, crocks of dried beans, peas, berries, plums, nuts… the joy of it. And not long before we can add cured pork.'

John laughed. 'You can always depend on pigs to reproduce at a rate.' They stood, hand in hand, surveying their home: pewter glinting in the firelight, a rocking chair either side of the hearth, a handsome oak chest spread with a crisp white cloth. Priscilla pulled John round to face her.

'We'll be needing another item of furniture.'

'Yes, I aim to start on a settle.'

She placed a finger on his lips. 'We'll be needing a cradle.'

1624

Chapter 53

Spring 1624

Reverend Lyford arrives

One on each side, John and Susanna supported Priscilla as they stood waiting on the harbor shore. With only two months before she was due to give birth, her belly was big and heavy; she was unsteady on her feet over rough ground. However, she was determined to greet passengers from the *Charity*, arrived from England, anchored by Clark's Island.

'I pray Edward is returned, please God,' Susanna said as the shallop drew in toward shore. 'There he is!' Priscilla held onto Peregrine as Susanna pushed forward. She watched as Winslow waded through shallow breakers to enfold his wife in his arms. They stood wrapped together as if no one else existed. When they disengaged and Winslow moved to greet John and Priscilla, Bradford joined them.

Knowing the governor's unspoken question, Winslow said, 'The investors refuse to send any of our friends from Holland. Instead they've sent more folk not of our church and an Anglican minister, name of Lyford, with a colleague, Oldham.'

'A lot more children,' Priscilla said.

'Lyford has brought five.' Winslow thumbed toward a rowdy, heckling group. 'But I did manage, with some difficulty, to get stuff for trade with the Indians, some basic provisions, clothes and a load of fishing gear. And,' Winslow punched the air, 'three heifers and a bull! That should get us started.' He grinned.

Priscilla smiled at the endearing gap between his front teeth.

'No sheep?' Susanna implored. 'Oh, to work soft fleece and spin wool, not only harsh, dusty flax.'

'His Majesty won't allow sheep out of the country – desperate to keep competition at bay. I'd have had to smuggle them. Couldn't risk it.' Winslow turned to Bradford. 'I've engaged a good boat-builder and a chap who promises he is an expert salt-maker.'

Bradford raised an eyebrow. 'Let's hope so.'

As John was occupied stowing provisions, Winslow and Susanna escorted Priscilla back up the hill. She took deep breaths of the tangy salt air. *With any luck we should soon have a grist mill and salt pans. We'll have fine flour to bake a cake, and seasoning.*

'Bradford is fuming,' John said as he came in next day for the midday meal. 'Winslow brought reports from the London investors which say that some of the folk who have settled here have sent letters with lists of complaints that long.' He held his arms straight out sideways at shoulder height. 'They complain about the church's strict religious ways; that church leaders unfairly impose their practices on everyone. They say they're denied the sacraments; duties needed for decency are neglected on the Lord's Day, endless religious disputes, children not even taught to read. There's thieving, laziness, foxes, wolves, mosquitoes. On and on.'

'Not taught to read?' Priscilla asked. 'Hmm. I wonder.'

After their meal, John went hunting and Priscilla called on Governor Bradford.

'Mistress Alden. Come in.' He motioned her to a chair on one side of the hearth, embers smoldering, while he took the other. 'What?'

'Sir.' Priscilla wasted no time. 'I've seen, with the newcomers, how many children there are, often at a loose end, looking for mischief. As you can see, I am far advanced.' She drew a hand across her belly. 'I can't labor as before, and I thought I might be of use starting a school. It would advance us if our young ones had some learning, even just to read and write.'

Bradford's lips formed a thin line. 'It is a worthy offer. And I will consider it in due course. For the present it is best that all the children, boys and girls, be put to work doing whatever task their age permits.' He stood.

'I understand.' Priscilla rose to take her leave. On her way home she called on Susanna and told her about her interview with the governor.

In the evening, sitting with John by their hearth, mending and rocking gently, Priscilla told him of Bradford's refusal to allow her to teach the younger boys.

'It was a good idea. Answered the complaint that children aren't taught to read. I wonder why?' John shook his head. 'Strange. Surely he would want the youth to learn to read the Bible.'

'Perhaps not,' Priscilla said, darning a sock. 'Perhaps he prefers they accept his church's way blind, not reading or thinking for themselves.'

'But that way is...'

'Exactly.' It's why they left the Church of England. They want to read the Bible and discuss and think and worship as *they* feel is right.' Priscilla put down the sock and looked at John. 'It is as if our leaders have decided that allowing any sort of worship different from their own would be like an infection, bringing disease, spreading rot.'

John leaned forward, elbows on his knees. 'Brewster says that is why King James persecuted our leaders. He felt they were an infectious disease, would cause his kingdom to rot.' He stood. 'Ironic. But we've more important matters at hand.' He put an arm round Priscilla's shoulders, drawing her close and tenderly stroked her belly. 'Kicking?'

'Every day, at certain times. Always the same, especially at night. A lively mite.' She chuckled. John tilted her face to his and kissed her.

Next week to the day, disregarding Bradford's wishes, Priscilla and Susanna welcomed eight boys into the Alden home.

'Come in, come in. There, now sit on the floor in a circle.' Priscilla showed the lads where to sit. She and Susanna sat on stools at the top of the circle. Francis sat next to her, the Lyford and Oldham lads together, the others in between.

That Lyford lad looks a mess: hair all in tangles, snot and dirt on his face. The Oldham boy is not much better. Interesting. Their fathers are mates, always together.

'I see several of you have brought slates,' she said. 'I have one, Hopkins, Lyford and Oldham… that gives four to share. Lyford, would you please lend yours to Francis?'

'I ain't lettin' him touch mine!' Lyford pointed at Francis. 'He be a witch!'

Francis leapt to his feet.

'Sit down,' Priscilla said. 'Whatever makes you say such a thing?' she demanded sharply.

'Because I seed 'im in the witch's house, that Mistress Brewster. One tooth top of her mouth sticken out under her lip,' he demonstrated. 'Long straggly hair, wanderin in the swamp, shriekin' and moanin' – she's a witch hag. And anyone goes in a witch's house is one. My father says all you crazy ones – ye're all witches. If he touches my slate he'll give me the mange.' He pointed again at Francis and viciously scratched his arm.

'How dare you speak like that? In this room you show respect for your elders. Like as not you'll have only one tooth left if you live as long as she.' As Priscilla delivered her reprimand she glanced round the circle and struggled not to laugh at the study of mouths agape, eyes staring. 'Now let me see your arm.' She stood and pushed back the sleeve covering the proffered arm. The flesh was covered in red spots, raw and bleeding. 'You already have the mange. Hasn't your mother made an infusion?'

'Naw, she don't know how.'

'I'll make up a lotion and bring it down later. Now, there'll be no more talk of witches. Utter nonsense. Dreadful.' Priscilla took Lyford's slate and gave it to Francis.

An hour later they'd learned the alphabet as far as 'L', an hour passed in absorbed concentration and ended in pride. Witches seemed to be forgotten.

'Our time is up,' Priscilla said. 'You've done well, very well. See you again same time next week.' She returned the borrowed slates to their owners.

'Thank you, Mistress,' Francis said. 'It were a good lesson.'

'Thank you,' chorused the others as they filed out.

'Well I never!' Susanna exclaimed. She and Priscilla stared at one another in amazement. 'Edward said last night Reverend Lyford has beseeched Bradford to accept him into our church; that he goes down on his knees thanking God for this chance to gain purity.'

'Bradford has given him our biggest house and a servant; that nice lass who came on the *Anne* and has been helping Alice.' Priscilla shifted her weight. 'Do you think they really call us witches, as his boy said?'

Susanna frowned and wiped her brow. 'Either Reverend Lyford is a most dreadful hypocrite or his lad is lying. Time will tell. I'd best be off; Edward will be in to eat.'

'Thank you, Susanna.' Priscilla took hold of her friend's hands. 'This wouldn't have happened without you.'

'You know I've always wanted to. And Edward approves – that helps.' She winked.

'Edward approves of what?' John asked as he came through the door, left open to receive the fresh spring air and light.

'I must be off. Your wife will explain.' Susanna dropped a curtsy and skipped across the track.

'I'll be glad when I can skip again,' Priscilla said. *If I survive.* 'Winslow approves of Susanna and me teaching the young lads. Once a week only, so as not to keep them from helping with building and planting. He says he'll soothe any objection Bradford may have.'

'Well done! You are a clever lass. You and Susanna – a formidable pair.' Chuckling, John went to the lean-to for a wash.

★ ★ ★

As promised, Priscilla brewed an infusion of plants, chiefly scabious, to treat the Lyford boy's mange. Carrying the bottle, she took care with her steps. She didn't want to trip on a root or a rabbit hole. *This has become a noisy place, with all the hammering and sawing and children running here and there, and folk shouting above the din.*

The Lyford house was down near the harbor, a prime spot. Priscilla knocked, again and again, and was about to give up when the door opened.

A tall, matronly woman, frowning and sullen asked, 'What do you want?'

'I've brought a bottle of remedy for the mange. Your lad…' As she spoke, Priscilla noticed Alice Bradford's servant huddled on a stool in the far corner, head down, wiping her eyes.

Following the direction of Priscilla's focus, Mistress Lyford took the bottle. 'Thank you.' She shut the door.

'Twas only the second Sabbath after the *Charity* arrived; there was the Reverend Lyford, sharing the position of preacher with Elder Brewster, and so fervent – the rise and fall of his loud voice, arms waving; one would think him possessed. Not many days after that Bradford invited him onto the council. However, Lyford and Oldham were often seen with a group of malcontents, talking in low voices, sniggering behind their sleeves. And one day Susanna brought news Lyford had held a private Anglican baptism for a newborn babe. Bradford was furious but seemed to let it go.

When the group of lads next came to the Alden house for their lessons, the Lyford boy boasted, 'My pa, he can read and write really well. He's writing hundreds of letters. All day long he writes letters.'

That evening Priscilla told John.

'It fits,' John said. 'Bradford has asked Howland and me to have a look through their windows.'

'To spy,' Priscilla said.

'Tonight, after dark,' John replied. 'The *Charity* is set to sail tomorrow, late afternoon when the tide begins to ebb.'

Chapter 54

Spring 1624

A trial

John heaved the last bundle of beaver pelts into the shallop and turned to the little family waiting to board: father, mother and their small girl. 'So you're risking crossing the ocean again.' John gave a hand to the woman and lifted the little girl on board.

'Anything is better than staying here. It is dire. Nothing like the fine descriptions.' The woman's tone was hard with bitterness. John climbed aboard and turned to take the ropes.

'Wait, wait!' Reverend Lyford came running, pushing through the crowd. 'Wait,' he panted. Almost tripping and falling into the shallop, he handed a small packet to the father of the departing family. 'Give this to the captain.'

John looked across to where Bradford stood, feet slightly apart, hands behind his back, his eyes fixed mid-distance as if on some imaginary object out on the waters; impassive, no hint of recognition.

I'll follow his example. Pretend to know nothing. John unfurled the sail, took the tiller and looked back to wave to Priscilla, standing beside Susanna. She waved, one hand resting on her belly. *I'm a lucky man. Pray God the birth goes well.*

★ ★ ★

That night after dark, John sailed with Bradford and Winslow out beyond the sand spits where the *Charity* was hove to for the night. Bradford persuaded the captain to relinquish Lyford's packet of letters and the three men stayed all night copying enough of them to give evidence of sedition. Bradford kept a few of the originals but he didn't want the London investors to know he'd seen what Lyford was plotting. Not yet.

John was proud to be asked to participate and grateful to Standish for teaching him to write. But he had to promise to say nothing – not even to Priscilla.

Days passed into weeks. John kept a keen watch on Reverend Lyford and Oldham. Lyford continued to preach, vociferously, brazenly, as if he were Church of Christ to the core. But he and Oldham also held their scarcely hidden cabals and strutted and commanded as if they themselves were governors. Still Bradford did nothing, said nothing.

A sun-filled morning greeted John as he stepped across his threshold. Soaking up the warmth falling onto his shoulders he stretched, standing tall, pleased Bradford was trusting him in the troubles with Lyford. He strode with an easy gait down the track, and as he reached the clearing he spied Standish, poised to knock on Oldham's door. Increasing his pace he drew level as the door opened.

Oldham stood, disheveled and scowling. 'What do **you** want?' he sneered.

'It is your turn to stand watch,' Standish commanded, drawing himself up straight and tall as he could muster.

Oldham stepped forward so his face was almost touching Standish's. 'Beggarly rascal! Little Captain Shrimp! Stupid boy. I'll not take orders from you.'

Standish didn't move. 'It is your turn to stand watch.'

Suddenly, John saw a blade flash. A knife was at Standish's throat. John leapt forward. 'Rogue!' He grabbed the arm holding the knife, throwing Oldham to the ground. 'No, Miles!' he yelled as Standish drew his sword. Across the track Bradford rushed from his house and leapt to catch Standish's sword arm as he was about to slice at the scrambling, kicking Oldham. Standish reluctantly re-sheathed his sword and he and Bradford helped John secure Oldham's hands behind his back.

'The best place for you is a cell in the fort,' Bradford said, 'at least until you've come to your senses.' He then addressed the gathering of curious, babbling onlookers. 'Go from here and get on with your day's work.'

Bradford on one side, Standish on the other and John behind, they marched Oldham, cursing and snarling, up the hill. Lyford was nowhere to be seen.

The next day was the Sabbath. John and Priscilla joined the Winslows to assemble for the march to the fort. Since the day the fort was completed, every Sabbath and every Thursday, which was lecture day, the colonists gathered by the beat of the drum at Standish's house at the foot of Fort Hill. Every man carried his musket and Bible. In silence, led by a sergeant, they marched three abreast up the slope. Bringing up the rear were Governor Bradford, wearing a long robe, with Elder Brewster on his right and on his left, Captain Standish, cloaked, bearing his side arms and carrying a small cane in his hand. Solemnly and quietly the congregation gathered in the meeting room. 'Where's Reverend Lyford?' John whispered. Lyford was not in his usual place as preacher beside Elder Brewster.

Bradford pushed through to John. 'Could you please find him?'

'Yes, sir.' John ran down the hill through the empty settlement to Lyford's house. He crept around the side to peer in through the oiled parchment window. Difficult as it was to see clearly, it was obvious the room held a large gathering, with Lyford standing facing his audience, preaching, exhorting.

'Cast in your lot with me. I've written to London asking them to send more folk like us. We'll hound out these lording-it Church of Christ leaders. Have a tolerant colony with a proper church, in God's name, as our Almighty Father intended.'

John had heard enough. Bradford waited at the doorway of the fort, and John reported what he'd seen.

'That does it,' Bradford said. 'Tomorrow I'll summon those two wretches to stand trial for seditious plotting and disturbing the peace. But don't say anything, not until after I've summoned them.'

★ ★ ★

'I know, I know.' John tried to soothe Priscilla, frustrated beyond endurance that she couldn't attend the trial.

'Trust this to happen now, when I can hardly move.'

'I'll tell you everything that happens but you know you couldn't stand so long. You could give birth any day.'

'I'll have to wait,' Priscilla sighed.

John kissed her tenderly, on the nose, on her pouting lips. 'The drums.' Drum beats and the clamor of voices carried up the hill, growing louder. 'Goodbye.' He kissed Priscilla again and hurried out the door.

An excited chattering crowd marched behind an armed military company escorting the two prisoners, hands chained behind their backs. Seeing Howland and Lizzie, John fell into step beside them.

'Wonder how they'll try to wriggle out this time?' Howland tramped as if a soldier himself.

'And what the punishment will be.' John glanced up at Wituwamat's bleached skull, glaring down from its pike.

The procession paraded up to the fort. Bit by bit, pushing to get good viewing positions, folk funneled into the large meeting room, its gloom broken only by narrow shafts of light piercing slits high in the walls. Bradford and his associates seated themselves along one side of a long table, facing the crowd. Bradford bade silence. Overhead sounded the tramp, tramp, tramp of the sentry.

Bradford rose and read the indictment, clearly declaring the falsity of the prisoners' accusations. His voice was calm and strong, stature erect, demeanor quiet. When he had finished speaking the prisoners scoffed.

'Nonsense! Where's the proof? All trumped up.' Lyford turned toward Oldham, closing one eyelid. Oldham hopped from one foot to the other. "T'isn't just... not right... high and mighty.' Spittle gathered round his laboring mouth and dribbled into his beard.

Looking straight ahead at no one, Bradford slowly drew a bundle of papers from his pouch. Oldham clammed up. John thrilled as the governor read from the copies of the intercepted letters.

'The ruling clique at Plymouth matched the Jesuits for policy... only one way to break their high-handed hold; send an overwhelming number not of their church who would have the right to hold office. Keep back all the Leiden company.' Bradford held up another sheet of parchment. 'If that captain you spoke of should come here as general, I am persuaded he would be chosen captain, for this Captain Standish looks like a silly boy, and is in utter contempt.'

Silence. Tramp, tramp, tramp. As a unit, with military precision, all heads turned from an 'eyes straight ahead' position facing Bradford, to the left toward Standish. The captain's posture did not alter. He said nothing.

Well done, Miles. John silently applauded.

Oldham now jumped about like a fighting cock. 'Scurrilous rascals!' He shook his fist at Bradford. 'How dare you open our letters! Low-down, thieving spies, you are.' Turning toward the crowd he called out, 'Come, my friends. Billington, you have often complained. Now is the time. Let us seize control. I am your man. Stand to arms, Billington!'

Silence. Not a murmur. Waiting. As if on cue, Lyford raised his voice, wailing, tears streaming down his cheeks. 'It was John Billington and his lot complained and deceived me. I have wronged you, who have done me such kindness. The letters are false – worth nothing.' Down he went on his knees. 'How can I ever make amends? Help me, God! I am a miserable wretch, unsavory salt.' He moaned and swayed, and banged his head on the floor, wrists secured behind his back.

I don't believe I'm seeing this. I thought we'd left charlatans behind in England. John remembered his friend who had probably died in prison because he had followed a charlatan priest. He looked at the table and saw a furrow appear on Brewster's forehead. The Elder leaned toward Lyford with a concerned gesture. Now the crowd consulted in groups of twos and threes. 'Get rid of the lot.' 'But Lyford is so remorseful. And the tears...' 'All sham, I swear, all sham.'

Bradford commanded silence. 'Oldham is to leave this colony immediately. His wife and children may stay until he can remove them suitably.' He looked over at Lyford, still huddled on the floor. After a brief consultation with Brewster, he said, 'You, because of your contrition, may have a six-month reprieve. If your repentance proves sound, you may stay.'

Signaling his goodbye to Howland, John pushed his way through the babble and crush of bodies to hurry back to Priscilla. Over their midday trencher of fish stew he recounted the proceedings. Priscilla listened, rapt, forgetting to eat. When John told of Lyford's reprieve, she pushed on the tabletop to rise to her feet. 'They should have sent him packing. How can they be so soft?'

'Mustn't be hasty.' John ate his last mouthful. 'The few London investors who still back us chose him and we need their support.'

'What support?' Priscilla stood straight, knuckles on hips. 'They've sent us virtually nothing 'til now, and now when they do we have to pay exorbitant prices. They have us over a barrel and are taking advantage. Care nothing for our welfare. Just want their money back – quick.'

'Well of course. With the recession over there what do you expect?'

'You say to me, "be patient, we can't expect to get rich quick" but we've been nearly starving. Worked to the bone to send the *Fortune* back fully laden; could have paid off half our debt. Not our fault the French grabbed her!' Priscilla's voice rose. She took the trencher and spoons and tankards from the table.

'Priscilla…'

'They haven't sent anything like enough good stuff to trade with. How can we get the furs to pay the debt?' She moved slowly and jerkily to the washing pail.

'Calm down,' John said. 'You'll do yourself an injury getting so worked up.' He stepped over behind her and put his hands on her shoulders. Priscilla stepped aside, turning to face him, throwing the dishes into the pail. John jumped back from the splash.

'And they send all these makeshift feckless people. How are we to build a colony fit to be a home for our children? A home such as Father wanted us to have.' Priscilla's eyes brimmed.

'Priscilla,' John implored.

'Why can't they sign on good responsible citizens, like Mother and Father? Folk needn't belong to the Church of Christ, they just need to be decent.' She put her hands over her face. 'Wretched vermin!'

'Priscilla, please.' John put an arm round her shoulders, drawing her close, but his voice was firm. 'They are not all feckless. We now have a salt-maker and a boat-builder. With a fishing fleet and plenty of salt we can send shiploads of cod to Spain. Fetches a pretty price there.'

Priscilla wiped away her tears. She looked across at the waiting cradle. 'I hope you are right.'

John sighed. 'The reality is we are not strong enough to stand on our own. We have only Massasoit and his tribes to trade with, and our debt is very large. But we'll do it. Don't lose heart.'

★ ★ ★

Walking past Howland's house on his way to the stores, John became aware of a commotion on the harbor shore. Hurrying to investigate, he found Hopkins directing a rowdy group of men to stand in two rows, each man with his musket. Then Standish arrived, hauling Oldham, still shackled, hands behind his back.

'This'll teach you. We'll give you the send-off you deserve.' Giving his victim a shove, the captain said, 'Run the gantry.'

Oldham had no choice but to obey, running, stumbling through the tunnel of jeering men buffeting him with the butt ends of their muskets, his destination a rowing boat anchored out just beyond the shallows. He departed Plymouth colony with naught but the clothes he was wearing. John watched as the small boat slowly crossed the harbor toward the sand spits. *Poor idiot.*

Chapter 55

Spring 1624

Lyford's second chance

In the cool dusk of a spring evening, John tramped from the marsh to deliver two brace of duck to the Brewster household. Finding the door open, he knocked and entered.

The Elder sat reading. 'Ah. Thank you, Mr Alden. What would we do without your contributions to our pot?'

'I'm pleased to help, sir.'

Laying his book aside, not losing his page, the Elder said, 'Reverend Lyford does seem to have truly repented. I think the trial brought him to see his errors. It is two weeks now and I believe he is sincere in his piety. I'm glad we gave him another chance.'

'Yes, sir. He is behaving just as he should.'

'One must always try to seek out the good in a man, in his soul. There is always a spark of good – in children of God.'

'Yes, sir. And do you agree one should take special care with children – not be too harsh? Spare the rod?'

Brewster looked at John with a surprised, quizzical frown. 'Spare the rod? Without the rod children would grow into beasts. No. 'Tis the rod produces God-fearing Christian men.'

As John left the Brewster house, Standish leapt out from the shadows.

'Miles! What are you doing?'

'John, I think Lyford is conniving again. This afternoon I saw him opening his door to Billington, and then a few more and a few more. Looks like he's holding secret meetings in his house. I propose that you and I, and perhaps Howland, organize our rosters to keep a round the clock watch.'

'And here was Brewster saying just now he thinks the scoundrel's reformed, truly reformed!'

'Bradford is hoping so,' Standish said. 'He'd like a quiet life for a change.'

John took the first after-dark watch. Peering through the opaque window, he could discern Lyford's form, bent over his table, scribbling rapidly by the light of a pine knot. The quill flew across the page, line after line, page after page, with never a pause for deliberation, only for sharpening his quill or mixing more ink. Hour after hour this continued.

How many letters? Or is he writing a treatise?

Standish and Howland reported the same. Also, all three noticed surreptitious comings and goings from the Lyford house. After four days of these observations, John suggested they'd seen enough to report to Bradford. As Howland was scheduled to go fishing and Standish was committed to hunting, it fell to John to call on the governor.

'Mr Alden, come in.' Bradford motioned to a chair by the hearth. 'Sit down.' He took his own seat opposite. John surveyed the room, more spacious since the governor's marriage to Alice, and with evidence of a woman's presence: pewter ware set out on the table and chests, spinning wheels in one corner, a curtained 'bedchamber' in another. A cooking pot hung over the fire, its odors stirring John's hunger.

'What brings you?' Bradford asked.

John had got as far as describing Lyford's excessive night-time writing and was starting to describe the suspicious gatherings when there was a loud insistent knock on the door.

'Whoever?'

John twisted to see as Bradford opened the door. 'Mistress Lyford!' John rose to offer her his chair.

'No, thank you, this won't take long.' Lyford's wife stood straight, frowning, lips drawn tight, a picture of resolute determination. 'I am concerned for your servant girl, Mr Bradford. For her own sake you must take her back.'

Bradford raised his eyebrows. 'Why?'

'Because my husband is meddling with her. He is a lecher, Mr Bradford. He forced me before we were married and I cannot count the times I've caught him in bed with a servant girl.' She folded her arms emphatically. 'I'll not have your girl endure any more distress. I daren't leave the house or he'll be after her.'

Bradford paled. He bowed his head and stroked his brow, as if to wipe away yet another miserable episode. 'Thank you, Mistress Lyford. I appreciate your difficulty in having to go behind your husband's back. Thank you.' He looked at her with searching sympathy. 'I fear this means you will all have to leave Plymouth.'

'I know,' she replied, straightening her back. 'I'll take my leave now. I've already taken the lass to your wife.'

Bradford opened the door and bade her good day. He sank into his chair. 'That's it. They'll be sent away tomorrow.'

'I'm sorry, sir. I know you hoped he would reform.'

'Scurrilous rascal.' Bradford thumped his knee. 'Thank you for all your efforts, Mr Alden.'

John found Priscilla and Susanna in the front yard pounding and stirring a cauldron of clothes and linen steaming over a fire; laundry day.

'Leave that,' John called. 'Come indoors for a rest. I've news.'

'Good riddance!' Susanna said when she'd heard. 'Nothing but trouble, that man.'

Priscilla clapped her hands. 'I told you so. I knew he was – horrid.' She spat out the word and John knew she'd have uttered a more lurid description but for manners. 'But I feel sorry for his poor wife. She has to go with him – and the children. How she must suffer.' Priscilla shivered. She looked at John and smiled in gratitude and love. She put her hands on her belly.

'I'll help Susanna with the laundry,' John said. 'You shouldn't be pounding and stirring that heavy wash.' He felt rather taken aback when the two women looked at him in astonishment, staring, mouths agape.

'You'll never!' Priscilla said. 'Laundry is women's work. I'm quite capable, with Susanna's help.' She heaved herself up from the stool and waddled to the yard.

'I'll see she doesn't overdo it.' Susanna lowered her voice. 'But 'twas a fine offer. You're a good man, John Alden. Now be off and hunt us some meat.' She stepped briskly to join Priscilla.

As he took down his musket from its pegs over the door he heard Susanna say, 'When we've done this we must bake the groaning cakes. Have you got plenty of beer? Groaning cakes and groaning ale – I reckon you'll have a party of about a dozen.'

John shuddered.

When he returned at dusk with two brace of duck, Priscilla welcomed him with an exuberant kiss.

'It's a lovely thing, to do the washing and have it all dry and smelling sweet from the sun on such a day as this. Could you set out the barrels of ale please? Best to be ready.'

He knew her cheerfulness was forced; that she'd be missing her mother, even with Susanna as midwife. John took her in his arms. 'You're a brave lass.'

'John! John!'

Priscilla shaking his shoulder; he jumped from a sound sleep.

'It has started – the pains.' She gasped. 'I'll walk about. Mother said to walk and count.'

'I'll fetch Susanna.'

Winslow opened the door to John's hammering.

'It's started.'

'Come in, man.' Winslow put an arm round John's shoulder.

Susanna appeared, already dressed. 'I heard. Bed down there, John.' She indicated a pallet. 'Until daybreak. Then you'd best spend the day hunting.'

John could not sleep. Consumed with restlessness, he quietly eased himself out of the Winslows' house. Beginning to pace up and down the track, he heard Priscilla's cries and the high-pitched chatter of women's voices. 'When 'twere my time.' Groaning inwardly he strode down to the harbor. Finding a flat-topped boulder he sat, looking out over the moonlit water, praying fervently that Priscilla would be safely delivered. *Please, God, please don't take her from me. I love her, need her to stand by me. No one else, only Priscilla.* He prayed as he'd never prayed in his life, remembering how she'd suffered living with the Brewsters, the sight of her in the Indian camp, unable to stand, reaching for him, their wedding night. Never had he known such happiness. And now, giving birth to the result of their hours of bliss. *Please, God, don't take her.*

At the first dawn lightening of the sky, John set off to the forest, following a trail that crossed the brook, thus avoiding proximity to his home and the sound of Priscilla's pain.

That evening when he returned, all was quiet. He knocked on his own door. Susanna opened and beaming, led him into the bedchamber.

Priscilla sat against the bolsters, holding a babe to her breast. 'John, come see your daughter.' She smiled, though her voice was tired and weak.

John knelt beside the bed. He stroked Priscilla's brow and stared. This was the first newborn babe he'd ever seen. She came from his loins. Her tiny fists curled tight with the effort of sucking; blond wisps covered her head and he perceived a faint throbbing like a heartbeat at the center of her skull. A powerful tenderness pulsed through him. 'She is beautiful.'

'Your wife did well, especially for a first,' Susanna said. 'She's to stay abed. I'll be back at first light.' Stooping to gather up a bundle of soiled linen she said, 'The rest should be like shelling peas.'

1627

Chapter 56

Summer 1627

Dorothy's son

Priscilla caught her breath. *The same gray-blue eyes, soft light brown hair, delicate features; so like Dorothy.* Now six years later, here he was, brought from Holland to live with his father and stepmother in this strange new land.

Hand outstretched, Bradford strode forward as the lad climbed out of the shallop onto the landing rock. 'Son.'

John Bradford shook his father's hand. 'Sir.'

Alice Bradford stepped forward. 'I'll take him to the house to meet William and Joseph. Come with me, John.' She put an arm round the boy's shoulder and hurried him away from the hustle and chatter of the crowd on the shore.

Priscilla remembered Dorothy in their cramped quarters aboard the *Mayflower*, grieving for her son.

'I help Father.' Elizabeth darted away from Priscilla's side, heading for John, unloading trunks and gear from the shallop.

'Elizabeth! No!' Priscilla called sharply, struggling after her, holding onto their son John, called 'Jack' to avoid confusion with his father.

Winslow intercepted the small girl, her blond curls bobbing in the light wind, catching the sunlight. He scooped her up and brought her to her mother. Elizabeth squirmed, her chubby, rosy arm stretched toward John.

'She does adore her father. Thank you, Master Winslow.' Priscilla spoke to her daughter's upturned face. 'Father is busy. Now come along. He'll be up for dinner soon.'

Susanna, heavily pregnant again, eased her way to join them. She took Elizabeth's hand and stroked her head. 'You can help me with a batch of cornbread.'

Morning chores and dinner completed, Priscilla left Elizabeth and Jack to play with Lizzie Howland's girl, Elizabeth's age. She smiled thinking of the two small 'mistresses' already playing at 'goodwife', setting Jack his chores. He was amazingly willing. Tomorrow she would do the same for Lizzie.

Swinging her basket she set out for the brook to gather sallet and wild leeks. The sun shone warm, not too hot. A soft wind brought a fall of late blossom. Entering the copse, out of sight of far-seeing eyes, she stopped and caught petals in her open palm. *There should be a good crop of plums.* Drawing in deep breaths of sea air scented with the tang of pine, she leaned against a tree trunk, relishing the quiet solitude. *How deliciously sinful it feels to linger.* Ambling along the familiar meandering path Priscilla studied darting insects and spiders' webs revealed in streams of sunlight filtering through hazel and birch boughs. Following their routine of a midday rest, the birds offered only an occasional chirrup amongst softly rustling leaves. At her feet, violets nestled in the protection of mossy rocks. Ferns thrust strident fronds. Through the lethargic repose the brook announced its hurrying presence. Following a sharp curve as the path led round a boulder, Priscilla stopped short. His back to her, a lad stood looking into the water. She waited, not moving, but her basket scraped against the boulder. The lad whirled round.

'John! John Bradford! Good day, John.' Priscilla introduced herself. 'I was close friends with your mother.'

'I can't remember her. I wish I could live in Holland. If only Pastor Robinson hadn't died.' John looked at his feet and drew the back of his hand across his eyes. 'First they leave me behind, and then they make me come here.'

'Your mother didn't want to leave you, John. She longed for you. Missed you so much.' Priscilla put an arm round the shaking shoulders.

'How did she die? Was it the scurvy?'

'She fell overboard. It was the middle of the night and no one realized until morning.'

'Where was my father? Why wasn't he with her?'

'He was on an exploring expedition. When they found this place to settle.'

'I don't like this place.'

'No. I understand. But you might grow to like it.'

'I've been sent to gather brushwood.' He kicked the basket beside him. 'If I was living with Pastor Robinson he'd be teaching me to read and write. Father's always too busy. Says it isn't important – not yet.'

'Your father is our governor; he carries a heavy load.'

'He's always in meetings,' John said.

Priscilla showed him her basket. 'I've come to fetch sallet and leeks. Then I'll help you carry the brushwood.'

When both baskets were full, Priscilla took one handle of the brushwood basket, John the other. 'When you've delivered this to Mistress Bradford, would you like to come by our house? I have a few books might interest you.'

'Aye, please.'

'Only if Mistress Bradford doesn't need you, mind.'

A timid knock on the open door made Priscilla jump. She looked up from spinning flax to see Dorothy's son hovering uncertainly in the doorway. 'John, come in,' she met him, hands outstretched. Elizabeth and Jack, seated on the floor, looked up from their task of transferring nuts from one pile to the other, scattering them, and crawling to retrieve them.

'Here.' Priscilla motioned for John to sit at the table. 'Have a piece.' She placed a plate of cornbread in front of him. She stepped over to the book box, pushed the heavy polished lid back on its hinges, and took out her gardening book and copy of *Hamlet*. Sitting beside the boy, with her own little ones in view, she opened both books to the first page. 'Can you read either of these?'

'January: snowdrops, icy wind blows. Song thrush sings. Put straw over turnips to protect from frost,' John read slowly, halting.

'You **can** read,' Priscilla said.

'May I look further?'

'Of course.'

He turned to May and June. 'Where are we now? Sow parsnips. Crop beans. Plant squash. Gather early peas. May I see your garden?'

Priscilla laughed. '*Hamlet* can wait for another time.' She replaced the books in the box, gathered up Elizabeth and Jack, and led the way through the lean-to out into the acre of garden at the back of the house.

'It's beautiful!' John exclaimed.

A small grove of plum trees in blossom beckoned from the far corner. Rows of raspberries, plantings of vegetables, clumps of hollyhocks, columbine dancing everywhere, rosemary, rue, sage. 'You have an English garden,' the boy said. 'Mistress Robinson planted a knot garden in Leiden.' He looked up at Priscilla. 'I used to help Mistress Robinson tend her garden. May I help you?'

Priscilla looked into his sad, pleading eyes; tired eyes for one so young; deep bluish pockets above gaunt cheekbones. 'As long as Mistress Bradford agrees.' She pointed to the red ball descending the western sky. 'Look where the sun is. You'd best be getting back. Time for prayers soon.'

★ ★ ★

Priscilla walked slowly from an afternoon of caring for Mary Brewster, to collect her little ones from Susanna. Gazing up into the full leafed trees, deep green against the bright blue sky, she thought of the ripening corn, of their brood of freshly hatched chicks, of her own healthy 'brood', and of John becoming ever more respected as one of the colony's leaders. Her thoughts returned to Mary, once so proud, now wasting away in torment. She and Susanna had tried every potion and poultice they could think of; Dr Fuller applied leeches mercilessly.

Knocking, she stepped through Susanna's open door, her feet following a shaft of sunlight into the comfortingly dim room. Order and calm. Susanna sat in her rocker with Jack on her lap, playing hand games. Elizabeth was too absorbed with her hessian dolls – making them a house under the table – even to look up.

'How is she?' Susanna raised her eyes. 'Sit down awhile.'

Priscilla gratefully settled into the other rocking chair. 'I fear Dr Fuller's blood letting is making her worse. So weak. She hardly has the strength or the will to take a sip of broth. And the worst is, she believes her illness is God's punishment – or at best a test, making her fight Satan and go through hell now to cleanse her soul so she can earn her passage to heaven when she dies.' Priscilla stood and dusted her apron in agitation. 'She won't allow me to comfort her; brushes all kind words aside.'

Susanna shook her head wearily. 'It's so harsh; all the soul searching and checking on one another, and shovelfuls of suffering and punishment heaped on a body.'

'When life brings enough hardship as it is.' Priscilla sat down again. 'Imagine dying without a priest to say the last rites. So frightening. The Church of England is kinder, and has merry feast days.' She sighed wistfully.

'Speaking of merry, has John told you of the settlement sprung up north of Wessagussett, that they call Merrymount?'

'No.'

'Well,' Susanna shifted Jack to the other side of her lap. 'Pat-a-cake, pat-a-cake. Edward's been up there on a visit, and the report he brought back has incensed Bradford.'

'Do say.'

'The leader is Thomas Morton; a barrister, learned, can read and write in Latin and Greek. And an Anglican – firmly.'

'Why did he come over?'

'Seems he relishes the chance to build his own estate on his own terms, not answerable to anyone, and gets on very well with the Indians.'

'The tribes we routed at Wessagussett?'

'The same. They have drinking parties. All dance together, wives as well, round an eighty-foot high maypole!'

'That's wonderful!' Priscilla exclaimed and clapped her hand over her mouth, looking furtively over her shoulder at the open door. 'Oh, I wish we had a maypole,' she whispered.

'Edward brought back a couple of Morton's poems he'd copied out. They were very saucy.'

Priscilla giggled. 'Bradford would disapprove – mightily.'

'Morton doesn't keep the Sabbath; prefers to go hunting with his falcon. But the worst is, he's cleaning up the fur trade with the Indians as far north as Maine.'

'That is serious,' Priscilla said.

'The Indians favor Morton because he sells them guns.' Susanna frowned. 'He goes against the King's proclamation. Edward is working with Bradford, writing to Morton to remind him of this.'

'Bradford and his assistants have a hard time of it,' Priscilla mused. 'It's hard enough for them keeping folk in line here. I can see the set-up at Merrymount would be seductive, and threatening. Ah well, I must get back. John Bradford will soon be coming.'

'Does he come to you every day?'

'Doesn't often miss,' Priscilla said. 'Helps me in the garden, and then we have an hour reading and writing. He is quick!'

'Expect he finds it hard in the Bradford house with his father's new wife and family.'

'I think so, though he doesn't speak of it.' Priscilla took Jack from Susanna's lap and persuaded Elizabeth to bring her dolls and build them a house under the table at home. Holding her son's hand, with Elizabeth trailing behind, she bade Susanna goodbye.

Priscilla and John Bradford were coming to the end of their reading hour, studying *Hamlet*. 'To thine own self be true...' John moved his finger along under the words.

'You are becoming more fluent every day,' Priscilla said.

A rapid, severe knocking made her leap up from the table and hurry to the door. There stood Mistress Bradford.

'Is John here?'

'Aye, aye, didn't you know?' Priscilla asked, turning to look back at John.

The lad jumped up from the table and came to stand beside Priscilla. He looked at the floor.

'Is this where you've been, day after day when I couldn't find you?' his stepmother demanded.

'Yes, ma'am,' John mumbled.

'You didn't know he was here?' Priscilla repeated.

'No. I did not.' Mistress Bradford's expression was keen and hard.

'It's my fault. I should have asked your permission. I thought – please don't blame the lad.'

'He is old enough to know better. Come along now. You can explain yourself to the governor.'

'Oh no, please – I'll call on Governor Bradford in the morning,' Priscilla pleaded.

Footsteps on the track. It was John.

'Good day, Mr Alden.' Mistress Bradford took her stepson's hand and led him down the track.

On hearing of the misunderstanding with Alice Bradford John groaned. 'I work closely with the governor, and Brewster, Winslow and Standish. I need to have their respect. I do not need this kind of – shenanigans.' He stopped pacing and looked directly at Priscilla. 'You must go to the governor, now before prayers, and apologize.'

In a turmoil of regret, Priscilla hurried to the Bradford house, arriving in time to hear John's whipping. Cringing, her head throbbing, she waited. When the lash of the cane and the stifled sobs had stopped, she knocked.

Bradford opened the door and stepped back, startled. 'Mistress Alden.' His voice was quiet and cold. 'Enter.' He did not invite her to sit down.

Priscilla's apology ended with a promise to leave John Bradford alone. The boy must integrate with his new family. She dragged herself back up the track, abject with misery. *This wretched place. So harsh.*

She pushed open her door to see John with Elizabeth on one knee and Jack on the other, playing bouncy, bouncy, the children chortling and shrieking with delight.

He stopped. 'Well?'

'I apologized and promised to have nothing more to do with the boy.' In a silent, hard fury, she fed the children, put them to bed and dished up a trencherful of pottage for John. Setting it down before him she said, 'I'm not hungry,' and sat herself in her rocking chair with her mending.

'Priscilla, please. I'm sorry but you must understand.'

'I understand. I understand very well. There is no place in these strict people for ordinary kindness. The lad is unhappy, missing the Robinsons, transported to this crazy, strange land – and he is **Dorothy's** son!' She darned furiously. 'But no – that counts for nothing. He must fit in, be just like the rest, whipped like the rest.' She broke down, sobbing. 'Poor Dorothy, poor John.' She turned toward her husband. 'And you, John Alden, are becoming like them. You didn't used to be. But now.'

'Priscilla, that is not just.' John rose from his stool. 'You know you want me – want us – to rise to a position in this colony.' His voice reverberated with indignance. 'You want your pudding and eat it. You don't seem to accept there is a cost.'

Neither spoke for several minutes. Then John drew up his stool beside her. 'Leave it a little while. I'll try to find a moment to speak to Bradford when the dust has settled. Or perhaps do it through Brewster or Winslow. We'll work it somehow for you to be friends with Dorothy's lad.'

Chapter 57

Summer 1627

The debt

Early morning in high summer; Priscilla crept barefoot into her garden, relishing the quiet and the feel of cool, dewy grass. Over to the chicken coop; all still there; eight balls of cheeping, legged yellow fluff. She laughed out loud. A swell of contentment surged through her as she inspected the healthy beans and squash, the raspberry canes, the gooseberry bush that had come on a ship in the spring. Her children shone with health, and thanks to her diplomatic husband, she was now friends with John Bradford – and his stepmother Alice.

Was that a knock? Already at this hour? She'd barely cocked an ear when Susanna was beside her. 'What brings you?'

'She died in the night.'

'Oh.'

'The Elder was with her.'

'Do you know – was it peaceful?'

'Judging from the Elder's grief, no. He blames himself that he couldn't help her find some peace. It seems she was terror stricken to the last.'

'Poor Mary. Poor woman. Shall we go in and sit awhile and pray for her? The little ones are still asleep.'

Priscilla and Susanna sat together quietly at the table, thinking of Mary and praying to God to receive her gently.

Mary's death fell heavily on the Pilgrims. All the colony gathered at her graveside in respect.

That evening John and Priscilla sat together by the hearth. 'Sixty years,' Priscilla said, 'and what she suffered. All for…'

'For her husband and the Church of Christ,' John answered.

'If only, if only… those beliefs tormented her so. It was terrible, John, how the constant examination of her own soul tormented her.'

'It does make you wonder.'

'If only she could have prayed to the Blessed Virgin Mary, who brings gentle comfort and mercy.'

'You may be right, but don't ever breathe such a thought to anyone in this colony, not even Susanna, or heaven knows what would happen to you.'

★ ★ ★

Priscilla quickly fed Elizabeth and Jack and tucked them into their trundle bed in the bedroom. She wanted no distractions when John returned from the meeting. The debt. It gnawed away, the worry of it churning and churning; a millstone dragging them down, never getting lighter. They *must* find a solution.

John strode into the room and hung his hat on its peg. Priscilla kissed him. Once they were seated with a trencher full of stew, they said grace.

'The meeting – anything decided? Any hope?'

John took several mouthfuls before he spoke. 'I am very hungry and this is delicious. Tastes better every day.' Catching his wife's eye he put down his spoon and took Priscilla's hands in his. 'Aye. We made an important decision.' He breathed deeply. 'I've agreed, along with seven others, to undertake the colony's debt.'

Priscilla gasped, snatching back her hands. 'But – but – it's such a risk! If things go wrong and we're wiped out – nothing left.' She pushed back her stool and stood, fists clenched. 'This is not what Father intended. All very well pulling together, but this – this goes way beyond that!'

'This colony is for us, not for your father,' John began.

'Yes it is! He put all his money into it, his dream, a place where our children would be safe; safe and free from the evil ways of the old country.'

'Priscilla, listen.'

'No. You listen. Father wanted us to prosper, become established, eminent. Surely we want that too. I want it, and I thought you did.'

'Ssh. You'll wake the children.' John stood by the table. 'Yes, I want us to prosper. You know I do.' He spoke quietly, his voice firm and hard to the point of being harsh. 'But we cannot know what your father would have done if he were here now.' He drew his hand across the back of his neck. 'Whatever – we have to deal with the situation as it is, not for the dreams of those who have died.'

Priscilla recoiled, cheeks flushed. Tears sparkled in her eyes. 'He died a miserable death; he and Mother and Joseph, and all the others. I want to honor my father and mother. No… no… Mother was right. We should never have…'

'Priscilla! You must not say those words. It will be alright. We are to have a monopoly on all the fur trade. Reckon to pay off the debt in less than ten years.'

'A monopoly on the fur trade? How? However will you enforce it? After Wessagussett 'tis only Massasoit's tribes trust us. None of the other tribes are likely to favor us with their trade.'

'Howland is one of us eight. He and I reckon to build a trading post up in Maine. On the Kennebec River. Fur trade is good up there.'

'Promises, promises. I thought we were to pay off the debt with fishing, salt-packed cod to Spain. Still not a sign of a salt pan. The useless man doesn't know what he is doing.' She struck her forehead. 'The Kennebec River? Maine? That is miles and miles away. You'll be gone for weeks and Howland's Lizzie is expecting any time soon.' She sank into her rocker, staring into the fire.

'We'll wait 'til after she's delivered. It has to be done. This confounded debt.' John paced back and forth. 'I'm beginning to think there's something untoward going on, something awry. In spite of all our efforts the debt doesn't shift.' He faced Priscilla. 'Allerton's been mixing his private dealings with the colony's for several years now.'

'What?' Priscilla shrieked, jumping up. 'What do you mean?'

'Sssh.' John put a finger to his lips. 'Not a word. I hope I'm wrong, especially with Brewster's girl married to him.'

'You **must** find out. We'll not be financing any man's fiddling!' Priscilla turned her back. 'We'll be poor forever more. Scraping by with two little ones, a third on the way and God knows how many more.' She buried her face in her apron, mute, shaking.

'Priscilla, you never said. Another? When? Please calm yourself.' He came behind her and held her shoulders. 'It **will** be alright. I'll do my best. You know I will. But you must stand by me.'

Priscilla stepped back facing her husband. 'I am your wife. I must obey you. It is the law.' She walked round the table. 'But I trusted you... you promised you would talk to me... consult, especially on important matters.' She wept again. 'We... we were to be different.' She caught her breath in a sob. 'You've broken your promise.' She raised her chin. 'You say I must stand by you? No. I'll do as you say but you cannot command my feelings.'

'Priscilla!' John clutched his hair. 'You don't understand!' He turned on his heel, took down his musket and hat and left the house.

July 1630-July 1632

Chapter 58

June 1630 - July 1631

Roger Williams comes to Plymouth

He promised, he promised. I thought he would be different from other men. The phrases ran through Priscilla's mind like circling wasps. Gradually she brought herself round and now, three years later she gave herself wholeheartedly to the challenges of everyday home life: her four children's needs, expanding her knowledge of remedies and with Susanna, teaching a small group of boys once a week. Bradford never interfered. It seemed he pretended not to know.

Her love for John remained strong and she was proud of him. He worked hard, gave his all to the colony, and it was clear Bradford and the other leaders valued his judgment and depended on him.

'Oh look! Joseph, you've got mud on your stocking. Elizabeth, please find him a clean one – quick. We must be on time. It's Sabbath.' Jack and Joseph bounced about, punching, pinching, shoving. Priscilla struggled to pull Pris' arms through the sleeves of her baby's gown; Pris, protesting with howls, wriggling her arms and legs every which way. John stood quietly by the door, waiting.

'There. At last. Sssh.' Priscilla soothed her unhappy babe. 'Elizabeth, have you got the sachet of herbs ready? Caraway, dill, fennel. Mustn't have you falling asleep.'

'Yes, Mother.'

The Alden family hurried, walking and running to join the congregation assembled at the foot of Fort Hill.

'Now hush,' Priscilla gasped. Trying to regain some dignity they walked the last few paces, flush-faced and breathless.

Excited, barely audible whispers rippled through the gathering. 'Arrived last night... wife and two little ones...'

'Who?' Priscilla whispered to the woman beside her.

'New teacher. From Salem.'

At the roll of the drums, the procession moved forward, solemn and sedate, whispers gradually extinguished.

Because they were late, the Aldens were at the back of the meeting room, John on the men's side, and Priscilla with the women and children. She had to stand on tiptoe to get a view of the new teacher. He stood between Elder Brewster and the most recent pastor, facing the congregation. He was tall, with thick dark hair, deep brown eyes set back under arched eyebrows, a prominent well-shaped nose and full lips. Following the way of preachers, he was clean shaven. He had an air of gentle calm. Even before he spoke, Priscilla liked him.

'Brethren.' Elder Brewster raised his hand. 'May I introduce our new teacher, Master Roger Williams, come to us from Salem. He has chosen to come here because we Pilgrims, unlike our Puritan brothers, have separated from the Church of England. Mr Williams will lead us in our afternoon prophesying, but would like to say a few words now.'

'Brothers.' Roger Williams stepped forward. 'Already I feel I have come among friends, kindred spirits, who believe that to engage honestly in the work of God, one must remove oneself from all doctrine, liturgy and sacraments of the Anglican way. I look forward to open and devout seeking amongst us.' He stepped back, gesturing for the pastor to begin.

The pastor's sermon droned on with moments of dramatic effect: raised voice, waving arms, subsiding again into theological meanderings. Priscilla's attention wandered to a spider residing in its web in the rafters. She watched as an unsuspecting fly flew into the trap and struggled to extricate itself as the spider traveled along the strands of its home and ate its prey.

Pris whined. Priscilla rocked to soothe her and saw Elizabeth and Joseph were falling asleep on their feet. She handed them each some caraway and fennel to chew and gave Jack some dill.

The room was becoming hot and stuffy in the summer sun. There was a rustle and murmur. Just in front, Lizzie Howland, expecting a second babe, clutched onto the woman standing beside her to stop herself swooning.

She's big with child. She shouldn't be here. The rules are too harsh.

They had a break at noon for a picnic lunch before the afternoon session.

'Why do we have to hurry so?' Jack asked, dawdling with his cornbread. 'I don't want to be even one extra minute in the meeting room. They go on and on.'

'Come along now,' Priscilla said. 'I don't want to be stuck at the back.'

They joined the Winslows near the front. Priscilla listened to the chatter and bustle as the room filled behind her. The religious leaders processed slowly down the aisle and took their places facing, as before. Elder Brewster brought the meeting to order and invited Mr Williams to present his topic.

'I propose we meditate on Verse 6 from Matthew, Chapter 6. "But thou, when thou prayest, enter into thy closet, and when thou hast shut thy door, pray to thy Father which is in secret; and thy Father which seeth in secret shall reward thee openly".'

Then, following the established order, the pastor spoke briefly before Mr Williams gave his interpretation. 'It seems to me that this, and the preceding verse about giving alms, indicate that we are each intended to have our own private communication with God; to follow our own conscience in the way we pray. Jesus says to pray in secret; not as human authority dictates, but in the way we each feel is right. The way we worship is between us and God.'

Priscilla drank in his quiet, strong voice, his straightforward manner, his earnestness. *He isn't like the others. He is so clear!* She shifted from one foot to the other in her excitement. Governor Bradford discoursed with reference to Hebrew texts. Elder Brewster spoke at length, then several men in the congregation, and finally Master Winslow.

'Well, what do you reckon?' John asked as they walked back.

'I could understand Mr Williams, but when Governor Bradford quoted Hebrew and the others spoke I got lost in all the theology and doctrine.' Priscilla paused and looked up at John. 'But Mr Williams made sense – more sense than anyone else I've heard. Don't you think so?'

'Hmm, perhaps.'

In the morning, on her way to the brook to gather sallet, Priscilla spied Mr Williams clearing his plot of tree roots and coarse grass. As she drew level he stopped.

He greeted her. 'Mistress Alden?'

Priscilla nodded and half curtsied. 'Sir.'

'No, not "sir". Simply Mr Williams. Did I see you at the prophesying meeting?'

'I was there.' Priscilla looked into his soft brown eyes. 'I... I.'

'Go on.'

'I could understand when you spoke, but all the rest was confusing. I want to understand.'

Roger Williams leaned on his fork. 'I have a suggestion. I hear you teach a small group of boys to read and write. With all there is to be done,' he looked round the plot to be cleared, 'I haven't time to teach my lad. If he could join your group; an hour a week is it? I'll give you instruction from time to time.'

'Oh! I should be very grateful.'

Roger Williams' son joined Priscilla's young scholars that week. She reckoned he was about eight years old, and he had his father's dark hair and eyes. He was a bright lad; she could see he learned more quickly than his companions but took pains not to let it show. Wanting to respond to his eager, inquisitive mind, she asked Susanna to tutor the others while she contrived particular challenges for the son of the man whose teaching on Sabbath afternoons brought her mind alive.

Nigh on a month had passed when Roger Williams hailed Priscilla as she was passing by his house on her way to the brook.

'Mistress Alden.'

She stopped and waited as he made his way from the far side of the plot, picking his way among stumps and hummocks of grass.

'My lad is coming on well,' he said, slightly out of breath. 'Says you make him want to learn more and more. Quotes *Hamlet*. Good book.' He smiled. 'I have some free time on Wednesday afternoon. Would you like to come for an hour's further study of Jesus' teachings?'

'Yes please. Yes. I'll ask Mistress Winslow if she can look after my little ones for a bit. If she can I'd be glad to come. Thank you.'

Priscilla knocked nervously on Mr Williams' door and stepped back as it opened wide.

'Come in, Mistress Alden. Come and sit down.' He gestured to a stool drawn up by a rough-hewn table in the far corner of the small earthen floored room; not next to the hearth where his wife stirred the cooking pot.

She nodded toward Priscilla, smiling. 'Good day.'

Priscilla returned the greeting with a hesitant smile and sat where Mr Williams had indicated. She kept her shaking hands in her lap. A quick glance around the room told her that this was a poor dwelling. No chairs, only stools and apart from the table, not another stick of furniture. A pallet was set against the wall near the hearth and another across the room.

'I thought to start we might take up the parable of the sower. You know it?'

'Oh, aye, aye.' Priscilla looked into his kind gaze and began to feel a little more steady and warm, in spite of the draught.

'An important parable as it is found in Matthew, Mark and Luke. I'll read it out from Matthew.'

Priscilla listened, taking in the measured, rhythmical recitation of the parable and Jesus' explanation to his disciples.

'So the question is,' Mr Williams said, 'how can we cultivate the fertile soil within us? Just sit and contemplate a minute. It is not a test. Let something come into your mind; it won't be wrong.'

Still feeling nervous, Priscilla closed her eyes and waited. 'It is about listening and seeing. Listening to Jesus' words... I know. Psalm Four. "Stand in awe and sin not; commune with your own heart upon your bed and be still." We must be still and listen.'

'Well said. I've not connected Psalm Four with the parable. You've help me to see in a new way.' He sat quiet a moment, his hands folded on the table. 'The seeds of God's truth are inside us. We have to listen to a voice from within which will resonate with Jesus' words, as you just have, and a good harvest will grow.'

The hour sped by in discussion and listening.

Walking slowly home, Priscilla pondered. This was a type of instruction she'd never known. This wasn't having rules and doctrines pounded into you to memorize. This was finding something inside which led you on to search deeper. She felt a flickering, an awakening, and clutched herself as if to be sure whatever it was didn't fly off. *Thank you, Mr Williams. I feel as if you've cast a spell on me, and I don't want it to end.*

Not every week, but whenever he could, Roger Williams gave Priscilla instruction. Focusing on Jesus' teachings, Priscilla's task was to ponder a passage and prepare a response which described what she 'heard' and 'saw' in it to apply to her own life. She set aside an hour in the early morning before the children woke.

At first she tried to talk to John about this new way of learning, but John was mistrustful; said he preferred to rely on the wisdom of men who were Bible scholars. Therefore Priscilla kept her adventure in her own private place.

During her hours with Roger Williams all else ceased to exist. Although his wife was in the room she seemed to disappear. Mr Williams always paid close heed to Priscilla's ideas, and most wonderful, said she helped his own understanding to grow. She felt she could melt into his eyes; stay in the comforting reassurance of his presence forever. Sometimes when they were studying a passage in the Bible, both leaning across the table, their heads almost touched. She felt his warm breath, sweet like a kiss on her cheek. If their hands brushed the feel of his skin sent shivers through her and she had to fight to keep hold of her thoughts. After a meeting with Roger Williams, Priscilla had a spring in her step, a song on her lips, a renewed warmth toward her family. She instinctively knew he had found something in her she had never known was there; a knowing which infused her with a new exhilaration, and she guarded it closely, not sharing it even with Susanna.

The months marched on: braking and hackling the flax, harvest, winter, spring, with the tasks, discomforts and pleasures that accompanied each season. For the most part Priscilla managed to balance herself between her family life and her secret life. However, occasionally she slipped.

Of an evening, she and John sat in their rockers by the hearth, Priscilla knitting, John recounting the agenda of a council meeting. Priscilla's thoughts sometimes drifted to an imagined conversation with Mr Williams; her knitting slowed to rest in her lap.

'Priscilla. Are you ailing? You haven't heard a word of all I've said.'

'I'm sorry. I drifted off. Busy day.'

'I asked if you'd seen Mr Prence about recently. He's been giving me odd looks.'

Priscilla's antennae stretched. 'No… no… not for a long time. Surely now our colony has grown he is too busy checking up on folk to be bothering us.'

'Hope so. I detest his watching, spying.' John drew deep on his pipe and puffed a chain of smoke rings. 'Standish has suggested the two of us go hunting farther afield; camp out two or three nights.'

'Do you want to?'

'Aye. It's a long time now since Wessagussett. Must be getting on for ten years. The memories aren't so vivid and Miles is a stalwart friend. 'Twill be good to get away from the colony for a few days. Wish we would take down Wituwamat's skull.'

'You'll need your knapsack packed.'

Chapter 59

September 1631

Seeds of discontent

With little Pris wriggling in her arms, Priscilla and her three older children waved goodbye as John and Standish set off in the early morning sun, on one of their increasingly frequent hunting trips up north. They would be gone several days. *Please come back safe*, she prayed silently. 'In we go; on with the chores. Elizabeth, please tidy the pallets and sweep the floor. Jack and Joseph, collect the eggs and clean out the coop.'

Mid-morning, she delivered her brood to Susanna and restraining herself from skipping, walked along the path to Roger Williams' house with a lilting, dance-like gait. Soft air; a light breeze stirring the leaves; birds singing strong as if happy to be alive.

An hour later Priscilla bade Mr Williams goodbye with a brief accidental touch of their hands. Her heart full, she walked slowly along the path, head bowed, replaying in her mind every word, every gesture, every intonation of their time together.

'Mistress Alden.'

She jumped. 'Mr Prence!' She felt her cheeks flush hot.

'I've disturbed your... reveries?'

'What do you wish of me?'

'I was only passing. Couldn't resist the pleasure of a few moments in your company.' Prence fell into step beside her. 'I've noticed you are a regular visitor to the Williams' home.'

Priscilla stepped away from him to the side of the path, keeping her eyes on her feet. *He's been spying.* 'I do call on Mistress Williams from time to time. She is a good devoted soul. Is Patience well?'

'Very well. She thrives in our marriage. Blossoms.'

Priscilla knew that Patience was growing thin and haggard. Rarely smiled. She hurried her pace, avoiding Prence's probing eyes.

'You and Mr Alden must sup with us of an eve.'

Priscilla did not reply. At last. 'Good day, Mr Prence.' She knocked on the Winslows' door.

Over the next few days Priscilla became increasingly distracted, alternately inhabiting a world with Roger Williams and worrying about Mr Prence. She forgot about the children's chores. Whilst stirring the stew she pondered and forgot to add the onions. Whilst hoeing her garden she pondered and didn't notice little Pris crawling into the strawberry patch, pulling up the plants. Whilst mending she let her hands fall into her lap, still, as she stared into the hearth. She forgot when to expect John.

The door opened and her husband walked in on pandemonium. Pris sat on the floor under the table, whimpering as Elizabeth tried to pull her out. Jack and Joseph were engaged in a grand boxing match over by the lean-to; Priscilla was seated in her rocking chair mending, and miles away.

'Priscilla!' John thundered. 'Why aren't these children in bed? Have they been fed?'

Priscilla started and quickly discarded her mending. 'Just trying to assemble my thoughts before… I meet with…'

'Before meeting with Roger Williams. Strewth! This is going too far. Now get the children to bed.'

Thank heavens at least they are fed. Priscilla switched back into matron mode.

John strode over and grabbed both his sons by the collar. 'Stop this! To bed with you.' He gave them a push toward the bedchamber.

Priscilla got down on her knees and pulled Pris from under the table. 'There, there.' In the bedchamber they all knelt to say prayers before undressing down to their smocks.

'In you get.' Priscilla tucked the covers round and uttered soothing words. Emerging into the main room, closing the inner door behind her, she went to the hearth and dished up stew for supper. 'You must be very hungry,' she said as John sat at the table.

He ate several mouthfuls and said, 'This doesn't taste right.'

Priscilla looked up from her spoon. ' Ah, you're right. It is bland. I must have forgotten the onions and peas.'

'Priscilla.' John put down his spoon. 'Since you have been meeting with Mr Williams the household has fallen into disarray. This is not like you. What is the man doing to you?'

'I'm sorry, John, but he is showing me a new way of learning, of understanding the teachings of Jesus. Helping me discover – it is exciting, John, and will help me to…'

'Help you to what? Follow his fanciful ideas about each person following his own conscience? There lies chaos, Priscilla. Utter chaos.' He stood, face flushed, and wiped his brow. 'Be careful, Priscilla. Don't be led astray by this man.'

Frozen in her seat, Priscilla stared at John.

In a more gentle tone he said, 'I have news. On our hunting trips Standish and I scouted the area further north, across the Jones River. 'Tis more fertile up there. We found an excellent place for a settlement and have purchased a goodly parcel of land from the Indians. We'll have acres and acres, Priscilla. More than we could ever have here.'

Priscilla's head reeled. *No, no*, she silently screamed. Unsteadily, she stood to clear the table. 'You say you purchased the land. How? Did you give the Indians a handful of worthless trinkets or did you pay a fair price?'

John banged his fist on the table so hard the last of the stew spilled from the trencher. 'Confound that Roger Williams! These are his notions you are spouting. If it were unwise for us to settle there, or if we did wrong, Hobbamock would have said. And he hasn't.' He paced around the room. 'Why have I done all this?' He gestured to the settle, the polished chests, the rocking chairs, table, cradle. 'For you I've done it. And then you ask if…what has got into you? You want to prosper. Your father's dream… where has that gone?'

'I…' Priscilla sank back onto her stool.

Whimpering came from the bedchamber. John turned on his heel and stormed out.

Priscilla pulled herself up and ghostlike, crossed to the bedchamber to comfort the children. When she'd settled them to sleep again she shakily made her way to her rocking chair. Never had John been so furious. She felt churned up, turned inside out. *I must think. He is right. I have been neglecting our household. But every time I speak of Mr Williams' views he explodes. Oh Lord. I am not going to stop seeing Mr Williams. He understands me in a way no one else ever has – not even Susanna. I can speak of Mary Brewster's torment, of Catherine Carver's wish to die, and her gift; or my longing for fun and merry-making; of any doubts and troubles and he doesn't judge. No. I'll not give him up. But I love John and he works so hard for me, for us, and he is right – I do want us to prosper. But I will not move away from here. I'll keep my pondering private. I'll show John I love him. I'll put home life first. Then perhaps he'll forget about this notion of moving or leave it 'til years hence. Perhaps Susanna and Edward Winslow could persuade him to stay, remind him Plymouth Colony needs him.*

Priscilla waited and listened for the sound of the latch lifting. Hours went by. She dozed and started awake. Not the latch, only a log spluttering. Worry kept her awake. Where had he gone? Had something happened to him? As the night wore on, worry gave way to guilt; what had she done?

The first twitterings of pre-dawn birdlife came to her ears as the latch lifted. Priscilla shot up and rushed to the door. 'I've been so afraid. Thank God you're back. I'm sorry.'

'Come. No more words. Come to bed. We've only an hour or two before daybreak.'

In the morning, although slightly dizzy and with eyes hot from lack of sleep, Priscilla felt more buoyant, resolved that she would not try to combine 'pondering' with household tasks. To her relief John was cheerful again and gave her a hearty kiss as he set off to the fields.

Having set her older children to their tasks and given Pris the *Mayflower* hessian dolls to play with, Priscilla was settling to pluck a brace of duck when a knock on the door preceded Susanna's entry.

'Let me give a hand,' she said as she disentangled herself from Elizabeth's energetic embrace. 'How's my favorite girl? Chopping pumpkin and squash for the pot?' Pulling up a stool beside Priscilla she took a second duck onto her lap.

'I'm so glad you've come across,' Priscilla said. 'Elizabeth, could you go and pick a basket of beans?'

When Elizabeth had gone into the garden Susanna said, 'We could hear John's anger last night. He was very loud.'

'It was about Roger Williams. He is so against his ideas and hates me being influenced.'

'Don't you think perhaps he's jealous?' Susanna looked sideways at Priscilla. 'I've noticed you seem far away at times. And, Priscilla, tongues are starting to wag.'

'But that's ridiculous. Only once a week, and sometimes not that often Mr Williams gives me instruction, and Mistress Williams is always there in the room, stirring the pot.'

'I don't have to tell you. It doesn't take much to get the gossip started. More's the pity.'

'Susanna, how can I explain? Mr Williams' way of teaching is different, kind and gentle. He says to be still and listen, instead of the harsh judging that tormented Mary Brewster.'

'I know Edward thinks highly of Mr Williams, and says he is right about our taking the Indians' land for trinkets. We should pay a decent price. But keep this to yourself.' Susanna stopped plucking and put a hand on Priscilla's arm. 'The important thing is, don't let there be hard feelings between you and John. He loves you so much. It hurts him to see you so enthralled with Mr Williams.' She sat quiet, staring at the duck. 'I fear if word gets about there is discord between you and John, Elder Brewster will summon you for counseling.'

Priscilla shuddered. 'I know you are right. But I won't stop thinking and searching as Mr Williams has taught me. It feels right and I won't stop.' She choked, abandoned the duck and drew the back of her hand across her brow. She wept. 'John says he and Standish have bought land up north. He wants to leave Plymouth and settle there. Please can you and Master Winslow persuade him it would be a mistake?'

Susanna put an arm round Priscilla's shoulders and hugged her. 'I don't want to lose you. Would be like losing a sister. Of course I'll speak to Edward.'

With Susanna's promise, Priscilla felt more hopeful and set to preparing a flavorsome pottage and making their home tidy. As a special touch she strewed the floor with branches of hyssop to give a pleasing scent when trod on.

As John entered the doorway she hurried to give him a welcoming kiss and stopped, recoiling from his dark frowning glare.

'We've been summoned by the Elder to be counseled.'

'No!' Priscilla stepped back.

''Twas Mr Prence had the pleasure of informing me. Seems "someone" overheard our angry words.'

★ ★ ★

Even as she and John stood outside the Brewsters' door, waiting for an answer to John's knock, Priscilla could not believe this was happening. Nor could she stop shaking. She clasped John's arm. She must not swoon.

The door opened. 'Come in.' Unsmiling, Elder Brewster motioned them to sit on two stools facing his own chair. On a stool beside the Elder's chair sat Mr Prence. John didn't move.

'I insist this interview be held in private,' John said. 'Unless Mr Prence leaves the room we will bid you good day.'

'Mr Prence is here to learn how these interviews are conducted. He is preparing to take on my role.'

'I will not remain in the room unless Mr Prence leaves. Nor will Mistress Alden.'

'Very well,' the Elder said. 'I have other matters to attend to this morning. We need to be brief. Will you please go, Mr Prence. I will come to your house when I have need of you.'

Priscilla still hung onto John's arm. He guided her onto the stool beside his. She clasped her hands tight.

The Elder lowered himself into his chair. 'This is a sad day, to hear of anger and strife between you. We believe it is God's will that husbands and wives should live in harmony, making whatever sacrifices are needed to this end. Disharmony undermines the foundation of our colony. Our very survival depends on each family working as a strong team.'

'I understand and agree,' John said. 'I know Mistress Alden does too. We suffered much in order to marry, as you know.' Priscilla saw him give the Elder a keen look. 'We are pledged to one another and neither of us would ever put our marriage in jeopardy. An occasional disagreement does not imply a serious rift, and can sometimes clear a misunderstanding.'

'My informant said what he heard was rather more than a "disagreement" as you put it, and he surmised that Mr Williams was somehow involved.'

'If you tell me who your informant is I'll be pleased to correct his perception. He heard a few words and blew them up from a pinprick into bloodshed.' John snorted.

Elder Brewster drew back. He turned to Priscilla. 'Is it true you are receiving religious instruction from Mr Williams?'

Priscilla gained strength from John's stout defense. Calmly, she said, 'Very occasionally, while I am helping his goodwife with her chores. She has much to do and Mr Williams is paid so little.'

The Elder shifted uncomfortably, placing the tips of his fingers together. 'Ah. Our coffers are low.'

'My husband speaks true,' Priscilla said. 'We are devoted and always will be.' She looked at John believing at that moment she was speaking the truth.

'Thank you.' Elder Brewster rose. 'I know life here can be a strain and you have contributed much, Mr Alden. Long may it continue.' He showed them to the door.

Back in their own home, with the door closed, Priscilla took John in her arms. 'Thank you. You spoke strong and true. I have been wrong to ignore our home life.'

'Please come back to me, Priscilla. You've been absent so long.'

'I am yours.' Priscilla took his face in her hands, running her fingers over his eyebrows, eyelids, following the contours of his cheeks, his lips, as if she were a blind person seeing with her fingers. She kissed him, finding her John again.

Late in the afternoon while she was adding to the stew, waiting for John to return from hunting, Priscilla pondered. *Roger Williams and John. I need them both. I must be careful. I lost my balance, my devotion. I want things to settle down. I want John to be happy, to forget about moving away. To lose Roger Williams and Susanna...* she wiped away tears.

★ ★ ★

Reluctantly, John left Priscilla's embrace and shouldered his musket to hunt for the pot. He wanted to take her to bed and love her all afternoon and night long, make her his again and again. He was angry; angry with Roger Williams, angry with Prence, low-down weasel, angry with Elder Brewster for his sanctimonious blindness, angry with Bradford, encouraging Prence to snoop, angry with the Church of Christ for its holier than thou intolerance. If he'd had any hesitation before, he had none now. The solution was to move. Standish was for it. They would start a new settlement and it would grow. He was not alone in wanting more land, and in wanting to be free of the Plymouth leaders' dictatorial ways; their constant 'observing' of folks' behavior. He would remain committed to serving on Plymouth's council and the magistrates' court; committed to trapping and lumbering to pay off the colony's debt. The new settlement would depend on Plymouth prospering. However, he wanted more for his family than a constrained religious colony whose primary purpose was prayer. Above all, he wanted Priscilla to forget about Roger Williams.

Chapter 60

July 1632

John's surprise

A year passed. Priscilla's household returned to its former orderly routine. As John and Standish often went on three to four day hunting trips, it was easier for her to arrange her day around visits with Roger Williams. But she never again forgot to be ready to welcome her husband on his return.

'Priscilla!' John's hat flew into the room, circling before landing beside the table. His children screamed with delight as their father strode across the room, took his wife from the hearth and danced her round the table. 'It's almost finished – our new house – and there's a surprise in it for you.'

In shock, Priscilla sat down hard. 'I knew not... so soon? I thought it would be years. *Hopefully never.* Where?'

'I wanted to give you a surprise. On our hunting trips Standish and I have labored hard, clearing land, putting up farm buildings, and our house.'

'But I thought...' Priscilla put her face in her hands. 'Off!' she snapped at Pris, pulling at her skirts and stood, hands on hips. 'You never asked my view. You promised you would consult... how soon... how far?'

She pressed her fingers against her temples. Roger Williams' face filled her vision.

'Reckon about two months.' John bent down to Elizabeth's imploring arms, dancing her round in a circle. 'Up beyond the Jones River. About ten miles.'

'Ten miles! Much too far.'

'The land is better farther north. We're near a marsh, perfect for shooting fowl; they flock there by the hundreds. Standish and I are calling it "Ducksburrow".'

'I'll lose my friends... the children... no one to play with. We might as well be crossing the ocean again.' She sank onto a stool, head in her hands. 'I'll be left in a wilderness full of Indian savages and wild beasts. We could all die; be eaten alive. That is not what Father wanted.'

'Calm down, wife. Listen, for once, please listen.' John grasped her shoulders, put a hand under her chin. 'Look at me. This move **is** what your father wanted. For us to prosper, our children to advance, have new opportunities. This is a chance to produce more, take advantage of all those newcomers in Boston – they need everything we can supply: corn, livestock, and they'll pay well.'

Priscilla jerked her face out of his hand. 'No. It's starting all over again. Clearing, digging the fields. No... too much, too far away.'

'Boston: massive deep harbor, rivers going inland, good land – Boston will prosper. So we must take advantage as best we can.' John punched the palm of his hand with his fist. 'With more land and our trading post in Maine, we'll have furs to send to England and produce for Boston. The road to prosperity. You know that won't happen here in Plymouth.'

'Why not?'

'You know why not. The land here is poor and there's not enough of it. And Bradford is not interested in prosperity. He wants to worship and commune with his soul. You feel held back. You know you do.'

'I'd rather be held back and live, thank you.' Priscilla paced, the table between them. 'You are a cruel man, John Alden.'

'I know you lost your family. It won't happen again, I promise.'

'Promise! Meaningless, useless word.' Priscilla stamped and clenched her fists. 'You promised, before we were wed, you would consult me. But you don't. Without consulting me you signed to be an undertaker of the debt and it has taken five years to ferret out Allerton's cheating!'

'Priscilla, listen.'

'Now you've decided we'll move far away to the north, not giving me a single thought. Don't ever speak the word "promise" to me again – ever.'

'Priscilla, this **is** for you. I do think of you.'

'I thought you were different from other men, but no. I see now you are just the same.' She collapsed onto the stool, head in her arms on the table, sobbing. 'I'm trapped in this godforsaken land, with children to care for. Before they came I could have gone back to England – but now.'

'This is crazy talk. Stop it.'

The children stood silent, not moving.

'I won't leave you in the wilderness. Standish and Barbara are coming, and Elder Brewster, and several other families. They all see this is the way to go.'

'The Winslows?'

'No – later perhaps.'

'I'll lose Susanna.' Priscilla rocked from side to side. 'No, no, no, I won't go without Susanna.'

'This is impossible.' John looked at the rafters. 'What about your longing to have a proper school in a schoolhouse? Bradford forbids it. Where we are going he cannot stop you.'

'Susanna. I need Susanna to help me with the teaching.'

'Hopeless. We must say prayers and eat. Standish is coming with me tomorrow, first light. We'll be away four days. Speed the building along. I'll need a good supply of victuals.'

At daybreak John kissed Priscilla goodbye. She whispered, 'Come home safe,' bowed her head and turned away.

It is a soft day. Priscilla stepped into her garden for a moment's quiet before her children woke. Her eyes rested on the small stakes marking her buried snowdrop bulbs. Her primrose seeds couldn't grow in this harsh climate, but the snowdrops. *I must remember to dig them up to take. A new garden to plant, and John Bradford won't be there to help.*

A blond curly head came into her line of vision. 'Elizabeth!' Priscilla hugged her girl close. 'I never heard you. Come, you'll get cold with only your smock on.'

'Has Father gone to build our new house?'

'Yes.'

Her children washed, dressed and breakfasted with cornmeal porridge, Priscilla set Elizabeth to weed the beans; Jack and Joseph to pick raspberries and strawberries, and clean out the chicken coop, gathering the dirty straw and droppings into a pile to use as manure. When she had swept the floor and put the bedding to air, Priscilla spun flax. Like Susanna, she longed for the day when the colony had sheep, giving soft wool; so much gentler and easier to work.

'Hello? Hello?'

'Susanna!' She threw herself into Susanna's arms. 'Last eve John said we'll be leaving here soon. In about two months. Please come too. Can you not persuade Master Winslow?'

'I'll try, but I fear he'll feel duty bound to stay and support Governor Bradford. Oh Priscilla. I'll miss you terribly, terribly much.'

'Please bide with me awhile.'

'Give me some mending.'

Sitting with Susanna by the hearth, Priscilla put down her sewing. 'I'm afeard. Now I know how Mother felt. She did not want to cross the ocean. I was impatient with her.' She brushed away tears. 'Poor, brave Mother.'

'She was a good woman, so kind and skilled with her remedies and birthing,' Susanna said. 'I was glad she birthed me on the ship. Safe hands. I was in safe hands.'

Priscilla sobbed. 'That is what you are. Safe hands. And I'm losing you. I don't know if I can…'

Susanna took Priscilla in her arms. 'You will be brave; you will cope. I know you will. You are strong.'

'But I'll be alone. All alone. With none but beasts and Indians around when John is away… often… the council and court here in Plymouth. He says Captain Standish and Barbara will come, but not 'til the harvest is in, and our homesteads will be far apart – at least a mile.'

Priscilla clutched Susanna's arm. 'And Barbara isn't **you** – there, just across the track – you. She isn't you.'

'Surely you'll come on Sabbath days. Sail across the harbor. Much quicker that way.'

'I suppose so. But it isn't the same.' Priscilla stared, as if suddenly hit by a thought. 'I'll be entirely dependent on John to come here. Oh, it will be so lonely. You won't be there to help me set up house – that was such fun – and…' Priscilla wept heavily. 'I'm with child again and I won't have you.'

'I'll come and stay. When the date draws near I'll come. I'll come for long visits. I'm sure Lizzie Howland will take my little ones.' Susanna held Priscilla's hands.

'Mother,' Elizabeth called. 'We've done all the chores.'

'I must be gone. Edward will be in for midday meal and I've not yet plucked the fowl.'

Priscilla wiped her eyes, blew her nose, and tried to compose herself. Susanna wiped tears from her own eyes.

Next morning Priscilla set Elizabeth, Jack and Joseph to do their chores, left Pris with Susanna and followed the path to the brook. As she drew near Mr Williams' house she could see him, forking over his plot to a fine tilth.

He looked up and came over to the fence. 'Good day, Mistress Alden. Off to the brook?'

'Aye. To pick strawberries and gather groundnuts,' Priscilla said. 'That's nice loamy soil you've got. Should grow a good crop.'

'I'm turning it to get it soft for my goodwife to plant in case I'm not returned by the spring.'

'Oh?' Priscilla's tone betrayed her alarm.

'I've arranged to live with the Indians – Massasoit's tribe – for a spell. I want to learn their language and ways.' He looked into Priscilla's eyes. 'I look forward to hearing your thoughts and questions when I return.'

Priscilla grabbed hold of the fence and fought back her tears. She tried to keep her voice steady but her eyes swam. She felt a hole opening up in the pit of her stomach. 'I – that is, we – most likely won't still be here. John says our home lot is almost ready. We'll be moving away up north soon. I never knew 'til now.'

'He didn't tell you?'

'No. Wanted to surprise me.' She took a deep breath.

'Is it far?'

'Ten miles.'

'Too far for you to walk here and back in one day.'

'We'll come by shallop on the Sabbath, I'm sure.'

Roger Williams did not speak. He held Priscilla with his eyes. Tears escaped her own.

'Mistress Alden, I shall miss our meetings. You have a fine mind and spirit. Don't give up. Please come to Plymouth on the Sabbath.'

'We will. Thank you, Mr Williams.' She couldn't say more. He clasped her hands and she curtsied slightly. As he turned back to his forking she carried on down the path, feeling her heart would dissolve. She hurried, wanting to run. *I hope there's no one else at the brook.* There wasn't. She crossed over and paced slowly along the bank, sinking in to the quiet sounds of high summer: birds idly chirping, the brook burbling, its springtime rushing spent. A buzzard lazily soared high above. She savored the cool touch of soft moss on the boulders. Would she ever feel comforted?

Seeing a flat boulder she sank onto the mossy seat. Sunlight whitened the birches and softened the grass, the lichen and granite. *I wish I could drift away. I'm frightened. Frightened of the move. Frightened of what has happened to me with Roger Williams. I think I love him yet I cannot tell a soul, not even Susanna. He is going away and might never come back. He could be killed. Anything. I don't want to go, but perhaps it will help. And another babe on the way. Oh Mother of Christ, have Mercy.* She buried her face in her hands and swayed, imagining Mother holding and rocking her when she was a little girl. Memories of early years in Dorking enveloped her: helping Mother, playing with her cousins, festive gatherings, sitting on Father's knee as he told stories of olden times. *This will never do. The children. I must think of them and get on with work. Plenty of it.*

Part 3

1632–1687

September 1632-January 1633

Chapter 61

September - October 1632

Another journey

In the dawn of a fine mid-September morning the Alden family said goodbye to Plymouth. John and Priscilla, with their new dog, Zach, took their places beside the ox pulling a cart laden with their possessions, cats and four children. After a last farewell wave to their friends, Priscilla did not look back.

All through the morning they plodded on. As the track skirted Plymouth Harbor, it led through the familiar mix of pines and hardwood, and to the right, scrub leading to harbor-side marshes. In this month of September the foliage wore the heavy green of high summer, except for the maple leaves whose tinge of scarlet encroached on summer's green. It was time to stop and eat and let the children run about. Priscilla was tired. She placed one foot in front of the other, head down to keep an eye out for tussocks of grass, holes or large stones. This track was terribly rough; if one could call it a track.

'What is that sound?' she asked. 'Running water?'

'The Jones River ahead; bridge of logs across it,' John replied.

Priscilla looked in horror as they approached the expanse of fast flowing water. The log bridge barely cleared the rippling current and was only just wide enough to take the cart. 'I'll walk behind,' she said, going to the back. 'Hold tight, Elizabeth. Don't let go of Pris.'

Tentatively, the ox set a foot on the logs, and drew back. It started to shy away.

'Gee up,' John commanded sharply, cracking the whip across its shoulders.

The beast started across, lowering its horns this way and that. Priscilla stayed close behind, inching forward. A log turned under her foot and the cart lurched. Pris screamed. Priscilla commanded Zach to 'Stay' and scooched round to help John steady the cart. Zach stayed. The log stopped shifting; the ox steadied, and balance was restored.

'Easy now, easy, easy.' John coaxed the beast forward.

'Hush now, quiet. Everything is alright.' Priscilla soothed the whimpering Pris. 'We'll soon be across and then we'll stop a bit.' Elizabeth, Jack and Joseph were pale and wide-eyed. 'You did well not to cry out. Thank you.' Priscilla congratulated her children. 'And you are a very good dog.' She patted Zach and stroked behind his ears. 'Not so far now; we're over halfway.'

In the lengthening shadows of late afternoon, John guided the ox over rough ground through a copse of trees. The cart lurched and lunged. The half-asleep children were thrown awake and hung onto whatever they could grab. Pris started to cry.

The cart stopped. 'There,' John said, nodding toward the scene in front of them. Sheltered under the branches of a large elm tree, a house waited, standing in an acre of cleared ground. To the right of the front door was a small raised bed, soil dug over and ready for planting.

Priscilla clasped her face in her hands. 'Is that our home?'

'That is our home,' John said.

'It is so big – so long! I've never seen!'

'Thirty-eight and a half feet long, ten feet wide; a hall and a parlor, with the chimney between the two. Come, let's unload.'

Priscilla gave each of the children something to carry and she gathered up a bundle of bedding.

When she crossed the threshold, John took her hand. 'Your surprise.' He led her round to the kitchen side of the huge deep chimney and there was a bake oven, built into the chimney. 'You don't have to do your baking out in the yard.'

'John!' Priscilla dropped the bedding and turned into his arms. 'Thank you so much! I declare I am the only woman in these parts to have such an oven. And with a wrought iron door! How did you?'

'Aha – secret dealings.' John laughed and hugged her. 'There is a good cellar below and two bedrooms above – proper bedrooms.'

Priscilla rose before dawn to fill John's knapsack and bid him goodbye.

'I'll be back tomorrow evening with a cartload. Ferry the livestock another day.' John hugged her, and waved as he disappeared with the ox and cart.

Priscilla sat on a flat tree stump to await the sunrise, Zach at her feet; a young brindle bulldog raised from a pup by Francis. His parting gift. The farewells. Francis. Young scamp, set the *Mayflower* on fire, grown now into a fine young man, helpful and kind. John Bradford. She'd grown to love Dorothy's son. Susanna. Brought back memories of saying 'goodbye' to folk in Dorking; the men overly hearty with claps on the shoulder and promises of 'We'll be next'. Mother and the aunts unashamedly weeping. They knew. It was the final parting. 'I'm glad to have you.' She stroked the dog and talked to him. 'We are all alone here. Not another soul. Even when the Standishes and others do come, they won't be close by, as in Plymouth. Father complained that Dorking was too crowded and land too scarce. We have endless land here, but in Dorking the peddlers and market traders brought news. Of London, France, Spain and Holland. And folk – friends, cousins – were close by to help and have parties with. Ah Zach, it is lonely here. In Plymouth we lived in houses all huddled together, and folk helped each other, but so much spying. A tiny, isolated colony in a wilderness of beasts and Indians. Now, because John wants more land; he is so proud of this place he's built. But I've never been so alone. I'm frightened.' She wondered how Roger Williams was faring amongst the Indians. Would she ever see him again? Dawn was breaking, bringing birdsong to full voice. Wrenching herself from these musings she said, 'Come on, Zach. Let's feed you and the children and get to work.'

'Please may we explore?' Elizabeth, Jack and Joseph wriggled on their stools. Joseph accidentally kicked Zach, sitting under the table. The dog yelped and ran to the cover of Priscilla's skirts.

'You must take care,' Priscilla said. 'Zach is important to us here. He'll guard us against wolves.'

'Wolves? Nearby?' Elizabeth asked, suddenly still and wide-eyed.

'I'm sure there aren't any about now. Elizabeth, help me wash the trenchers and then we'll all explore.'

Trenchers washed and put away, Priscilla said, 'The first thing is to find the spring. I think I heard burbling water close by, in the copse yonder, out the front.' Priscilla led her four children, she, Elizabeth and Jack each carrying a pail. A two-minute walk brought them to a brook tumbling over waterfalls, and at its head the spring.

'Oh, isn't it lovely!' Elizabeth cried, dropping her pail.

'May we wade?' Jack asked.

'Please,' Joseph added.

Little Pris put her thumb in her mouth and stared.

'It is a splendid brook; a beautiful spot.' Priscilla smiled. 'Your father chose a good place to build, with the brook close by. Another day we'll come wading but now we must fill our pails, then explore, and then finish unpacking.'

Once the pails of water were set in place back at the house, Priscilla opened the kitchen door onto a large expanse of garden: row on row of raised beds, cleared, dug over to a fine tilth. 'Look, all prepared for planting! Look,' Priscilla said. 'There is a gate at the far end and beyond that…' Excitement chased apprehension. Picking up Pris, she walked through the garden to the gate and spied a clump of maples. 'Our very own, for sap and syrup and sugar! We won't have to venture up into the woods.'

A stockade bordered the garden and the farm buildings, fencing them off from a large field which stretched behind.

'Look at the barn!' Jack exclaimed. 'It's huge.' He ran into the large building. 'This must be the cow yard at the side.' Behind the barn was an orchard and more fields.

'These sheds,' Priscilla said, 'a good lot of storage for tools. We'll put the chicken coop beside the shed nearest the house.'

'It's huge, huge!' Elizabeth and Jack and Joseph danced about, waving their arms like windmills. Priscilla stood gazing out over acres and acres of cleared land and the forest beyond. On the edge of the forest, standing clear, a magnificent hornbeam spread its branches, hosting grapevines all entwined.

★ ★ ★

'We've done well; our produce and the livestock all here, and garden and orchard started,' Priscilla said, rocking gently. 'Now we need a spell of soft rain.' She and John sat in their rocking chairs by the hearth, their two cats, descendants of Bibs, curled up as feline cornerstones, whilst Zach lay with his head on John's foot. 'It is quiet here,' Priscilla commented. 'So quiet; a silence I've never known, not even in Plymouth.'

'Reminds me of when our building party first came off the *Mayflower*,' John said. 'No wind in the rigging, or sailors' calls, or moans of the sick. No sound at all except the wind and the rain, and then the Indians started.'

Zach growled softly and the hair on his neck bristled. Then came the distant howl of a wolf, to be joined by more and more. The dog stirred himself and paced.

'All right, Zach. Good dog. They're far away. Come lie down.' John spoke quietly and Zach obeyed. 'He'll be good protection, along with my gun. I must teach you how to shoot. I have a second musket in the roof.'

Priscilla said nothing. She hated the sound of wolves howling. She didn't want to think of nights here alone with the children. And she did not want to learn to shoot.

★ ★ ★

Priscilla stopped to lean on her hoe, thankful for the less punishing heat of early autumn. She surveyed her garden: raspberry canes planted, strawberry patch and herb garden started, clumps of snowdrop bulbs by the front door. Little Pris toddled close by, picking up lumps of earth to feed her doll. *I should be pleased. Hard work but rewarding. Why do I feel like lead inside? And I'm always afraid.* She shaded her eyes, looking across the fields to the woods for her boys. *What is that? I'm sure I saw movement – and now nothing. Just young Jack and Joseph gathering brushwood.* She resumed her hoeing. *More and more, when I fetch water, sometimes in the garden, shadows, shapes that appear and melt away. I hate being so alone. Am I going mad?*

'Fa-fa?' Pris tugged at her skirt.

'Father is away building more houses. He'll be back soon.'

'Fa-fa.'

Priscilla felt a surge of anger. *Always building for Standish and Brewster. Good, but they'll not be close by. If anything happened.* 'We must be strong.' Mother's words sounded in her head. *I wish she were here, and Susanna, and Roger Williams. No time to ponder in this place. I'm bitter. Never have I felt so bitter and afraid. My young pupils – gone. Please God I'm not going like Mary Brewster. I'm drowning in bitterness and mustn't let the children see, or John. Be strong. Another baby on the way.*

'Hie! Hie! Jack and Joseph called as they emerged from the woodland, laboring with their heavy basket. Priscilla watched with relief and pride as her two young lads crossed the unplanted clearing and tugged their load through the orchard into the cow yard.

'Come along, Pris, we've hoed enough today.' She glanced up at the woodland, shadows slanting low. *Again, a shape… I'm sure. Gone now.* She shivered. Taking Pris by the hand and grasping her hoe to use as a staff she hurried to the cow yard as quickly as Pris' two-year-old legs would permit.

'Well done,' she said admiring the basketful of kindling. 'You've brought some juniper. Lovely. Now let's get the chickens in and the goat tethered close by the house.' She forced her voice to sound strong and hearty. 'No foxes or wolves are going to get our animals. I'll shut the pigs in the sty.' She also double-checked to be sure Bessie and her calf were secure in the cowshed.

In the house, Elizabeth had all in order. Stew simmering, hearth swept, table laid; Zach lying by the door, head on paws, waiting for his master; the two cats prowling, gazing hopefully at the young cook.

'You're a good lass.' Priscilla gave her daughter a heartfelt hug. 'All beautifully ready.'

'And I've been mending. Look, Father's shirt and breeches and the same for Jack and Joseph.'

Zach's ear twitched and he was on his feet, barking, tail wagging, wriggling all over, turning round and round in circles. Half a minute later John threw open the door.

The family was all together again: prayers, supper, stories and laughter, and bed. With John there Priscilla felt safe and dismissive of her half-seen apparitions. *Just fancies because I'm alone. I must pull myself together.*

The weeks traveled into autumn. Their harvest, brought from Plymouth, was stored in the barn, roof and cellar. Not an abundant harvest, but enough. Priscilla tried to ignore her unease and loneliness. Working hard had always been a way of dulling pain. She held Roger Williams in her mind, imagining sitting across the table from him, the feel of his presence, their conversations. However, she could not rid herself of the 'phantoms', the shapes, shadowy, then gone.

Late in the afternoon with shadows lengthening and an autumn chill in the air, Priscilla walked to the brook to fetch water. A few leaves left their branches, drifting down. She tightened her shawl. As she straightened with her full pail of water, she saw a face peering round a birch tree, an Indian face. She gasped a strangled cry, dropping the pail, and it was gone. But she heard a twig snap. Shaking, she refilled the pail and hurried back to the house.

All was quiet and in order.

That evening, as she sat with John by the hearth she determined to tell him of the incident.

'The Standish house and Brewster house are both finished. Great day! And lands cleared with another three houses on the way,' John said. He leaned down and stroked Zach, stretched at his foot. 'With Standish nearby we'll have Hobbamock; he'll stay by Standish wherever he goes. I reckon he's as good a protection against Indians as any palisade or fort.'

Zach bristled. Wolves howling. Every night, sometimes far away, sometimes closer. Priscilla shivered.

'Standish says I'm needed at a council meeting tomorrow.'

'Oh?'

'I'll set off early. Sail across. Reckon to stay the night and help Miles and Barbara with their first cartload next day. They'll be our neighbors soon – how's that?! Then Elder Brewster.'

'That **is** good news,' Priscilla said. She decided to say nothing about her 'phantoms'. *It would only worry him and he'd think I'm going mad like Mary Brewster.*

Chapter 62

October 1632

Joseph disappears

Only one night alone, and we have Zach, and I can shoot – sort of. Priscilla told herself to buck up. 'Elizabeth, we'll bake today; a good big batch.'

Elizabeth hopped with pleasure. 'My favorite task, using our splendid oven, and the delicious smell.'

Together they kneaded the dough and put it to prove. 'We'll grind meal for animal fodder and cooking whilst waiting for the loaves to rise,' Priscilla said. 'Oh for a good grist mill.'

'Aye. 'Tis such hard work with pestle and mortar.' Elizabeth settled herself with the mortar in her lap and a sack of grain at her side.

Priscilla set Jack and Joseph to shaking the boughs of the apple trees, gathering the fallen fruit. 'Mind you don't fall. No time for broken bones. When you've finished you may go to the edge of the forest to gather brushwood.'

The sun was well on its way to the horizon when Priscilla pulled the last loaves from the oven. 'There's a feast for supper,' she said, hot and flushed. 'We'd best get the animals fed and penned for the night.'

'Mother! Mother!' Jack ran into the kitchen, tears streaming down his cheeks. 'I can't find Joseph – and the pigs are out – way up across the field at the edge of the forest.'

'Elizabeth, stay with Pris. Zach, stay. Good dog. Stay with Elizabeth. Guard the house.'

Priscilla hurried after Jack, disregarding her swelling belly. 'Wait – we'll take a bucket of corn.' Carrying her extra burden, she half-lumbered, half-ran across the rough fields. 'Joseph, Joseph,' she called. The pigs were clustered, rooting in the trees bordering the fields. 'Find a couple of thin branches. You switch from behind while I lure them with the corn. Thanks be they're coming.' Priscilla shook the bucket, hurrying backwards. Being more interested in their evening feed of corn than the woods, the pigs followed eagerly. When she'd got them safely penned Priscilla looked in on Elizabeth. 'Good lass,' she said.

'Joseph?'

'I'm going back to search now. The pigs are shut in. Could you do the chickens?'

'Surely,' Elizabeth said.

Priscilla hoisted her skirts and ran back across the fields, panting and gasping.

Jack called, 'Joseph, Joseph.'

'Where were you? Do you have any idea which way he went?'

'We were here.' Jack pointed to the abandoned basket of brushwood. 'I was gathering over here, and when I'd got an armful and turned – he wasn't there.' Jack sobbed and wiped his eyes on his sleeve.

'So he was over here on the other side of the basket.'

'Aye.'

Priscilla looked for traces of footsteps in the pine needles and moss. Nothing. No broken twigs. *As if he's been spirited away. No.*

Don't think such a thing. The phantoms. I must keep calm. 'Joseph, Joseph,' she called. 'Jack, you stay here. Help me gather pine cones to use as markers. I'm going to search over this way. Don't go **anywhere**.' *The wind is getting up. Feels like a storm coming.* Her apron full of pine cones, Priscilla felt her way in the darkening shadows along a deer track. Calling, calling, she frequently looked back to remember landmarks and left a trail of pine cones. The wind whistled and thrashed the branches overhead, drowning the usual sounds of birds softly clucking and twittering as they roosted for the night. Her calls, 'Joseph, Joseph,' jarred in her ears. It seemed like forever, calling, calling, her steps taking her deeper into the forest. Scrubby saplings caught at her skirts. The wind whipped her shawl. Twiggy branches dislodged her coif. She tripped on a root and almost fell. 'Joseph, Joseph.' Only the raucous cawing of crows pierced the howling wind. It whipped tendrils of ivy curled round slender tree trunks. Storm clouds blew in high above. Priscilla stopped, and heaving a sob, turned back. She was anxious to reach Jack before dark closed in; before the storm broke. Still calling, she followed the markers back to Jack who waited, shivering, frightened. 'There's a storm coming. We'll search again in the morning.' Between them they carried the basket of brushwood back across the fields, pursued by rumbling thunder. A livid fork of lightning lit up the sky and heavy raindrops fell as they made their way across the cow yard.

'Joseph?' Elizabeth asked, as they pushed into the kitchen. The young girl tried to stand strong but her eyes welled and she crumpled onto a stool.

'We'll search again in the morning. Now we must pray.' Priscilla gathered her children round her by the hearth and offered fervent prayers for God to keep Joseph safe and bring him home. No one could eat; not even little Pris. The freshly baked bread sat on the table untouched. After she had tucked Elizabeth, Jack and Pris into bed Priscilla sat by the fire in her rocking chair with Zach at her feet. Too numb with terror and grief to weep, she passed the hours trying to pray, trying to chase away visions of young Joseph, only just turned five, being scalped, or made into a slave, tortured and shamed. All the worst things she'd heard about Indians swarmed into her head. The rain lashed down; lightning crackled and thunder rolled. Zach sat bolt upright, ears pricked. *He knows. He knows we are afraid.*

'Mother, I can't sleep,' Elizabeth stood in the doorway of the bedchamber.

'Of course you can't,' Priscilla said. 'Bring your quilt and come sit with me.'

'Me too.' Jack and Pris joined Elizabeth, all huddling together, waiting for morning, too frightened to speak or sleep. Only little Pris slumbered fitfully, cradled in Priscilla's arms.

Gradually the storm passed over, moving toward the ocean. Quiet. Before dawn quiet when not a bird or creature stirs.

Rap, rap... rap, rap. Insistent firm knocking on the front door. Priscilla handed Pris to Elizabeth.

'Quiet, Zach.' Zach stopped growling but his hackles bristled and he kept close to Pricilla's side. She took the musket from its place over the hearth and slowly walked to the door. Rap, rap. Louder. Lifting the latch, musket aimed, she opened the door a crack. In the shadowy murk, the dusky brown head of an Indian brave emerged, a small white arm clutching his muscular neck.

'Hello. Friend.'

'Hush, Zach.' She slowly opened the door wider. 'Joseph!'

'Yours?'

'Aye.' Priscilla dropped the musket and reached out to take her son. Half-asleep, Joseph clung tighter.

'C-come in.' Almost swooning, Priscilla invited the brave, carrying Joseph in his arms, to sit at the table. Elizabeth, Jack and Pris stood by, staring, silent.

In the firelight Priscilla studied the brave's face, dim recollections hovering in her mind until a memory crystallized. 'Tinsin?'

'Aye.' He smiled, nodding.

'Oh! Thank you. First me,' she pointed to herself, 'long ago…
now my son. Elizabeth, please fetch our special basket.'

Elizabeth crossed the room to a row of barrels standing against
the wall, an array of baskets and bowls resting on their lids. She
brought the special basket. Priscilla showed it to Tinsin; intricately
woven, beautifully patterned. 'From your wife.'

'Aye, aye.' Tinsin grinned, gently loosening Joseph's hold on his
neck. 'Aijana.'

'My friend,' Joseph murmured sleepily, clasping his arms
tighter.

'Joseph, let me hold you,' Priscilla held out her arms. Somewhat
reluctantly, her son climbed onto her lap.

'Would you like some bread?' She offered a loaf.

'Thank you.' Tinsin ate half the loaf. 'My son,' he gestured with
a beckoning motion. 'To our camp. Many miles.' He ate some more
bread. 'Your son very tired and hungry. He eat and sleep, and I bring
him.'

'Thank you, thank you. We thought.' She held Joseph tight.

'I know. He is safe.' Tinsin finished the loaf. 'We watch. We
watch when your brave goes.'

Priscilla smiled and wept. 'You are good, so good.'

Tinsin's consternation at her tears became a grin. 'We are friends.'

'Aye. Aye.' Priscilla nodded.

He detached a leather cord from round his neck and loosened
the drawstring of a finely beaded pouch. From it he withdrew a
small carving of a bird. 'A woodpecker. Our sacred bird. Fights to
the death to protect her young. Even against an eagle. For you. Keep
you safe.'

Priscilla gently stroked the fine carving. 'Thank you.' Tinsin gave
her the pouch. She carefully placed the woodpecker in its home. 'I
will keep it with me always.'

'I go.' Raising his hand, Tinsin went to the door and walked out
into the opaque pre-dawn light.

John came home to a clamorous welcome. Zach barked, the children shouted, 'Father, Father… Joseph… and Indian.' Gradually the story was told.

John did not smile. 'It ended well,' he said. 'Tinsin, you say. The same brave who found you in the forest all those years ago?'

'Aye,' Priscilla said.

'We are fortunate to live near friendly Indians. But Joseph, all of you, must never, *never* go off into the forest without an adult you know. **Never**. His voice was stern.

Later after the children were in bed John and Priscilla sat by the hearth.

'I'll ask Standish if he knows Tinsin and his Indians,' John said. 'Did you know they were watching you?'

'I kept seeing shapes that disappeared. I feared I was going mad.'

'You said nothing.'

'I didn't want to worry you.'

'Priscilla, you must tell me if something is troubling you. What a terrible ordeal. My brave wife.' He left his rocking chair, knelt beside her, and held her hands. 'I know it is hard for you being here alone. Susanna sends her love.'

Priscilla couldn't hold back her frightened misery. Tears fell onto the mending. John held her hands and stroked her belly. 'The next one.' She held onto his rough, strong hands, unable to speak.

John cleared his throat. He slowly stood and returned to his rocking chair. Priscilla looked at him, alarm flickering in her heart.

'I have sorry news,' he said. 'The Standishes have decided at this last minute to delay moving here until spring.'

'Oh no.' Priscilla gasped.

'Barbara doesn't want to face a winter here until they've had time to settle and more families come. Especially as she never knows when Miles will be off on a mission.'

Priscilla put her head in her hands. *I don't believe it. Surely not true.*

'Bradford pushed for them to stay in Plymouth longer. With pressure from two sides, Miles surrendered.'

'So – no Hobbamock? No one. Just us. All winter.'

'Don't worry. We have Zach. And you know Susanna has promised—'

'I know.' Priscilla cut him off. 'When my time comes she'll come and bide awhile.' Her voice filled with bitter resignation. 'If things go as planned. Hah. How likely is that?'

'Priscilla, please. Be strong. I've never heard you speak so darkly.' John lifted her to her feet. 'Come to bed. A new day tomorrow.'

Dumbly, head bowed, Priscilla allowed John to guide her to the bedchamber.

'What? What has happened?' Priscilla opened her eyes to shafts of sunlight. She sat up, pulled herself out of bed and hurried to the hearth.

'Good morning, Mother.' Elizabeth stood stirring the cooking pot. 'Father said to let you sleep. Porridge?'

'A minute. I'll wash and dress. Where is your father?'

'Gone hunting. Jack and Joseph are giving the apple trees a last shake.'

Bless them. It is a new day. And Sabbath day after tomorrow. I'll see Susanna. I wish Mr Williams was safely returned.

Chapter 63

January 1633

Elizabeth is midwife

I pray the kind weather holds, please God let it hold, at least 'til I'm delivered. Priscilla rocked gently by the hearth. The first day of January 1633. She stood and opened the door to inspect the night. A full moon shone bright in a clear black sky. The air was still. Good. Wolves howling echoed from a distance. Zach growled. She returned to the warmth of the hearth. *John will return tomorrow with Susanna. Please God, let nothing happen to prevent her from coming.* She fetched her psalter. Psalm 23. 'The Lord is my shepherd...' Reassuring, comforting. Time for bed. But she felt strangely restless. *I must sleep.* She took a good draught of distillation of chamomile.

Oh, no, no, please God no. Wide awake, Priscilla waited. *Perhaps not.* She tried to pretend the roaring wind wasn't really so ferocious. There came another pain. No question. She rose from her bed and dressed. Rain thrashed down and the wind blew a tempest. John could not possibly sail in such a storm. *I must prepare.*

Opening the lid of the linen chest she took out the old quilt and linen she used for birthing. She spread a clean cloth on the closed lid to hold the items she would need: a bowl of soft butter for lubrication, phials of betony syrup for pain, plenty of soap, a scrubbed bowl of hot water to wash in, a sharp knife. She would sterilize it over the fire nearer the time. *Oh.* She clutched at her belly. *Keep track of how long...* She prepared a poultice of hyssop to protect the umbilical cord from infection.

'Be merciful unto me, O God, be merciful unto me; for my soul trusteth in thee: yea in the shadow of thy wings will I make my refuge...' (Psalm 57).

Priscilla recited the words of the psalm over and over, like a mantra, as she moved slowly, methodically, putting things in place. The storm howled and battered relentlessly. Pacing, hanging a cauldron of water over the hearth to heat, preparing hasty porridge for breakfast, tasting the chicken broth. After-birth food. A strange calm came over Priscilla. *Poor little Elizabeth, only nine years old, early to act as midwife. And no wet nurse. Birthing turns the milk bad; needs a few days to get right. Pray it goes smoothly; less harm done.*

'Be merciful unto me...' Without thinking Priscilla began to recite prayers to the Virgin Mary.

Holy Queen, Mother of Mercy
To thee do we cry
Turn then
Thine eyes of mercy toward us
O clement, O loving,
O sweet Virgin Mary.

She held in her mind the statue of the Virgin in the old church in Dorking. *Have mercy, have mercy.* The Virgin's face changed into Mother's face, smiling, encouraging, calm.

The black of night slowly morphed into the gray of dawn. Still the winds raged. No birdsong. The children stirred. The pains came more frequently, sharper.

'Mother!' Elizabeth stared at Priscilla and the chest lid all laid out.

'Aye. It has started. Now help me prepare the bed.' Elizabeth took one side of the bed, Priscilla the other and together they rolled up the bedding. 'Stack the bolsters – so – I'll lean against them – and we just lay out the quilt and several sheets. My little midwife.' Priscilla stroked her daughter's fair curls. 'I can probably manage most of it myself; this **is** the fifth. But I'll need you to cleanse the knife over the hearth flames when I say.'

By now Jack and Joseph were dressed and present, staring. Pris, still in her night shift, clamored for her porridge.

Priscilla gasped and gripped her belly.

Elizabeth took over caring for her brothers and sister without being asked. 'Jack, go milk Bessie. Joseph, feed the chickens.'

'Thank you, lass, thank you,' Priscilla breathed as Elizabeth wiped her brow and gave her a whittled stick to bite on. 'Merciful Mother of God, save me, for my children; Mother, save me,' she whispered as she pushed.

Remarkably soon it was accomplished. Exhausted, Priscilla leaned back against the bolster, her squalling baby boy cradled against her breast. She held Elizabeth's hand. 'You were wonderful. Never faltered, did exactly as I bid.' She smiled at Jack, Joseph and Pris standing close by, peering at the babe. Pris stretched out her chubby arms. 'Me, me.'

After a few sucks at her breast, the babe slept, breathing easily. Priscilla laid him in the cradle by her bed, leaned back into her pillows and closed her eyes.

A fearsome shrill shrieking jerked her awake. Clenching his tiny fists, his face contorted, her babe screamed. Priscilla gathered him to her. He wouldn't suckle. She could not soothe him, not rubbing his back, or his tummy, nor rocking; nothing helped his awful pain. She'd never known a babe suffer thus.

Jack and Joseph gawped fearfully and went outside. Little Pris whimpered; then wailed. Elizabeth hugged and soothed her; tried to distract her playing house games. Seeing her children suffer exacerbated Priscilla's misery and mounting sense of helpless panic. Was it the storm raging outside affected the babe thus? She knew not. After hours of screaming he fell limp and slept until the pain woke him. So it went on for two days and nights. On the morning of the third day the tempest abated. Priscilla held her infant, stroking his forehead, murmuring. He quietened, shuddered and lay still.

'No, no.' Priscilla choked, trying to jostle her babe back to life. 'No,' she wailed.

Elizabeth threw her arms round her mother's neck. For her children's sake Priscilla controlled her grief. 'It is finished,' she said. 'I'll keep him here by me awhile. Thank you, Elizabeth.' She kissed her young midwife and held her close.

That evening John arrived with Susanna. Zach's barking was the only sound welcoming them. Elizabeth opened the door. John and Susanna walked into a room of quiet, downcast children. In Susanna's comforting embrace they allowed themselves to cry.

John strode to Priscilla in the bedchamber. 'My love. My poor love.' He held her close.

'You've come,' Priscilla said weakly. 'Our boy was to be called William for Father. 'Twas terrible.' She turned her head away, looking down at the lifeless body lying in the cradle. 'The poor mite. For two days and nights he screamed.'

John lifted the small bundle, gazed into his dead son's face, and cradling him in his arms, stumbled from the room.

Enveloped in Susanna's motherly arms, Priscilla wept.

When her friend could weep no more, Susanna said, 'I'd best have a look at you; see if everything is as it should be.' She turned to the four silent, watching children. 'Off you go now, to the other side of the chimney until I call you.'

Her inspection completed, Susanna said, 'You are clean. Perfect. I promise you, Priscilla, it wasn't the birthing, nor your milk was the problem. Your babe had something awry inside him. There was a babe born in Holland was similar. A mystery. I don't know. But I do know, even if I'd been here 'twould have been no different.' She wiped tears from her cheek. 'But I'm sorry you were alone. Terrible. My Priscilla.'

Priscilla didn't argue against Susanna's words but in her heart she felt sure that if they had remained in Plymouth her babe would have been healthy. She believed that even if the birthing wasn't to blame, the journey or most probably the struggle to re-pen the pigs and fright of Joseph going missing caused the unborn babe harm. Perhaps a sign from God. A sign saying John was wrong to move to this place.

The morning shone fine, unusually warm for January. John carried the small coffin. Jack and Joseph walked beside their father. Behind them Priscilla leaned on Susanna's arm whilst Elizabeth held Pris' hand and clustered close to Susanna. The silent procession made its way amongst newly planted fruit trees to the grave.

Thanks be the earth isn't frozen solid. Hearing a fluttering of wings Priscilla looked up. A vivid red crested bird perched in a young apple tree, its sparkly black eyes staring at the grave. *It should be a robin. Our small English robin, in our orchard in Dorking.* She saw her little brother Joseph climbing the old apple tree to pick the highest branches, she and Mother picking the fruit they could reach. They chattered about preparations for the harvest feast with aunts, uncles, cousins. She clutched the arm holding hers; felt a hand press over her own. A warm freckled hand.

'Ashes to ashes…' John recited the Anglican prayers of committal, his voice breaking. The small family stood mute as he shoveled soft earth into the grave.

Susanna stayed for the month of January. With the support of her friend, Priscilla threw herself into domestic work; at this time of year hour upon hour of spinning flax and grinding corn. She took refuge in hearing the gossip from Plymouth and discussing medicinal plants and remedies. Susanna said Hobbamock told her of a tea the Indians make from the bark and roots of sassafras which prevents the scurvy.

'Would do us well to learn more Indian remedies,' Priscilla said. 'They have long known how to use the plants that grow in these parts.'

'Perhaps. But I'm afraid they make potions that drive a body out of his wits,' Susanna said, 'or are poisonous.'

The day came when John Bradford called to take Susanna back to Plymouth. Priscilla clung onto her friend, willing her to stay.

'It has been so good, biding with you,' Susanna said, gently disengaging herself. 'Weather permitting you'll be coming soon for the Sabbath.'

'Aye, that we will,' John said.

Priscilla choked and nodded. She hoped they could go if not this Sabbath, the next. She longed for Roger Williams to be there. She needed him, his comfort and understanding.

1634-1635

Chapter 64

April 1634

Misery on the Kennebec

Home. Three nights in Plymouth. Good to be back. As the track emerged from woodland into their clearing John stopped. *A home to be proud of.* Priscilla's roses growing by the door, her garden bursting with vegetables, flowers and herbs, fences neat and straight, barns in order, pigs rooting in their pen, cow and calf tethered in the orchard. *Ah, it is good.* Zach's welcoming furor greeted him, followed by Priscilla with their four healthy children. John shook hands with his two sons, man fashion, and ruffled their hair. He kissed Elizabeth on the cheek as befitting a young lady and scooped Pris into his arms. *I wish I didn't have to go off again so soon.*

'We've prepared a special meal.' Elizabeth took her father's hand and hopped and skipped. 'We baked bread today, and put cranberries in.' She looked up enticingly, swung John's arm and tripped on a root. John laughed and steadied her. Elizabeth continued with her speech. 'There's your favorite succotash, and pumpkin… two pies, blackberry and plum, and for later before bed, roasted apples…'

'Ah, I know,' John interrupted and stooped to hug his firstborn. 'Roasted apples to dip in beer. A treat fit for a king.'

He kissed Priscilla. 'What man could ask for more?' Priscilla squeezed his hand and dropped a half-curtsey.

When the children were all in bed John and Priscilla drew their rocking chairs to the hearth. John lit his pipe and Priscilla took up her knitting.

'So good to be back. You've made a beautiful happy home. Staying with the Bradfords – not at all the same. All a bit stiff.' He pulled on his pipe and exhaled a contented sigh. 'John Bradford sends his regards. Says he's a mind to join us.'

Priscilla stopped knitting and looked up at her husband. 'Really? It would be good to have him here. But tell, what news? What happened in the court session?'

'Nothing too dire. A servant brought a case against his master for not providing enough clothing, and won. Another servant is to be whipped because he ran away for five days.'

'Why did he run away?'

'Not clear. Beyond his discontent at being a servant. I doubt whipping and the stocks, all the corporal punishment, does any good. At least the man will be whipped in private. Two couples were sentenced to the stocks and whipping for conceiving before marriage.'

'So harsh and humiliating,' Priscilla said.

'You'll be pleased to hear, permission has been granted for a grist mill on Town Brook. We'll be grinding our own corn and wheat at last. Hopkins was fined for drinking with servants and friends at home – again. And tax. Tax is to be paid on corn last day of November – five shillings per basket – and if a man doesn't pay he'll be fined twice the amount he owes.'

'Our tax?'

'One pound and four shillings – we're in the top fifteen because we're worth a lot.'

'I'm proud of you, John.' Priscilla stopped knitting and putting her flax yarn and needles aside she left her chair to sit on John's lap, arms round his neck. John laid his pipe aside to hold her. 'You've become one of the leaders. Assistant governor, court assistant. You and Howland setting up the trading post.' She kissed him. 'If only you didn't have to be away so much.' She nestled her head against his shoulder. 'Mind, 'tis not so bad with Miles and Barbara only two miles away, and Hobbamock with them.' She sat up and looked at John, a quizzical furrow on her brow. 'Hobbamock and Miles. A strange pair. Couldn't be more different. Why is Hobbamock so devoted to Miles?'

'I've wondered,' John said. 'Hobbamock never trusted Squanto, nor did Miles. But Squanto is long gone. Hobbamock is pinese to Massasoit. Perhaps he sees Standish as a more reliable ally – unencumbered by church beliefs, not so tied up with Boston. I expect he likes him, and reckons he can more easily be sure Massasoit's interests are served working through him than Bradford.'

'Hmm.' Priscilla nestled again into John's embrace.

'Standish is a good man,' John mused. 'I reckon we'll build a prosperous town here. More and more families are moving up this way from Plymouth.'

'Aye. I wish the Winslows would come. Poor Susanna, with Edward sailing back and forth to England. You are away a lot, but at least not so far and on the dangerous ocean.' John cleared his throat. Priscilla sat up straight and looked at him. He pretended not to notice her expression of alarm.

'About the trading post. Word has come there's a party of English, led by a man called Hocking, anchored above our post, intercepting the Indians, taking our trade.'

Priscilla stood abruptly, and smoothed her skirts. John crossed his legs and took up his pipe. 'There's nothing for it. Howland and

I will have to sail up there and sort it. I'm sure it won't take much. With Howland and me both there as partners – will add weight. Reckon they're chancing their luck and will back off if we say "no go".' In truth John wasn't so sure Hocking would co-operate, but he didn't want Priscilla to worry. He stood and emptied his pipe ash onto the hearth. 'We need that fur trade badly, to settle the debt. And we've been granted the right, by Jove. Until we can settle the debt and cut all ties with the London investors we'll not be able to prosper as is our right.'

Priscilla sat down again and resumed her knitting, needles gaining speed.

'We plan to set off in about a week,' John said.

'Shouldn't you wait? The smallpox is up there, raging through the Indians. What if you get infected?'

'No. We daren't leave it. Need to nip this in the bud.'

'It is so far; way up the coast. How long?'

'I don't know. About three weeks. I'll try to arrange for Francis and John Bradford to visit and help. Miles and Barbara will call often and Hobbamock and Tinsin will make sure you are safe. I'm sorry. I don't want to leave you again so soon.'

★ ★ ★

'That's everything.' John heaved the last sack of corn up onto the bark. He stepped from the landing rock into the vessel and with Howland at the bow took his place in the stern to catch the ropes. Grasping the tiller he told the crew to hoist the sails as a small shore party waved good wishes. Dozens of careering, cawing gulls escorted the small vessel across the harbor. John thought of Captain Jones' lessons in seamanship and said an inward 'thank you'. 'Bless this southerly wind,' he said to Howland, now seated beside him. 'Hope it holds.' He looked up at the sails pulling taut, white against a hot blue sky. 'Also hope dealing with Hocking is plain sailing.'

'So do I,' Howland said.

'I reckon you should take command. Your diplomatic skills are better than mine. Captain Howland, your word will be obeyed.' John saluted.

With the wind behind, they sailed through the nights, making good time. At sunrise of the fourth day John sailed the bark into the wide mouth of the Kennebec River, a calm expanse with flat deep green lands extending on both sides. From previous trips he knew there were no rapids ahead, or unseen hazards. With the sun at their backs, the still air quickly gained heat and within the confines of the river, humidity. There was no breeze to dry off the sweat. A raucous cawing sounded from a coven of crows circling above the treetops, big black shapes wheeling and fighting. High above them vultures soared. *So many. Must be carrion somewhere.* Howland and the crew were quiet, their silence adding to John's growing uneasiness. *There is probably no reason to worry. It is just this hot sticky weather, unusual for April.* He shifted position and adjusted the sails to take advantage of every breath of wind. Almost noon. Rounding the bend that led to the cove which housed their trappers' outpost, they faced another bark, resting at anchor.

John drew up alongside, shouting, 'Ahoy, Ahoy!'

An ill-shaven man emerged from below. His shirt was covered in tobacco juice and the remains of many meals; his pot belly protruded over breeches barely hanging onto his hips. He strutted and swayed, brandishing a carbine, a pistol tucked into his belt. 'Hocking here. Wha'd be yer business?' he shouted, his voice thick, words slurred. One by one his crew appeared on deck.

Howland called to him. 'Sir. Perhaps you were unaware, but you have anchored in our waters.'

'Wa'd'ya mean **your** waters?' Hocking swayed from side to side and stumbled.

'We have the legal right to all fur trade on this river. Have you not been informed? I am sorry if there has been a misunderstanding.'

'Bollocks!' Hocking shouted, rocking back on his heels. 'Bollocks! Says who? We're here,' he rotated onto the balls of his feet, 'and here to stay.'

'Aye, aye!' His crew yelled, shaking their fists in the air.

'He's drunk,' John said. 'Drunk and stubborn.'

Howland stood quiet, looking down the river from whence they'd come. 'No good trying to reason. Reckon we should wait. Perhaps try again in the morning, though I doubt he'll be any more sober.'

'Aye,' John said. 'I don't like being within range of a crowd of drunkards waving their pistols about.'

Moored upstream in the lee of the shore, John and Howland listened to boisterous yelling and singing traveling over the water from Hocking's bark. All afternoon it continued. Dusk cast her shadows into a still evening. On the river, fishing birds roosted in the trees or settled in shore nests. Nature's quiet was disturbed only by the noise downstream.

'Reckon they're drinking hard liquor,' John said. 'If they carry on like this they'll not be sober in the morning. Like as not even more belligerent.'

'Aye. We could be here days, trying to persuade, getting nowhere.'

'What do you say we cut their cables. Let the current take Hocking down the river to the sea. That'll sort him.'

'Right. Good plan,' Howland said. 'We'll wait 'til dark. If their bawling continues we'll drift down and moor opposite; shortest distance for a canoe to slip across. I'll send three men, two to maneuver the canoe and one to cut the cables. Hocking thinks we're upstream. They'll be a good way down the river before he realizes what has happened.'

Under cover of moon-lit darkness and the noise across the river, John and Howland moored as planned and helped three crew into the canoe, knives sharpened. An owl hooted and received an answering call.

Remaining on the foredeck, John and Howland watched closely as the canoe nudged up to the stern of the bark. One cable almost cut through. Then the current caught hold and pushed the canoe back out into the river. The bark hadn't budged.

'We couldn't cut with only two left to hold the canoe against the current,' one of the crew said as they drew up alongside.

'Right,' Howland said. 'Looks like Hocking still doesn't suspect anything. The canoe will hold four.'

'I'll go,' John said.

'No,' Howland said.

'Surely 'tis better I take the risk.'

Howland flushed. His eyes glinted. 'I forbid it. I want you here.'

'Please let me.' Moses stepped forward; a handsome muscular young man with a mop of curly black hair. 'I'm deft with a knife.'

Again, John and Howland watched closely, ready with their muskets. The canoe drew up alongside the fore cable. Hocking stamped up onto the foredeck. He lumbered and swayed to the rail, yelling, 'Hey dogs… Wha'd ya think ye're doin?' His crew scrambled from below, reeling, brandishing pistols. Hocking slouched over the rail waving his carbine. And then, as if drawn by a magnet, the barrel found its way to Moses' head.

Howland shouted, 'Stop. Shoot me. He's only obeying my orders. Stop! Shoot me!'

As if he'd heard nothing, Hocking pulled the trigger. Moses' dark head fell forward. His body slumped down below the gunnels.

A shot was fired from behind John and Howland. Hocking fell. His crew gathered round. They probed, prodded; one knelt putting his ear against the inert chest. 'He's dead!'

'My God, my God,' Howland moaned. 'Who fired that shot?'

'I couldn't help it, sir.' One of the crew stepped forward. 'He killed our man. He might have killed others as well.'

Hocking's crew yelled obscenities, firing their pistols at Plymouth's bark.

'Go below,' Howland ordered his crew. He and John attended to their approaching canoe. John's stomach turned as they lifted up poor Moses, his head a bloody mess. *My God. I wish I had gone.* Unbidden, his mind returned to the Wessagusset massacre. *I hate this killing in cold blood. 'Tisn't honest warfare. 'Tis bad.*

'Look,' Howland said. 'They've weighed anchor. They're going.' He bent over Moses' body. 'He was a fine young man. Killed by a drunken lout, an English drunken lout.' He brought his fist down hard on the deck.

John called down to the crew for a blanket. He and Howland gently wrapped Moses' body and carried it forward to the bows. He put an arm round Howland's shoulder. 'We'll have to bury him here, quickly tomorrow morning. Then head back. But now you need a good tot or two of brandy. Make you sleep.'

Howland, John and their crew rose at dawn. John could take no pleasure in the glorious sunrise bringing the river and its inhabitants to life. Rather, it felt a mockery, and he was not alone in his mood. Apart from necessary commands, no one spoke. The bark weighed anchor and sailed upstream a mile or so to the trading post John and Howland had built shortly after agreeing to take on a share of the colony's debt. The small shingled dwelling was still there; a dwelling similar to the smallest houses in Plymouth. John was pleased how well it withstood storms and the fearsome Maine winters.

'Ahoy!' Howland's call brought forth the three trappers.

'You're a glum looking lot,' one said.

John was taken aback at how unperturbed the trappers were on hearing of the double murder. 'Happens all the time. It's the battle for fur. What have you brought us? We're damn near empty of supplies.'

Still mute, the crew ferried supplies to the trading post. Sacks of cornmeal, wheat flour, rye, barley, sugar. Crocks of pickled onions, beans, and dried berries, apples, peas and turnips.

'Hey! This is a good lot.' A trapper guffawed as he hoisted crocks and sacks from the canoe. 'And a side of pork – ah – hickory cured. The best,' he said, giving the pork a good sniff.

John spoke quietly to Howland. 'Sooner this is finished and we're off the better.' He felt a dead weight in his chest of sorrow and foreboding.

'Here's the best,' one of the crew said, as he and a mate heaved up barrels of beer and a keg of rum.

'Thank ye, thank ye. Come. We've cooked up breakfast.'

John knew he should eat, and tried to make himself, but the trappers' fare of hasty porridge, pork and beans and hardtack stuck in his throat.

'Were you aiming to stay and truck with the Indians?' a trapper asked.

'We were,' Howland said. 'But now, after these shootings…'

'I wouldn't if I were you, in any case,' the trapper said. 'Smallpox has been bad in these parts. Spread like wildfire among the Indians, poor sods. We was afeared to go near them.' He wiped his hand over his eyes. 'Thing was, we could hear their cries. 'Twas eerie; Indians wailing and wolves howling in the night.' He paced up and down. 'We thought on it, didn't we?'

'Aye, we did,' his comrades nodded.

'Reckoned weren't Christian to do nothing, whatever the risk.' He tucked his thumbs into his braces and hiked his breeches. 'So we did the Godly thing. Went to the aid of those poor pagan creatures. Terrible it were. Blood and pus runnin' and sticking them to their mats, being bare skinned as they are, and then their skin flays off.'

John shook his head and laid his spoon aside. *Not now. Don't want to hear this now.*

'And in the freezing cold,' the trapper went on. 'A mess of gore. So weak they couldn't tend each other or fetch water or wood. Ran out of food. Burning their dishes and bows and arrows to make a fire.'

'So we fetched wood and water, and gave them what comfort we could,' his comrade said, 'and buried the dead.'

John looked at Howland. His head was bowed; his food also scarcely touched.

'Praise God, we escaped catching it,' the trapper said. 'Seems it ran its course. But I wouldn't risk lingering.'

'No. Thank you, we won't,' John said.

'Crew, would you fetch Moses' body please,' Howland said.

As he left the room with Howland to find a suitable place for a grave, John noticed the trappers scoffing the food he and Howland had been unable to eat. No time to plank logs for a coffin. They dug a deep grave. The trappers, from somewhere, provided a winding sheet. Together, John and Howland gently swaddled the strong body and shattered head. Then with ropes they lowered Moses into the deep pit. One of the crew made a rude cross and the small company stood, heads bowed, silent. John cleared his throat, and trying to keep his voice steady, offered a short prayer. As he finished he looked up and saw Howland grimacing, eyes screwed tight to keep back the tears.

The return journey to Plymouth was tedious as they were now sailing into the wind. Neither John nor Howland, nor the crew wanted to talk. As their bark sailed across Plymouth Harbor, John could make out Governor Prence and Standish standing, waiting to greet them. When he disembarked he could only respond to Standish's hearty welcome with a numb handshake and an unsmiling 'Thank you'. He could not look at Prence. Governor Prence. He'd weaseled his way into this favored position, magnanimously offering to give Bradford a rest, and no one else wanted the job.

'Howland, Alden, come to my house and give your report. You are invited to sup, of course,' Prence commanded.

No one else, apart from John and Howland was present when Prence heard their story. Howland recited accurately all that had happened. John sat hunched over the table, head bowed, looking at his hands. When Howland had finished there was a long silence. John looked up into Prence's eyes. They gleamed with triumph. The governor leaned back in his chair, then stood to deliver his pronouncement.

'This is a sorry affair. You are responsible for the murder of an Englishman. Dread to think of the consequences for our relations with Boston if word gets back to Winthrop.' Prence paced back and forth. 'Having decided to cut Hocking's cables, you, Howland, did right to stay on board your bark. But surely you should have tried harder to negotiate with Hocking, given it more time. He is, was, an Englishman. And if you could not persuade him, refer back to us in Plymouth.'

From the corner of his eye John glanced at Howland; saw his jaw lock, unlock, his lips clamped in a grim line.

'However, you, Howland, did at least beg Hocking to shoot you instead of poor Moses. But you, Mr Alden, why did you need to stay on the bark? To keep yourself out of harm's way? Why did you not go in the canoe instead of Moses? You must have known the risks, intelligent man that you are,' Prence sneered, 'and you preferred to risk the life of a simple soul, Moses. I've a mind to bring you before the court and charge you with cowardice.'

John felt himself coloring as he knew he did when enraged. He clenched his fists under the table.

Howland jumped to his feet. 'Mr Prence. I protest. This is outrageous. I ordered Alden to remain on the bark. Furthermore, no others on the council are present to give their views. Alden and I are assistant governors. It would be wrong to charge Mr Alden without the agreement of the other assistant governors.'

The table blurred before John's eyes. He blinked, trying to focus, get his mind straight.

Howland continued. 'We thank you for your offer to sup, but we would not want to add to your dear wife's burdens. My Lizzie will be happy to look after us. Goodbye, Mr Prence.'

Shakily, John stood. He stared at Prence, a hard disdainful stare. Saying nothing he followed Howland out the door. Waiting until they were well out of earshot of Prence's house, he said, 'Thank you. The man is a scoundrel, out to get me any way he can.' The two walked in heavy silence. Halfway across the clearing John stopped. 'Why don't you move up to Ducksburrow; get away from this strict place and Prence's hot air. You'd be heartily welcomed in our settlement, where a man can prosper and breathe freely.'

'Thing is, I have a good place here, with a large portion of the best land. We're prospering well enough and I think Lizzie wouldn't want to leave.' Howland stared at the ground, poked at the turf with the toe of his boot. 'Mind, after this miserable business I think I'll keep myself to myself more. Finish this year on the council and then bow out.'

'Sorry to hear it,' John said. 'We need your solid good sense.'

Chapter 65

April 1634

Prison in Boston

A week later John prepared to set sail again. This time alone in his shallop filled with sacks of corn: his, Standish's and Howland's. Destination, Boston to trade. Before casting off he pulled three sheets of parchment from his pouch and looked over Standish's careful, exact, up and down script, Howland's slightly haphazard scrawl, and Priscilla's beautiful sloping hand. All there. Lists of items to bring back.

As he sailed across Massachusetts Bay, John gave thanks for the bracing spring day, cloudless blue sky, sun warm on his back. The sails filled; the shallop sped through small whitecaps. He wanted to complete this journey as quickly as possible and get back to Ducksburrow; get on with the spring planting, and when time permitted, building houses. Ducksburrow was growing. He thought of Priscilla expecting another child. *Pray God this one lives, and Priscilla lives. Must be sure to fetch Susanna in plenty of time.*

Sailing into Boston Harbor John thrilled to the place as he did every time he journeyed there. Large oceangoing vessels moored alongside the wharf. Houses and warehouses were set back around a market square and everywhere there was the noisy hurry and hustle of folk doing business.

As John pulled alongside the wharf and lowered his sails a stevedore called down to him. "Ere – let's 'ave yer ropes. Hey Thomas, fetch a cart,' the man yelled as he caught the stern lines.

'Thank you. Thank you kindly,' John said as he tossed the final sack from the boat onto the heap to be towed to market, and climbed up onto the wharf. He straightened his doublet and bent to tie his bootlace. *Need a new pair. These are nearly worn through.* As he started to raise his head he beheld five pairs of black shoes sparkling with polish. Slowly regaining a standing posture he found himself facing Governor Winthrop and four other Boston worthies, two on either side. Despite his surprise at seeing them there, he thought how only men of high status and rank would be dressed all in black and only the governor would be wearing a suit of fine velvet with slashed sleeves, cuffs of delicate white lace, a starched white neck ruff. His trademark, a pair of gossamer gloves so thin you could see through them, were not worn but carried. His companions' dress was suitably, deferentially opulent.

The governor proffered a manicured, unhardened hand.

Shouldn't think he's ever held an axe.

'Mr Alden.'

'Sir. To what do I owe this honor?'

'There is a matter we wish to speak with you about. How is Mr Bradford? Well I trust and Mistress Bradford?'

'Both quite well, and if Mr Bradford had known I would meet with you he would have sent his regards, I'm sure. What is your concern, Mr Winthrop?'

'Please come to my house. We'll discuss it there,' the governor said. 'May I introduce my assistants?'

What can this be? They are so stiff, severe. Walking beside the governor,

John's mind scouted. *All the times I've come here with corn he's never appeared. Is there a problem with Prence? With Plymouth? What can he want?* Outwardly he spoke admiringly. 'A fine town. Established, prosperous after only four years. Thriving under your leadership, Mr Winthrop.'

'I thank you for your praise, Mr Alden.' Winthrop halted. 'This is my home.'

John stared. *It's grand: two stories, gabled, glass windows. I wish I could give Priscilla a house like this.*

Winthrop pushed open a heavy oak door into a large dim room. In the middle stood a substantial rectangular oak table, highly polished, with carved legs. A grand fireplace was set into the left wall. No fire flickered to dispel the chill hanging in the dusky air. In the far right-hand corner stood a small writing desk and chair. The governor offered no refreshment, not even a tankard of ale. He and his assistants maintained their stern demeanor. John stood still, looking at the governor. His throat was dry; his palms sweated, and his stomach had that particular ache of fear. *But this is daft. I've done nothing wrong. The governor is known for being dour.* He tried to reason his way into calm.

'Please be seated, Mr Alden.' Winthrop took his position at the head of the table and gestured to a single chair placed mid-point on his left. John slipped into his seat, his back to the empty fireplace. The four assistants placed themselves in a row across from John. The chair legs scraped the flagstone floor as they took their seats. John looked from one face to another, all expressionless masks, to the point of all looking alike. *Why do they not speak? Why so strange, so grim?*

'Mr Alden,' the governor spoke. 'I understand you are joint manager with Mr Howland of the trading post on the Kennebec River.'

'Yes, sir.'

'We have received news of the incident there and Mr Hocking's death.'

'Mr Hocking shot our man at point-blank range, sir.'

'Mr Alden. Mr Hocking was in the employ of Lord Say and Sele. When word of this reaches England, we'll be seen to be cutting one another's throats for beaver. Before we know it we'll have a Royal Governor over here, effecting an iron hand. We must be seen to mete punishment for such behavior. Therefore I must detain you here in prison to await settlement of the affair. I'll write to Governor Prence informing him.'

John gazed into Winthrop's cold, gray eyes. *He cannot do this, surely.* He rose from his seat, hands placed firmly on the table. 'Sir. I protest. I did not shoot Hocking. Witnesses will attest to that. As you well know, I am not without standing: assistant governor and serving on Plymouth's panel of court justices. You have no right to treat me like a common criminal.'

The governor stood, his unblinking gaze fixed straight ahead. 'I have every right, Mr Alden. As governor of this most prominent colony in all the region, I will do what I must to keep good relations with those in England whose investments support us. Gentlemen,' he looked to the men on his right. 'Escort Mr Alden to his cell.'

'My corn. Sacks of corn to trade. Sir.' John packed all the disdain and venom he could muster into his parting word.

'I'll see it's put in store. Goodbye, Mr Alden.' Governor Winthrop continued to stare at the door, not altering his pose as the four black-clad dignitaries led John into the street, two grasping his elbows, two following behind.

Fie. Fie on you all. John seethed inwardly. Blinded with rage and disbelief, his eyes misted over. The long meandering walk passed unseen. *Where are they taking me? Where is this prison?* Finally, up a set of steps, through a grand door into a large room with a dais and benches at one end where, John surmised, the jury sat. Linseed oiled parchment windows kept the room dim. *The courtroom.*

'Downstairs.' A worthy held open a door. With the four men behind him, John tentatively made his way down a dark narrow staircase, almost falling over a sharp spiral turn. Unable to see, he braced his arms against the walls. The air became increasingly dank and cold. He counted fifteen steps before he could put one foot in front of the other on a level floor. A narrow corridor was dimly lit from slits at ceiling height, letting in a few shafts of light.

'Stop,' came the barked command. A key graunched in a lock, a door swung open and an arm pushed John into his cell, a space only big enough to hold a pallet and a pail on an earthen floor.

'You'll be brought victuals at even.' The door banged shut and the key turned in the lock.

Incensed, John paced, three steps forward, three back. *Who does Winthrop think he is? Behaving like a tyrant king. He has no right. Damn him. I've worked and striven, learned to read and write. My opinions are held in high regard – and now clapped in a prison cell!* He hugged himself against the damp and cold. *They haven't even given me a blanket. I'll request one. Why couldn't they detain me in someone's house? Damn humiliating.*

Unable to see the sky, John had no way of gauging the hour. Eventually the key turned in the lock. A swarthy man in breeches and tunic entered holding a trencher of cornmeal and a spoon. "Ere.' He jabbed his arm forward keeping his eyes averted to the side before withdrawing his hand with such haste the trencher almost fell on the floor.

'Thank you,' John said. 'Could you bring me a blanket please?'

The jailer shifted from one foot to the other, eyes on the floor, a smirk hovering on his lips. 'I'd 'ave to get permission, see. An all's gone 'ome now.'

'Well, see what you can do.' Impatient fury hardened John's tone. The jailer's exit was slow paced. The door banged shut. 'Stupid half-wit.' John snarled at the locked door.

As he expected, the cornmeal was tasteless, coarse and dry so it stuck in his throat. Nothing to drink, not even a beaker of water. His ache of hunger reminded him of earlier years, building the palisade and houses, sometimes on only one small portion of meal a day.

He tried to steady his mind with the thought that as soon as the assistant governors got word he was being held here, someone would come to his rescue. He knew there would be no help from Prence. That wretch would be happy to see him perish. Cold, hungry, in a nightmare of apprehension, John could not sleep. He paced, tried to doze, paced again. *What if Prence keeps Winthrop's letter secret? How long before alarm will spread? Priscilla. Priscilla with child. She works so hard, planting, hauling pails of water, doing a man's work as well as caring for the children and the household.* The night was a never-ending torment.

With the morning victuals, his jailer brought a folded blanket, delivered as if it was burning his hands. This time he was in a hurry to leave.

'Wait. A beaker of ale please.'

The jailer slowly turned. 'Oh – don't know about that,' he drawled.

'Confound you. Bring me ale or I'll report you.'

'How's that?' his captor sneered. 'Being as you're shut up 'ere.' He pulled the door to with extra force.

John shook out the blanket to wrap it round his shoulders. Threadbare hemp. Fleas jumped out. He groaned out loud.

The days and nights dragged on, deliveries of food the only markers preventing the hours becoming an amorphous continuation. Day and night he shivered, wondering if a fever was setting in; wondering why hadn't someone come yet from Plymouth?

Seven days. Perhaps Winthrop had decided to settle matters himself; use John as a scapegoat, refuse to release him. What would happen to Priscilla? Left alone with the children, not knowing; he thought of her torment. If only he had taken her advice and commissioned Hopkins to bring the corn, as others do: Bradford, Winslow. But Hopkins takes a big cut, and charges a fortune for the goods he sells. *Oh God. This is driving me mad.* He searched his mind for a comforting verse from the Bible and found none.

Day after day these thoughts circled and re-circled through his mind. As time went on he sat, for hours, staring at the plank and daub walls of his cell, tracing the plank edges, gazing into their shapes. *Where is Priscilla now? What is she doing?* Standish – the ambush at Wessagussett – horrifying images permeated his mind. Was this a punishment? He forced himself to stand and pace, back and forth, and sank again onto his pallet, staring.

His only sleep was to doze in fits and starts, a few minutes at a time. *Have I been left to rot? To be hanged in Boston – to appease the English investors? Does Prence agree with Winthrop? After all the struggles, taking on the debt, to be hanged?* He turned on his side, face in his hands, trying to hide, disappear.

On the tenth day, as he was listlessly pacing, trying to escape his thoughts, John thought he heard voices, as if far off, then footsteps. *Is this it? The gallows – get it done quickly.* A cold sweat seeped through every pore; his hands freezing wet with fear. A trickle of shit ran down his leg. The key in the lock. The door slowly opened and…

'Miles! Miles! Thank God!' John fell on the captain's neck. Miles hugged him close and recoiled.

'You poor rascal. You are a mess and you stink. Let's get you out of here. Priscilla sent a change of linen – and look!' Standish unwrapped a parcel to reveal a pie. 'You're lucky I didn't eat it. No one bakes as good a pie as Priscilla.'

'How is she, and the children – are they well? Have they managed?'

'Priscilla's been nearly out of her mind. You should have seen her when she heard you are still alive and I was coming for you. Come on. We'll talk later. This place is vile.' He poked at the jailer, standing by the door, posture straight in pretense of authority. 'You oaf. You lousy, flea-ridden piece of vermin.'

'Sir!' the jailer protested.

'Fie!' Miles shot back before leading John out of his cell.

John stumbled after Standish, limbs stiff, feet numb with cold, back down the corridor before climbing the unseen stairs. His knees ached. His balance was tipsy. He tripped, almost fell and tried to grip the walls. *God give me strength.*

They emerged into the dim courtroom and then out into a day of bright sunshine. He blinked and rubbed his eyes.

'There's an inn down the street. We'll stay the night there. Now a tankard of ale and you can wash and change your linen before we use the afternoon to trade. Set sail at daybreak.'

In a daze, John relaxed into Miles' care. 'We'll share my pie,' he said.

They retrieved John's corn and after a successful afternoon's trading, sat down to a meal of venison pie and ale. 'Food here is superior to anything our inns have to offer,' John said.

'They have a grist mill, so flour aplenty for pies, cakes, dumplings,' Miles said. 'Also, Boston imports spices, sugar, all sorts.'

When he'd finished eating John asked, 'Miles, why did it take so long before you came?'

'I sailed up the second day you were overdue. Winthrop would not even let me see you. I was in a lather of fury. Knew I'd get no backup from Prence. That man would as soon see you hang.'

'I know.'

'So I persuaded Bradford to write to Winthrop. Got him to see that although he is not serving as governor this year, Winthrop does respect him; will give him an ear over anyone else. 'Twas Bradford obtained your release. The moment he received Winthrop's letter of pardon I set off.'

'I owe a great debt to Bradford, and to you, Miles. Thank you.'

Even at a distance, as they tacked across Plymouth Harbor, John and Miles could hear echoes of cheers. As they approached the landing rock, 'Hooray! There's Alden! God be praised! Well done, Standish. You've brought him back. Thanks be you're safe, John.'

Eager hands pulled John from the shallop. He was so weak and giddy he could hardly stand. He stumbled into the crowd, wordless, overcome with joy, relief and exhaustion. *Steady, get a grip*, he said to himself as he and Miles, with keen helpers, unloaded the shallop. He felt a hand on his shoulder. 'Howland!'

'Thank God you're safe,' Howland's voice shook as he thumped John's shoulder.

'Aye – and here are your goods,' John replied, helplessly grinning. 'And your list.' He retrieved Howland's list from his pouch. 'You can check.'

'Bother the list. You are the important item. Couldn't care about the rest.'

By now the western sky was offering a display of red and orange waves, shifting, drifting, now and again tinged with blue, gray, making way for a ball of red.

'Fine day tomorrow,' Miles said.

Tomorrow, Priscilla.

Bradford pushed through the welcoming crowd. 'You must both stay the night with us,' he said. 'I'll invite Winslow and Howland to sup. They'll want to hear all.' Prence was not to be seen.

Although he was grateful to stay in the Bradford home, John was restless, restless to get back to Priscilla. All through his recounting of what had happened, his mind was in another place, with Priscilla in their home. Later, exhausted as he was, he could not sleep.

★ ★ ★

At noon the next day, John and Miles sailed into Ducksburrow Harbor. Together they walked the half-mile to the Standish home. They talked of Ducksburrow, their pride and plans for the settlement to become a town, with its own meeting house and school, independent of Plymouth. On reaching his house Miles called and Barbara rushed out, enveloping him in her voluptuous embrace and kisses.

John said goodbye, thanked Miles again and continued along the two-mile trek to his home. Through the copse he heard Zach barking and then there was Priscilla, flying to meet him, children hurrying behind; Elizabeth wearing her own goodwife's apron, Jack with his long manly stride, Joseph leaping cavorting, windmilling his arms as only Joseph could, and little Pris running, stumbling, running to keep up. His Priscilla and their children. He ran to her, held her close into his body and wept.

Chapter 66

August 1635

Turbulence

'This dreadful heat.' Priscilla talked aloud to herself. 'And so humid. Saps my energy, makes us all bad tempered.' She kneaded and thumped the bread dough. 'The one time I'd be happy to have a bake oven in the yard. I'll be glad when the day is done. Mind, nights aren't much better. Mustn't talk to myself like this. They'll think I'm mad. It's the heat.'

That night Priscilla lay awake, tossing and turning in sweat soaked linen whilst John lay breathing deeply, evenly, oblivious. The children were quiet, even baby Sarah close by in her cradle. Zach lay curled in his usual place on the floor at the foot of the bed. Priscilla dozed fitfully and eventually drifted into sleep.

'What?' she started awake. Zach was pacing, whining and growling softly deep down in his throat. The hair on the back of his neck bristled. 'Ssh – what is it, Zach?' she whispered. 'Settle down. Sit.' The dog tried to obey but couldn't. Then, of a sudden came a roar of wind thumping into the corner of the house. The timbers shook. The children, awake and frightened, ran to the safety of their parents' bed.

'Bad storm,' John said.

The wind didn't just howl and roar; it thumped and banged. Rain hammered against the walls like waves pummeling the deck of a ship. They heard a huge crack and splintering. Priscilla held her breath as a tree crashed to earth, its branches brushing the walls of the house.

'To the cellar,' John said.

Priscilla quickly gathered up blankets to keep them warm and guided the children to the cellar hatch. John went down the ladder first and then helped his children climb down into the dark, damp storeroom, to sit among sacks of turnips, parsnips and carrots. Priscilla came last carrying baby Sarah. John climbed back up to fetch Zach. 'Poor dog.' Shivering and whining, Zach sat on his master's lap.

'Will the house fall down?' Jack asked. 'We'll be buried alive if it does.' Another mighty crack and splintering crash.

'Hope the chimney stack holds,' John said. 'We're safer here than anywhere else. We can always climb through the rubble if need be.'

'Shall we sing?' Priscilla said.

In answer John sang, ''Twas in the month of Maying…' Priscilla joined, and then Elizabeth, Jack, Joseph and Pris. Eighteen-month-old Jonathan clapped. Priscilla and John sang every song and nursery rhyme they knew and started again, their children joining, not flagging, until they were so tired they dozed, in spite of the horrendous noise above. Hour after hour.

'Reminds me of the storms at sea.' Priscilla sat huddled beside John.

'Hmm. Only thing missing is the wind shrieking in the rigging. I never want to hear that sound again,' John said. He put his arm round Priscilla, pulling her close.

'Thanks to you we didn't go to the bottom,' she said.

He tapped her nose. 'You exaggerate, but thank you.'

'I must have dozed off.' Priscilla woke to silence. She nudged John. 'It's quiet. Is the storm over?'

John rubbed his eyes and emptied Zach off his lap. He climbed up and opened the hatch. Light. The children woke and eagerly scaled the ladder. Priscilla handed Zach up into John's arms. Then she passed up Sarah before climbing the ladder herself. 'Amazing! Everything is still standing.'

'Please may we go out,' Jack and Joseph clamored.

'We'll have a look before breakfast,' John said.

The front doorway was blocked by the branches of the beautiful old elm tree that had stood a little way to the southeast, torn up by its roots.

'The door to the garden.' Priscilla opened onto devastation. Through the limbs of a large branch she saw branches and bits of roofing strewn over her beds of vegetables, herbs and flowers. 'Oh no,' she wailed.

'At least the house is standing.' John stood beside her. The children were silent. 'You'd best cook up some breakfast while I get chopping.'

Happily, a few embers still glowed in the hearth and by the time Priscilla had got a blaze going and prepared hasty pudding and bean soup with pork, John had cleared a way out of the front door.

Bent double, John and Priscilla tunneled through the branches. The children followed. The sight was numbing. Trees down everywhere. Tall pines broken off in the middle, young oaks and walnut trees twisted and scoured. The biggest trees, like the elm, down with roots exposed. Priscilla stood stricken. 'It's as if they've been tortured.'

'We won't have to worry about a tree falling on our house in the future,' John said. 'They're all down now. Look how they're lying. Reckon the storm blew up from the southeast. It'll be headed Boston way. Give King Winthrop something to deal with.'

In the farmyard the barns were still intact, but the roof was off the pigsty and the chicken coop was blown to bits. Peering through branches, they saw the corn flattened in the fields, beaten down by the wind and rain.

'This wasn't just a storm,' John said. 'I reckon it was a hurricane like they have down in the Indies. Never seen anything like this before.'

Priscilla put her arm through John's. 'And you worked so hard to build our homestead.'

'Ah well – Praise God the house is unscathed,' John said. 'And mercifully my family are all in one piece. You too, Zach.' He bent down and stroked the dog standing by his leg. 'It'll take a while, sorting this lot. What I wouldn't give for a man servant to help. Our corn crop – at least it was ripe. Hope we can salvage some.'

The night of the day after the storm, as Priscilla and John stood by their door to bid the day farewell, there came a great eclipse of the moon.

'John.' Priscilla clutched his arm. 'What does it mean? These strange happenings: the insect plague and fever the year Jonathan was born, the terrible storm and now this. Are they portents? Warnings from God? I'm frightened.'

'I don't know. I'll be looking in on Elder Brewster tomorrow – see if he needs help. I'll ask him what he makes of it.'

'He'll probably say "It's God's will. Testing us." Seems to be the answer to everything,' Priscilla said. 'In any case there's nothing for it but to pick up the pieces and carry on. I hope we'll have enough left of our crops to last the winter.'

★ ★ ★

It was the close of the day, a cherished time; the children abed in the room the other side of the chimney, Priscilla and John sitting by the hearth in their rocking chairs with Zach and the two cats.

''Tis good now our place is back in order, and our neighbors' homes. Two whole months' hard labor but we've done it; harvest in, poor as it is, and enough firewood to last years.' John drew several draughts on his pipe, rocking gently. 'It **will** take years to log all the trees blown down.'

'Time to go blackberrying, and nutting,' Priscilla said, 'and pick the grapes top o' the field. A miracle the hornbeam didn't come down, its branches all twirled with vines – and think of the wine we'll make. Lovely stuff.'

'Hmm.' John blew a smoke ring. 'I've been talking with Standish. We reckon the time is right to go west and buy a good lot of land from Massasoit; enough for a farm. Massasoit is keen to sell; about twenty-five miles from here.'

'You'll be away.'

'Not for long. About a week.'

Priscilla stopped knitting. She looked at John. 'Are you sure it's right, we settlers buying so much land from the Indians, cheap, knowing they don't see owning the land as we do?'

John laid down his pipe and stood abruptly. 'Roger Williams again. Rue the day he ever came to Plymouth. Bradford is right. The man has a windmill in his head. Wish he'd stayed away with the Indians.'

Priscilla's cheeks flamed and her knitting needles flew. 'Bradford too says we shouldn't keep buying more and more land, and Hobbamock says as well, when the Indians sell us land they think they're only selling the use of it. They believe the land is for everyone to use, and care for. They don't understand that our way of owning means everyone else keep out, for evermore. Standish knows this.'

'Priscilla. This is fanciful talk.' John paced back and forth in front of the hearth. 'What would you have us do? What about our children?'

Disturbed by John's raised voice, Zach roused himself and stood, ear cocked, whining.

'It's alright, Zach. Lie down.' Two circles to the right, one circle to the left and a collapse into his sleeping position, head on paws. Lowering his voice, John continued. 'How are we to prosper and have lands to leave our children? The land is their future. Would you condemn them to a mean and miserable life of struggle? Don't you believe in our purpose? To build a new England? Why have we fought so hard? What for?' He stopped and stood looking down at Priscilla, her eyes cast down on her knitting. 'The Indians can learn **our** ways. Why shouldn't they? They want our guns. They need our corn. They can do as we do.'

An inner shudder ran through Priscilla. She stiffened so as not to let it show. What could she say? Nor did she have the heart. John was only doing his best. 'I'll not argue it,' she said. 'But I hope they stay peaceful.'

Sitting down again, John said, 'In any case there is a movement of Indians becoming Christian, in the praying towns, learning English. It is our destiny to prosper in this land and if I don't buy what I can, I'll be left out.'

'I can see that,' Priscilla said. She tried to shake off her feeling of foreboding, and decided to change the subject. 'I'll invite Susanna to come and stay while you're gone. My supplies of medicines are low and she is such a good help with that, and it is hard for her with Edward off in England securing more supplies, and two of their boys dead from the fever.' *And she'll more likely listen to me. I wish I'd not said anything. It's only upset John and spoiled our hour together.*

'Good plan,' John said. 'Folk tell me how they value your way with medicines, and with Ducksburrow growing you'll need plenty. Our Ducksburrow doctor.'

'I've had good teachers. Mother and Susanna.'

'Now come, lovely wife. To bed. Let me chase all your crazy thoughts away.'

Priscilla gave John her hand. 'Aye. And you will, husband. You always work magic on me.' *And then another child.*

Chapter 67

August – September 1635

No longer there

Priscilla stood at the barnyard fence as John and Standish, knapsacks on their backs, muskets in hand, crossed the harvested cornfield and disappeared into the forest. She stood in the early cool quiet, trying to shake herself out of the tremors of fear that John might not return; a fear that beset her every time he stayed away overnight. *I hope Susanna comes. She promised.* She walked across the farmyard; pigs rooting, chickens crowing and clucking, and Bessie and her daughter calling 'milk me'.

In the kitchen she found the children were up and dressed, ready to do their pre-breakfast chores: Elizabeth milking, Jack feeding the pigs and cleaning the pigsty, Joseph collecting eggs with Pris helping.

While they ate breakfast Priscilla addressed her troop. 'This week we're going to harvest berries to store and herbs and plants for medicines. Elizabeth, you know which flowers and herbs to pick. Jack and Joseph, blackberries, currants, cranberries and late strawberries. If there's still time you can shake the orchard but that can wait. Pris. What are you doing with those eggs?'

'Putting them in groups – counting.' Pris sat on the floor arranging the eggs in groups of four.

'Mind – you'll break them. Now fetch a basket to put them all in and then you'll help me with the cooking and sweeping.'

Pris did as she was bid, carefully placing the eggs in a basket. 'Please may I help Joseph and Jack pick berries? I don't like cooking.'

'No. You're five years old; time you learned to cook and we'll want to have the house clean and fresh and a good stew over the hearth for Susanna. Reminds me. Elizabeth, would you please bring enough hyssop to strew some on the floor. It does smell lovely, and Jack – juniper branches for the fire.'

'We're getting ready for Susanna, Susanna, Susanna!' Elizabeth led a chorus of excitement.

'I'll make a berry pie,' Priscilla said, 'top crust with white flour. Special treat.' Zach ran this way and that as if asking for a job to do. 'You mind little Jonathan, Zach. See he doesn't come to any harm.' Zach trotted over and stood by the toddling lad making for the table. *My word. He understands.*

The morning flew by. Priscilla drew her pie from the bake oven. *Does look good.* Baskets of berries and herbs rested on the tops of barrels of peas, beans and meal placed along the end wall. The floor was scrubbed, strewn with hyssop, and Priscilla's best cloth covered the table. Jack and Joseph staggered in with a large basket of juniper, and Elizabeth sorted and labeled the herbs. *She's learned well.* Priscilla watched her eldest with love and pride. She stepped across to the hearth to stir the stew, stooping to pick up Jonathan and carry him back to Elizabeth. 'Keep him with you. He's always crawling toward the hearth. Zach, you've gone from your...'

Zach stood in the doorway, bristling, ears forward, softly growling. He barked. Priscilla came to look, shading her eyes. Was it? Two figures; a woman and a man. She ran back, scooped up

Jonathan and ran down the path. 'Susanna! Oh, Susanna! And John Bradford.' She thrust Jonathan into John Bradford's arms and hugged Susanna as if to never let her go. Tears escaped. 'You're here.' She closed her eyes dissolving into the warmth and love of Susanna's strong arms. Then the children made their claim, the girls demanding hugs and kisses, Jack and Joseph, handshakes. Priscilla turned to John Bradford, clasping his arm. 'I'm so glad 'tis you brought her. You'll stay?'

'Thank you,' John said. 'Just for the night. We're still rebuilding after the storm. So much damage.'

After dinner Jack and Joseph led John Bradford all round the homestead before he set to cutting logs from fallen trees.

Priscilla, with Elizabeth helping, set out the baskets of herbs and flowers, pestles and mortars, jars, and linen for poultices. She settled Pris and Jonathan under the table, playing with the hessian dolls. 'Please mind Jonathan, Pris. Don't let him go near the hearth.'

'Those dolls have seen a thing or two,' Susanna said. 'Not many dolls can say they sailed across the ocean.'

'What a journey it's been,' Priscilla said. She pulled two stools by the table. 'Now sit down and tell me the news. How is life in Plymouth?'

'Trogs along.' Susanna ground sage leaves. 'First thing you should know is Roger Williams submitted his resignation, pending the council's decision.'

'No! Why?' Priscilla stopped mashing and looked at Susanna.

'He senses many in Plymouth don't like his ideas – which is true. But there are almost as many who do agree with his views, and value his open questioning way. Edward for one. And I.'

'I don't want him to leave. I cannot imagine a more helpful, kind teacher.' Priscilla sighed. 'But John doesn't like his views.'

'I know. Well, he will be going. The council was split, half for, half against. Elder Brewster decided it. Said Mr Williams stirred too much division.'

Priscilla sat motionless, staring. She'd been so relieved and happy when her teacher returned safely from his sojourn with the Indians. Although she could never have hours of instruction with him as before, it was good hearing him teach when they went to Plymouth on the Sabbath, and good knowing he was there.

'Priscilla?' Susanna put a hand on Priscilla's. 'I know you feel deeply for him. I'm sorry.'

'Where?' Priscilla asked.

'Where what?'

'Where is he going?'

'Says he aims to return to Salem. They want him back. You know he is against infant baptism. I reckon that was the last straw, on top of his insisting everyone should be free to worship as he feels is right.'

'It's his way of looking into things. Just sitting quiet and dwelling on a passage from the Bible, or a problem, to see the meaning,' Priscilla said.

'What you call "pondering"?'

'Yes. But with the endless work, no close neighbors to help with the children, without you, I never have time to ponder.'

'I've never been given to sitting quiet like that, doing nothing. I like being busy.'

A wail. Priscilla leapt up. In two strides she reached the hearth and grabbed Jonathan. She plunged his arm into a pail of cold water. 'Fetch a poultice, quick, Elizabeth. You know – rum, onion, cornmeal. I'm sure we have one left.'

Elizabeth moved almost as fast as her mother, opening the lid of the medicine chest. 'Two left.' She brought the poultice and a strip of linen.

'Now will you learn?' Priscilla scolded the whimpering boy. 'There, there. It'll feel better soon.' She softened as she bound the burn. *Praise God it isn't bad. Must have been a spark spit out onto his arm.* 'Bring a piece of cornbread, Elizabeth. Take his mind off it.' She handed Jonathan into Elizabeth's care and shakily made her way to the table. 'Pris, I told you to mind him. What were you doing?'

'I'm sorry, Mother. Making a house for the dolls.' Priscilla looked and saw juniper and hyssop twigs arranged as walls; upended beakers and bowls served as tables and chairs.

'But I told you to watch Jonathan. He could have been badly burned. You are a naughty child. Go sit in the corner until I say.' Priscilla put her head in her hands. 'Can't leave off watching him for a second. Can't even have a conversation with you and I hardly ever see you now.' She wiped her eyes.

'It's hard for you here – alone. No one to help look after the little ones.' Susanna took Priscilla's hands in hers and gave a squeeze. 'It's hard for the children too. Having no one close by to be friends. Mind, they are good. Helping all they can.'

'Except sometimes,' Priscilla said, looking over to where Pris sat on a stool in the corner, her back to them, shoulders shaking.

'Poor little lass,' Susanna said. 'Shall I…?'

'Leave her be. She's got to learn.'

'You'll be needing more poultices.' Susanna placed her hands flat on the table, and pushing herself upright, went to the strings of onions looped on the wall and twisted off five. 'Nice looking onions. I'll get chopping.'

Jonathan was still whimpering, trying to tear off the poultice. 'Give him a few drops of St John's wort oil and a small cup of chamomile tea,' Priscilla instructed Elizabeth. 'It'll ease the pain and make him drowsy.' She joined Susanna chopping onions and soon there was a hefty pot simmering over the fire.

'Do you see Barbara Standish often?' Susanna asked as they took up pestles and mortars again.

'Only from time to time, usually if one of their children is poorly. Brought their lad Alexander the other day. He had a cough; his hair was dry, skin pasty, dark circles under his eyes. Had a listless way about him. I dosed him with syrup of tansy and sure enough, he retched up an enormous long tapeworm.'

'That is shocking,' Susanna said.

'Hmm. She's kind hearted; a warm snugly sort of mother. Reckon she means well – but – always coming here for remedies. I don't think she ever has any of her own,' Priscilla said.

'Dangerous.' Susanna pounded harder. 'Sounds like you're the doctor here.'

'Aye, as you are in Plymouth with Dr Fuller gone, and your two lads. I'm so sorry.'

Susanna shook her head. 'That fever. Is it two years since? So strange. First the plague of those horrid insects, big as bumblebees, came from the forest, filled our houses and fields, day and night. The Indians warned that following the insects the fever would come. Sure enough, in the hottest months it hit.'

'We were lucky to be spared up here,' Priscilla said. 'How is it the Indians always seem to know?'

'They've lived in these parts so long – we're new. Don't know the ways of this strange land,' Susanna said. She stopped mashing sage leaves and put a hand on Priscilla's arm. 'I have a special piece of news. Edward has decided to move near here, in Marshfield.'

Priscilla jumped up and clapped her hands. 'Praise be! Only five miles from here; an easy walk. But why not in Ducksburrow?'

'Not sure. Edward reckons Ducksburrow will soon grow much bigger than now. Many in Plymouth are chafing at the church's strict ways and they also want more fertile land than is available in the old colony. I'm wondering if he wants to be more remote for protection against the spread of diseases like that fever.' Susanna scraped her mashed leaves into a bowl and replenished her pestle. 'I do know he wants to build a large estate with a manor house to be called "Careswell", like the one he left behind in England. Trouble is, he is so often away.' She stared at the door. 'How I miss him and when he sails for England I always fear he'll not return. And of course he isn't here to supervise the building. My own two lads will do most of the work, but they aren't skilled, so I fear it will take forever.' She looked over at Pris, still seated on a stool in the corner. 'Surely…'

'Aye.' Priscilla addressed her daughter's back. 'You can come back now, Pris, but you must try harder to be helpful.'

Her face streaked with tears, Pris walked slowly across the room and stood beside her mother. 'I promise I'll try harder.' She hiccupped a sob.

'Clear up the mess under the table and then you may go see if Elizabeth needs help before prayers and supper.'

'Yes, Mother.'

It was the last night of Susanna's visit.

'I wish you could stay longer,' Priscilla said. She and Susanna sat in the two rocking chairs by the hearth, knitting and mending. 'You've been a wonderful help, with the garden, the children, and my medicine chests are full, ready for the winter.' She stood and put another log and branch of juniper on the fire, and paused, taking in the picture of Susanna, head bowed over the mending, fingers moving quickly and deftly.

Susanna looked up. 'It has been a joy for me, being here. I know it's lonely for you, so far away, but for me it's been a welcome release from all the gossip and interfering in one another's affairs. And to have time with you, Priscilla, and your lovely, lively children – oh, I've loved it.'

'I've not felt so peaceful and happy since we came here; the chance to confide, discuss, talk of womanly things. I miss you terribly.' Priscilla sat down again.

'I'd bide longer if I could,' Susanna said, 'but four days was all my older lads could manage, even with Howland's and Hopkins' wives helping.'

Priscilla put a hand to her brow. 'I want to remember all my questions before Francis comes to fetch you tomorrow. The minute you've gone I'll think of something.' She tried to be cheerful, to push away the encroaching sadness. 'Oh – here's a curious complaint.' She carried on knitting. 'A young woman came along wanting to speak privately. She was weaning her first babe and I thought it would be a problem with her breasts or underparts.' She looked over to Susanna. 'But no. She wanted a remedy to bring her to full pleasure when...'

'I know,' Susanna said. 'Because we're told from the day our bleeding starts that we won't conceive unless we have full pleasure.'

'The poor thing was in tears over it. Said her husband is frustrated and angry with her. But the strange thing is, she had conceived even without...'

'I've heard of this before. What did you do?'

'I gave her a jar of very dilute lavender water.' Priscilla put her knitting down. 'And maybe this was wrong, but I told her that to keep her husband happy she should pretend, and gave her a few hints. I told her she is probably very fertile and we had a laugh.'

Susanna chuckled. 'Clever advice. Do you know if it worked?'

'I know she conceived again, with or without full pleasure. And she hasn't asked for any more lavender water.'

After a quiet few moments, Priscilla said, 'I have a thought. Is it alright if I ask John to gather some men and help work on Careswell? So you could move up here sooner?'

'I didn't want to ask. I would be so grateful, but only if he can spare the time. I know he's very busy with meetings and court sessions in Plymouth.'

'Good. I feel better already. I know John will want to do everything he can.'

'Priscilla, I couldn't ask for a better friend. Thank you. Edward will be grateful too, I'm sure.' Susanna folded the mending and laid it aside. She stepped over beside Priscilla and bent to kiss her cheek. 'Time for bed I think.'

Zach barked and danced, pulling at Priscilla's skirt. She obediently followed him to the front door to see Francis bounding through the copse. Recognizing his first master, Zach went into joyful contortions of barking, jumping, twisting, not settling until Francis bent down to stroke him and say 'Hello'.

'Just in time for dinner,' Priscilla laughed, hugging him.

'I've got some splendid news but I want Susanna to hear it too.' His grey eyes twinkled and he hopped a step or two in anticipation. 'There she is.'

Susanna hurried along the track, carrying baby Sarah.

Francis exploded. 'Sheep – we have sheep! At last!'

'Oh joy! How?' Susanna and Priscilla chorused.

'Bought them from the Dutch down in New Amsterdam. Arrived in Plymouth yesterday. Forty. Fine looking animals.'

'John and Miles will be cock-a-hoop,' Priscilla laughed.

'Susanna,' Francis put an arm round her shoulder. 'Your little ones are all well and eager to have their mother home again.'

'Praise God. Thank you, Francis.' Susanna tilted her head, smiling up at him.

'This is a splendid meal, Mistress Alden. Splendid.' Francis rested his spoon on his trencher and put his hands in his lap.

'Thank you, Francis,' Priscilla said. 'It is so good to have you here. I miss you.'

Francis cleared his throat. 'I have more news.'

'Oh?' Priscilla responded with a questioning frown.

'I'm to wed.'

'Congratulations!' Priscilla relaxed into a grin.

'We've decided to move to Yarmouth.'

'Yarmouth! That's miles and miles away.' Priscilla stood and went to the hearth to hide her shock. 'I always thought, hoped, you would move here.'

'Aye,' Francis said. 'That was my intention, before. But with every year the governor and his assistants become more strict; pass more laws against this, against that. A fellow can hardly turn round without having a fine slapped on him. Ducksburrow isn't far enough away, especially with Prence thinking to move here.'

'Oh Francis. That it should come to this.' Priscilla returned to the table and slumped down onto her stool. 'I've missed you... known you since...'

Francis stood, came round behind her and put his hands on her shoulders. 'You've been like a mother, or the best older sister, encouraging, taught me my letters; Mr Alden too. Believed me when I found the sea. Always kind, both of you.' He sighed and paced. 'But I can't take it any more, being within reach of Prence's spying eye. Hopkins is coming too. Yarmouth'll be the place for us renegades.'

'Can't say I blame you,' Susanna said.

Priscilla tried to be brave when she said goodbye to Susanna and Francis.

'Come again soon.' She squeezed Susanna's hands and kissed her cheek. 'Good fortune be with you, my renegade.' She hugged the young man, feeling she was bidding a son farewell, probably forever.

'Thank you.' Francis' voice was husky. 'For everything.'

Priscilla waved to their backs until she could no longer see them. Feeling weighed down by a heavy emptiness she said brightly to her children, 'We'll harvest squash this afternoon.'

Walking slowly across the fields, basket in one hand, holding Jonathan's hand in the other, she bowed her head, thinking of Susanna, and of Francis and Roger Williams, both leaving Plymouth. No longer there.

1637-1645

Chapter 68

Spring 1637

The Pequot War

Sitting on her milking stool, Priscilla leaned her head against Bessie's side, hoping that the rhythm of milking would calm her nerves, push her fears away. She had wanted to savor this fresh sweet smelling day; there wouldn't be many more before the heat of summer set in. But she was frightened and angry. Late afternoon, another day gone and still John hadn't returned. Why couldn't Bradford stand up to Winthrop? He had given in to the Boston governor's demand for a troop from Plymouth to join in an attack on the Pequot Indians. So, although Plymouth had no quarrel with the Pequot, John had dutifully joined the military company. He could be killed, or horribly wounded.

Ruth's hungry yelling roused her. She got to her feet and carried her pail indoors. Pris stood rocking the cradle.

'Come little bundle, number seven.' She gathered the babe to her breast and sat rocking as Ruth sucked, frantic at first, then relaxing into a peaceful rhythm. Elizabeth pulled a batch of cornbread from the bake oven. Then she checked the stew and stirred the beans.

'You are good,' Priscilla said, as her daughter laid out the trenchers, spoons and beakers. Jack and Joseph carried in logs to keep the fire going during the night.

'Will Father be home soon?' Jonathan asked. 'I want to show him the baby lamb. A surprise.'

'I don't know. He said there was so much to do in Plymouth, so many cases brought to the court, he could be gone a long time.' Priscilla had decided she would not tell the children their father was sent to fight the Indians. 'Gather round and we'll say prayers. Elizabeth – you read – there's a marker where we finished this morning.'

By the time Jack had said a closing prayer, asking for Father to come safely home, Ruth was asleep.

'Now we can eat,' Priscilla said as she tucked her babe into the cradle. 'Dark already. And the wolves – every night and dawn – never stop.' She shuddered. Zach bristled and growled. 'It's alright, Zach. They're far away.' She stroked the dog's head, felt his velvety ears and gave him a pat. He settled. 'This is a splendid stew, Elizabeth. Delicious.' She ate eagerly.

'Were there wolves in the old country?' Jack asked.

'No. I grew up in a town. So did your father, although a different town to me. Wolves didn't come into the towns. But women and children all stayed indoors after dark anyway. A town crier would walk up and down the streets with a lantern, crying out the hour and "All's well". There weren't wolves but thieves might have been about and there were poor vagrants coming in from the country, starving because they had no work.'

'Why? We have too much work,' Joseph said.

'Farmers were changing from crops to sheep. Wool fetched more money and as you know, caring for sheep doesn't need as many folk as planting and tending crops. So the workers had no jobs, no money to buy food. They came into the town begging and sometimes broke into houses to steal food.'

'Poor people. That is terrible,' Elizabeth said.

'Yes. Hard times. One of the reasons my father decided to come to this new land.'

'Tell us the story of sailing on the *Mayflower*,' Jack said. He pretended to be the ship's captain. 'Hoist the sails. Weigh the anchor. All hands.'

'That is for another evening. Time for bed.' Fleetingly, in Jack, Priscilla saw the face of her young brother, Joseph.

Later, as she sat knitting by the firelight, listening to the wolves, Priscilla thought of Joseph, so keen and lively, so proud of learning seamanship from Master Jones.

Next day, around midday, Priscilla sat spinning while Elizabeth prepared dinner. Zach, in his usual position by the door, cocked his ears and growled softly, then leapt into his welcoming dance. Pris clapped, Jonathan yelled, Sarah waved her arms about and Elizabeth laughed.

'It's your father. Let Zach go, Elizabeth. We'll follow. Call Jack and Joseph.' Her babe in one arm, lifting her skirts with the other hand, Priscilla hurried, looking out for roots and stones as her children ran ahead and behind.

'Father, Father!' Jack and Joseph sprinted toward the tall figure, approaching quickly with his long, loping stride.

Then she and the babe were in John's arms, her face held in his hands, receiving kisses. He stepped back.

'How's the little one?' He tenderly stroked Ruth's cheek. She gurgled and latched onto his proffered finger.

'She's glad to see you,' Priscilla said. 'Praise be you're back safe.'

As Zach led the procession to the house, Jonathan hopped up and down, pulling on his father's tunic. 'Please come – come see our surprise.' John tousled his son's hair.

'We'll all come,' Priscilla said.

Jonathan pulled John by the hand, out the back door, through the farmyard and into the sheep's field. He ran to a wobbly legged lamb that was pulling on its mother's udder. 'Just born – only two days,' he said, gently stroking its back.

'Fine work,' John said. 'Did the ewe do it herself or did she need help?'

'She needed help,' Priscilla said. 'A breach. Elizabeth brought it out.' She put an arm round her daughter. 'She'll be a fine midwife, she will.' She saw admiration and fatherly pride in John's eyes and the look of a man recognizing that his daughter was becoming a young woman, a beautiful young woman.

Priscilla put her arm through John's as they walked back to the house. Elizabeth hurried ahead, keeping up with two-year-old Sarah, by now quick and agile on her feet.

'Our eldest is growing up fine,' John said. 'Won't be many more years 'til she's courted.'

After dinner, Elizabeth took Pris and Sarah into the garden; Jack and Joseph set off to collect brushwood, Jonathan tagging along behind. Ruth slept in her cradle.

Hand in hand, John and Priscilla walked through the farmyard to the orchard. 'A beautiful sight,' John said, 'apple and plum trees in full blossom, blue sky.'

Priscilla leaned against her husband. 'I've been so afraid. Are you really safe and well? Not wounded? Seems a miracle.'

'Aye. I'm as fit as when I left, because we arrived too late to fight. But not too late to watch the carnage.' John drew a hand across his eyes. 'I'm not sure I should tell you of it.'

'You must. I'll give you no peace until you do.'

'Come. We'll sit on your bench.'

Seated, holding Priscilla's hand, he took a deep breath. 'The Indians were all gathered in their encampment, believing there was an agreement that women and children would be safe, spared. Winthrop's men surrounded the encampment and attacked, setting fire to their wigwams, shooting, hacking the Indians to pieces. Wind fanned the flames; the place was an inferno. Poor creatures burned to death. The screams, the stench.

Priscilla gasped.

'Are you alright?'

She nodded. 'Go on.'

'We left immediately and by the time we'd sailed back to Plymouth, Bradford had received a report from Winthrop. He related that about four hundred Indians perished; more burned to death than were killed with swords, rapiers, or were hacked to death with tomahawks. About as many as perished were taken prisoner; men and boys to be shipped to slavery in the West Indies; women and children to be divided among Winthrop's soldiers. When he'd finished reading, Bradford offered a prayer of thanksgiving to God for a "sweet sacrifice" which brought a speedy and complete victory. Prence said "Hear! Hear! Thanks be to God." His cheer was met with silence. Even Standish seemed shaken.'

'It's atrocious,' Priscilla said. 'The cruelty and the betrayal. The Indians trusted their women and children would be safe.' She choked. 'Unbearable.'

John put an arm round her shoulder. 'I didn't want to tell you. I shouldn't have.'

'No. You did right. I wanted to know the truth of it; not be spared.'

'The day before this slaughter the Pequot were the most powerful tribe on these shores. There goes another source of trade, you can be sure. Like what happened after Wessagussett.' John rested his elbows on his knees and stared at the ground. 'The Indians inflict horrible tortures but they don't kill hundreds at once and they honor their promises. It was a dastardly thing to do. Dread to think what will come of it.'

John and Priscilla sat awhile without speaking. From the farmyard came the sounds of pigs grunting, the cock crowing, the goat bleating and Elizabeth ordering her siblings.

'She's only thirteen and already the little house mistress. Runs our household as well as I do,' Priscilla said.

'This is a good place,' John said.

'Aye, and we have good neighbors.'

'So far, but Prence says he aims to move here.'

'Francis said as much two years back. I was hoping perhaps it wouldn't happen.'

'Thanks be for Standish. He'll keep him under control.' John stood, took Priscilla's hands and pulled her to her feet. 'Work to be done.'

Chapter 69

Spring 1638

Submerged agitation

Priscilla pulled an apple bough to her face, breathing in the scent, caressing her cheek with the delicate blossom, gazing deep into the perfectly formed pale pink flower. The day was soft with a gentle heat in spite of the noon day hour, and a quiet breeze stirred her hair. She looked across the fields, some freshly planted with corn, pumpkin, beans and squash; others with barley, rye, wheat, peas; reaching up to the forest. *A fine achievement. Must take a hoe and begin weeding this afternoon.*

What? Who? A lone woman appeared at the edge of the forest and hurried across the fields, away to the left of their land. *A woman alone in the forest? Surely not. Far too dangerous. Strange.* Priscilla made her way back through the orchard, keeping an eye out for fallen twigs – good for kindling. Without knowing why, she decided not to tell John about the woman.

As she walked into the kitchen she jumped. 'John! Husband!'

He stood by the table, a wild beast draped round the back of his neck. 'What is that? I never heard Zach bark. Where is he?'

Jack and Joseph burst in. 'Zach ran off. We were gathering groundnuts by the hornbeam. Zach got a scent and wouldn't come when we called.'

'First time he's done that,' John said. 'I'll have to give him a thrashing.'

Priscilla cringed and went to call Elizabeth and the younger children from the garden.

John laid his burden on the butchering table.

'Father, what is that creature?' Jack tentatively poked at it.

When the rest of his brood came in John addressed his excited audience.

'This is a wildcat. First one I've managed to shoot. And I'll tell you how. These beasts know how to hunt geese. They come into the marshes. See this bobtail?' He flicked the short tail. 'Looks just like the neck of a goose. It hides down in the reeds and sticks its tail up. A goose flying over thinks it's another goose, flies in to land, and whoosh! The cat's on it and our dinner is gone.'

'Horrid beast,' Joseph said.

'Well, this creature didn't fool me. I crouched down low and crept along, bit by bit. Within range I stopped and waited. Sure enough, a goose flew down, the cat sprang and I got 'im.' John crescendoed in triumph and punched the air.

'Hooray. Hooray.' Even stately Elizabeth joined in the chorus. Amidst their cheering, they heard the distant sound of an animal howling, yelping.

'Is it Zach?' Priscilla dashed out the door. 'Oh Zach. Poor dog.' Zach ran to her, yelping and pawing at his nose, studded with porcupine quills. John pinned their dog between his knees and held his head while, as gently as she could, Priscilla pulled out the quills one by one with her tongs. The children watched, rapt, and when the operation was over, comforted and petted their canine friend as he whimpered, turning in circles, not knowing what to do with himself, until he flopped down by the hearth, head in his paws, gazing at them mournfully.

'Guess he doesn't need a thrashing,' John said. 'Reckon that was punishment enough.'

After dinner the children went about their chores. Priscilla sat at the table with her pestle and mortar to grind medicinal herbs and seeds, having settled Sarah underneath to play with the hessian dolls. John was sharpening the butchering knife and hatchet, to skin and butcher the wildcat.

'Good meat I'm told,' he said.

'Tell me the news,' Priscilla said. 'I want to know all the gossip.'

John drew breath, keeping his eyes focused on parting the pelt from the spine. 'The first thing was the task of writing to Roger Williams.'

'Oh?'

'You know he went to Salem after here. Well, Salem belongs to Massachusetts Bay and, as you can imagine, Winthrop did not like Williams' ideas influencing the folk of Salem; said he must go. But if he stopped preaching he could stay until spring.'

Priscilla stopped grinding her herbs. She sat still, eyes on John.

'But Williams carried on preaching regardless, and Winthrop threatened to send him back to England.'

Priscilla caught her breath, John looked up, and then down again, resuming his bloody task. 'So Williams fled. Left wife and children behind in Salem and fled into the wilderness. Survived three months – God knows how – helped by Indians I suppose. Speaks their language.'

'Heavens above.' Priscilla paled and lowered her face, resuming her pestle and mortar work.

'He is now starting a settlement with a few followers on a piece of land belonging to Plymouth – up near Massasoit's place. Bradford said, and we all agreed, that our relations with Massachusetts Bay would be compromised by him being there. So Winslow has written asking him to move on – with our good wishes.'

'Oh really. That does take the cake!' Priscilla saw John's hand tremble. His wrist flicked in spasm. He didn't look up and paused to get a firmer grip.

'I feel sorry for the man,' John said. 'But why didn't he stop preaching for a time, before the spring? Would have saved all that hardship – and think of his wife and children. Just left – not knowing if he was dead or alive.'

Priscilla sat still, staring at John. 'Brewster, Bradford and Winslow didn't stop preaching when King James threatened. They fled. Brewster was always in hiding, leaving Mary and the children behind, not knowing.'

John stopped and looked at his wife. His face colored. 'It's not the same. Our leaders had an established sect – large following. They'd formed a doctrine of their own. Williams is a loner with some daft ideas and a few crazy followers.'

Priscilla put aside her pestle and mortar to grasp the table. The room swam. *Don't argue any more. Get steady. He's only just come home.* She focused her eyes on her mortar and breathed deeply. Ruth began to cry. As she stood, she said, 'That's a lovely lot of meat you've cut up.'

John wiped his hands and the knife. As he scoured the butchering bench he said, 'I'll go and check my fences. A man in Plymouth had his pigs and sheep mauled by wolves. His fences weren't high enough. Need to be five feet. Wolves can't jump that high. Then he let his dog go for the wolves and they tore it to bits. Stupid man.'

'It's a blessing you know what you're doing.' Priscilla rocked as she fed the babe.

'Aye. We've seven mouths to feed now. And all healthy, thanks to my skillful hardworking wife.' Priscilla looked up and smiled as John came and kissed her forehead.

Throughout the afternoon and evening Priscilla absently performed chores, absently responded to the children and John. Distraught, she wondered, *Where will Roger Williams go? What will happen to him? I wish he could live close by.* Putting the children to bed she told herself she must not be so distracted. Perhaps hearing of other happenings would help. John settled himself in his rocker, lit his pipe and crossed his legs. Zach settled himself on his master's floor-bound foot. The two cats curled up on either side of the hearth.

'I'll give the stew a final stir,' Priscilla said. She stepped up near the fire, taking a long handled stirring stick. Round and round she stirred. The broth, with bits of fowl and venison, became a whirlpool, drawing her into its center. She stared as the dark liquid became the sea with bits of flesh and flotsam floating round and round – which transformed into Dorothy's face – light brown hair floating out, frightened wide-open gray eyes. Then Catherine Carver's thin elegant features, rich dark hair, sad brown eyes – and Roger Williams' strong earnest face, drawing her in.

'Priscilla! I'm telling you the news – you're not listening. What is the matter?' John's sharp tone broke through.

She started. 'Ah, just, just…' The stew was a stew again.

'Are you alright? You're pale. Are you ailing?' John leaned forward, as to stand.

'Don't get up. I'm fine. Just drifted for a minute. Sorry. I do want to know everything the council discussed.' Priscilla moved slowly, trying to disguise her inner trembling. She seated herself in her rocker and took up her knitting.

John wiped his brow and drew on his pipe. He crossed his legs, frowning slightly.

'Nothing very bad, I hope?' Priscilla said.

'A case of murder. A man from Plymouth and three indentured servants, returning from a trading expedition, came upon a lone Indian. They attacked him, took his wampum belt and left him for dead. But the Indian lived a few days – long enough to describe the men who fell on him. The question is, should the attackers hang?'

'What do you think?'

'I think they should. It was a dastardly thing to do – and there's fear of the Indians deciding to avenge him, especially after the Pequot carnage.'

'I agree,' Priscilla said.

'It will be decided at the court session in two weeks. The other major item was a letter from that crazy woman, Anne Hutchinson, the woman tried and excommunicated – exiled from Boston.'

'What was her crime?'

John cleared his throat and leaned forward. He looked down and stroked Zach. Priscilla stopped knitting.

'She – behaved like a man.'

'What? How?'

'She preached a different doctrine. She challenged the minister and magistrates. She drew followers like a magnet. She dominated her husband. She challenged the governor! She reckoned her mind and thoughts were the equal of any man's.'

Priscilla said nothing and resumed her knitting. After a minute or two she spoke, her voice quiet, 'Do you remember, John, before we married, 'twas when we were trysting in the storeroom.' She smiled at him.

John leaned back. 'I remember,' he said, and drew a hand though his hair.

'You said then that you liked a woman to speak her mind – and her husband would do well to listen.'

John leaned forward again. His face tensed, cheekbones set. 'I still hold by that. But she has to keep her ideas in the house, for her husband and perhaps her children. She has to defer to her husband. It's God's law, Priscilla. You know that. It's not God's will for a woman to go against a man.'

Priscilla felt a burning in her chest. She brushed a hand across her hot cheeks. 'What was in the letter?'

'She settled with her family and some followers on land she thought belonged to Plymouth – was asking permission to stay there. But it isn't our land so we wrote to say Plymouth has no objection.'

Priscilla decided to say nothing more. Her knitting needles gained speed.

'There's a good piece of news,' John said. 'Ducksburrow has been granted town status. We are a town in our own right – only in law responsible to Plymouth.'

'Well done, John. You've worked so hard for that – and with our own meeting house, tavern and trading house – and lots more people – so we should be a town.' Priscilla put away her knitting. 'I'll give Ruth a last feed before bed.' Lifting the babe from the cradle she kept her manner composed. Inwardly, her mind and feelings churned. *Anne Hutchinson. What a woman! I wish I could meet her.*

Chapter 70

Summer 1638

Mary Mendome

The next two weeks flew past. Priscilla felt contented during this time, when she, John and the children all worked hard; in the garden and fields, keeping domestic life in its rhythm. John often went hunting, sometimes taking Jack with him. Priscilla used some of these hours to give Elizabeth and Pris practice with their reading and writing.

'Here, Pris. I know you like the almanac, with its numbers.' Priscilla set the big book in front of her daughter. 'You have the slate and pencil.' She then took her gardening book from the book box. 'For you, Elizabeth, you can kill two birds with one stone.' She set out quills, ink and parchment for her eldest.

'Mother, couldn't I copy from *Hamlet* instead? Jack has read it twice and he's only twelve.'

Priscilla paused. 'I suppose so. But you'd best not speak of it. Women are supposed to use our knowledge for the home.' She gave

Elizabeth the small volume, with a mixture of pleased pride and misgivings. Elizabeth eagerly opened the book at the page where there was a marker. 'Why is there a marker here?'

'Perhaps Jack wanted to come back to that place.'

Elizabeth read a passage aloud. '"This above all, to thine own self be true, And it must follow\as the night the day\Thou canst not be false to any man." Mother, this is beautiful. "To thine own self be true…" What does it mean? Is it the same as when Mr Williams says to look to your own conscience for the way to God's will?'

Priscilla stared over Elizabeth's blond head. She saw Catherine Carver, weak, nearing death, handing her the book, reading aloud, '"To thine own self…" This is for you. With my Bible.'

'We can't discuss it now. Just do your copying – it will soon be time for dinner.'

★ ★ ★

Next morning John departed for Plymouth; another session on the magistrates' court. After dinner Priscilla left Elizabeth to mind the house and went to the orchard. She needed time to think. *Where is Elizabeth heading? Question after question she asks. John will worry if he knows. What should I do? I admire her wish to learn but I fear where it might take her.* She looked up into the plum trees. Blossom gone. She pulled a branch down to inspect. *Ah, the tiny fruits beginning to form – and soon there will be the first signs of grapes on the vines.* Looking up toward the hornbeam, host to the vines, she started. An Indian – a brave – standing by the tree. As if alerted by her gaze he disappeared. *Why? What is going on? Please God, don't let it be trouble. Not while John is away.* She hurried back to the house.

Elizabeth and all the children were working in the garden and farmyard. Even little Sarah. *Good. They're all safe.* Baby Ruth stirred. Time for her feed. Priscilla settled with the babe at her breast. All was quiet. *Why do I feel so on edge? Zach is here.* The trusty dog, curled up by the hearth, twitched an ear as if he'd read her thoughts. By the time she'd fed Ruth and changed her linen, Priscilla reckoned, seeing how low the sun was in the sky, it was mid-afternoon. She lifted the cloth covering a large bowl of bread dough. Proved – ready for baking.

Flouring her hands she tipped the dough onto the table. 'Gather, pull, down and push.' She hummed. 'Gather, pull, down and push...'

Hammering on the door. A woman's voice. 'Help, please quick, help.'

Dusting her hands on her apron, Priscilla dashed to open the door.

A young woman, distraught, hands clasped in pleading, gasped, 'Please, please hide me – they're after me.'

'Come in. I'll hide you in the cellar.' Priscilla shut the door on the distant shouting of men's voices. Zach growled. She pulled the woman by the arm to the hatch and wrenched it open. 'Stay down there.' She closed the hatch, and heaving and pushing, rotated a barrel of cornmeal into place to cover it and spread some branches of hyssop all around. She wiped the sweat from her brow, dabbed her hot cheeks with a little dilute lavender water, and resumed her kneading. Tense with listening she worked the dough. *Perhaps they won't think to come here. Why should they? Gather, pull, down and push...* Zach growled low in his throat, cocked his head to one side, listening. 'Hush, Zach,' Priscilla commanded. A stave battered the door. Zach at her side, Priscilla opened the door a crack. A man's ugly whiskery face pressed close to her. Stinking breath. She cringed backwards. 'What do you want?'

'Lookin' for me poor dear wife,' he said. 'Gone missing an I'm afeard for 'er. Afeard some Indian carried 'er off.'

'I've seen no one,' Priscilla said.

The man peered over her head into the room and pushed the door with one arm, shoving Priscilla aside with the other. Zach lunged, digging his teeth into the man's calf. He yelled, swore, kicked and tried to beat the dog with his stave. Baby Ruth wailed.

'I told you, I've seen no one. Now be gone.'

'Call your dog off – call 'im off,' he screeched. 'I'll go.'

'Here, Zach.'

Zach obeyed and withdrew his teeth, growling, hackles up.

'Go, or I'll set him on you again.'

Moaning and swearing, blood dripping from his leg, the man limped off, using his stave as a cane.

'Come, Zach,' Priscilla called. Still growling, her protector reluctantly left his post and came indoors. Priscilla slammed the door shut and pulled the latch through to the inside. She soothed her crying babe. 'There, there – quiet now.' When the wails subsided and Zach had stopped growling she stood still and listened. Mercifully the children hadn't heard. She looked out the back door and spied their shapes at the far end of the garden near the maple grove. Back to uncover the hatch. Push, turn, shove; barrel back against the wall, hyssop branches taken away, she opened the hatch and helped the ashen faced, trembling woman up into the room.

'Sit down,' Priscilla said. 'Here, at the table. I'll fetch you a beaker of ale.' She gave the woman a drink. 'Who are you? What is this all about? Are you the woman I've seen crossing the fields?'

Opposite her sat a slim, fine featured young woman. Deep blue eyes, black curls escaping from her coif. Priscilla noticed her hair had a healthy sheen and her skin was fair. Even in her distraught state, licking her lips, twisting her hands distractedly, she was beautiful.

'Yes, I am Mary Mendome.' Unable to sit still, she stood, walked a few steps one way and back again. 'My husband. He is a brute. He beats me. If you could see my back.' She sat down again and looked at Priscilla. 'One day I happened to call in on Mistress Standish, delivering a few items from the store, and I met Tinsin, one of Massasoit's braves, Hobbamock's son. It was instant. We both knew. Hobbamock knew.' She hugged herself, arms round her waist, stood and paced again, unable to keep even her head still, looking up and from side to side. 'We trysted in the forest. He built us our own little house.' She sobbed. 'So sweet. He's good, and gentle and kind. He put healing ointments on my wounds; took me to meet his squaw and daughters and they were friendly and caring.'

'My dear,' Priscilla stood and put an arm around her shoulder. 'I am so sorry. But you must be quick.'

'My husband got suspicious, came searching with a troop of men and dogs. Tinsin heard them long before I did. We ran, crisscrossing streams to confuse the hounds. He brought me to the edge of your fields and said to come here, because you are good, kind people. He also said to run in all different directions to fool the dogs.'

'You've done well. You are a strong, brave lass. But you mustn't stay here. And you must not tell **anyone** you were here,' Priscilla said. She hurriedly fetched a basket of berries she'd picked that morning. 'Take this, try to calm yourself, and behave as if you've been innocently picking berries all morning. Be nice to your wicked husband and give him whatever he wants. God bless you.' She kissed Mary's check and escorted her out the door. Tears coursed down her own cheeks as she watched the young woman hurrying away down the track. She wiped her face, closed the door and started to tremble, shaking, shivering as if with a fever. *What have I done? What have I done? Harbored a woman who has lain with an Indian. If I'm found out it will be the end of us here. We'd be exiled for sure and they'd probably whip me. But I couldn't turn her away. I couldn't.* Her heart was thumping. She felt dizzy. She sat on a stool and put her head down to her knees. When the dizziness cleared she walked slowly to the barrel of ale and poured a beaker. She made her way to her rocker, and lowering herself, leant against the supportive high back. Slowly she sipped the ale. Gradually the shaking subsided and her heart quietened. She knew she was ashen from the cold sweat on her brow. Zach sat by her knee, whimpering. 'Good dog,' she said stroking him. 'Good dog.' Resting her head against the high back of the rocker, she closed her eyes and waited for her strength to return.

'Mother! Are you aright, what happened?' Elizabeth's cry roused her. Her daughter came beside her and put a hand on her brow. ''Tis cold and damp.'

'Ah, 'tis nothing,' Priscilla said. 'I just had a funny turn.'

On the morrow, late afternoon, Priscilla went again to the orchard and looked up to the forest. *Not a sign of anyone and it has been quiet all day. Perhaps the whole thing has blown over. I pray so.* As she walked back toward the house, Zach came running to her, whining, bristling. He tugged at her skirt. 'What is it, Zach?' She hurried after him, fear mounting. Then she heard what Zach had heard before her. A low rumbling noise, as the ground began to shake. She ran, calling to the children but they were ahead of her, in the house huddled together under the table. They'd even pulled the cradle under. Dishes crashed off the shelves, the barrels of meal and peas and beans danced and bounced. As in the hurricane, Priscilla and her children and Zach climbed down into the cellar and waited until the sound of falling objects ceased and the house was steady and quiet. Cautiously they climbed out and set to replacing fallen utensils and dishes. Then came another rumbling and shaking, not so fierce or prolonged as the first. Dishes wobbled but remained on the shelves. On inspecting the farmyard they found only the chicken house was dislodged and Jack would repair it.

Although relieved the damage hadn't been worse, Priscilla was frightened. Never in her life had there been such strange, destructive happenings. Were they omens? Punishments? Signs of God's wrath against people like Anne Hutchinson and Roger Williams disturbing the order of things? Against the Pequot war? Buying Indian land cheap? Should she not have hidden Mary Mendome? She wished she could ask Mother or Catherine Carver or Roger Williams.

With his barking dance, Zach signaled John's return. Even from a distance, Priscilla could see that all was not well. Where was the buoyant spring in his step? His heavy stride presaged his downcast, frowning face. She hugged him, clasping him longer, as if to chase out the trouble. Once inside the house she sent the children to work outside until dinner.

'What is the matter?' she asked.

He slumped down on a stool, elbows on knees, hands hanging limp, staring at the floor.

'The session was filled with no end of minor disputes and misdemeanors – except for the case of the Indian murder. Finally at the close of the second day we sentenced the man and his accomplices to be hanged. Thought we were finished. Bradford started to adjourn when a man burst in. "I have a case against my wife," he shouted. "Where are you from?" Bradford asked. I'd never seen him before. Bradford told him to take the stand and state his case. So he did. He was rough looking, unkempt, beard all ragged, clothes stained, and the way he swayed and smelled, he'd definitely been at the bottle. "My wife has been fornicating – with an Indian," he said.'

'Do you know, Priscilla,' John looked up. 'He was enjoying himself. His voice rose in triumph when he made this pronouncement.'

Priscilla clenched her hands underneath her apron, determined to appear calm.

'Bradford and I both questioned him closely, asking how did he know. What evidence did he have? He said he set the dogs after her and they found a little Indian wigwam in the forest. "Was she there, with the Indian?" we asked. "No" he said, "but we know'd she had been." He said he'd been suspicious and heard whisperings and folks sniggering at him. "I know'd" he said.'

Priscilla could hardly breathe.

John went on, staring at the floor. 'Then, all the jury, except for me, Bradford and Winslow, they all took his side. No proof. Just hearsay. They wanted the maximum punishment. I pleaded, argued, told them to come to their senses – all to no avail. So this poor woman is sentenced to be dragged behind a cart up and down the streets of Plymouth, receiving a whipping all the while. And to wear AD sewn into her sleeve for the rest of her life. Her wretched husband did quite skip and dance from the courtroom.' John straightened up.

'Priscilla, you've gone pale as chalk – are you alright?'

'It's just too terrible,' she said. 'Too terrible. I don't understand the jury.'

'I wonder if it was because we'd sentenced three Englishmen to hang for murdering an Indian. There were some who thought we shouldn't. They think that Indians are vermin, barbaric savages. A kind of tit for tat.'

Priscilla shuddered. 'As if this poor woman's punishment isn't barbaric. And they don't even know for sure she's guilty. Oh John,' she wept. 'It's unbearable.'

'The hanging and cart whipping are on the same day, two days hence. I'll have to be there as a witness,' he said.

Priscilla gripped his hand.

★ ★ ★

It's been three days. Surely they've got it over with by now. Priscilla stopped trying to be cheerful, and, apart from feeding Ruth, left the little ones to Elizabeth while she dug and weeded. *What state will that poor woman be in when they've finished with her? She's a pretty young thing. And stuck with that brute husband. What if he made her admit she'd been here? I hate having a secret from John, but it would put him in a terrible quandary if he knew, with his position.* There! Zach's bark.

'John! Are you unwell?' Priscilla clasped her husband to her as he stumbled toward the house, his face by turn suffused into deep red flushes, then pale as birch bark. Indoors he sank heavily onto a stool and made as if to retch. 'Nothing left,' he gasped. Elizabeth brought a little broth in a beaker. John brushed it away. 'It was horrific.' He hid his face in his hands. 'Animals they were, baying and cheering. God Almighty.' He groaned. 'That poor woman… hanging's more merciful.'

Priscilla gathered him to her. 'Try to have some broth – strengthen you. Lie down a minute and then we'll walk in the fields.'

Dumbly, John did her bidding.

In the night Priscilla was startled awake by John's hoarse, strangled cries. As she shook him he moaned. 'Drenched in her own blood, lashed, lashed, she didn't utter a sound, her body twitching, dragged on the ground, her clothes ripped to shreds, dirt filling the gashes. On and on. I begged Bradford to make them stop.'

Priscilla stroked his face and forehead. 'There, there, you did everything you could. I'll fetch some syrup of lavender to help you sleep.'

The next morning, Priscilla was pleased to see the beneficial effects of her potion. John was still subdued, but he ate a good breakfast and set off with Jack and Joseph to check the fences. *Dare I ask it?* She feared John's answer to her plea. *Could the woman stay here to recover?*

After dinner she did ask. John stared at her. 'Priscilla, what are you thinking of? I am an assistant governor and magistrate. I would be flouting Bradford – and all of them. I would be flouting the law. A wife is under the authority of her husband.'

'But it is also expected that the husband should respect his wife and treat her decently.'

'I know. But we cannot have her here. It would be like… setting a keg of gunpowder alight. Her lover was an *Indian*.'

'But John, her wounds. They'll fester – cause gangrene – she could die if she's not treated.'

'Can someone else do it? I know. You're the doctor here.' John paced back and forth. He stared at the floor then looked up at the ceiling. He stopped and turned to Priscilla. 'You can treat her in her own home, and I'll go with you. I'll not have you going into the company of that man alone. And who knows what rabble are about.'

'Thank you, thank you, husband.' She put her hands on his shoulders and laid her head against his neck.

John carried the small medicine chest with Priscilla's selection of ointments, poultices, syrups and lotions. Priscilla carried a pile of clean linen sheets and cloths. As they walked along Ducksburrow's main street John asked a passerby to point out the house. 'Along there,' the man pointed, 'opposite the tavern.'

'It's a hovel,' Priscilla said.

John rapped on the door. It opened a crack. A surly snarling face, stinking of drink, said, 'Wha'd want?'

'My wife has come to treat your goodwife's wounds.' Priscilla noticed John put his foot in the crack. 'Please let us in.' He pushed and the man staggered back.

Priscilla almost retched at the filth and stench. She crossed the small room and bent down over the huddled, moaning form lying on the bare earth floor. John set the medicines down beside her.

'Where is her pallet?' Priscilla demanded.

'Over there – I dumped her down – doesn't deserve better.'

John brought the pallet and helped Priscilla ease the woman onto it. He stood back.

'I need clean water,' Priscilla said, looking into the pail of scummy mess.

'Off you go,' John ordered. 'To the brook. See you come straight back.'

Priscilla started to remove the blood and dirt encrusted clothes. The woman was listless, barely conscious. 'It's Mistress Alden here...' A flicker of recognition.

With great effort the woman mouthed, 'I... didn't... tell.' Priscilla heard a scrape and thump behind her. She turned. John had half-fallen onto a stool. He sat, elbows on his knees, head in his hands. 'Are you alright?' she went to him.

'Yes, yes, just had to sit down. Don't mind me,' he said.

The woman's husband brought in a pail of fresh water. He thumped it down, spilling some onto the floor, then retreated to his corner.

'I'm sorry. This will be painful,' Priscilla whispered into the woman's ear. 'But I must clean out all the dirt and grit. Have a sip of this.' She put a beaker to the woman's swollen, split lips.

For the next two hours, Priscilla carefully bathed, cleaned and applied ointments and poultices. She bound strips of linen round the wounds and gave the woman a syrup to help her sleep and ease the pain. Wearily she stood, gathering up the torn clothes. 'Where are her garments?' she demanded of the man. He pointed to a chest. Opening the lid, Priscilla found a clean shift and also took out three blankets. Trying her best not to cause more pain, she eased on the shift and wrapped the woman in the blankets. 'She must stay warm,' she told the husband. He snarled.

John stood. They opened the door to face a crowd of silent, staring faces. A man shook his fist.

'Fornicator, Indian whore, fornicator.' He was joined by another, and another; men, women and children, chanting.

'Quiet,' John thundered. 'Be gone and stay away or I'll call up the army.'

Priscilla began to shake and grasped his arm. John put his hand over hers. 'We'll wait until they've gone.'

When the street was empty they started home. 'I reckon we'll stop off at Standish's house,' John said.

'Come in, come in,' Barbara chortled. 'I'll fetch my pie – just out of the oven.'

'What has happened?' Miles asked. 'You look as if you've had an awful fright – been through the mill.' He eyed the medicine chest and bundle of clothes. 'Here, sit down.' He placed stools round the table.

Still feeling faint, Priscilla left it to John to explain. 'Thing is, the woman needs treatment, and left with that brutish husband… but if I continue to escort Priscilla there it will be taken I approve the woman's crime, if she did it.'

Standish stood and stroked his beard. He walked twice around the table, paced the length of the room, came back and sat down. 'I have it. I'll speak with one of her husband's mates I know. Make him take the wretched man on a hunting or trapping trip. Get him away from here a week or two – hopefully longer. The problem of the rabble – a military matter. I'll escort Priscilla to the woman's house, and install myself in the tavern.'

'Mind you don't drink too much,' Barbara said.

'That way I can listen to the gossip and mood – and if any folk look like causing trouble – the military steps in.'

Priscilla felt her head clear. She breathed a great sigh of relief. 'Thank you, Captain Standish.'

John clapped Miles on the shoulder. 'I knew you'd sort it.'

'And I'll send good healing food – chicken broth, and eggs and cornbread,' Barbara pronounced.

'Thank you, Barbara,' Priscilla put a hand on the plump, rosy arm.

Continuing their walk home, John said, 'Strange thing happened when I saw the poor woman's wounds. A picture came into my mind of a lad I saw being carried off a ship – I was only a lad myself. He'd been keelhauled… wounds even worse than… more dead than alive. I'd forgotten about it, 'til that moment. That's when I had to sit down.'

Priscilla stepped out into the first morning of autumn. *It has happened so suddenly. When I went to bed it was summer; now there's an autumn chill and tingle. Time to gather the grapes.*

Carrying a large basket, in the late afternoon she crossed the fields to the Hornbeam. *It's so beautiful decked with full ripe grapes, seems a pity to pick them.* She popped a few into her mouth. *Sweet.*

She picked and picked until the sun was low, gathering her shawl closer against the cooling air. *Just a few more…* She felt a presence close by. Slowly she stopped picking, numb with fear, and turned round. 'Tinsin!'

'How is she?' he asked, his face drawn, tense. 'I should not have…'

'She is much better. I've been treating her wounds and she is now up and walking.'

Tinsin let out a deep sigh, 'Thank you.'

'Do not think you did wrong. Mary loves you. It's we English who have done wrong.'

'Tell her I love her. Thank you.' Tinsin smiled a grief stricken smile, bowed his head and disappeared into the forest.

Chapter 71

Spring 1640

Priscilla's frustrations

Alone in her large ordered kitchen, Priscilla stepped forward and back, forward and back to the turn of her spinning wheel. She gave thanks for wool and thought of Susanna, at her home in Marshfield at last. Building their big house had taken forever. She longed to visit. Only five miles, but the walk there and back took a big chunk of the day, with so much work and another babe on the way. She reckoned about four months hence. This would be the eighth. Surely she must stop child-bearing soon. Bless Elizabeth. Now a grown, competent young woman and at this moment taking charge of her siblings; older ones sowing crops in the fields and little Sarah and Ruth helping her in the vegetable garden. With John gone hunting Priscilla had a rare moment alone with her thoughts. Her mind drifted back, back to the first year and memories of Catherine Carver, her gifts, *Hamlet* and the fine mirror, now resting in her box of treasures. Not once, since the day Catherine gave it to her, had she found a minute when she dared take it from the velvet bag and look at her own image. 'Look within,' Mistress Carver had said. Roger Williams said the same thing. She'd not heard a word about him; his whereabouts, alive or dead, nothing since Plymouth refused him permission to settle near Massasoit. How was it, after all these years, how many? Must be nearly eight since her last Bible lesson with him, and her memories, her sense of him, her need for him remained as acute as ever. She did not long for him to replace John, but he had awakened some part of herself and understood her in a way John never could.

'Mother! I cannot find Pris and Jonathan anywhere.' Elizabeth rushed in, her face scarlet. 'I've searched and called, through the fields, in the maple grove, along the brook. They've disappeared.'

'That child, why can she not stay put and do as she's told? Have you gone up to the hornbeam and called into the forest?'

'Aye. I don't think she'd go into the forest. She knows about Joseph getting lost.'

'The brook?'

'As far as our boundary.'

'We'll follow it further.'

Priscilla and Elizabeth with Sarah and little Ruth picked their way along the brook, swollen and boisterous in its spring rush. The day was hot so it was a relief to be walking in the shade of the wood, especially as Ruth begged to be carried. Underfoot spring growth pushed up through the torn remains of autumn's fallen leaves. On the rocks, new moss sprouted vivid green against its dull hued parent and birds shouted their usual nest-building clamor. Priscilla tried not to let her fear show; fear of finding her children's bodies, drowned. So many children perished that way. But almost worse was the fear of wandering Indians, seeking revenge for the Pequot massacre. She and Elizabeth searched in the undergrowth, calling. After an hour's trek they crossed the Alden boundary. Still no sign, no answer. The brook was becoming smaller as it neared its source. Had they been carried off by Indians? Panic brought on a bout of dizziness. Priscilla put Ruth down; she swayed, caught hold of a tree trunk.

'BOO!'

She whirled around. 'Jonathan, what do you think you are doing? Where is Pris?'

'We wanted to show you a surprise.' Pris' tousled head appeared around another tree trunk. 'We've built a house.'

Overwhelmed with fury Priscilla grabbed Pris, yanking her arm. 'Do you have any idea of the trouble and worry you've caused? You are **ten** years old. Too old to be taking your brother off and playing in the woods when there's work to be done. Furthermore, it is not safe to go so far away from our house.'

'But, Mother. We found the perfect spot. Please come see,' Jonathan begged.

'Alright, show us,' Elizabeth said.

About fifty yards into the wood on the left they pushed through a thicket of hazel into a clearing. Priscilla caught her breath.

Beside a flat moss-covered boulder Pris and Jonathan had built a replica of an Indian hut, bending saplings, covering them with juniper branches.

'Look, Mother.' Jonathan crawled in, beckoning. Priscilla knelt and peered in. Piles of acorns, walnuts and pine cones of varying sizes and shapes. Jonathan picked up an oblong tightly knit pine cone. 'These are sugar cones. This is a storehouse – like Father's in Plymouth.'

Priscilla looked at Pris, remembering how she loved to sit on John's knee while he told her of 'his' storehouse with barrels of beer, wine, grain, on and on. Pris knew every last item in that storehouse. Wearily Priscilla stood. She put her aching head in her hands. *I must not soften. Pris must learn her lesson. She needs to learn how to run a home, not a storehouse.* She glared at her daughter. 'You and Jonathan are supposed to be helping your brothers plant the corn. Why aren't you?'

'They're too bossy,' Pris said.

'You deserve a beating, dreadful child. Lucky for you your father refuses to use the rod. I would. Anything to bash some sense into your head. Now come.'

It was a long silent walk back home.

Her hoped-for time alone shattered, Priscilla listlessly chopped onions and turnips to add to the pottage. Still unrecovered from tremors of fear for Pris and Jonathan, weary from the drudgery of never-ending household tasks and weary from childbearing, she leaned against the chopping bench, longing to sit and do nothing. Looking out the open kitchen door at the life-enhancing spring day, she could not feel its beauty. Her mind turned to another worry. A few Sabbaths back she had overheard her Elizabeth talking with Elizabeth Prence about Anne Hutchinson. The Prence girl said her father had delivered a tirade against Mistress Hutchinson, decrying her behavior and ideas. Both Elizabeths expressed excitement, said they wished they could meet this amazing woman who dared to confront men. Priscilla did not know what to do. Should she admit to eavesdropping and caution Elizabeth, or do nothing and hope the fascination would die? She wished she didn't feel the need to squash her daughter's desire to reach out, break the bonds, but she feared where such impulses might lead.

Interrupting her thoughts, John tramped in carrying two brace of duck. Priscilla barely said 'Hello'. *More plucking. I hate plucking.* John slumped onto a stool.

'Poor reward for a morning's shooting. Would have done better to work in the fields.' He stood and leaned against the door frame, looking out across his lands. 'Trouble is I spend so many days in Plymouth – I'm not keeping up with trading our crops, and breeding. Need to get a ram up here and borrow a bull from someone.' He turned to face Priscilla. 'On top of everything, the price of cattle and corn has nose-dived. Damn. Only so much a man can do.'

'Why have prices fallen?'

'One reason is King Charles has put an embargo on any more Puritans emigrating. Says England is losing too many capable folk. But I reckon the main thing is with the Puritan rebellion growing – Cromwell leading – they sense a different future coming, one that gives them power. So they want to stay. And you see, with fewer folk coming over and the Massachusetts Bay folk now producing most all they need, I can't see how we'll ever get the market again – how I'll ever be able to prosper... build us a bigger house.'

Priscilla did not know what to say. John's words caused her to feel even more crushed. She tipped the onions and turnips into the pottage and stirred with extra force as bitterness surged through her. They wouldn't be in such straits if John hadn't agreed to take on a share of the colony's debt – which still wasn't paid off – after – she did a quick calculation – thirteen years. She swallowed her bile.

'I know the children are helping all they can,' John said. 'Pris, bless her, you realize she's taken on all the farmyard duties so Jonathan can work more in the fields, though he's still only a boy.'

'Pris was very naughty this morning. Elizabeth had set her to working in the fields and of a sudden couldn't find her anywhere.' Priscilla told John all that had happened. 'I think you should punish her severely. I need all the children to do their jobs, else things will start to fall apart.'

'I'll have stern words with her.'

'How that girl will ever run a home I can't think. She hates spinning and carding – wool always ends up in a snarl. Doesn't like sewing. A miracle she's avoided infection from always having a pricked finger.'

'She's got wonderful spirit and energy. I'm sure when she is grown and finds a man she likes she'll change. Elder Brewster says Jack is coming on apace. He's offered to give him another half-day every week.'

Priscilla looked up from the pot of pottage. 'That is good. Is Jack pleased?'

'Aye. Of course it means he'll have less time to work our land –
extra reading and that.'

Priscilla resumed stirring the pottage. Staring into the cauldron
she was quiet a moment. Then she said, 'Are there no young men
in Plymouth who'd be wanting work? Could we pay a low wage in
addition to food and lodging?'

'Good idea.' John squeezed Priscilla's shoulder. 'If he was keen,
such a man might soon improve our income.'

'Reckon this is cooked. I'll ring the bell.'

'Wait,' John said. 'I want you to know I was hoping to take you to
Marshfield; to visit with Susanna for a few days, but I cannot spare
the time.'

'I know. Thank you for thinking of it.' Priscilla forced a smile.
'Perhaps next year.'

★ ★ ★

When John returned from his next court session in Plymouth he
brought a young man with him.

'Arthur? Is it young Arthur Howland?' Priscilla held out her
hands. 'Haven't seen you for years – how you've grown. You were a
lad – now a man. Come in, welcome.'

John scooped up a beseeching Ruth, holding her above his head
as she screamed with delight, kicking and waving her arms about.
The five older children stood in a dignified manner; Mary, now
two, crawled round and round in circles, chortling her welcome,
but Sarah jumped about, begging for John's attention. When Zach
had stopped barking and the children quietened John said, 'Arthur
here has agreed to come help us farm.'

'Marvelous,' Priscilla smiled. 'Is your father willing to spare you?'

'He has three indentured servants, and Uncle John will help out
if need be. He's no longer involved in the council or court.'

''Tis our loss,' John said. 'Howland made good suggestions. But
he's not been the same since the Hocking incident. Although it
wasn't his fault.'

'It's not only that,' Arthur said. 'Don't pass this on but neither my father nor Uncle John can stand being in the same room as Mr Prence. And he is always assistant governor and magistrate. They cannot swallow his puffed up, intolerant strictness. Always reckons he's right.'

'Hmm,' John said. 'Well I sympathize.'

'So rather than run the risk of punching the stupid windbag, they stay away.'

'Well, well,' Priscilla said. 'Tomorrow is Sabbath, and I've hardly started preparing. To dinner.'

All afternoon, Priscilla, Elizabeth, Pris and Sarah cooked, cleaned, and made sure Sabbath garb was mended, washed and starched. They laid out Arthur's pallet and bedding.

'I hope he'll be what we need,' Elizabeth said.

'We'll have to see.' Priscilla straightened from tucking in blankets. 'But I reckon your father will have been assessing him. Seems intelligent. If he knows his farming.'

★ ★ ★

Sitting in the Ducksburrow meeting house, Priscilla was on the women's side, furthest from the aisle, with her daughters and younger children lined up beside her; John was on the other with his sons and Arthur.

Priscilla longed for pews so she could rest her back. Having to sit straight, on a flat bench, holding Mary hour after hour was so tiring. She turned to hand the child to Elizabeth and noticed her daughter's gaze directed across the aisle. Following its track Priscilla saw the gaze of a young man traveling back to Elizabeth. *That is William Peabody!* Looking sideways she saw Elizabeth blush. *Well, how long has this been going on?* Priscilla continued to hold Mary herself.

Tap, tap. She heard the approach of the tithingman, tapping his long staff on the floor as he walked up the aisle, checking, searching for a sleeping man or woman or a misbehaving young person.

Priscilla struggled not to laugh out loud at this pompous, strutting specimen with his almighty staff – knob at one end to strike a man, fox tail at the other to tickle a sleeping woman. Now his step quickened purposefully, stopping beside the bench where John and the boys were seated. He raised his staff and brought the knob down squarely on Joseph's head. Priscilla almost cried out. Joseph uttered a loud, surprised 'Ow'. The preacher didn't miss a beat. The tithingman took hold of Joseph's collar and dragged him out past Jack, marching him to the back to sit on the gallery steps with the younger lads. *Why?* Priscilla was angry. *He wasn't making a noise.*

An eternity later, the preacher ceased and the gathering stood to disperse for the noon hour. As Priscilla waited to take John's arm she noticed William Peabody hang back as other men jostled by. Elizabeth did the same. Walking out with John, Priscilla glanced back over her shoulder. William and Elizabeth were walking out together. *Well I never. Elizabeth hasn't said a word.* Once outside she saw Elizabeth leave William and seek out Elizabeth Prence. Now her attention turned to Joseph's disgrace. 'John,' she said, 'what was he doing? He never made a sound.'

John drew a ball of twine from his pouch. 'Our son left this on the floor. As he was sandwiched between Arthur and Jack I didn't see him. He was playing cat's cradle and tying knots. Old sharp eyes got him.'

'Oh it's too ridiculous,' Priscilla said. 'These hours and hours of meaningless words. I'm surprised no one set fire to the meeting house – just for some relief from the bone creaking boredom.'

'Quiet,' John spoke sharply.

'Ah. There's Susanna.' Priscilla peered through folk spreading their picnics. 'I'll go to her – see if she'd like to join us.' Weaving through gathering families, Priscilla reached her friend and hugged her. 'It is so good to see you. Seems like forever.'

'I've been away past two Sabbaths, visiting my eldest and his wife in Scituate.'

'Are they well? Is everything alright?'

Priscilla and Susanna had been chatting about domestic matters for some minutes when Priscilla asked, 'Have you heard any news of Anne Hutchinson, or Mr Williams?'

'No news of Anne Hutchinson.' With a questioning frown, Susanna said, 'Hasn't John told you? Mr Williams has started a colony in Rhode Island.'

'No. John never told me.' Priscilla put a hand to her blushing cheeks. 'I wish him well. Hope it succeeds and grows, becomes a settlement where folk can be less restricted than here, free to follow their own convictions.' She bowed her head.

'You seem fraught. Are things hard just now?' Susanna asked with concern.

'Aye. But I must be strong, as Mother used to say.' Priscilla lifted her head, standing straight. 'Please join us to eat. We're just over there.'

On the walk home, Elizabeth said, 'Mother, I've invited Elizabeth Prence to come visit tomorrow afternoon. I hope that's alright. We so enjoy talking and Sabbath noon hour is never long enough. We thought we could read and copy together.'

'I could see,' Priscilla said. 'You didn't want to bother coming to eat. Of course she may come. Why doesn't she come for dinner? I think Father has an errand or two in the town tomorrow morning. He could call by for her.'

'Thank you!' Elizabeth skipped a few steps.

Priscilla decided she would say nothing about Anne Hutchinson, hoping that the attentions of William Peabody would lessen her daughter's interest in this extraordinary woman.

★ ★ ★

'Is there anything else?' John read through Priscilla's list. 'Flour, a sugar cone, barley, thread. Is this really all?'

'All for the moment,' Priscilla said. 'And don't forget to call for Elizabeth Prence. Shall I write her down?'

'Cheek,' John said as he kissed her and strode off to the town, whistling.

Priscilla turned to begin baking for the day's meals. Bread, pudding, pies. 'There will be how many?' She counted up. 'Eleven at table!'

All morning she, Elizabeth and Pris baked and cooked over the hearth. Just past midday Zach barked and leapt about. Elizabeth ran to the door and along the track to greet her friend.

'Come in, welcome. How lovely you could come,' Priscilla took Elizabeth Prence's hands. 'Perfect timing. Dinner is ready. John, could you call Arthur and our lads please?'

'Mother sent you this.' Elizabeth held out a basket. Priscilla lifted the cloth. 'Oh, my dear – a pie! Tell her thank you so much.'

Splashing and the sound of male voices came from the lean-to. 'Good – everyone is here,' Priscilla said as John and his workmates came to the table. 'Have you two met? Elizabeth Prence – Arthur Howland.' She saw Elizabeth blink, and lower her eyes and then look up though long, dark lashes. She curtsied slightly.

Arthur blushed and half bowed awkwardly. 'Pleased, pleased.'

'Now all be seated,' John said, and led his gathering in prayers.

All through the meal Priscilla watched as first Arthur and then Elizabeth Prence glanced furtively across the table at one another. Elizabeth ate almost nothing; her Elizabeth, sharing her trencher, obligingly ate both portions. Arthur abandoned his portion to Jack.

My oh my – what have we here? Priscilla felt the thud of fate land in her heart. *With Arthur's and Elizabeth's fathers sworn enemies.*

Chapter 72

December 1643

Young vs Old

John bowed his head against the wind-blown snow, the first snowfall of the winter, early December. He could feel the temperature plummeting as he hurried along Ducksburrow's main street to the tavern. From fifty yards he heard the babble of raised voices and he pushed the door open into the musty warmth of a press of men all talking at once.

Across the room Mr Peabody raised his arm and beckoned, 'Mr Alden.' Pushing and shoving his way through, avoiding contact with Mr Prence, John reached his friend, father of his daughter Elizabeth's betrothed.

'Why the furor?' John asked.

'William and I have found a good clearing for a hunting party. Only about five miles into the forest. Now's the time, with the temperature heading for freezing. As you can see, our men are raring to go.'

'When?'

'First light tomorrow. There'll be about twelve of us. Standish will bring his ox and a cart to carry the carcasses back.'

★ ★ ★

'Please, Father. Please may I come? I'm almost as old as Jack,' Joseph pleaded.

'Sorry, lad. Need you to stay and look after your mother and sisters. Perhaps next year.'

'Yes, Father.' Joseph scowled and looked at the floor.

John kissed Priscilla, holding her close. 'Only two nights.' Then he and Jack shouldered their knapsacks and flintlocks and stepped out into the freezing, gray pre-dawn light.

They hadn't gone far when a call hailed them from behind. 'Hie, hie!'

'Miles!' John stopped and waited until Standish, with his ox and cart, caught up. It was good, trudging along with Standish beside him, discussing the Indian threat and the worrying increase of crime within the colony.

'Seems like a spiral,' Miles said. 'The more restrictive the laws our governors pass, the more crime increases, leading to more punishing laws.'

'Aye. Ironic,' John said.

'One thing is sure,' Miles said. 'We'll always need a strong military. And I reckon there should be a domestic force to keep law and order. So the rule of law would prevail just the same, whether the militia is at home or off somewhere else.'

'Thanks be for you, Miles. We can trust you to keep order, stability.'

Judging by the position of a bleary sun, John reckoned it was mid-morning when the forest path opened into a large clearing. John asked Arthur Howland and his father to help him and Jack erect two large shelters. By noon the camp was set up with the two shelters on the edge of the clearing. In the center, they scraped a circle of earth clean for a fire and erected a tripod and spits to take cooking pots and game.

While most of the hunting party tramped into the forest for a shoot before dusk, Mr Winslow and Mr Peabody volunteered to shoot for the pot and prepare an evening meal.

Refusing to abandon their pursuit of a deer, John and Jack were among the last to return to the campfire, where the men were seated round in a circle. Jack sat down beside young Arthur and John made a space between Arthur's father and Standish.

Winslow stood to lead them in prayers.

John looked at the sky. *Full moon, stars, owls hooting, wolves howling in the distance, a clear night. Probably won't go below freezing. I hope Priscilla is safe.* He looked around the circle of men. Prence and sons to Standish's right. Then Winslow, Mr Peabody and William. *William and Elizabeth. The new generation.*

'Amen.' Winslow closed prayers.

'Food at last. Looks good.' John turned to Arthur Howland Senior. 'Thank you for allowing young Arthur to work at my place. A fine worker. Sure you can spare him?'

'I have enough hands. You give so much time to the business of governing, and they don't come fairer than you. Seems only right to help you out. Hear you had a big hand negotiating for the Confederation; there's a good thing – a pledge among our English settlements to act as one in the face of any threat. Suppose Rhode Island had to be left out to satisfy Winthrop.'

'Aye,' John nodded. 'We can blame that on Mr Williams.'

The low pitched murmuring of men's voices was punctured by someone calling out from the shadows on the other side of the circle.

'Congratulations, Mr Prence, Mr Winslow, on settling the Confederation.'

Another voice. 'Aye – but why is Rhode Island not included?'

'I'll tell you why.' Prence rose to his feet. John could see he was in oration mode: feet firm and set astride, thumbs tucked into his belt, head thrust forward. *No, no. Not now*. John bent his head.

'Mr Williams and his colony are a threat to stability and therefore a threat to our survival. Mr Bradford, Mr Winslow, Mr Brewster all agree with Governor Winthrop; Mr Williams is not quite right in the head.' John watched Prence contort his features in mockery. 'His crazy ideas would lead to chaos – every man worshipping in his own way, governors responsible to the *people* – did you ever hear anything so daft?' He rolled forward onto the balls of his feet and back again, pausing for effect. 'Madness.'

'Why is it madness?' a voice from across the fire.

'Aye, why is it madness?' Arthur Howland Senior called out.

Prence turned on him. 'Would you be governed by a rabble? The majority are ignorant louts. Not capable of the judgments required to govern. No. Government must be in the hands of a few religious stable men in their right minds.' He paused, drew breath, 'And you, Mr Howland, are clearly not such a man, nor is your son.'

Then, to John's astonishment, Jack spoke. 'Surely the way ahead lies in all males becoming educated – educated to think and debate. I'm sure if men were thus free to explore different ways of thinking they would behave better, contribute more. And another thing, cruel Old Testament punishments are not appropriate here.'

John stared at his son. *Is this Brewster's influence? Can't be*. Stunned, he said nothing.

As if on cue, William Peabody said, 'I agree. We need to revise the laws to suit our situation – and everyone should be subject to the law in equal measure. Take Mr Brewster. What good was it to him that because of what his servant did a host of his valuable livestock were slaughtered? And his servant didn't commit murder. Should he really have to pay with his life just because he buggered a load of animals? We are not the Hebrews. We are Englishmen, developing a new society.'

'Hear, hear.' A voice, joined by others, from the darkness.

Prence rose again. John looked up at him. His face was a picture of florid rage. Sweat beaded on his forehead and ran down his cheeks into his neck. His sons, sitting cross-legged beside their father's quivering legs bent their heads, hands over their ears as if not wanting to see or hear.

'You young fools. Renegades. You are proof that with your way lies chaos. We must have one way, one religion, enforced by law, resolutely followed by all. Therein lies stability. And what have we older ones risked everything for, if it isn't stability?!' His voice rose almost to a shriek as, with a final flourish of his arm, he sat down.

As the sky began to release another fall of snow, Winslow rose. 'Gentlemen. I think we should sleep.'

The camp settled. John was comfortable enough, the silence of the snowy night disturbed only by the snuffling and snoring of his companions in the shelter. However, it was long before he slept, and then only fitfully, troubled as he was by Prence's bitter tirades. *The young do have a point, our punishments are too harsh – we need new laws. But I fear a growing opposition between young and old. We old ones – we need to be a bit more tolerant. I wish Pricilla was here. Reckon she'd relish the adventure, sleeping out on such a night. I want her in my arms. I want to hear her say she loves me... as before... before when? She says kind things, doesn't fight, but... I fear there's something missing.* He tossed and turned, his mind going round in circles, and wanting Priscilla.

At dawn the men emerged from their shelters into a landscape covered in a foot of snow. Through the trees shone a sky of red and gold streaks and with breakfast the sun rose, full, yellow and hot, into a vivid blue sphere. Lumps of snow dropped off bare branches and white avalanches slid from evergreen boughs. *'Tis glorious.* He stretched. Needing to relieve himself he crossed the clearing. As he was about to search for a private place amongst the trees, Prence followed and stood in front of him.

'What has got into your son? Educating and revising laws – phah! And how can you allow that William to court your Elizabeth?' He pressed a forefinger against John's chest. 'Him saying our laws aren't suitable? Who does he think he is?'

John stepped back abruptly. He felt his throat and face growing hot. Through tight lips, his voice steely and controlled, he said, 'Mr Prence. It is not your place to question my son or my choice of son-in-law. They are both good young men. I know for a fact they too want a stable future. They are searching for the best way to achieve that. Perhaps we would do well to listen. Now, if you will excuse me.'

'And another thing,' Prence continued. 'That young Howland – working at your place.'

John turned his back and hurried on into the forest. Almost shaking with rage, he fastened his attention on the ground. *Mustn't trip on a root or stone, hidden under the snow*. He felt his way with his feet.

That evening, a sinking, watery sun cast lingering shadows of tree trunks across the snow as John and Jack and Standish trudged toward camp, each with a deer slung round his shoulders; Jack carrying a raccoon as well. Tired and pleased with their day's hunt, they said little. Except for a few clucks from roosting birds the only sound was of their boots crunching the snow. Dusk encroached by the minute.

'Hope we haven't got far to go. I forget how quickly dark comes in the forest,' Standish said.

'And I'm starving,' Jack added.

Of a sudden there was a shriek – and another – crack – gunshot. John dropped his deer and ran, following the sound. Carrying the game, Jack and Standish hurried after. They found Prence clinging onto a tree, a gash down his face, doublet ripped, leg clawed. A wildcat lay dead. Young Howland stood with his flintlock.

'Well done, Arthur. You saved his life.' John put an arm around Prence's waist then circled his other arm around his own neck and slowly began to walk him to camp.

'Thank you, Howland,' Prence muttered through teeth clenched against the pain, head hanging.

'How?' Jack asked Arthur.

'I'd spied Prence ahead and kept well back, not wanting to cross his path. He went out of sight and when I heard the shriek…'

'Good man,' Standish said.

Back at camp, Winslow cleaned and bandaged Prence's wounds as best he could. John addressed Prence's son. 'Take your father home in the morning. Then fetch Mistress Alden to treat him. And be sure you escort her there and home again properly.'

After the evening meal, John stood by the fire. Men were gathering in small groups. He caught phrases. 'Folk need incentive.' 'Surely some religious tolerance.' 'Not surprising folk are leaving Plymouth.' 'Not only for more land.' 'Fit the yolk too tight and…'

He sought out Standish and found him leaning against a tree on the edge of the clearing.

'Ah John. Quite a drama we had there. Reckon Prence wasn't watching out for cats in the trees. Should have known better.'

'Thank God young Howland came to the rescue.'

'An irony there,' Miles chuckled. 'The very man Prence banished. "Never set foot across my threshold. No contact with my daughter".'

'Wasn't as if young Arthur had behaved dishonestly,' John said. 'He asked Prence for permission to court his daughter, as is the custom. Got sent away as if he'd committed a crime. Pity Prence is so rigid. Causes a lot of misery, and makes the young rebel. Feels shaky, inside the colony and with the Indians. Pity Hobbamock is gone. He kept things stable with Massasoit; knew what all the tribes were up to.'

'Aye. Almost a year since he passed on and it feels just as bad,' Standish said.

'And Brewster. Sad month, April. Times I didn't agree with his judgment; never figured how he could be so taken with Prence. But Prence never showed the Elder his true colors. Devious devil.' John looked up into the starry night sky. 'Brewster was often wise, had a broad view of things. Jack was very fond of him.'

Standish put a hand on John's shoulder. 'We'll be the old ones soon. We must do our best.'

The next day's hunting passed without incident and on the morning of the third day after breakfast, the hunting party struck camp. With Standish's ox pulling the cart, now loaded with carcasses of deer, raccoons, a few wolves and young Arthur's wildcat, the troop followed the track leading back to Ducksburrow.

On the trek home John found a chance to take Jack off to one side, about twenty feet distance from the others. 'I need to have a word about your speech the other night.' His son was silent. 'I agree we need to revise our laws, and every man should be equal under the rule of law.' Still no response. 'But Jack, wherever did you get these notions about all men being educated? Every man having the vote? I've never heard of such a thing – nor has anyone else I know.'

'These notions, as you call them, are abroad more than you realize, Father. I am not the only man to have these views,' his son replied.

'But where are they coming from?'

'From abroad.'

Jack wouldn't say more.

'Whatever.' John tried to stay calm. *Reckon I know where they're coming from. Rhode Island.* He kept his tone measured. 'I hope you can appreciate my predicament. Your words are an attack on Bradford, Prence, Winslow – and the others I serve with. If they think I am putting these notions into your head, I'll lose their respect and trust.'

'I do see that, Father. And I'll not say more.'

John and his son faced one another. 'Thank you,' John said. However, he saw a look pass across the earnest face. The look of a decision taken? He felt uneasy.

Chapter 73

Spring 1645

Leaving the nest

Priscilla, together with Elizabeth, Pris, Elizabeth Prence, Sarah and Ruth, sat gathered round the hearth sewing. Linen tablecloths, pillowslips, shifts, petticoats – and Priscilla sewing the wedding dress. Deep ruby red taffeta. A gift from Susanna. *She knows we are strapped for money.*

'You'll look a picture in this, with your fair skin and blond curls.' Priscilla's needle traveled along a seam.

'Last chance to wear low-cut,' Elizabeth Prence said, 'before you're a married matron with high collars.' She sighed. 'How I wish…'

'It will happen one day, I know it will,' Priscilla said. 'Now – a turn in the garden I think, before Elizabeth has to go back home.' All five girls went to work in the vegetable garden while Priscilla headed for the orchard to signal Arthur to come from the fields. When she had reached the gate between the farmyard and the orchard, she heard Zach suddenly barking fiercely, and hurried back to see who could be coming. *Mr Prence! I thought he was in Plymouth!* She ran to the garden. 'Elizabeth, quick, hide in the barn under the haystack. Your father...'

Both Elizabeths fled as Priscilla, smoothing her skirts, motioning to Pris, Sarah and Ruth to say nothing, went to answer the hammering on the door.

'Mr Prence. What a surprise!'

'I'm looking for my daughter. Is she here? If she is anywhere near that Howland...'

'I've not seen her – not for a long time, Mr Prence. I'm sorry you're so bothered. Perhaps she's gone gathering sallet and leeks. If I should see her I'll tell her you're looking for her.'

'Obliged,' Prence growled.

Zach growled.

'Ssh, Zach.'

Prence doffed his hat and bowed. 'It is so rare to have the pleasure of your company, Mistress Alden.' His eyes altered from glittering hard to soft and beseeching. 'I had hoped, as we are neighbors.'

Priscilla, transfixed and repulsed at the sight of the ugly mole, was abrupt in her reply. 'You will appreciate, Mr Prence, that at this time of year we have much to attend to. Now if you will excuse me.'

'Good day, Mistress Alden. Another time perhaps.' Prence bowed again, hesitated as if resisting his dismissal; then, with a slow measured step, made his way back down the track.

Priscilla waited until she was sure he was gone, then closed the door. *Phew – a close one. Too close.* She wiped her brow. Feeling shaky and weary she went to the barn. Not a sign. 'You can come out now.' The two young women emerged, covered in hay. 'Elizabeth, we'll get you cleaned up, give you a basket of sallet, and then you must get on home.' She called to Sarah. 'Off you go – pick a good lot of sallet by the brook, and take care. Too many have drowned in that brook.' Then she called the waiting Arthur. 'You've not got long. Her father was here.' *How is he back from Plymouth before John? So strange. That Prence. Barely a word of gratitude to Arthur for saving his life. Dreadful.*

★ ★ ★

When John returned from Plymouth he was in a somber mood, unsmiling, unresponsive to the usual clamor of welcome. In response to anxious questions he would only say, 'I'll explain after dinner.'

When the meal was over, dishes washed and put away, John sat in his rocking chair by the hearth, Priscilla in hers. The family gathered and were quiet.

'When I took my place in the court, I could see Bradford had a document spread before him on the table. He convened the session and then explained this was a petition, come from the magistrates of Scituate – a petition for religious tolerance. The majority of deputies on our council were in favor and drew up a motion, which Bradford read aloud, to grant full and free tolerance of religion to all who abide by the law and submit to the government. This to include Jew, Turk, Papist, or any other. The court was about to pass the motion when Prence shillyshallied. Said it should be given more time. So Bradford said we would consider at greater length and reconvene in two days.' As he talked, John became agitated. He stood and emptied his pipe bowl – then walked away from the hearth around the table. 'I could see Prence circulating, working on men to persuade them against. He and Winslow lodged with Bradford. I stayed with Howland. Wish Howland was on the court. Damn shame. He said he knows many Plymouth families who want to leave, not only for better land – they feel they're under a dictatorship.'

'And they're right,' Jack interjected.

'When we reconvened Prence wasn't there. Sent apologies – apparently urgently needed at home. The fox. Didn't want to be seen as the "no-tolerance" leader. Winslow did the dirty work. Asked for a postponement. Said more time was needed to consider. Bradford granted his request quicker than that.' John wearily returned to his chair. 'It's enough to demolish a man. I'm all for the rule of law and folks pulling together. But I'm not so daft I can't see that if folks feel dictated to against their will they won't stay. We worked ourselves nearly to death building Plymouth Colony. There's folk saying we fled from intolerance and are becoming no better than the monarchy we left behind.'

'Father,' Elizabeth scraped her stool forward. 'What does Captain Standish say?'

'Ah. Standish. An ally. He too thinks the motion for tolerance should have been adopted. He says now we need to concentrate on Ducksburrow. Points out we've got a good lot of forward thinking men up here.' John looked at Arthur and Jack. 'As long as they keep their feet on the ground.'

'I reckon Prence will be mighty unpopular around here,' Priscilla said. 'Can't think who amongst us would support him. But I'm sorry to hear Winslow's become so rigid. He wasn't like that before.'

'Nor was Brewster,' John said. ''Twas more in his old age he feared dissension – wanted everyone to think and worship alike – the Pilgrims' way. I miss him. He may have become less tolerant but he was always kind – had a gentle way about him.'

'And a scholar,' Jack said. 'He taught me so much. He loved his books. Had a good variety.'

'We need the next generation to be strong and fair if our colony is to live,' John said.

★ ★ ★

Priscilla and Elizabeth stood by the hearth stirring a large kettle of milk with dried rennet, waiting for the curd to form. 'There. It's well on its way.' Priscilla crossed the room to where Ruth was embroidering clothes for Elizabeth's marriage. She looked at the young head – a mass of deep auburn curls – bent over the gardening book and her work. *How she loves that book.* Priscilla watched her daughter transfer its drawings to her sewing. *Pity those curls have to be hidden under a coif.*

'Oh bother!' A moan of frustration came from the spinning wheel.

'Let's have a look.' Priscilla went to her namesake. 'This is a right tangle. I'll sort it,' she said, trying to keep her irritation hidden. 'You knead the dough. Reckon it's proved by now.'

'Yes, Mother,' Pris said. Her dejection showed in her unsmiling face and slumped shoulders. Her tall, willowy stature stooped and shrank.

What is to be done? Priscilla worried.

There was a fierce knocking at the door. Priscilla opened. 'Elizabeth! Come in, child. Whatever is the matter?'

Elizabeth Prence's face was red and tear-stained; she wrung her hands and clasped her arms around her middle before falling into Priscilla's embrace. 'We're going – Father – to Nauset – soon.'

'But that's way round the other side of the cape – miles away from Plymouth. Come, sit down.' Priscilla guided the sobbing young woman to a stool by the table.

'Father says he doesn't want to stay here. Doesn't like the company.' Elizabeth buried her head in her arms on the tabletop. 'He wants to start a new settlement – with folks who follow his ways – and where there is plenty of good land.' She was now sitting up straight. 'And there's another reason; to remove me far away from Arthur and you.'

A coil of anger rose in Priscilla's belly such as she'd not felt since discovering Mary Brewster's designs to keep her away from John. She said, 'Well. He'll not succeed. We will find a way. Providing you and Arthur remain true, he'll not succeed.'

★ ★ ★

Sabbath. Priscilla had one thing on her mind. *I hope Susanna will be there. Please, let Susanna not stay away.* She hurried her children and John, wanting to arrive before the meeting began. Food packed for the noon hour – bother – Elizabeth would have seen to all this. Her eldest, married, gone. In her mind's eye Priscilla saw Elizabeth, radiant in her red taffeta gown, standing proud beside William Peabody, son of one of Ducksburrow's foremost citizens. She sighed. Why did these folk have such a dour wedding ceremony? One could hardly call it a ceremony – it was simply sealing a contract. At least Elizabeth was permitted to wear her red gown and there was a small party in the spacious home William had built for his bride. But the gathering had to be discrete and secretive to keep hidden from Prence's prying eyes and avoid a fine for wrongful revelry. Pulling herself back into the moment, she distributed baskets of food and herded her family into the fresh June morning.

'You don't usually hurry like this,' John said. 'Is something up?'

'Surely you understand I want time for words with Elizabeth – mother, daughter words – and with Susanna if she's there.' *Pity I must keep this secret from John but he'd be compromised – his position, his all-important position.*

'Women's ways,' John said.

Priscilla scanned the cluster of folk gathering outside the meeting house. *There she is.* Quickly she approached Elizabeth and William. He smiled, the picture of a proud husband. As she pulled Elizabeth over to a space away, Priscilla whispered, 'Is it alright? Does William agree?'

'He does, and we've fixed a time for tomorrow when we know Mr Prence is going to Nauset to stake out his homelot.'

'Praise God. Thank you, William,' Priscilla breathed. They walked sedately back. Elizabeth, now Mistress Peabody, entered the meeting house on her husband's arm. Once over the threshold, William went to the men's side, Elizabeth to the women's. The Aldens followed not far behind; Priscilla looked around trying to spot Susanna. *Oh why isn't she here?*

The assembled meeting sat attentively, waiting while Reverend Partridge planted himself in a speaking position. There was a rustle at the back. Knowing she shouldn't, Priscilla turned to look. *Susanna.* She smiled.

This is going on forever. Priscilla could not concentrate. When not occupied with keeping her little ones quiet, she let her mind go here, there, and mostly it rested on young Arthur Howland and Elizabeth Prence.

'We will now adjourn for noon hour.'

Priscilla turned to Pris. 'Will you please lay out our food. Be with you in a trice.' She pushed her way to the back. 'Susanna.'

Susanna clasped her hands.

'Come with me please, a way apart,' Priscilla said. When they were far enough off, she continued. 'You know about young Arthur Howland and Elizabeth Prence?'

'Oh yes, and now Mr Prence is moving to Nauset. He is dead set against all the Howlands. Doesn't want one anywhere near his daughter.'

'I want to know if you approve, for I have a plan.' They walked further away, Priscilla keeping her voice low. 'Mr Prence is going to Nauset tomorrow. Elizabeth and William have agreed to witness a pre-contract between Arthur and Elizabeth. It only needs two witnesses – am I right? And they're as good as married – legally?' She looked at Susanna apprehensively. 'I know I'm interfering but I'm determined Mr Prence should not get his way over this. He ruined the tolerance vote. That's enough. These two love one another; it is obvious they belong together.'

Susanna chuckled. 'Splendid idea. But I'll better it. I'll be the second witness, along with William. That way none of the Aldens can be implicated. It won't affect Edward. He's above reproach and in any case he's sailed off to England – again.'

'Oh, praise be. Thank you!' Priscilla beamed and heaved a sigh. She put a hand on Susanna's arm. 'I'm sorry Edward has set sail again. You must stay with us a spell, beginning tonight.'

'That would be a treat.' As they turned to walk back to the gathering, Susanna said, 'I have some disturbing news. You know Anne Hutchinson left Rhode Island? Took her family into the fearsome Mohawk territory in New York. All massacred by

Indians. Except for one girl, escaped.'

Massacred. Images of a hand grabbing her hair, pulling her head back and then a tomahawk slicing her scalp made Priscilla shudder. Her stomach churned and she drew a hand across her brow. 'Why did she leave Rhode Island?'

'Edward says she was continually getting into squabbles, attacking the magistrates, don't remember who else. I suppose even Roger Williams was losing patience, though I can't imagine he'd have asked her to leave.'

Roger Williams. Priscilla longed to know how he fared. She wondered what Rhode Island was like. 'I'm sure it's a happier place than here,' she inadvertently murmured.

'What's that?' Susanna asked.

'Lord have mercy,' Priscilla said. 'I'm thankful our Elizabeth is with William. He thinks broadly but his feet are well on the ground. Good to see her so happy.'

'Hmm, I recall you were worried your Elizabeth and the Prence lass were overly interested in Anne Hutchinson. An inspiring woman, exciting new views, attracted followers, but she was not sensible. Seems she became half-crazed.' After a moment Susanna went on, 'And another instance of a woman must be crazy or gripped in melancholy… just the other day a woman living only a pace down the road from us murdered her own small daughter. Cut her throat with a knife.'

'No! Why?' Feeling unsteady, Priscilla grabbed Susanna's arm.

'No one knows for sure. But the child was by a first husband.'

Priscilla didn't speak, numbed by the horror. A massacre, a murder. Both women half-crazed. She and Susanna drew near the noon hour gatherings.

'Come join us,' Priscilla said, taking comfort in this ordinary scene. 'Look. The food is all spread out on a blanket.'

'Thank you I will. Where's Peregrine?' Susanna searched the clusters of folk for her son. 'Ah – over there with the young men. He's got his food. Don't know what I'd do without Peregrine, with my eldest and his wife living in Scituate.'

'Aye, he's a good young man and forever being trounced on by Prence for some minor "crime".' Priscilla noticed the Prence family were on their own. 'Who is that young couple? Susanna, I've not seen that pair before. With the fine clothes.'

'They'll be the Lathams; not long come to Marshfield. She is Edward's niece. Her father is a wealthy merchant and assistant governor in Boston. Strange thing is they have no land, so perhaps her father pays for their fine apparel and servants. Gossips say she doesn't deign to lift a finger.'

'Ah, to sit on a cushion and sew a fine seam,' Priscilla said. 'Would be nice.'

★ ★ ★

Even with Susanna's support for her plan, all the next day, Priscilla was in a state of nerves. She dropped a ladle, burnt her finger, got cross with Mary and Rebecca.

'Calm yourself,' Susanna said. 'It will work out.'

Dinner was almost finished when John said, 'I nearly forgot. Arthur, William Peabody asked yesterday if he might borrow you this afternoon to help with his fencing. Of course I said yes.'

Looking down into his trencher Arthur nodded and mumbled assent.

As Priscilla cleared the table, Susanna and Arthur departed.

Pray God, nothing goes wrong. Priscilla repeated to herself all afternoon, burying herself in the weeding, leaving Pris to manage the children and make sure they performed their tasks. The afternoon wore on. She came indoors to check the stew and beans, and stood staring into the pot, praying.

Zach barked. The door opened.

'Elizabeth.' Priscilla grasped Elizabeth Prence's hands. 'Arthur?'

'Success,' Elizabeth said.

Arthur didn't need to say anything. Head held high, beaming, he said, 'Thank you, Mistress Alden, and Mistress Winslow.'

Priscilla sank onto a stool, weak-kneed with relief and happiness.

'I told you it would be fine,' Susanna said, her smile rivaling Arthur's.

All through the evening meal Priscilla felt a warm glow. But she puzzled that Jack and Joseph seemed subdued, didn't say much. After the meal, when the family had gathered round the hearth to share the day's events, Jack stood.

'There's something I need to say.' He looked straight ahead, eyes focused on the lintel over the hearth.

Oh no, what is coming? Priscilla clasped her hands tight.

'You know I've always wanted to go to sea. Well, I've decided to go to Boston to learn seamanship. It's the place to go to become commander of a ship.'

Priscilla looked at her eldest son, seeing him as if for the first time, a man; tall, straight, with his father's strong angular face, light brown wavy hair, serious hazel eyes. She depended on him. When John was away Jack became man of the family. *I've always known deep down he wanted to go to sea, but I hoped, persuaded myself that he would change his mind and stay.* She looked at her husband; pale, hands trembling, he almost dropped his pipe.

'I should have seen it coming... but so soon?' John stared at the floor, then raised his eyes to his son. 'Could you not wait? A year or so? Until our farm is better recovered?'

Sensing John's distress, Zach, old and stiff in his joints, struggled from his place by the hearth and with a whimper, lay down, resting his head on his master's boot. John reached down and stroked his dog behind the ears.

'I'm sorry, Father,' Jack said, 'but I have already delayed past the best age to apply for a place on a ship. And this intolerance vote clinches it.'

'But you would become a leader here in Ducksburrow, along with William.'

Priscilla watched her husband slump in his chair, hand over his eyes. Jack sat down and stared at the hearth. No one spoke.

Joseph stood. He too fixed his eyes on a place above the lintel.

'Like Jack, I too want to move away – start my own farm – on the land you and Standish bought – if Standish agrees.' He spoke hurriedly as if to expel his unwelcome message as quickly as he could.

'But why?' John pleaded. 'I can see your brother wants to go to sea, but you, Joseph, you know we need you here.' He leaned forward in his insistence. 'Arthur is… I don't know how we'd manage without Arthur. Pris helps, but she is a woman, and Jonathan is only twelve. And just when we've paid off the London debt and have a chance to prosper…'

'John! Is it true?' Priscilla leapt up and took John's hands, kissed his cheek. The girls clapped and laughed. 'Congratulations, Father. Many congratulations.' Jack and Joseph punched the air.

'Can this not persuade you to stay, Joseph?' John said.

Joseph drew his stool closer to his father; all the family stopped their noise to listen.

'I've been thinking for some time that the yoke is too tight in Plymouth. And now, I'm seeing how just a few men have the power to control the direction; seeing how the vote for intolerance was swung. And no. I don't like it.'

'But Ducksburrow could be different. There's you and William and Arthur. You all could lead the way here.'

'Father, you know that's not possible. We have to follow Plymouth's laws,' Joseph said.

John shook his head, as if he still could not believe what he was hearing.

'I'll stay 'til next year's planting is done. And it will be some time afore I've cleared the land to farm it. I'll come back when you're stretched.'

'You mean well,' John said. 'Thank you. I'll speak with Standish about it tomorrow.' In spite of his victory with the London debt, he spoke as a man defeated.

Later, when they were in bed, Priscilla hugged John close and stroked his brow. ''Tis a sad loss. But Joseph will come and help when needed, I'm sure. Sadly, Jack – 'twas bound to happen. And at last – no more London debt! Well done, husband. Feels like a weight lifted.' She did not let him see the ache and misery she felt, losing her two eldest boys; Jack going to sea, the dangerous sea, and her charming mischievous Joseph, so far away. And with the ache of loss she felt a tug, a longing for a new place, to live amongst folk who were more tolerant, not so rigid, free in their minds. She didn't blame Joseph for wanting to leave. She wished…

1649-1657

Chapter 74

Spring 1649

Pris makes a decision

'A feast day! Bradford has declared a feast day to celebrate.' Priscilla ran to meet John as he bounded along the track shouting his news.

'Why? What has happened?'

'King Charles is dead. News came this morning. Beheaded. Cromwell will form a parliament. Puritans in power. Incredible.'

'Heavens above. A disturbance of the divine order,' Priscilla said. 'Aren't you pleased?'

'Oh yes – well I don't like the thought of anyone being beheaded, but a wonderful happening. Has Bradford named the day?'

'April 7th – next week.'

'Two feast days this year; spring and harvest.'

'And another thing. Governor Winthrop has just died.'

Priscilla looked at John; held his eye. 'Another king gone,' she said quietly. 'Wonder if the Boston government will loosen up.'

'I hope,' John said.

As Priscilla and John crossed the threshold of their home they heard splashing in the lean-to.

'Strange,' Priscilla frowned. 'We haven't rung the bell for dinner. Joseph!' She ran to be enveloped in a bear hug.

John clapped his son on the shoulder. 'This is a surprise. Did you get word of our feast?'

'Aye. The news is everywhere. Cheering. Puritans governing England. Hard to believe.'

Priscilla rang the bell. The younger girls and little David came from the garden; Jonathan, Arthur and Pris from the fields. With gasps, cheers, hurrahs, they greeted Joseph. As the family group settled for prayers Priscilla could see Arthur was bursting with some hidden satisfaction. He waited about half a minute after John's 'Amen' and broke into the excited hubbub of questions directed at Joseph. 'May I please speak? I have news.' An expectant silence waited. 'Elizabeth and I called on Mr Prence at Nauset. We confronted him with our intention to wed. Pointed out we've been true for seven years. Both of us swore we would never marry another. When he still said no, Elizabeth told him, very well, we'll run off away where you have no power and show you up for the rascal you are. That did it. He grumbled his assent. I'm so proud of Elizabeth.'

Priscilla led clapping and congratulations, exchanging a special look with Arthur.

'Well done, both of you,' John said.

'I wondered, Mr Alden, could you arrange for us to be married here in Ducksburrow, among friends, instead of Plymouth. Seeing as both you and Captain Standish are magistrates here.'

'I'll have a word with Standish,' John said. 'I'm sure he'll be as delighted as I am.'

As ever, dinner was rapidly consumed. No lingering when it came to filling hungry bellies. Trenchers washed and put away, the Alden family with Arthur gathered round the hearth. Priscilla cast her eyes round the assembled faces. *A fine family.* She gazed a time at John. *We have been through so much.* Then she looked at her namesake. *She's nearly twenty; lovely young woman, tall, willowy, hazel blue eyes, soft brown hair, good natured. Can't understand; doesn't seem to want to marry. Sarah, so like Elizabeth, blond curls, blue eyes, pretty; she'll be an excellent home maker. Ruth, beautiful and gentle. Mary, the plainest, but so hardworking, a generous heart. Rebecca with her mass of dark curls, dark sparkling eyes, dances through the day. Little David, only five, stocky and strong, determined to do a man's work. Her men: Jonathan, handsome, charming, and Arthur, for he is like one of the family; his earnest boyish freckled face.* She wondered how Jack was faring in Boston and then gave all her attention to Joseph, sun-browned, bigger, stronger than she remembered. He was describing his farm, the settlement.

'More and more folk coming west; fertile land you bought, Father. Doing well. Tell you what – there's an unusual person made a good life in Taunton.'

'Why unusual?' Priscilla asked.

'Because the person is a woman. Never married. Must be around sixty. All on her own, apart from a brother. She's built up a tidy estate; two houses, nearly two hundred acres of land, manages it all, travels on horseback and I'm told she has shares in the ironworks in Taunton.'

'Such a thing could never happen in England,' Priscilla said, 'except among the nobility. For ordinary folk a woman's life is dependent on her marriage. If she doesn't marry she's a burden and treated as inferior. When I was a girl I saw women for sale in Dorking market.' She shifted restlessly. 'Do you ever meet this woman?'

'I do. She comes over to Bridgewater time to time. Calls in to compare methods. Keen to learn, find out how folks do things. And of course I go over to Taunton.'

Pris leaned forward. 'Joseph, could I come and stay with you awhile? I should like to meet this woman. I could do your cooking and washing, as you haven't yet got a wife.'

'Absolutely fine by me, if you can be spared here,' Joseph said. 'Come with me when I return.'

'Father? Mother?'

Priscilla hesitated, looking across to John. *What if she got into danger? What if she fell in love with a man out there? No, I mustn't hold her back.* 'I suppose so – not too long mind. Can you spare the time to bring her home, Joseph? Will you be sure she's safe?'

'I'll do everything in my power to keep her safe, and yes, I can spare the time for another visit back here.'

'Oh Father, please,' Pris pleaded. 'I'll be sure to come back safe.'

'I'll sleep on it,' John said.

All during the week before the feast, Priscilla was filled with a wistful happiness, having Joseph at home, part of the family again. With his help the fields were now prepared for planting, so John was less careworn, more good humored. Like all the goodwives of Ducksburrow, she and her daughters were immersed in a frenzy of preparing food.

Happily April 7th was a fine warm day, not too hot. Folk from Ducksburrow and nearby Marshfield gathered on Ducksburrow common and watched a parade of the militia which ended with the musketeers firing a celebratory volley.

'Three cheers!' Standish led a rousing chorus of shouts before folk began their feasting.

Walking home that evening, Priscilla put her arm through John's. Joseph and Pris walked ahead, deep in conversation, the other children straggling here and there. 'It was a happy occasion,' Priscilla said. 'The feast and Arthur and Elizabeth's wedding. I'm glad you were prepared to marry them here. A happy couple.' She slowed her pace, enjoying the scents of the spring evening, the quiet cluckings and twitterings of roosting birds. 'Have you decided yet, about Pris?'

'I feel uneasy about it,' John said. 'But she clearly wants to go. I saw her face light up when Joseph described this woman.'

'I feel the same,' Priscilla looked at the ground. 'But she is twenty.'

'Alright, I'll say yes. On a different subject, I think it is time to build a bigger house.'

'John! Here in Ducksburrow? I'm all… akimbo in my nerves.'

John laughed. 'I like unsettling you – with good things. Doesn't often happen.' He put his arm round her.

★ ★ ★

'I knew we should not have allowed Pris to go.' John pounded a fence post into the ground with such force Priscilla flinched. She stood by with a basket of eggs.

'Joseph said they wouldn't be back before the fortnight and it's only three days beyond that now,' she said, trying to keep the worry out of her voice.

'If they haven't returned by day after tomorrow I'll ask Standish to come with me and bring her back.'

The next two days crept by. On the morning of the third day John set off to fetch Standish while Priscilla packed his knapsack. 'Don't worry, Mother,' Sarah said. 'I'm sure Joseph wouldn't let any harm come to Pris.'

Ruth ran in from the garden. 'They're back. I'm sure it's them, crossing the fields. Jonathan's run up to meet them.'

'Praise be!' Priscilla hurried through the farmyard and orchard where she could see. 'Yes. Yes.' Picking up her skirts she ran and stumbled between corn heaps. Pris ran and hugged her close.

'Mother. You're crying.'

'It's just – we were so worried.' Priscilla wiped her cheeks. 'Jonathan, run after your father. Try to catch him before he fetches Standish.'

'I'm sorry you've been upset,' Joseph said. 'We decided to make one last trip to Taunton.'

Full of happy relief Priscilla chattered. 'We'll have a special meal; succotash with chicken in, pumpkin, venison stew, cornbread and berry pies.'

In the kitchen, Pris looked in the barrel of flour. 'It's very low. Would you like me to go to the store in town?'

'Ah. Thank you. We also need a sack of beans and a cone of sugar.'

'And a spool of strong thread,' Sarah called from the hearth.

★ ★ ★

Some days after Joseph had gone back to Bridgewater, Priscilla and Pris kneaded dough together on the scrubbed kitchen table. Sunlight shone through the open door, reaching into the farthest corner of the room where Sarah was dutifully spinning, alternately wool and flax. Ruth supervised Mary and Rebecca, planting and weeding the garden.

A feeling had been growing in Priscilla that Pris was only half present. Even when engaged in jobs she liked she would stop and stare as if into a distant place. She did so now, suddenly halting in her stroke, looking fixedly at the dough.

'Pris, is there something troubling you?' Priscilla asked.

'Not troubling exactly, but I've come to a decision.'

Priscilla's heart contracted. *Has she met someone in Bridgewater? Does she want to leave?*

'Over several years I've been thinking I don't want to marry and have babies. Not because of you; you are so good a mother and goodwife, but I want something different and I do not want to be the property of a man. And you know I'm not good at housewife tasks. When I met the woman in Taunton, successful, running farms, and not married, I saw it could be done.'

Priscilla stopped kneading and waited.

'I know now what I want.' Pris looked her mother in the eye. 'When I went to the store in town the other day I found it is up for sale. It is in a perfect spot, a small house, fair distance from the tavern. The owners are moving up to Scituate so its stock is run down, making it a good price. I know I could make it a success. Mother, more than anything, I want to own the store.'

Feeling punched, Priscilla resumed her kneading. 'We cannot always have what we want, Pris. The woman in Taunton has given you crazy notions. Would you live in the store? Alone? Without protection? Father would never agree. Even if he could afford to buy the property, and I'm not sure he can.' Priscilla thumped the dough extra hard. Glancing up, she saw her daughter biting her lip, cheeks flaming, a tear hovering, about to fall. She stopped kneading and put an arm round Pris' waist. 'I'm sorry. I sympathize. And it isn't as if you can't read and write and do numbers. You're excellent in those skills. Why don't you have a school? We'll always need a school.'

Pris' shoulders drooped. 'It's hopeless. I... I'd be no good as a teacher. I don't much like small children, or large ones. Doubt I could keep discipline.' She stepped over to the door and stood looking out into the garden. 'Joseph says they need a store in Bridgewater.'

Priscilla gasped, reeling backwards. 'Pris, you wouldn't!' *That's blackmail. The sly minx. She knows John and I would be distraught.* 'I'll talk to your father.'

'Jonathan is keen to help me,' Pris came back to the table. 'And John Bradford. They have no children and their house is right next to the store. His wife says she would love to help me serve customers – the perfect chance to pick up all the gossip.'

Priscilla resumed her kneading. *How weary I feel of a sudden. Never a moment's peace.* She looked up, listening. Rough, Zach's replacement, whimpered and whined. 'Not like him. Sssh.' There was a feeble thump on the front door and then a thin, barely audible wail. 'Stay back.' Priscilla motioned to the dog and opened the door.

A lad collapsed at her feet. Half-clad in rags revealing a back that was red-raw with whipping stripes, bone thin, matted hair, scalp bald in places. 'Pris,' she called. Together they lifted him into the house. 'Sarah – a pallet – there beside the barrels. Clean water, linen strips.' Easing him gently onto the pallet she saw he had a black eye and bruises on his cheeks, arms and chest. His feet were cracked and bleeding. 'Could you fetch a clean shift, Sarah?' She and Pris undressed and washed the floppy, weak body. 'He's half-dead. I wonder where he's come from?' Priscilla mused as she smoothed calendula ointment into the open wheals and yarrow on the bruises. 'There's a pot of chicken broth over the fire. When he's had some of that perhaps he'll recover enough to tell us. Mind, how we'll manage to get anything through those cracked, swollen lips...'

Pris brought a bowl of broth and the smallest spoon she could find.

'Thank you. Now, could you raise him up a bit, hold him steady, while I...' Slowly Priscilla spooned some of the broth into the battered mouth, relieved the lad was able to swallow.

At noon hour John and Jonathan strode in from the fields. 'We'll sow the two fields up by the forest with hay.' They stopped short.

'I recognize him,' Jonathan said. 'He's a servant, belongs to the Latham couple up in Marshfield.'

'My God,' John said. 'Whatever?'

'He collapsed on the doorstep. He'll not be able to return until he's recovered enough to walk.' Priscilla got to her feet.

'He's obviously been suffering ill treatment for a long time,' Jonathan said. 'Has he not complained to the court, Father?'

'No. Don't suppose he dared, with Mistress Latham being Winslow's niece, and her father a powerful man in Boston.'

'So much for equality before the law,' Jonathan said.

'I cannot bear to send him back to receive more ill treatment. There must be something we can do,' Priscilla implored.

'Sadly, no. Only if the Lathams agree to sell him, and I am certain they will not.'

Priscilla sighed and shook her head. 'We'll let him be now. He needs to rest quiet. Sarah has dinner ready.'

After dinner, Priscilla sent all her daughters and David to work in the garden, or help Jonathan in the fields. 'Please come and sit awhile,' she said to John. 'You do nothing but work.' She looked across at the pallet. 'He's sleeping. Good.'

'I miss young Arthur mightily.' John eased himself into his rocker.

'Such a pity Francis decided to move to Yarmouth. He'd have helped. What about asking John Bradford, or Alexander Standish?'

'I'll have a word with Miles about Alexander. John is married, has his own place to see to, like Arthur.'

Priscilla knitted and rocked a minute. She waited while John lit his pipe. When he'd drawn several long draughts she said, 'Pris and I were talking this morning. She is desperate to have the store in town. You know the owners are moving up north. She reckons she could run a profitable little business.'

John stood, his face flushed. 'Why can't she get a husband and have a family? That is what women are meant to do.' He paced and turned on his heel. 'I'll not have a daughter of mine engaged in commerce! It isn't right. It's that confounded Taunton woman. Should never have let her go.'

'John, listen. You know Pris has never been any good at housework. Hopeless with a needle and spinning, not interested in remedies. She manages cooking, but doesn't like it. Takes no pleasure or pride.' Priscilla let her knitting fall. She looked intently at her husband. 'The prospect of having her own business has caught her spirit. She has it all worked out; says Jonathan will help her.'

'I need Jonathan here,' John exploded. 'Can't have him wasting time on some useless…'

Priscilla stood. 'I feel the same. But Pris has said if she can't have a store here she'll go to Bridgewater. She doesn't want a life of child rearing and says she doesn't like children well enough to teach.'

'Well she can learn to like children. Other women do.'

'John, don't you see?' Priscilla placed her hands on his shoulders and looked into his eyes. 'If we don't let her have a store here we'll lose her. She'll go. She is strong minded.'

John wiped his brow and slumped down into his chair, head in his hands.

'Don't be like Prence, or Bradford, so rigid. Their children left them to escape.'

'Feels all wrong, a woman running the store. What will people think? What about my standing? Would she really go off to Bridgewater? My God I don't want to lose her. My beautiful Pris. Surely she wouldn't do that?'

'I fear she would go. I know she would. You underestimate how stubborn she is.'

John moaned. 'I'm cornered. Looks like I have to say yes.' Head down, shoulders drooping, he trudged off up to the fields.

Chapter 75

1655

Priscilla's resolution

'Priscilla, I'm sorry, but we cannot hold a house-warming party on Christmas night,' John said.

'But why? We would only invite folk like ourselves who aren't ridiculously strict.'

'Because the Plymouth council has just passed a law forbidding any activity on Christmas other than work and prayer. Anyone who is seen or reported to break that law will be fined, just as folk are fined for not attending church.' John took his hat from its hook. 'If word got back we were partying on Christmas night I'd be fined, humiliated, reprimanded like a naughty child.' He twisted his hat round and round. 'Tell you what. We'll wait until January 1st, if it doesn't fall on the Sabbath. Well clear of Christmas. Then we'll show off our new home.'

'I'm happy with that. I'll check the almanac.'

John took his rifle from its place over the door. 'Off to shoot for the pot. Anything you need from Pris' store? I'll call by on my way home.'

'A sack of white flour and I'm running low on cotton thread again,' Sarah called from her seat by the fire, a pile of mending by her side.

John kissed Priscilla goodbye and opened the door to a world of swirling snow.

'Sky looks full of it,' Priscilla shuddered as she hurried to the hearth.

★ ★ ★

January 1st. Blue sky. The morning sun glinted off two feet of fresh hard crusted snow. Glorious day. On her way to the barn Priscilla breathed in the sparkling air. *The light is almost blinding. Hope Bessie and Bonnie can give us enough milk. Pray Susanna can get here. Should manage, now they have a horse. Peregrine can give John a hand with chopping logs.*

She returned with a good pail-full of fresh milk. *Hoped for more, but we'll make it do.* Her spacious hall was already bathed in enticing smells: pies, gingerbread, cakes. Bowls of sauces, nuts and dried berries and plates of cornbread stood on every available surface and two massive turkeys spit-roasted over the hearth. Priscilla took the pail of milk to the buttery and returned to the hearth to check the pots of venison stew, fish stew, succotash, beans and pork. She addressed her daughters. 'You are doing splendidly.' Sarah, Ruth, Mary and Rebecca, all flush faced with excitement and exertion, chopped: onions, turnips, carrots and pumpkin.

'Will we have a pumpkin filled with milk? Could we even try a pumpkin pie?' Sarah asked. 'Pris gave us a recipe brought down from Boston – remember?'

'It needs spices,' Priscilla said. 'I'll see what we have.'

'Pris gave us spices too, I've already looked,' Sarah said. 'We've nutmeg, ginger and cloves. Her store is bursting. Whenever I go there she has something new.'

'Well then – thanks to Pris we'll have a pumpkin pie!' Priscilla did a hop and a skip. 'Where's the recipe?'

'Here.' Sarah drew a folded parchment from her apron pouch. 'It says to first prepare a pastry shell. Ruth, you are the best pastry maker, even from coarse flour. You make the pastry while Mother and I do the second step.'

Priscilla interrupted. 'For this special occasion we'll have the upper crust made from white flour.'

Sarah continued with the recipe. 'Slice the pumpkin and fry with sweet herbs, spices, sugar and beaten eggs. Yum.'

Priscilla felt a surge of pleasure and fun. A new recipe, Sarah telling her what to do. She surveyed the room. Boughs decking beams and hearth. 'Oh – juniper boughs for the fire. I almost forgot. Jonathan… David…'

'I've already sent them out,' Sarah said. 'Rebecca and Mary, we need you to slice apples.'

She is so like Mother; hustling, knowing just what has to be done, everything in hand. For an instant Priscilla was back in the large Dorking kitchen, helping to prepare Christmas dinner: a table laden with stuffed partridge, a massive roast goose or two, pigs' feet laid on apples, thatched cottage pie, mince pies; and the cousins would soon arrive bearing pies and puddings, singing Wassail. A merry time. She snapped back into now. 'This is a luxury. Hope we don't run out of eggs. Perhaps Susanna will bring some.' Priscilla and Sarah fried the sliced pumpkin with the herbs and spices. 'Ah, the aroma! I wish it would last forever. Pastry ready? Apples ready? And we need some currants.'

'Place alternate layers of pumpkin mixture and apples and currants in the pastry shell,' Sarah read. 'There. Into the oven. If it is good can we make another?' she asked.

Rough barked as Jonathan and David came in the back door with baskets full of snow covered juniper branches. There was a knock on the front door.

'Susanna! Come in. Come in. And Peregrine with your lovely

wife. You're just in time for the noon meal; John should be back any minute.'

Jonathan greeted Peregrine. 'I'll help stable your horse. This way.'

Susanna hugged Priscilla and held out a basket. Priscilla lifted the cloth. 'Mince pies! How did you get the meats and spices?'

'Your Jonathan brought them from Boston when he went to buy supplies for Pris' store. Cost a penny or two but worth it for a treat. Just like the old country – hey.'

'I can scarce believe my eyes,' Priscilla said.

'And here.' Susanna gave her another basket.

'Eggs! Oh thank you. I was afraid we'd run out. I'm forgetting. Let me take your shawl – all snowy. Come warm yourself by the fire.'

'When I've thawed out, I'm longing to see round your house. It must be twice the size of the other.'

'I hardly know myself.' Priscilla inspected the venison stew. 'Four bedrooms, a large parlor, the long table set in there for dinner and Jonathan has lit a fire. Proper buttery – a big cellar. Yes it feels strange and wonderful.'

The last of the shadows of dusk were disappearing into a clear, starlit sky. Full moon.

'Look, Susanna, the gown you made me to celebrate the end of child-bearing.' Priscilla twirled, showing off the deep green taffeta, a close fitting waist and bodice with buttons of black velvet, a full skirt, exquisite broad lace collar and cuffs and the black sash Father gave her when they left London.

'It is lovely, if I do say so,' Susanna said.

'My beautiful wife.' John beamed, took her hand and bowed.

Priscilla curtsied. She glanced round her family, all dressed in their finest clothes. *They are a handsome lot.*

There was a knock on the door signaling more guests arriving. They came and came: Miles and Barbara Standish and four sons, the Howlands, Pris, and Elizabeth and William with their children and a guest.

'My friend John Bass.' William introduced a tall, dark-haired, slim young man. 'From Braintree. Here on a visit.'

'Welcome,' Priscilla said. ''Twill do us good to have someone from foreign parts bringing us fresh news. Meet Captain and Mistress Standish.'

'Ah – we all know of Captain Standish,' Mr Bass said.

'Have you brought your flute, Miles?' Priscilla asked.

'I made sure he did,' Barbara said. 'I know we'll want a merry tune, I told him.'

'Well done,' John said. 'Reckon everyone is here. It's just Jack and Joseph – too far away. We'll gather round the table for prayers.'

Priscilla took her place at one end of the table, resplendent with their feast and now, bedecked with candles. Bayberry candles. At the other end sat John. *My John. Still strong, standing straight, handsome, and all by his own efforts, he has risen from a cooper to a prominent position in our government.*

All evening the gathering feasted, paused to converse, feasted again. Priscilla watched Mary and Rebecca under Sarah's command, making sure serving dishes were passed and replenished. *I'm so proud of them, and I can be at ease.* She wasn't sure but she reckoned John Bass cast his eye often on Ruth. *She does look fetching in my wedding gown, that deep blue with her auburn curls and fair skin. Pity she's so shy, and quiet.*

Peregrine, sitting on her left, nudged Priscilla to attention. 'You know the Latham servant? The lad you treated in the summer?'

'Yes. Poor young man.'

'He's dead.'

'Dead?'

'I found him. Was on my way to deliver supplies from Pris' store. There he was by the track. A great log fallen on top of him. Like he'd been trying to carry it. An awful state he was in. Rags, no shoes, feet frostbit, bones poking through his skin, all bruised and wounded.'

Priscilla held onto the table to steady her dizzy head. She didn't want another mouthful of food. 'If only – if only I'd done more; tried harder to get him placed in another home.'

'But you couldn't have.' Peregrine placed a hand on her arm, frowning in concern. 'Mistress Latham, being Winslow's niece, is untouchable. But they can't stop the body being submitted to the coroner.'

Pris, sitting on Priscilla's other side said, 'But we should all be equal before the law, and she isn't royalty.'

'Plymouth doesn't want to upset Boston. Her father's position there… we need to be in Boston's good books. Trade, protection.'

Priscilla gazed down the table, watching the laughing, talking, pouring of ale. There were autumn hues of roasted fowl, baked pie crusts, gingerbread, cornbread. She gazed and heard as if from another world. She was kneeling by the broken and bruised body lying frozen in the snow, looking in from outside on this scene of merry warmth. Gradually the voices grew dim, the liveliness more distant.

'Mother. Are you alright?' Pris' voice broke through.

Priscilla turned and slowly her daughter came into focus.

'You're pale,' Pris took her hand. 'You're cold.'

'I'm so sorry,' Peregrine said. 'I hope I haven't distressed you.'

'No. Don't worry. Must be the warmth. Not used to it. I'll go check on Susanna's mince pies warming.' She left the table and concentrating on keeping her balance walked carefully through the kitchen and out through the back door into the quiet, clear night. Dark branches glistened with frost and snow in the moonlight. An owl called. So cold. How many birds would be lying dead on the snow in the morning? Frozen, fallen from their perches. Nature's lethal beauty. *At least he's out of his misery. May his soul rest in peace.* Roger Williams' face came into her vision; his kind searching eyes. *Such a thing would not happen in Rhode Island.* She shook her head, trying to bring herself back into the present. *We are having a party.*

Slowly, she returned to the kitchen and took two of Susanna's pies from the oven. Now her skin was flaming hot. Adopting a smile she carried the pies into the parlor. Sarah followed bringing the two pumpkin pies and a third mince pie.

John rose, raising his beaker of ale. 'To all our good women for this glorious feast.'

'Hear, hear! Salutations!' Standish led the chorus of men scrambling to their feet.

The table cleared and moved back against the wall, Standish withdrew his flute from his pouch. As he played, John, Priscilla, Barbara and Susanna all taught the young ones the steps of folk dances from the old world: *The Winding Dance, Maiden's Dance, Hay Dance*. Growing up in Plymouth's world, there was no opportunity to learn to dance. Only John Bass knew all the steps.

'How did you learn?' Priscilla asked.

'My father and mother are not strict Puritans,' he said. 'They believe merriment is good for the soul.' His dark eyes twinkled as he skillfully maneuvered himself to take a place beside Ruth.

He is charming. Priscilla smiled.

John crossed the room to join her. 'Look,' he said quietly, nodding slightly in the direction of Sarah, welcoming Alexander Standish by her side.

All the guests had departed except for the Standishes. John and Miles sat by the hearth.

Barbara joined Priscilla washing the trenchers. 'I need to ask you,' she said. 'Miles has been complaining of pains in his chest. Doesn't say much but I think it has been going on for some time.'

Priscilla questioned her about the symptoms.

'He doesn't like to speak of it – and then, when he doesn't know I'm watching, he'll wince and clutch himself.'

'Indigestion?'

'I ventured to ask him. He says not.'

Priscilla suspected stones but didn't want to say so. It was a difficult cure and if not got rid of caused a long, painful death. *Pray not. John loves Miles like a brother.*

'Here's a bottle of sperage.' She wrote out the dosage. 'Follow this exactly and if there's no improvement in two weeks we'll try something else. Let's join our men by the hearth awhile.' Priscilla fetched her knitting. She and Barbara arranged themselves on the settle.

'Steady stream coming over,' Miles was saying. 'Fleeing persecution in England. Strange folk. No church buildings. They meet in houses and sit in silence until someone is "moved" by the holy spirit to stand and speak.'

'Then what happens?' John asked.

'The person sits down when he's finished. Then there's more silence until someone else is "moved". That's what they call it. Or so I'm told. Young John Bass was telling me. He's gone to one of their meetings in Boston – out of curiosity.'

'Sounds very odd,' John said.

'Oddest thing – women are allowed to speak!'

'No!'

'You can imagine they're not popular in Boston. Quakers, they're dubbed, because sometimes when they're speaking they tremble.'

'What is their belief?' Priscilla intervened.

'Absolute simplicity. No sacraments. Not even baptism. Call themselves "Friends". No hierarchy, no doctrine. Just every person being open to God. Peaceful. Refuse to fight.'

'Chaos,' John said. 'Folk need preaching; to be told what to believe or at least to follow the scriptures – otherwise, chaos.'

'Mr Bass said there's three been hanged recently and a woman, Mary Dyer, exiled.'

'On what grounds hanged?' Priscilla asked.

'Sedition, rebellion, presumptuous obtruding.'

'But those aren't hanging offenses.'

'I guess they reckon sedition and treason are the same thing. Well, my dear Barbara, I reckon 'tis time we were off.'

'I'll bring your horse and cart round,' Jonathan said. Alexander went with him, casting a goodbye glance at Sarah, sitting beside her mother.

Priscilla stood with John in the doorway, waving the Standish family farewell. As they disappeared into the wood John put his arm round Priscilla and walked her back to the hearth.

'A splendid party,' he said. 'My clever wife. 'Twas a merry feast.'

'Aye, a merry evening,' Priscilla said aloud. *With a wound running through it. We should have done something to help the lad, not just accepted.* Her stomach tightened and she clenched her fists. *Never again. Never again will I just accept. I'll not spoil John's pleasure now. Tell him tomorrow.*

Chapter 76

Spring 1656

John is shaken

Priscilla on his arm, John walked with measured pace along the street to Ducksburrow's meeting house; the meeting house he and Standish had built years ago; at this moment covered with wolves heads nailed onto the external walls, showing the men of Ducksburrow were vigorous in their efforts to protect livestock.

The Aldens passed through the clusters of folk gathered outside, exchanging greetings. As they stepped through the doorway John scanned the congregation. *All the usuals but, Miles and Barbara not here?* Priscilla removed her arm from his and took a seat by Elizabeth. John sat across the aisle beside William and his father.

Miles must be worse. First time he hasn't managed Sabbath – and for Barbara to be absent too… Disquiet filled him. *Everyone in black. Though we always wear black on Sabbath.* A raucous cawing of crows penetrated the preacher's drone. He shuddered with foreboding and told himself to shake it off. *Listen to the preacher.* But his mind drifted, back to the early years with Miles: building the first houses in Plymouth, Miles suggesting how to lay out the colony, taking charge, organizing, practical. Above all, loyal. *I know he hasn't got long, but 'til now I'd hoped.* Beside him William stood. Prayers.

The preacher, as always, prayed and preached on and on. The hour glass showed an hour gone. John kept his eyes on the preacher, but the rest of his being was elsewhere, traversing the years, the adventures: finding Plymouth Harbor, the huggery, near shipwreck in the squall, troubles with Squanto, Massasoit's fury, building the wall, then the fort...

The preacher stopped, mouth agape, eyes staring straight down the aisle.

'Woe, woe. Parson! Thou art an old fool.' A woman's voice. John turned. Three disheveled women made their way up the aisle, the first discarding her scant hessian dress as she came. 'Parson! Thy sermon is too long. Sit down. Thee has already said more than thee knows how to say well. Thee speaks nonsensical doctrine. Gibberish!' By the time she had reached as far as John's seat she was naked. The preacher covered his eyes with his hands. His flock stared, wide-eyed.

'What creature is this?' screeched a goodwife, swooning into ready arms.

John, William and the tithingman escorted the woman and her companions back down the aisle and out the door.

'Get dressed and be gone,' John said. 'Before you are put in the stocks or worse.'

The naked woman held her hessian frock over her front. She looked John in the eye. In the instant he was held by a clear, honest blue-gray gaze. 'All those words and doctrines get in the way. If you really want God's truth you must be still and listen.' She spoke quietly.

Silence. John didn't know how many seconds, minutes had passed while she held him with her eyes. He shook his head and shoulders as if to shake off a cumbersome cloak. 'Begone! Begone, I say. No more of your crazy ways.' He turned and strode back into the meeting.

Seated again, he had difficulty holding still. He wanted to go... go to his friend. When the Sabbath meeting finally came to a close he hurried through the excited, babbling crowd to Priscilla, talking with Susanna. 'Good day, Susanna. Excuse me interrupting.' Taking Priscilla's elbow he said, 'Miles isn't here. I'll go call in on him now, come home after.'

Barbara answered his knock. 'John. Come in. Do come in.'

My Lord, she looks ill as well. Probably distress and worry. John followed Barbara to the hearth where Miles sat in his rocker, a rug over his knees, his face soft and gray.

The captain's eyes lit up in welcome. 'My friend.' Then, seized in pain, he ground his clenched teeth. Beads of sweat broke out on his ashen face. The spasm passed.

Barbara mopped his face with a cloth. 'As you can see, it's much worse, just since we saw you last – a week?'

'Aye,' John said.

Miles smiled faintly. 'I'm glad you've come. What news? Do take a seat.' He gestured to the other rocker.

'Just today,' John said, 'there we were standing all quiet during the prayers, when up the aisle came three crazy women, shouting "woe, woe, woe" and would you believe it one took off her dress. Stood stark naked in front of the preacher, uttering blasphemy.'

Miles shook his head, a smile hovering. 'Entertaining. Livened things up I'll wager.'

'William and I hustled them out and sent them packing. Quakers, I reckon they were. A pestilence. A disruptive pestilence. Crazy people. All this about preaching being a waste of time; just be still and listen, they say. Worse than Roger Williams if 'twere possible.' John leaned forward, elbows on his knees, staring at the floor. 'They're too unsettling. Folk need leaders, strong men like you to keep control. Else all we've struggled and worked for could dissolve.' He looked imploringly at Miles.

'Don't worry,' Miles said. 'It will blow over. They'll go on their way when they see they're not getting anywhere.' He looked John in the eye. 'The time is coming for me to go on my way too.' He stopped to endure another bout of pain. When it subsided he said, between breaths, 'I'd like you... to witness my will. In the drawer of my desk.' He feebly waved a hand in the direction of his desk standing against the wall.

John found a parchment scroll tied with a black ribbon, and handed it to Miles. The captain untied the ribbon and unrolled the scroll. 'It is important you know what you are signing,' he said, and started to read.

John sat again in the rocker. The reading was long and painful. '...And finally, I give unto my son and heir apparent, Alexander Standish, all my lands as heir apparent by lawful descent in England and the Isle of Man, including the estate of Duxbury Hall... usurped from my line of the family by my great-grandfather.'

'Miles! In all these years you have never mentioned these lands,' John said.

'Ah well, you see, I have always been aware folk thought me pompous.' Miles stopped to gather his strength. 'And perhaps I was, a little. So I decided to say nothing lest it be turned against me as further evidence of my pomposity.'

'Duxbury Hall.' John stood and paced in front of the hearth. ''Tis but a small change from Ducksburrow to Duxbury. I want this town to be named Duxbury in honor of you.'

'To be sure, I would be honored,' Miles replied, his voice now barely a whisper.

'You are spent,' John said. He rested the will on Standish's Bible on his lap. When Miles had signed and John had witnessed, John replaced the document in the desk. 'I'll call on you again tomorrow,' he said, laying a hand on Miles' shoulder. The weary head nodded and a withered hand clasped John's.

'Ah. Wait.' Standish lifted his hand. 'Barbara... please fetch... *Iliad*.' He gestured toward his bookshelf. 'I want you... to have it, John... fond memories.'

'Thank you, Miles. I'll treasure it always.' John's eyes swam with tears.

Head down, he trudged through the open door of his house. Priscilla rose from reading the Bible aloud to their six grown children.

'You look sad. Bad news?'

John nodded. 'He's made out his will; asked me to witness it. He is in terrible pain. White with it. Teeth clenched and grinding.'

'Nothing I've given him has worked,' Priscilla said. 'If only we had a doctor.'

'I doubt a doctor could have helped him any more than you; most likely have made it worse. I don't know how he can go on like this much longer. Skin and bones. Barbara says he won't eat.'

'We must send Jonathan to Boston for some opium,' Priscilla said, turning toward their son.

Jonathan stood. 'Surely I'll go. Pris needs some supplies, but I'd go in any case.'

★ ★ ★

A light breeze stirred young leaves on this fair, fresh spring morning.

'Safe journey and bring us word of your brother,' John said. He and Priscilla waved as Jonathan and Alexander, riding Standish's two mares, set off.

'Alexander said Barbara had a list, and he had a yen to go in any case,' John said.

Indoors, discussing the day's chores, Priscilla said, 'Elizabeth has asked if she could borrow Ruth today to help her with the children. You know she's about to give birth any minute.'

'She is enormous.'

'She also let slip John Bass is staying. I have a hunch he'll be calling on you soon.'

'He seems a good man. Father well established and respected – a Deacon.' John drew his hand across the back of his neck and wiped his brow. 'I'll be off to the fields. It's a race to get the crops in.'

John walked slowly through the orchard. Beautiful plum blossom, woodland unfolding soft spring green. *Miles is dying. My truest friend. How many years? Must be thirty-five. Always loyal and forgiving. Hot-headed at times, could be cruel in battle, but as a friend always talked straight, eager to help, great problem solver. God how I'll miss him.* He looked up, scanning the far field. David and Arthur were ploughing with Miles' oxen. *Thanks be Arthur comes to help when he can.*

Come dinner time, John, David and Arthur tramped through the farmyard toward the kitchen, savoring smells wafting through the open door.

'Welcoming odors,' John said as he stepped into the kitchen. He stopped. Seated at the table, eating, were a young man and a woman and a boy child, dressed in plain gray, no collars or cuffs. Quakers. 'Who? Why are they here?' he demanded, almost shouting.

'John. They've had nothing to eat, walking all the way from Boston. Banished with threat of hanging,' Priscilla said. 'The lad fell on a sharp rock; has a deep cut in his leg. Folk in the town sent them here.'

'I'll not have them in my house. Someone else can look after them. Lunatic fanatics. NEVER in my house. Out!'

'We'll go. Thank you, Mistress,' the man said. Silently, patiently, the three bowed their heads as Priscilla escorted them to the door.

John strode to the book chest and lifted out his Bible. 'Prayers,' he said. Without hesitation he found the page he wanted. His voice was unhurried but stern. 'Psalm 144. "Rid me and deliver me from the hand of strange children, whose mouth speaketh vanity, and their right hand is a right hand of falsehood." Now we may eat.'

During the meal no one spoke. Glancing round the table, John saw all eyes focused on their trenchers, Priscilla's as well. He ate rapidly. His family and Arthur kept up with him, finishing when he did. The girls hurried out to the garden. He said to Arthur and David, 'Go on ahead. I'll be along shortly.' Only Priscilla remained.

'Priscilla, listen to me.'

She stopped with her armload of trenchers and turned to face him.

'As your husband, I command you, following the Holy Word. You are **never** to allow another Quaker to set foot inside this house. They are wolves in sheep's clothing, using clever ways to subvert all we have strived for and hold to be God's will and true. Heretics. You saw those crazy Quaker women come into our Sabbath. 'Twere best they were purged from the land, plague and pestilence that they are.'

Priscilla turned and dumped the trenchers into the washing pail. With her back to him she said, 'I will do as you say, John, because you commanded me to.' Turning back to face him, hands on her hips, she continued, 'But I cannot agree. I cannot believe you are so hard hearted against these poor persecuted people who…'

A firm, steady knock on the door, meant to be heard but not a hammering.

John opened. 'Mr Bass! Do come in.'

'Good day, Mr Bass,' Priscilla answered his greeting. 'I'll leave the two of you to your business. I will be in the garden if you have need of me.'

John invited Mr Bass to be seated in Priscilla's rocking chair, whilst taking his own place. He crossed his legs.

Mr Bass sat, elbows on knees, leaning forward, hat in hand. 'I'll come straight to the point, Mr Alden. I've come to ask permission to court your daughter Ruth.'

John met his eyes, deep brown, looking straight at him. 'Well, Mr Bass.' He leant back in his rocker and lit his pipe. 'I know nothing about you, except that you're a friend of William's and your father is a Deacon.'

'He is, but not of the Pilgrim's persuasion. I have a farm – around three hundred acres, and a substantial farmhouse. Do you mind that we are not of your church?'

John leaned forward. 'Mr Bass. Captain Standish is Anglican. A better man you won't find in all Christendom. No; it's the wretched

Quakers I detest.' He leaned back again. 'But about Ruth. I have to tell you she isn't quite as strong, robust as my other girls. I'm not sure how well she would cope with a life of heavy farm tasks.'

'I have servants, Mr Alden. House servants to fetch water, do the laundry, butchering, digging. Ruth is so kind and gentle and modest; I'm sure all my family would want to care for her and make her happy, as I do.'

'That does make a difference.' John studied the earnest, hopeful young man and felt moved by his warmth and commitment. 'You may court Ruth, Mr Bass, provided she consents.' He stood. Suddenly realizing his beautiful Ruth would be leaving them, he wanted to end the interview. He rather abruptly escorted Mr Bass to the door. 'Fare you well. We'll see you again soon, no doubt.'

He strode off up to the fields without telling Priscilla, needing to be alone. *Standish dying. Jack and Joseph both gone. Elizabeth married, and now Ruth, and she'll be going so far away. I don't want her to go so far. Pray God he'll care for her.*

When John came back to the house for supper Ruth had come in from the garden.

'Hello, Father,' she said.

He saw the question in her face and took her hands in his. 'Mr Bass called this afternoon. He asked permission to court you. I said yes, if you agree.'

Ruth looked down at her hands, enclosed in her father's protective clasp. 'Yes, I agree,' she whispered.

John gathered her to him and held her tight. He felt his heart would break. *Why haven't I paid her more heed? And now – she'll be gone.* Aware the room was silent, with no pre-meal bustle, he stepped back. 'Ruth is to be courted by John Bass.' He watched as Priscilla and the girls kissed her. David and Arthur voiced hearty congratulations.

'I must be going now, Mr Alden,' Arthur said.

'Tomorrow?' John asked. *Still four fields to sow.*

'I'm sorry. I can't tomorrow. I'm late getting my crops in.'

'Of course.' *Of course. He is married, with his own land. I'm not thinking straight. Alexander will help when he and Jonathan return. So much disturbance.* 'Of course, Arthur. Thank you for all your help.'

★ ★ ★

'I'll call in on Miles,' John told Priscilla next morning. 'We've been talking about the early years, the trials and successes. Helps take his mind off the pain.'

'Jonathan should be back today. Pray he got some opium.' Chopping onions, Priscilla didn't raise her eyes.

'Anything you need from Pris' store?' He shrank from Priscilla's cold, held-in anger. Worse than when she stormed. *Why does she think we should care for lunatic Quakers?*

'A small packet of currants, if she has some.' Priscilla turned her back and carried the platter of chopped onions to the stew pot.

Shrugging his shoulders, John trudged down his track, oblivious to the sounds and sights of an exuberant spring morning.
Leaving his dying friend, John tried to comfort Barbara. Fraught, distracted, she twisted her hands, dabbed wet cheeks with her apron. 'I don't know what to do... what to do.'

'There, there, Barbara. You are doing all you can. He's a brave man and you are a good wife. Take comfort knowing he loves you dearly.'

'Will Priscilla come soon?' Barbara asked. 'I've used up almost all the syrup she gave me.'

'I'll tell her. I'm sure she'll be along tomorrow. Goodbye for the moment.' He placed his hands on her shoulders and gave a squeeze.

Walking through the grove surrounding Standish's house along the track leading to the town, John's legs felt heavy; his head was fuzzy with fatigue and sadness. *Must try to perk up for Pris. Who's that ahead? It can't be.* 'William Bradford!' He called out, quickened his step, ran a few paces then walked fast again. 'Bradford, Bradford.' Catching up, breathless, he gasped, 'What brings you to Ducksburrow? This is a first visit, is it not?'

'It is, and not a happy one.'

'Oh?'

'I'm on my way to Marshfield. I've received a letter informing me of Edward Winslow's death – last year. On an English expedition against the Spanish in the West Indies. Yellow fever. Died and was buried at sea, with honors, off Jamaica. It is my sad duty to tell Susanna.'

'You look weary, sir. Would you like me to go instead?'

'Thank you, but no. I must do this.' Bradford's head drooped. 'So sad. No. I'll be fine. Please give my regards to Mistress Alden.'

'I will. Goodbye, sir.' John raised his hat and walked on, his heart constricting. *Winslow dead. Our leaders – all our courageous leaders – going.* He stopped briefly at Pris' store, and told her the news. 'I must hurry back and tell Priscilla. Most likely she'll invite Susanna to bide with us awhile.' He kissed his daughter. 'You're a good lass.'

When John told Priscilla of Winslow's death she sat down heavily. 'He was a good, kind man. Susanna never stopped hoping that one day he would come home and not go away again.' She looked at John. 'Thank you. Yes. I'd love her to come here for a time.'

'I'll go to Marshfield in the morning,' John said. 'I hope Jonathan comes soon, and pray he's been able to buy the opium. Barbara says she's hardly any of your syrup left.'

'Tomorrow morning I'll take her another jar of syrup,' Priscilla said. ''Tis a heavy hearted time.'

★ ★ ★

John stood in front of the Winslows' door, a door of thick oak panels, a large wrought iron knocker. He rapped. No answer. He rapped again with greater insistence. The door opened. Josiah stood there, silent and stern. This was the first time John had looked closely at Winslow's eldest son. His long face was bisected by straight lines; dark hair cropped in a straight fringe across his brow, eyebrows unarched, meeting at the bridge of his nose, mouth fixed in a thin line; all this set on a long neck with an Adam's apple the size of a walnut.

'Mr Alden, what can I do for you?' As Josiah spoke and swallowed, it was as if the 'walnut' were trying to dislodge itself.

John focused his gaze on his host's gray eyes. 'I've come with condolences, and to ask your mother if she'd like to bide with us awhile.'

'It is best Mother remains here. My sister needs her presence, and I want her here until the will has been read and Father's estate dealt with.'

'Josiah – who is that?' John heard Susanna's voice.

''Tis Mr Alden.'

Susanna hurried into view. 'Mr Alden. Do come in. We're about to have dinner.'

Josiah, rather ungraciously, John thought, stepped aside.

Although he was glad of a meal, it was a silent, half-hearted repast. Preparing to take his leave John took Susanna's hands in his. 'Priscilla sends her love. She would welcome a visit from you.'

Susanna looked at Josiah. 'I'll bide here a week, and then yes. Peregrine will bring me; a week today.' She smiled at John. 'Thank you.'

The evening light was beginning to fade. 'I'm surprised Jonathan and Alexander aren't here yet. On horseback, if they started early… it's time for prayers.' John paced the floor. Priscilla, the girls and David gathered round the table. John opened the Bible. He began to speak and stopped. 'What was that?' Rough barked. 'Hush, Rough. Quiet.' Through the silence, a whinny.

'They're back, they're back.' Shouting, barking, the family and Rough rushed out.

Jonathan and Alexander trotted to the front door and dismounted. *They aren't smiling. Something is wrong? They look…* John searched the clouded faces.

'Father,' Jonathan said, 'I'm sorry there is bad news. Jack is in prison, in Boston. He's been locked up for two weeks, doesn't know when he'll be released.'

'No,' John croaked. 'How? Why?'

The girls and David gathered round, silent.

'Took a time to piece it together. He's done nothing wrong. He was just returned from a sea voyage; has his own ship now. He was standing in the street talking with a couple of Quakers and the constable hustled them all into prison.'

'Damn those Quakers!' John thundered. 'He could hang – just for being seen with them. They are a curse; a curse, a curse.' He punched his palm with his fist. 'My son!'

Alexander handed Priscilla a small pouch. 'The opium.'

'Thank you,' she said, taking the pouch with shaking hands.

'I'll stable the horses. David, give me a hand,' Alexander said.

'You'll stay for a meal?' Priscilla put a hand on Alexander's arm.

'Aye, thank you,' he said, gathering the reins.

'I'll go to Plymouth first light; get someone to go to Boston – now – get him released.' John strode indoors. 'If only Standish were well. He'd do it. Or Bradford, but he's not up to it. Oh, who is there?' He circled the table. 'If only Winslow...' He halted. 'Prence. The only man I can think of. I reckon Governor Endecott would listen to Prence. He too hates the Quakers. Could vouch Jack isn't one.' He looked at Priscilla. 'You agree?'

'I can't think of anyone else.'

'Decided. Court session begins tomorrow. I'll speak to Prence before we convene. Now,' he addressed his waiting family. 'Prayers and supper.'

As he began to read, the words swam. *Get hold*, he said to himself, steadying his voice. He knew the psalm so well he could recite it. 'Make haste, O God, to deliver me; make haste to help me, O Lord...' (Psalm 70).

Priscilla and Sarah served up a stew of fowl: pigeons, partridge, goose, duck. The familiar food looked strange. He ate without tasting, thinking of his son, festering in the kind of prison cell he knew so well; the dark cramped space, cold fetid damp, fleas, lice and vile jailer. After supper he couldn't settle. It was impossible to sit in his rocker. While Sarah and Ruth washed the trenchers and Priscilla took her place at the spinning wheel, John paced.

'Wretched Quakers. Jack could hang,' he said to no one in particular.

'But John,' Priscilla stopped spinning. 'It isn't their fault. They were only having a conversation.'

John rounded on her. 'How can you be so blind, disloyal? Your own son. Winslow dead. Standish dying. Bradford soon to go. Hope to God Prence can save him. If those lunatics weren't in Boston, our Jack would not be in prison. Maybe to lose his life!' He clenched and unclenched his fists, wiped his hot brow. 'I'm going to check on the livestock.'

Chapter 77

Spring 1656

Jack's story

Wearily, after a sleepless night, Priscilla prepared John's knapsack. Apart from prayers, no one spoke until Priscilla bade John goodbye. 'I'll be thinking of you, praying Prence is willing to help. I'm going to call on Standish this morning, with opium and digitalis. That should help with the pain.'

'Good.' John kissed her cheek and turned to go on his way.

Priscilla was restless, numb with worry, ready to weep thinking of Jack in prison; the cruelty and misery. *Must focus. Must get this mixture right. Too much will kill him. Must make Barbara understand – only one dose per day.*

It was noon by the time she returned from the Standishes, weary and sad, admiring the captain's silent endurance. Sweating and twisting, he'd bitten on a stick, never crying out.

As she opened the front door she fell backwards. A hunched figure sat at the table, his back to her. From his heaving shoulders she could see he was breathing heavily. *From running? Not a Quaker. Isn't dressed like a Quaker.* She slowly approached. He turned round. 'Jack!' She grabbed him; clutched him close. 'My boy, my boy.' She leaned back to look again. 'Is it really you? You got away?'

'They helped me escape – the Quakers – I'll tell you but I'm starving. Only just ran in.'

Hearing voices the girls came in from the garden. They stared, mouths agape in silent disbelief; then clapping hands, calling out, hurried to supply food.

'Mary, fetch Jonathan. He'll need to go to Plymouth to stop Prence going to Boston.' Priscilla asked Jack, 'Would you prefer food first, or to get clean?'

'Just a hunk of cornbread. Then I'll wash.'

'Sarah, fetch a suit of John's clothes. I'll prepare a solution to deal with the lice and fleas.'

By the time Jack was clean and in fresh clothes it was the hour for prayers and dinner. When he had assuaged his hunger he told his story.

'I was standing on the main street of the town, talking with two Quaker men. "Friends" they call themselves. Having not a few hours returned from a long sea voyage I didn't know of the hatred against them and was simply interested to find out their beliefs. Before I knew what was happening two constables had grabbed us, herded us to prison and clapped us, all three of us, in a minute cell.' He stood and paced out the area. 'We moldered there, the jailer mocking, treating us badly every chance he got. Often he'd throw our victuals in so the mess landed on the floor. "Clean it up" he'd say jeering. "Eat it off the floor." Or he'd pour the trencherful over our heads. I got furious and railed at him, but the other two were always patient and kind. Never lost their temper. I asked them how they could not be angry. "Wait, wait on the Lord," was always their response. To be frank, I couldn't understand. Then, gradually, the jailer seemed to grow tired of his tormenting games. He became curious. Speaking to him as if he were intelligent and worthy of respect, they explained their belief;

that every person is worthy in the sight of God, no matter how bad they have been. Every person has a place inside himself where Christ lives. Every person can be guided by His light. He has only to be still, and wait, and God will speak.

'They invited him and me to sit with them in silence. We did. From that moment the jailer's behavior changed. He sat with us often. The spirit and goodwill of the two Friends seemed to seep into him. Morning before last he announced that he wanted to help us escape.' Jack looked down and wept. 'Their response was to tell him to set me free but not them. They told him if he set us all free and we were caught, I would be branded as one of them and hanged with them for sure. I begged them. Please, please, I said. Please come. We'll head for Ducksburrow. But no. So under the cover of dark, the jailer led me out of there, through back streets and set me on the road to here, saying at last he'd done something good in his life, wishing me well.'

There was silence. All heads bowed.

'A miracle,' Priscilla said.

'Truly good people,' Jack said. 'They suffer horrible cruelty in Boston.'

'Quakers are given refuge here by some,' Priscilla said, 'and hated by others.' She looked down at her folded hands resting on the table. 'I must warn you, your father is one who hates them. Holds them responsible for you being thrown in prison, and could have been hanged.'

'No – that is wrong!' Jack banged his fist on the table. 'I chose to speak with them. They didn't force me.' He stood.

'Please try not to argue and upset him,' Priscilla said. 'Captain Standish is dying. Winslow is dead. He'll be so happy you are here safe.'

'I'll try. Now I'll make myself useful.' He put an arm round David's shoulder. 'Show me what to do, little brother. You're a big lad now.'

Overwhelmed with joy and relief for Jack, grief for Standish and Susanna, revulsion at the torture of the Quakers, a jumble of feelings all at once, Priscilla could hardly stand. 'Must get on with the spinning,' she mumbled, taking steps toward the wheel.

'I'll spin this afternoon,' Sarah said. 'You go do something in the garden or orchard. Bide there awhile.'

'Thank you,' Priscilla said.

Next morning Priscilla woke, joyful with disbelief. *Jack is home, with us. In the family again.*

'How long will you stay?' she asked, when they were gathered for breakfast.

'I reckon until things have settled down in Boston; less of a rampage. Then I'll captain a trading expedition. No hanging at sea. Not on my ship.'

'I'm so glad to hear it, Jack. Your father will be too. You know he doesn't like corporal punishment, even for the Quakers.'

Jack took his younger brothers to plant field crops. Priscilla allocated the daily tasks among her daughters. 'Ruth, would you please go into town and tell William, Elizabeth, and Pris that Jack is here and invite them all to dinner. Also, stop in to see Captain Standish on your way home and check that Barbara is giving him the correct dose.' She sighed. 'We'll prepare a big dinner while you're gone, and in any time left to spare, do the garden. Spinning and mending can wait.'

With the family gathered round the table, excited and happy to welcome Jack, dinner was a happy time of storytelling and reminiscing. Elizabeth and William's four children frolicked and mercilessly petted and kissed Rough, patient in his old age. Elizabeth was full in her pregnancy. *She does well in her child-bearing, and raising them.* Priscilla admired her hearty daughter, still beautiful with her clear skin and blond curls. *Only Joseph and their father not here. Pity.* Rough growled and stiffly got to his feet, discarding loving hands. There was knocking, timid, weak.

Jack opened the door and stepped back.

'They said to come here,' a tired voice rasped.

'C-come in,' Jack said.

Priscilla gasped. A woman staggered into the room, diminutive in gray, with blood soaked linen wrapped over her head and under her chin, bandaging her ears, holding the hand of a man, cheek oozing raw burns. 'Oh my God in heaven,' Priscilla moaned.

With Elizabeth, Pris and Sarah helping her she bathed and dressed the ghastly wounds: gashes where ears should have been, burns from hot irons, backs savaged from flaying with tarred ropes. Bits of tar had to be scraped out. Long and painful. When the job was accomplished, Priscilla asked, 'Do you want to eat?'

Mute and shaking with pain the couple shook their heads 'No.'

'Try a little stew. Give you some strength.'

William left off his subdued conversation with Jack. 'They can't stay here.'

'I know,' Priscilla said. 'John has ordered... no question...'

'We'll take them back with us. There's many folk in town offering refuge.'

'A steady stream coming from Boston,' Pris said. 'I have a small family staying. The Quakers all gather in my back room to hold meeting for worship.' She stood straight. 'I can't find any harm in the Friends. None at all. And the women take part.'

'Please don't let your father know you think this way,' Priscilla said. 'He is terribly upset just now. If he knew his own family were harboring Quakers...'

'We'll say nothing, of course.' William guided the injured couple to the door.

★ ★ ★

Priscilla woke to the sound of rain, fine steady rain. She stretched. *Good. Not too heavy, not stormy, perfect timing with most of the plants in and corn sown in the fields.* She rose, made up the fire, swept the hearth and checked the bake oven. Bread today. Rough roused himself, pressing his white muzzle against Priscilla's leg and then lay down again. 'Good dog. You are elderly. Not so good of hearing these days. Pain in the joints?' Priscilla scratched him behind the ears.

The household set about its daily routine: men in the fields, rain or no, women indoors, cooking, mending, spinning. Sarah spun flax; Ruth and Mary started on piles of mending while Rebecca helped Priscilla at the hearth. Beautiful loaves of bread and fruit pies soon streamed from the bake oven.

'Smells so good,' Mary looked longingly at a pan of cornbread.

'Cornbread and maple syrup for supper,' Priscilla said.

'Halloo, halloo,' John came bounding through the door, greeted by Rough's belated bark. 'Where is my son? I must see him.'

Priscilla smiled at her husband. 'Up in the fields. Almost time for supper.' John disappeared out the back door.

When supper was cleared, the family sat round the hearth waiting for Jack to tell his father of his escape and to listen to John's news of the court session. When Jack had come to the end of his story he looked at his father and said, 'They are good people.'

'Good or bad they are disruptive lunatics,' John said. 'I know Boston have tortured them and I don't approve of that. We don't torture them here; not beyond a whipping, but they have to go. A contamination, like the plague, we must get rid of them.'

Silence hung over the room.

'Tell us the news. What happened in the court session?' Priscilla asked.

'The usual fines for fornication: four or five. Our friend Peregrine was one. Fornicated with his fiancée before marriage. I'm sure there are more crimes than in the early years. A woman was sentenced to whipping for unclean behavior by her husband and for lying with her brother. A woman was brought before the court for chopping her stepfather in the back with an axe. As she is with child she was given the choice between a ten pound fine or to be publicly whipped when her condition permits. There were several cases of servant abuse, and last, we heard the coroner's report on the Latham servant.' John stood and knocked out his pipe over the fire. Priscilla ceased mending and leaned forward. John sat down, lit his pipe again and drew breath. 'It was appalling. We sentenced Latham to death and indicted his wife for cruelty and neglect. However, Latham, clever fox, claimed benefit of clergy, which is that if the accused can read verse 1 of Psalm 51, asking for the mercy of God, he can escape being hanged. This was granted! Never before in this colony has it been granted! So he'll get away with having his hand burned and, as he has no lands, all his goods confiscated. As for his wife, no one has come forward to prosecute her so the case will be struck from the records. It is what I've said from the beginning. It's because she is Winslow's niece.'

'Wrong. So dreadfully wrong,' Priscilla left her seat and circled the table. 'For such atrocious cruelty to be treated so lightly.'

John waited until his wife sat down again. He cast his eye round his family. 'I sailed on the *Mayflower* strong in the belief we would build a society where there was equal justice for all, servant and master, no lords and ladies.' He looked at the floor, shaking his head. 'It is worrying, so much crime and disturbance. So much jostling and maneuvering as to who is higher and lower; so much unrest, and the Quakers stirring no end of mischief.' He drew a sheet of parchment from his pouch. 'This is a letter sent to me from a Quaker we banished about a month ago. He went to Rhode Island and has now popped up again. Stupid fool. Prence brought him before the court accusing him of "many offenses against God". So we sentenced him to be whipped. But the punishment couldn't be carried out because he refused to pay the marshal his whipping fee. So we banished him again and on leaving he gave me this.' John's hands trembled as he held the parchment out to read.

'John Alden, I have weighed thy ways, and thou art like one fallen from thy first love: a tenderness once I did see in thee, and moderation to act like a sober man, which through evil counsel and self-love thou art drawn aside from... like a self-conceited fool, puffed up with the pride of his heart because he hath gotten the name of a magistrate... In love this is written, to dishearten thee in time before the evil day overtook thee; let it be so received from thy friend.'

'Did you ever hear such malicious, devious slander? Goes to show they're lunatics. The court decided to appoint our William, and Alice Bradford's son, Southworth, to sit in on Quaker meetings here in Ducksburrow and through argument persuade them of the wrong of their ways, and to go far, far away and never return.'

Priscilla looked at John with concern. *He is terribly agitated, unsettled. Longing for stability and security. We all do. With so many deaths and the Quaker disruptions, it feels a bit like an earthquake.*

That night in bed John whispered, 'I didn't speak of it to the family, but the worst is, Prence refused to go to Boston on Jack's behalf. He and Bradford refused that anyone should go.'

'Impossible,' Priscilla gasped. 'Why?'

'They don't want to do anything to cause ripples in Boston. Say we are too in need of Governor Endecott's goodwill and support, both for trade, and protection in case of trouble with the Indians. 'Twas horrible to see the look of satisfaction on Prence's face as he delivered the decision.'

Priscilla shivered.

★ ★ ★

John led the procession following Captain Standish's coffin. Immediately behind him Priscilla supported Barbara, now thin and wasted, weeping. Behind and surrounding Priscilla and Barbara, every soul in the town had come to pay their respects. Priscilla admired the coffin, John's work, polished elm, inscribed 'To Miles Standish from his friend John Alden'.

After the committal John addressed the gathered crowd. He spoke briefly of his admiration of Standish and of their friendship and then proposed that in light of Standish's estate in the old country, Duxbury Hall, the residents of Ducksburrow change the name of their town to 'Duxbury'; not much of a change and a fitting way to honor their founder.

'Aye, aye,' Elizabeth's William called out, leading to unanimous approval.

Priscilla felt proud of her husband and all that he and Captain Standish had accomplished. If only, if only his views... she sighed. *The poor Quakers.*

Chapter 78

February 1657

Ruth's marriage

Priscilla rose before first light. Her family all still abed, she made up the fire and inspected the myriad of pots suspended over the hearth. *Pray God they're good people. Pray God they like us. I hope this will be enough food. Must put the turkeys on the spit soon.* After stirring, tasting, putting a batch of cornbread in the oven along with a berry pie, she opened the door a crack. A misty blue light hovered over the crisp surface of snow. *Only an inch or so. Not enough to cause trouble. They'll be starting out about now.* Hearing steps she turned to see Ruth coming down the stairs. They kissed good morning.

'My last day,' Ruth said with a tremor in her voice. 'Hard to believe.'

Priscilla squeezed her daughter's hands. 'Aye.' She cleared her throat and spoke softly. 'Your wedding day. Let's check through your trunk while we're alone; be sure you have everything.'

Ruth started at the top, working her way down through bed and table linens, clothes, blankets, cleansing and bandaging linens, various household items and prettily embroidered petticoats and shifts – gifts from her sisters. Priscilla waited. When Ruth straightened up she put the gardening book into her hands.

'I want you to have this. You love it more than anyone. I've watched you pore over the diagrams for knot gardens. With servants to help in the house you may have time to create a corner of ordered beauty from the old world.'

'Mother! Thank you.' Ruth pressed the book to her cheek.

Then she handed Ruth the purple velvet bag tied with a black silk cord. 'This too is from the old world.'

Ruth untied the cord and drew out the elm hand mirror. 'What is this? How?' She stared, open mouthed.

'It was given me from a beautiful friend – our first year in this land. She was dying.'

'But Mother. To look at oneself in a mirror – 'tis vain.'

'It is not vain, Ruth. Not if you remember your beauty is a gift from the Lord. "It is He who has made us…" It is not wrong to see how beautiful you are – and ponder your inner beauty.'

Ruth swayed a little and grasped Priscilla's arm. 'Thank you… I… it is a treasure. I'll put it in my trunk now, in a safe place.'

When Ruth had carefully placed the velvet bag deep down amongst the soft linens, Priscilla said, 'And I want you to have this.' She opened a small leather bag intricately decorated with beads and withdrew the woodpecker carving. 'You remember the story, how Tinsin gave it to me when he brought Joseph home, all those years ago.'

'Aye. Because the female woodpecker will fight to the death to protect her young.' Ruth stroked the carving, and fell into Priscilla's arms sobbing. 'I… I love John Bass, but I don't want to leave. I wish…'

Priscilla gathered her close, held her tight, stroked her hair. 'My precious one.' She wiped tears from Ruth's cheeks and her own.

Now, one after another, the family descended the stairs. John embraced Ruth as if to never let her go. Sisters and brothers, all knew now was the moment to say goodbye before the busyness of preparations and forced cheerfulness when John Bass and his parents arrived. Priscilla felt she would never recover. Elizabeth wed, but close by; Jack and Joseph gone, but they were men, not so in need of their mother. But Ruth. *She is a delicate flower. As I can't be with her I want her to have all my treasures. Mary, Mother of God, please keep her safe,* she prayed.

After prayers and breakfast came welcome distracting tasks: feeding the animals, fetching water and logs and juniper branches, cooking and baking until every surface of the kitchen was covered.

'Time to change,' Priscilla announced.

As Priscilla and her four daughters came down the stairs in their fine gowns, John stood waiting in his Sabbath day best. 'A posy of beauties,' he exclaimed. 'David, Jonathan, hurry.'

Elizabeth and William with their children and Pris crunched along the track on foot. One by one, they all bade Ruth goodbye.

The sun was high. Dinner was ready. Was that a tinkling in the distance? Two handsome roans harnessed with sleigh bells trotted round the bend pulling a trap with a ledge on the back for Ruth's trunk. As they drew up outside the Aldens' front door John Bass leapt down from the driver's seat, and strode to greet Ruth.

Priscilla watched intently as a portly gentleman, hearty and merry, helped his dimpled smiling wife down from the trap. John Bass introduced his father and mother.

'Welcome, Mistress Bass.' Priscilla held out her hands, hoping she didn't show how tense she felt.

'Good day. So happy to be here, and this is Ruth.' Ruth dipped a slight curtsy. 'Oh my dear, you are every bit as lovely as John says.' She turned to Priscilla. 'I promise we will do everything we can to ensure she is happy and well cared for. Losing a daughter is... I know.'

'I can see… I feel sure you will,' Priscilla said. 'Now do come in.' She overheard Deacon Bass saying, 'You never saw a man so love struck as our John and I can see why.'

John Bass took Ruth on his arm and following John Alden, led her into the parlor where a table was laid with the wedding register. Alden took his place, back to the glowing hearth. Ruth and her betrothed stood facing him.

Gazing at her daughter, Priscilla felt she'd never seen so beautiful a woman. *Ruth, in my mother's gown, the gown I wore when John and I were wed; her deep blue eyes reflecting the indigo taffeta. But it would hardly matter what she was wearing, her inner beauty would shine through. 'Tis only fitting she should have a handsome husband who is also gentle and kind.*

Deacon and Mistress Bass and the Alden family gathered round to witness as John conducted the brief civil ceremony of marriage. He recorded the marriage in the town register, Deacon Bass and Elizabeth's William signing as witnesses.

'Now to the feast.' Alden led folk into the large front room where a long and substantial oak table was laid out for the wedding dinner.

Sarah and Mary took care of serving and replenishing the splendid fare as folk ate and drank with gusto and merriment. Only Ruth, Priscilla noticed, did not tuck in with her usual appetite. *She's nervous of what's to come, nervous of bedtime.* Nor did Priscilla relish her food.

When even Jonathan and David could not eat another slice of pie, Deacon Bass stood. 'May I raise a toast to our wedded couple and to our generous hosts, Master and Mistress Alden. You have given us a warm welcome and a stupendous feast. To all assembled here I say "God bless you now and evermore".' When the shouts of 'Hear, hear' had quietened he said, 'Sadly the moment has come when we must depart if we are to reach our halfway stop before nightfall.'

While Jonathan and John Bass loaded Ruth's trunk onto the trap Priscilla wrapped her daughter in furs. She held her tight in a last embrace and whispered in her ear, 'Try to relax and it will be wonderful.' Ruth nodded and hastily wiped a tear from her cheek before turning to be enfolded in her father's arms. John Bass stood respectfully apart until Ruth put her arm through his. He helped her up into the trap to sit between his father and mother, and ascended to the driver's seat. With a flick of the whip and a chorus of goodbyes, the trap, jingling merrily, disappeared into the late afternoon winter's sun.

I think she'll have a good home. They are kind and merry, and of good means. But how I shall miss her. Braintree is so far. When will I see her again? Ever?

1658-1660

Chapter 79

Spring 1658

Priscilla writes a letter

'I reckon it's clean at last,' Elizabeth said as she fetched ointments and poultices to disinfect and heal.

'We've almost finished.' Priscilla wiped the sweat from the woman's face. 'You are very brave.' In the background, Elizabeth's children quietly recited the alphabet and their numbers. *This is a good home.* Priscilla felt a quiet pride in her eldest daughter.

As they were wrapping the wounded arm in clean linen, William entered. 'How is she?'

Priscilla always felt warmed, reassured, in William's presence. He had a calm, competent energy expressed in his earnest, finely chiseled features.

'Pray it heals and knits.' Elizabeth brought a bowl of gruel from the hearth and helped the woman sip from a spoon.

'I bring good wishes from your companions,' William greeted the woman. 'They will soon be meeting for worship and will pray for you.'

'I would like to attend.' The woman tried to stand and sank back. 'My head will clear in a moment.'

'But my dear, are you strong enough? Shouldn't you rest here awhile? I'll bide with you.' Priscilla put a restraining hand on her shoulder.

'No, thank thee. God will give me strength.'

'I am attending,' William said. 'I've been appointed to attend and reason these folk out of their convictions. Mind, I cannot find anything to reason them out of. Are you coming, Elizabeth?'

'Aye.' Taking the woman's good arm Elizabeth helped her to stand. 'We'll support you. Mother, won't you come? Just this once. Father is in Plymouth. Can't do any harm.'

'I... I'm not sure... yes.' Priscilla put her arm around the woman's waist.

'You look after the little ones 'til we're back.' Elizabeth instructed her eldest daughter.

In the backroom of Pris' store a group of gray clad men, women and children stood or sat in silence, on stools, chairs, upturned barrels. Priscilla and Elizabeth helped the woman to a chair. They sat on stools. William stood, back against a wall. No one spoke as more Quakers quietly filed in heads bowed.

To Priscilla it felt very strange. No one said 'Meeting will now begin.' No one spoke at all. Never had she experienced a group of people sitting in silence, and so still, not like statues exactly, but still. No fidgeting, no coughing, no swatting mosquitoes. Just still. It made her nervous, fearful of a tickle in her throat, or stomach rumbling. She was hungry. No sound at all to cover a cough or a sneeze. A huge bluebottle buzzed round the bodies looking for flesh to bite. It chose a large nose belonging to a man sitting close by. Whether it bit or not, Priscilla didn't know. One second, two seconds, three seconds; the nose twitched. The fly flew off. She lowered her eyes fixing her gaze on her hands folded in her lap. Gradually her thoughts quietened, and the silence felt less threatening. Someone's stomach rumbled. It didn't matter. Sitting quiet like this could be a chance to rest. No tithing man to reprimand restive children. Even the children seemed calm. She breathed deeply, easily and settled into the quiet, the peace, becoming dimly aware that this silence was not just a lack of sound – there was something in it; an intangible, rich substance. She let go, let it hold her, and lost all sense of time.

'Brethren.' A woman's voice. 'We have suffered much torment, some even hanging. I am minded by God to give thanks for these good people who bind our wounds and give us refuge.' Priscilla looked up and met the woman's clear, kind gaze. Her voice melodious, measured in its passion, she went on.

'It is hard, friends, but in our suffering we must remember God lives in our persecutors. God created all creatures and lives in each of us. Just as we have aspects of our earthly fathers and mothers in us, so there is a quality of God in everyone, and we must seek that quality of God even in those who harm us. There are no chosen few; no damned. God's love is too huge for that. Earthly status of high born, low born counts for nothing with God. Christ, God's own says, "The Kingdom of God is within you." He means within everyone, rich and poor, high and low, sinners, the lost, the broken hearted, the sick, in body and soul. Look within, friends. Listen to an inner voice; a voice that will lead you to work for goodness and justice born of love for *all*, as God loves all!'

Silence.

At once uplifted and shattered, Priscilla clenched her hands together. This was a woman speaking – like – like a preacher only not a preacher. Better than a preacher because it wasn't doctrine; it was truth from her own heart. And everyone there, men, women and children listened. She tightened her muscles against shaking. It was too much, too wonderful, too frightening.

When the meeting ended Priscilla said hurried goodbyes, needing to get away, to try to think. The delicious warmth of late afternoon did little to calm her jangling mind. One thing was clear. These Quakers were good people and very sane. She was certain any outlandish behavior was a desperate effort to jolt folk out of their complacent ways. She was in awe of their courage and refusal to hate, hit back, seek revenge. They were truly trying to follow Christ's way. Therefore, those who persecuted the Quakers were no better than those who persecuted Christ Jesus and sentenced Him to death on the cross. Moreover, their message about equal justice and love for all, regardless of status – was that not what John believed in? What irony. *I must do something to help them. I know. I must. It is not enough to treat their wounds. I want to prevent the torturous wounds and hangings.*

Rob's welcoming bark startled her. Nearly home. Gathering herself, feigning composure, she kissed Mary, 'Hello.'

'Supper is ready.'

'Ah. Ah, thank you. I'll be there in a moment. Call David and Jonathan and the girls and start.' Priscilla cast her shawl aside. Seated at her writing table she took a sheet of parchment from the drawer, sharpened a quill, prepared a saucer of ink, and began to write.

Chapter 80

Spring 1658

The betrayal

How long had they been sitting here? Prence droned on and on in his high pitched grating voice, undeterred by noises of fidgeting: shuffling feet, the odd cough, elbows shifting position on the long oak table; undeterred by flies buzzing round his sweat hued face, the whine of a mosquito landing on his mole. John looked across at the motes of dust dancing in shafts of sunlight. Glass windows now. The colony had prospered enough to fit the common house with glass windows. He wanted this interminable meeting to end so he could get home to his planting. *How am I to prosper enough to fit glass windows in my own house… Give Priscilla…*

His gaze shifted to the hearth. He saw her lying by the Brewsters' hearth, that first winter, collapsed on her pallet, exhausted, starving. She'd struggled to stand. She needed him, leaned on him then. A mist of memories.

'And finally.'

At last. John looked eagerly into the stony face.

'We have a troublesome matter. This morning I received a letter from Governor Endecott.' Taking a sheet of parchment from his pouch Prence looked at John. 'He requests Mistress Alden come to Boston to be examined for witchcraft.'

'What?' John leaned back, laughing. 'That is a crazy mistake. The governor has the wrong person; or is he addled in the head?'

'He goes on,' Prence raised his voice and read from the sheet. 'If we find evidence, she will be tried, and if found guilty, hanged. If she is not found guilty of witchcraft, she will be banished for seditious and sacrilegious behavior.'

'Why?' John thundered, knocking back his chair to tower over the table, slamming down his fist. He felt the stunned silence of his fellow assistant governors.

'It seems your wife, Mr Alden, has written to Governor Endecott demanding he cease persecuting the Quakers. She has had the temerity to advise Endecott that they are a righteous, Godly people and that he would do well to listen to their message.'

His head spinning, John heard gasps, guffaws, saw wagging heads. He felt his face glowing hot and broke out in a sweat. He glared, enraged at the tight lipped triumph on the governor's face. His voice low, hard, measured, he said, 'I'll look into this. Governor Endecott can wait. He cannot force my wife to go to Boston.'

'I do not wish to displease the governor of the Massachusetts Bay colony. We need his favor – as you well know, Mr Alden. We will do what Governor Endecott wishes. You should have kept control of your wife.'

John turned his back on the excited self-righteous questions and exclamations of concern. He strode from the room. Once outside he struggled to stand. Gasping as if punched, his knees buckling, he stumbled down the incline to the harbor. With shaking limbs he waded out to his shallop, weighed anchor and hoisted the sails.

Lurching down the track leading to his home, John sought to balance his mind. *She couldn't have. Impossible she would do such a thing, betray, humiliate me – why – has she gone mad? She can't have. Endecott has got her confused with someone else, another woman called Priscilla. My own Priscilla would never do such a thing.* He tried to reason his way out of his fear and misery.

Rob barking, scampered to greet him. Priscilla followed, holding up her skirts, hurrying in welcome. He held her away, at arm's length. His voice catching, strangled, he asked, 'Did you? Did you write to Governor Endecott? The Quakers?'

She looked aside, at the ground. 'Yes.'

'How could you? You fool. You crazy fool,' John bellowed, pushing her away. 'You have gone behind my back, betrayed me. I am a laughing stock. "You should keep your wife under control," they snigger.'

'But John, listen.' Priscilla stepped toward him.

He held his arm at an angle across his face as if to ward off a blow. The birds, in full-throated nest-building song mocked him. 'Priscilla, I trusted you. I have always trusted you.' He turned away, looking to the sky and faced her again. 'Endecott demands you go to Boston to be tried for witchcraft.'

Priscilla gasped and covered her mouth to stifle a cry.

'What did you think he would do? Search his soul? You know he hates anything smacking of Quakers. Brands them all witches. Is vicious.' He paced back and forth. Rob sat on his haunches, head cocked on one side, whimpering. 'Of course he would accuse you. Or did you think he would make an exception because I am an assistant governor?'

'I... I don't know.'

'More likely *I'll* be implicated because of *you*.'

Priscilla twisted her hands. 'But John, everyone knows I am not a witch.'

'Do they?' John grew hoarse. 'Counts for nothing. If Endecott wants evidence, they'll find it. Then you'll be tried. If found guilty, hanged. And if by God's grace, you are not hanged you will be banished, as Anne Hutchinson was, for seditious activities. What do you think of your heroine Anne Hutchinson now?' John railed, shaking his fist.

Rob clambered round his legs, whining, begging.

'Damned Quakers!' John kicked him away and turning on his heel stumbled back down the track, away from home.

★ ★ ★

Stunned, blinded with tears, Priscilla groped her way back to the house. Rob whimpered and pressed against her so she almost tripped and fell. Indoors she sank onto a stool, clutching her waist with her arms.

'Mother. What is wrong?' Mary dropped her ladle on the floor, and hurried to Priscilla's side, an arm round her shoulder.

Priscilla shrugged her off. 'No matter.' Her tone was sharp. She rocked back and forth, her lips shaping soundless words. *I hate these stupid, cruel people. Wrong, wrong. Not what we came here for; not a just society. I don't care. Let them hang me. What's the point? If I'm banished, I'll go with the Quakers to Rhode Island, Roger Williams. He'll protect me.* She shook herself, put her face in her hands and wept. *But I love John, my children. Please God save me. I shouldn't have done it. I should have known. He's right; I'm a crazy fool to imagine Endecott would...* She moaned and rocked.

Mary knelt beside her, taking her hands. 'Mother, please. What has happened? Where is Father?'

'Stop babbling,' Priscilla snatched her hands away. 'I'll not speak of it now.'

Hours passed. Time for prayers and supper. David and Jonathan and Rebecca came into the kitchen from a day of planting corn. They stopped. 'What?'

'I'd have fetched you,' Mary said. 'But I didn't dare leave her. She won't tell me.'

'Mother.' Priscilla's children gathered round her. She waved them off and sat tight lipped, silent, clutching herself, rocking and moaning softly; the only sound in a heavy silence.

Dark enveloped the house. Priscilla refused to move, impervious when Mary gently placed a shawl round her shoulders. Rob lay at her feet; her children clustered by the hearth. Waiting. Wolves howled in the distance. Rob growled deep in his throat. The hair on the back of his neck bristled. He stirred, and jumped up, barking, whining, scratching at the door. Priscilla remained still, head bowed, not daring to look up. She heard John dump his knapsack on the floor, hang his hat and place his musket on its pegs while the children accosted him with questions and concern. He brought a stool and sat by her. She noticed his bootlace was untied.

'Priscilla.' He took her hand. 'Can you tell me why? How could you... if you love me... did you really not see the risk?' He pleaded.

'No... I don't know,' she muttered, eyes still fixed on her lap.

'Look at me.'

Cautiously she raised her eyes to his; saw his hurt.

'I love you, Priscilla. God knows I don't want to lose you. I went to see William and together we called on his father. You remember he's good friends with Deacon Bass, and, a glimmer of hope for us, they are both long standing acquaintances with Endecott. Mr Peabody is setting out for Braintree first light. The plan is for him and Deacon Bass to go to Boston and try to talk Endecott round.'

Priscilla drew a deep shuddering breath. 'Thank you. I am sorry. Thank you.'

John pressed her hand. 'All we can do now is pray. You must not go near any Quakers. Curse the lot. First they land our son Jack in prison and now this.' He flared and thumped his knee with his other hand. 'Promise me, Priscilla, if we ever get through this, you will never do anything beyond domestic duties without seeking my permission. Our livelihood depends on trade with Massachusetts Bay. That means we *do not* displease Endecott. He is a powerful man and extremely rigid.

'I promise,' Priscilla whispered, head bowed.

Priscilla wandered along the brook, forgetting to pick sallet, her insides throbbing, red-raw. Almost a month and no word from Mr Peabody. Weakened with hunger, starved of sleep, she gazed into the hurrying cascades, caught up in the rush of spring, and walked on. *Let them hang me... serve John right. Said he believed in equal justice for all... but not now... oh no... but if I am hanged... my children... Roger Williams' face... calm, gentle... Catherine Carver... to thine own self be true... please save me... John's eyes, pleading, hurt, angry.* She tripped and fell.

Something tugging at her ankle. Barking in her ear. Rob. Cries. 'Mother, Mother... where are you? Oh, Mother.' Rebecca hugged her close. 'We couldn't find you. You've come far into the forest. Here. Put your arm round my neck.' Carefully, slowly, Rebecca helped Priscilla to sit and then stand. Nothing broken or sprained. Priscilla took Rebecca's arm. Head bowed she studied the path, absently wary of tripping on a root. 'I'm sorry,' she mumbled. 'Can't walk any faster.' She tightened her grip and stopped. 'I feel... I feel... I'm going under.'

'Mother. Poor Mother.' Rebecca's voice caught. Priscilla felt her child's strong arm around her waist. She leaned into the youthful body. 'So tired.' Her eyes blurred and she gave herself up to the enveloping fuzzy fog.

'Where am I?' Her eyes saw hanging folds of deep blue cloth. Ah, the feel of linen next to her skin, head cushioned... *our bed.* Through the walls of the bedchamber she heard subdued male voices; then John saying 'Goodbye, thank you,' and the grating click of the latch.

John entered the bedchamber carrying a stool. He placed it where he could sit facing her. 'It is bad news. Endecott refuses to budge. On receipt of a summons you must go to Boston where you will be examined for evidence of witchcraft and then...'

'I know. Then hanged or banished.' Priscilla's tone was flat as if she no longer cared.

'I've given this much thought. I will not deliver you to the Boston magistrates. I will take you to Roger Williams' settlement in Rhode Island.' John's voice rasped, faltered. 'He will give you refuge.' He grabbed Priscilla, held her close and then threw her back down onto the pillows. 'I command you to eat. You will need strength for the journey and God knows what hardships will befall you there. Mary will pack your clothes and victuals. The children and Susanna are all sworn to secrecy. If asked they will say you are ill and need to be alone. No one will know you've gone. Thanks be we don't live in the town.'

Priscilla grasped John's hand. 'When?'

'First light tomorrow.'

Chapter 81

September 1658

John pleads with Endecott

All through the hot summer months John struggled to recover his balance. He strove to appear calm, steady, working on his farm and going to Plymouth for court sessions where he endured and ignored thinly disguised sniggers and taunts. 'Wife a witch... can't control his woman.' Inwardly he reeled with shock, disbelief, shame. *How could she betray me thus?* Never in all his years in this new land had he felt so lonely. Priscilla not with him. Elder Brewster, Standish, Winslow, Bradford – all passed away. He was sure Bradford, despite his subservience to Massachusetts Bay, would not have been so harsh and vindictive as Prence. He would have tried to change Endecott's mind.

Of one thing he was certain. He loved Priscilla and had to bring her home before winter closed in. He could not leave her to freeze in the Williams' shack of a house, two tiny rooms and an earthen floor. In her weakened state she could perish. Eventually, he decided. He would go to Boston and plead her case with Endecott. He consulted with the elder Mr Peabody in preparation. Together they worked out a case and rehearsed the argument, Mr Peabody taking the part of Endecott, challenging. John learned to watch Mr Peabody's face closely for the slightest change in expression, without appearing to do so.

★ ★ ★

John knocked and waited. He rapped the wrought iron knocker harder. As he was about to knock again the heavy oak door opened.

'Mr Alden.'

'Governor Endecott. Thank you for receiving me.' John faced a man not quite as tall as he, with an overwhelmingly gray presence, punctuated by his plain black garb. Shoulder-length gray hair, a gray face and stone gray eyes staring with an unflinching gaze.

Unlike Winthrop, no lace collar, no gossamer thin gloves. Work hardened hands.

'Please be seated.' The governor motioned to a chair at the side of a polished oak table, before placing himself in the armchair at the table's head. 'Your purpose?'

'I have come to ask your pardon, sir, for Mistress Alden.'

Governor Endecott leaned back in his chair, pushing against the table.

'Your grounds?'

'First, let me assure you that I share your views about the Quakers. They are a pestilence, an evil influence, and we need to be rid of them.'

'Pity your wife and son do not agree.'

'My son had no interest in the men who addressed him. Before he could leave your constables arrested him.'

'His story.'

John decided to avoid an argument about his son. 'Mistress Alden,' he continued, 'is a simple soul, and like all women is lacking in powers of reason. She cannot bear to see anyone suffer and is not able to understand why it may be necessary to inflict suffering. But she is not a witch, this I promise.'

'Her behavior and her letter to me indicate she has been infected with Quaker beliefs, and they *are* witches. That she should *dare* to tell me I should listen to them. Perfidious! The work of the devil.' Governor Endecott spoke in a cold, quiet tone, his rage betrayed only by white knuckles as he grasped the edge of the table.

'The fault is mine.' John looked into the hard eyes. 'Being in Plymouth so often I lapsed in vigilance and control. She is a foolish woman, and until now I have not seen how foolish. Have you not ever experienced the difficulty of controlling a foolish woman?' Endecott stared into John's eyes, with never a blink. However, a faint flush crept up his neck. John bowed his head, pretending not to notice. 'I promise, sir, in future I and all my family will watch Priscilla closely. I assure you she hasn't the wit to understand or pronounce heretical doctrines – unlike those scourges, Hutchinson and Williams. I fear for her sanity – her very life. In her terror of a trial she neither sleeps nor eats. She has become a listless wandering shade. I beg of you, sir.' John kept his head bowed in supplication, listening, listening for some sound of movement, of human reaction. At last, the scrape of the governor's chair. John raised his head. Stiff backed, Endecott walked slowly to his desk. Sitting with his back to John he opened the drawer and drew out a sheet of parchment, a quill and a dish of ink. He wrote. The scratch of quill on parchment grated in John's head. He clenched his fists, wiped the sweat from his forehead. He watched as Endecott wrote, on and on until he'd filled the sheet. He put the sheet in the drawer and drew another. *Whatever is he writing? Surely neither a pardon nor a summons can be this long.* John wiped his forehead again as the governor put down the quill, blotted the sheet, carefully rolled it and tied it with a black ribbon. With rigid deliberation Endecott came and stood looking down on John. He handed John the scroll.

'I bid you go.'

John stood and inclined his head in a slight bow. 'Good day.'

Feeling humiliated and angry, John staggered to the dock and into his shallop. Hands shaking, he untied the black ribbon and unrolled the sheet of parchment.

Mr Alden,

Concerning your wife Priscilla. In view of her weak character and instability of mind, I accept your plea that she is innocent of witchcraft at this moment. However, I will appoint citizens of Duxbury who have experience in identifying witchcraft to watch over your wife and report to me. Below is a list of behaviors which are indicative of witchcraft...

'No wonder he took so long writing,' John mumbled. He scanned down to the final paragraph.

If Mistress Alden is deemed to be engaged in any of the above behaviors, she will be summoned. Before writing the above, I wrote a summons and placed it in my desk drawer, with instructions to anyone serving in my place.

Thank God. A reprieve. But she'll have to stay within the confines of home. She daren't go into the town for many months.

John sighed and looked out over the harbor; billowing white clouds reflected in the still blue water. *That it should come to this. My feisty spirited Priscilla, clever, wise even; that I should have to portray her as ignorant, unable to reason. She can reason as well as any man. So dangerous!* He hoisted his sails, loosed his mooring lines and caught the westerly breeze.

★ ★ ★

John moored his shallop alongside Plymouth rock. When he attended the magistrates' court tomorrow he would tell Governor Prence of Endecott's decision. He was looking forward to this moment; to seeing the governor's angry disappointment. Prence would have been delighted if Priscilla were banished or even hanged. His grudges seemed to know no bounds. John shuddered.

He decided that before going to John Howland's home for the night he would take a turn by Town Brook, always a cheery, peaceful spot, and a site of happy memories.

Standing in a glade of birches, watching the last rays of sunlight sparkle the tumbling water, John remembered times when he met Priscilla here for secret rendezvous; hurried fervent embraces before helping her carry pails of water up to the Brewster home. So long ago. Gradually he became aware of a presence nearby. He turned and started. A Quaker woman stood motionless.

'Mr Alden?'

'You, you are?'

'Aye. 'Twas I interrupted your Sabbath nigh on two years ago. Please believe me; we don't set out to cause chaos. We just want to startle folk out of their rigid, selfish ways.'

She spoke softly. Those same blue-gray eyes held him as before in a gaze of calm penetration. He stood mute, unmoving. He heard the brook as a melodic pulsing, the evening chirps and clucks of roosting birds, a slight rustle of leaves, as if from a great distance. His whole attention was absorbed into this graceful young woman, now clad in a soft dove-gray gown, close fitting bodice, skirt falling in gentle folds. She looked directly at him, clear eyes, cornsilk hair touching her shoulders, a few freckles scattered over her cheekbones; standing still, hands easily clasped at her waist. 'Perhaps you wonder how I come to be here. A small group of us reside in Duxbury, where we are welcome. Word spread about Mistress Alden's troubles with Governor Endecott. Knowing you would be here for the magistrates' court tomorrow I hoped I could find a moment to speak with you alone. Mistress Alden took a great risk for us and we want you both to know we are grateful from the bottom of our hearts. We pray she'll escape harm.' She lowered her eyes and after a brief moment raised them again to meet John's. 'We know you for a good man, Mr Alden. Word goes about you care deeply for your wife and family. Prithee, don't allow the harsh ways of Plymouth's religion to deaden your compassion for all God's creatures. We are all God's creatures and should treat one another thus, with justice and mercy. Our Lord gave His love to the persecuted, the outcast. I know deep inside yourself you feel this to be true, as Mistress Alden does.' She leaned toward him, pleading with her eyes, a small earnest frown creasing her forehead.

John stood, unable to speak. Even in her pleading the woman had an unearthly calm, as if she inhabited an oasis of peace. He felt drawn, wanting to join her in this strange serene place. He took a step toward her.

She held up her hands. 'It is God within you, you feel. Stay. Be still.' She turned and walked away, slowly, easily.

John gazed after her until the last fold of her gown disappeared in the foliage. He began to shake. He trembled and wept. Pressing his forehead against the rough bark of an oak he grasped hold of the trunk. *My God, my God, what is happening to me?* When his tears were spent he sat a long time by the brook, staring into the hurrying water, not thinking, numb. '...a tenderness once I did see in thee... which through evil counsel and self-love thou art drawn aside from...'; the Quaker's letter, the persecuted Quaker. He shook himself. *Damn Quakers. Was she bewitching me? I am so tired. That is when witches get hold.*

Trudging slowly to Howland's home, John recalled the moment he parted from Priscilla, leaving her with Roger Williams and his wife. Although she was weak, John sensed Priscilla was not sorry to be left in their care. She did not cling to him as in the old days when they parted. *Will she be glad to see me, glad to come home? Surely she cannot have enjoyed living in that hovel? Or will she be further infected, reignited with that man's crazy ways and ideas?* The pit of his stomach knotted. *Damnation. To have to seek recourse to Roger Williams for my wife's safety. How Prence would gloat and make mischief if he knew.* A root caught the toe of his boot. He stumbled and grabbed hold of a tree trunk. He stood a moment trying to clear his mind. *Go steady.*

Day after the morrow, he would set off for Rhode Island, first light.

Chapter 82

Spring 1660

Susanna's anger

At home again in Duxbury, Priscilla daydreamed, dwelling in her memories. From the moment she first saw Roger Williams' house her heart felt lighter. It was an attractive shingled house framed by two grand trees, a beech on the right and a walnut tree on the left. Though small, with a packed earth floor, it was not a hovel, as John had called it. There were two rooms with a fireplace between and a lean-to built along the outside back wall. She didn't know why, but it felt light and airy.

She remembered Mr Williams' surprise and delighted welcome. His wife too received her with kindness and warmth. They invited John to stay for a meal and the night but he declined, departing after explaining Priscilla's need for refuge. The moment he left she relaxed into the Williams' sympathy and care.

Mr Williams was so busy governing his colony there wasn't time for lessons with just herself and him, but he held weekday study groups and he showed particular interest and admiration for her contributions. Sometimes their eyes met in unspoken understanding. It thrilled her to feel that after so many years, she was still special to him.

She also had liked Mistress Williams and enjoyed helping her in her garden, making remedies and of course there was never-ending cooking and mending. Although she was worn and thin, Mistress Williams seemed a cheerful contented person, quietly proud to be her husband's wife. And Priscilla felt proud and happy that she was helping to make a pleasant home for her teacher. She didn't worry about her own home, knowing Mary and Sarah would take good care of John and the other children, but she did suffer a pang when she thought of Susanna.

Wistfully she recalled the freedom and acceptance in Mr Williams' colony. Folk could worship as they wished without fear of reprimand, counseling or punishment. They held meetings for worship in one another's houses and governors had no authority over religious matters. For Priscilla this was a joy. Why should governors, magistrates and the clergy have the authority to decide what is God's will? Why should they have such power as they do in Plymouth and Boston? Folk of all beliefs came there, including Indians, and most exciting, two women Indian sachems from nearby tribes. Imagine! Indian men obeying women chiefs.

Priscilla remembered stories she'd heard about Mr Williams' courage, his forays into Indian tribes, living with the vermin-ridden natives in their smoky huts to learn their way of life: how they hunted, planted, cooked, raised their children, worshipped, and their medicines and language. She learned that his remarkably muscled physique was earned from days of canoeing from tribe to tribe in scorching, humid heat and freezing wind. He was a strong man in every way, and gentle, and Priscilla tried to smother her longing for him, a tormenting mix of desire and guilt.

Living in Providence had been intoxicating. She could stretch, breathe, say what she thought, test her views. She felt at home there and she was sure that if John were the same man she'd met on the *Mayflower*, he would too.

She shook herself. John was not the same man, but her life was with him and she was now confined again to their homestead. For how long?

Time for the midday meal. Slowly she walked through the orchard and farmyard. 'Mary,' she called. No response. In the kitchen Mary stood with Susanna, heads bowed.

Susanna looked up. 'Mary Dyer's been hanged. Quakers are pouring into Duxbury.'

Feeling unsteady, Priscilla lowered herself onto a stool. 'Poor woman... so unjust... so wrong.'

'Well she was banished several times. She must have known of the Quaker men who were hanged,' Susanna said. 'She shouldn't have gone back to Boston. A stupid thing to do.'

'How can you say that? She was so brave... living for what she believed... she was right and true... like Mr Williams.' Priscilla stood, hands on hips, eyes hard. 'I sometimes wish I could... run away. It is like being in prison. Nigh on eighteen months, never allowed in town except on the Sabbath, escorted by John, pinioned on a pew by my daughters, escorted home again. I can't even talk with Elizabeth and Pris unless they come here.'

'Priscilla!' Susanna grabbed Priscilla's shoulders. 'I could shake you. Would to God I could shake some sense into you. Have you so soon forgotten you might have been hanged, or banished? How do you imagine you would have fared?' She pushed Priscilla away. 'Listen to me. John took you to Mr Williams, a man he detests, to keep you safe. He prostrated himself before Endecott, begged; to save you – because he loves you. Most husbands would have turned their backs on a wife who betrayed and humiliated them as you did. But no. He endured more humiliation. He has always held and protected you – and what thanks does he get?'

'But Susanna – he is so rigid – stupid in his hatred of the Quakers. He was not like that in the early years... I thought...'

Priscilla sat down again and wiped her eyes. 'I thought… he promised he would always listen to me… pay heed to my views. He doesn't. He hasn't for so long.' She flared up. 'Don't you see? He has betrayed *me*.'

'I do think you have gone mad, Priscilla. Wake up. Pull yourself together. You are a grown woman – a grandmother, behaving as if you are twenty. You are disappointed. That is not the same as betrayal. Think of someone else beside yourself. Think of the times we're in, of all John has to cope with… Bradford, Brewster, Standish, my Edward; all his supportive friends have died. And now even his own wife wants to run away?' Susanna wiped her brow. 'Thanks be he is in Plymouth. It would break his heart to hear you speak thus.' Stepping toward the door she said, 'I'll not stay longer.'

Priscilla felt drained, weak at the knees. She hastened to sit and spin flax. Mary chopped fowl and vegetables, and baked a pie, preparing dinner. Neither spoke. When the sun was high Mary went to fetch the others in from the fields and garden. Priscilla stopped spinning and closed her eyes, sinking into the solitary quiet, reeling from Susanna's harangue. She sighed. She would do as Dorothy did all those years ago. Put her feelings aside. Behave as she should; she could not bear to lose Susanna's love. Nor did she want to mar the happiness of Sarah's wedding. In only two weeks' time she would wed Alexander Standish.

Rob barked and pawed at the door. Priscilla did not stand. John strode in, his face somber, lips clamped shut.

'Massasoit is dead.'

Priscilla felt riven, as if by lightning. Dimly she heard John speak.

'There is probably no cause for fear. Things are quiet on the Indian front. His sons have taken Christian names: Alexander and Philip. They have reaffirmed our ancient treaty with their father. Pray they have Massasoit's negotiating skills.'

Priscilla said nothing.

'There is other news.' John faltered and cleared his throat. 'Endecott has hanged Mary Dyer.'

'I know.'

'I wish the Quakers had never come to these shores. But hanging. That is going too far. It is wrong.'

Priscilla resumed her spinning.

1662-1671

Chapter 83

July 1662

Sachem Alexander dies

Hot, weary and feeling perturbed after the court session in Plymouth, John gratefully stepped into the cool of his spacious parlor. 'Priscilla,' he called.

'Ah, you're back,' she hurried from the garden through the kitchen. 'Come, sit down. I'll pull you a beaker of ale. She sat across from him at their parlor table. 'What news?'

'Nothing of great importance, except that...' John stood and wiped his brow. 'I don't like the tone Josiah Winslow and Prence take; high handed, dictatorial, especially when speaking of the Indians. It seems Sachem Alexander has ignored our agreement with his deceased father and twice sold land to a Rhode Island settler; not permitted as Rhode Island isn't included in the Confederation.

Priscilla raised her eyebrows and stiffened. 'Perhaps Sachem Alexander doesn't know Rhode Island is not in the Confederation.

Perhaps he does not understand what the Confederation is, or why Rhode Island is excluded. Why would he understand the ridiculous prejudices against Roger Williams and his settlement?'

John decided to ignore Priscilla's anger. He did not want to pursue an argument concerning Roger Williams' views. 'Also there are rumors Alexander is making proposals to the Narragansetts about joining forces against the English. Prence has summoned him to appear in court. He hasn't responded. So Prence has sent Josiah Winslow to bring him in.'

'How dare he?' Priscilla pushed her stool back and leaned, hands on the table. 'How dare he treat a sachem thus? Alexander is chief. Did we ever summon Massasoit?'

'No,' John paced. 'How different Josiah is from his father. Edward Winslow treated Big Chief Massasoit with utmost respect. He was deferential and skilled in diplomacy. But now, his son is on a mission to fetch Alexander; force him to attend our court – set to convene here in Duxbury tomorrow.'

★ ★ ★

A hammering on the door interrupted the Aldens' midday meal. John opened to a messenger. 'They're coming. Court to convene.'

With a hasty goodbye to Priscilla, John grabbed his hat and flintlock and ran to keep up with the lad. About half a mile hence they caught up with a small procession, English on horseback, Indians on foot. Josiah Winslow rode in front. John fell in behind the Indian women at the rear.

'Hurry along, hurry along.' One of Josiah's men prodded the young chief and his brother with the barrel of his gun.

'I walk at the pace of my women,' Sachem Alexander said.

On reaching the courthouse, Josiah and his men dismounted. They ordered the Indians to leave their bows and arrows outside and ushered them in, motioning the women to sit in a corner on the floor. John took his place on the benches beside Prence. Alexander, Philip, their interpreter and their half dozen braves stood facing.

'Order.'

The session was short. Alexander acknowledged he shouldn't have sold the land, promised not to do it again and assured the magistrates that rumors of an alliance with the Narragansetts were groundless. 'In truth, they have always been our enemies,' he said.

John looked into the inscrutable faces for signs of duplicity. *Can't tell. But Prence and Winslow seem satisfied.* He and Prence joined the group accompanying the Indians to Winslows' home in Marshfield for a meal, and to stay the night.

Greeted by Mistress Winslow and ushered by a servant, John took his seat at a long rectangular table. The room glowed in candlelight; pewter and silver glimmered. Josiah, at the head of the table, flicked his wrist to indicate where the Indians should be seated. Women to the kitchen. Servants brought in platter after platter of every sort of fowl, a pigeon pie, bowls of venison stew and fish stew. Not much talk. Full attention was given to eating. John looked across from time to time at Alexander and Philip sitting opposite. He noticed beads of sweat on Alexander's brow. His skin took on a strange hue. Of a sudden he clutched his belly and cried out. Philip and his attendants helped the stricken chief to lie on a pallet. Josiah sent for a surgeon, who when he arrived, said, 'He needs a strong purgative,' and administered a large dose.

A few minutes later, Alexander was writhing in agony, unable to control his bowels – mess and pandemonium.

Philip begged Josiah, 'Please, please let us take him home – he needs to be at home.'

'Permission granted,' Josiah said.

Alexander's attendants lifted their chief up onto their shoulders. The Indian grimaced, clenched his teeth, his fists, determined not to make a sound. In spite of the pain and the foul smelling mess issuing from his bowels, he held still. John marveled at his control. The chief was dignified in his own stink, filth and agony. *I have to get away from here.* He did not want to stay in this opulent house now reeking of shit. He bowed his head, impervious to the surrounding babble. When the Indians had departed he thanked his arrogant host and took his leave.

Only five miles, full moon; he knew the track and had his flintlock. The night was warm and still. Wolves howled in the distance. John kept watch along the undergrowth and overhanging limbs for wildcats' eyes. Disturbed by the recent events he could not share Prence's complacent assurance that Alexander and Philip know their place. Why would they? They see themselves as kings; not as subservient to a mere governor. As he walked, John's restless thoughts turned to Priscilla. There was something not right. She was more contended now the Quakers were gone and she could go freely into the town. But for a long time and especially since her sojourn in Rhode Island she'd had a reserve; was not with him in the wholehearted way he longed for. The memory of fetching her from Roger Williams' home haunted him still. When he arrived she seemed startled. He was surprised at how well she looked; plump again, rosy cheeks, a happy way about her. She did not throw herself into his arms. The moment of parting with Roger Williams; the lingering, searching meeting of eyes, brush of hands and Priscilla's flush of color; he wished he could blot out the picture forever. She was beautiful in a way he'd not seen since... he dared not let his thoughts go further. The pain of estrangement ate at him. When they made love he could imagine she was his, but in the morning...

Not far now. He heard Rob barking. The front door opened showing a candle flame. He almost broke into a run. 'Priscilla,' John gathered her into his arms. 'My God, I love you, and our home.' He removed her coif, buried his face in her rich auburn hair. Not a streak of gray. She stepped back, out of his embrace. 'You are not abed,' John said, 'though you weren't expecting me 'til morning.'

'I couldn't settle; don't know why.' She led him into the kitchen. 'Come. Sit awhile. Tell me all.'

Settled in his rocker, pipe lit, John recounted all that had happened.

'The surgeon should not have given him a strong physic...'twill weaken him. He'd expel naturally if it were something he ate.'

John was quiet a moment. He leaned forward, elbows on his knees; head bowed looking at the floor.

'I remember going with Edward Winslow on his visit to Massasoit. When we took the red coat and copper necklace. We endured the flea and lice ridden wigwam, nothing to eat, festivities going on and on. But Winslow knew Massasoit was King and he had the sense to treat him like one. And Massasoit, the King, paid homage to our King James. Winslow understood. We needed Massasoit's allegiance, and as it turned out, he needed us too. All that is now in danger. That trust built up – through sticky patches over the years. Remember the problems over Squanto?'

Priscilla chuckled. 'I remember! Massasoit's furious braves suddenly appeared. I had to run find Bradford. I was terrified.'

'But now? The younger ones – Josiah – certainly, and some of us older – Prence; they forget we've ever owed the Indians anything. Forget that without their help we'd not have survived. How can they forget – so soon? I'm afraid we'll pay.'

★ ★ ★

Four days later John went into the town, to call on Pris and stop in at the tavern; pick up on any news. In the dim light of the ale house half a dozen men stood drinking. He asked the keeper for a tankard full, twisted round and was glad to see William had come in. The two stood apart from the others.

'How is Elizabeth and all the children?'

'All eight are well praise God. Elizabeth seems to have her mother's gift for bestowing health and happiness!' William said.

'Drink to that!' John grinned. 'Who's that filthy wretch just come in?' he asked, lowering his voice.

William looked toward the door. 'That's the rat-husband of the poor woman who was dragged and whipped. Always in here.'

'I've got news,' the man said. 'That Indian was here – he's dead.'

John stepped up to him. 'The Indian chief? Son of Massasoit? Called Alexander?'

'Yep.'

'How do you know?'

'Been out hunting – over near Mount Hope. That's where his camp is.'

'I know, I know.'

'I say,' drawled the twisted mouth. 'Let a man get to his drink.'

John stood aside. The man saunter-swaggered over to the beer barrels. 'Hey! Hi! Keeper!' he called. 'Ale!'

The owner emerged from the back. 'Hah!' he said. 'Yer an't paid nigh a month gone. I an't gi' any more 'til yer pay yer due.' He wagged a finger in the man's face. 'And if ther's trouble – I'll throw yer out!'

'On me.' John pressed a coin into the keeper's hand.

'Why thank ye,' the man said.

'Now. Tell me where you got your news.'

'Hang on. Let a man ha' a sip.' He downed the tankard in one go. He grinned, displaying one upper front tooth set approximately at right angles into his brown blotchy gum. 'Hardly wet the whistle,' he said, stroking his bristly neck. 'Could do wi' another.'

'After you've told me.' John forced a calm demeanor. *I'd like to shake it out of him.*

The man gazed on John from underneath shaggy eyebrows, pausing to consider. 'Well I been huntin and trappin in those parts many a year. An I know another trapper does the same. He come from up in northern parts – where Indians are fearsome – an he done learn their ways – o' trappin an huntin – an he says the squaws are...' the man wriggled and sniggered.

'We don't need to know that,' John said.

'Well, as I were tryin to say, this mate o' mine, he knows Indian tongue.' The man paused. 'He knows the Mount Hope Indians.' Another long pause.

'Go on,' John said.

'My throat's parched,' the man said.

'Not until you've finished.'

The man tilted his head to one side and then the other, peering at John. 'Don't I know you from somewhere?'

'You've likely seen me around,' John said. 'Your mate knows Chief Alexander's Indians?'

'Aye. An they tell 'im their chief died – terrible it were – terrible pain in t'belly.' He grabbed at his abdomen and writhed.

'So his young brother Philip will be chief,' John said.

'An thing is – they say Philip is mad. Sure his brother was poisoned.'

John groaned.

'My drink,' the man thrust his face up next to John's.

'Phew!' John stepped back and gave him a coin at arm's strength.

'So baby brother's chief.'

'Barely weaned.'

'He'll not be any trouble.'

John caught the remarks coming from the group across the room. He turned back to William. 'Shall we go?'

Walking with his son-in-law along the main street John said, 'Have you heard the story about Edward Winslow rushing to Massasoit when the chief was sick?'

'Can't say as I have.'

'It was in 1623. Winslow received urgent summons – Massasoit was dying. Taking Hobbamock he set off. When they arrived, Winslow undertook the unpleasant task of de-furring the chief's mouth – gave him a concoction to get his bowels moving – fed him nourishing broth – and Massasoit recovered.' John walked a few paces in silence. 'It occurs to me that it is a bitter irony. Josiah's father credited with saving Massasoit's life; Massasoit's son accusing Winslow's son of poisoning his brother.'

'Only in one generation,' William said. 'Not good.'

Chapter 84

1670

Rhode Island calls

Priscilla knocked and pushed open Susanna's door, left slightly ajar to let in air and light. 'Good day.' Susanna sat by the hearth carding wool.

'Priscilla! Lovely surprise.'

'Let me help.' Priscilla drew up a stool. She sat quiet a moment, taking in the calm of the small kitchen, neat and plain, table and floor scrubbed and polished.

'Thank you,' Susanna handed her two cards.

'I love this room,' Priscilla said as she worked the wool to prepare it for spinning. 'So calm, peaceful.'

'Aye. I am happy in this little house, near you and your children. Elizabeth and William – I feel almost like another mother to them, whereas with Josiah I feel rather like an unwanted encumbrance.'

'Susanna.' Priscilla put aside her carding and clasped her friend's hands. The hands of an old woman; wrinkled, knuckles swollen and red. Of a sudden, she realized Susanna had lost height, was stooped, hair gray. How had she not seen before? 'Please come and stay with us awhile. I need help making up remedies.'

Susanna sat quiet, resting her hands. Then she said, 'Do you remember I said awhile back my eyes were not quite so good anymore? Recently they've got a lot worse, rapidly. I cannot see well enough to make up remedies. Don't know what plants I'm picking – only by smell and feel – and that is not careful enough. Your Elizabeth comes and picks and gives me the leaves and flowers to grind. She makes up the remedies for me.'

'That is what Mary and I will do. Please, please say you'll come.'

Susanna raised her misted blue eyes. 'Aye, I'll be glad to – perhaps I could stay on after Ruth's visit.'

'Perfect.' Priscilla hugged Susanna. 'I must go now, if I'm to call on Pris and Elizabeth and be home in time for dinner.'

Priscilla waited while Pris served a customer. She loved her daughter's store; goods all labeled and placed in order on shelves or in barrels on the floor. Breathing in deeply, the smells of spices, wood, grain reminded her of the smell of the cargo hold on the *Mayflower*. John's cargo hold. She drifted back trying to feel again the excitement, intoxication of burgeoning love. *John was so different then; ardent in his beliefs, beliefs new to me which I came to share. What had happened?*

'Mother.' She was enveloped in Pris' hug. 'Do you have a list?'

'Aye,' Priscilla took a small sheet of parchment from her pouch. As Pris gathered the items together they chatted. 'How is Mary Mendome?' Priscilla dropped her voice. 'Poor woman, whipped and dragged. I can still see that huddled mangled body tossed in the corner like a dead beast.' She drew her hand across her eyes.

Pris pulled up two stools. Speaking barely above a whisper she said, 'Again and again she asks me to thank you for treating her wounds. She's healed wondrously well, only a small scar on her chin. You ask how she is. Surviving. Would you believe it, even after all these long years folk gather to stare and point at her shack. "She be a witch. Indian fornicator, whip and drag her, drown her." She daren't open the door even a crack or they'd be after her, drag her out. If he is at home her husband rants at them, brandishing a stave – not that he cares for her. He's always beating her. But she's his property.'

'The beatings, the wounds?'

'I wait 'til he's gone, which is most of the time, and fetch ointments and linen from Elizabeth. Sneak across after dark and do what I can.'

'You're a good woman,' Priscilla said. 'You take her food, too, and don't ask for payment.' Pris' cat rubbed against her leg; she bent to stroke it.

'Sometimes, after dark, when I'm sure there's no one about and there's no moonlight, I take her and her daughter out for a step in the fresh air. She says she longs to run away, take her daughter to live with Tinsin's tribe. She still loves him. Doesn't blame him for what happened.'

'It was a good love. Tinsin loved her too. He told me.' Priscilla began to stand and sat down again. 'Tinsin used to come often, bringing braves to help John with the crops. They became friends; used to see them standing at the fence, talking, using a lot of gestures. I think Tinsin helped fill the hole after Standish died. But we never see him now, with the Indian troubles, Josiah Winslow and Prence causing terrible bad feeling.' She stood. 'But Ruth will be coming soon and we'll have a big family party. Oh, I can't wait!'

'Aye.' Pris grinned. 'It will be such fun and wonderful, wonderful to see Ruth.'

'I must be off; call on Elizabeth before dinner. Please give Mary Mendome my best wishes when you next see her.' Priscilla kissed her namesake goodbye, feeling light and tingly, like a child waiting for Christmas Day. *Ruth... Ruth is coming... Ruth.*

Elizabeth opened to Priscilla's knock. Grandchildren hurled themselves into her, as if they hadn't seen her for months. 'My darlings.' She stooped and gathered them close. Straightening, she joined Elizabeth adding to the stew cooking over the fire. 'I've been with Susanna. She said how she appreciates you and William – feels part of the family. It seems Josiah and his wife don't have much time for her. She is so grateful – loves you very much.' Priscilla looked at Elizabeth. 'Why so solemn? Elizabeth? Is something the matter?'

'Sit down, Mother,' she motioned to a rocking chair. Priscilla did as she was bid. Elizabeth asked her eldest to look after the younger children. She sat in the rocker across from Priscilla.

'William and I didn't want to tell you and Father before Ruth's visit. However, we didn't want anyone else to tell you.'

'What is it?'

'We've been discussing, thinking on it for years. William and I have decided to move – to Rhode Island.'

'But Elizabeth! How can you? You are mainstays here! Both of you.'

'Surely you've seen the direction of things over the years. A small group of men dictating the laws, coercing with fines and punishments to suit themselves. It is a few imposing a rod of iron over us all. We were hoping that with the new generation things might change – but Josiah Winslow is set to take over after Prence. Arrogant beyond belief. No respect for the Indians. Appalling. William can't stand him – nor can I. Plymouth is becoming a puppet. Strings pulled by Massachusetts Bay. We feel it is wrong and we do not want our children to grow up in such a climate. We long to live in a place which values freedom of thought and worship. That place is Rhode Island. Roger Williams has asked William to be his assistant governor. The population has grown hugely and he is away a lot, negotiating between Indian tribes and with the other colonies. He can't keep up with all the domestic affairs. Elizabeth and Arthur Howland are coming too. You can imagine how they rile against the dictators. And others. Alexander Standish's great friend, Benjamin

Church, is leaving; not going to Rhode Island but he wants to live far away from here.'

Priscilla leaned her head back and closed her eyes. The world was swimming, a blur. *Rhode Island. Roger Williams. Reach inside yourself for the meaning. The Quakers. Be still. Listen. Let God speak to you.* She drifted. The cacophony of children's voices echoed. Gray clouds floated slowly through her mind.

'Mother?'

Priscilla opened her eyes. She took a deep breath. 'I wish…'

'You wish… Mother?'

'Nothing. I understand your reasons. But Elizabeth – to lose you. Is there no other way? Your father will be beside himself. I think he looked to William to step into his shoes. I pray Alexander and Sarah don't leave.'

'Mother!' Elizabeth knelt beside Priscilla, laid her head on her lap. 'I don't want to leave you,' she wept. 'God knows I don't.'

Priscilla stroked her blond curls. 'My first. My little midwife. Do you remember? When William was born. You never lost your head. I might have known this day would come. From the moment you wanted to read *Hamlet* – were so enthralled with Anne Hutchinson.'

'If only we could take you with us.'

'That is wrong,' Priscilla said. 'You should think of your father. All his efforts, hard work. He is a good man. My place is with him. I do love him, Elizabeth.'

'Your love for father,' Elizabeth raised her head, sat back on her haunches, 'is deeper than your love for all you know to be right and true? Father always does what Prence and Winslow want, even if he doesn't agree. How can you bear it?'

'That does not matter. I must not leave him.'

Shakily Priscilla stood. 'Soon be dinner time. I'll be going.'

Priscilla stumbled from Elizabeth's house, her mind reeling. This could not be true. With Elizabeth she'd shared the Shakespeare folios William brought from Boston; she could freely voice her thoughts without fear of upsetting John. She envied the harmony between

Elizabeth and William, a meeting of minds. What she'd hoped for with John. Rhode Island. She clenched her fists. She absolutely could not and should not leave John. And what would happen to Susanna? How could she persuade them to stay? But she knew it was useless, if they'd been pondering the decision for years.

So many of the young ones leaving – the good ones. Francis Billington, and then John Bradford, Dorothy's son, left ten years ago – all the way to Connecticut. She missed them.

Walking up toward the main street, Priscilla passed a group of young boys playing catch and kick with a ball, and skipping rope. *Good. 'Tis good they play thus.* As she reached the corner, the tavern door burst open and the keeper pulled a woman after him, screaming and struggling to get free.

'Into the stocks wi' ya, drunken slut.' Three other men mauled and pinioned her arms and legs. They hoisted her into her humiliating prison, clamping down the limb enclosing planks.

The young boys stopped their games and ran to begin their sport, finding large tufts of grass and earth, hurling them at the woman. They also threw stones.

'Stop that! Don't you dare!' Priscilla shouted and knocked the clods of earth from their fists. 'You could kill her, throwing stones, and then you'd be hanged. Now get on back to your games and leave her alone.' She hurried home. John was already washed, ready to eat dinner.

'John, the tavern keeper and fellows hauled a drunken woman out and fastened her in the stocks. Young lads threw clods of earth and stones. Surely she should be brought before the court to decide her punishment.'

'Aye, of course. I'll go see to it now.'

He returned, angry. 'Young scamps at it again. Took her home. Told the tavern keeper he should bring her to court, not punish her himself.' He sat down heavily. 'I sometimes think we're on the edge of lawlessness. Needs a strong and just hand at the helm.'

Priscilla toyed with her food. When John had finished eating she said, 'I have some news – from Elizabeth.'

'No one sick I hope? You look worried.'

'Elizabeth and William have decided to move to Rhode Island.'

'What? Impossible!' John leapt up. 'They cannot mean it – it's crazy – the place is full of crazy Quakers.'

'John, please come sit by the hearth and let me explain.'

After Priscilla had put Elizabeth and William's case as best she could, John said, 'There must be some way to persuade them to change. The colony needs men like William. I was sure he would commit to the government here. I know how he feels about Josiah. So do I. But he shouldn't run away – damn!'

'They've been thinking it over a long time. I reckon their decision is final,' Priscilla said.

Rob barked, hackles bristling. Priscilla stood to see who was at the door. John opened to a messenger.

'I've come from John Bass. Says he regrets but reckons with the Indian unrest it wouldn't be safe to bring Ruth and the children so far from home.'

Priscilla collapsed onto a stool, head in her hands.

Chapter 85

March – April 1671

John takes a stand

The fort was dim, lit only by shafts of March sunlight filtering through slatted windows, briefly disturbing the dusty shadows. John shivered in the damp cold, as yet unpenetrated by spring warmth. The magistrates mingled, exchanging news and gossip before the court convened. John joined Prence, Winslow and Bradford's son William, interrupting guffaws of laughter.

'Good day, Mr Alden,' Winslow said. 'We were recounting sightings of the Indian "King"; how he struts and swaggers as if he was our very own King Charles; decks himself in robes and large belts of wampum and necklaces, all reckoned to be worth at least twenty pounds.' He nudged Prence. 'When greeting him his subjects must say "My service to you," while stroking both the King's shoulders.' Winslow mimicked the obeisance, doing homage to Prence. 'Mind, if he doesn't pay heed, he'll find his kingdom is shrinking,' Winslow went on. 'I sued the son of King Philip's sister for the money he owed on a horse. Only way he could pay was to mortgage a tract of land. I used the mortgage to get an even larger tract. Clever coup I reckon.' Winslow tossed his head, congratulating himself.

'Aye,' Bradford said. 'I've gained a lot of land that way. Heard they're even selling land from their reservation on Mount Hope.'

Prence chuckled. 'Their loss, our gain if they get into debt and have to pay with land. Good way for us to get rich.'

'You've also been selling them flintlocks for land, going against our own law. What happens when they have no more land to sell?' John asked.

'They can move on – go somewhere else. Always been their way,' William Bradford thumbed over his shoulder.

John held his anger in check. *It has not always been their way. I'd expect this contemptible exploitation from Winslow and Prence, but that Bradford's own son, his namesake, should behave like this.* He had difficulty sitting through the court session amongst these men he was coming to detest. *Strict laws against Quakers and crime and religious laxity are one thing – but this disrespect, gloating, putting the Indians in a hopeless predicament – have they no memory of the early years?* His mind was only half on the interminable proceedings. He wanted to get away. The moment finally arrived when Governor Prence rose to say, 'Court adjourned.'

'Wait!'

John looked toward the voice. A man pushed through the standing crowd to face Prence. 'From Swansea,' he panted. 'Thought you should know; Indians flocking to Mount Hope, from all directions. Philip led a march of sixty armed warriors right up to the edge of our settlement.'

'I've heard rumors the "King" has been wooing the Narragansetts,' Winslow said, 'but we've heard that one before. There's also rumor of a plot to kidnap our governor and extract a great ransom.' He threw back his head laughing. 'I'd like to see him try. Reckon it's all puffed up posturing.'

'Nevertheless,' Prence said, 'I think he should be summoned to a meeting.'

'Aye, but not here,' Bradford said. 'Reckon we should choose somewhere neutral.'

'Taunton?' Winslow suggested.

'Good idea,' Prence said as he stood to close the meeting. 'It's not too far from here. Reckon we should invite a delegation from Massachusetts Bay to lend weight, and with them as witnesses we cannot be accused of unfair practice. The pesky Indians will have to do as we command... or else. Ha!'

★ ★ ★

Across miles of rough fields they marched; scrubby fields, cleared but not yet ploughed, bristling, cracking in the scorching April sun. Such a sun as killed Deacon Carver, John remembered. As fit at seventy years as many younger than he, he was nevertheless glad their march wasn't a long one and had no steep inclines. He marched in the front line; Bradford, Winslow, Prence and himself, leading the Plymouth militia to Taunton. He was marching alongside Prence, the man who had been his enemy for fifty years. Sweating and itchy, swatting at flies and mosquitoes, he commented, 'Reckon the Indians have got it right, wearing nothing but bear grease and a loincloth.'

'Filthy pagans,' Prence snorted.

John said nothing. He hoped for a good outcome from this meeting with Sachem Philip and his warriors, but his mood was somber, pervaded by foreboding. He felt closed in, suffocated by the press of men around him, the rancid smell of sweat soaked garments, the occasional clash of muskets, and the raucous babble. Crows, glistening black, cawed and fought overhead. Buzzards soared high in the vivid blue. Hearing coarse shouts and guffaws behind, he looked over his right shoulder. A small group of ruffian types, slovenly in dirty tobacco spattered garb, were putting on a theatrical display as they marched. One acted the part of "King" Philip, mincing, issuing commands. Another did obeisance while half-a-dozen jostled, spat, brandished knives.

'Prence!' John grabbed the governor's arm, 'Look – that behavior is intolerable.' He started to push his way toward the group.

Prence pulled him back. 'Leave them. Only having a bit of fun. Bradford will sort them if need be. He's commander, not you.'

John decided he must try to persuade this man to see reason. 'Mr Prence, you and I have served our colony from the early years. Not many of us old-comers left now.'

'We've done well I reckon. Strong, prosperous.'

'Complacent and greedy too. Could throw it all away if we continue to take Philip's land by trickery and extortion. Do you really think the Indians won't seek revenge?'

'You talk nonsense. They know we're too strong for them. Barbaric pagans. We'll cow them into submission until they slope off – to pastures new.' Prence quickened his stride, staring straight ahead.

'We are behaving like barbarians,' John raised his voice. 'Surely you remember the first years; our struggle to survive; Squanto and Massasoit saved us. Have you forgotten how Bradford and Winslow worked to build trust – the treaty?' Heads close by turned toward the pair. *We were weak then. Now we are strong and using our strength against Massasoit's son. And Bradford and Winslow's own sons lead this... this perfidious betrayal – and you, Prence, you betray us all.* John glanced at Prence's profile, that large red mole, sprouting a single hair. His jawbone locked, unlocked, locked. His thin lips clamped tight. John pleaded, 'Why can we not cease taking unfair advantage? Allow them to share this land?'

'You fool.'

'Be warned. The way we are following can only lead to war.'

Prence glared at John. 'You just want to return to former times – old man. That was then. Now is now. Have you forgotten it is God's will for us, his saints, to occupy this land? Therefore it is God's will for us to be rid of anything that stands in our way. It was God's will that Massasoit should help us. That was in the past. Nothing to do with now.'

'Wrong, wrong. You are wrong to forget a past debt. You are wrong to treat the Indians as if... as if they are pests to be exterminated.'

'That is exactly what they are, and it is our mission either to convert them to our way, which I don't trust, or harry them away – far away where they can do no harm.'

'Please see sense,' John placed his hand on Prence's shoulder. He felt the muscles tighten and twitch. 'You know they are people – intelligent people. Some have gone to Harvard; learned English so they can read the Bible. They serve as interpreters. What you are saying is madness.'

Prence stopped, throwing off John's hand. 'Enough, Alden. Watch your words!'

John dropped back. He trudged along, eyes downcast, inwardly seething. *I risked my life coming to this land to build a just society. Priscilla lost all her family. And now we're in danger of being no better than what we fled from.*

Taunton Green. The words reminded John of cool, lush green swards in English towns and villages. *No time for nostalgia.* He reprimanded himself. This 'green' was a small field of rough grass littered with tree stumps. Sunlight bounced off the fresh, quiet leaves of surrounding woodland. No sign of an Indian or the Massachusetts Bay men.

'Order! At arms!' Bradford stood facing.

Grumbling, men hustled and jostled into formation.

'March!'

Why are we doing this? John wondered silently. *To intimidate I suppose.* A man next to him repeatedly drew his dagger and re-sheathed it as if practicing.

To the right, at the far end of the green, the men from Boston, a few at a time, stumbled amongst the trees, sloughing off knapsacks heavy with pallets and provisions needed for their long march. They fanned their faces with their hats. Several sat down and removed their boots to examine sore feet.

John was thankful Plymouth to Taunton was only about twenty miles, an easy two-day trek. He scanned the bordering woodland across the green for Indians. No sign. The Massachusetts Bay commander gave his men time to stretch, swig from their jugs, put their shoes back on. Then, 'Order! Attention!' The command carried across the green. His men regrouped in formation and as if on cue, unseen Indians emerged from amongst the trees. Sachem Philip, short as Standish, his long rich red robe draped round his shoulders, with dignified, measured step, hand raised, greeted the Massachusetts Bay commander. John mused, *Good thing the Boston militia are here. Philip seems to trust them. Doesn't trust us an inch and I don't blame him.*

Sachem Philip and the Massachusetts Bay commander spoke briefly. A messenger strode across the green and announced, 'Philip demands you surrender hostages before he will parley.'

Of course, he's afraid of a trap. John watched as Philip's warriors, faces painted, clustered together. About as many as the Plymouth militia, he guessed.

'Never! Advance! Finish them off. Hayee!' A band of about a dozen Plymouth militia rushed forward, some brandishing daggers, others charging with muskets ready to fire.

'Stop! Idiots!' John yelled, running after them. After only a few paces he felt his arms grabbed on both sides, pulling him back. With horror he saw Philip's warriors advancing, firearms poised to shoot. At a brief command from Philip they fell back to stand among the trees as the Massachusetts Bay troop ran forward, firearms aimed at the unruly band from Plymouth. 'Halt. Or we shoot!' The Boston soldiers buffeted them about the head and shoulders with the butt ends of their muskets, hustling them back to Bradford. 'Keep your men under control.'

'Shameful,' John muttered as Bradford politely delivered a reprimand. 'Shameful.' He couldn't resist calling out, 'They should be put in shackles – and the stocks when we return!'

Prence kicked John's left ankle and glared at him. Josiah Winslow stepped out from Prence's other side. 'With all respect, Mr Alden,

I think you should keep your counsel to yourself.' Transfixed by the sight of Josiah's 'walnut' Adam's apple, jerkily moving up and down, John then stared into the bulging cold, gray eyes. *You sniveling lout... puffed up toad... land grabbing swine.* Eventually Josiah averted his gaze. With an arrogant turn on his heel he joined Bradford.

The time dragged on. John waited fidgeting. 'What's the problem, Prence?' he asked, as for the third time the messenger started back across the green to Philip.

'Bradford says Philip doesn't want to parley here on the green. Fears another attack.'

'There's a meeting house in the town. Why not there? Easier to keep control in a building,' John said.

Prence nodded and turned to Bradford. By now the sun's rays were slanting, at a blinding angle. The messenger returned and took another message back to Philip. The Sachem held up both hands and bowed slightly.

'He agrees!' Bradford stood facing the Plymouth militia. 'Order!' He squawked as if his throat were sore. 'We will meet with Philip and his braves in the Taunton meeting house; English on one side, Indians on the other. I command order – anyone who disobeys will be punished.'

Empty threat. John joined Winslow, Prence and Bradford to lead the march into town. Not wishing to converse with his companions, he thought of Priscilla. *I hope she is safe, with only David and women in the house.* Jonathan and Alexander Standish were in the crowd of men behind him. *Perhaps Tinsin has delegated a few braves to keep watch. Tinsin – is he here?* John wiped his brow. *This damned scorching sun.*

★ ★ ★

The large timber meeting house, sheltered under the arching branches of a tall elm tree, offered a promise of shade and calm. Perhaps now the Plymouth men would quieten, behave less like an unruly mob. However, as they marched into the hall, the men behind John pushed, jostled, laughed, cursed. Someone shoved him. He stumbled, swung round and roared, 'Quiet! Order!' For a brief moment no one uttered a sound. John helped Bradford assemble the militia in orderly rows facing forward on the left-hand side of the aisle. He then took his place in the front row on Josiah's left, Prence on Josiah's right, next to the aisle.

'Here comes the little "king",' Winslow nudged John. As a unit the militia maneuvered to watch Philip lead his warriors into the hall.

'Tinsin!' John grunted and clenched his fists. Tinsin marched on Philip's right, heading the single file of warriors, all carrying flintlocks, marching quietly, eyes facing forward, aligning themselves on the right side of the aisle. John's thoughts raced. *Of course! Why didn't I realize? Tinsin, a pinese like his father Hobbamock... pinese to Philip, as Hobbamock was to Massasoit.* His head swam with rage at the taunts and threats ricocheting round the hall. He stood in stunned admiration that the Indians did not respond, and heaved a sigh of relief when the Massachusetts Bay commander bellowed from the rear, 'Order. Silence!'

Still air, fetid with sweat, tobacco and bear grease; bear grease which sent insects recoiling, back to the unprotected Englishmen.

Winslow beckoned to Prence for a brief whispered conference. John waited, frowning.

Prence stepped into the aisle. He threw back his shoulders and straightened his torso. 'Come forward, little "king".' He beckoned to Philip. As the sachem slowly left his place to stand before Prence, John sought and met Tinsin's eyes.

'Reports have come to us that you are soliciting the Narragansett tribe to join with you and attack Plymouth. Is this true?'

'Hey little "king". Trying to become a big "king" – ha!' a man called from behind John's head.

'Silence you cur!' John wheeled round thrusting his clenched fist up against the man's jaw.

Philip replied, 'No, it is not true. Our allegiance is with Plymouth as stated in the treaty between my father and your fathers.'

Prence stamped his foot. 'We hear you are plotting to kidnap our governor, myself that is, to get ransom money. Do you deny this?'

'A false rumor.'

'You deny these reports. Can you tell me where they come from?'

'No, I cannot.'

'Are you saying it is we who are lying?'

'No.'

'But someone is lying.'

Josiah high-stepped forward to stand beside Prence. John dug his nails into his palms.

'Little "king".' Josiah's tone was mocking, sing-song. 'Ignorant as you are, you must see someone is lying. As it is not us, it has to be you.' He paced a few steps, hands behind his back, head high.

For pity's sake, Josiah, John thought. *You know Philip hates you. Don't fan the flames.* Sweat stung his eyes. He slapped the back of his neck as a mosquito bit deep.

'Therefore,' Josiah went on, 'we have prepared a document for you to sign.' He held his right hand out to the side for Bradford to place a scroll on his open palm. Unrolling the scroll, Josiah continued. 'In this document you confess to the naughtiness of your heart.'

Philip remained still, erect, staring straight ahead, looking at no one. 'You have been causing trouble, little "king", threatening war. Therefore we demand you surrender all your warriors' weapons. By signing this document you promise to be peaceful.' Josiah stepped close to Philip and mockingly fingered his robe. 'A fine rich robe. The robe of a "king".' Philip did not move. 'You should be grateful to us, little "king", that we bestow upon you this opportunity to regain our favor so we may allow you, savage heathens, to remain on your reserve.' Still fingering Philip's red cloak, Josiah held out a quill and jerked the robe from the sachem's shoulder.

As he watched, John had a vision of the young Quaker woman standing in the grove of birch trees. *We are all God's creatures and should treat one another with justice and mercy.* Meeting Tinsin's gaze, he leapt forward, grabbed Josiah's shoulders from behind and pulled him round. 'You listen to me, and you.' He glared at Prence. He pushed Josiah in amongst the militia. 'All of you,' he thundered. 'Shame! Shame on you all. You commit despicable acts and claim it is God's will because we are his saints.' John clasped his hands and bowed his head as if in prayer. 'You say, then is then,' he mockingly tilted his head and hands to the left. 'Now is now.' He tilted to the right and looked at Prence. 'But you are wrong.' He stared full at the militia. 'You should know. This tribe of Indians,' he gestured to Philip, 'helped us colonists survive the early years. Because of their goodwill, teaching us how to plant corn and trap fish, we are here today. We were starving, dying. They saved us. And the peace treaty. Trust. Is there to be no recognition? No respect? No honoring what we owe them?' John pushed his forefinger into Josiah's chest. 'You milk-sop whelp. You sniveling proud wretch. Your father would weep for shame. You have taken – yes taken – more land from the Indians than anyone. And you, William,' he stared into the eyes of young Bradford. 'Are you really your father's son? You proud fools. You spit on all your fathers' good work; tear it to shreds.'

'Enough, Alden.' Josiah beckoned and several militia men seized John by the arms, forcing him back into his place.

'Be quiet, old man,' a voice called, setting off a chorus. 'Be quiet, old man… quiet, old man.'

John sought Tinsin's gaze and saw gratitude, admiration, in his eyes.

Prence held up his hand for silence. John heard him say to Winslow, 'Raving like a madman, stupid old fool.'

'To resume,' Josiah again held out a quill to Philip.

'You are wrong to dishonor us with your false accusations.' The sachem took the quill. 'But to satisfy your evil hearts and show we are honorable, I will sign.' He bent to make his mark on the parchment.

Crash. A war-whoop. John whirled round to see one of the warriors banging his flintlock on the floor. 'I will never fight for this sachem. He is only a white-livered cur.'

Philip never flinched. With his eyes and the lift of his forefinger he commanded silence. He made his mark on the parchment and led his warriors, slowly, single file from the meeting house.

As he watched them go, John silently vowed, *So help me God, as long as there is breath in my body I will try to make our leaders see sense. They can snub me, mock me; if they don't regain the Indians' trust and restore some of their land, there will be war, a savage war. Must talk with Tinsin. If there's war we'll need protective Indians, loyal to our family. Can he be loyal to both us and Philip?*

★ ★ ★

John dragged his heavy legs. He felt drained, suffering a tiredness he'd not known, even after fifteen, twenty hour stretches laboring in the fields. All the long trek back from Taunton he'd been shunned, by everyone except Jonathan and Alexander Standish, and although they walked with him they didn't have much to say.

Arriving at the borders of Duxbury, Jonathan and Alexander went into the town, Jonathan to call on his betrothed, Abigail. John turned down the track leading to home. Blinded by the late afternoon sun he stumbled, grabbed at tree trunks, the white birch bark peeling off in his hand. Priscilla… Priscilla… he would tell her all. *She was right all those years ago when she warned against exploiting the Indians. I'd got sucked into a wrong way of thinking. Well – she'd have been proud to see me stand up for Sachem Philip and his tribe. Ah! Rob's bark.* The dog came running, jumping and barking all round his knees. But no Priscilla. He and Rob entered the open door of his home.

'Susanna!'

The old woman ceased kneading dough and felt her way to meet him. She took his hands in hers. 'Priscilla is in the orchard.'

Good to be back in his home, to cross his farmyard, hogs snuffling, chickens scratching and clucking, goats tethered to a walnut tree. He leaned on the gate to the orchard, breathing in the scent of apple, plum and cherry blossom. Peering through the pink haze he spied Priscilla sitting on her bench, head bowed. 'Priscilla,' he called, weaving through the trees.

'Priscilla?'

She looked up. 'Ah – John – you're back – and safe.'

But it was as if she was looking beyond him, scarcely saw him.

'Priscilla, are you ailing? Is that why Susanna...' He sat beside her.

'Elizabeth and William left yesterday. Susanna has come to live with us.'

'Oh, I see. I was always hoping they might have a change of heart,' John said. 'This is a sad moment. But Priscilla, you'd have been pleased.' He took her hand. 'I stood up to Prence and Bradford and Winslow on Philip's behalf – and Tinsin was there.' He poured out the story, reliving every detail, and pounding his fist on his knee, proclaimed his resolve to never stop trying to make them see sense.

Priscilla shook her head. 'Why don't we move to Rhode Island? Get away from all this wrong headedness. Start afresh, build a good place. Please. Please let us go. We'll take Susanna with us.'

'What? What are you thinking of? How can you say such a thing – abandon all we have built over the years – Standish and I. Run away? Stop trying?' John stood and stared at Priscilla. He ran his hand through his hair, looked up to the sky. 'I could shake you. You know Rhode Island is not in the Confederation – has no protection. No. This is our place. We must change it from within – not run away!'

Priscilla put her hands to her cheeks as if she'd been slapped and burst into tears. 'Elizabeth – my own – and all her children – I'll be lost without her. We are like twins.'

John felt helpless. He sat down again, put an arm round his wife's shoulders. 'I'm sorry... I know...'

'No you do not. You do **not** know.' Priscilla shrugged him off and stood, eyes blazing through her tears. 'You live in a make believe world if you think you can change our governors.'

'Priscilla, I told you. Rhode Island is unprotected. If the Indians… you cannot expect them to say "Oh those English in Rhode Island are good. We'll leave them alone." No, we have no control over what the Indians might do. Not now.'

'As you wish,' Priscilla said. 'I shall always do as you wish, I promised.' The bell rang for prayers and supper. Priscilla turned her back and walked toward the house. John followed, slowly, as his wife strode ahead. *Damn Rhode Island*. He kicked hard at a hummock of turf and reeled back as a sharp pain shot up through his shinbone. *Damn. A hidden rock*. Gingerly he limped on. *Thank God nothing broken*, but he was beginning to feel something cracking inside him.

1674-1676

Chapter 86

1674

John Bass calls

Long shafts of mid-morning sun shone into Priscilla's kitchen. She sat with her circle of boys, all absorbed in concentration as they bent over their slates, copying from sheets of parchment she had prepared with quotations from the Bible; no sound apart from the scratching of chalk on slate and nature's conversations entering through the open doors and windows. Priscilla looked across to where Susanna sat rocking, knitting, her wrinkled honey face lit in the sun, her favorite cat sharing her lap with the growing garment. Bright blue eyes clouded over, unable to see, Susanna could still knit and spin, and as ever, advise the best remedies for myriads of ailments. *It is so good to have her here with us, a mother and sister to me all through the years.* Priscilla's thoughts drifted back to the early times. Susanna preparing a festive wedding for her and John; always there for the birthings, except William.

Hark. She listened. 'Susanna. Do you hear? I'm sure I hear a horse's hooves. Who?' Curious and slightly apprehensive, she went to the front door. 'Mr Bass!'

John Bass dismounted. 'Good day, Mistress Alden.'

The sadness in his eyes, the set of his mouth, sent a shock of alarm. 'Come in... do come in.' She left him to tether his horse and hurried to fetch a beaker of ale. The scratching on slates ceased. The boys stared expectantly. Priscilla's hands trembled as she drew the ale. Returning to the front room she found John Bass standing.

'May I speak with you alone?'

'Yes, aye, yes. Come into the parlor.' She led him into the smaller front room; the room where he and Ruth were wed. 'Pray be seated.' She motioned him to sit in an armchair alongside a small desk while she sat on the other side. 'Is... is something amiss, Mr Bass? You seem... not your usual cheerful self.'

'I've come to say...' He stopped; passed his hand over his eyes; took a deep breath. 'Ruth... Ruth...' His voice caught. 'Passed away the day before yesterday.'

Priscilla gasped. She felt cold, as if a shard of ice had passed down through the top of her head to her feet. She clutched and twisted her apron; held it to her face. 'No... no...' She stared into space. 'I'll dismiss the boys.' As if she were a wooden doll being propelled by a child she walked into the silent, waiting kitchen. John Bass followed close behind, ready to support her if need be.

'Dismissed.'

The boys filed out in silence.

'Please sit down.' John Bass pulled a stool to the kitchen table and guided Priscilla to sit.

'Susanna. It's Ruth... died.'

Susanna replied with a soft moan.

'How... what...?' Priscilla asked, staring at the tabletop.

John Bass sat across from her. 'She'd given birth, to a healthy little girl. She was weak, but doing fine. Then after a few days the fever set in.'

Priscilla groaned; put her head in her hands.

Mary bounced in from the garden, her basket full of cabbages and leeks. 'Time to prepare—'

'Ruth. Dead,' Priscilla said.

'I'll fetch Father and David.' Mary dropped her basket and ran to the fields.

'Mother did all she could to ease her pain.' John Bass looked beseechingly at Priscilla.

'I'm sure.'

'I wish I'd risked bringing Ruth for a visit, those years back. But I was worried about the Indians, the rumors.'

'You weren't to know, Mr Bass.'

John strode in followed by David and Mary. 'Is this true?'

John Bass rose. 'Aye.'

John took the younger man's hand. Then he wiped his brow, his face blanched, stricken. He inhaled as if summoning all his strength. 'And the child?'

'She fares well.'

'Please stay to dinner, Mr Bass – and the night. You don't want to be journeying in the dark with the Indians so restive,' John said.

'Thank you, no. If I go now I should reach our friends' house in Scituate by dark.'

'I'll make up a parcel of cornbread and pie,' Mary said.

'Thank you kindly. I'll go up to Boston tomorrow to give Jack word.'

Mary handed John Bass the parcel of food and a small jug of ale. 'Safe journey.'

John went with him to unhitch his horse.

Priscilla sat slumped over the table, numb. Returning, John sat with her, an arm round her shoulder. She stared into the distance, seeing images of Ruth, a little laughing, dancing sprite holding up the freshly plucked flower of a forget-me-not. Then a lass, head of auburn curls bent over her treasured gardening book, lost in the drawings, learning to read the instructions. Beautiful in the deep blue wedding dress. 'No, no, it cannot be,' she said aloud. She turned from John and stood looking over to Susanna. 'If I'd been there it wouldn't have happened. Susanna – if you had been there she'd have been well. The after birth. Mistress Bass wasn't good enough.'

'Priscilla, you cannot know,' John said.

'I know. I do know. Susanna helped me birth ten children. Not William but she checked me the day after. I lived. I helped Elizabeth with thirteen. All alive. Mother taught me. Susanna knows. Ruth... Ruth. Poor Ruth.'

Susanna carefully felt her way from her rocking chair over to Priscilla. She sat on the other side of her from John and put an arm around her, gently rocking.

Priscilla wept. 'I want her back. I want her here, a grave here. To visit her. My Ruth. She's **mine**.' Susanna held her as she became enveloped in a gray mist. Then she felt herself being gently shifted into John's arms. She leant her head against his chest. 'Ruth, come back. God. Ruth.' She shivered, teeth chattering.

'Here, sip this.' Susanna put a beaker to her lips. Arms lifting her, guiding her, everything hazy, outer garments off. 'Blankets. She mustn't get a chill.' Distant voice. Lying in bed, hands pulling blankets close up, all round her.

Priscilla woke. Dawn birdsong, cock crowing. Time to rise. She remembered. John's arms were around her. She felt his shivering, his silent, clenched grief broken by a wrenching sob. She lay staring into the gray light, into nothing. Tears spent left a hollow place inside.

★ ★ ★

The weeks of summer passed in a mist. With only a dim awareness of John, Susanna, and the children, Priscilla performed household tasks mechanically, responding to faraway voices telling her what to do. She lived in an inner space where she dwelt with anguished images of Ruth in feverish pain, calling for her. She wasn't hungry, nor did she sleep, refusing Susanna's bedtime potion.

One day she endeavored to lift the cauldron of pottage down from the lug iron. Its weight pulled her over into the fire. She heard Mary scream. Strong arms pulled her and laid her flat. Her hand burned. Faces swam above her. 'I'll get a poultice. Thanks be it isn't bad.' They carried her to her bed. In spite of her hand throbbing, she closed her eyes, disappearing into her own dark place.
A slap on her cheek, and another, harder, painful. Susanna!

'Wake up, Priscilla. Drink this.' She held a beaker of broth to Priscilla's lips. 'Now eat this, all of it.' A small slab of cornbread. 'This has gone on too long. You cannot bring Ruth back. What about all of us? We are alive and need you. Poor John. Seared with grief. But he carries on being with us, living.'

Chapter 87

January – June 1675

An unfair trial

Aijana and Chitsa

After Susanna had shocked her back into life, Priscilla rejoined her family and worked hard at the tasks of late summer and autumn, preparing remedies, harvesting and storing fruit and vegetables, and ending the year with the Aldens' annual secret celebration of Christmas, a treasured vestige of the old world.

In January news came of two deaths. The first was that of Mr Prence. John and Priscilla could not resist a cheer and a celebratory dinner with wine.

'Wonder how his brother Charles fared? If he's still living. I still cannot believe how unjust our elders were.' John growled in disgust.

The second death was cause for concern. Alexander Standish called in with the news that Sachem Philip's interpreter, Sassamon, had visited Josiah Winslow to say Philip was joining with other tribes, preparing to wage war against the English. 'At first Winslow dismissed this as Indian tittle-tattle. Then, several days later, Sassamon's body was found under the ice in a nearby lake; musket, hat and coat left on the shore. Looked like suicide. But the Indian who pulled the body ashore said no water came from the mouth. And his head and neck were bruised and swollen.'

'You reckon he was murdered by one of Philip's braves?' John asked.

'Probably, but we don't know. Josiah has ordered an investigation, searching for culprits and witnesses.'

'This will fan the flames,' John said. 'Winslow has always said he doesn't want war with Philip, and believed Philip didn't want it either. But now...'

★ ★ ★

John straightened up and leaned against the massive hornbeam. Another sack emptied. He wiped the sweat from his forehead. So far behind; mid-May and only a third of his fields sown. He sighed as he stretched his aching back. *So many trips to Plymouth. Can't work as I used to. The boys help when they can. Indians used to help. Haven't seen an Indian in months, not even Tinsin. Sun high. Time for dinner.* He hauled himself across his fields to the house, splashed his face and sank onto a stool at the table. Got up again to fetch the Bible. Prayers. With David now married they were a small group: John, Priscilla, Susanna and Mary. They ate in silence.

'Please sit awhile,' Priscilla begged him.

'No. Must use every hour of daylight.' John returned to the fields. Doggedly he carried on, seeking refuge in his labor from painful visions of Ruth, gentle, smiling, inviting.

Next morning, breakfast over, the front door opened.

'Pris!' What are you doing here?' John asked.

'I've come to help.'

'But your store…'

'David's Mary is tending the store. She loves serving. So I'll join you in the fields, Father, if I may?'

John took Pris in his arms. Tears pricked his eyes. 'Come to help your old father.'

Pris rested her hands on his shoulders. 'Old or not, you have too much to cope with.'

John fetched sacks of corn from the barn and marveled as Pris heaved one over her shoulder and grabbed another in her free hand.

'Beautifully tilled,' she said as they trudged across the prepared fields. 'If only these skirts… they do get in the way.' She kicked the long flounces this way and that.

Starting where John had left off, father and daughter rhythmically cast barley seed, working in tandem. Out of the corner of his eye John appraised his wife's namesake. Gracefully slim, not an ounce of extra flesh and so strong. *She does the work of a man.* He was mystified and proud. Judging by the position of the sun, John reckoned they'd only been working an hour when the unremitting heat and glare were sapping their strength.

'Time for a drink.' As he handed Pris a beaker of cool spring water, John said, 'Thank you, Pris. You are a grand girl. I'm… I'm so proud… of you.' His voice shook.

'Father, I'm glad if I can help.' Face flushed and streaked with sweat, Pris adopted a 'man to man' pose, legs astride, hand on hip, her small bosom rising and falling from exertion. She stood a moment thus and then hugged him close.

With Pris coming every day and the boys helping as often as they could, crops were in by June 1st – the day set for the trial.

★ ★ ★

Priscilla bent over the open trunk; *a clean smock, doesn't know how long he'll be gone. Wish I didn't feel so agitated. David will be here with his Mary.* She prepared parcels of pie, cheese, cornbread, and a large wedge of ginger cake.

John strode in from the farmyard. 'Hogs dealt with, tethered the goats and the cows.' He stood beside Priscilla. 'I fear this trial is going to be messy. Only one witness – an Indian who already has a grudge against the accused. Poor blighters. Three Indians: the main so-called culprit and his son and a friend. Probably all innocent. If they're found guilty and hanged it could take a while.'

'But if they're innocent, and if it's a fair trial... and by law they need two witnesses. Even I know that,' Priscilla said.

'It seems our governors bend and change the law to suit themselves. I'll try to send word back if it's longer than three days.' John kissed her tenderly, lingering, and shouldered his knapsack.

Priscilla watched his receding back. When he was out of sight she turned to seek diversion in domestic duties. 'Mary,' she called into the garden. 'Shall we start a batch of cheese? The milk is rich. Good spring grass.' Mary left her weeding. Together they prepared a pan of milk and hung it over the fire to curdle.

'Fine day,' Mary said. 'Father should have an easy sail. I'll start dinner. David and Mary will be here soon.'

Priscilla joined her daughter at the chopping table. 'Lots of carrots.'

'They need using up,' Mary said. 'On the way out. Turnips keeping well but not the carrots. Thought I'd bake a pumpkin and apple pie, for a treat. Apples need using too.' Mary went to the hearth to check on the milk. 'Almost ready.'

Chopping carrots together, Priscilla said, 'You are such a good housekeeper, don't you wish for a home of your own?'

'In a way, yes. But I'm plain. Can't see as any man would want me, and more than that, I'm so frightened of birthing. If I didn't have you, or Susanna...' Ruth's death hung in the air. 'I'd much rather help you and Father here, and later, I'm sure one of my brothers or sisters will take me in.'

Priscilla stopped chopping. Only the sound of Susanna spinning wool, a hum like an echo of wind, stirred the quiet of the kitchen. She put her hands over Mary's. 'Look at me. You are not plain. You are beautiful inside, like my mother. She wasn't dashingly pretty, but she had a truly lovely nature and was a good housewife, like you. My father loved her dearly. Please don't think yourself plain, Mary.'

'Thank you,' Mary said. She kissed Priscilla and rushed to the hearth. 'Just in time.'

★ ★ ★

'He's been gone over a week.' Priscilla ground sage in her pestle and mortar.

'He did send word. You know he had to wait for the hangings,' Susanna reminded her.

Priscilla sighed. ''Tis worrying.' She leaned across the table and peered into Susanna's bowl. 'That looks good and fine.' She sifted a handful of ground hyssop leaves through her fingers. 'Spiky tough leaves transformed.'

Mary brought in another basketful of leaves and flowers.

'We aren't keeping up with your picking,' Priscilla said. Mary settled to help.

Thump, thump. Their new sheepdog, Pyke, spread out by the hearth, thumped his tail with increased vigor and scrambled to his feet. Barking, he ran to the door.

'John, John's back.' Priscilla leapt from her stool and dashed out. *He's exhausted, laboring.* She ran to him. He stopped and took her in his arms.

'Terrible. Wretched. Disgraceful.'

'Come. Mary has dinner ready.'

John ate in silence, but after their meal the family gathered round the hearth to hear his story.

Seated in his rocker, pipe lit, Pyke's head resting on his knee, John began. 'As you know, the jury of eighteen gathered in the fort to try the accused Indians. There was only one witness; an Indian who had been forced to give up his coat to the main "culprit" to pay off a gambling debt. At this point I protested and backed out;

refused to serve. In spite of this shabby set up, the jury, to a man, declared the three accused all guilty.'

'Were you frowned on for refusing to be part of it?' Priscilla asked.

'Got some dirty looks, but they know my views by now. Josiah said if I'd stayed on the jury and been the only "not-guilty" vote they'd have thrown me off anyway.'

'That is dreadful, so unjust!' Mary said.

'Worse to come.' John drew on his pipe. 'On June 8th the three men were marched to the gallows, swearing they were innocent. The main culprit was hanged first, then his friend. When the son's turn came the rope broke before the noose had done its work. The lad fell to the ground. He shakily got to his feet, and saw the bodies of his father and the friend hanging, still twitching.' John bowed his head.

'Poor lad,' Priscilla said.

'Winslow told him that if he confessed, he'd be granted a reprieve. So he "confessed". Said he stood helplessly by as his father killed Sassamon. Instead of letting him go, Winslow ordered him back to the cells. The rat. As we were filing out of the fort Winslow said to me, "If there is war we'll shoot him." I protested. "You all know he is innocent. All three are innocent. This is shameful." When we'd got outside I tried again. I pleaded with him. "Can you not see which way the wind is blowing? Why did you make it legal to sell arms to the Indians? It was always against our law. But you changed the law. Arms for land; your greed for land." Winslow turned his back and stomped off.'

''Tis wrong and dangerous,' Priscilla said.

'What does Winslow imagine the Indians are planning to do with all their flintlocks?' Mary asked.

'Winslow's answer to that is, they wouldn't dare fight us and if they do we'll finish them off. If only Benjamin Church were still here and William. They would have influence. I am a lone voice and no one listens.'

Please may we go to Rhode Island, Priscilla pleaded silently, not daring to say the words aloud.

★ ★ ★

The following afternoon Priscilla went alone to her garden to weed. Shielding her eyes against the western sun she scanned the fields. There was John, hoeing round the mounds of corn, also planted with squash and beans. *As Squanto taught us.* Somewhat stiffly, she lowered herself onto her hands and knees, arranging her skirts to keep them out of the way. Priscilla relished weeding. There had been enough rain so the soil was moist and the weeds pulled easily. She sifted a handful of friable earth through her fingers and breathed in the scents of her herbs: rosemary, lavender, thyme, marjoram… marjoram for melancholy. Engrossed in the plants Priscilla could forget the time, forget everything. The sun traveled its road down the sky.

A shadow fell across the ground in front of her. She froze. Her heart thudded. *Am I about to be hatcheted?* She struggled to her feet. 'Tinsin!' The Indian put a finger to his lips. Whispering, he introduced the two women at his side.

'My squaw, Aijana and daughter, Chitsa.'

'Is it… Aijana… from when I ran away?'

Aijana smiled and nodded.

'They stay here. War coming,' Tinsin said. He pointed to his daughter's leg, limping to show she was lame. 'My English squaw – well?' he asked.

'Healed, but unhappy,' Priscilla said. 'Very bad husband.'

Suddenly, looking past Priscilla's shoulder, Tinsin raised his hand in greeting. Priscilla turned as John came loping through his crops. Obeying Tinsin's signal, he kept his voice almost a whisper. 'Tinsin, Tinsin, welcome.' He grasped Tinsin's hand. 'Yours?' He nodded toward the women.

'Tinsin has asked if his squaw and daughter might seek refuge here. His daughter is lame and cannot run,' Priscilla said.

'Run?' John asked.

'War,' Tinsin said. 'I am very sad. Philip does not want war, even after that trial.' He spat in disgust. 'But our sachem cannot control his warriors. They thirst for revenge. Want to take back their land.'

John nodded. 'I understand. Of course your women are welcome here. We'll do everything we can to keep them safe.'

Tinsin briefly bowed his head in gratitude and sprinted away, keeping himself hidden among the trees bordering the Aldens' fields.

John returned to his hoeing.

Priscilla took Aijana and Chitsa indoors to meet Mary and Susanna.

Susanna held out her hands. 'Welcome, welcome.' She searched the unseen faces.

When Susanna let go of her hands, Aijana looked round the room. 'Ah.' She pointed.

'The basket!' Priscilla said. 'Yes, this is the basket you gave me so long ago.' She put the basket, full of nuts, into Aijana's hands. Aijana murmured Indian words, remembering the time their tribe had sheltered Priscilla until John appeared.

Once Mary had recovered from the shock, she set about preparing a small secret home for the refugees. Rearranging barrels and containers in the buttery, she created a hidden room. Priscilla fetched two pallets and blankets. Mary spread them on the floor. 'There. Cozy and snug.'

Priscilla examined Chitsa's foot. A deep cut, not properly healed. Using sign language she got Aijana's permission to treat it. The young woman was brave during the painful process of getting out the dirt and grit. She clenched her teeth and held tight onto the corner of the tabletop. *Amazing. I am a stranger and she holds still – doesn't cry out.* Priscilla applied a poultice on the cleansed wound and Chitsa, limping, joined her mother to help Mary chop vegetables for the pottage.

When John came in for evening prayers and supper he said he reckoned it was safe for Aijana and Chitsa to eat at table. 'No one likely to come by at this hour, and the door is closed.'

Indian mother and daughter were mystified when presented with a trencher and spoons. Mary made a game of it, bringing giggles and laughter as they learned how to eat the English way.

'It's a happier, livelier house with our newcomers.' Priscilla sat at her flax wheel as Susanna spun wool.

'I can hear the laughter and jolly babbling,' Susanna said.

'They make up games, games that also get the work done. Reminds me of when the Indian squaws and children came to Plymouth the first year, to help with the planting. So merry they were.'

'I remember,' Susanna said. 'And you were becoming sick with misery because John ignored you. Praise God it finally came right.'

'So long ago,' Priscilla said. 'Aijana keeps asking to help John in the fields. He says no; he's afraid she'd be seen. This morning when he went to start hoeing the next acre he found it had already been done!'

'I never!' Susanna said. 'She wants to say thank you.'

'It was touching, watching John trying to thank her. I think Aijana understood in her own modest way.'

When she next went to town Priscilla told Pris about Tinsin's squaw and daughter.

'Surely Mary Mendome would want to know,' Pris said.

'Seems only right. She loves Tinsin and said she is very fond of his family.' Priscilla kept her voice low and looked over her shoulder to be sure no one had entered unnoticed. 'And if she knows they are here she will want to visit, I'm sure. Perhaps when her husband is away trapping?'

'Mercifully he is away more than he's here,' Pris said.

'But John still doesn't know about Tinsin and Mary. I would have to tell him all, and he would know that his Indian friend has fornicated with one of our own. I fear he'll be terribly angry.'

'You must risk it.' Pris looked into her mother's eyes. 'Trust Father. It was a very long time ago. He has changed. Has much more sympathy and admiration for the Indians. And he hates cruelty and despises that beastly husband of Mary's. Please, Mother. You must.'

★ ★ ★

Her heart beating fast, hands clammy, face blushing, Priscilla stood at the orchard gate. She chided herself for being so silly, but ever since the Endecott eruption she'd feared another onslaught of John's rage. *Please don't be angry*, she begged silently. 'John, husband,' she called. 'I need to ask something of you.' She watched him closely as, using a hoe for a stave, he crossed the fields to oblige her. When they had sat down side by side on Priscilla's bench she turned to him. 'There is something I must tell you. Something I've feared to tell you 'til now. But now I must.' She clenched her hands at his look of alarm and began. She told him the whole story; that she'd hidden Mary Mendome and knew of the love between her and Tinsin. 'And now she stays hidden away with her daughter in that hovel. Pris takes her food after she's shut up her store and there's no one about. I'm sorry. I didn't like keeping it secret, but feared knowing would have put you in an impossible position.'

John sat quiet for what seemed like an eternity. Priscilla twisted her hands, chewed her lip, studied a stain on her apron. Her stomach churned.

'You did right not to tell me. If I'd known I was friends with an Indian who had fornicated with one of our women...' John shuddered. 'Even now it doesn't sit easy. But Tinsin is a good man, loyal and true. That I know. And Mary Mendome's husband is vile. Vile and cruel.' He took Priscilla's hand. 'I wish... I don't like to think you keep secrets from me. But I see in this case you had to. You did right to shelter the poor woman. You say Pris takes her food?'

'Aye.'

'She's a good woman, like her mother.'

'John.'

'I know that note in your voice. What now?'

'Could we possibly, when the horrid Mendome man is away, bring Mary and her daughter to see Aijana and Chitsa? She knows them. I'm sure she'd want to visit with them.'

'What? You said she never dares leave her house.'

'Under cover of darkness – in disguise – Pris could find a way.'

John pondered. Shook his head. 'What next? If you and Pris can work out a safe way, alright. Poor woman.'

With their parents' blessing, Pris and Jonathan contrived whatever ruses were needed to bring Mary and her daughter Constance to the Alden house after nightfall. Priscilla's anxious waiting dissolved into joy as Aijana and Mary greeted each other like sisters and introduced their daughters. ''Tis wonderful, truly wonderful. All talking as if they've been friends from way back.' Then came a stab of worry. She turned to Pris. 'I'm afraid Constance might say something. Give them away if perchance she should be questioned.'

'Haven't you noticed?' Pris said. 'Listen.'

Priscilla paid close attention. 'She isn't speaking English.'

'No. She has a strange language all her own.'

Chapter 88

Summer – Autumn 1675

War

'Priscilla!' There was a loud urgency in John's tone. *He's returned from the tavern. Sallet can wait.* She hurried back to find him in the kitchen, pacing.

'We are at war,' he said, sitting down heavily. Priscilla drew up a stool beside him. 'Word has come of an Indian raid on a settlement out near Mount Hope. Two houses burned to the ground. Mercifully no one was killed as it was Sabbath and everyone was gathered in the meeting house.' He stood, pacing restlessly. 'Most folks living there, fearing the worst, had already moved to a nearby garrison. Winslow has ordered militia from all Plymouth's towns to rendezvous at Taunton and then march on to Swansea, near Mount Hope.'

'Lord have mercy, no. Our boys, all the young men, God knows what might befall them.'

'Winslow will take command of all our troops. General Josiah Winslow.' John snorted. 'Hard to believe that arrogant, puffed-up young man is the son of Edward and Susanna. He's asked Benjamin Church to be his aide. Alexander thinks Church should be commander in chief. Knows how to fight in the wilderness, and would know better how to keep neutral and friendly Indians on our side.'

★ ★ ★

The Duxbury families all gathered next morning in the town center to wish their men Godspeed. Priscilla did her best to offer a hearty, encouraging farewell, but her heart shivered, heavy as a millstone.

Immediately the militia had departed, Josiah Winslow called for attention. To a subdued audience of old men, women and children he said, 'I am proclaiming this Thursday coming, June 24th, to be a day of fasting and humiliation. These troubles with the Indians are a sign that we are not in God's favor. No doubt we are being punished for crimes toward one another, for laxity in religious duties, for no one could be more innocent toward their neighbor than we. We have dealt magnanimously with these wanton, senseless beings sent by God to test our perseverance in establishing His kingdom here in this land. They are like the pestilences of old, sent as opportunities for the Israelites to renew their faith and trust in one God. Like the Israelites of old we must pray and don our swords against the barbarian pagans.'

When John and Priscilla had reached the safe confines of their own home, Priscilla exploded. 'Of all the perfidious, disingenuous, utterly dishonest... appalling, utterly appalling.' Then, seeing the expressions of surprised fright on Aijana's and Chitsa's faces, she tried to comfort and soothe. 'It isn't you... not your fault... these troubles.' Turning to John she said, 'The visits with Mary and Constance. How? With Jonathan gone?'

'I'll take his place,' John said.

'You're not worried about your position? If you're found out?'

'I reckon I've already compromised my position. A bit more won't matter.'

'Thank you. Thank you,' Priscilla said. 'You are a good man, John Alden. Pris says the only time Mary is happy is when she and Constance are here.'

'Not surprising.' John rested his hands on Priscilla's shoulders and kissed her brow.

The visits carried on, even as war hysteria swept through the settlements. John came home from trips to the tavern with fragmented reports of battles and Indian atrocities. Only when he knew Aijana and Chitsa were out of earshot would he relate what he'd heard, keeping his voice low.

'A group of twelve troopers rode into an ambush; Indians getting the better of us with sporadic attacks from nowhere; routing villages. One village was burned to the ground. Still smoking. Our men saw pieces of paper wafting in the air. They were the torn pages of a Bible. A few miles further on they came upon the remains of eight Englishmen; heads, scalps and hands mounted on poles planted along the roadside.'

Although sickened by reports of Indian atrocities, Priscilla knew the English could be equally barbaric. Also, she realized the reports coming through could be biased. 'I don't want all the dreadfulness to poison our feelings for Aijana and Chitsa,' she said.

'Nor do I,' John replied. 'Do you know, those two take me back to my trek with Edward Winslow to Massasoit's camp, when we took the red coat and copper necklace. All along the way we met delightful, helpful Indians. Squaws and children dancing round us, playing, sparkling with fun. And the braves helpful every step of the way. Even carried some of our load – we were so hot and heavily laden.'

'A tragedy it has come to this.'

'I remember Squanto explaining about the memory holes; markers in the ground where important events had happened. It was the duty of each generation to remember.' John slowly shook his head. 'We've ruined all that. They will want revenge to be sure.'

'Trouble is, we've gone so far down this road of grabbing and destroying, it feels there's no going back. It is now a question of us or them.'

'Aye. There's a rampage against Indians – all Indians. I wish Aijana wouldn't go working in the fields at night. I'm very grateful, but it would be terrible if something happened to her. Is there any way to get her to understand?'

Priscilla sighed. 'I'll try. Do you know, several mornings, we've found a parcel by the back door. Always the same. Large pieces of hide, porcupine quills, beads and sewing thong.'

'I reckon Tinsin is leaving it so she can make clothes for herself and her daughter,' John said.

Throughout the summer and harvest time Priscilla worked close by Susanna's side. She needed physical closeness with her friend to feel calmed, protected. Susanna helped her persuade Aijana not to work in the fields at night. At harvest, when families helped one another and folk arrived without warning, Susanna was the first to hear an approach and give the alert so Aijana and Chitsa could hide. Susanna always knew what to do, but more than anything practical, Priscilla welcomed her comforting embrace. Susanna's arm round her shoulder soothed her churning, frantic worry.

'Why?' Priscilla muttered sleepily, awoken in the night freezing cold. *Yesterday was warm and full of sunshine.* She retrieved more blankets from the trunk and scampered back to bed, snuggling in close up against John's warm body. In the morning, as soon as she opened her eyes, she knew. That special acid light – snow. She opened the door. Four inches and not yet November.

Week after week the wind cut like ice and the ground stayed frozen hard, covered in snow. Priscilla and Susanna sat by the hearth, wrapped in shawls, mending and remaking clothes. 'Praise be our harvest was good,' Priscilla said. She rested her hands in her lap and looked up. 'Do you know, I reckon this is the first year we've not had a Thanksgiving festival since 1621. 'Twould be a mockery in any case with the carnage going on.'

'I fear for our men,' Susanna said. 'Can't remember it ever freezing so early as this. They'll be suffering frostbite for sure.'

A blast of cold air swept through the room as John came in, stamping snow from his boots. Hearth flames wavered.

'News?' Priscilla asked.

'Not many at the tavern. Only us old-timers, and few of us left. Reports that we've had sporadic battles with the Indians – vicious but not successful. The aim was to confront Philip in his camp on Mount Hope and fight him there. But by the time our troops arrived there wasn't a soul in sight; only hogs rootling around, vast acres of corn growing. Our men pulled it all up.' John held his hands to the fire. 'Church reckoned he knew where Philip had gone – Pocasset – and with a small troop chased after him. General Winslow and the bulk of our men stayed behind, waiting for reinforcements to arrive from Massachusetts Bay and Connecticut, and fighting bloody skirmishes against the Indians. Church returned. Philip had slipped his grasp. Then, of all the stupid things to do,' John stamped his foot. 'Winslow decided to go after the Narragansetts. I cannot think why. The Narragansetts hadn't thrown in their lot with Philip. They were still neutral.'

'Did Church agree?' Priscilla asked.

'I don't know, but I cannot imagine he would be that stupid.' John slumped into his rocker. 'No one at the tavern knew many details, only that it was an horrific bloodbath. Their camp torched. Like the Pequot war. Word has it we won. Won't know what happened 'til the boys come home.'

Priscilla shuddered. She dropped her sewing on her chair and stirred the cauldron of stew with forced jerky strokes. Her stomach heaved.

Nights were the worst. In the daylight hours Priscilla could work, keep her mind on her tasks, talk with Susanna, enjoy learning to communicate with Aijana and Chitsa. With Mary Mendome's husband away fighting, she and Constance were able to visit almost every evening, whenever Pris and John could escort them. It was a joy to see Mary unfold, her pinched, frightened face relaxing into girlish happiness as she chatted and laughed.

One evening the snow was falling heavily and fast. Priscilla asked John if Mary and Constance could stay the night and the morrow. John agreed, reckoning the husband wouldn't return until the war was over. As she often did, Mary offered to spin flax. She sat at the flax wheel while Priscilla spun wool. They worked in silence for a time and then Priscilla asked the question she'd been wanting to ask for weeks. 'Only one child?'

The flax wheel stopped. Mary bowed her head, hands in her lap, cheeks aflame. 'After I was discovered... ever since then he can't...' She flopped her wrist limp.

'Ah,' Priscilla said, persevering with her wheel, keeping the hum going.

'So he uses other things.' Mary was barely audible. 'Broomstick, even the poker once.'

'My dear!' Priscilla gasped.

'So I never had another and now I'm too old.'

That night in the privacy of their bed Priscilla told John. 'Isn't there something we can do to get her away from that man? He could kill her.'

'If she'd not been sentenced and branded, she could have brought him to court. Not now. The only thing would be to buy her from him. We could try, but I'm sure he'd not agree. Wretched spiteful louse.'

Chapter 89

February – May 1676

Indian raids and the ague

'First week in February and still it stays above freezing.' Priscilla stood with John at the back door. John dug his shovel into the ground and turned over a clod of earth. 'Reckon I could begin ploughing.'

'John.' Priscilla peered across the fields, shading her eyes. 'What's that? Moving across the edge of the forest? Men!' She grabbed John's arm and pointed. They looked and waited. English.

'By God in heaven!' John shouted. Pyke barked. 'By God in heaven. It's Church… and… our boys! Our boys!'

Priscilla ran inside. 'Mary. Our boys are back. Food. Medicines.' She stopped, seeing the questions on Aijana's face. 'You and Chitsa will have to stay hidden while they are here. We'll find a way to bring you food.'

Aijana nodded and took Chitsa to their hidden home.

Priscilla hurried out to see how near the men were and fearfully, who. *Jonathan, Alexander, Susanna's sons... where is David?* Her heart contracted. *Ah. There at the back, limping badly.* She tried to run, stumbling over hummocks, to meet her boys.

Drawing near, she recoiled. Church could barely stand. He was being dragged along, his arms over the shoulders of two comrades. The men were filthy. They stank of the flux and suppurating wounds; their faces were gray and gaunt.

'Haven't had a meal in weeks,' Jonathan swooned.

'Reached Marlborough,' Church gasped. 'Winslow disbanded. Men too wounded and starved to fight.'

'The Massachusetts Bay and Connecticut troops were fresher. Many more of them,' Alexander said.

Priscilla gave David her arm and John wrapped Jonathan's arm over his shoulder so he didn't fall. Slowly the ravaged men crossed the fields to the house.

Mary and Susanna had converted the large front room into a hospital; pallets and blankets laid out, medicine chests at hand, piles of linen bandages and poultices. Priscilla and Susanna washed and cleaned out wounds, applied ointments and poultices. Susanna did not need to see. She could do it all by touch. Mary cooked a large pot of chicken broth, made up more poultices and cut worn undergarments into bandage strips.

Next day, fed gently with broth and porridge, wounds cleaned and dressed, the men went to their own homes.

'Joseph?' Priscilla asked Jonathan. 'Do you know?'

'He is alive, starving. Wounds not too bad. Headed back to Bridgewater.'

'And Elizabeth and William?'

'Don't know. Never saw William. As Rhode Island remained neutral we can only hope.'

'If the folk of Rhode Island are safe it is because Roger Williams took the trouble to learn the Indians' language and their ways. He has treated them with respect, as we should have.'

'Aye. I suppose you have a point,' Jonathan said. 'Now I'll be getting back to my dear wife. Thank you, Mother, for all your care.' He took her hand and kissed it. 'Goodbye.'

As often as they could, Jonathan and Alexander came to help John with the ploughing. They brought news of Indian raids on towns in the north, starting with Lancaster, war-whooping, burning, massacring and taking captives.

Jonathan found a moment to speak with Priscilla alone. 'Pris says Mary Mendome's husband is returned, wounded and starving. He won't be going anywhere for a time.'

'Poor Mary.' Priscilla sighed.

With March came news of more massacres, further south, the latest at Medfield and Wessagussett. Together, John and Priscilla gave thanks every day that their boys had not been called again to fight.

The parcels of leather, quills, beads and sewing thong continued to arrive regularly, about every fortnight.

'May I see?' Priscilla asked Aijana.

'Aye.' The squaw showed her the top half of a tunic, so carefully sewn she couldn't see the stitches; the rounded neck decorated with beads.

'That is beautiful! For you?'

Aijana smiled.

As Mary Mendome's husband had a blood lust to kill Indians, he took himself off as soon as he could stand. Mary and Constance were able to resume their clandestine visits.

Priscilla waited anxiously for John to return from the tavern. Reports abounded that Indians swarmed, attacking town after town. Scituate, so close, sacked and burned. Taunton, Middleborough. Would Duxbury be next? She worked in her garden, hoping that planting would calm her, but she found she was sowing seeds in the wrong places.

Pyke barked. She hurried into the kitchen. John stood by the table, his expression grim. 'Church is taking Alice and their son away, to Rhode Island. Says he'll lead our troops from there.' John paced wearily to the hearth and reached for his pipe. 'Alice's parents begged him to leave Alice and the boy with them in Plymouth, to stay in the safety of Clark's garrison, at least 'til she's given birth in May. Church was adamant he'd take Alice and their son with him. They left today.'

'He must know something,' Priscilla said.

'He believes Duxbury and Plymouth will be next.'

Aijana, chopping turnips and onions for the stew, vanished. She returned, holding out a strip of flattened birch bark. She gave it to John.

'Where did this come from? Tinsin?'

Aijana nodded.

John held it for Priscilla to see. A picture. A town with a circle around it, and one house on the northern edge of the town with a double circle round. Outside the circles stick figures of Indian warriors ran brandishing muskets. None came inside the circles. Priscilla looked at Aijana.

'Duxbury?' She pointed to the town.

Aijana nodded 'Yes'.

'Our house? Here?' She pointed to the circled house.

Aijana nodded 'Yes' again.

'Safe? No Indians?'

Aijana shook her head. 'No Indians.'

Priscilla took the squaw in her arms. 'Thank you.'

In spite of the reassuring picture, Priscilla grew more and more frightened as the day wore on. The house was silent. John continued planting the corn. *I wish he would stay indoors. Probably no safer, but...* Nothing happened all that day. No distant war cries, nothing but the usual sounds of farmyard life and bird life and a breeze stirring the spring leaves. The night of wakeful waiting went on forever. The morning was peaceful; a fine sunny day.

Perhaps they won't come. Perhaps we really are safe. Priscilla hardly dared think it. Still the house was silent. John came in from the fields for dinner. *Comforting to say prayers. The only talk that makes any sense.*

> Because thou hast made the Lord, which is my
> refuge, even the most high, thy habitation;
> There shall no evil befall thee, neither shall
> any plague come nigh thy dwelling.
> For he shall give his angels charge over thee,
> to keep thee in all thy ways.
>
> (Psalm 91)

Of a sudden, no warning, war whoops, shrieking, such a pitch and crescendo, as if right outside the house. Priscilla froze. The back of Pyke's neck bristled. He whined and growled and cowered under the table. On and on the whooping and shrieking. Priscilla saw Mary go white, begin to swoon. Susanna held her while Priscilla fetched a bottle of distilled lavender water. Gunshots.

'Lord have mercy. Our Father which art in heaven.' John prayed, his voice low and soft. On and on he prayed, prayer after prayer, measured calm, holding them in the blanket of his words.

Eventually, when the sun was halfway down the western sky the cries, shrieks, gunshot, receded until all was quiet again. Aijana smiled as if to say, 'I told you'.

Priscilla began to shake. She couldn't use her hands. Her teeth chattered. She felt cold. Susanna wrapped her in a blanket and brought her to sit by the fire. 'You've been clenched up tight so long,' she said. 'Sip this down. I'll give you some more before bed. Help you sleep.'

'Susanna, Susanna.' Priscilla clutched hold of Susanna's hands. 'Don't leave me.' She sobbed like a child, her face pressed into Susanna's skirts.

The cock crowing woke Priscilla into the dawn. She lay still, listening to the chickens clucking quietly; then the triumphant announcement of an egg laid. In the lulls of birdsong demarking territories and calling a mate, she could hear the hogs snuffling. The comforting ordinary sounds of animal life. John stirred beside her. She turned in to him. They lay clasped together, not speaking. She'd almost drifted off again when the sounds of the hearth being swept, pots hung on the grid iron, propelled her into wifely duties. Whilst lying in bed she could forget her age, but rising brought on the aches of a stiff back. As she stretched she felt a load had lifted; they were all still alive, in their home, life going on.

Mid-morning, Pris burst in, unexpected. 'They attacked Plymouth,' she said. 'Burned Clark's garrison to the ground. Eleven killed, most of them women and children.'

Priscilla swayed and groped for a stool.

★ ★ ★

At least the chickens are laying well, Priscilla said to herself, emerging from the hen coop with a basket of big brown eggs. She fastened the gate to the coop – turned – *Who is that? Alexander. Why has he come?* She hurried to the house. 'Welcome. What brings you?' She tried to keep the worry out of her voice.

''Tis Sarah. She's bad sick. The ague,' he said.

'I'll come with you now.' Priscilla handed Alexander her medicine chest to carry. She found Sarah in a bad state; high fever, shivering, too weak to stand. Even raising her head brought on dizziness. Her smock and bed linen were soaked in sweat.

'My poor girl.'

'Mother.'

'We'll put you right,' Priscilla soothed as she changed the bed linen and put Sarah into a fresh smock. She instructed Alexander the dosage to give her. 'I'll send Mary down to help with the children and the chores.'

Taking her medicines, she called on Pris. 'Are you well?'

'Aye. So far. But folk are falling like flies. Mary Mendome's got it, bad.'

'Is her husband at home?'

'No. Still fighting. Could you give me a remedy and I'll call on her after dark,' Pris said.

'Of course, with my good wishes. Praise God Winslow kept our boys back to guard the town. Alexander in command! The rest of our family alright?'

'So far,' Pris said.

As the spring crept on Priscilla felt increasingly weary, stretched between tending the sick in the town, taking on more of the chores at home with Mary away caring for children and cooking for stricken families, and trying to keep up in her garden. Susanna took on more too. Whenever Alexander or David called in unexpectedly, there was a panic to keep Aijana and Chitsa hidden. Priscilla knew she was fraying. She snapped and was sorry. How could she be cross with John and Mary, with reports coming in of bloodbath encounters between the Indians and the English; the English more often losing, being pushed onto the back foot.

Into the second week in April the temperature shot up. 'I fear this heat will spread the fever.' Priscilla sweated as she and Susanna prepared a batch of bread.

'Never imagined it possible to be so hot.' Susanna wiped her brow and mopped her face with her apron.

At dinner time, John returned from a visit to the tavern, his head high, step buoyant. 'Reckon we've made a dent at last.'

'How is that?' Priscilla asked.

'We captured and killed the Narragansett chief. Could be the beginning of a chance to dismember the Indians' alliance. He was the forceful leader, not Philip. Without him...' John drew up a stool and sat down. 'However, bad news. I have to make five more coffins.'

'Any of ours?' Priscilla scrunched her apron.

'No, though David's Mary is bad.' He looked over at Susanna, leaning against the table, got up and guided her to a stool. 'Take the weight off your feet. You'll be pleased to know your brood are all well.'

Susanna smiled and laid her hand on his. 'Thank you, John.'

Gradually the fever ran its course. By the second week in May, Priscilla reckoned it was safe to bring Susanna down into the town for a visit with Pris. It was good to see the main street come alive again; folk bustling, gossiping, sloughing off the pall of sickness.

'Susanna! So good to see you. Feels like an age since you were last here.' Sarah and David's Mary called, pushing through a large gathering of women. Mary hugged Priscilla.

'Thanks to you and Mary we've all survived, and we did have it very bad.'

'Thank Susanna too,' Priscilla said. 'She taught me all the remedies I used.' She put an arm round Susanna's shoulder. 'We're on our way to Pris' store.'

'We are too; we'll come with you,' Sarah said.

'Mother, Susanna, Mary, Sarah,' Pris welcomed them. 'All together!'

Pris' store was full of women buying, talking, enjoying their new-found health in an exuberance of gossip ranging from witches to the war.

Priscilla asked Sarah, 'Has Alexander heard news of the war? Progress?'

'Aye. He reckons the tide could be turning in our favor. We've been winning more skirmishes, but the main reason is Benjamin Church is back. You know he bowed out for three months? Winslow refused to accept his strategy, and as Alice was expecting he stayed with her. But now the babe is born he has returned, vowing to hunt down Philip. What's more, he is friends with the Sakonnet Indians who will help him.'

'Pray it is over quickly,' Priscilla said. 'This has been the most vicious, evil war. I fear God will punish us. We have been wicked.'

'Mother, please do not think black thoughts. Not now. We must get through it and recover,' Pris said.

Chapter 90

May - August 1676

Susanna falls ill

'How different this is from our knot gardens in England,' Priscilla said. 'No time for those here. Herbs and flowers grow higgledy-piggledy among everything else.' Absorbed, chattering, Priscilla did not see Susanna fall. She heard a thump.

'Susanna!' She clambered to where Susanna lay. She cradled her head, patted her cheeks. Susanna opened her eyes. 'Ah. What happened? Did I faint?'

''Twas the hot sun. Mary...' Priscilla called. 'Come quickly!' With Mary helping, Priscilla lifted Susanna to her feet. Together they held her up, leading her indoors and onto her bed. 'Water. Spring water and beer.' Supporting Susanna's head, Priscilla held the beaker to her lips. A swallow or two and Susanna sank back onto the pillow, her face flushed. 'Brow hot. Blankets.' Priscilla sat holding Susanna's hands. Not many minutes passed before the shivering started. 'Oh no. It's the ague,' Priscilla moaned softly.

Day and night, for five days, Priscilla tended Susanna, giving her every potion she could think of, soothing away the sweat, easing her into fresh linen, piling on blankets when the shivering started again. *If only Elizabeth were here. She might know another remedy. Aijana might know an Indian cure but that would mean going into the forest and we cannot risk it, none of us.* She prayed. Prayed to God, to the Virgin Mary. 'Have mercy. Don't take her. Please don't take her from me.' But even as Priscilla prayed, Susanna became delirious, thrashing, calling out, 'Edward. Save me...' Her eyes bulged in terror as if she saw a fearful monster. Priscilla gave her the smallest dose of belladonna, remembering her mother taking their last drops to give the bosun. Susanna's delirium subsided but the fever didn't break. On the morning of the sixth day as the birds heralded the dawn, Susanna passed away. Priscilla gazed at her friend's face. 'No. No. It cannot be.' She gently closed her eyelids, covering the clouded blue eyes. She kissed Susanna's cheek, clutched her hands, buried her face in the inert, still soft stomach, and wept. *I should not have taken her to town. Oh why did I take her to town?*

A hand on her shoulder. 'Mother. I'm so sorry. Here. Drink this down.' Mary offered her a beaker.

'No. I'll not be drugged. If I'm drugged she'll leave me. I must keep her. Make her live.' Priscilla pushed Mary away. She sat holding Susanna's hands all day, refusing to move, to eat, willing Susanna to open her eyes, be alive. She heard John sawing, hammering, making a coffin and refused to believe.

Mary and Jonathan had to prize her away, hold her back as John lifted Susanna, cradling her in his arms.

For days Priscilla wandered as one possessed, not in this world. Aware of Mary hovering close by she turned and snapped. 'Get away. You don't belong here.' She gravitated to the spot in the garden where she and Susanna were working together before... and sat there, in the hot sun, in the rain. Only when dark came and the wolves howled would she leave that spot. During these days she created her own imaginary world which held four people: herself,

Susanna, Mother and Roger Williams. No one else was real. She was dimly aware of John trying to comfort her, drawing her close in bed. She pushed him away. And she absolutely refused all of Mary's potions.

Gradually she resumed her daily tasks, but in her own world. When she went into the garden she saw Susanna bent over, checking the herbal shrubs were in good health after the winter. She saw Susanna of long ago, picking plums by Town Brook; sparkling cornflower blue eyes, honey skin, merry, comforting, wise. Then, unbidden, Susanna became Mother. Deep warm eyes, working hard and cheerfully, tending the sick, loving Father whilst hating the voyage. *She was brave. Poor Mother. I couldn't save her. I couldn't save Susanna.* Then she told Roger Williams everything, her most private feelings, and he understood.

One day all the Alden family and Susanna's sons, Josiah and Peregrine, came to the house. Priscilla left Mary to provide a meal and sat alone in her rocker. She dimly registered Josiah was reading Susanna's will. She had few belongings, but her one substantial possession, her house, she left to Mary. Priscilla started and almost cried out. Susanna knew. She had overheard her conversation with Mary when Mary said she wanted to remain a maid. Dear Susanna.

Spring became summer. Hot dragging summer. Overwhelmed with lassitude, becoming ever weaker, Priscilla went through the motions of the daily routine. Increasingly, Mary bade her sit, out of the way. Priscilla didn't resist. She half-heard conversations, stories about the war: slave ships, carnage, betrayal. At times she covered her ears. There was just one happening which drew her attention. Aijana found another parcel of leather and beads. She knew then that Tinsin was still alive and was glad.

That same morning Pris rushed into the house. 'Mother, Father! Winslow has just now ridden through town saying there's fear of an attack on Bridgewater and Taunton. Indians about to cross the river.'

'Joseph!' Priscilla wrapped her arms around her waist.

Late in the afternoon Alexander and Jonathan called in to say Church was in town collecting men and provisions. 'We'll join his troop,' Alexander said.

'I'm going too,' John said. 'Mary, pack my knapsack please.'

'But...no... you cannot,' Priscilla gasped in bewilderment.

'I'm no use to you, Priscilla. You've left me. You live somewhere else, in your own world. I cannot rest here another minute. I may be old but we have a commander my age. I'm going.'

'David and Rebecca's Thomas will stay,' Jonathan said. 'They'll work in the fields and protect you.'

John gave Priscilla a goodbye kiss on her cheek.

Chapter 91

August 1676

John goes to fight and rescues a child

'Not far now to Bridgewater.' Alexander passed word from Benjamin Church to John, marching in the front line with Jonathan and Alexander. It was the second afternoon of their march and he still felt a spring in his step, buoyant and pleased to be in the company of young men, away from farm duties, and away from Priscilla. She seemed to care nothing for him anymore, for their life together. Where had she gone? Who inhabited her secret world? He felt helplessly shut out, and was weary with the pain of it, weary from knocking on a door that never opened.

He looked up through the treetops, stirring in a hot late afternoon breeze. Buzzards soared high. John recalled walking along this same track – how many years ago? – with Standish on their way to buy land from Massasoit. Land that Joseph now farmed. Now to fight Massasoit's son.

What was that in the distance? Shielding his eyes he made out small figures which gradually grew into men.

'Firearms at the ready,' Church commanded. A further hundred yards revealed the white English flag. In response to burgeoning 'Hoorahs' Church commanded, 'Quiet! We could be surrounded by Indians for all we know.'

As the Bridgewater militia drew near, John spied Joseph in the front. Big, ungainly, head like a tree stump, Joseph reminded John of a friendly bear. As the two front lines met John was enveloped in an enormous silent hug.

'Not far to the river,' Joseph spoke to Church.

The joined up troops continued their silent march about half a mile. Church ordered the bulk of the men to stay back while he led the front line forward to the riverbank. John was grateful to Hobbamock for teaching him how to be silent on his feet like an Indian. As he peered through the tall grasses he saw two Indians sitting on a huge tree felled across the river. He could see one of them had gray hair and wrinkly skin. A shot and the old Indian fell into the river. The young Indian disappeared like a shadow into the night before Church could fire again. He sent Alexander to bring up the troops and ordered them to hunt down the Indians and shoot to kill. Fighting zeal propelled John into action – soon over. It didn't require much ferreting to rustle the Indians from their hiding. John gawped at their pitiable state. Bone thin, stunned and terrified, their arms trembled so they could not fire their muskets. Church's men shot. John raised his musket but could not bring himself to fire. Ten warriors fell dead. The others threw down their arms in surrender.

Light was fading. Church's troop marched their captives back to a clearing by the river.

John was put in charge of making camp. First he gathered twigs and small branches and struck a fire.

'Still the fastest man alive to strike a fire,' Joseph said.

Then he detailed men to gather more brushwood for the fire and took a crew with him to cut saplings. By the time a pot of victuals was heated through, shelters and a corral for the prisoners had been erected.

Sitting with Jonathan, Joseph and Alexander by the fire, John said, 'If it weren't for the purpose of our being here, this could be fifty years ago on a trek to Massasoit's camp. Making shelters as taught by the Indians. We'd be eating fish, cornmeal, boiled acorns provided by the Indians, and kept awake as they sang themselves to sleep.' He shook his head. 'They were friendly, wanting to help us, wanting our friendship.'

'That was a different time,' Joseph said. 'You can see the terrible state they're in. Been chased from swamp to swamp. Their raids are horrific but don't kill many. Whereas we... given a chance we slaughter hundreds.' He put down his hunk of cornbread. 'Do you know, it is said that fleeing from place to place, always fleeing, the Indian children hindered their escape, unable to keep up or stay quiet. So they had to kill them – kill their own children. Some say it was too much for the parents. They could not do it. So a cruel woman was found. She killed a hundred in one day.'

John and his sons sat silent, heads bowed.

In the morning Church chose a select group of English soldiers and friendly Sakonnet Indians to go in pursuit of the disappeared Indian, whom one of the Sakonnets recognized as Philip. Among those chosen were Joseph, Jonathan and Alexander. John was detailed to guard the prisoners.

The day was long and hot. John felt on edge, fearful for his sons. The prisoners were parched and starving. John shared some of his ale and food and persuaded his comrades to do the same.

With the sun almost below the horizon, John took his musket and ventured into the forest for more firewood. Gathering up his load, he heard voices and cracking branches. He dropped the wood and raised his musket.

'Church!' John waited as the troop tramped toward him with a host of Indian prisoners. He fell in at the rear. A hundred paces on he heard a musket fire and felt a piercing pain in his right calf. He whirled and fired at a moving body. An Indian fell. The man beside John strode to the body and shot him again. Church halted the troop, ordered, 'Guard the rear,' and, 'March on.' After a brief inspection John reckoned he'd escaped with a graze and ignoring the pain tried to keep up. He fought off bouts of dizziness and was dimly aware of clumps of flies gathering in the bloody wound.

When they reached camp, Joseph tore a clean linen towel into strips, cleansed the wound and bound it tight.

In the meantime Church and the leader of the Bridgewater militia decided the only place large and secure enough to hold so many prisoners was the Bridgewater pound.

Another short march. John's leg was throbbing. Jonathan and Joseph marched with him at the rear. When they reached the town John was pleased to see Church organizing plenty of food and drink for the captives and their Sakonnet guards.

Later, in lodgings with Jonathan, Joseph and Alexander, John smiled to hear laughter echoing up from the pound.

'Hear we took one hundred and seventy-three prisoners,' Joseph said.

'Listen to them.' Jonathan tilted his head toward the open window. 'Merry on food and safety.'

'They have no idea what lies in store, poor innocents,' John said. 'Unless perchance they've heard of the slave ships in Plymouth Harbor, waiting for their cargo.'

No one spoke for several minutes.

Alexander broke the pall. 'Church is a good man. A great warrior when he has to fight, but is for fairness and against undue cruelty. I keep trying to persuade him to stay in Duxbury.'

'Aye,' John said. 'We need him there.'

'My Sarah will miss his Alice terribly,' Alexander said, 'but he is adamant he doesn't want to live in a town; prefers the wilderness;

is settling way down south in the southeastern most tip of the Narragansett Bay. Unpopulated except for Quakers, Baptists and Sakonnet Indians.'

'Do you reckon Church will ever catch Philip?' Jonathan asked. 'He seems expert at slipping one's grasp.'

'Sure of it,' Alexander said. 'Almost had him last night. Church's Sakonnet guides found Philip's camp. Church and about ten of us set a snare and camped close by. Everything set. Then our guard took a nip too many, stupid drunkard, and caused noisy chaos. Wanted to shoot him.' Alexander stood and stretched. He poured everyone another tankard of ale. 'But you can bet your life on it. Church, with the help of his Sakonnet friends will get Philip. It is only a matter of time. Provided of course Church doesn't get himself shot first. He takes fearful risks. Has had quite a few close shaves.'

John and his sons talked long into the night, recounting stories of raids, battles, burnings, and speculating gloomily about the outcome. Would the English and the Indians ever be able to achieve co-operation, with customs so different and this breakdown of trust?

'One thing I'll say,' Joseph said, 'the Indians deliver some of the most gruesome tortures you can imagine. Long, drawn out…' He shuddered. 'But unlike us they never rape their women captives, whereas some English rape their own wives.'

In the morning John had difficulty walking. With troops and prisoners mustered, the moment came to bid Joseph farewell. Tears came to John's eyes. 'Come for a visit if you can. 'Twould do your mother good.'

'Aye. When all this is over, I'll come.'

John gripped Joseph's hand.

'Forward, march!' Church commanded.

Jonathan and Alexander walked with John at the rear. When at last time came to make camp for the night John collapsed. Ten miles had seemed forever. Ten more tomorrow.

★ ★ ★

'Reckon we're about halfway. Have a drink, Father.' Jonathan handed John his jug of beer. The sun was high overhead, mercilessly hot.

'Thank you.' About to take a sip, John lowered the jug. 'Listen.' Buzzards soared and crows cawed in the silent heat.

'It's only the birds,' Alexander said.

'No. There. Again. That's a human cry. Over to the left.' John ignored Jonathan and Alexander's protests and slowly limped toward the sound, dragging his right leg. Jonathan and Alexander could but help him.

'Ssh,' John said. The cry ceased. His efforts to creep silently were hampered by his bad leg but he insisted they go on.

Two hundred yards into the forest they came upon an Indian boy, bound to a tree, eyes wide and glazed with terror.

'No fear. Friend.' John spoke the Indian words Tinsin had taught him. 'We help.'

Recently dried blood and pus covered a head wound, and a gash on his lower left calf suggested a cut hamstring. John cut through the vine ropes and grasped the boy's arms firmly as he struggled to get away. Jonathan and Alexander pinned him between them and he fell limp.

'We'll take him with us,' John said.

'But Father, we are already far behind the troop,' Jonathan said. 'This will slow us down even more. We'll have no protection from vengeful Indians. Surely it's better to leave him to be rescued by his own.'

'You know that won't happen. We take him.' *Perhaps a child to care for will bring Priscilla back.*

Hobbling on, well-nigh crippled by the searing throbbing in his leg, John felt sick at heart. Where was there any goodness or sense in this war? Why had they all been so blind, himself and Standish included, determined not to see that no good could come of stealing the Indians' land? For that is what they had done. And now, so much blood spilt. How could it be right? How could a just God approve of this? And Priscilla. Would she ever come back to him? Open her arms to him again? What would it take?

Chapter 92

August 1676

Pris' sadness - the war ends

'John's gone.' Priscilla sat stunned for a moment and then stepped over to her spinning wheel, seeing Susanna, spinning, spinning, back and forth with a light deft step, not needing eyes.

Pris and David bounded in through the open door. Pris kissed Priscilla, giving her shoulders a squeeze. 'We've come to help. Father said he's left a deer he shot yesterday. Needs butchering.'

'Good day, ladies,' David waved as he loped out the back door to the fields.

Pris and Mary set to skinning and butchering while Aijana, Chitsa, Mary Mendome and Constance worked at the table, chopping vegetables and making pies for the midday meal.

Priscilla slowed her spinning to watch Pris and Mary. She saw Pris glance in her direction and heard, 'Is she any better?' Mary shook her head, 'No.' Priscilla spun faster. *What do they mean 'better'? I'm not sick.* Again she slowed and listened.

'Are things going well in the store?' Mary asked. 'No difficult customers?'

'Not really, I suppose, and David's Mary is a great help.'

'Do you see much of Abigail? She never comes up here. Will she be alright with Jonathan gone off to fight again?'

Pris jerked the last stretch of pelt from the deer. 'I don't know how she'll cope, but I hope she doesn't take it out on me.' She vigorously slit the rib cage. 'She comes into the store and says dreadful things, in front of customers.'

'What does she say?'

'That I should leave Jonathan alone – find myself a husband – as a woman should.' With her bloodied hand Pris wiped her eyes. 'She keeps Jonathan away. Won't let him near me. He has always stood up for me, been on my side, helped me – we had such fun together – the laughs.' She covered her face. 'I've lost him. Lost my favorite, closest brother.'

The sight of Pris in distress jolted Priscilla out of her bubble. She hurried to her daughter, wiped the blood off her face. 'There, there. It's probably just because of the war. I'm sure it will pass.' She returned to her spinning, to her world with Susanna.

Pris brought the butchering hatchet down so hard she almost split the bench. Mary put an arm round her sister's shoulders. 'I'm sure Jonathan feels it too.'

Days passed. Priscilla neither knew nor cared how many. She drifted through time with no sense of urgency, undertaking the tasks Mary set her but often abandoning them partially completed. She registered that Mary was frustrated but did not see why. Pris and David came and went, sometimes with Thomas, Rebecca's husband. Rebecca, her youngest daughter, reminded her of a brook in spring, running, leaping through the days.

Priscilla was seated in her rocker, knitting, thinking of Susanna. David ran in from the fields. 'Our troop! I'm sure it's our troop marching along the border of the far field. I'll go meet them.'

Priscilla struggled to remember. *Our troop... oh yes.* She continued to rock; she dozed. Images of Father and Mother, Joseph and Captain Jones; Joseph, Father and Mother so ill and John Alden carrying...

'It was Church's men.' David's voice pulled her into now. 'But Father, Alexander and Jonathan weren't with them. Father's wounded.'

'Wounded? Father? Who?' Priscilla's question was met with silence. She sank back into her reverie. The effort of existing in two different worlds was too taxing. She declined supper, listening to prayers from where she sat. She knew it was night when the wolves howled, sounding closer. She covered her ears.

Pyke's hackles bristled. He growled deep in his throat. Armed with pitchforks and muskets David and Thomas went to see the animals were safe.

The women gathered round the hearth and waited, knitting and mending in silence, listening to the crackle and hiss of logs against the everlasting background of howling wolves. Pyke lay still, ears cocked. Priscilla's cat curled on her lap. Her sister chose Mary.

Of a sudden Pyke jumped up, barked loudly and pawed at the back door as if to tear it down. A hammering. David's voice. 'It's us. Open.' Mary lifted the latch. Jonathan and Alexander, supporting John, fell into the room, followed by David, carrying the Indian boy.

Priscilla hung back. 'John?'

'Mother,' Mary said. 'Father is wounded. You must treat his wound.'

'Aye,' Priscilla said. 'Of course.' She applied herself to the task and did not leave off before she had carefully cleaned and bound the wound. Then she returned to her rocker, leaving the Indian boy to the ministrations of Aijana and Chitsa.

★ ★ ★

'Mother,' Mary called.

Priscilla straightened from her hoeing as Mary threaded her way through rows of vegetables made festive with bright calendula, zinnias, nasturtiums.

'Fancy. I want to make pies with a white flour upper crust to celebrate our men coming home safe and I've run out of flour. Could you go to Pris' store for me?'

Priscilla wrapped her summer shawl close. She was always cold, even in the August heat. Taking her basket she dutifully set off. In the town, passing the meeting house, she noticed freshly severed wolves' heads nailed to the walls. *Good. Wretched creatures.*

'Mother! Good day.' Pris gave her mother a hearty kiss and hug. 'Here. Sit on a stool. What can I get for you?'

'Five pounds of white flour please and…'

A cluster of women entered. 'Reckon that strange creature's a witch… seen dark cloaked shapes come out o' her shack at nightfall… an' then me little Sally felt a pinch o' the night and were in a screamin fit.'

To Priscilla the words were a far off irritation. She batted them away. 'I'll go into the garden 'til you're not busy.' She went from the store into the back room. *Where the Quakers held their meeting for worship,* she recalled and vaguely wondered where the Quakers had gone. Out the back door into a garden of vegetables, herbs, flowers, all neatly planted in rows; not a weed to be seen. At the back of the garden a gate opened into an orchard: apple trees, plum, damson, cherry, all bearing ripening fruit. Under an apple tree was a bench. *Ah. I'll sit here awhile.* On the back was carved 'From Jonathan'. *How kind. This is like the bench John made for me. Dear Jonathan.* Priscilla sat quiet in the afternoon sun. Butterflies flitted on the lavender, a few seconds here, a few seconds on another blossom. *Pity there are no honeybees in this land. They would love the lavender.* Birdsong sounded far away. She closed her eyes, cushioned in the warmth. Drowsiness drifted into sleep.

Priscilla dreamt she was walking across a wide, open space, a grassy field without borders. Susanna was on one side of her, Mother on the other. She clutched their hands. 'Stay. Don't go. Keep me safe,' she implored. She looked from one to the other, beseeching their kind silent faces. Then, gradually they began to snarl and turned into wolves. She ran, tripped and fell. Something lifted her. She uncovered her eyes. Susanna faced her, slowly walking backwards. 'Stop clinging. Go to John. Let the dead go.' She faded.

Priscilla woke with a start, wondering where she was. She realized she was shaking. She sat quietly until the shaking stopped and slowly stood. *Only a dream.* Making sure she was steady, she retraced her steps back to the house and into the storeroom. Opening the door a crack she saw Abigail.

'We really would rather you didn't call round. Jonathan is with me in this. If there are any parcels of supplies, barrels, crates, our servant will cart them here.' Abigail's steely eyes bored into Pris. 'How many times? Why don't you get your own man? Cease being a burden.'

Other customers stared and murmured behind their hands. 'Wait 'til Goody Warren hears this.'

'And Goody Bridges.'

Priscilla burst into the room. 'Abigail, come outside with me. I want to talk with you.' She led Abigail down the main street to the edge of the town where they were alone. 'Why do you taunt Pris? What are you afraid of, telling her to keep away from Jonathan? She is his sister. They have always been close. Why do you have to ruin it? You are behaving like a fiend. And to talk like that with other women in the store. For shame!' Priscilla stopped walking. 'Look at me.'

Abigail looked away. 'Jonathan is married now, to me. Surely you agree it isn't right for Pris to interfere. He belongs with his wife and children.' Then, eyes downcast, she said, 'I think Jonathan loves Pris better than me. If she weren't his sister he would marry her. I think he wishes he could be married to her and not me. I wish she would go away.'

'My dear,' Priscilla said. 'I know how in love Jonathan was with you when you married. He could talk of no one else. If anyone has a right to be jealous it is Pris. But I warn you, the way you are behaving now, you are on track to destroy his love. Do you not see how ugly you have become? An inner ugliness. You may have fine features, but they won't save you.'

Abigail said nothing for several long minutes. She shook herself as if to wrench herself free from something clutching hold of her.

'I'll try. But can you not see how hard it is? They've been close all their lives. She can make him laugh in a way I cannot. They're so easy together. They fit hand in glove. I feel second best, left out when she is with us.'

Priscilla put a hand on Abigail's arm. 'Aye. I do see. But there are different kinds of love. You love Jonathan or you would not be so jealous. It is you who has a family with him. Do you not feel how he loves you, not as a sister but as a wife? If only you could trust. One love does not replace the other, or chase it away. I do believe if you could open your heart a little more, and perhaps even love Pris as a sister, all of you would be much happier.'

'You make it sound easy.'

'I know it isn't easy, and you've rather backed yourself into a corner. But I reckon Pris would meet you halfway. I've never known her bear a grudge.' Priscilla placed her hands on Abigail's shoulders. 'You're a fine, intelligent young woman. Don't shrivel yourself into a shrew.'

Abigail looked up and met Priscilla's eyes. 'Thank you.'

Engrossed in her conversation with Abigail, Priscilla hadn't noticed the street behind them filling with folk and the rising excited voices. A man called out, 'Hoorah! Here he comes, Captain Church with King Philip's head.' The street exploded in celebration as Church rode through the crowd bearing Philip's head aloft. 'The war is over… it's over… we've won!' Folk shouted and danced.

Abigail punched the air and shouted, 'Hoorah for Captain Church!'

'Goodbye, Abigail.' Priscilla kissed her daughter-in-law and hurried along the track back toward home. *It isn't good what we've* done. *It is bad. We should have gone to Rhode Island.* She halted. *Bother. I've forgotten the flour. I'll have to go back.* She skirted behind the crowd and met Pris, standing and cheering outside her store. 'I forgot the flour.'

In the quiet of Pris' store Priscilla gave vent. 'It is good the war is over, but it is our fault it happened. To parade and exult… dreadful. We should be hanging our heads in remorse.'

'But Mother, Captain Church fought long and hard, took fearful risks to capture Philip. Surely you can allow him some glory. He didn't start the war, but he has ended it.'

'We should have gone to Rhode Island. They didn't fight.'

'Mother. I could shake you. Will you please stop pining for some place you imagine is a perfect world; a world that doesn't exist. I know losing Susanna is terrible, and Elizabeth was always your favorite, but you've gone away, from Father, from us all, and we need you. Father loves you. He is distraught.'

'He can come to Rhode Island. I've asked him to.'

'Mother.' Pris raised her voice and thumped a barrel. 'Do you care nothing for all Father has done? He and Captain Standish founded this town. Father has built you a wonderful large house. Almost all our family live here in Duxbury, and Father is still deeply committed to governing Plymouth. Besides, he has changed. He defended Philip against all Plymouth's leaders. And all you can think of is to go to Rhode Island because you miss Elizabeth and care for Roger Williams. Do you think we haven't noticed? And just to let you know, reports have come that the Indians did attack Rhode Island.'

Priscilla put her hands to her burning cheeks. Her head swam. She sought a stool.

'I'm sorry,' Pris said. 'I know I was harsh and I didn't want to hurt you, and Alexander says Elizabeth and William were not hurt. I'll walk you home and carry the flour.'

News of Church's parade through Duxbury had reached the Alden household before Pris and Priscilla. Although shocked by

Pris' scolding and already weak, Priscilla's first thoughts were for Mary Mendome and Constance. 'I fear this means your husband will soon return. I wish you could stay with us always.'

John left his talk with Alexander and put his arm round Priscilla's shoulder. She leaned against him. 'There'll be skirmishing awhile yet,' John said. 'I'm sure Mendome won't want to miss out. Reckon Mary and Constance can bide here awhile longer, and if Mendome should surprise us, well – I'll deal with him.'

'Thank you, Mr Alden.' Mary curtsied and Constance copied her mother.

'Thank you, Mr Alden.' Priscilla looked up into John's face and smiled.

That night after bedtime prayers, Priscilla kissed Aijana, Chitsa, Mary and Constance goodnight, as she did every night, even when she was in her own world. A tear ran down Aijana's cheek, hastily brushed away. *She's worried about Tinsin. Pray he's survived.*
Priscilla woke before dawn. She felt different. She ran her hands along the folds of the bed curtains, brushing against the thick, rough texture. The only sound she could hear was the dawn twitterings of birdlife. Her thoughts turned to the tasks of the day: early milking, draw ale for breakfast, stir up the fire under the porridge pot. John slept on. She rose, relishing the cool of early morning before the sun began its hot assault. *Strange. I feel I've come back into life. First I'll say good morning to my herbs and vegetables and watch the sun rise.* Stepping softly past the buttery she peeked behind the barrels. Empty pallets. No one. Not a soul anywhere. Priscilla gasped, covering her mouth to stifle a scream. What was that bundle tucked up beside a barrel? She picked it up and shook out Mary Mendome's dress and shawl, and Constance's. Out of the folds fell an exquisite bead belt. *They've gone. Did Tinsin come in the night? Was it all planned? Of course. The leather tunics were for Mary and Constance. They're going to live with the Indians.* She gazed at Mary's dress with the letter 'A' stitched into the sleeve. *She's free. As long as Tinsin can keep them safe. Please God, please let them live and be happy.* She buried her face in

the dress and wept. Then she stirred the embers in the hearth, got a blaze going and burned the clothes left behind. There must be no trace. She contemplated the dresses being eaten in the flames, relived the ghastly punishment inflicted on Mary, her appalling wounds. *A miracle she recovered. Plymouth did wrong to treat her thus. Plymouth has gone bad.* A movement beside her made her start. It was the Indian boy, Kekut. His face was contorted, stricken, though not a tear escaped his eye. Priscilla gathered him close. 'They've gone to a good safe place with Tinsin. We'll miss them horribly but they would not be safe staying here,' she said. 'But we can keep you safe, Kekut. You are a child. We will be your mother and father, your family. Mr Alden can make the English understand.' *But if we lived in Rhode Island there would be no need to make the English understand.*

Chapter 93

August 1676

An honorable man

A pounding on the door made Priscilla jump. She'd barely opened when a strange man stormed in.

'Alexander. Sarah says he's here. I must speak with him.'

'In the fields… the harvest.' Priscilla called over her shoulder, 'Quick, Mary – fetch Alexander.'

'I thank you. Mistress Alden? I am Benjamin Church.' He removed his hat, bowed slightly and wiped his flushed face. 'Honored to meet you.'

Priscilla was interested to set eyes on this man she knew Alexander admired. He was stocky, not tall but not as short as Standish. He paced impatiently, running his fingers through light brown hair. His beard was a shaped stubble running from ear to ear along thick jowls. He had finely shaped eyebrows and, incongruous for a warrior Priscilla thought, a rather effeminate bow-shaped mouth.

'Benjamin! What brings you?' Alexander ran into the kitchen.

John, Jonathan, Pris, David and young Kekut followed close behind.

'Winslow promised. He **promised**,' Church said. 'I return from Boston and what greets me? Their heads on spikes, with Philip's. Did you know of this?'

'I don't know what you're talking about,' Alexander said. 'Whose heads? Wait. We're starving. After dinner when we can pay attention tell us what happened.'

The meal was consumed hurriedly, in silence. Church drained his beaker of ale.

'Come by the hearth,' John said, gesturing to the captain to sit in Priscilla's rocking chair. He took his own customary seat. The men pulled up stools. Priscilla, Mary and Pris listened as they cleared away trenchers and beakers. Then, sitting at a discreet distance, they mended and sewed quilts; quiet tasks enabling them to hear.

'When I brought Philip's head to Plymouth,' Church began, 'Winslow requested I hunt down his two most trusted and powerful warriors, old Annawon and Tuspaquin. He said we wouldn't be safe until they were killed.'

'But Annawon was surely too old to do any harm. I remember him from Massasoit's days,' John said.

'I said the same, but no. Winslow wanted him dead. With six men I finally tracked him to his camp cleverly set at the base of a steep rock face with swamp all round. The only way to get into the camp was down the rock face. With two Sakonnet Indians shielding me, we made the descent. Annawon's son looked up and seeing who we were, cowered in a heap, his blanket over his head. He was lying beside their muskets propped against the branch of a tree. I waved my hatchet and grabbed the muskets. With his son's life at stake, Annawon gave in. His warriors all gave themselves up. Not a shot was fired, not a drop of blood spilled.'

'Praise God,' Alexander said. 'Amazing.'

'Their food was cooking over the campfire. I said I would like to eat. Annawon was pleased to share a meal. I promised clemency for his people as long as they co-operated. However, his own fate would be in the hands of the Plymouth court. Annawon nodded his acceptance.' Church stood and paced up and down, hands clasped behind his back. 'I hadn't slept for two days; was desperate for sleep. Posted men to keep watch. Lay down. Couldn't sleep. Looked around. All Annawon's Indians and my men were sleeping soundly. Only Annawon and I were awake. We lay on either side of the fire looking at each other. Suddenly he got up and left the tent, weaponless of course. I thought he needed to... you know. But minutes went by. I rose quietly and stood over beside his son, ready to use him as hostage.' Church shook his head. 'You'll never believe this.' He stopped pacing. 'Annawon returned carrying a woven basket. He knelt before me, holding the basket for me to take. Then he said, in English, "Philip adorned himself with these items when he sat in state. You have killed Philip. The war is over. You have won. Therefore these things are rightfully yours." I thanked him.'

Priscilla let her mending fall in her lap. Rapt, she focused entirely on Church. Not a sound in the room.

Church continued. 'He lifted out a belt of wampum, must have been nine inches wide, designs of animals, flowers, birds. A beautiful thing. He draped it over my shoulders and it reached all the way down to my ankles. Other wampum belts, a fine, richly woven red blanket – so soft – and two glazed powder horns.' He paused, wiped his brow and eyes. 'I tell you I have never felt so honored, nor will I ever again.' He looked directly at Priscilla. 'An honorable man – to be so dishonored at our hands.' He sat down. 'We sat talking all night. He told many stories from his years serving Massasoit. He revered the sachem of old times. As to this terrible war, he blamed Sassamon and the over-zealous war-lusting warriors. We talked of the soul, the spirit. Annawon believed there is one God that rules over all men everywhere and in the after-time, any wrong a man has done to any person, Indian or English, man, woman or child, will be visited upon him in turn.' Church stayed quiet a moment. 'I'd had a notion that both Annawon and Tuspaquin could be a great aid in helping the Massachusetts Bay soldiers in their ongoing fight with a hostile tribe in Maine. Governor Endecott has asked me to lead a squadron of their men. When I arrived in Plymouth with Annawon I put this to Winslow. I persuaded him to promise clemency for Tuspaquin should he give himself up, and of course for Annawon.'

John interjected, 'Seems a good idea to me.'

'Then I got word to go to Boston – urgent.' Church put his head in his hands. 'Should have stayed. I return...' He could hardly speak. 'Annawon's head... Tuspaquin's... on spikes. A fine old Indian. Wise. Loyal. Would have been a good friend, ally, negotiator. He trusted me. Tuspaquin would have followed his lead.' Church stood. 'I want nothing more to do with Plymouth Colony. Better off on the edge of the wilderness with the trustworthy Sakonnets and tolerant English and refugee Baptists and Quakers. At least they stay true to their word. Come with me, Alexander. This town is full of petty falsehoods. Winslow is a hypocrite.' Priscilla glanced at Mary, sadly nodding in agreement. 'Come with me, all of you. You would be near Elizabeth and William. The Alden tribe.'

Priscilla noticed John crossing, uncrossing his legs, looking uncomfortable.

'I would join you tomorrow,' Alexander said. 'But we're all settled here with growing families. Besides, if we all came it would soon be another town – and you'd be moving again to escape us.' He put a hand on Church's shoulder.

'I'm coming with you.' Priscilla stepped forward.

'You'll be most welcome, Mistress Alden,' Church said. 'But...' He looked at John, now standing.

'Priscilla, no,' John said, his face flushed dark red, hands clenched.

'I am going. Mary, please start packing my trunk. At what hour tomorrow should I be ready, Captain Church?'

'Mother. Don't be ridiculous,' Pris commanded.

'Daylight, Mistress Alden. Thank you for a delicious meal.' Amid the furor of protestations and efforts to dissuade Priscilla, Church took his leave.

Priscilla turned her back on her family and walked out the kitchen door. She half-ran through the garden and into the copse, following the path that led to the brook. Checking to see no one was behind her she walked rapidly, absently staring into the sparkle of little waterfalls. *I will go to Rhode Island. I will. I will.* If she went, John would come, and if he refused she could live with Elizabeth and William. John has Mary to care for him, and all the family. *In Rhode Island I can breathe freely, speak freely.* She chose to ignore Susanna's intrusive voice. 'John has always loved you, risked everything for you... been loyal even when you betrayed him.' *That was then; this is now. That was then; this is now.* The phrase became a chant in her head, hurrying her footsteps. She hoped Mary was packing her trunk. If not, no matter. She would go as she was and Alexander could bring it later.

Squawking above caught her attention. Without slackening her pace she looked up, shielding her eyes. A female woodpecker battled an enormous black crow. She thought of the woodpecker carving given her by Tinsin, and followed the fight as the woodpecker flew from tree to tree. *Please, please win, brave mother.* Her foot went down a rabbit hole and she fell, crying out as her head hit something sharp.

Priscilla came awake into the motion of being carried, cradled, warm wet drops falling onto her cheeks.

'Thank God you are alive. Please, Priscilla. Please stay. Let me care for you.'

She drifted off into a daze, hearing John's words, recognizing it was he who was carrying her. In a hinterland of dim awareness she felt him lay her carefully on their bed so she leaned against the bolsters. Mary brought chicken broth and lavender water. Priscilla accepted both. Pris, Jonathan and David stood at the foot of the bed. 'Is she alright? What happened?'

'We'll let her rest,' John said, dismissing them. He remained, sitting quietly beside Priscilla, holding her hands.

Priscilla did not go with Benjamin Church in the morning. Her head throbbed. Trying to perform daily tasks she suffered dizzy spells and stumbled. By midday she had given in to Mary's plea to sit in her rocker and knit.

After several days she began to be steady on her feet and able to function. She recalled Benjamin Church exhorting them to come to Rhode Island, and felt restless. But she was also tired, taken over by a deep weariness, and she didn't enjoy the refreshment that comes with a sound night's sleep. Memories of Susanna, Mother, of her stay with Roger Williams no longer brought her alive.

As weeks passed, Priscilla regained her ability to perform household duties. Outwardly she was the same capable wife, mother, Duxbury doctor she'd been before Benjamin Church's visit. Inwardly she followed Dorothy's resolve to shut out her feelings and desires. She no longer yearned for Susanna or Roger Williams. She no longer wanted to move to Rhode Island. Nor did she allow herself memories of Mother and Father and Joseph, and her early life. Too painful. Books Jonathan had brought her from Boston, Shakespeare's plays and sonnets, Newton's *Opticks*, lay unopened.

Her pleasure came from her garden, her well stocked medicine chest and her flourishing family. She taught her grandchildren to read and write and instructed the girls in the preparation of remedies. She gave her evenings to spinning, weaving, knitting and sewing garments for her grandchildren.

Without fully knowing it, Priscilla was gradually burying that part of herself Roger Williams had awakened: her desire to be still and listen, to ponder, to learn, her searching. Those desires only led to trouble. Better to concentrate on the daily tasks required to run a successful household, which she did admirably.

Chapter 94

Autumn 1677 – March 1678

Kekut

Over the months John continued to suffer from Priscilla's surface, somewhat brittle, 'goodwife' behavior. Where had her honest passionate love gone? He found some solace in the growing affection between him and Kekut. Kekut had always helped in the fields and now they often went hunting together; John with his flintlock, Kekut armed with his bow and a sheaf of arrows, though John reckoned the lad would soon be strong enough to use a rifle. He had gained inches in height over the past year and was becoming well-muscled.

However, especially gratifying for John was Kekut's desire to learn carpentry and furniture making. The lad was patient and careful; he learned how to plane and fit strips of wood, how to make tenon joints, how to finish surfaces so they shone like glass, and he developed his skill in carving. John admired the intricacy of his work. Together in the barn the two developed their craft, not saying a lot, but Kekut's black eyes sparkled as if a flame burned behind, and John's heart warmed so he sometimes got a lump in his throat. The harvest was in. Trees were donning their vivid autumn colors: reds, yellows, orange, burnished gold. The summer's heat gave way to clear crisp air, ethers that put a spring in one's step.

John and Kekut tramped across fields of stubble, their mission to hunt deer. Kekut led the way into the forest, finding tracks John would not have seen. The forest shimmered with autumn tinted light, leaves rustling in a light breeze, squirrels leaping from branch to branch, chattering, gathering acorns, scattering squawking birds. Kekut stopped. He pushed away fallen leaves to reveal a memory hole. 'A sachem of old had a mighty battle with a huge black bear, a legend in the forest. For hours they fought until finally, though badly wounded, his skin ripped, the sachem plunged his knife into the beast's heart. The memory hole is to remind us of the victory and to give thanks to the spirits of the forest and to the bear.' Kekut had taught John that the Indians respect the animals they kill and thank them for the food, clothing, and tools they provide.

As they turned to resume their trek, they faced a solitary Indian brave. He wore only the traditional loin cloth and carried a bow and arrows. John was relieved to see he wasn't adorned with war paint. He spoke to Kekut and gestured that the lad should come with him and John should stay.

'No,' John said, holding onto Kekut's arm. John searched Kekut's sensitive face; taut, cheek and jaw bones clenched, a slight furrow between his black eyebrows, and his eyes – the sparkle gone, expressionless, flat. A solitary golden leaf floated gently along a shaft of sunlight and landed in the triangle formed by their three sets of feet. John's stomach knotted, his head fizzed.

Kekut looked John in the eye. 'I go. My father is sick – to die.'

'But you will return. Please say you will come back to us. You are still young. Mistress Alden and I, we love you, want to care for you.'

Kekut's gaze did not change. 'I go. I must go.'

John begged the brave, 'Please keep him safe.'

The brave stared, impassive, inscrutable.

'Kekut, tell him we want you to be safe.' John looked into Kekut's eyes, searching. *All the child in him has been shut out.*

The brave grunted, jerking his head, beckoning, impatient. Kekut raised his hand to John and followed the brave. John stood, fixed, watching until the lad's back disappeared round a bend.

The year ended; a new spring arrived. In his barn, John worked on, catching the last hours of daylight. He was making a chest of drawers to hold clothes and linen so Priscilla would not have to bend over and dig down into a trunk. Their three cows peered over the doors of their pens, softly munching hay; their breath and bodies providing the only warmth. It had been a winter of deep snows; even now, early March, snow swirled from gray skies. John worked mechanically. The barn felt empty. The house felt empty. He veered between hope and despair, trying to accept that Kekut would never return but each morning hoping this day would bring a miracle.

The light was gone. Another day ended. John put away his tools and stepped out into snow falling thick and fast, big flakes, piling as they landed.

After prayers and supper, John and Priscilla sat in their rockers by the hearth as they did every evening. Priscilla took up her mending. John half-heartedly whittled. Patch, their fourth dog, settled himself at John's feet and their two cats curled up in their places either side of the hearth. No sound but the low hum of the wheel as Mary spun, the crackle of burning logs and the distant howling of wolves.

John's mind churned as it did every night. *Is he alive or dead? Is he safe with his tribe? Have they persuaded him to hate us as we're English? When they tell him of the terrible things we've done, of the slave ships, why wouldn't he hate us? But would Kekut not see we are different? We saved him and kept Aijana and Chitsa safe. And why has he refused to tell us how he came to be tied to the tree?* Forgetting himself, John groaned out loud.

'John. Are you ailing?' Priscilla looked up from her knitting. Patch whined, looking up at his master. The dog pricked up his ears and, barking loudly, jumped up. He made such a noise John and Priscilla barely heard the knocking on the back door. 'Quiet, Patch. Who?' Fetching his rifle, John cautiously opened. 'Kekut!'

There he stood, the Indian lad, still a lad though he'd gained an inch or two over the five months gone. However, his features belied his age, stronger, more defined: a high clear brow, black eyes spaced and serious, prominent cheekbones, his mouth still sensitive but with a resolute expression, betraying a wisdom beyond his years. His sleek black hair reached his shoulders and he wore Indian leggings and a tunic, and moccasins.

'Come in, come in. Come sit by the hearth.' Almost speechless John welcomed him. Mary dashed to fetch a trencher of pottage and cornbread. Priscilla stood, arms outstretched, her knitting falling to the floor. 'Oh Kekut. How wonderful. 'Tis a miracle. You are alive and well.' As Kekut took a seat by the fire, trencher in hand, Priscilla sat down again, watching him eat, unable to take her eyes off his face.

Mary, unable to stop beaming, pulled up a stool. 'I am so happy. So happy you are here.'

When Kekut finished eating John asked, 'Can you tell us what happened? What is your story, Kekut? Will you stay?'

Kekut hesitated. 'I couldn't say this until now because I was ashamed. When we were fleeing the English I was careless; climbed a tree to scout for the enemy and fell. My people depended on me as I was quick and agile, silent. I hurt my leg and was lame, so I had to be among the children chosen to be killed.'

'What?' Priscilla leaned forward. 'They killed the children?' John recounted what he'd learned in Bridgewater. Priscilla blanched.

'My father couldn't do it; gave the task to my uncle. He almost did. Took me away, put his knife to my throat and then dropped his arm. Tied me to the tree where you found me.'

John let out a moan and a whistle.

'Tinsin told my family I was here; told them you are good people and would keep me safe. He told them about Mr Alden's defense of the Indians in the Taunton meeting and that you kept Aijana and Chitsa hidden. So my father was content for me to be here. But when he knew he was dying he wanted to see me. I am his only living child. All the other children...' Kekut faltered, struggling to keep his composure. 'He asked me to forgive him, forgive them all. He said their survival depended on fleeing and hiding, keeping silent and unseen. He asked me to stay with the tribe but said it was my choice. He took so long to die. It was long and painful. Then I stayed for the mourning and had many pow-wows trying to decide where I should be.'

John and Priscilla and Mary bowed their heads.

'I decided here.'

John's eyes misted. 'Thank you. Thank you, Kekut.' He put a hand on the Indian's shoulder.

Priscilla impulsively hugged her Indian 'son' and Mary hugged herself, doing a jig of joy.

Then John asked, 'Do you not hate us, after all the terrible things we English have done?'

'Yes, I do hate the English. They have destroyed us. But you are not like those English. It is good here. You are good people. You are my father and mother and sister now.' He gestured to his tunic and leggings. 'My English clothes – too small.'

Priscilla laughed joyously. 'You shall have a new set of English clothes.'

Chapter 95

July 1678

John and Priscilla visit the family graves in Plymouth

On his return from his tribe, Kekut showed a keen interest in learning to read and write English, so the small family sat around the table for a time every evening after supper to read and copy from the Bible. Kekut especially liked the stories of the tribes in the Old Testament and the psalms. He learned quickly and taught John, Priscilla, and Mary words and phrases from his own language.

'Stand in awe and sin not: commune with your own heart upon your bed and be still.' As Priscilla searched for ways to explain the passage to Kekut, trying to think of instances in his own Indian lore which conveyed the same message, she was overcome by memories of sitting with Roger Williams at his table. Her eyes brimmed and she abruptly removed to the hearth to take up her knitting. John and Kekut stayed on at the table, studying, murmuring against the background hum of Mary's spinning.

Slowly rocking, Priscilla let her thoughts go where they would, back into the past, calling up memories of loves lost and passed away. As sadness threatened to engulf her, she stood to stir the stew pot. As she stirred she heard the words, 'So you, Hector, are father and mother and brother to me, as well as my beloved husband. Have pity...' Startled, she glanced over at the table and saw John looking at her. Her hands trembled and she felt slightly dizzy. Looking at the floor she eased herself back into her rocker. Those words. She hadn't thought of them for... how many years? The passages from Standish's copy of the *Iliad*... the words John read to her on their wedding night. He'd learned to read and write as a gift to her. She recalled the happiness of that night and she remembered saying to John, 'You are father and mother and brother to me.' She leaned her head against the back of the rocker and closed her eyes. When some minutes had passed she grasped the arms of her chair, slowly stood, and walked to the table. 'I wish to visit our graveyard in Plymouth. We are old. A visit before we pass away.'

'The weather is set fair,' Kekut said.

'Very well. Tomorrow,' John said. 'But I fear the sight of the Indian slaves will be too distressing.'

'I want to go.'

That night Priscilla's dreams were full of disturbing voices: Susanna – 'John took you to a man he detests to keep you safe... begged Endecott, to save you... he loves you.' Pris – 'Father has changed... defended the Indians...' Catherine Carver – 'To thine own self be true...' John – 'You don't understand...' Voices from the past demanding to be heard.

★ ★ ★

A hot midday sun beat down as John and Priscilla lowered their boat's sail and climbed out onto Plymouth's dock. Already feeling queasy from the heat, Priscilla hung onto John's arm trying to steady herself against the overpowering stench of Indians covered in bear grease. Immediately in front of them was a large pen, about fifty feet square, crowded with Indian males and some females, all roped together at the waist. Silent, sullen, most stared at the ground. A few gazed straight ahead, looking out across the harbor, refusing to flinch from the taunts and flicking whips of the English guards. One young Indian brave turned his head to look directly at Priscilla and John. Priscilla gasped at his disfigured face. One eye was missing; in its place a red pulpy socket. Beneath the socket barely healed scars ran down his cheek and neck to his breast.

'Come.' John put an arm round Priscilla's shoulders. Placing himself between her and the pen he hurried her along the track leading up to the hill fort where the display of three heads, King Philip's, and his two trusted chiefs, brought further distress. Priscilla trembled. Without John's support she would have buckled. John led her to a flat boulder behind the fort, in the shade of its high wall. He uncorked a jug of ale. 'Drink.'

'Did... did we inflict those wounds?'

'Looked more like the type of mutilation warring Indians do to one another. Perhaps he was guilty of betraying his own people. Reckon our men would have sliced his head with an axe and killed him outright – if they hadn't shot him.'

Priscilla sat quiet, sipping her beaker of ale. She heaved a deep sigh.

'Why? Why? Why?'

'Do we have some bread and cheese?' John asked. 'You need food to feel stronger. Then we'll go to the graves.'

When they had eaten, John took Priscilla's hand and led her along a deer track to the clump of birches that sheltered the tiny graveyard.

'John! The crosses are smooth and clean, and the lettering, still crisp. Clear as ever it was!'

'Aye. Whenever I come for a court session I make sure they're in good order.'

'And these birches. They were only saplings when we moved to Duxbury.' Priscilla shaded her eyes, looking up through the dappled branches. She took John's hand. 'Thank you, husband.' She bowed her head. 'Mother, Father, Joseph and Master Jones. May you rest in peace.' She stood quiet, remembering, and wiped a tear from her cheek. 'What would Mother and Father have thought about all this?' She turned, sweeping her arm toward the harbor.

''Tis a blessing they don't know,' John said. They gazed down on the harbor scene. Plymouth constables called out, 'On wi ya – get on there – step lively!' as they herded chains of Indians into the shallop that would carry them to the slave ship, anchored where Master Jones had anchored the *Mayflower* by Clark's Island.

Priscilla faced John, clutching his arms. 'Why? Why are we treating them so horribly?' She shook him as if to shake out an answer.

'This war cost a fortune. We need money to pay the debt. At the same time it clears all these lands of Indians – so we English can settle farther and farther without threat, and our governors can ease their consciences thinking slavery is kinder than mass execution. Though I'm not so sure.' John looked down at the silent, straight standing Indian cargo. 'They are a proud people. I wonder if they wouldn't prefer death.' He took Priscilla's arm. 'Come sit in the shade a time before we go. Have another drink. The sun is fierce.'

They returned to the flat boulder and sat, backs against the wall of the fort, looking through the birch grove across acres of rough grass to the forest beyond. The rasping song of cicadas almost drowned out distant shouts from the harbor. A slight breeze soothed Priscilla's cheek.

'I've been thinking,' John said, 'perhaps we should have moved to Rhode Island. Perhaps we still should.'

Priscilla put down her beaker and stared at him. 'What did you say?'

'Every time I come here to Plymouth I listen to Josiah Winslow and young William Bradford gloating over all the land they are acquiring; even tracts on Mount Hope, the Indians' last home.' He stood and paced. 'Roger Williams was right about paying the Indians a fair price for their land. I wish I'd followed his advice.' He stood still, studying the ground. 'And I'm thinking he is right that all men should be educated, learn to think for themselves, follow their own conscience. Especially when their governors have no conscience at all.' His voice rose. He thumped his fist into the palm of his hand. Saying nothing for a few moments he looked out across the harbor. Turning back to Priscilla he drew a deep breath. 'Priscilla, tell me true. Are you in love with Roger Williams? Is that why you have been so remote? Is that why you want to move to Rhode Island?'

Priscilla said nothing, looking down at her hands twisting the cloth of her gown. She looked up into John's eyes, saw the questioning hurt. 'Perhaps, for a time, but not now. He awakened something in me – the desire to search inside myself, rather like the Quakers – it felt so exciting and so right, and Roger Williams wanted to know what **I** thought; even said he learned from me, and that is what I thought we would have – you and I, our special secret, different from other couples. Then when you made big decisions, like undertaking the debt and moving to Duxbury and you didn't even discuss it...' her voice shook and she wiped her eyes with the back of her hand. 'So... so I imagined I had a secret knowing with Roger Williams. I've wanted to move to Rhode Island because folk are free to say what they think, be merry, without being examined and punished. And Indians visit – the women sachems – think on it – Indian men obeying women chiefs. And I miss Elizabeth.'

John sat down beside her and took her hand. 'There is another decision I made I've never spoken of for shame. In the time of the troubles over Squanto I confronted Bradford; told him he was risking the lives of us all for the sake of one devious Indian. He was furious. Said he was following God's will and if I wanted to advance my position I would not challenge again.' John bowed his head to the side. 'More important to me than anything else was to build a stable, prosperous life for us and our children. So I never challenged him again, always did what was expected, and he grew to trust me. Reckon I didn't want you to question, unsettle things. Then when Standish and I found Duxbury – it was a chance to get away, build our own town – and I did not want you to disagree. I wanted you to want it too. But I see now, reckon I knew it even then, I betrayed something in myself – did it again when I didn't stand up for Charles Prence – and I let you down.'

Priscilla moaned. 'I'm confused and it is so hot. But I do see I've been selfish doing what I thought was right and not thinking how it might affect you, especially with the Quakers. And I've been crazy and cruel to push you away – you have always loved...' Priscilla broke down. 'It was when I heard you read those words last night... those words... our wedding night... you've been true, all the years... how could I... how could I...'

John put his arm round Priscilla and she leaned into him. They sat quiet for a time. Priscilla drew deep shuddery breaths and gradually, in the shelter of John's body, relaxed into calm. Then, with a perplexed frown, she sat up straight. 'I don't understand. Catherine Carver lived by Shakespeare's verse: "...to thine own self be true, and it must follow, as the night the day, thou canst not then be false to any man." I thought I was being true to myself when I pondered, hid Mary Mendome, helped Arthur and Elizabeth, and especially writing to Endecott about the Quakers. But I was being false to you.'

'We went in different directions,' John said, 'and stopped confiding in each other. And times have been hard, so hard. You've been wondrous brave. Those early years: sickness, starving, living in hovels, a tiny settlement surrounded by wilderness and Indians.'

'Aye.' Priscilla gave a slight rueful laugh. 'A little colony led by some peculiar folk. There were a few fine souls: Deacon and Catherine Carver, Susanna, Edward, Standish in his way, even Bradford – and **you**, John. They should have paid you more heed; not been conned by that wretched Mr Prence. To think, he was governor for years.' She shook her head. 'Perhaps 'tis best not to think on it.' She sat quiet, gazing up into the boughs of the trees. 'I thought when we came to this land we would build another England, only better, without the poverty and evil doings. Father's dream. I thought we would build a town like Dorking, with larger houses and family all close by. Wonder if any of the cousins are still alive. This land is strange, wild, harsh climes. Beautiful, but always, I am fearful. But you have made us a fine home and founded Duxbury. I see now why you became more rigid, hostile to anything that threatened disturbance. Even the poor Quakers.'

'Aye. The poor Quakers.' John stood, looking across the colony, the harbor and to the forests all round. 'I followed Prence and Winslow's lead, until their treatment of Alexander and Philip. I could not stand by and say nothing, but no one paid any heed. We have prospered, are set to possess all this land. But the price. Blood. Oceans of blood. Who will cross those oceans?'

'We must not despair. We must not. We started something that could have been good. We have to hope and trust our children will make things better.' She stood, smiling into John's tanned face, his features still strong, set in a shock of white hair. She put her arms round his neck. 'I love you, John Alden.'

Chapter 96

November 1680

Thanksgiving

In the clearing outside the Aldens' front door a 'U' of trestle tables bore a cornucopia of pies, breads, cheeses, chutneys, berries and large pots of stews: seafood, poultry, pork, venison and mutton. Jonathan and David ministered spits roasting deer and turkeys. Children scampered about playing hide and seek, tag and leap frog, occasionally grabbing slabs of cornbread, handfuls of berries and nuts. Priscilla contemplated her children, all in their middle years, seated at table, eating, reminiscing and discovering one another's fortunes since they'd last been together. Elizabeth and William, Jack, Joseph; she smiled to see Pris and Abigail chatting like sisters. As she sat quiet these few moments she felt Susanna's presence, like a guardian spirit, among them all. Priscilla never stopped missing Susanna, her loyal friend from the beginning. Susanna had birthed all her children and many of the grandchildren and they all lived, mothers and babes. Only William and Ruth perished, without Susanna. She shook herself and basked in the gentle early November sun. Sitting at the head table with John on her left and Kekut on her right, she drew in deep breaths of clear autumn air with its tang of salt and pine. Every year she gazed in surprised wonder at the shimmering collage of autumn's display. A solitary maple leaf slowly descended onto her trencher. She looked closely into the hues of red, the veining, and touched John's arm.

He turned to her. 'Maple.'

'Do you remember, when we first sighted land and sailed down along the coast? A day like today. Crisp and blue and a warm autumn sun – and banks of these amazing colors. I thought we'd come to paradise!'

'Aye. Then we hit the shoals.'

'Master Jones saved us by turning back,' Priscilla said.

'We've hit many shoals along the way. So many times our settlement might have been wrecked.' John spoke quietly and his eyes took on a faraway look.

'Aye. But husband, we survived. Hard to believe we nearly starved those first three years. Look at us now! Tables groaning, surrounded by all our family, except William and Ruth.' Priscilla looked over to where John Bass sat with her daughter's seven children. As if it were yesterday, she saw Ruth dressed in the wedding gown she herself had worn and her mother before. She saw herself pressing the precious gardening book, the elm hand mirror, and the woodpecker carving into Ruth's hands, and then Ruth, radiant and trembling, luxuriant auburn curls dancing round her shoulders, holding out her hands to greet her betrothed. Eyes welling with tears, Priscilla looked away, over toward the copse. 'John, John! Look there, in the trees.' She clutched John's hand. 'It's Tinsin! Tinsin, welcome!' Swinging her legs over the bench Priscilla ran to greet their friend. From the shadows behind stepped Aijana and Chitsa, and Mary Mendome with Constance.

'All well.' Tinsin bowed to his women. 'All well.'

'Aye, aye,' Priscilla laughed and wept. 'All well. All is well. Come and eat.' She beckoned to Kekut. 'Have you met Tinsin? He and his women will eat with us.'

'I have heard many stories about you.' Kekut responded to Tinsin's greeting.

The bell sounded and Jack stood. Parents gathered and hushed their children. Jack, the firstborn son, stood straight and tall. His jacket and breeches were of a superior cut; he wore a fine linen shirt and his boots shone. Priscilla realized with a start she'd never seen her son was so handsome, with an air of quiet authority. Her heart beat faster with pride. Their Jack was living little Joseph's dream. 'I be a sea captain when I'm grown.' Jack spoke. 'This is our final day gathered here in celebration of the *Mayflower* anchoring in Cape Cod sixty years ago. We are also celebrating our mother and father and I want to say some words of tribute to them. We all know the story of their voyage on the *Mayflower* and the beginnings of their love and life together. It is our great fortune they both survived the first years of hardship and went on to build our family, Plymouth Colony and then Duxbury. Father, you have always been on the governing council of Plymouth. Having resided many years in Boston where folk live under the iron rod of fanatical governors, I appreciate your pleas for religious tolerance, less vicious punishments, and recently your efforts to prevent maltreatment of our Indian allies.

'Our mother, as well as keeping our home, has always labored tirelessly tending to the sick and wounded, has striven to educate boys and girls, and has championed several risky causes where she felt injustice and cruelty were intolerable. Father, you too have always hated cruelty and supported Mother whenever you could whilst staying within the bounds of the law. There was just one instance when Mother's unswerving, almost unthinking dedication to the Quaker cause nearly brought the house down. You managed to prevent Mother being sentenced to death or permanent banishment and together you pulled through.

'Together you believe in equal justice for all, freedom of thought and now education for all men.' Jack smiled at his father. 'You've changed, Father. Remember the hunting trip?' John grinned and nodded.

'Some of us have remained here in Duxbury, others have moved farther afield. But I know that we all want to lead our lives following Father and Mother's example. They started out on a grand adventure sixty years ago, an adventure into the unknown. We too cannot know what lies ahead in this vast strange land. But we will live the adventure and I believe we all want to work to repair the damage inflicted by our terrible recent war. A toast. To Father and Mother.'

As the toasts dimmed, Kekut stood and motioned for silence. Carrying a cloth sack he walked round the table to face John and Priscilla. He laid the sack on the table and withdrew a small wooden chest, made of elm, polished to a reflecting hue. The lid was embellished with a carving of a male and female woodpecker standing guard over a nest of eggs, all encircled with a garland of ivy leaves. 'For you, Mistress Alden.'

Priscilla stared at the beautiful object, took it into her hands, stroked the carving. Looking into Kekut's eyes she said, 'Thank you. This is a treasure.' Kekut bowed, then reached into the sack again.

'Master Alden.' He handed John a carved woodpecker totem. 'I want to thank you both for protecting and caring for me.'

'Aye, aye.' Joseph stood and clapped, leading a chorus. 'Our protectors.'

John stood and bowed.

Priscilla stood beside him, leaning on the table to steady herself. Her voice faltering, she said, 'Thank you, Kekut, for your beautiful gifts, and thank you all for making the journey to come here; Tinsin, with your women, our dear friends. You have given us a store of happy memories to last the rest of our days. As Jack has said, John and I set out on the *Mayflower*, knowing the voyage would be an adventure. I think none of us had an inkling of how many would perish, nor did we foresee the strange challenges and difficulties we would face. But I especially want to say that without your father's support and devotion through all our trials,' she turned to John and took his hands in hers, 'I doubt I'd have survived. And all of you,' she scanned the gathering, 'have been a blessing from the moment each of you came into our lives.' She looked directly at Tinsin and his women. 'I would like to raise a toast to everyone here and to four people who are no longer with us, but whose presence John and I continue to feel and treasure.' She raised her beaker. 'To Captain Miles Standish, Susanna Winslow, Ruth, and baby William.'

The gathering all rose and called out their love.

When dusk brought a chill to the air and shapes became shadowy, Priscilla begged Tinsin to bring his wives and daughters to sleep in the Alden house. 'Mary and Pris and I are longing to talk with our friends, and I am sure Kekut would like to talk with you further.' Tinsin agreed.

As she expected, when she and John finally retired to their own bedchamber Tinsin and Kekut stayed sitting cross-legged by the hearth, talking, talking.

'Reckon the time has come for Kekut to decide whether he wants to stay with us or live with the Indians.' John kept his voice low.

'I know we've always said he must go back to his people if he wishes, but how I'll miss him if he does,' Priscilla said. 'I wonder if his gifts were parting gifts.'

John softly groaned.

★ ★ ★

Priscilla and John stood by their front door in the early morning sun, waving goodbye as their family drove away in horse-drawn carts and traps, or set off for Duxbury town on foot. Priscilla wiped the tears from her cheeks. *The far away ones, Elizabeth, Jack, Joseph, I might never see them again.* John coughed and cleared his throat. They waited and watched as the last cart disappeared through the copse. Turning to go back into the house they faced Tinsin and Kekut. Tinsin put his arm around Kekut's shoulder. 'A good man. Good Indian.' Priscilla clutched John's hand. 'We have pow-wow all night until sunrise.'

Kekut looked from Tinsin to John and Priscilla. 'Tinsin has helped me to decide. I stay here with you.'

'Oh! Oh thank you,' Priscilla cried.

'We are very grateful and happy.' John shook Kekut by the hand.

'I stay with you and go to Harvard. Already I read Shakespeare and *Opticks*.'

John whooped. 'Hoorah! Excellent.' He clapped Tinsin on the shoulder. 'My friend. Thank you.'

'Oh, Kekut!' Priscilla impulsively hugged the young Indian. ''Tis wonderful news. Jonathan will bring more books from Boston. We'll all study and prepare you for Harvard. ''Twill be an adventure.'

Chapter 97

June 1685

Priscilla's bench

Slowly, gingerly, Priscilla picked her way through the tuffocky, blossoming orchard. She stopped to accommodate a sharp twinge in her knees. *Bother.* She waited. *There. It's passed. Not three years ago I didn't have any of this trouble.* She drew her handkerchief from her pouch and wiped the beads of sweat from her brow. Leaning against a tree trunk she savored the scent and spring beauty of plum and apple blossom, leaves still young in their early light green. She could see her destination about a hundred yards hence; her bench, under the boughs of the first apple tree she and John had planted on moving to Duxbury.

There. At last. Good to sit in the gentle late afternoon sun. She watched John planting peas in the adjoining field. He straightened up, saw her and waved. Putting down his sack, treading carefully between planted rows, he came through the gate to sit beside her. Priscilla smiled. She stroked the weather polished oak arm of the bench.

'My bench. You made it for me in our first wedded year.' John put his arm round her shoulder. She leaned into him. 'About this time we were wed. First week in June. A happy time in spite of hunger and Susanna and Edward's babe dying.'

'Aye,' John said. 'I remember wondering if the day would ever come. That year of being supervised went on forever.'

'You placed my bench in our garden where I could sit hidden from the prying eyes of gossips eager to accuse me of sin – must never be idle; mustn't waste a second of God's time.'

'Amazing we're still here. In our eighties. Be gad. When you think of all we've been through. It's been a strange life. Not what I'd hoped. I wanted to give you a grand house, like the Winslows'. And I never dreamt we would suffer so much hardship and strife.'

'Hmm.' Priscilla looked into the distance. 'I had visions of grand houses with walled gardens, of fine gowns and silver on the table – and servants. Reckon I was rather uppity and proud.'

They sat quiet for a time. The voices of Mary and Kekut carried across the fields, Kekut 'home' from Harvard to help with the sowing. Surrounding them were the birds' evening roosting chirrups and the hum and scratch of insects.

'We may not have as grand a house as the Winslows', but we've made a good home, good in ways that count.' Priscilla stroked John's arm. 'I love our home. I think I might even grow to love this rough, wild land, except for the wolves. I'll always hate the wolves.' She shuddered.

John took her hand. 'Do you not still regret… that we don't live in Rhode Island?'

Priscilla placed her other hand over his. 'Now I can't move about easily, I have plenty of time to ponder. And John,' she drew him to look at her, 'the reading and learning with Kekut, and him bringing his friends here for visits, I reckon we've made our own little Rhode Island.'

John gathered her to him and stroked her hair, still auburn and thick. He kissed her tenderly. 'I love you.'

'I love you, John Alden, even more than the day we wed.' Priscilla held him close, letting go into the cradle of his arms. Minutes passed before they drew apart. John held her face in his hands, drew his thumb across her brow.

Priscilla looked after him as he strode back to the field, his stride easy and strong, back straight, head high. 'My John.' She spoke the words aloud, remembering their first encounter on the *Mayflower*; his raised eyebrow taking her in, her rescuer. Closing her eyes, she lifted her face to the soft sun. A warm glow of peaceful happiness flooded through her. Something brushed her cheek. She looked to see an apple blossom fallen onto her lap. Holding it gently she gazed into the pale pink petals veined with deeper pink and a touch of green. The blossom drew her in so she became aware of nothing else, drifting, drifting, carried away in the delicate pink basket.

Epilogue

Priscilla's coffin was John's last creation in wood. After her burial he put his woodworking tools away and never touched them again.

He continued to serve on Plymouth's council and magistrates' court and participated in matters of Duxbury's governance. Whilst working in the fields he would sometimes stop and gaze at Priscilla's bench in its place under the apple tree, but he never sat on it.

The only outward sign of his grief was his refusal to lie in the bed he and Priscilla had shared. All night he sat in his rocker by the hearth, Patch at his feet. He stared into the embers, sometimes dozing.

Although John took pleasure in watching his grandchildren develop and enjoyed talking with them, his greatest comfort was Kekut. The young Indian gentleman often came to stay, bringing news of Harvard and Boston, and especially of Jack's well-being and fortunes.

When John began to ail, and his sickness worsened, Kekut stayed by him, gently nursing his elderly friend and uttering soothing Indian phrases. In his pain and delirium John grasped Kekut's hand as if never to let him go. The Indian was holding him when John whispered his last words, 'Priscilla, my Priscilla.'

Afterword

Records show that John and Priscilla attended Duxbury's Sabbath meeting in 1680, Priscilla on John's arm. At the time of John's death, September 12th, 1687, he was eighty-eight years of age. The date of Priscilla's death is uncertain. For the purposes of my story she dies two years before John.

In the year 1691 Plymouth Colony was absorbed into the bounds and jurisdiction of Massachusetts Bay.

The Pilgrim Fathers did as the Lord God of Abraham and Isaac commanded. They went forth and multiplied. Hence the descendants of John and Priscilla Alden number in the thousands. My family's line comes from Ruth who married John Bass and went to live in Braintree, Massachusetts.

Acknowledgements

My thanks go to the many friends, colleagues and family who have helped bring *The Mayflower Marriage* to fruition.

Firstly, to Jane Robotham who persuaded me to set sail and has provided invaluable ballast throughout the journey. To Jess Thompson who came to the rescue when the ship was foundering, tirelessly re-reading, making suggestions, teaching me what writing a novel was about.

 I am indebted to a crew of editors, advisers, and readers who have helped with research, historical accuracy, sharpening and polishing: Judy Ferretter and Mary Strover for advice and editing, Helen Rogers, Pam Flesner, Robert Stevens and Anne Graf for reading; Claire Porter of Chapter House Books, Sherborne, Dorset and Christina Walkley for help with research, and Mary Doble for her constant support.

To Janet Gelerntner for her helpful tuition in the early stages. To Helen Baggott who has been a superb copy editor, proofreader, and extremely generous with supportive advice.

To Tom Hay who guided my research and escorted me to the 'Plimoth Plantation' and the Alden House in Duxbury.

A special thanks goes to Conran and Sandra Hay; Conran for his assiduous editing for historical accuracy and Sandra for her professional formatting and proofreading with her astute eye for discrepancies. Any historical inaccuracies are entirely my own.

To Esther Robotham for launching me into the world of social media, and to Liz Gordon for her knowledgeable and enthusiastic work on promotion and navigation in the seas of the publishing world.

To Harvey Robotham who drew the map and provided many unexpected but timely insights.

Finally, to the team at Matador who have been professional, available and endlessly patient from the initial enquiry stage to the finished product.

My grateful thanks to all.